The [illegible] as

Also by Ellis Peters

BROTHER CADFAEL MYSTERIES
A MORBID TASTE FOR BONES
ONE CORPSE TOO MANY
MONK'S-HOOD
SAINT PETER'S FAIR
THE LEPER OF SAINT GILES
THE VIRGIN IN THE ICE
THE SANCTUARY SPARROW
THE DEVIL'S NOVICE
DEAD MAN'S RANSOM
THE PILGRIM OF HATE
AN EXCELLENT MYSTERY
THE RAVEN IN THE FOREGATE
THE ROSE RENT
THE HERMIT OF EYTON FOREST
THE CONFESSION OF BROTHER HALUIN
THE HERETIC'S APPRENTICE
THE POTTER'S FIELD
THE SUMMER OF THE DANES
THE HOLY THIEF
BROTHER CADFAEL'S PENANCE

THE FIRST CADFAEL OMNIBUS
THE SECOND CADFAEL OMNIBUS
THE THIRD CADFAEL OMNIBUS
THE FOURTH CADFAEL OMNIBUS

INSPECTOR FELSE MYSTERIES
A NICE DERANGEMENT OF EPITAPHS
BLACK IS THE COLOUR OF MY TRUE LOVE'S HEART
THE KNOCKER ON DEATH'S DOOR
RAINBOW'S END
FALLEN INTO THE PIT
DEATH AND THE JOYFUL WOMAN
THE GRASS WIDOW'S TALE
THE HOUSE OF GREEN TURF

Ellis Peters writing as Edith Pargeter:

THE HEAVEN TREE TRILOGY
THE HEAVEN TREE
THE GREEN BRANCH
THE SCARLET SEED

THE MARRIAGE OF MEGGOTTA

MOST LOVING MERE FOLLY

Ellis Peters

The Fifth Cadfael Omnibus

The Rose Rent
The Hermit of Eyton Forest
The Confession of Brother Haluin

Brother
CADFAEL

WARNER FUTURA

A *Warner Futura* Book

First published in this omnibus edition in Great Britain in 1994 by
Warner Futura
Reprinted 1995

THE ROSE RENT first published in 1986 by Macmillan
Published by Futura in 1987
Reprinted 1987, 1988, 1989, 1990, 1991
Published by Warner Futura in 1992
Reprinted 1993

THE HERMIT OF EYTON FOREST first published by Headline in 1987
Published by Futura in 1988
Reprinted 1991
Published by Warner Futura in 1992
Reprinted 1993

THE CONFESSION OF BROTHER HALUIN first published by
Headline in 1988
Published by Futura in 1989
Reprinted 1991
Published by Warner Futura in 1992
Reprinted 1993

A CIP catalogue record for this book
is available from the British Library

ISBN 0 7515 0949 3

Photoset in North Wales by
Derek Doyle & Associates, Mold, Clwyd.
Printed and bound in Great Britain by
Clays Ltd, St Ives plc

Warner Futura
A Division of
Little, Brown and Company (UK)
Brettenham House
Lancaster Place
London WC2E 7EN

Contents

The Rose Rent

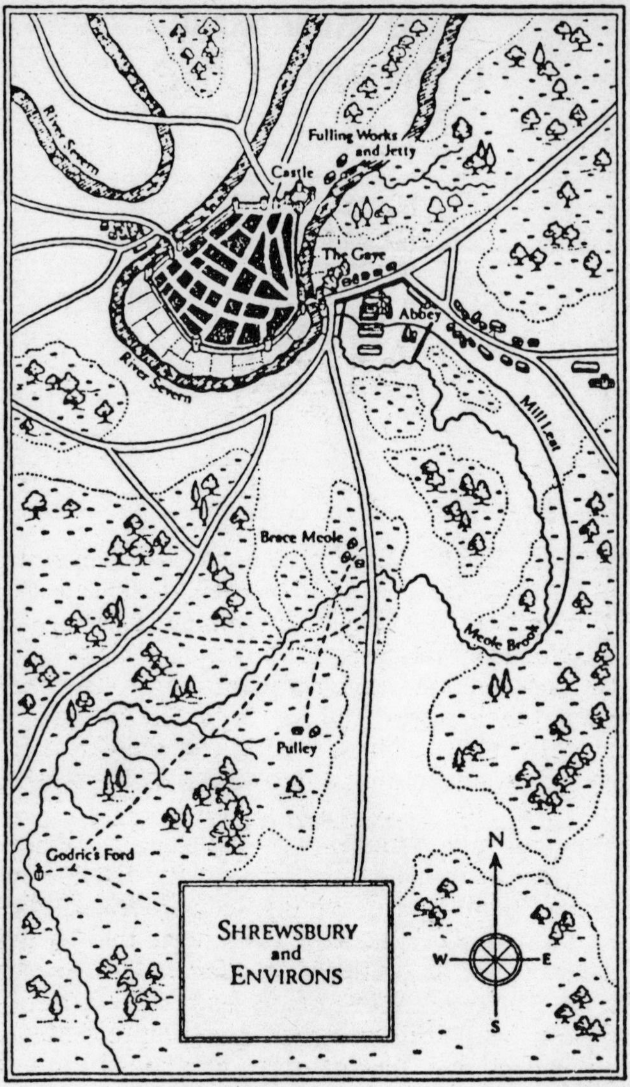
River Severn
Fulling Works and Jetty
Castle
The Gaye
Abbey
River Severn
Mill Leat
Brace Meole
Meole Brook
Pulley
Godric's Ford
SHREWSBURY and ENVIRONS
N
W
E
S

Chapter One

BY REASON of the prolonged cold, which lingered far into April, and had scarcely mellowed when the month of May began, everything came laggard and reluctant that spring of 1142. The birds kept close about the roofs, finding warmer places to roost. The bees slept late, depleted their stores, and had to be fed, but neither was there any early burst of blossom for them to make fruitful. In the gardens there was no point in planting seed that would rot or be eaten in soil too chilly to engender life.

The affairs of men, stricken with the same petrifying chill, seemed to have subsided into hibernation. Faction held its breath. King Stephen, after the first exhilaration of liberation from his prison, and the Easter journey north to draw together the frayed strings of his influence, had fallen ill in the south, so ill that the rumour of his death had spread throughout England, and his cousin and rival, the Empress Maud, had cautiously moved her headquarters to Oxford, and settled down there to wait patiently and vainly for him to make truth of rumour, which he stubbornly declined to do. He had still business to settle with the lady, and his constitution was more than a match for even this virulent fever. By the end of May he was on his way manfully back to health. By the early days of June the long sub-frost broke. The biting wind changed to a temperate breeze, the sun came out over the earth like a warm hand stroking, the seed stirred in the ground and put forth green blades, and a foam of flowers, all the more exuberant for having been so long restrained, burst forth in gold and purple and white over garden and meadow. The belated sowing began in jubilant haste. And King Stephen, like a giant breaking loose from some crippling enchantment, surged out of his convalescence into vigorous action, and bearing down on the port of Wareham, the most easterly still available to his enemies, seized both town and castle with hardly a graze to show for it.

'And is making north again now towards Cirencester,' reported Hugh Beringar, elated by the news, 'to pick off the empress's outposts one by one, if only he can keep up this storm of energy.' It was the one fatal flaw in the King's military make-up that he could not sustain action for long if he failed to get instant results, but would abandon a siege after three days, and go off to start another elsewhere, squandering for no gain the energy devoted to both. 'We may see a tidy end to it yet!'

Brother Cadfael, preoccupied with his own narrower concerns, continued to survey the vegetable patch outside the wall of his herb-garden, digging an experimental toe into soil grown darker and kinder after a mild morning shower. 'By rights,' he said thoughtfully, 'carrots should have been in more than a month ago, and the first radishes will be fibrous and shrunken as old leather, but we might get something with more juices in it from now on. Lucky the fruit-blossom held back until the bees began to wake up, but even so it will be a thin crop this year. Everything's four weeks behind, but the seasons have a way of catching up, somehow. Wareham, you were saying? What of Wareham?'

'Why, that Stephen has taken it, town and castle and harbour and all. So Robert of Gloucester, who went out by that gate barely ten days earlier, has it slammed in his face now. Did I not tell you? The word came three days since. It seems there was a meeting back in April, in Devizes, between the empress and her brother, and they made it up between them that it was high time the lady's husband should pay a little heed to her affairs, and come over in person to help her get her hands on Stephen's crown. They sent envoys over to Normandy to meet with Geoffrey, but he sent back to say he was well disposed, no question, but the men sent out to him were unknown to him, name or reputation, and he would be uneasy in dealing with any but the Earl of Gloucester himself. If Robert will not come, says Geoffrey, no use sending me any other.'

Cadfael was momentarily distracted from his laggard crops. 'And Robert let himself be persuaded?' he said, marvelling.

'Very reluctantly. He feared to leave his sister to the loyalties of some who were all but ready to desert her after the Westminster shambles, and I doubt if he has any great hopes of getting anything out of the Count of Anjou. But yes, he let himself be persuaded. And he's sailed from Wareham, with less trouble than he'll have sailing back into the same port, now the king holds it. A good, fast move, that was. If he can but maintain it now!'

'We said a Mass in thanksgiving for his recovery,' said Cadfael absently, and plucked out a leggy sow-thistle from among his mint. 'How is it that weeds grow three times faster than the plants we nurse so tenderly? Three days ago that was not even there. If the kale shot up like that I should be pricking the plants out by tomorrow.'

'No doubt your prayers will stiffen Stephen's resolution,' Hugh said, though with less than complete conviction. 'Have they not given you a helper yet, here in the garden? It's high time, there's more than one's work here in this season.'

'So I urged at chapter this morning. What they'll offer me there's no knowing. Prior Robert has one or two among the younger ones he'd be glad to shuffle off his hands and into mine. Happily the ones he least approves tend to be those with more wit and spirit than the rest, not less. I may yet be lucky in my apprentice.'

He straightened his back, and stood looking out over the newly turned beds, and the pease-fields that sloped down to the Meole Brook, mentally casting an indulgent eye back over the most recent of his helpers here in the herbarium. Big, jaunty, comely Brother John, who had blundered into the cloister by mistake, and backed out of it, not without the connivance of friends, in Wales, to exchange the role of brother for that of husband and father; Brother Mark, entering here as an undersized and maltreated sixteen-year-old, shy and quiet, and grown into a clear, serene maturity of spirit that drew him away inevitably towards the priesthood. Cadfael still missed Brother Mark, attached now to the household chapel of the Bishop of Lichfield, and already a deacon. And after Mark, Brother Oswin, cheerful, confident and ham-fisted, gone now to do his year's service at the lazarhouse of Saint Giles at the edge of the town. What next, wondered Cadfael? Put a dozen young men into the same rusty black habits, shave their heads, fit them into a single horarium day after day and year after year, and still they will all be irremediably different, every one unique. Thank God!

'Whatever they send you,' said Hugh, keeping pace with him along the broad green path that circled the fish-ponds, 'you'll have transformed by the time he leaves you. Why should they waste a simple, sweet saint like Rhun on you? He's made already, he came into the world made. You'll get the rough, obdurate, the unstable to lick into shape. Not that it ever comes out the shape that was expected,' he added, with a flashing grin and a slanted glance along his shoulder at his friend.

'Rhun has taken upon himself the custody of Saint Winifred's altar,' said Cadfael. 'He has a proprietorial interest in the little lady. He makes the candles for her himself, and borrows essences from me to scent them for her. No, Rhun will find his own duties, and no one will stand in his way. He and she between them will see to that.'

They crossed the little foot-bridge over the leat that fed the pools and the mill, and emerged into the rose-garden. The trimmed bushes had made little growth as yet, but the first buds were swelling at last, the green sheaths parting to show a sliver of red or white. 'They'll open fast now,' said Cadfael contentedly. 'All they needed was warmth. 'I'd begun to wonder whether the Widow Perle would get her rent on time this year, but if these are making up for lost time, so will her white ones be. A sad year, if there were no roses by the twenty-second day of June!'

'The Widow Perle? Oh, yes, the Vestier girl!' said Hugh. 'I remember! So it's due on the day of Saint Winifred's translation, is it? How many years is it now since she made the gift?'

'This will be the fourth time we've paid her her annual rent. One white rose from that bush in her old garden, to be delivered to her on the day of Saint Winifred's translation –'

'Supposed translation,' said Hugh, grinning. 'And you should blush when you name it.'

'So I do, but with my complexion who notices?' And he was indeed of a rosy russet colouring, confirmed by long years of outdoor living in both east and west, so engrained now that winters merely tarnished it a little, and summers regularly renewed the gloss.

'She made modest demands,' observed Hugh thoughtfully,

as they came to the second plank-bridge that spanned the channel drawn off to service the guest-hall. 'Most of our solid merchants up in the town value property a good deal higher than roses.'

'She had already lost what she most valued,' said Cadfael. 'Husband and child both, within twenty days. He died, and she miscarried. She could not bear to go on living, alone, in the house where they had been happy together. But it was because she valued it that she wanted it spent for God, not hoarded up with the rest of a property large enough to provide handsomely even without it for herself and all her kinsfolk and workfolk. It pays for the lighting and draping of Our Lady's altar the whole year round. It's what she chose. But just the one link she kept – one rose a year. He was a very comely man, Edred Perle,' said Cadfael, shaking his head mildly over the vulnerability of beauty, 'I saw him pared away to the bone in a searing fever, and had no art to cool him. A man remembers that.'

'You've seen many such,' said Hugh reasonably, 'here and on the fields of Syria, long ago.'

'So I have! So I have! Did ever you hear me say I'd forgotten any one of them? But a young, handsome man, shrivelled away before his time, before even his prime, and his girl left without even his child to keep him in mind . . . A sad enough case, you'll allow.'

'She's young,' said Hugh with indifferent practicality, his mind being on other things. 'She should marry again.'

'So think a good many of our merchant fathers in the town,' agreed Cadfael with a wry smile, 'the lady being as wealthy as she is, and sole mistress of the Vestiers' clothier business. But after what she lost, I doubt if she'll look at a grey old skinflint like Godfrey Fuller, who's buried two wives already and made a profit out of both of them, and has his eye on a third fortune with the next. Or a fancy young fellow in search of an easy living!'

'Such as?' invited Hugh, amused.

'Two or three I could name. William Hynde's youngster, for one, if my gossips tell me truth. And the lad who's foreman of her own weavers is a very well-looking young man, and fancies his chance with her. Even her neighbour the saddler is looking for a wife, I'm told, and thinks she might very well do.'

Hugh burst into affectionate laughter, and clapped him boisterously on the shoulders as they emerged into the great court, and the quiet, purposeful bustle before Mass. 'How many eyes and ears have you in every street in Shrewsbury? I wish my own intelligencers knew half as much of what goes on. A pity your influence falls short of Normandy. I might get some inkling then of what Robert and Geoffrey are up to there. Though I think,' he said, growing grave again as he turned back to his own preoccupations, 'Geoffrey is far more concerned with getting possession of Normandy than with wasting his time on England. From all accounts he's making fast inroads there, he's not likely to draw off now. Far more like to inveigle Robert into helping him than offering much help to Robert.

'He certainly shows very little interest in his wife,' agreed Cadfael drily, 'or her ambitions. Well, we shall see if Robert can sway him. Are you coming in to Mass this morning?'

'No, I'm away to Maesbury tomorrow for a week or two. They should have been shearing before this, but they put it off for a while because of the cold. They'll be hard at it now. I'll leave Aline and Giles there for the summer. But I'll be back and forth, in case of need.'

'A summer without Aline, and without my godson,' said Cadfael reprovingly, 'is no prospect to spring on me without preamble, like this. Are you not ashamed?'

'Not a whit! For I came, among other errands, to bid you to supper with us tonight, before we leave early in the morning. Abbot Radulfus has given his leave and blessing. Go, pray for fair weather and a smooth ride for us,' said Hugh heartily, and gave his friend a vigorous shove towards the corner of the cloister and the south door of the church.

It was purely by chance, or a symbol of that strange compulsion that brings the substance hard on the heels of the recollection, that the sparse company of worshippers in the parish part of the church at the monastic Mass that day should include the Widow Perle. There were always a few of the laity there on their knees beyond the parish altar, some who had missed their parish Mass for varying reasons, some who were old and solitary and filled up their lonely time with superogatory worship, some who had special pleas to make, and sought an extra opportunity of approaching grace. Some, even, who had other business in the Foregate, and welcomed a haven meantime for thought and quietness, which was the case of the Widow Perle.

From his stall in the choir Brother Cadfael could just see the suave line of her head, shoulder and arm, beyond the bulk of the parish altar. It was strange that so quiet and unobtrusive a woman should nevertheless be so instantly recognisable even in this fragmentary glimpse. It might have been the way she carried her straight and slender shoulders, or the great mass of her brown hair weighing down the head so reverently inclined over clasped hands, hidden from his sight by the altar. She was barely twenty-five years old, and had enjoyed only three years of a happy marriage, but she went about her deprived and solitary life without fuss or complaint, cared scrupulously for a business which gave her no personal pleasure, and faced the prospect of perpetual loneliness with a calm countenance and surprising supply of practical energy. In happiness or unhappiness, living is a duty, and must be done thoroughly.

A blessing, at any rate, thought Cadfael, that she is not utterly alone, she has her mother's sister to keep the house for her now she lives, as it were, over her shop, and her cousin for a conscientious foreman and manager, to take the weight of the business off her shoulders. And one rose every year for the rent of the house and garden in the foregate, where her man died. The only gesture of passion and grief and loss she ever made, to give away voluntarily her most valuable property, the house where she had been happy, and yet ask for that one reminder, and nothing more.

She was not a beautiful woman, Judith Perle, born Judith Vestier, and sole heiress to the biggest clothiers' business in the town. But she had a bodily dignity that would draw the eye even in a market crowd, above the common height for a woman, slender and erect, and with a carriage and walk of notable grace. The great coils of her shining light-brown hair, the colour of seasoned oak timber, crowned a pale face that tapered from wide and lofty brow to pointed chin, by way of strong cheekbones and hollow cheeks, and an eloquent, mobile mouth too wide for beauty, but elegantly shaped. Her eyes were of a deep grey, and very clear and wide, neither confiding nor hiding anything. Cadfael had been eye to eye with her, four years ago now, across her husband's death-bed, and she had neither lowered her lids nor turned her glance aside, but stared unwaveringly as her life's happiness slipped irresistibly away through her fingers. Two weeks later she had miscarried, and lost even her child. Edred had left her nothing.

Hugh is right, thought Cadfael, forcing his mind back to the liturgy. She is young, she should marry again.

The June light, now approaching the middle hours of the day, and radiant with sunshine, fell in long golden shafts across the body of the choir and into the ranks of the brothers and obedientiaries opposite, gilding half a face here and throwing its other half into exaggerated shade, there causing dazzled eyes in a blanched face to blink away the brightness. The vault above received the diffused reflections in a soft, muted glow, plucking into relief the curved leaves of the stone bosses. Music and light seemed to mate only there in the zenith. Summer trod hesitantly into the church at last, after prolonged hibernation.

It seemed that brother Cadfael was not the only one whose mind was wandering when it should have been fixed. Brother Anselm the precentor, absorbed into his singing, lifted a rapt face into the sun, his eyes closed, since he knew every note without study or thought. But beside him Brother Eluric, custodian of Saint Mary's altar in the Lady Chapel, responded only absently, his head turned aside, towards the parish altar and the soft murmur of responses from beyond.

Brother Eluric was a child of the cloister, not long a full brother, and entrusted with his particular charge by reason of his undoubted deserving, tempered by the reserve that was felt about admitting child oblates to full office, at least until they had been mature for a number of years. An unreasonable reserve, Cadfael had always felt, seeing that the child oblates were regarded as the perfect innocents, equivalent to the angels, while the *conversi,* those who came voluntarily and in maturity to the monastic life, were the fighting saints, those who had endured and mastered their imperfections. So Saint Anselm had classified them, and ordered them never to attempt reciprocal reproaches, never to feel envy. But still the *conversi* were preferred for the responsible offices, perhaps as having experience of the deceits and complexities and temptations of the world around them. But the care of an altar, its light, its draperies, the special prayers belonging to it, this could well be the charge of an innocent.

Brother Eluric was past twenty now, the most learned and devout of his contemporaries, a tall, well-made young man, black-haired and black-eyed. He had been in the cloister since he was three years old, and knew nothing outside it. Unacquainted with sin, he was all the more haunted by it, as by some unknown monster, and assidous in confession, he picked to pieces his own infinitesimal failings, with the mortal penitence due to deadly sins. A curious thing, that so over-conscientious a youth should be paying so little heed to the holy office. His chin was on his shoulder, his lips still, forgetting the words of the psalm. He was gazing, in fact, precisely where Cadfael had been gazing only moments earlier. But from Eluric's stall there would be more of her to see, Cadfael reflected, the averted face, the linked hands, the folds of linen over her breast.

The contemplation, it seemed, gave him no joy, but only a brittle, quivering tension, taut as a drawn bow. When he recollected himself and tore his gaze away, it was with a wrench that shook him from head to foot.

Well, well! said Cadfael to himself, enlightened. And in eight days more he has to carry the rose rent to her. That task they should have allotted to some old hardened sinner like me, who would view and enjoy, and return untroubled and untroubling, not this vulnerable boy who surely can never else have been alone in a room with a woman since his mother let him be taken out of her arms. And a pity she ever did!

And this poor girl, the very image to wring him most painfully, grave, sad, with a piteous past and yet composed and calm like the Blessed Virgin herself. And he coming to her bearing a white rose, their hands perhaps touching as he delivers it. And now I recall that Anselm says he's something of a poet. Well, what follies we commit without evil intent!

It was far too late now to devote his mind to its proper business of prayer and praise. He contented himself with hoping that by the time the brothers emerged from the choir after service the lady would be gone.

By the mercy of God, she was.

But she was gone, it seemed, no further than Cadfael's workshop in the herb-garden, where he found her waiting patiently outside the open door when he came to decant the lotion he had left cooling before Mass. Her brow was smooth and her voice mild, and everything about her practical and sensible. The fire that burned Eluric was unknown to her. At Cadfael's invitation she followed him in, under the gently swaying bunches of herbs that rustled overhead from the beams.

'You once made me an ointment, Brother Cadfael, if you remember. For a rash on the hands. There's one of my carders breaks out in little pustules, handling the new fleeces. But not every season – that's strange too. This year she has trouble with it again.'

'I remember it,' said Cadfael. 'It was three years ago. Yes, I know the receipt. I can make some fresh for you in a matter of minutes, if you've leisure to wait?'

It seemed that she had. She sat down on the wooden bench against the timber wall, and drew her dark skirts close about her feet, very erect and still in the corner of the hut, as Cadfael reached for pestle and mortar, and the little scale with its brass weights.

'And how are you faring now?' he asked, busy with hog's fat and herbal oils. 'Up there in the town?'

'Well enough,' she said composedly. 'The business gives me plenty to do, and the wool clip has turned out better than I feared. I can't complain. Isn't it strange,' she went on, warming, 'that wool should bring up this rash for Branwen, when you use the fat from wool to doctor skin diseases for many people?'

'Such contrary cases do happen,' he said. 'There are plants some people cannot handle without coming to grief. No one knows the reason. We learn by observing. You had good results with this salve, I remember.'

'Oh, yes, her hands healed very quickly. But I think perhaps I should keep her from carding, and teach her weaving. When the wool is washed and dyed and spun, perhaps she could handle it more safely. She's a good girl, she would soon learn.'

It seemed to Cadfael, working away with his back turned to her, that she was talking to fill the silence while she thought, and thought of something far removed from what she was saying. It was no great surprise, when she said suddenly, and in a very different voice, abrupt and resolute: 'Brother Cadfael, I have thoughts of taking the veil. Serious thoughts! The world is not so desirable that I should hesitate to leave it, nor my condition so hopeful that I dare look for a better time to come. The business can do very well without me; Cousin Miles runs it very profitably, and values it more than I do. Oh, I do my duty well enough, as I was always taught to do, but he could do it every bit as well without me. Why should I hesitate?'

Cadfael turned to face her, the mortar balanced on his palm. 'Have you said as much to your aunt and your cousin?'

'I have mentioned it.'

'And what do they say to it?'

'Nothing. It's left to me. Miles will neither commend nor

advise, he brushes it aside. I think he doesn't take me seriously. My aunt – you know her a little? She's widowed like me, and for ever lamenting it, even after years. She talks of the peace of the cloister, and release from the cares of the world. But she always talks so, though I know she's well content with her comfortable life if the truth were told. I live, Brother Cadfael, I do my work, but I am not content. It would be something settled and stable, to take to the cloister.'

'And wrong,' said Cadfael firmly. 'Wrong, at least, for you.'

'Why would it be so wrong,' she challenged. The hood had slipped back from her head, the great braid of light-brown hair, silver-lit like veined oak, glowed faintly in the subdued light.

'No one should take to the cloistered life as a second-best, and that is what you would be doing. It must be embraced out of genuine desire, or not at all. It is not enough to wish to escape from the world without, you must be on fire for the world within.'

'Was it so with you?' she asked, and suddenly she smiled, and her austere face kindled into warmth for a moment.

He considered that in silence for a brief, cautious while. 'I came late to it, and it may be that my fire burned somewhat dully,' he said honestly at length, 'but it gave light enough to show me the road to what I wanted. I was running towards, not away.'

She looked him full in the face with her daunting, direct eyes, and said with abrupt, bleak deliberation: 'Have you never thought, Brother Cadfael, that a woman may have more cause to run away than ever you had? More perils to run from, and fewer alternatives than flight?'

'That is truth,' admitted Cadfael, stirring vigorously. 'But you, as I know, are better placed than many to hold your own, as well as having more courage than a good many of us men. You are your own mistress, your kin depend on you, and not you on them. There is no overlord to claim the right to order your future, no one can force you into another marriage – yes, I have heard there are many would be only too pleased if they could, but they have no power over you. No father living, no elder kinsman to influence you. No matter how men may pester you or affairs weary you, you know you are more than equal to them. And as for what you have lost,' he said, after a moment's hesitation as to whether he should tread so near, 'it is lost only to this world. Waiting is not easy, but no harder, believe me, among the vexations and distractions of the world than in the solitude and silence of the cloister. I have seen men make that mistake, for as reasonable cause, and suffer all the more with the double deprivation. Do not you take that risk. Never unless you are sure of what you want, and want it with all your heart and soul.'

It was as much as he dared say, as much as and perhaps more than he had any right to say. She heard him out without turning her eyes away. He felt their clear stare heavy upon him all the time he was smoothing his ointment into its jar for her, and tying down the lid of the pot for safe carriage.

'Sister Magdalen, from the Benedictine cell at Godric's Ford,' he said, 'is coming to Shrewsbury in two days' time, to fetch away Brother Edmund's niece, who wants to join the sisterhood there. As for the girl's motives, I know nothing of them, but if sister Magdalen is accepting her as a novice it must be from conviction, and moreover, the child will be carefully watched, and get no further than her novitiate unless Magdalen is satisfied of her vocation. Will you speak with her about this? I think you already know something of her.'

'I do,' Judith's voice was soft, and yet there was a shade of quiet amusement in the tone. 'Her own motives, I think, when she entered Godric's Ford, were scarcely what you are demanding.'

That was something he could not well deny. Sister Magdalen had formerly been, for many years, the constant mistress of a certain nobleman, and on his death had looked about her with single-minded resolution for another field in which to employ her undoubted talents. No question but the choice of the cloister had been coolly and practically made. What redeemed it was the vigour and loyalty she had devoted to it since the day of her entry, and would maintain, without question, until the day of her death.

'In no way that I know of,' admitted Cadfael, 'is Sister Magdalen anything but unique. You are right, she entered the cell seeking not a vocation, but a career, and a career she is making, and a notable one, too. Mother Mariana is old and bedridden now, the weight of the cell falls all on Magdalen, and I know no shoulders better fitted to carry it. And I do not think she would say to you, as I said, that there is but one good reason for taking the veil, true longing for the life of the spirit. The more reason you could and should listen to her advice and weigh it carefully, before you take so grave a step. And bear in mind, you are young, she had said goodbye to her prime.'

'And I have buried mine,' said Judith very firmly, and as one stating truth, without self-pity.

'Well, if it comes to second-bests,' said Cadfael, 'they can be found outside the cloister as well as within. Managing the business your fathers built up, providing employment for so many people, is itself a sufficient justification for a life, for want of better.'

'It does not put me to any great test,' she said indifferently. 'Ah, well, I said only that I had been thinking of quitting the world. Nothing is done, as yet. And whether or no, I shall be glad to talk with Sister Magdalen, for I do value her wit, and know better than to discard unconsidered whatever she may say. Let me know when she comes, and I will send and bid her to my house, or go to her wherever she is lodged.'

She rose to take the jar of ointment from him. Standing, she was the breadth of two fingers taller than he, but thin and slender-boned. The coils of her hair would have seemed over-heavy if she had not carried her head so nobly.

'Your roses are budding well,' she said, as he went out with her along the gravel path from the workshop. 'However late they come, they always bloom equally in the end.'

It could have been a metaphor for the quality of a life, he thought, as they had been discussing it. But he did not say so. Better leave her to the shrewd and penetrating wisdom of Sister Magdalen. 'And yours?' he said. 'There'll be a choice of blooms when Saint Winifred's feast comes round. You should have the best and freshest for your fee.'

The most fleeting of smiles crossed her face, and left her sombre again, her eyes on the path. 'Yes,' she said, and nothing more, though it seemed there should have been more. Was it possible that she had noted and been troubled by the same trouble that haunted Eluric? Three times he had carried the rose rent to her, a matter of . . . how long . . . in her presence? Two minutes annually? Three, perhaps? But no man's shadow clouded Judith Perle's eyes, no living man's. She might, none the less, have become somehow aware, thought Cadfael, not of a young man's physical entrance into her house and presence, but of the nearness of pain.

'I'm going there now,' she said, stirring out of her preoccupation. 'I've lost the buckle of a good girdle, I should like to have a new one made, to match the rosettes that decorate the leather, and the end-tag. Enamel inlay on the bronze. It was a present Edred once made to me. Niall Bronzesmith will be able to copy the design. He's a fine craftsman. I'm glad the abbey has such a good tenant for the house.'

'A decent, quiet man,' agreed Cadfael, 'and keeps the garden well tended. You'll find your rose-bush in very good heart.'

To that she made no reply, only thanked him simply for his services as they entered the great court together, and there separated, she to continue along the Foregate to the large house beyond the abbey forge, where she had spent the few years of her married life, he to the lavatorium to wash his hands before dinner. But he turned at the corner of the cloister to look after her, and watched until she passed through the arch of the gatehouse and vanished from his sight. She had a walk that might be very becoming in an abbess, but to his mind it looked just as well on the capable heiress of the chief clothier in the town. He went on to the refectory convinced that he was right in dissuading her from the conventual life. If she looked upon it as a refuge now, the time might come when it would seem to her a prison, and none the less constricting because she would have entered it willingly.

Chapter Two

THE HOUSE in the Foregate stood well along towards the grassy triangle of the horse-fair ground, where the high road turned the corner of the abbey wall. A lower wall on the opposite side of the road closed in the yard where Niall the bronzesmith had his shop and workshop, and beyond lay the substantial and well-built house with its large garden, and small field of grazing land behind. Niall did a good trade in everything from brooches and buttons, small weights and pins, to metal cooking pots, ewers and dishes, and paid the abbey a suitable rent for his premises. He had even worked occasionally with others of his trade in the founding of bells, but that was a very rare commission, and demanded travel to the site itself, rather than having to transport the heavy bells after casting.

The smith was working in a corner of his shop, on the rim of a dish beaten out in sheet metal, pecking away with punch and mallet at an incised decoration of leaves, when Judith came in to his counter. From the unshuttered window above the work-bench the light fell softly sidewise upon her face and figure, and Niall, turning to see who had entered, stood for a moment at gaze with his tools dangling in either hand, before he laid them down and came to wait upon her.

'Your servant, mistress! What can I do for you?'

They were barely acquaintances, merely shopkeeper-craftsman and customer, and yet the very fact that he now did his work in the house which she had given to the abbey made them study each other with a special intensity. She had been in his shop perhaps five times in the few years since he had rented it; he had supplied her with pins, points for the laces of bodices, small utensils for her kitchen, the matrix for the seal of the Vestier household. He knew her history, the gift of the house had made it public. She knew little of him beyond the fact that he had come to her erstwhile property as the abbey's tenant, and that the man and his work were well regarded in town and Foregate.

Judith laid her damaged girdle upon the long counter, a strip of fine, soft leather, excellently worked and ornamented with a series of small bronze rosettes round the holes for the tongue, and a bronze sheath protecting the end of the belt. The bright enamel inlays within the raised outlines were clear and fresh, but the stitching at the other end had worn through, and the buckle was gone.

'I lost it somewhere in the town,' she said, 'one night after dark, and never noticed under my cloak that girdle and all had slipped down and were gone. When I went back to look for it I could find only the belt, not the buckle. It was muddy weather, and the kennel running with the thaw. My own fault, I knew it was fraying, I should have made it secure.'

'Delicate work,' said the smith, fingering the end-tag with interest. 'That was not bought here, surely?'

'Yes, it was, but at the abbey fair, from a Flemish merchant. I wore it much,' she said, 'in earlier days, but it's been laid by since the winter, when I lost the buckle. Can you make me a new one, to match these colours and designs? It was a long shape – thus!' She drew it on the counter with a fingertip. 'But it need not be so, you could make it oval, or whatever you think suits best.'

Their heads were close together over the counter. She looked up into his face, mildly startled by its nearness, but he was intent upon the detail of the bronzework and inlay, and unaware of her sharp scrutiny. A decent, quiet man, Cadfael had called him, and coming from Cadfael there was nothing dismissive in that description. Decent, quiet men were the backbone of any community, to be respected and valued beyond those who made the biggest commotion and the most noise in the world. Niall the bronzesmith could have provided the portrait for them all. He was of the middle height and the middle years, and even of the middle brown colouring, and his voice was pitched pleasantly low. His age she thought, might be forty years. When he straightened up they stood virtually eye to eye, and the movements of his large, capable hands were smooth, firm and deft.

Everything about him fitted into the picture of the ordinary, worthy soul almost indistinguishable from his neighbour, and yet the sum of the parts was very simply and positively himself and no other man. He had thick brown brows in a wide-boned face, and wide-set eyes of a deep, sunny hazel. There were a few grizzled hairs in his thick brown thatch, and a solid, peaceful jut to his shaven chin.

'Are you in haste for it?' he asked. 'I should like to make a good job of it. If I may take two or three days over it.'

'There's no hurry,' she said readily. 'I've neglected it long enough, another week is no great matter.'

'Then shall I bring it up to you in the town? I know the place. I could save you the walk.' He made the offer civilly but hesitantly, as though it might be taken as presumption rather than simply meant as a courtesy.

She cast a rapid glance about his shop, and saw evidences enough that he had in hand a great deal of work, more than enough to keep him busy all through the labouring day. 'But I think your time is very well filled. If you have a boy, perhaps – but I can as well come for it.'

'I work alone,' said Niall. 'But I'd willingly bring it up to you in the evening, when the light's going. I've no other calls on my time, it's no hardship to work the clock round.'

'You live alone here?' she asked, confirmed in her assumptions about him. 'No wife? No family?'

'I lost my wife, five years ago. I'm used to being alone, it's a simple enough matter to take care of my few needs. But I have a little girl. Her mother died bearing her.' He saw the sudden tension in her face, the faint spark in her eyes as she reared her head and glanced round, half expecting to see some evidence of a child's presence. 'Oh, not here! I should have been hard put to it to care for a newborn babe, and there's my sister, out at Pulley, no great distance, married to Mortimer's steward at the demesne there, and with two boys and a girl of her own, not very much older. My little lass stays there with them, where she has other children for playmates, and a woman's care. I walk over to see her every Sunday, and sometimes in the evenings, too, but she's better with Cecily and John and the youngsters than here solitary with me, leastways while she's still so young.'

Judith drew breath long and deeply. Widower he might be, and his loss there as bitter as hers, but he had one priceless pledge left to him, while she was barren. 'You don't know,' she said abruptly, 'how I envy you. My child I lost.' She had not meant to say so much, but it came out of her naturally and bluntly, and naturally and bluntly he received it.

'I heard of your trouble, mistress I was mortally sorry then, having known the like myself not so long before. But the little one at least was spared to me, I thank God for that. When a man suffers such a wound, he also finds out how to value such a mercy.'

'Yes,' she said, and turned away sharply. 'Well . . . I trust your daughter thrives,' she said, recovering, 'and will always be a joy to you, I'll come for the girdle in three days' time, if that's enough for you. No need to bring it.'

She was in the doorway of the shop before he could speak, and then there seemed nothing of any significance to say. But he watched her cross the yard and turn into the Foregate, and turned back to his work at the bench only when she had vanished from his sight.

It was late in the afternoon, but still an hour short of Vespers at this season of the year, when Brother Eluric, custodian of Saint Mary's altar, slipped almost furtively away from his work in the scriptorium, crossed the great court to the abbot's lodging in its small fenced garden, and asked for audience. His manner was so taut and brittle that Brother Vitalis, chaplain and secretary to Abbot Radulfus, raised questioning eyebrows, and hesitated before announcing him. But Radulfus was absolute that every son of the house in trouble or need of advice must have ready access to him. Vitalis shrugged, and went in to ask leave, which was readily given.

In the panelled parlour the bright sunlight softened into a mellow haze. Eluric halted just within the doorway, and heard the door gently closed at his back. Radulfus was sitting at his desk near the open window, quill in hand, and did not look up for a moment from his writing. Against the light his aquiline profile showed dark and calm, an outline of gold shaping lofty brow and lean cheek. Eluric went in great awe of him, and yet was drawn gratefully to that composure and certainty, so far out of his own scope.

Radulfus put a period to his well-shaped sentence, and laid down his quill in the bronze tray before him. 'Yes, my son? I am here. I am listening.' He looked up. 'If you have need of me, ask freely.'

'Father,' said Eluric, from a throat constricted and dry, and in a voice so low it was barely audible across the room, 'I have a great trouble. I hardly know how to tell it, or how far it must be seen as shame and guilt to me, though God knows I have struggled with it, and been constant in prayer to keep myself from evil. I am both petitioner and penitent, and yet I have not sinned, and by your grace and understanding may still be saved from offence.'

Radulfus eyed him more sharply, and saw the tension that stiffened the young man's body, and set him quivering like a drawn bowstring. An over-intense boy, always racked by remorse for faults as often as not imaginary, or so venial that to inflate them into sins was itself an offence, being a distortion of truth.

'Child,' said the abbot tolerantly, 'from all I know of you, you are too forward to take to your charge as great sins such small matters as a wise man would think unworthy of mention. Beware of inverted pride! Moderation in all things is not the most spectacular path to perfection, but it is the safest and the most modest. Now speak up plainly, and let's see what between us we can do to end your trouble.' And he added briskly: 'Come closer! Let me see you clearly, and hear you make good sense.'

Eluric crept closer, linked his hands before him in a nervous convulsion that whitened the knuckles perceptibly, and moistened his dry lips. 'Father, in eight days' time it will be the day of Saint Winifred's translation, and the rose rent must be paid for the property in the Foregate . . . to Mistress Perle, who gave the house by charter on those terms . . .'

'Yes,' said Radulfus, 'I know it. Well?'

'Father, I came to beg you to release me from this duty. Three times I have carried the rose to her, according to the charter, and with every year it grows harder for me. Do not send me there again! Lift this burden from me, before I founder! It is more than I can bear.' He was shaking violently, and had difficulty in continuing to speak, so that the words came in painful bursts, like gouts of blood from a wound. 'Father, the very sight and sound of her are torment to me, to be in the same room with her is the pain of death. I have prayed, I have kept vigil, I have implored God and the saints for deliverance from sin, but not all my prayers and austerities could keep me from this uninvited love.'

Radulfus sat silent for a while after the last word had been said, and his face had not changed, beyond a certain sharpening of his attention, a steady gleam in his deep-set eyes.

'Love, of itself,' he said at last with deliberation, 'is not sin, cannot be sin, though it may lead into sin. Has any word of this inordinate affection ever been said between you and the woman, any act or look that would blemish your vows or her purity?'

'No! No, Father, never! Never word of any sort but in civil greeting and farewell, and a blessing, due to such a benefactress. Nothing wrong has been done or said, only my heart is the offender. She knows nothing of my torment, she never has nor never will give one thought to me but as the messenger of this house. God forbid she should ever come to know, for she is blameless. It is for her sake, as well as mine, that I pray to be excused from ever seeing her again, for such pain as I feel might well disturb and distress her, even without understanding. The last thing I wish is for her to suffer.'

Radulfus rose abruptly from his seat, and Eluric, drained with the effort of confession and convinced of guilt, sank to his knees and bowed his head into his hands, expecting condemnation. But the abbot merely turned away to the window, and stood for a while looking out into the sunlit afternoon, where his own roses were coming into lavish bud.

No more oblates, the abbot was reflecting ruefully, and thanking God for it. No more taking these babes out of their cradles and severing them from the very sight and sound of women, half the creation stolen out of their world. How can they be expected to deal capably at last with something as strange and daunting to them as dragons? Sooner or later a woman must cross their path, terrible as an army with banners, and those wretched children without arms or armour to withstand the onslaught! We wrong women, and we wrong these boys, to send them unprepared into maturity, whole men defenceless against the first pricking of the flesh. In defending them from perils we have deprived them of the means to defend themselves. Well, no more now! Those who enter here henceforward will be of manhood's years, enter of their own will, bear their own burdens. But this one's burden falls upon me.

He turned back into the room. Eluric knelt brokenly, his smooth young hands spread painfully to cover his face, and slow tears sliding between the fingers.

'Look up!' said Radulfus firmly, and as the young, tortured face was turned up to him fearfully: 'Now answer me truly, and don't be afraid. You have never spoken word of love to this lady?'

'No, Father!'

'Nor she ever offered such a word to you, nor such a look as could inflame or invite love?'

'No, Father, never, never! She is utterly untouched, I am nothing to her.' And he added with despairing tears. 'It is I who have in some way besmirched her, to my shame, by loving her, though she knows nothing of it.'

'Indeed? In what way has your unhappy affection befouled the lady? Tell me this, did ever you let your fancy dwell on touching her? On embracing her? On possessing her?'

'No!' cried Eluric in a great howl of pain and dismay. 'God forbid! How could I so profane her? I revere her, I think of her as of the company of the saints. When I trim the candles her goodness provides, I see her face as a brightness, I am no more than her pilgrim. But ah, it hurts . . .' he said, and bowed himself into the skirts of the abbot's gown and clung there.

'Hush!' said the abbot peremptorily, and laid his hand on the bowed head. 'You use extravagant terms for what is wholly human and natural. Excess is blameworthy, and in that field you do indeed offend. But it is plain that in the matter of this unhappy temptation you have not done ill, but in truth rather well. Nor need you fear any reproach to the lady, whose virtue you do well to extol. You have not harmed her. I know you for one unfailingly truthful, insofar as you see and understand truth. For truth is no simple matter, my son, and the mind of man is stumbling and imperfect in wisdom. I blame myself that I submitted you to this trial. I should have foreseen its severity for one as young and unpractised as you. Get up now! You have what you came to ask. You are excused from this duty henceforth.'

He took Eluric by the wrists, and hoisted him firmly to his feet, for he was so drained and trembling with weakness that it seemed doubtful if he could have risen unaided. The boy began to utter stumbling thanks, his tongue lame now even upon ordinary words. The calm of exhaustion and relief came back gradually to his face. But still he found something to fret him even in his release.

'Father . . . the charter . . . It will be void if the rose is not delivered and the rent paid.'

'The rose will be delivered,' said Radulfus forcibly. 'The rent will be paid. This task I lift here and now from your shoulders. Tend your altar, and give no further thought to how or by whom the duty is undertaken from this day.'

'Father, what more should I do for the cleansing of my soul?' ventured Eluric, quivering to the last subsiding tremors of guilt.

'Penance may well be salutary for you,' admitted the abbot somewhat wearily. 'But beware of making extravagant claims even upon punishment. You are far from a saint – so are we all – but neither are you a notable sinner, nor, my child, will you ever be.'

'God forbid!' whispered Eluric, appalled.

'God does indeed forbid,' said Radulfus drily, 'that we should make more of our virtues or our failings than is due. More than your due you shall not have of, neither praise nor blame. For your soul's ease, go and make your confession as I have ordered, with moderation, but say to your confessor that you have also been with me, and have my countenance and blessing, and are by me delivered from the duty which was too heavy for you. Then perform whatever penance he may give you, and beware of asking or expecting more.'

Brother Eluric went out from the presence on shaky legs, emptied of all feeling, and dreading that this emptines could not last. It was not pleasure, but at least it was not pain. He had been dealt with kindly, he who had come to this interview looking upon success and release from the ordeal of the woman's nearness as the end of all his troubles, yet now this void within him was like the house swept clean in the Bible, ready for residence, aching to be filled, and as apt for devils as for angels.

He did as he had been bidden. Until the end of his novitiate his confessor had been Brother Jerome, ear and shadow of Prior Robert, and from Jerome he could have counted on all the chastisement his over-anxious soul desired. But now it was to the sub-prior, Richard, that he must turn, and Richard was known to be easy and consoling to his penitents, as much out of laziness as kindliness. Eluric did his best to obey the abbot's injunction, not to spare himself but not to accuse himself of what he had not committed, even in his secret mind. When it was done, penance allotted and absolution given, still he kneeled, with closed eyes and brows painfully drawn together.

'Is there more?' asked Richard.

'No, Father . . . No more to tell of what is done. Only I am afraid . . .' the numbness was beginning to melt, a small ache had begun in his guts, the empty house would not long be uninhabited. 'I will do all I may to put away even the memory of this illicit affection, but I am not sure . . . I am not sure! How if I fail? I go in dread of my own heart . . .'

'My son, whenever that heart fails you, you must go to the source of all strength and compassion, and pray to be aided, and grace will not fail you. You serve the altar of Our Lady, who is perfect purity. Where better could you turn for grace?'

Where, indeed! But grace is not a river into which a man can dip his pail at will, but a fountain that plays when it lists, and when it lists is dry and still. Eluric performed his penance before the altar he had newly trimmed, kneeling on the chill tiles of the floor, his whispering voice half-choked with passion, and kneeled still when he was done, with every nerve and sinew of his body imploring plenitude and peace.

Surely he should have been happy, for he was vindicated, delivered from the weight of mortal guilt, saved from ever having to see the face of Judith Perle again, or hear her voice, or breathe the faint sweetness that distilled out of her clothing as she moved. Free of that torment and temptation, he had believed his troubles were at an end. Now he knew better.

He knotted his hands into pain, and burst into a fury of passionate, silent prayers to the Virgin whose faithful servant he was, and who could and must stand by him now. But when he opened his eyes and looked up into the mellow golden cones of the candle-flames, there was the woman's face radiant before him, a dazzling, insistent brightness.

He had escaped nothing, all he had done was to cast away with the unbearable pain the transcendent bliss, and now all he had left was his barren virgin honour, this grim necessity to keep his vows at all costs. He was a man of his word, he would keep his word.

But he would never see her again.

Cadfael came back from the town in good time for Compline, well fed and well wined, and content with his evening's entertainment, though regretful that he would see no more of Aline and his godson Giles for three or four months. Doubtless Hugh would bring them back to the town house for the winter, by which time the boy would be grown out of all knowledge, and approaching his third birthday. Well, better they should spend the warm months up there in the north, at Maesbury, in the healthy caput of Hugh's modest honour, rather than in the congested streets of Shrewsbury, where disease had easier entry and exaggerated power. He ought not to grudge their going, however he was bound to miss them.

It was a warm early twilight as he crossed the bridge, matching his mood of content with its mild and pleasant melancholy. He passed the spot where trees and bushes bordered the path down to the lush riverside level of the Gaye, the abbey's main gardens, and the still silver gleam of the mill-pond on his right, and turned in at the gatehouse. The porter was sitting in the doorway of his lodge in the mild sweet air, taking the cool of the evening very pleasurably, but he also had an eye to his duties and the errand he had been given.

'So there you are!' he said comfortably, as Cadfael entered through the open wicket. 'Gallivanting again! I wish I had a godson up in the town.'

'I had leave,' said Cadfael complacently.

'I've known times when you couldn't have said that so smugly! But yes, I know you had leave tonight, and are back in good time for the office. But that's all one for tonight – Father Abbot wants you in his parlour. As soon as he returns, he said.'

'Does he so, indeed?' Cadfael echoed, brows aloft. 'What's afoot, then, at this hour? Has something wild been happening?'

'Not that I know of, there's been no stir about the place at all, everything as quiet as the night. Just the simple summons. Brother Anselm is sent for, too,' he added placidly. 'No mention of the occasion. Better go now and see.'

So Cadfael thought, too, and betook himself briskly down the length of the great court to the abbot's lodging. Brother Anselm the precentor was there before him, already ensconced on a carved bench against the panelled wall, and it appeared that nothing of too disturbing a nature was towards, for abbot and obedientiary were provided with wine-cups, and the like was offered to Cadfael as soon as he had reported himself in response to the abbot's summons. Anselm moved up on the bench to make room for his friend. The precentor, who also presided over the library, was ten years younger than Cadfael, a vague, unworldly man except where his personal enthusiasms were concerned, but alert and subtle enough in anything that concerned books, music or the instruments that make music, best of all the most perfect, the human voice. The blue eyes that peered out beneath his bushy brown eyebrows and shock of shaggy brown hair might be short-sighted, but they missed very little that went on, and had a tolerant twinkle for fallible human creatures and their failings, especially among the young.

'I have sent for you two,' said Radulfus, when the door was firmly closed, and there was no fourth to overhear, 'because a thing has arisen that I would as lief not bring up in chapter tomorrow. It will certainly be known to one other, but through the confessional, which is secret enough. But else I want it kept within here, between us three. You have both long experience of the world and its pitfalls before you entered the cloister, you will comprehend my reasons. What is fortunate is that you were also the abbey witnesses to the charter by which we acquired the Widow Perle's house here in the Foregate. I have asked Anselm to bring with him a copy of the charter from the lieger-book.'

'I have it here,' said Brother Anselm, half-unfolding the leaf of vellum on his knee.

'Good! Presently! Now the matter is this. This afternoon Brother Eluric, who as custodian of the Lady Chapel altar, which benefits from the gift, seemed the natural person to pay the stipulated rent to the lady each year, came to me and requested to be excused from this duty. For reasons which I should have foreseen. For there is no denying that Mistress Perle is an attractive woman, and Brother Eluric is quite unpractised, young and vulnerable. He says, and I am sure truly, that no ill word or look has ever passed between them, nor has he ever entertained a single lustful thought concerning her. But he wished to be relieved of any further meeting, since he suffers and is tempted.'

It was a carefully temperate description, Cadfael thought, of what ailed Brother Eluric, but mercifully it seemed the disaster had been averted in time. The boy had got his asking, that was plain.

'And you have granted his wish,' said Anselm, rather stating than asking.

'I have. It is our work to teach the young how to deal with the temptations of the world and the flesh, but certainly not our duty to subject them to such temptations. I blame myself that I did not pay sufficient attention to what was arranged, or foresee the consequences. Eluric has behaved emotionally, but

I believe him absolutely when he says he has not sinned, even in thought. I have therefore relieved him of his task. And I do not wish anything of his ordeal to be known among the other brothers. At best it will not be easy for him, let it at least be private, or confined to the few of us. He need not even know that I have confided in you.'

'He shall not,' said Cadfael firmly.

'So then,' said Radulfus, 'having rescued one fallible child from the fire, I am all the more resolved not to subject another equally unprepared to the same danger. I cannot appoint another boy of Eluric's years to carry the rose. And if I nominate an elder, such as yourself, Cadfael, or Anselm here, it will be known all too well what the change means, and Brother Eluric's trouble will become matter for gossip and scandal. Oh, be sure I know that no rule of silence keeps news from spreading like bindweed. No, this must be seen as a change of policy for good and canonical reasons. Which is why I asked for the charter. Its purport I know, but its exact wording I cannot recall. Let us see what the possibilities are. Will you read it aloud, Anselm?'

Anselm unrolled his leaf and read, in the mellifluous voice that rejoiced in swaying hearers in the liturgy:

' "Be it known to all, present and future, that I, Judith, daughter of Richard Vestier and widow of Edred Perle, being in full health of mind, give and bestow, and by this present charter confirm to God and to the altar of Saint Mary in the church of the monks of Shrewsbury, my house in the Monks' Foregate, between the abbey forge and the messuage of Thomas the farrier, together with the garden and field pertaining to it, for an annual rent, during my lifetime, of one rose from the white rose-bush growing beside the north wall, to be delivered to me, Judith, upon the day of translation of Saint Winifred. By these witnesses recorded: as to the abbey, Brother Anselm, precentor, Brother Cadfael; as to the town, John Ruddock, Nicholas of Meole, Henry Wyle." '

'Good!' said the abbot with a deep, satisfied breath, as Anselm lowered the leaf into the lap of his habit. 'So there is no mention of who is to deliver the rent, merely that it must be paid on the fixed day, and into the donor's own hand. So we may excuse Brother Eluric without infringing the terms, and as freely appoint another to bear the rose. There is no restriction, any man appointed may act for the abbey in this matter.'

'That's certain,' agreed Anselm heartily. 'But if you purpose to exclude all the young, Father, for fear of bringing them into temptation, and all of us elders for fear of exposing Brother Eluric to suspicion of, at least, weakness, and at worst, misconduct, are we to look to a lay servant? One of the stewards, perhaps?'

'It would be perfectly permissible,' said Radulfus practically, 'but perhaps might lose something of relevance. I would not wish to diminish the gratitude we feel, and should feel, for the lady's generous gift, nor the respect with which we regard the gesture of her choice of rent. It means much to her, it should and must be dealt with by us with equal gravity. I would welcome your thoughts on the matter.'

'The rose,' said Cadfael, slowly and consideringly, 'comes from the garden and the particular bush which the widow cherished during the years of her marriage, and tended along with her husband. The house has a tenant now, a decent widower and a good craftsman, who has cared for the bush, pruned and fed it ever since he took up household there. Why should not he be asked to deliver the rose? Not roundabout, through a third and by order, but direct from bush to lady? This house is his landlord, as it is her beneficiary, and its blessing goes with the rose without further word said.'

He was not sure himself what had moved him to make the suggestion. It may have been that the evening's wine, rewarmed in him now by the abbot's wine, rekindled with it the memory of the close and happy family he had left up in the town, where the marital warmth as sacred in its way as any monastic vows gave witness to heaven of a beneficent purpose for mankind. Whatever it was that had moved him to speak, surely they were here dealing with a confrontation of special significance between man and woman, as Eluric had all too clearly shown, and the champion sent into the lists might as well be a mature man who already knew about women, and about love, marriage and loss.

'It's a good thought,' said Anselm, having considered it dispassionately. 'If it's to be a layman, who better than the tenant? He also benefits from the gift, the premises suit him very well, his former quarters were too distant from the town and too cramped.'

'And you think he would be willing?' asked the abbot.

'We can but ask. He's already done work for the lady,' said Cadfael, 'they're acquainted. And the better his contacts with the townsfolk, the better for trade. I think he'd have no objection.'

'Then tomorrow,' decided the abbot with satisfaction, 'I will send Vitalis to put the matter to him. And our problem, small though it is, will be happily solved.'

Chapter Three

BROTHER VITALIS had lived so long with documents and accounts and legal points that nothing surprised him, and about nothing that was not written down on vellum did he retain any curiosity. The errands that fell to his lot he discharged punctiliously but without personal interest. He delivered the abbot's message to Niall the bronzesmith word for word, expecting and receiving instant agreement, carried the satisfactory answer back, and promptly forgot the tenant's face. Not one word of one parchment that ever passed through his hands did he forget, those were immutable, even years would only slightly fade them, but the faces of laymen whom he might well never see again, and whom he could not recall ever noticing before, these vanished from his mind far more completely than words erased deliberately from a leaf of vellum to make way for a new text.

'The smith is quite willing,' he reported to Abbot Radulfus on his return, 'and promises faithful delivery.' He had not even wondered why the duty should have been transferred from a brother to a secular agent. It was in any case more seemly, since the donor was a woman.

'That's well,' said the abbot, content, and as promptly dismissed the matter from his mind as finished.

Niall, when he was left alone, stood for some minutes gazing after his departed visitor, leaving the all but completed dish with its incised border neglected on his work-bench, the punch and mallet idle beside it. A small sector of the rim left to do, and then he could turn his hand to the supple leather girdle rolled up on a shelf and waiting for his attention. There would be a small mould to make, the body of the buckle to cast, and then the hammering out of the fine pattern and the mixing of the bright enamels to fill the incisions. Three times since she had brought it in he had unrolled it and run it caressingly through his fingers, dwelling on the delicate precision of the bronze rosettes. For her he would make a thing of beauty, however small and insignificant, and even if she never noticed it but as an article of apparel, a thing of use, at least she would wear it, it would encircle that body of hers that was so slender, too slender, and the buckle would rest close against the womb that had conceived but once and miscarried, leaving her so lasting and bitter a grief.

Not this night, but the night following, when the light began to fade and made fine work impossible, he would close the house and set out on the walk down through Brace Meole to the hamlet of Pulley, a minor manor of the Mortimers, where his sister's husband John Stury farmed the demesne as steward, and Cecily's boisterous children kept his own little girl company, made much of her, and ran wild with her among the chickens and the piglets. He was not utterly bereft, like Judith Perle. There was great consolation in a little daughter. He pitied those who had no children, and most of all such as had carried a child half the long, hard way into this world, only to lose it at last, and too late to conceive again. Judith's child had gone in haste after its father. The wife was left to make her way slowly, and alone.

He had no illusions about her. She knew little of him, desired no more, and thought of him not at all. Her composed courtesy was for every man, her closer regard for none. That he acknowledged without complaint or question. But fate and the lord abbot, and certain monastic scruples about encountering women, no doubt, had so decreed that on one day in the year, at least, he was to see her, to go to her house, to stand in her presence and pay her what was due, exchange a few civil words with her, see her face clearly, even be seen clearly by her, if only for a moment.

He left his work and went out by the house door into the garden. Within the high wall there were fruit trees bedded in grass, and a patch of vegetables, and to one side a narrow, tangled bed of flowers, overcrowded but spangled with bright colour. The white rose-bush grew against the north wall, tall as a man, and clutching the stonework with a dozen long, spiny arms. He had cut it back only seven weeks before, but it made rapid and lengthy growth every year. It was old; dead wood had been cut away from its stem several times, so that it had a thick, knotty bole at the base, and a sinewy stalk that was almost worthy of being called a trunk. A snow of white, half-open buds sprinkled it richly. The blooms were never very large, but of the purest white and very fragrant. There would be no lack of them at their best to choose from, when the day of Saint Winifred's translation came.

She should have the finest to be found on the tree. And even before that day he would see her again, when she came to fetch her girdle. Niall went back to his work with goodwill, shaping the new buckle in his mind while he completed the decoration of the dish for the provost's kitchen.

The burgage of the Vestier family occupied a prominent place at the head of the street called Maerdol, which led downhill to the western bridge. A right-angled house, with wide shop-front on the street, and the long stem of the hall and chambers running well back behind, with a spacious yard and stables. There was room enough in all that elongated building, besides the living rooms of the family, to house ample stores in a good dry undercroft, and provide space for all the girls who carded and combed the newly dyed wool, beside three horizontal looms set up in their own outbuilding, and plenty of room in the long hall for half a dozen spinsters at once. Others worked in their own homes, and so did five other weavers about the town. The Vestiers were the biggest and best-known clothiers in Shrewsbury. Only the dying of the fleeces and fulling of the cloth were put out into the experienced hands of Godfrey Fuller, who had his dye-house and fulling-works and tenterground just down-river, under the wall of the castle.

At this time of year the first fleeces of the clip had already been purchased and sorted, and sent to be dyed, and on this same day had been duly delivered in person by Godfrey. Nor did he seem to be in any hurry to be off about his business, though he was known for a man to whom time was money, and money very dear. So was power. He enjoyed being one of the wealthiest of the town's guildsmen, and was always on the look-out for an extension to his realm and influence. He had his eye, so the common gossip said, on the almost comparable wealth of the Widow Perle, and never neglected an opportunity of urging the benefits of bringing the two together by a match.

Judith had sighed at his staying, but dutifully offered refreshment, and listened patiently to his dogged persuasions, which at least had the decency to avoid any semblance of loving courtship. He spoke solid sense, not dalliance, and all he said was true. His business and hers, put together, and run as well as they were being run now, would become a power in the shire, let alone the town. She would be the gainer, in terms of wealth at least, as well as he. Nor would he make too repulsive a husband, for if he was turned fifty he was still a presentable figure of a man, tall, vigorous, with a long stride on him, and a thick crop of steel-grey hair capping sharp features, and if he valued money, he also valued appearances and refinements, and would see to it, if only for his own prestige, that his wife went decked out as handsomely as any in the county.

'Well, well!' he said, recognising his dismissal and accepting it without resentment, 'I know how to bide my time, mistress, and I'm not one to give up short of the victory, not one to change my mind, neither. You'll come to see the rights of what I've said, and I'm not afraid to stand my ground against any of these young fly-by-nights that have nothing to offer you but their pretty faces. Mine has seen long service, but I'll back it against theirs any day. You have too much good sense, girl, to choose a lad for his dainty seat on a horse, or his pink and yellow beauty. And think well on all we could do between us, if we had the whole of the trade brought together in our hands, from the ewe's back to the cloth on the counter and the gown on the customer's back.'

'I have thought of it,' she said simply, 'but the truth is, Master Fuller, I do not purpose to marry again.'

'Purposes can change,' said Godfrey firmly, and rose to take his leave. The hand she gave him resignedly he raised to his lips.

'Yours, too?' she said with a faint smile.

'My mind won't change. If yours does, here am I waiting.' And with that he did leave her, as briskly as he had come. Certainly there seemed to be no end to his persistence and patience, but fifty can ill afford to wait too long. Very soon she might have to do something decisive about Godfrey Fuller, and against that massive assurance it was hard to see what she could do but what she had been doing all along, fend him off and be as constant in denial as he was in demanding. She had been brought up to take good care of her business and her labourers, no less than he, she could ill afford to take her dyeing and fulling to another master.

Aunt Agatha Coliar, who had sat a little apart, sewing, bit off her thread, and said in the sweet, indulgent voice she affected sometimes towards the niece who kept her in comfort: 'You'll never rid yourself of him by being too civil. He takes it for encouragement.'

'He has a right to speak his mind,' said Judith indifferently, 'and he's in no doubt about mine. As often as he asks, I can refuse.'

'Oh, my dear soul, I trust you can. He's not the man for you. Nor none of those youngsters he spoke of, neither. You well know there's no second in the world for one who's known joy with the first. Better by far go the leave of the way alone! I still grieve for my own man, after all these years. I could never look at any other, after him.' So she had said, sighing and shaking her head and wiping away a facile tear, a thousand times since she had kept the storehouse and the linen here, and brought her son to help manage the business. 'If it had not been for my boy, who was young then to fend for himself, I would have taken the veil that same year that Will died. There'd be no fortune-hunting lads pestering a woman in the cloister. Peace of mind there'd be there.' She was off upon her best theme, and sometimes seemed almost to forget that she was talking to anyone but herself.

She had been a pretty woman in youth, and still had a round, rosy, comfortable freshness, somewhat contradicted by the alert sharpness of her blue eyes, and the taut smile that visited her mouth very often when it should have been relaxed and easy in repose, as if shrewd thoughts within wore her soft outward seeming like a disguise. Judith could not remember her own mother, and often wondered if there had been much resemblance between the sisters. But these, mother and son, were the only kin she had, and she had taken them in without hesitation. Miles more than earned his keep, for he had shown himself an excellent manager during the long decline of Edred's health, when Judith had had no thought to spare for anything but her husband and the child to come. She had not had the heart, when she returned to the shop, to take back the reins into her own hands. Though she did her share, and kept a dutiful eye upon everything, she let him continue as master-clothier. So influential a house fared better with a man in the forefront.

'But there,' sighed Agatha, folding her sewing on her spacious lap and dropping a tear on the hem. 'I had my duty to do in the world, there was to be no such calm and quiet for me. But you have no chick nor child to cling to you, my poor dear, and nothing now to tie you to the world, if it should please you to leave it. You did speak of it once. Oh, take good thought, do nothing in haste. But should it come to that, there's nothing to hold you back.'

No, nothing! And sometimes the world did seem to Judith a waste, a tedium, hardly worth keeping. And in a day or two, perhaps tomorrow, Sister Magdalen would be coming from Godric's Ford, from the forest cell of the abbey of Polesworth, to fetch away Brother Edmund's niece as a postulant. She could as well take back with her two aspiring novices as one.

Judith was in the spinning room with the women when Sister Magdalen arrived, early the following afternoon. As heiress to the clothier's business for want of a brother, she had learned all the skills involved, from teasing and carding to the loom, and the final cutting of garments, though she found herself much out of practice now at the distaff. The sheaf of carded wool before her was russet-red. Even the dye-stuffs came seasonally, and last summer's crop of wool for the blues was generally used up by April or May, to be followed by these variations on reds and browns and yellows, which Godfrey Fuller produced from the lichens and madders. He knew his craft. The lengths of cloth he would finally get back for fulling had a clear, fast colour, and fetched good prices.

It was Miles who came looking for her. 'You have a visitor,' he said, reaching over Judith's shoulder to rub a strand of wool from the distaff between fingers and thumb, with cautious approval. 'There's a nun from Godric's Ford sitting in your small chamber, waiting for you. She says they told her at the abbey you'd be glad of a word with her. You're not still playing with the notion of quitting the world, are you? I thought that nonsense was over.'

'I did tell Brother Cadfael I should like to see her,' said Judith, stilling her spindle. 'No more than that. She's here to fetch a new novice away – the infirmarer's sister's girl.'

'Then don't you be fool enough to offer her a second. Though you do have your follies, as I know,' he said lightly, and clapped her affectionately on the shoulder. 'Like giving away for a rose-leaf the best property in the Foregate. Do you intend to cap that by giving away yourself?'

He was two years older than his cousin, and given to playing the elder, full of sage advice, though with a lightness that tempered the image. A young man very neatly and compactly made, strong and lissome, and as good at riding and wrestling and shooting at the butts by the riverside as he was at managing a clothier's business. He had his mother's blue, alert eyes and light-brown hair, but none of her blurred complacency. All that was, or seemed, vague and shallow in the mother became clear and decisive in the son. Judith had had good cause to be glad of him, and to rely on his solid good sense in all matters concerning commerce.

'I may do as I please with myself,' she said, rising and laying her spindle down in safety with its cone of russet yarn, 'if only I knew what *does* best please me! But truth to tell, I'm utterly in the dark. All I've done is to say I should be glad to talk to her. So I shall, I like Sister Magdalen.'

'So do I,' agreed Miles heartily. 'But I should grudge you to her. This house would founder without you.'

'Folly!' said Judith sharply. 'You know well enough it could fare as well without me as with me. It's you who hold up the roof, not I.'

If he disclaimed that, she did not wait to hear, but gave him a sudden reassuring smile and a touch of her hand on his sleeve as she passed, and went to join her guest. Miles had a ruthless honesty, he knew that what she had said was no more than truth, he could have run everything here without her. The sharp reminder pricked her. She was indeed expendable, a woman without purpose here in this world, she might well consider whether there was not a better use for her out of the world. In urging her against it, he had reopened the hollow in her heart, and turned her thoughts again towards the cloister.

Sister Magdalen was sitting on a cushioned bench beside the unshuttered window in Judith's small private chamber, broad, composed and placid in her black habit. Agatha had brought her fruit and wine, and left her to herself, for she went in some awe of her. Judith sat down beside her visitor.

'Cadfael has told me,' said the nun simply, 'what ails you, and what you have confided to him. God forbid I should press you one way or the other, for in the end the decision is yours to make, and no other can make it for you. I am taking into account how grievous your losses have been.'

'I envy you,' said Judith, looking down into her linked hands. 'You are kind, and I am sure you are wise and strong. I do not believe I am now any of these things, and it is tempting to lean upon someone who is. Oh, I do live, I do work, I have not abandoned house, or kinsfolk, or duties. Yet all this could as well go on without me. My cousin has just shown me as much by denying it. It would be a most welcome refuge, to have a vocation elsewhere.'

'Which you have not,' said Sister Magdalen shrewdly, 'or you could not have said that.' Her sudden smile was like a ray of warmth, and the dimple that darted in and out of her cheek sparkled and was gone.

'No. Brother Cadfael said as much. He said the religious life should not be embraced as a second-best, but only as the best – not a hiding-place, but a passion.'

'He would be hard put to it to apply that to me,' said Sister Magdalen bluntly. 'But neither do I recommend to others what I myself do. If truth be told, I am no example to any woman. I took what I chose, I have still some years of life in which to pay for it. And if the debt is not discharged by then, I'll pay the balance after, ungrudging. But you have incurred no such debt, and I do not think you should. The price comes high. You, I judge, will do better to wait, and spend your substance for something different.'

'I know of nothing,' said Judith bleakly, after a long moment of thought, 'that I find worth buying in this world now. But you and Brother Cadfael are right, if I took the veil I should be hiding behind a lie. All I covet in the cloister is the quiet, and the wall around me, keeping the world out.'

'Bear in mind, then,' said the nun emphatically, 'that our doors are not closed against any woman in need, and the quiet is not reserved for those who have taken vows. The time may come when you truly need a place to be apart, time for thought and rest, even time to recover lost courage, though of that I think you have enough. I said I would not advise, and I am advising. Wait, bear with things as they are. But if ever you need a place to hide, for a little while or a long while, come to Godric's Ford and bring all your frets in with you, and you shall find a refuge for as long as you need, with no vows taken, never unless you come to it with a whole heart. And I will keep the door against the world until you see fit to go forth again.'

Late after supper that night, in the small manor-house of Pulley, in the open scrubland fringes of the Long Forest, Niall opened the outer door of his brother-in-law's timber hall, and looked out into the twilight that was just deepening into night. He had a walk of three miles or so before him, back to his house in the Foregate of the town, but it was a familiar and pleasant walk in fair weather, and he was accustomed to making the trip two or three times in the week after work, and home in the early dark, to be up and at work again betimes in the morning. But on this night he saw with some surprise that there was a steady rain falling, so quietly and straightly that within the house they had been quite unaware of it.

'Bide overnight,' said his sister at his shoulder. 'No need to get wet through, and this won't last the night out.'

'I don't mind it,' said Niall simply. 'I shan't hurt.'

'With all that way to go? Get some sense,' advised Cecily comfortably, 'and stay here in the dry, there's room enough, and you know you're welcome. You can be up and away in good time tomorrow, no fear of oversleeping, these early dawns.'

'Shut the door on it,' urged John from the table, 'and come and have another sup. Better wet inside than out. It's not often we have time for a talk among the three of us, after the children are all abed and asleep.'

With four of them about the place, and all lively as squirrels, that was true enough; the grown folk were at the beck and call of their young for all manner of services, mending toys, joining in games, telling stores, singing rhymes. Cecily's two boys and a girl ranged from ten years old down to six, and Niall's own chick was the youngest and the pet. Now all four were curled up like a litter of puppies on their hay mattresses in the little loft, fast asleep, and round the trestle table in the hall the elders could talk freely without disturbing them.

It had been a good day for Niall. He had cast and decorated and polished the new buckle for Judith's girdle, and was not displeased with his work. Tomorrow she might come to fetch it, and if he saw pleasure in her eyes when she took it, he would be well rewarded. Meantime, why not settle here cosily for the night, and get up with the dawn to a newly washed world, and a sweet green walk home?

He slept well, and was roused at first light by the usual wild, waking rapture of the birds, at once sweet and strident. Cecily was up and busy, and had small ale and bread ready for him. She was younger than he, fair and benign, happy in her husband and a born hand with children, no wonder the motherless child thrived here. Stury would take nothing for her keep. What was one more little bird, he said, in a full nest? And indeed the family was well provided here, keeping Mortimer's little manor prosperous and in good repair, the cleared fields productive, the forest well managed, the small coppice ditched against the invading deer. A good place for children. And yet it was always an effort to set out for the town, and leave her behind, and he visited often for fear she should begin to forget that she was his, and not the youngest of the Stury brood, fathered and mothered here from birth.

Niall set out through an early morning moist and sweet, the rain over, seemingly, for some hours, for though the grass sparkled, the open soil had swallowed up the fall, and was beginning to dry. The first long, low beams of the rising sun lanced through the trees and drew patterns of light and dark along the ground. The first passion of bird-song gradually softened and lost its belligerence, grew busy and sweet and at ease. Here also the nests were full of fledgelings, hard work day-long to feed them all.

The first mile was through the edges of the forest, the ground opening gradually into heath and scrub, dotted with small groves of trees. Then he came to the hamlet of Brace Meole, and from there it was a beaten road, widening as it neared the town into a cart-track, which crossed the Meole Brook by a narrow bridge, and brought him into the Foregate between the stone bridge into the town and the mill and the mill-pond at the edge of the abbey enclave. He had set off early and walked briskly, and the Foregate was still barely awake; only a few cottagers and labourers were up and about their business, and gave him good day as he passed. The monks were not yet down for Prime, there was no sound in the church as Niall went by, but faintly from the dortoir the waking bell was ringing. The high road had dried after the rain, but the soil of the gardens showed richly dark, promising grateful growth.

He came to the gate in his own burgage wall, and let himself through into the yard, set the door of his shop open, and made ready for the day's work. Judith's girdle lay coiled on a shelf. He held his hand from taking it down to caress yet again, for he had no rights in her, and never would have. But this very day he might at least see her again and hear her voice, and in five days' time he surely would, and that in her own house. Their hands might touch on the stem of the rose. He would choose carefully, wary of offering her thorns, who had been pierced by too many and too sharp thorns already in her brief life.

The thought drove him out into the garden, which lay behind the yard, entered by a door from the house and a wicket in the wall from the yard. After the indoor chill left from the night, the bright sunlight embraced him in the doorway, a scarf of warmth, and gleamed moistly through the branches of the fruit trees and over the tangled flower-bed. He took one step over the threshold and halted, stricken and appalled.

Against the north wall the white rose-bush sagged sidelong, its thorny arms dragged from the stone, its thickened bole hacked in a long, downward gash that split away a third of its weight and growth dangling into the grass. Beneath it the soil of the bed was stirred and churned as if dogs had battled there, and beside the battlefield lay huddled a still heap of rusty black, half sunk in the grass. Niall took no more than three hasty steps towards the wreckage when he saw the pale gleam of a naked ankle jutting from the heap, an arm in a wide black sleeve flung out, a hand convulsively clenched into the soil, and the pallid circle of a tonsure startingly white in all the blackness. A monk of Shrewsbury, young and slight, almost more habit than body within it, and what, in God's name, was he doing here, dead or wounded under the wounded tree?

Niall went close and kneeled beside him, in too much awe, at first, to touch. Then he saw the knife, lying close beside the outstretched hand, its blade glazed with drying blood. There was a thick dark moisture that was not rain, sodden into the soil under the body. The forearm exposed by the wide black sleeve was smooth and fair. This was no more than a boy. Niall reached a hand to touch at last, and the flesh was chill but not yet cold. Nevertheless, he knew death. With careful dread he eased a hand under the head, and turned to the morning light the soiled young face of Brother Eluric.

Chapter Four

BROTHER JEROME, who counted heads and censored behaviour in all the brothers, young and old, and whether within his province or no, had marked the silence within one dormitory cell when all the rest were rising dutifully for Prime, and made it his business to look within, somewhat surprised in this case, for Brother Eluric rated normally as a model of virtue. But even the virtuous may backslide now and then, and the opportunity to reprove so exemplary a brother came rarely, and was certainly not to be missed. This time Jerome's zeal was wasted, and the pious words of reproach died unspoken, for the cell was empty, the cot immaculately neat, the breviary open on the narrow desk. Brother Eluric had surely risen ahead of his kin, and was already on his knees somewhere in the church, engaged in supererogatory prayer. Jerome felt cheated, and snapped with more than his usual acidity at any who looked blear-eyed with sleep, or came yawning to the night-stairs. He was equally at odds with those who exceeded him in devotion and those who fell short. One way or another, Eluric would pay for this check.

Once they were all in their stalls in the choir, and Brother Anselm was launched into the liturgy – how could a man past fifty, who spoke in a round, human voice deeper than most, sing at will in that upper register, like the most perfect of boy cantors? And how dared he! – Jerome again began to count heads, and grew even happier in his self-vindication, for there was one missing, and that one was Brother Eluric. The fallen paragon, who had actually won his way into Prior Robert's dignified and influential favour, to Jerome's jealous concern! Let him look to his laurels now! The prior would never demean himself to count or search for defections, but he would listen when they were brought to his notice.

Prime came to its end, and the brothers began to file back to the night-stairs, to complete their toilets and make ready for breakfast. Jerome lingered to sidle confidentially to Prior Robert's elbow, and whisper into his ear, with righteous disapproval: 'Father, we have a truant this morning. Brother Eluric was not present in church. Nor is he in his cell. All is left in order there, I thought surely he was before us into the church. Now I cannot think where he may be, nor what he is about, to neglect his duties so.'

Prior Robert in his turn paused and frowned. 'Strange! He of all people! Have you looked in the Lady Chapel? If he rose very early to tend the altar and has lingered long in prayer he may have fallen asleep. The best of us may do so.'

But Brother Eluric was not in the Lady Chapel. Prior Robert hurried to detain the abbot on his way across the great court towards his lodging.

'Father Abbot, we are in some concern over Brother Eluric.'

The name produced instant and sharp attention. Abbot Radulfus turned a fixed and guarded countenance. 'Brother Eluric? Why, what of him?'

'He was not in attendance at Prime, and he is nowhere to be found. Nowhere, at least, that he should be at this hour. It is not like him to absent himself from the office,' said the prior fairly.

'It is not. He is a devoted soul.' The abbot spoke almost absently, for his mind was back in the privacy of his parlour, facing that all too brittle devotee as he poured out his illicit and bravely resisted love. This reminder came all too aptly. How if confession and absolution and the release from temptation had not been enough? Radulfus, not a hesitant man, was still hesitating how to act now, when they were interrupted by the sight of the porter coming down from the gatehouse at a scurrying run, skirts and sleeves flying.

'Father Abbot, there's one here at the gate, the bronzesmith who rents the Widow Perle's old house, says he has dire news that won't wait. He asks for you – would not give me the message –'

'I'll come,' said Radulfus instantly. And to the prior, who would have made to follow him: 'Robert, do you have someone search further, the gardens, the grange court . . . If you do not find him, come back to me.' And he was off at a long, raking stride towards the gate, and the authority of his voice and the vehemence of his going forbade pursuit. There were too many interwoven threads here – the lady of the rose, the house of the rose, the tenant who had willingly undertaken the errand Eluric dreaded, and now Eluric lost from within, and dire news entering from without. A woven pattern began to appear, and its colours were sombre.

Niall was waiting at the door of the porter's lodge, his broad, strongly boned face very still and blanched with shock under its summer brown.

'You asked for me,' said Radulfus quietly, viewing him with a steady, measuring stare. 'I am here. What is this news you bring?'

'My lord,' said Niall, 'I thought best you should know it first alone, and then dispose as you see fit. Last night I lay at my sister's home overnight because of the rain. When I came back this morning I went into the garden. My lord, Mistress Perle's rose-bush has been hacked and broken, and one of your brothers lies dead there under it.'

After a brief, profound silence Radulfus said: 'If you know him, name him.'

'I do know him. For three years he came to the garden to cut the rose for Mistress Perle. He is Brother Eluric, the custodian of Saint Mary's altar.'

This time the silence was longer and deeper. Then the abbot asked simply: 'How long since you discovered him there?'

'About the length of Prime, my lord, for it was nearly the hour when I passed the church on my way home. I came at once, but the porter would not disturb you during the office.'

'And you left all as you found it? Touched nothing?'

'I lifted his head to see his face. Nothing else. He lies just as I found him.'

'Good!' said Radulfus, and winced at using the word even for one right act, where everything else went grimly awry. 'Then wait but a moment, while I send for certain others, and we will go back with you to that garden.'

Those he took with him, saying nothing as yet to any other, even the prior, were Brother Anselm and Brother Cadfael,

witnesses for the abbey to the charter drawn up with
Perle. They alone had been told of Brother Eluric's tr
and shared the sorry knowledge that might be relevant
The young man's confessor was silenced by his office, an
any case Sub-Prior Richard was not the man Radulfus wo d
have chosen as a wise counsellor in such dark matters.

The four of them stood in silence round the body of Brother Eluric, taking in the pitiful heap of black folds, the outflung hand, the mangled tree and the bloody knife. Niall had withdrawn a few paces to leave them alone, but stood watchful in attendance, to answer whatever they might ask.

'Poor tormented child,' said Radulfus heavily. 'I doubt I failed him fatally, his disease was worse than I knew. He begged to be relieved of his task, but surely he grudged it to any other, and has tried here to destroy the bush. And himself with it.'

Cadfael was silent, his eyes roving thoughtfully over the trampled ground. They had all refrained from treading too close, nothing had been disturbed since Niall went on his knees to turn the pallid face up to the light.

'Is that how you read it?' asked Anselm. 'Are we to condemn him as a suicide? However we may pity?'

'What else can it be? Surely this involuntary love had so eaten into him that he could not bear another should take his place with the women. Why else should he steal out by night and come here to this garden, why else should he hack at the roots of the tree? And from that it would be but a step, in his despair, to the unholy temptation to destroy himself with the roses. What could fix his image more terribly and for ever in her memory than such a death? For you know – you two do know – the measure of his desperation. And there lies the knife beside his hand.'

It was not a dagger, but a good, long-hafted knife, sharp and thin, such as any practical man might carry on him for a dozen lawful purposes, from carving his meat at the table to scaring off footpads on a journey, or the occasional wild boar in the forest.

'Beside it,' said Cadfael shortly, 'not in it.'

They turned their eyes on him cautiously, even hopefully.

'You see how his hand is clenched into the soil,' he went on slowly, 'and there is no blood upon it, though the knife is bloodied to the hilt. Touch his hand – I think you'll find it is already stiffening as it lies, clutching the earth. He never held this knife. And if he had, would not the sheath be on his girdle? No man in his senses would carry such a knife about him unsheathed.'

'A man not in his right sense might, however,' said Radulfus ruefully. 'He needed it, did he not, for what he has done to the rose-bush.'

'What was done to the rose-bush,' said Cadfael firmly, 'was not done with that knife. Could not be! A man would have to saw away for half an hour or more, even with a sharp knife, at such a thick bole. That was done with a heavier weapon, meant for such work, a broom-hook or a hatchet. Moreoever, you see the gash begins higher, where a single blow, or two at the most, should have severed the stem, but it swerves downwards into the thick of the bole, where dead wood has been cut away for years, and left this woody encrustation.'

'I fear,' said Brother Anselm wryly, 'that Brother Eluric would hardly be expert with such a tool.'

'And there was no second blow,' said Cadfael, undeterred. 'If there had been, the bush would be severed utterly. And the first blow, I think, the only blow – even that was deflected. Someone interrupted the act. Someone clutched at the arm that was swinging the hatchet, and sent the blade down into the thick of the bole. I think – I *think* – it stuck fast there, and the man who held it had not time to get both hands to the haft and pull it out. Why else should he draw his knife?'

'You are saying,' said Radulfus intently, 'that there were two men here in the night, not one? One who tried to destroy, and one who tried to prevent?'

'Yes, that is what I see here.'

'And that the one who tried to protect the tree, who caught at the attacker's arm and caused his weapon to lodge fast – and who was struck down instead with the knife . . .'

'Is Brother Eluric. Yes. How else can it have been? Certainly he came here secretly in the night of his own will, but not to destroy, rather to take a last farewell of this wild dream of his, to look for one last time on the roses, and then never no more. But he came just in time to see another man here, one who had other thoughts, and for other motives, one who had come to destroy the rose-bush. Would Eluric endure to see that done? Surely he leaped to protect the tree, clutched at the arm wielding the hatchet, drove the blade down to stick fast in the bole. If there was a struggle, as the ground shows, I do not think it lasted long. Eluric was unarmed. The other, if he could not then make use of his hatchet, carried a knife. And used it.'

There was a long silence, while they all stared at him and thought out slowly the implications of what he was saying. And gradually something of conviction came easefully. For if Eluric was not a suicide, but had gone to his end faithfully bearing his burden and seeking to prevent an evil act, then his resting-place in the cemetery was assured, and his passage through death, however his account might stand for little sins needing purging, as safe as a prodigal son re-entering his father's house.

'If it were not as I've said,' Cadfael pointed out, 'then the hatchet would still be here in the garden. It is not. And certainly it was not our brother here who carried it away. And neither did he bring it here, I pledge my word on that.'

'Yet if this is true,' said Anselm consideringly, 'the other did not stay to complete his work.'

'No, he lugged out his hatchet and made off as fast as he could, away from the place where he had made himself a murderer. A thing I daresay he never intended, done in a moment of alarm and terror, when this poor lad in his outrage lunged at him. He would run from Eluric dead in far greater horror than he ever need have done from Eluric living.'

'Nevertheless,' said Abbot Radulfus strongly, 'this is murder.'

'It is.'

'Then I must send word to the castle. It is for the secular authorities to pursue murderers. A pity,' he said, 'that Hugh Beringar is gone north, we shall have to wait for his return, though no doubt Alan Herbard will send to him at once, and let him know what has happened. Is there more that we here must do, before we have Brother Eluric carried home?'

'We can at least observe, whatever is here to be seen, Father. One thing I can tell you, indeed you yourself will see it, what happened here happened after the rain stopped. The ground was soft when they came together here, see how they've marked it. And back and shoulder of the boy's habit are dry. May we now move him? There are witnesses enough here as to how he was found.'

They stooped in all reverence and lifted the stiffening but not yet rigid body, and laid him out on the grass, stretched on his back. From throat to toes the front of his habit was dark with the moisture from the earth, and the great dark stain of his blood clotted the cloth over his left breast. His face, if it had borne the stamp of sudden anger, dread and pain, had now lost that tension, and eased into the smoothness of youth and innocence. Only his eyes, half-open, retained the frowning anxiety of a troubled soul. Radulfus stooped and closed them gently, and wiped the mud from the pale cheeks.

'You take a load from my heart, Cadfael. Surely you are right, he did not take his own life, it was rapt from him cruelly and unjustly, and there must be a price to pay for it. But as for this child here, he is safe enough. I would I had known better how to deal with him, he might still have been living.' He drew the two smooth hands together, and folded them on the bloodied breast.

'I sleep too well,' said Cadfael wryly, 'I never heard when the rain ceased. Did anyone mark the end of it?'

Niall had drawn a little nearer, waiting patiently in case anything further should be required of him.

'It was over by about midnight,' he said, 'for before we went to our beds, there at Pulley, my sister opened the door and looked out, and said that the sky had cleared and it was bidding to be a fine night. But it was too late to start out then.' He added, putting his own interpretation on the way they turned to look at him, after so long of forgetting his presence: 'My sister and her man and the children will tell you I stayed the night over, and left in the dawn. It might be said a family will hold together, however. But I can tell you the names of two or three I said good day to, coming back along the Foregate this morning. They'll bear me out.'

The abbot gave him a startled and preoccupied look, and understood. 'Such checks and counter-checks are for the sheriff's men,' he said. 'But I make no doubt you've told us simple truth. And the rain was over by midnight, you say?'

'It was, my lord. There's but three miles between, it would surely be much the same here.'

'It fits well,' said Cadfael, kneeling over the body. 'He must surely have died about six or seven hours ago. And since he came after the rain stopped, when the ground was soft and moist to tread, there should be traces they've left after them. Here they've stamped the ground raw between them, there's nothing clear, but by one way or another they walked in here in the night, and one walked out again.'

He rose from his knees and rubbed his moist palms together. 'Hold your places where you stand, and look about you. We may have trampled out something of value ourselves, but at least all of us here but one wear sandals, and so did Eluric. Master Bronzesmith, how did you enter here this morning, when you found him?'

'Through the house-door,' said Niall, nodding in that direction.

'And when Brother Eluric came each year to fetch the rose, how did he enter?'

'Through the wicket from the front yard, as we did now. And was very quiet and modest about it.'

'Then this night past, coming with no ill intent, though so secretly, surely he would come as he always came. Let us see,' said Cadfael, treading carefully along the grass to the wicket gate in the wall, 'if any but sandalled feet came that way.'

The earth path, watered into mud by the rain, and again dried into a smooth, soft surface, had taken all their entering footprints and held them clear to view, three pairs of flat soles, here and there overlaid one on another. Or were there four pairs? With these common sandals size meant nothing very helpful, but Cadfael thought he could detect, among all those prints entering and none leaving, one which had trodden deeper than the rest, having entered here while the ground was wetter than now, and by lucky chance escaped being trodden out of shape with their morning invasion. There was also a broad, sturdy shoe-sole, recent like the sandals, which Niall claimed for his, and showed as much by fitting his foot to it.

'Whoever the second was,' said Cadfael, 'I fancy he did not come by the front way, as innocent men do. Nor leave by it, either, having left a dead man behind here. Let us look elsewhere.'

On the eastward side the garden was hemmed in by the wall of the house belonging to Thomas the farrier, on the west by Niall's workshop and dwelling; there was no way out there. But to the rear, on the other side of the north wall, lay a paddock, very easily entered from the fields, and no way overlooked by any building. A few paces along the wall from the mutilated rose-bush there was a vine growing, crabbed and old and seldom fruitful. A part of its twisted trunk had been pulled away from the wall, and when Niall approached it closely he saw that where the trunk turned sidelong and afforded a foothold, a foot had indeed scored it, mounting in panic haste.

'Here! Here he climbed. The ground is higher outside in the paddock, but leaving he needed a holt on the way.'

They drew close, peering. The climber's boot had scatched the bark and left soil in the scratches. And below, in the exposed earth of the bed, the other foot, the left, had stamped a deep and perfect print as he lunged upwards, for he had had to reach high. A booted foot, with a raised heel that had dug deep, but less deep on the outer edge at the back, where the wearer habitually trod his boot down. By the shape his footgear had been well made, but well worn also. There was a fine ridge of earth that crossed from below the great toe diagonally half across the sole, narrowing to vanishing point as it went, left by a crack in the leather. Opposite the downtrodden heel, the toe also had left an imprint shallowing slightly. Whoever the man was, he trod from the left of the heel clean to the right of the toe with this left foot. His spring from the ground had forced the print in deep, but his foot had left the soil cleanly, and the wet earth, gradually drying, had preserved the perfect mould.

'A little warm wax,' said Cadfael, half to himself, intently staring, 'a little warm wax and a steady hand, and we have him by the heel!'

They were so intent upon that single spot, the last remaining trace of Brother Eluric's murderer, that none of them heard the light footsteps approaching the open house-door from within, or caught in the corner of an eye the slight gleam of the sun upon movement and colour, as Judith came into the doorway. She had found the workshop empty, and waited some minutes for Niall to appear. But since the door into his living quarters was wide open as he had left it, and the shifting green and gold of sunlit branches stirring showed in reflection across the room within, and since she knew the house so well, she had ventured to pass through to find him in the garden, where she judged he must be.

'I ask pardon,' she was saying as she stepped into the doorway, 'but the doors were open, I did call –'

She broke off there, startled and bewildered to see the whole group of them swing about and stare in consternation at her. Three black Benedictine habits gathered beside the old, barren vine, and one of them the lord abbot himself. What errand could they possibly have here?

'Oh, forgive me,' she began haltingly. 'I didn't know . . .'

Niall sprang out of his shocked stillness and came running, putting himself between her and what else she might see if once she took her eyes off the abbot. He spread an arm protectively to urge her back into the house.

'Come within, mistress, here's nothing to trouble you. I have the girdle ready. You're early, I hadn't expected you . . .'

He was not good at providing a flood of reassuring words. She held her ground, and over his shoulder she swept the enclosed space of the garden with dilated eyes blanched into the chill grey of glass, and found the still body lying aloof and indifferent in the grass. She saw the pale oval of the face, the pale cross of the hands on the breast of the habit, the hacked bole of the rose-bush, and its sagging branches torn from the wall. As yet she neither recognised the dead youth, not understood at all what could have been happening here. But all too well she understood that whatever befell in this place, between these walls which had once been hers, somehow lay heavy upon her, as if she had set in motion some terrible procession of events which she was powerless to stop, as if a gathering guilt had begun to fold round her, and mock her with her purity of intent and the corruption of its consquences.

She made no sound at all, she did not shrink, or yield to Niall's awkward, concerned pleading: 'Come, come within and sit you down quietly, and leave all here to the lord abbot. Come!' He had an arm about her, rather persuading than supporting, for she stood quite still and erect, not a quiver in her body. She laid her hands on his shoulders, resisting his urging with resigned determination.

'No, let me be. This has to do with me. I know it.'

They were all drawing anxiously about her by then. The abbot accepted necessity. 'Madam, there is here matter that must distress you, that we cannot deny. I will not hide anything from you. This house is your gift, and truth is your due. But you must not take to yourself more than is customary from any godly gentlewoman in compassion for a young life taken untimely. No part of this stems from you, and no part of what must be done about it falls to your duty. Go within, and all that we know – all that is of consequence – you shall be told, I promise it.'

She hesitated, her eyes still on the dead youth. 'Father, I will not further embitter what is surely hard enough for you,' she said slowly. 'But let me see him. I owe him that.'

Radulfus looked her in the eyes, and stood aside. Niall took away his arm from about her almost stealthily, for fear she should suddenly become aware of his touch in that instant when it was removed. She crossed the grass with a firm and steady step, and stood looking down at Brother Eluric. In death he looked even younger and more vulnerable than in life, for all his immovable calm. Judith reached over him to the dangling, wounded bush, plucked one of the half-open buds, and slipped it carefully into his folded hands.

'For all those you brought to me,' she said. And to the rest of those present, raising her head: 'Yes, it is he. I knew it must be he.'

'Brother Eluric,' said the abbot.

'I never knew his name. Is not that strange?' She looked round them all, from face to face, with drawn brows. 'I never asked, and he never told. So few words we ever had to say to each other, and too late now for more.' She fastened last and longest, and with the first returning warmth of pain in her eyes as the numbness passed, on Cadfael, whom she knew best here. 'How could this happen?' she said.

'Come within now,' said Cadfael, 'and you shall know.'

Chapter Five

THE ABBOT and Brother Anselm departed, back to the abbey to send men with a litter to bring Brother Eluric home, and a messenger to Hugh's young deputy at the castle, to warn him he had a murder on his hands. Very soon word would go forth through the Foregate that a brother was mysteriously dead, and many and strange rumours would be blown on the summer winds all through the town. Some carefully truncated version of Eluric's tragedy the abbot would surely make public, to silence the wildest tales. He would not lie, but he would judiciously omit what was eternally private between himself, the two brother witnesses, and the dead man. Cadfael could guess how it would read. It had been decided, on maturer reflection, that it would be more suitable for the rose rent to be paid direct by the tenant, rather than by the custodian of the altar of Saint Mary, and therefore Brother Eluric had been excused from the duty he had formerly fulfilled. That he had gone in secret to the garden was perhaps foolish, but not blameworthy. No doubt he had simply wished to verify that the bush was well cared for and in blossom, and finding a malefactor in the very act of destroying it, he had naturally tried to prevent the act, and had been struck down by the attacker. A creditable death, an honourable grave. What need to mention the conflict and suffering that lay behind it?

But in the meantime here was he, Cadfael, confronted with a woman who surely had the right to know everything. It would not, in any case, be easy to lie to this woman, or even to prevaricate. She would not be satisfied with anything less than truth.

Since the sun was now reaching the flower-bed under the north wall of the garden, and the edge of the deep print might become dry and friable before noon, and perhaps powder away, Cadfael had borrowed some ends of candle from Niall on the spot, melted them in one of the smith's small crucibles, and gone to fill in carefully the shape of the bootprint. With patient coaxing the congealed form came away intact. It would have to go into a cold place to preserve its sharpness, but for good measure he had also purloined a discarded offcut of thin leather, and made a careful outline of the print, marking where heel and toe were worn down, and the diagonal crack across the ball of the foot. Sooner or later boots come into the hands of the cobbler, they are far too precious to be discarded until they are completely worn out and can no longer be mended. Often they are handed down through three generations before finally being thrown away. So, reflected Cadfael, would this boot some day need attention from Provost Corviser or one of his trade. How soon there was no telling, but justice has to learn to wait, and not to forget. Judith sat waiting for him now in Niall's neat, bare and austere living room, the room of a man living alone, orderly and clean, but with none of the small adornments a woman would have added. The doors still stood wide open, there were two unshuttered windows, green of foliage and gold of sun came quivering in, and filled the chamber with light. She was not afraid of light, she sat where it played over her, gilding and trembling as the breeze quickened. She was alone when Cadfael came back from the garden.

'The smith has a customer,' she said with the palest of smiles. 'I bade him go. A man must tend to his trade.'

'So must a woman,' said Cadfael, and laid his moulded waxen form carefully down on the same floor, where the draught would play over it as the sunlight did over her.

'Yes, so I shall. You need not fear me, I have a respect for life. All the more,' she said gravely, 'now that I have seen death close to, yet again. Tell me! You said you would.'

He sat down with her on the uncushioned bench, and told her fully all that had happened that morning – the defection of Eluric, the coming of Niall with his story of finding the crumpled body and the broken bush, even the first grim suspicion of deliberate damage and self-murder, before sign after sign pointed another way. She heard him out with unwavering attention, those arresting grey eyes dauntingly wide and intelligent.

'But still,' she said, 'I do not understand. You speak as if there was nothing of note or consequence in his leaving the enclave by night as he did. But you know it is something utterly unknown, for a young brother so to dare. And he, I thought, so meek and dutiful, no breaker of rules. Why did he do so? What can have made it so important to him to visit the rose-bush? Secretly, illictly, by night? What did it mean to him, to drive him so far out of his proper way?'

No question but she was asking honestly. She had never thought of herself as disturber of any man's peace. And she meant to have an answer, and there was none to give her but the truth. The abbot might have hesitated at this point. Cadfael did not hesitate.

'It meant to him,' he said simply, 'the memory of you. It was no change of policy that removed him from being bearer of the rose. He had begged to be relieved of a task which had become torment to him, and his request was granted. He could no longer bear the pain of being in your presence and as far from you as the moon, of seeing you, and being within touch of you, and forbiden to love. But when he was released, it seems he could not bear absence, either. In a manner, he was saying his goodbye to you. He would have got over it,' said Cadfael with resigned regret, 'if he had lived. But it would have been a long, bleak sickness.'

Still her eyes had not wavered nor her face changed, except that the blood had drained from her cheeks and left her pale and translucent as ice. 'Oh, God!' she said in a whisper. 'And I never knew! There was never word said, never a look . . . And I so much his elder, and no beauty! It was like sending one of the singing boys from the school to me. Never a wrong thought, how could there be?'

'He was cloistered almost from his cradle,' said Cadfael gently, 'he had never had to do with a woman since he left his mother. He had no defence against a gentle face, a soft voice and a motion of grace. You cannot see yourself with his eyes, or you might find yourself dazzled.'

After a moment of silence she said: 'I did feel, somehow, that he was not happy. No more than that. And how many in this world can boast of being happy?' And she asked, looking up again into Cadfael's face: 'How many know of this? Need it be spoken of?'

'No one but Father Abbot, Brother Richard his confessor, Brother Anselm and myself. And now you. No, it will never be spoke of to any other. And none of these can or will ever think one thought of blame for you. How could we?'

'But I can,' said Judith.

'Not if you are just. You must not take to yourself more than your due. That was Eluric's error.'

A man's voice was raised suddenly in the shop, young and agitated, and Niall's voice replying in hasty reassurance. Miles burst in through the open doorway, the sunlight behind him casting him into sharp silhouette, and shining through his ruffled fair hair, turning light brown into flaxen. He was flushed and out of breath, but he heaved a great, relieved sigh at the sight of Judith sitting composed and tearless and in calm company.

'Dear God, what has been happening here? The tales they're buzzing along the Foregate of murder and malice! Brother, is it true? My cousin . . . I knew she was coming here this morning. Thank God, girl dear, I find you safe and well befriended. No harm has come to you? I came on the run as soon as I heard what they were saying, to take you home.'

His boisterous coming had blown away, like a March wind, the heavy solemnity that had pervaded the room, and his vigour had brought back some rising colour to Judith's frozen face. She rose to meet him, and let him embrace her in an impulsive hug, and kiss her cold cheek.

'I've taken no harm, no need to fret for me. Brother Cadfael has been kind enough to keep me company. He was here before I came, and Father Abbot also, there was never any threat or danger to me.'

'But there *has* been a death?' With his arms still protectively about her he looked from her face to Cadfael's, anxiously frowning. 'Or is it all a false tale? They were saying – a brother of the abbey was carried home from this place, and his face covered . . .'

'It's all too true,' said Cadfael, rising somewhat wearily. 'Brother Eluric, the custodian of Saint Mary's altar, was found here this morning stabbed to death.'

'Here? What, within the house?' He sounded incredulous as well he might. What would a brother of the abbey be doing invading a craftsman's house?

'In the garden. Under the rose-tree,' said Cadfael briefly, 'and that rose-tree hacked and damaged. Your cousin will tell you all. Better you should hear truth than the common rumours none of us will quite escape. But the lady should be taken home at once and allowed to rest. She has need of it.' He took up from the stone threshold the form of wax, on which the young man's eyes rested with wondering curiosity, and laid it carefully away in his linen scrip to avoid handling.

'Indeed!' agreed Miles, recalled to his duty and flushing boyishly. 'And thank you, Brother, for your kindness.'

Cadfael followed them out into the workshop. Niall was at his bench, but he rose to meet them as they took their leave, a modest man, who had had the delicacy to remove himself from any attendance on what should be private between comforter and comforted. Judith looked at him gravely, and suddenly recovered from some deep reserve of untouched innocence within her a pale but lovely smile. 'Master Niall, I grieve that I have caused you so much trouble and distress, and I do thank you for your goodness. And I have a thing to collect, and a debt to pay – have you forgotten?'

'No,' said Niall. 'But I would have brought it to you when the time was better suited.' He turned to the shelf behind him, and brought out to her the coiled girdle. She paid him what he asked, as simply as he asked it, and then she unrolled the buckle end in her hands, and looked long at her dead husband's mended gift, and for the first time her eyes moistened with a pearly sheen, though no tears fell.

'It is a time very well suited now,' she said, looking up into Niall's face, 'for a small, precious thing to provide me with a pure pleasure.'

It was the only pleasure she had that day, and even that carried with it a piercing undercurrent of pain. Agatha's flustered and voluble fussing and Miles's restrained but all too attentive concern were equally burdensome to her. The dead face of Brother Eluric remained with her every moment. How could she have failed to feel his anguish? Once, twice, three times she had received him and parted from him, with no deeper misgiving than a mild sense of his discomfort, which could well be merely shyness, and a conviction that here was a young man none too happy, which she had attributed to want of a true vocation in one cloistered from childhood. She had been so deeply sunk in her own griefs as to be insensitive to his. Even in death he did not reproach her. He had no need. She reproached herself.

She would have sought distraction at least in occupying her hands, but she could not face the awed whispers and heavy silences of the girls in the spinning room. She chose rather to sit in the shop, where, if the curious came to stare and exclaim, at least they were likely to come one at a time, and some at least might come honestly to buy cloth, not even having heard yet the news that was being blown round the alleys of Shrewsbury like thistledown, and taking root as blithely.

But even that was hard to bear. She would have been glad when evening came, and the shutters were put up, but that one late customer, coming to collect a length of cloth for his mother, elected to stay a while and commiserate with the lady in private, or at least as much privacy as he could contrive between the clucking forays of Agatha, who could not leave her niece unattended for many minutes together. Those brief intervals, however, Vivian Hynde knew how to use to the best advantage.

He was the only son of old William Hynde, who ran the biggest flocks of sheep in the central western uplands of the shire, and who for years had regularly sold the less select fleeces of his clip to the Vestiers, while the finest were reserved to be collected by the middlemen for shipping to the north of France and the wool towns of Flanders, from his warehouse and jetty downstream, beyond Godfrey Fuller's workshops. The partnership between the two families for business purposes had existed for two generations, and made close contact plausible even for this young sprig who was said to be at odds with his father, and highly unlikely to prove a third successful woolman, his talent being more highly developed in spending the money his father made. So much so that it was rumoured the old man had put his foot down heavily, and refused to pay any more debts for his son and heir, or allow him any more funds to squander on dice, and girls, and riotous living. William had bailed him out of trouble often enough already, but now, without his backing, Vivian's usual resources were far less likely to lend to him or give him extended credit. And easy friends fall off from an idol and patron who no longer has money to spend.

There was no sign of drooping as yet, however, in Vivian's bright crest when he came, with his considerable charm and grace, to console a dismayed widow. He was a very personable young man indeed, tall and athletic, with corn-yellow hair that curled becomingly, and dancing pebble-brown eyes in which a full light found surprising golden glints. He was invariably elegant in his gear and wear, and knew very well how pleasant a picture he made in most women's eyes. And if he had made no headway yet with the Widow Perle, neither had anyone else, and there was still hope.

He had the wit to approach delicately on this occasion, with a declaration of sympathy and concern that stopped short of probing too deeply. Excellent at keeping his feet on thin ice, indeed sensible enough to know himself a man for surfaces, not for depths, he also had the gall to rally and tease a little in the hope of raising a smile.

'And now if you shut yourself up here and grieve in private for someone you hardly knew, that aunt of yours will drive you ever more melancholy. She has you talked halfway to a nunnery already. And that,' said Vivian with emphatic pleading, 'you *must not do*.'

'Many another has,' she said, 'with no better cause. Why not I?'

'Because,' he said, glittering, and leaning closer to lower his voice for fear Agatha should choose that moment to enter yet again on some pretext or other, 'because you are young and beautiful, and have no real wish to bury yourself in a convent. You know it! And because I am your devoted worshipper, as well you know, and if you vanish from my life it will be the death of me.'

She took that as a well-intended if ill-judged flourish, and was even a little touched by his suddenly caught breath and stricken gaze as he realised what he had said, and how it must bite home on this of all days. He caught at her hand, voluble and honeyed in dismay. 'Oh, forgive me, forgive me! Fool that I am, I never meant . . . There is no blame, none, can touch you. Let me in to your life closer, and I'll convince you. Marry me, and I'll share out all vexations and doubts from you . . .'

She did begin to wonder, afterwards, if it was all calculated, for he was a subtle and persuasive young man; but then she was disarmed and self-doubting, and could not bring herself to attribute deceit or self-interest to any other. Vivian had often enough pressed his attentions upon her and made no impression. Now what she saw in him was a boy no more than a year older than Brother Eluric, one who might, for all his flattery and exaggeration, be suffering something of what

Brother Eluric had suffered. She had so lamentably failed to offer the slightest help to the one, the more reason she should deal considerately with the other. So she tolerated him, and made firm but gentle answers, longer than she would have done at any other time.

'It's foolish to talk so,' she said. 'You and I have known each other from childhood. I'm your elder, and a widow, by no means a match for you, and I do not intend to marry again with any man. You must accept that for an answer. Waste no more time here on me.'

'You are fretting now,' he said vehemently, 'over this monk who is dead, though God knows that's none of your fault. But it will not always be so, you'll see all very differently in a month or so. And for this charter that troubles you, it can be changed. You can, you should rid yourself of the bargain, and with it the reproach. You see now it was folly.'

'Yes,' she agreed resignedly, 'it was indeed folly to put a price, even a nominal price, upon a gift. I should never have done it. It has brought nothing but grief. But yes, it can be undone.'

It seemed to her that he was drawing encouragement from this lengthening colloquy, and that she certainly did not desire. So she rose, and pleaded her very real weariness to rid herself of his continuing assiduities as gently as possible. Vivian departed reluctantly but still gracefully, looking back from the doorway for a long, ingratiating moment before he swung about and went, lithe and long-legged and elegant, down the street called Maerdol towards the bridge.

But even when he was gone, the evening was full of echoes of the morning, reminders of disaster, reproaches of folly, as Agatha worried away at the past.

'You see now how foolish it was to make such a ballad-romance agreement, like any green girl. A rose, indeed! You should never have given away half your patrimony so rashly, how could you know when you and yours might have great need of it? And now see what it's come to! A death, and all at the door of that foolish charter.'

'You need not trouble any longer,' said Judith wearily. 'I do repent it. It is not too late to amend it. Let me alone now. There is nothing you could say to me that I have not already said to myself.'

She went early to her bed, and the girl Branwen, relieved of the carding that brought her out in a rash, and put to work for a time in the household, came to fetch and carry for her, fold away into the chest the gown her mistress discarded, and curtain the unshuttered window. Branwen was fond of Judith, but not sorry, on this occasion, to be dismissed early, for Vivian's serving-man, left behind to carry home the bolt of cloth for Mistress Hynde, was settled cosily in the kitchen, throwing dice with Bertred, the foreman of the weavers, and both of them were personable fellows with an eye for a pretty girl. Branwen was not at all averse to being the desirable bone between two handsome dogs. Sometimes she had felt that Bertred had ideas above his station, and was casting a greedy eye in the direction of his mistress, being vain of his sturdy, straight body and fresh, comely face, and a silver tongue to match. But nothing would ever come of that! And when he had Master Hynde's Gunnar across the table from him, plainly captivated, he might better appreciate more accessible meat.

'Go now,' said Judith, loosing the great sheaf of her hair about her shoulders. 'I shan't need you tonight. But call me very early in the morning,' she added with sudden resolution, 'for I'm going to the abbey. I'll not leave this matter lying one hour more than need be. Tomorrow I'll go to the abbot and have a new charter drawn up. No more roses! The gift I made for so foolish a fee I'll now make unconditional.'

Branwen was proud of her advancement into Judith's personal service, and fondly imagined herself closer in her mistress's confidence than in fact she was. And with two young men in the kitchen already interested in her and prepared to be impressed, what wonder if she boasted of being the first to be entrusted with Judith's plans for the morrow? It seemed a pity that Gunnar should so soon aftwerwards recall that he had to carry home Mistress Hynde's cloth, and might end with a flea in his ear if he delayed too long. And though that left her the attentions of Bertred, whom on the whole she preferred, his pricked sense of proprietorship in a woman of his household seemed to flag disappointingly once his rival was out of the house. It was not, after all, a satisfactory evening. Branwen went to her bed out of temper between disillusionment and dudgeon, and out of sorts with men.

Young Alan Herbard, Hugh's deputy, dutiful and determined though he was, drew the line at coping unaided with murder, and had had a courier on the road as soon as the news came to his ears. By noon of the next day, which was the eighteenth day of June, Hugh would surely be back in Shrewsbury, not in his own house, where only one elderly servant remained during the family's absence, but at the castle, where garrison, sergeant and all were at his disposal.

Meantime, Cadfael betook himself and his waxen footprint, with the abbot's blessing, into the town, and showed mould and drawing to Geoffrey Corviser, the provost, and his son Philip, the foremost shoemakers and leather workers in the town. 'For sooner or later every boot comes into the cobbler's hands,' he said simply, 'though it may be a year ahead or more. No harm, at least, in keeping a copy of such witness as you see there, and looking out for the like among any you repair.'

Philip handled the wax delicately, and nodded over the evidence it provided of its wearer's tread, 'I don't know it, but it will be easily seen if ever it does find its way in here. And I'll show it to the cobbler over the bridge, in Frankwell. Between us, who knows, we may run the fellow down in the end. But there's many a man patches his own,' said the good craftsman with professional disdain.

A thin chance enough, Cadfael admitted to himself on his way back over the bridge, but one that could not be neglected. What else had they to offer a lead? Little enough, except the inevitable and unanswerable question: Who could possibly have wanted to destroy the rose-bush? And for what conceivable reason? A question they had all voiced already, without profit, and one that would be posed all over again when Hugh arrived.

Instead of turning in at the gatehouse Cadfael passed by and walked the length of the Foregate, along the dusty highway, past the bakery, past the forge, exchanging greetings in at doorways and over hedges as he went, to turn in at the gate of Niall's yard, and cross to the wicket which led through into the garden. It was bolted fast on the inner side. Cadfael turned instead to the shop, where Niall was at work with a small ceramic crucible and a tiny clay mould for a brooch.

'I came to see if you'd had any further night visitors,' said Cadfael, 'but I see you've secured one way in, at least. A pity there's no wall ever built high enough to keep out a man determined to get in. But even stopping one hole is something. What of the bush? Will it live?'

'Come and see. One side may die off, but it's no more than two or three branches. It may leave the tree lopsided, but a year or so, and pruning and growth will balance all.'

In the green and sunlight and tangled colour of the garden the rose-bush spread its arms firmly against the north wall, the dangling trailers pegged back to the stone with strips of cloth. Niall had wound a length of stout canvas round and round the damaged bole, binding the severed wood together, and coated the covering with a thick layer of wax and grease.

'There's love been put into this,' said Cadfael approvingly, but wisely did not say whether for the bush or the woman. The leaves on the half-severed part had wilted, and a few had fallen, but the bulk of the tree stood green and glossy, and full of half-open buds. 'You've done well by it. I could use you inside the enclave, if ever you tire of bronze and the world.'

The quiet, decent man never opened his mouth to answer that. Whatever he felt for woman or rose was his business, no other man's. Cadfael respected that, and viewing the wide, wide-set, honest and yet reticent eyes, he took his leave and set off back to his proper duties feeling somewhat reproved, and curiously elated. One man at least in this sorry business kept his eyes on his own course, and would not easily be turned aside. And he, surely, looking for no gain. Somewhere in all this there was greed of gain more than enough, and little enough of love.

It was almost noon by this time, and the sun high and hot, a true June day. Saint Winifred must have been at work coaxing the heavens to do her honour for the festival of her translation. As so often happened in a late season, the summer had all but caught up with the laggard spring, flowers which had lingered shivering and reluctant to bloom suddenly sprang into fevered haste, bursting their buds overnight into a blazing prime. The crops, slower to take risks, might still be as much as a month late, but they would be lavish and clean, half their hereditary enemies chilled to death in April and May.

In the doorway of his lodge in the gatehouse Brother Porter was standing in earnest talk with an agitated young man. Cadfael, always vulnerable to curiosity, his prevalent sin, halted, wavered and turned aside, recognizing Miles Coliar, that tidy, practical, trim young fellow a great deal less trim than usual, his hair blown and teased erect in disorder, his bright blue eyes dilated beneath drawn and anxious copper brows. Miles turned his head, hearing a new step approaching, and recognised, through a haze of worry, a brother he had seen only the previous day sitting amicably with his cousin. He swung about eagerly.

'Brother, I remember you – you were of some comfort and help yesterday to Judith. You have not seen her today? She has not spoken again with you?'

'She has not,' said Cadfael, surprised. 'Why? What is new now? She went home with you yesterday. I trust she has met with no further grief?'

'No, none that I know of. I do know she went to her bed in good time, and I hoped she would sleep well. But now . . .' He cast a vague, distracted glance about him: 'They tell me at home she set out to come here. But . . .'

'She has not been here,' said the porter positively. 'I have not left my post, I should know if she had entered the gate. I know the lady from the time she came here making her gift to the house. I have not set eyes on her today. But Master Coliar here says she left home very early . . .'

'*Very* early,' Miles confirmed vehemently. 'Before I was waking.'

'And with intent to come here on some errand to the lord abbot,' concluded the porter.

'So her maid told me,' said Miles, sweating. 'Judith told her so last night, when the girl attended her to bed. I knew nothing of it until this morning. But it seems she has not been here. She never reached here. And she has not come home again. Midday, and she has not come home! I dread something ill has befallen her.'

Chapter Six

THERE WERE five of them gathered in the abbot's parlour that afternoon, in urgent conclave: Radulfus himself, Brothers Anselm and Cadfael, witnesses to the charter which had somehow precipitated these dire events, Miles Coliar, restless and fevered with anxiety, and Hugh Beringar, who had ridden south in haste from Maesbury with Eluric's murder on his mind, to find on arrival that a second crisis had followed hard on the heels of the first. He had already deputed Alan Herbard to send men hunting through the town and the Foregate for any sign of news of the missing lady, with orders to send word if by any chance she should have returned home. There could, after all, be legitimate reasons for her absence, something unforeseen that had met and deflected her on her way. But minute by minute it began to look less likely. Branwen had told her tearful story, and there was no question but Judith had indeed set out from home to visit the abbey. None, either, that she had never reached it.

'The girl never told me what my cousin had said, until this morning,' said Miles, twisting frustrated hands. 'I knew nothing of it, or I could have borne her company. So short a walk, down here from the town! And the watchman at the town gate said good day to her and saw her start across the bridge, but after that he was busy, and had no call to watch her go. And not a sign of her from that moment.'

'And she said her errand was to remit the rose rent,' said

Hugh intently, 'and make her gift to the abbey free of all conditions?'

'So her maid says. So Judith told her. She was much distressed,' said Miles, 'over the young brother's death. She surely took it to heart that it was her whim brought about that murder.'

'It has yet to be explained,' said Abbot Radulfus, 'why that should be. Truly it does appear that Brother Eluric interrupted the attack upon the rose-bush, and was killed for his pains, perhaps in mere panic, yet killed he was. What I do not understand is why anyone should wish to destroy the rose-bush in the first place. But for that inexplicable deed there would have been no interruption and no death. Who could want to hack down the bush? What possible motive could there be?'

'Ah, but, Father, there could!' Miles turned on him with feverish vehemence. 'There were some not best pleased when my cousin gave away so valuable a property, worth the half of all she has. If the bush was hacked down and all the roses dead by the day of Saint Winifred's translation, the rent could not be paid, and the terms of the charter would have been broken. The whole bargain could be repudiated.'

'Could,' Hugh pointed out briskly, 'but would not. The matter would still be in the lady's hands, she could remit the rent at will. And you see she had the will.'

'She *could* remit it,' Miles echoed with sharp intent, '*if she were here to do it.* But she is not here. Four days until the payment is due, and she has vanished. Time gained, time gained! Whoever failed to destroy the bush has now abducted my cousin. She is not here to grant or deny. What he did not accomplish by one way he now approaches by another.'

There was a brief, intent silence, and then the abbot said slowly: 'Do you indeed believe that? You speak as one believing.'

'I do, my lord. I see no other possibility. Yesterday she announced her intention of making her gift unconditional. Today that has been prevented. There was no time to be lost.'

'Yet you yourself did not know what she meant to do,' said Hugh, 'not until today. Did any other know of it?'

'Her maid owns she repeated it in the kitchen. Who knows how many heard it then, or got it from those who did? Such things come out through keyholes and the chinks of shutters. Moreover, Judith may have met with some acquaintance on the bridge or in the Foregate, and told them where she was bound. However lightly and thoughtlessly she had that provision written into the charter, the failure to observe it would render the bargain null and void. Father, you know that is true.'

'I do know it,' acknowledged Radulfus, and came at last to the unavoidable question: 'Who, then, could possibly stand to gain by breaking the agreement, by whatever means?'

'Father, my cousin is young, and a widow, and a rich prize in marriage, all the richer if her gift to you could be annulled. There are a bevy of suitors about the town pursuing her, and have been now for a year and more, and every one of them would rather marry the whole of her wealth than merely the half. Me, I manage the business for her, I'm very well content with what I have, and with the wife I'm to marry before the year's out, a good match. But even if we were not first cousins I should have no interest in Judith but as a loyal kinsman and craftsman should. But I cannot choose but know how she is pestered with wooers. Not that she encourages any of them, nor ever gives them grounds for hope, but they never cease their efforts. After three years and more of widowhood, they reason, her resolution must surely weaken, and she'll be worn down into taking a second husband at last. It may be that one of them is running out of patience.'

'To name names,' said Hugh mildly, 'may sometimes be dangerous, but to call a man wooer is not necessarily to call him an abductor and murderer into the bargain. And I think you have gone so far, Master Coliar, that in this company you may as well go the rest of the way.'

Miles moistened his lips and brushed a sleeve across his beaded forehead. 'Business looks to business for a match, my lord. There are two guildsmen in the town, at least, who would be only too glad to get hold of Judith's trade, and both of them work in with us, and know well enough what she's worth. There's Godfrey Fuller does all the dyeing of our fleeces, and fulling of the cloth at the end of it, and he'd dearly like to make himself the master of the spinning and weaving, too, and have all in one profitable basket. And then there's old William Hynde, he has a wife still, but by another road he could get his hands on the Vestier property, for he has a young spark of a son who comes courting her day in, day out, and has the entry because they know each other from children. The father might be willing to use him as bait for a woman, though he's drawn his purse-strings tight from paying the young fellow's debts any longer. And the son – if he could win her I fancy he'd be set up for life, but not dance to his father's tune, more likely to laugh in his face. And that's not the whole of it, for our neighbour the saddler is just of an age to feel the want of a wife, and in his plodding way has settled on her as suitable. And our best weaver chances to be a very good craftsman and a fine-looking man, and fancies himself even prettier than he is, and he's been casting sheep's eyes at her lately, though I doubt if she even noticed. There's more than one comely journeyman has caught his mistress's eye and done very well for himself.'

'Hard to imagine our solid guildsmen resorting to murder and abduction,' objected the abbot, unwilling to accept so readily a suggestion so outrageous.

'But the murder,' Hugh pointed out alertly, 'seems to have been done in alarm and terror, and probably never was intended. Yet having so far committed himself, why should a man stop at the second crime?'

'Still it seems to me a hazardous business, for from all I know or have heard about the lady, she would not easily give way to persuasion. Captive or free, she has thus far resisted all blandishments, she will not change now. I do understand,' said Radulfus ruefully, 'what force of compulsion the common report may bring to bear in such a case, how a woman might feel it better to yield and marry than endure the scandal of suspicion and the ill will between families that must follow. But this lady, it seems to me, might well survive even that pressure. Then her captor would have gained nothing.'

Miles drew deep breath, and ran a hand through his fair curls, dragging them wildly awry. 'Father, what you say is true, Judith is a strong spirit, and will not easily be broken. But, Father, there may be worse! Marriage by rape is no new thing. Once in a man's power, hidden away with no means of escape, if coaxing and persuasion have no effect, there remains force. It has been known time and time again. My lord Beringar here will witness it happens among the nobility, and I know it happens among the commonalty. Even a town tradesman might resort to it at last. And I know my cousin, if once her virtue was lost, she might well think it best to mend her sorry state by marriage. Wretched though that remedy must be.'

'Wretched indeed!' agreed Radulfus with detestation. 'Such a thing must not be. Hugh, this house is deeply committed here, the charter and the gift draw us in, and whatever aid we can lend you to recover this unhappy lady is at your disposal, men, funds, whatever you require. No need to ask – take! And as for our prayers, they shall not be wanting. There is still some frail chance that no harm has come to her, and she may yet return home of her own volition, and wonder at this fury and alarm. But now we must reckon with the worst, and hunt as for a soul in danger.'

'Then we'd best be about it,' said Hugh, and rose to take his leave. Miles was on his feet with a nervous spring, eager and anxious, and would have been first out at the door if Cadfael had not opened his mouth for the first time in this conference.

'I did hear, Master Coliar, indeed I know from Mistress Perle herself, that she has sometimes thought of leaving the world and taking the veil. Sister Magdalen talked with her about such a vocation a few days ago, I believe. Did you know of it?'

'I knew the sister came visiting,' said Miles, his blue eyes widening. 'What they said I was not told and did not ask. That was Judith's business. She has sometimes talked of it, but less of late.'

'Did you encourage such a step?' asked Cadfael.

'I never interfered, one way or the other. It would have been her decision. I would not urge it,' said Miles forcibly, 'but neither would I stand in her way if that was what she wanted. At least,' he said with sudden bitterness, 'that would have been a good and peaceful ending. Now only God knows what her dismay and despair must be.'

'There goes a most dutiful and loving cousin,' said Hugh, as Cadfael walked beside him across the great court. Miles was striding out at the gatehouse arch with hair on end, making for the town, and the house and shop at Maerdol-head, where there might by this time be news. A frail chance, but still possible.

'He has good cause,' said Cadfael reasonably. 'But for Mistress Perle and the Vestier business he and his mother would not be in the comfortable state they are. He has everything to lose, should she give in to force and agree to marriage. He owes his cousin much, and by all accounts he's requited her very well, with gratitude and good management. Works hard and to good effect, the business is flourishing. He may well be frantic about her now. Do I hear a certain sting in your voice, lad? Have you doubts about him?'

'No, none. He has no more idea where the girl is now than

you or I, that's clear. A man may dissemble very well, up to a point, but I never knew a man who could sweat at will. No, Miles is telling the truth. He's off now to turn the town upside-down hunting for her. And so must I.'

'She had but so short a way to go,' said Cadfael, fretting at the fine detail, which left so little room for doubt that she was gone, that something untoward had indeed happened to her. 'The watch at the gate spoke to her, she had only to cross the bridge and walk this short piece of the Foregate to our gatehouse. A river to cross, a short walk along open road, and in those few minutes she's gone.'

'The river,' said Hugh honestly, 'has been on my mind. I won't deny it.'

'I doubt if it need be. Unless truly by some ill chance. No man is going to make himself rich or his business more prosperous by marriage with a dead woman. Only her heir would benefit by that, and her heir – I suppose that boy must be her nearest kin? – is going out of his mind worrying over what's happened to her, as you yourself have seen. There's nothing false about the state he's in. No, *if* some wooer has determined on drastic action, he'll have spirited her away into some safe place, not done her harm. We need not mourn for the lady, not yet, she'll be guarded like a miser's gold.'

Cadfael's mind was occupied with the problem until Vespers and beyond. From the bridge to the abbey gatehouse there were but three footpaths leaving the Foregate, two that branched off to the right, one on either side the mill-pond, to serve the six small houses there, the other descending on the left to the long riverside tract of the Gaye, the main abbey gardens. Cover was sparse along the high road, any act of violence would be risky there, and the paths that served the abbey houses suffered the disadvantage, from a conspirator's point of view, of being overlooked by the windows of all six cottages, and in this high summer there would be no shutters closed. The old woman in one cot was stone deaf, and would not have heard even the loudest screams, but generally old people sleep lightly and fitfully, and also, being no longer able to get about as actively as before, they have rather more than their share of curiosity, to fill up the tedium of their days. It would be a bold or a desperate man who attempted violence under their windows.

No trees drew close about the road on that, the southern side of the Foregate, only a few low bushes fringing the pond, and the scrub-covered slope down to the river. Only on the northern side were there well-grown trees, from the end of the bridge, where the path wound down to the Gaye, to a grove some little way short of the abbey gatehouse, where the houses of the Foregate began.

Now if a woman could be drawn aside there, even into the fringe of shadow, at that early hour and with few people abroad, it would not be so difficult to seize a moment when the road was empty and drag her further into the grove, or down among the bushes, with a cloak twisted about her head and arms. But in that case the person involved, man or woman, would have to be someone known to her, someone who could detain her plausibly in talk for a matter of minutes beside the road. Which fitted in well enough with the suggestion Miles had made, for even an unwelcome suitor who was also a town neighbour would be encountered in the ordinary meetings of the day with tolerance and civility. Life in a walled and crowded borough cannot be carried on otherwise.

There might, of course, be other reasons for removing the girl from home and family, though they would have to have something to do with the matter of the charter and the rose-bush, for surely that could not be some lunatic accident, unconnected with her disappearance. There might! But with all the cudgelling of his brains Cadfael could think of none. And a rich merchant widow in a town where everyone knew everyone was inevitably besieged by suitors out to make their fortunes. Her only safe defence was the one Judith had contemplated, withdrawal into a convent. Or, of course, marriage to whichever of the contestants best pleased or least repelled her. And that, so far, she had not contemplated. It might well be true that the one who considered himself most likely to please had risked all on his chance of softening the lady's heart in a few days of secret courtship. And keeping her hidden until after the twenty-second day of June could break the bargain with the abbey just as surely as destroying the rose-bush and all its blossoms. However many roses survived now, unless Judith was found in time not one of them could be paid into her hand on the day the rent was due. So provided her captor prevailed at last, and drove her to marry him, her affairs would then be his, and he could refuse to renew and prevent her from renewing the broken agreement. And he would have won all, not the half. Yes, whichever way Cadfael viewed the affair, this notion propounded by Miles, who had everything to lose, looked ever more convincing.

He went to his cell with Judith still on his mind. Her well-being seemed to him very much the abbey's business, something that could not be left merely to the secular arm. Tomorrow, he thought, lying awake in the dim dortoir, to the regular bass music of Brother Richard's snores, I'll walk that stretch of road, and see what's there to be found. Who knows but there may be something left behind, more to the point than a single print of a worn boot-heel.

He asked no special leave, for had not the abbot already pledged Hugh whatever men or horses or gear he needed? It was but a small mental leap to establish in his own mind that if Hugh had not specifically demanded his help, he would have done so had he known how his friend's mind was working. Such small exercises in moral agility still came easily to him, where the need seemed to justify them.

He set out after chapter, sallying forth into a Foregate swept by the long, slanting rays of the climbing sun, brilliantly lit and darkly shadowed. In the shade there was dew still on the grass, and a glisten in the leaves as a faint, steady, silent breeze ruffled them unceasingly. The Foregate on which he turned his back was bustling with life, every shop-front and house-door opened wide to the summer, and a constant traffic of housewives, urchins, dogs, carters and pedlars on the move, or gathered in gossiping groups. In this belated but lovely burst of summer, life quitted the confines of walls and roof, and moved into the sunshine. Under the west front of the church and across the gateway the knife-edged shadow of the tower fell, but along the enclave boundary it lay close and narrow, huddled under the foot of the wall.

Cadfael went slowly, exchanging greetings with such acquaintances as he met, but unwilling to be sidetracked into lingering. This first stretch of the road she could not have reached, and the steps he was retracing on her behalf were those of a pious intent which had never come to fruit. On his left, the lofty stone wall continued for the length of the great court and the infirmary and school within, then turned away at a right-angle, and alongside it went the first pathway that led past three small grace houses to the mill, on this near side of the mill-pond. Then the wide expanse of the pool, fringed with a low hedge of bushes. He would not and could not believe that

Judith Perle had vanished into either this water or the waves of the river. Whoever had taken her – if someone had indeed taken her – wanted and needed her alive and unharmed and ripe for conquest. Hugh had no choice but to draw his net wide and entertain every possibility. Cadfael preferred to follow one notion at a time. Hugh would almost certainly have enlisted the help of Madog of the Dead Boat by this time, to pursue the worst possibilities of death by water, while the king's sergeants scoured the streets and alleys and houses of Shrewsbury for a live and captive lady. Madog knew every wave of the Severn, every seasonal trick it had in its power to play, every bend or shoal where things swept away by its currents would be cast up again. If the river had taken her, Madog would find her. But Cadfael would not believe it.

And if Hugh also failed to find her within the walls of Shrewsbury? Then they would have to look beyond. It's no simple matter to transport an unwilling lady very far, and by daylight. Could it even be done at all, short of using a cart? A horseman carrying such a swathed burden would need a horse powerful enough to carry the extra weight, and worse, would certainly be conspicuous. Someone would surely remember him, or even question him on the spot, human curiosity being what it is. No, she could not, surely, be far away.

Cadfael passed by the pool, and came to the second pathway, on this further side, which served the other three little houses. Beyond, after their narrow gardens, there was an open field, and at the end of that, turning sharply left, a narrow high road going south along the riverside. By that track an abductor might certainly retreat within a mile or so into the forest, but on the other hand there was no cover here along the riverside, any attack perpetrated there could be seen even from the town walls across the water.

But on the right of the Foregate, once the houses ended, the thick grove of trees began, and after that the steep path dived down sidelong to the bank of the Severn, through bushes and trees, giving access to the long, lush level of the Gaye. Beyond that, she would still have been on the open bridge, and surely inviolable. Here, if anywhere in this short walk, there was room for a predator to strike and withdraw with his prey. She had to be prevented from reaching the abbey and doing what she intended to do. There would be no second chance. And the house of the rose was indeed a property well worth reclaiming.

With every moment the thing began to look more and more

credible. Improbable, perhaps, in an ordinary tradesman, as law-abiding as his neighbours and respected by all; but a man who has tried one relatively harmless expedient, and inadvertently killed a man in consequence, is no longer ordinary.

Cadfael crossed the Foregate and went into the grove of trees, stepping warily to avoid adding any tracks to those already all too plentiful. The imps of the Foregate played here, attended by their noisy camp-following of dogs, and tearfully trailed by those lesser imps as yet too small to be taken seriously and admitted to their games, and too short in the legs to keep up with them. In the more secluded clearings lovers met in the dark, their nests neatly coiled in the flattened grasses. Small hope of finding anything of use here.

He turned back to the road, and walked on the few paces to the path that descended to the Gaye. Before him the stone bridge extended, and beyond it the high town wall and the tower of the gate. Sunlight bathed the roadway and the walls, blanching the stone to a creamy pallor. The Severn, running a little higher than its usual summer level, shimmered and stirred with a deceptive appearance of placidity and languor, but Cadfael knew how fast those smooth currents were running, and what vehement undertows coursed beneath the blue, sky-mirroring surface. Most male children here learned to swim almost as soon as they learned to walk, and there were places where the Severn could be as gentle and safe as its smiling mask, but here where it coiled about the town, leaving only one approach by land, the narrow neck straddled by the castle, it was a perilous water. Could Judith Perle swim? It was no easy matter for girl-children to strip and caper along the grassy shores and flash in and out of the stream as the boys did, and for them it must be a more rare accomplishment.

At the town end of the bridge Judith had passed, unhindered and alone; the watchman had seen her begin to cross. Hard to believe that any man had dared to molest her here on the open crossing, where she had only to utter a single cry, and the watchman would have heard her, and looked out in instant alarm. So she had arrived at this spot where Cadfael was standing. And then? As far as present reports went, no one had seen her since.

Cadfael began the descent to the Gaye. This path was trodden regularly, and bare of grass, and the landward bushes that fringed it drew gradually back from its edges, leaving the level, cultivated ground open. On the river side they grew thickly, all down the slope to the water, and under the first arch of the bridge, where once a boat-mill had been moored to make use of the force of the current. Close to the waterside a foothpath led off downstream, and beside it the abbey's gardens lay neatly arrayed all along the rich plain, and three or four brothers were pricking out plants of cabbage and colewort. Further along came the orchards, apple and pear and plum, the sweet cherry, and two big walnut trees, and the low bushes of little sour gooseberries that were only just beginning to flush into colour. There was another disused mill at the end of the level, and the final abbey ground was a field of corn. Then ridges of woodland came down and overhung the water, and the curling eddies ate away the bank beneath their roots.

Across the broad river the hill of Shrewsbury rose in a great sweep of green, that wore the town wall like a coronet. Two or three small wickets gave access through the wall to gardens and grass below. They could easily be barred and blocked in case of attack, and the clear outlook such a raised fortress commanded gave ample notice of any approach. The vulnerable neck unprotected by water was filled by the castle, completing the circle of the wall. A strong place, as well as a very fair one, yet King Stephen had taken it by storm, four years ago, and held it through his sheriffs ever since.

But all this stretch of our land, Cadfael thought, brooding over its prolific green, is overlooked by hundreds of houses and households there within the wall. How many moments can there be in the day when someone is not peering out from a window, this weather, or below by the riverside, fishing, or hanging out washing, or the children playing and bathing? Not, perhaps, so many of them, so early in the morning, but surely someone. And never a word said of struggle or flight, or of something heavy and human-shaped being carried. No, not this way. Our lands here are open and innocent. The only hidden reach is here, here beside the bridge or under it, where trees and bushes give cover.

He waded the bushes towards the arch, and the last of the dew darkened his sandals and the skirt of his habit, but sparsely now, surviving only here, in the deep green shade. Below the stone arch the water had sunk only a foot or so from its earlier fullness, leaving a bleaching fringe of grass and water-plants. A man could walk through dry-shod but for dew. Even the winter level or the flush of the spring thaw never came nearer than six feet of the crown of the arch. The green growth was fat and lavish and tangled, suckled on rich, moist earth.

Someone had been before him here, the grasses were parted and bent aside by the passage of at least one person, probably more. That was nothing very unusual, boys roam everywhere in their play, and in their mischief, too. What was less usual here was the deep groove driven into the moist soil uncovered by the recent lowering of the level, and prolonged into the grass above. A boat had been drawn aground there, and no long time ago, either. At the town end of the bridge there were always boats beached or moored, handy for their owners' use. But seldom here.

Cadfael squatted close to view the ground. The grass had absorbed any marks left by feet, except for the lowest lip of the land, and there certainly at least one man had trampled the moist ground, but the mud had slithered under him and obliterated any shape he had left behind. One man or two, for the spread of slippery mud showed both sides of the groove the skiff had made.

If he had not been sitting on his heels he would never have caught the single alien thing, for there under the arch there was no glint of sunlight to betray it. But there it was, trodden into the disturbed mud, a metallic thread like a wisp of reddish-gold straw, no longer than the top joint of his thumb. He prised it out and it lay in his palm, a tiny arrow-head without a shaft, bent a little out of shape by the foot that had trodden it in. He stooped to rinse it in the edge of the river, and carried it out into the sunshine.

And now he saw it for what it was, the bronze tag which had sealed the end of a leather girdle, a delicate piece of work, incised with punch and hammer after being attached to the belt, and surely not torn from its anchorage now without considerable violence and struggle.

Cadfael turned in his tracks, strode up the steep path to the road, and set off back along the Foregate at his fastest pace.

Chapter Seven

THIS IS hers,' said Niall, looking up from the scrap of bronze with a fixed and formidable face. 'I know it, though I did not make it. It belongs to that girdle she took back with her, the morning Brother Eluric lay here dead. I made the new buckle to match this design, this and the rosettes round the tongue-holes. I should know it anywhere. It is hers. Where did you find it?'

'Under the first arch of the bridge, where a boat had been hauled up in hiding.'

'To carry her away! And this – trodden into the mud, you say. See, when this was set in place it was hammered home into the leather with the pattern, it would not come loose easily, even after years, and with the leather softening and thinning from use, and perhaps a little greasy with handling. Someone was rough with the girdle to tear this away.'

'And with the lady also,' Cadfael agreed grimly. 'I could not be sure, myself, I hardly saw the girdle when she took it in her hands that day. But you could not be mistaken. Now I know. One step at least on the way. And a boat – a boat would be the simplest means of all of carrying her off. No neighbour passing close, to query such large freight, no one ashore to wonder at any passing skiff, they're common enough along the Severn. The girdle from which this came may well have been snatched to help to bind her.'

'And she to be used so foully!' Niall wiped his large capable hands on the rag of woollen cloth on his bench, and began purposefully unfastening and laying by his leathern apron. 'What is to be done now? Tell me how best I can help – where first to look for her. I'll close my shop –'

'No,' said Cadfael, 'make no move, only keep watch still on the rose-bush, for I have this strange fancy the life of the one is bound up fast with the life of the other. What is there you could do elsewhere that Hugh Beringar cannot? He has men enough, and trust me, they're all hard at it, he'll see to that. Stay here and be patient, and whatever I discover you shall know. Your business is bronze, not boats, you've done your part.'

'And you, what will you do now?' Niall hesitated, frowning, unwilling to be left with the passive part.

'I'm off to find Hugh Beringar as fast as I can, and after him Madog, who knows all there is to know about boats, from his own coracles to the freight barges that fetch the wool clips away. Madog may be able to tell what manner of boat it was from the very dent it left behind in the mud. You bide here and be as easy as you can. With God's help we'll find her.'

He looked back once from the doorway, impressed by the charged silence at his back. The man of few words remained quite still, staring into some invisible place where Judith Perle stood embattled and alone, captive to greed and brutality. Even her good works conspired against her, even her generosity turned venomous, to poison her life. The controlled and uncommunicative face was eloquent enough at that moment. And if those big, adroit hands, so precise on his tiny crucibles and moulds, could once get a hold on the throat of whoever has rapt away Judith Perle, thought Cadfael as he hurried back towards the town, I doubt if the king's justice would have any need of a hangman, or the trial cost the shire much money.

The porter at the town gate sent a boy hotfoot up to the castle in search of Hugh as soon as Cadfael came to report, somewhat breathlessly, that there was need of the sheriff down at the waterside. It took a little time to find him, however, and Cadfael made use of the interval by going in search of Madog of the Dead Boat. He knew well enough where to find him, provided he was not already out on the water somewhere, about some curious part of his varied business. He had a hut tucked under the lee of the western bridge that opened the road into his native Wales, and there he made coracles, or timber boats if required, fished in season, ferried fares on request, carried goods for a fee, anything to do with transport by water. The time being then past noon, Madog happened to be taking a brief rest and a solitary meal when Cadfael reached the bridge. A squat, muscular, hairy elderly Welshman, without kith or kin and in no need of either, for he was sufficient to himself and had been since childhood, he yet had an open welcome for his friends. He needed no one, but if others needed him he was at their disposal. Once summoned, he rose and came.

Hugh was at the gate before them. They crossed the bridge together, and came down to the waterside and under the dim, cool shadow of the arch.

'Here in the mud,' said Cadfael, 'I found this, torn off surely in a struggle. It comes from a girdle belonging to Mistress Perle, for Niall Bronzesmith made a new buckle to match the belt fittings only a few days ago, and this was the pattern he had to copy. That puts it past doubt, he knows his work. And here someone had a boat laid up ready.'

'As like as not stolen,' said Madog judicially, eyeing the deep mark in the soil. 'For such a cantrip, why use your own? Then if it's noted, and any man smells something amiss about where it's seen and what's within it, nothing leads towards you. And this was early in the morning, yesterday? Now I wonder if any fisherman or waterman from the town has mislaid his boat from its moorings? I know a dozen could have left this scar. And all you need do, when you'd done with the skiff, would be turn it adrift to fetch up where it would.'

'That could only be downstream,' said Hugh, looking up from the little arrow-head of bronze in his palm.

'So it could! Only downstream from wherever he had done with it. And even that would surely be downstream from here, if here he set out with such a cargo. Far easier and safer than heading upstream. Early in the morning it may have been, and few people yet abroad, but by the time one rower, or even a pair, had taken a boat all round the walls of the town against the stream, as they'd have to do to get clear, there'd be folks enough about the shore and the water. Even after turning away from the town they'd have Frankwell to face – a good hour's rowing before they'd be free of notice and curiosity. Downstream, once past his stretch of the wall and out from under the castle, they could breathe easily, they'd be between fields and woodland, clear of the town.'

'That's good sense,' said Hugh. 'I don't say upstream is impossible, but we'll follow the best chance first. God knows we've dragged every alley within the walls, and ransacked most of the houses, and are still hard at it in there finishing the work. Not a soul owns to having seen or heard anything of her since last she spoke with the watchman at the gate, and started across the bridge here. And if ever she went, or was taken, back into the town, it was not by the gate. The porter passed in no cart or load that could have been hiding her, so he swears. Still, there are wickets through here and there, though most of them into burgage gardens, and it would be no easy matter to get through to the streets without the household knowing of it. I begin to believe that she cannot be within the walls, but I've set men at every wicket that gives access to a street, and made entry to every house an order under the king's justice. What's the same for all cannot well be resisted or complained of.'

'And has not?' wondered Cadfael. 'Never once?'

'They grumble, but even that under their breath. No, not one has put up any objection, nor shuffled and contrived to keep anything closed. And all yesterday until dusk I had her cousin treading on my heels, probing here and there like a worried hound on an uncertain scent. He's set two or three of his weavers to help in the hunt for her. The foreman – Bertred they call him, a strapping young fellow all brawn and brag – he's been out and about with us again all day, nose-down. He's gone with a party of my men now, out along the Castle Foregate, searching the yards and gardens in the suburb, and round to the river again. All her household is biting its nails, frantic to find her. And no wonder, for it's she who provides a living for the lot of them – a matter of twenty families or more depend on her. And never a hair of her to be found, and never a shadow of suspicion against any other creature, so far.'

'How did you do with Godfrey Fuller?' asked Cadfael, recalling what rumour said of Judith's wooers.

Hugh laughed briefly. 'I remember, too! And truth is truth, he seems as concerned about her almost as her cousin. What does he do but hand me all his keys, and bid me make free. And I did.'

'His keys for the dye-works and the fulling sheds, too?'

'All, though I needed none, for all his men were at work, and every corner open to view, and as innocent as the day. I think he would even have lent me some men to join the hunt, but that he's too fond of money to let the work slacken.'

'And William Hynde?'

'The old woolman? He's been away sleeping the night over with his shepherds and flocks, so his household said, and came home early this morning. He knew nothing about the girl going astray until then. Alan was there yesterday, and Hynde's wife made no demur, but let him look where he would, but I went back there this morning and spoke with the man himself. He's off back to the hills before night. It seems he has some hoggets up there with a rot of the feet, he and his man came back only to get a supply of the wash to treat them. And more concerned about them than about Mistress Perle, though he did say he was sorry to hear such news of her. By this time I'm certain she's not within the town. So,' said Hugh briskly, 'we may well look elsewhere. Downstream, we're agreed. Madog, come back with us to the town gate and get us a boat, and we'll take a look at what offers, downstream.'

In midstream, running with the current, and with only a twitch of Madog's oars now and then to keep them on course, they had the whole expanse of Shrewsbury's eastern side unrolling past them, a steep bank of green under the wall, here and there a cluster of low bushes at the water's edge, here and there a trailing willow tree, but chiefly one long sweep of seeding summer grass, and then the lofty grey stone of the wall. Barely a single ridge of roof showed over the crest, only the top of Saint Mary's spire and tower, and more distant glimpse of the tip of Saint Alkmund's. There were three wickets in the wall before they reached the mouth of Saint Mary's water-lane, which gave access to the river from town and castle at need, and in places the householders had extended their gardens to the outer side, or made use of the ground, where it was level enough, for their stores of wood or other materials for their crafts. But the slope here made cultivation difficult except in favoured spots, and the best gardens outside the wall were on the south-west, within the great serpent-coil of the river.

They passed the narrow walled chute of the water-lane, and beyond was another steep slope of grass, more cloaked in bushes here, before the town wall drew closer to the river, flanking the level, cleared strip of green where the young men were accustomed to set up the butts and practise their archery on holidays and fair-days. At the end of this ground there was one last wicket, close under the first tower of the castle, and past that the ground levelled, a sweep of open field between the water and the high road that emerged under the castle gates. Here, as on the Welsh side, the town had spilled beyond the wall for a short way, and little houses, close-set, bordered the road, huddling under the shadow of the great hulk of stone towers and curtain wall that straddled the only dry-shod approach to Shrewsbury.

The open meadows stretched away, widening, into an undulating expanse of field and woodland, peaceful and serene. The only remaining reminders of the town were here close beside the river. Godfrey Fuller's sheds and fulling-troughs and tenterground, and a short way beyond, the substantial warehouse where William Hynde's best fleeces lay corded and ready, waiting for the middleman's barge to come and collect them, and the narrow, stout jetty where it would draw alongside to load.

There were men going busily in and out here about the fulling workshop, and two lengths of bright russet cloth stretched and drying on the frames. This was the season for the reds, browns and yellows. Cadfael looked back along the castle wall to the last wicket giving access to the town, and recalled that Fuller's house lay not far from the castle precinct, so, for that matter, though a little more distant, close to the high cross, did William Hynde's. This gate was convenient for both. Fuller kept a watchman here at night, living on the workshop premises.

'Small chance of ever hiding a captive lady here,' said Hugh resignedly. 'By day it would be impossible, with so many busy about the place, and by night the fellow who sleeps here is paid to keep a close eye on Hynde's property, too, and keeps a mastiff into the bargain. I don't recall that there's anything but meadow and woodland beyond, but we'll go a little further.'

The green banks drifted by on either side, encroaching trees overhanging both shores, but there was no thick woodland, and no building, not even a hut for half a mile or more. They were about to give up the hunt and turn back, and Cadfael was preparing to tuck up his sleeves and take an oar to help Madog back upstream, when Madog checked and pointed.

'What did I say? No need to go beyond this, here's what marks the end of the chase.'

Close under the left bank, where a curving current had hollowed the ground and exposed the roots of a small hawthorn, causing it to lean at an angle over the water, its branches had snared a fish of their own. The empty boat lay unevenly, its bow held between two thorn-boughs, its oars shipped, rocking gently in the shallows.

'This one I know,' said Madog, drawing alongside and laying a hand to the thwart to hold them together. 'It belongs to Arnald the fishmonger, under the Wyle, he moors it there at the town end of the bridge. Your man had nothing to do but row it across and hide it. Arnald will be raging round Shrewsbury clouting every lad on suspicion. I'd best do him a good turn and get it back to him, before he twists off an ear or two. He's had this borrowed once before, but at least they brought it back that time. Well, my lord, here it ends. Are you satisfied?'

'Bitterly unsatisifed,' said Hugh ruefully. 'but I take your meaning. Downstream, we agreed! Well, somewhere downstream from the bridge and upstream from here, it seems, Mistress Perle was put ashore and laid in safe-keeping. Too safe by far! For still I have no notion where.'

With the aid of a trailing mooring rope, which had been frayed to suggest that it had parted of itself, they took the stolen boat in tow, and turned to the hard pull upstream, Cadfael taking an oar, and settling himself solidly on the thwart to try and match Madog's experienced skill. But when they drew level with the fuller's workshop they were hailed from the bank, and down to the water's edge came two of Hugh's officers, dusty and tired, with three or four volunteers from among the townsmen holding off respectfully at a little distance. Among them, Cadfael observed, was that same weaver Bertred, all brawn and brag as Hugh had called him, bestriding the greensward with the large confidence of a man who likes himself well, and by the look of him not at all downcast at fetching up empty-handed at the end of his voluntary search. Cadfael had seen him occasionally in attendance on Miles Coliar, though he knew little of him but his appearance. Which was eminently presentable, fresh-coloured and healthy and beautifully built, with the kind of open face which may be just what it seems, or may be well adapted to conceal the fact that there is an inner chamber which is very firmly closed. Something slightly knowing about the apparently candid eyes, and a smile just a little too ready. And what was there to smile about in failing to find Judith Perle, close to the end of this second day of searching for her?

'My lord,' said the older sergeant, laying a hand to hold the boat still and inshore, 'we've been over well-nigh every tuft of grass between these two reaches of the river, both sides, and nothing to be found, nor a soul who owns to knowing anything.'

'I've done no better,' said Hugh resignedly, 'except that this must be the boat that carried her off. It was caught in thorn-branches, a little way downstream from here, but it belongs at the bridge. No need to look beyond here, unless the poor woman's been moved and moved again, and that's unlikely.'

'Every house and garden along the road we've searched. We saw you making down-river, my lord, so we took yet another look round here, but you see everything's open as the day. Master Fuller made us free of all his holding.'

Hugh looked about him in a long, sweeping, none too hopeful glance. 'No, small chance of doing anything here unperceived, at least by daylight, and it was early in the day she vanished. Someone has looked in Master Hynde's warehouse there?'

'Yesterday, my lord. His wife gave us the key readily, I was there myself, so was my lord Herbard. Nothing within but his baled fleeces, the loft all but full of them, floor to roof. He had a good clip this year, seemingly.'

'Better than I did,' said Hugh. 'But I don't keep above three hundred sheep, small coin to him. Well, you've been at it all day, as well take a rest and be off home.' He set foot lightly to the thwart and stepped ashore. The boat rocked softly to the motion. 'There's nothing more we can do here. I'd best get back to the castle, and see if by chance someone else has had better luck. I'll go in here by the eastern gate, Madog, but we can lend you two rowers, if you like, and help you back upstream with both boats. Some of these lads who've been on the hunt with us could do with a voyage back to the bridge.' He cast a glance round the group that held off respectfully, watching and listening. 'Better than walking, lads, after all the walking you've done this day. Who's first?'

Two of the men came forward eagerly to uncouple the boats and settle themselves on the thwarts. They shoved gently off into the stream ahead of Madog, and set a practised pace. And it might well be, Cadfael thought, noting how Bertred the weaver hung well back from offering his own stout arms, that his walk home from the nearby castle gate into the town was barely longer than it would have been from the bridge gate after disembarking, so that he saw small gain in volunteering. It might even be that he was no expert with an oar. But that did not quite account for the small, bland smile and the look of glossy content on his comely young face as he withdrew himself discreetly from notice behind his companions. And it certainly did not account for the last glimpse Cadfael had of him, as he glanced back over his shoulder from midstream. For Bertred had lagged behind Hugh and his henchmen as they set off briskly towards the road and the eastern gate of the town, had halted a moment to watch them as they breasted the rise, and then had turned his back and made off at a purposeful but unhurried pace in the opposite direction, towards the nearest stand of woodland, as though he had important business there.

Bertred came home for his supper only with the early dusk, to a distracted household which had lost its routine and limped through the day forgetful of work, meal-times, and every other factor that served to mark the hours in an orderly and customary fashion. Miles fretted from workshop to street a dozen times an hour, and ran out to accost any passing soldier of the garrison for news, of which there was none. In two days he had grown so tense and brittle that even his mother, for once daunted into comparative silence, tended to slip aside out of his way. The girls in the spinning room whispered and wondered far more than they worked, and foregathered with the weavers to gossip as often as his back was turned.

'Who'd have thought he cared so much for his cousin!' Branwen marvelled, awed by his strained and anxious face. 'Of course a man feels for his own kin, but – you'd have thought it was his bride he'd lost, not his cousin, he goes so grieved.'

'He'd be a sight less concerned for his Isabel,' said a cynic among the weavers. 'She'll bring him a passable dowry, and he's well enough satisfied with his bargain, but there are as good fish in the sea if she slipped off the hook. Mistress Judith is his keep and future and all. Besides, the two get on well enough, for all I could ever see. He's got every call to worry.'

And worry he did, in a nail-biting, brow-furrowing frenzy of concern and anxiety that continued unbroken through the day, and at night, when search was perforce abandoned, subsided into a mute, resigned dejection, waiting for morning to renew the hunt. But by this second twilight it seemed every corner of the town had been ransacked, and every house and garden and pasture in the suburbs at least visited, and where were they to look next?

'She can't be far,' Dame Agatha insisted strenuously. 'They'll surely find her.'

'Far or near,' said Miles wretchedly, 'she's too well hidden. And some villain holding her, for certain. And how if she's forced to give way and take him? Then what's to become of you and me, if she lets a master into the house?'

'She never would, and she so set against marrying. No, that she won't do. Why, if a man uses her so ill, more like by far, once she's free of him – as she will be! – to do what she's thought of doing so long, and go into a nunnery. And only two days now to the day of the rent!' Agatha pointed out. 'Then what's to be done, if that passes and she still lost?'

'Then the bargain's broken, and there's time to think again and think better, but only she can do it. Until she's found there's nothing to be done, and no comfort. Tomorrow I'll go out again myself,' Miles vowed, shaking an exasperated head over the failure of the king's sheriff and all his men.

'But where? Where is there left they haven't searched already?'

A hard question indeed, and one without an answer. And into this waiting and frustrated household Bertred came sidling in the dark, discreetly quiet and solemn about the continuing failure to find any trace of his mistress, and yet looking so sleek and bright-eyed that Miles was brutally short with him, not at all his usual good-tempered self, and followed him with a long, glowering stare when Bertred wisely made off into the kitchen. On warm summer evenings it was pleasanter to be outdoors than there in the dim, smoky room with the heat of the fire, even when it was turfed down for the night or raked out until morning, and the rest of the household had gone out on their own ploys. Only Bertred's mother Alison, who cooked for the family and its workers, was waiting there none too patiently for her truant son, with a pot still warming over the naked fire.

'Where have you been till this time?' she wanted to know, turning on him with the ladle in her hand as he tramped briskly in at the door and went to his place at the long trestle table. He gave her a casual kiss in passing, brushing her round red cheek lightly. She was a plump, comfortable figure of a woman with some worn traces still of the good looks she had handed on to her son. 'All very well,' she said, setting the wooden bowl before him with a crash, 'after keeping me waiting here so late.

And much good you must have done all day, or you'd be telling me now you've brought her home, and preening yourself like a peacock over it. There were some of the men came home two hours ago and more. Where have you been loitering since then?'

In the dim kitchen his small, self-satisfied smile could barely be seen, but the tone of his voice conveyed the same carefully contained elation. He took her by the arm and drew her down to the bench beside him.

'Never mind where, and leave it to me why! There was a thing I had to wait for, and it was worth the waiting. Mother . . .' He leaned close, and sank his voice to a confidential whisper. '. . . how would you like to be more than a servant in this house? A gentlewoman, an honoured dowager! Wait a little while, and I mean to make my fortune and yours, too. What do you say to that?'

'Great notions you always had,' she said, none too impressed, but too fond to mock him. 'And how do you mean to do that?'

'I'm telling nothing yet, not till I can say it's done. There's not one of those busy hounds out hunting all this day knows what I know. That's all I'm saying, and not a word to any but you. And . . . Mother, I must go out again tonight, when it's well dark. Never you worry, I know what I'm about, only wait, and you'll be glad of it. But tonight you mustn't say a word, not to anyone.'

She held him off doubtfully to get a better look at his smiling, teasing face. 'What are you up to? I can keep as close a mouth as any where there's need. But don't you go running your head into trouble. If there's ought you know, why haven't you told?'

'And spend the credit along with my breath? No, leave all to me, Mother, I know what I'm about. Tomorrow you'll see for yourself, but not a word tonight. Promise it!'

'Your sire was just such another,' she said, relaxing into smiles, 'always full of great plans. Well, if I spend the night wakeful out of pure curiosity, so be it. Would I ever stand in your way? Not a word out of me, I promise.' And instantly she added, with a brief blaze of unease and foreboding: 'Only take care! There may be more than you out about risky business in the night.'

Bertred laughed, and hugged her impulsively in long arms, and went away whistling into the dusk of the yard.

His bed was in the weaving-shed with the looms, and there he had no companion to wake and hear him rise and do on his clothes, more than an hour after midnight. Nor was it any problem to slip out from the yard by the narrow passage to the street, without so much as risking being seen by any other member of the household. He had chosen his time with care. It must not be too soon, or there would still be people stirring. It must not be too late, or the moon would be up, and darkness suited his purpose better. And it was dark indeed in the narrow lanes between the overhanging houses and shops, as he threaded the mass of streets between Maerdol-head and the castle. The town gate there on the eastern side was a part of the castle defences, and would be closed and guarded during the night hours. For the past few years Shrewsbury had been safe enough from any threat on the eastern approach, only the occasional brief Welsh raid from the west had troubled the peace of the shire, but Hugh Beringar maintained the routine watchfulness without a break. But the most easterly wicket, giving access to the river under the very towers of the fortress, was there to be used freely. Only in times of possible danger were all the wickets closed and barred, and sentries set on the walls. Horsemen, carts, market wagons, all must wait for the gates to be opened at dawn, but a solitary man might pass through at any hour.

Bertred knew his way in the dark as well as by day, and could tread as lightly and move as silently as a cat. He stepped through the wicket into the slope of grass and bushes above the river, and drew the wooden door closed after him. Below him the flow of the Severn made fleeting ribbons and glints of moving light, just perceptible as tremors in the darkness. The sky was lightly veiled and showed no stars, and was just sufficiently less dark than the solid masses of masonry, earth and trees to show their outlines in deeper black. When the moon came up, more than an hour later than this, the heavens would probably clear. He had time to stand for a moment and think out what he had to do. There was little wind, but he had better take it into consideration, it would not do to approach the watchman's mastiff at the fulling works downwind. He wet a finger and tested. The slight, steady breeze was blowing from the south-west, from upstream. He would have to move round the bulk of the castle virtually to the fringes of the gardens along the high road, and come about from downwind in a cautious circle to reach the back of the wool warehouse.

He had taken a good look at it in the afternoon. So had they all, the sheriff and his sergeants and the townsmen helping them in the search. But they had not, like Bertred, been in and out two or three times at that warehouse, when fetching away fleeces for Mistress Perle. Nor had they been present in Mistress Perle's kitchen on the night before her disappearance, to hear Branwen declare her mistress's intent to go to the abbey early in the morning and make a new charter, rendering her gift of property unconditional. So they had not seen, as Bertred had, Hynde's man Gunnar drink up his ale and pocket his dice shortly afterwards, and take himself off in some haste, though he had seemed to be comfortably rooted for the evening. That was one more creature besides Bertred who had known of that intent, and surely had slipped so promptly away to disclose it to yet one more. Which one, the old or the young, made no matter. The strange thing was that it had taken Bertred himself so long to grasp the possibilities. The sight of the old counting-house hatch, that afternoon, securely shuttered and barred on the outer side, and probably also made fast within, had been all that was needed to enlighten him. If he had then waited patiently in the cover of the trees until dusk, to see who slipped out from the wicket in the town wall, and exactly where he headed with his rush basket, it had been only a final precaution, to render certainty even more certain.

Heavy against his side, in the great pocket stitched inside his coat, he had a long chisel and a hammer, though he would have to avoid noise if he could. The outer bar across the hatch need only be drawn back out of the socket, but he suspected the shutter was also nailed fast to its frame. A year ago a bale of fleeces had been stolen by entry through this hatch, and as the small counting-house within was already disused, old Hynde had had the window sealed against any further attempt. That was one more thing the sheriff did not know.

Bertred came down softly along the meadow beyond the warehouse, with the gentle wind in his face. By then shapes of things showed clearly, black against faded black. The bulk of the building was between him and Godfrey Fuller's workshops, the very faint shimmer of the river a little way off on his left hand. And double his own height above him was the square of the shuttered hatch, just perceptible to his night eyes.

The climb presented no problems, he had made sure of that. The building was old, and due to this rear wall backing into the slope, the base of the wall of vertical planks had suffered wet damage over the years, and rotted, and old Hynde, never one to spend lavishly, had reinforced it with split logs fastened across horizontally on top of the massive sill-beam, affording easy toe-holds high enough for him to reach up and get a grip on the rough sill under the hatch, which was just wide enough to lend him a secure resting-place with an ear to the shutters.

He drew himself up carefully, got a hand firmly on the bar that sealed the hatch, and a thigh along the sill, and drew breath and cautiously held it, wary of the first strange and unexpected thing. The shutters fitted together well, but not quite perfectly. For about a hand's-length down the centre, where the two leaves met, a hairline of light showed, too fine to give a view of anything within, a mere quill-stroke of faint gold. Perhaps not so strange, after all. Perhaps they had had the grace at least to let her have a candle or a lamp in her prison. It would pay, surely, to accommodate her in as many harmless ways as possible, while trying to break down her resistance. Force need only be tried if all else failed. But two days without gain began to look very like failure.

The chisel inside his coat was jabbing him painfully in the ribs. He worked a hand cautiously into the pocket and drew out the tools, laying them beside him on the sill, so that he could ease himself a little nearer to the sliver of light, and lay his ear to the crack.

The sudden start he made all but toppled him from his perch. For a voice spoke up, firmly and clearly, quite close on the inner side of the shutters.

'No you will not change me. You should have known it. I am your problem. You brought me here, now get me hence as best you can.'

The voice that answered was more distant, perhaps at the far side of the room, in hopeless retreat, and the words did not come over clearly, but the tone was of desperate complaining and abject pleading, and the speaker was a man, though so unrecognisable that Bertred could not be sure whether he was old or young, master or servant.

His own plan was already awry. At best he must wait, and if he had to wait too long the moon would be up, and the risks more than doubled. The place was right, his judgement confirmed, the woman was there. But the time was ill-guessed, for her gaoler was there with her.

Chapter Eight

'YOU BROUGHT me here,' she said, 'now get me hence as best you can.'

In the narrow, bare room which had once been Hynde's counting-house, the small flame of the saucer lamp barely showed them to each other. He had flung away from her, and stood in the far corner, his back turned, his head bowed into the forearm he had braced against the wall, his other fist driving uselessly and painfully against the timber. His voice emerged muffled, its helpless rage degraded into a feeble wail: 'How can I? How can I? There is no way out now!'

'You could unlock the door,' she said simply, 'and let me go. Nothing could be easier.'

'For you!' he protested furiously, and swung about to glare at her with all the venom of which his nature was capable. It did not amount to much more than self-pity. He was not a venomous man, only a vain and foolish one. He wearied her, but he did not frighten her. 'All very well for you! And I should be finished, damned . . . thrown into prison to rot. Once out, you'd denounce me and take your revenge.'

'You should have thought of that,' she said, 'before you snatched me away, you and your rogue servant. You brought me here to this sordid hole, locked in behind your wool bales, without comfort, without decency, subject to your man's rough handling and your insolent pestering, and do you expect gratitude? Or even mercy? Why should I not denounce you? You had best think hard and fast. You will have to release me or kill me at last, and the longer the delay, the worse will be your own plight. Mine,' she said bitterly, 'is already bad enough. What has become by now of my good name? What will my situation be when I go back to my own house and family?'

Vivian came back to her with a rush, flinging himself on his knees beside the rough bench where she had taken what rest she could, and where she sat now erect and pale, her hands gripped together in her lap, her skirts drawn close about her as though to avoid not only his touch, but the very dust and desolation of her prison. There was nothing else in the room but the broken desk where once the clerk had worked over his figures, and a stone ewer with a chipped lip, and a pile of dust and debris in the corner. The lamp stood on the end of the bench beside her, its light now full on Vivian's dishevelled hair and woeful face. He clutched at her hands imploringly, but she withdrew them so sharply that he sat back on his heels with a great gulp of despair.

'I never meant such mischief, I swear it! I thought you had a fondness for me, I thought I had only to get you to myself a while, and it would all be agreed between us . . . Oh, God, I wish I'd never begun it! But indeed, I did believe you could love me . . .'

'No! Never!' She had said it many times in these past two days, and always with the same irrevocable coldness. He should have recognised from the first utterance that his cause was hopeless. But he had not even been deceiving himself into the conviction that he loved her. What he coveted was the security and comfort she could bring him, the payment of his debts and the prospect of an easy life. Perhaps even the pleasure of cocking a snook at his parsimonious father – parsimonious at least in Vivian's eyes, because he had finally tired of bailing his heir out of debt and trouble. Oh, no doubt the young man had found the prospect of marriage with her pleasurable in itself, but that was not the reason he had chosen that particular morning for his bid. Why let half a fortune slip through your fingers, when with one bold stroke you might have the whole?

'How have they accounted for my vanishing?' she asked. 'Is the worst said of me already? Have they been looking for me at all? Am I thought dead?'

One faint spasm of defiance and spite passed over Vivian's face. 'Looking for you? The whole town's turned upside-down looking for you, the sheriff and all his men, your cousin and half your workmen. Not a house but they've visited, not a barn but they've searched. They were here yesterday, towards evening. Alan Herbard and three of the garrison with him. We opened the doors to them, and showed the baled fleeces, and they went away satisfied. Why did you not cry out then, if you wanted rescue from me?'

'They were here?' Judith stiffened, chilled by this spurt of malice. But it was the last, he had done his worst, and could not maintain it long. 'I never heard them!' she said with resigned bitterness.

'No.' He said it quite simply now, all his resistance spent. 'They were easily satisfied. The room is quite forgotten, and all those bales shut out sound. They never questioned. They were here again this afternoon, but not asking for the keys. They'd found the boat . . . No, you might not hear them. Would you have cried out to them if you had?'

It was a meaningless question, and she did not answer it, but she gave it some thought. Would she have wished to be heard calling for help, and baled out of this mean prison, unprepared, dusty and stained, compromised, piteous? Might it not have been better to be silent, and make her own way out of this predicament? For the truth was that after the first confusion, indignation and alarm she had never been afraid of Vivian, nor in any danger of giving way to him, and now she would welcome as much as he would a solution which would smooth out of sight all that had happened, and leave her dignity and integrity independent of any other soul. In the end he would have to release her. She was the stronger of the two.

He ventured a hand to clutch at a fold of her skirt. The face he lifted to her, seen clearly thus close and lit by the yellow flame of the wick, was strangely vulnerable and young, like a guilty boy pleading in extenuation of some heinous fault and not yet resigned to punishment. The brow he had braced against the wall was smeared with dust, and with the back of his hand, sweeping away tears or sweat or both, he had made a long black stain down his cheek. There was a trail of cobweb in the bright, fair, tangled hair. The wide brown eyes, dilated with stress, glinted gold from the spark of the lamp, and hung in desperate appeal upon her face.

'Judith, Judith, do me right! I could have used you worse . . . I could have taken you by force –'

She shook her head scornfully. 'No, you could not. You

have not the hardihood. You are too cautious – or perhaps too decent – both, it may be! Nor would it have benefited you if you had,' she said starkly, and turned herself away to evade the desperate and desolate youth of his face, with its piercing reflections of Brother Eluric, who had agonised in silence and without hope or appeal. 'And now here we are, you and I both, and you know as well as I know that this must end. You have no choice but to let me go.'

'And you'll destroy me!' he said in a whisper, and sank his corn-gold head into his hands.

'I wish you no harm,' she said wearily. 'But it was you brought us to this, not I.'

'I know it, I own it. God knows I wish it undone! Oh, Judith, help me, help me!'

It had come to that, the bleak acknowledgement that he had lost, that he was now her prisoner, not she his, even that he was dependent upon her to save him from the trap he himself had set. He laid his head in her lap and shook as though with cold. And she was so tired and so astray that she had lifted a resigned hand to lay upon his head and quiet him, when the sudden tearing, rushing slither of sound outside the shutters at her back caused them both to start and freeze in alarm. Not a loud sound, merely like some not very heavy weight sliding down and ending in a dull fall into grass. Vivian started to his feet, quivering.

'For God's sake, what was that?'

They held their breath, straining into a silence as sudden as the sound, and as brief. Then, more distant from the direction of the riverside fulling-works, came the loud, savage alarm-baying of the chained mastiff; and after a few moments this changed abruptly into the deeper, more purposeful note of the chase, as he was loosed from his chain.

Bertred had trusted too confidently to old, worn, neglected wood, left too long uncared for on the weather side of the warehouse. The sill on which he was perched had been fixed in position with long nails, but at the more exposed end the nails had rusted in many rains, and the wood round them had rotted. When he shifted his weight further forward to ease an uncomfortable cramp, and get an ear more avidly to the crack, the wood splintered and parted, and the sill swung down before him, scraping the planks of the wall, and sent him slithering and clawing to the ground. Not a great fall nor a very loud sound, but loud enough in that depth of the night to carry to the fulling-works.

He was on his feet as he reached the ground, and leaned for a moment against the wall to get his breath back and steady his legs under him after the shock of the fall. The next moment he heard the mastiff give tongue.

Bertred's instinct was to run uphill towards the houses along the high road, and he set off in that direction, alerted to terror, only to check a moment later in the despairing knowledge that the hound was far faster than he could be, and would overhaul him long before he reached any shelter. The river was nearer. Better by far make for that, and swim across to the open spur of woodland at the end of the Gaye. In the water he could more than match the hound, and surely the watchman would call the dog off rather than let it pursue further.

He turned, and began to run in wild hare-leaps downhill across the tussocky grass, full tilt towards the river-bank. But both dog and man were out after him now, roused to a thief-hunt in the small hours, when all honest folk should be in their beds, and only malefactors could be abroad. They had traced the sound of his fall only too accurately; they knew someone had been clambering round the warehouse, and surely with no good intent. A detached part of Bertred's mind somehow had time to wonder, even as his legs and lungs strained for the speed of terror, how young Hynde managed to go back and forth by night without raising the same alarm. But of course the mastiff knew him, he was one of the guarded, an ally in the protection of property here, not an enemy and a threat.

Flight and pursuit made strangely little noise in the night, or disturbance in the darkness, and yet he felt, rather than saw, man and hound converging upon his path, and heard the rush of movement and the purposeful in-and-out of breath drawing close from his right flank. The watchman lunged at him with a long staff, and caught him a glancing blow on the head that half-stunned him, and sent him hurtling forward out of balance to the very edge of the river-bank. But he was past the man now, and could leave him behind, it was the dog, close on his heels, that terrified him, and gave him the strength for the last great leap that carried him out from the grass spur overhanging the water.

The bank was higher than he had realised, and the water somewhat lower, exposing shelving faces of rock. Instead of clearing these into deep water, he fell with a crash among the tilted stones, though his outflung arm raised a splash from the shallows between. His head, already ringing from the watchman's blow, struck hard against a sharp edge of stone. He lay stunned where he had fallen, half-concealed beneath the bushy overhang, wholly shrouded in the darkness. The mastiff, no lover of water, padded uneasily along the grassy shelf and whined, but went no further.

The watchman, left well behind and out of breath, heard the splash, caught even a brief shimmer in the fitful pallor of the river's surface, and halted well short of the bank to whistle and call off his dog. The would-be thief must be half across the river by now, no use troubling further. He was reasonably sure that the felon had not succeeded in making an entry anywhere, or the dog would have raised the alarm earlier. But he did walk round the warehouse and the dye-sheds to make sure all was in order. The dangling sill under the dark shutters hung vertically, like the planks against which it rested, and the watchman did not observe it. In the morning he would have a thorough look round, but it seemed no harm had been done. He went back contentedly to his hut, with the dog paddling at his heels.

Vivian stood rigid, listening, until the dog's baying grew more distant, and finally ceased. He stirred almost painfully out of his stillness.

'Someone was prowling! Someone guesses – or knows!' He wiped sweat from his forehead with a dirty hand, prolonging the smears already there. 'Oh, God, what am I to do? I can't let you go free, and I can't keep you here any longer, not another day. If someone suspects . . .'

Judith sat silently, steadily watching him. His soiled and disillusioned beauty moved her against her will, as he could never have moved her at his most decorative and elated, the finest cock on the midden. Afraid to go on with his over-bold scheme, unable to retreat from it, frenziedly wishing he had never embarked upon it, he was like a fly in a cobweb, tangling himself ever more inextricably.

'Judith . . .' He was on his knees again at her feet, clinging to her hands, pleading, cajoling, but passionately, like a child, quite forgetful of his charm and stripped naked of his vanity. 'Judith, help me! Help me out of this! If there is a way, help me to find it. If they come and find you, I'm ruined, disgraced . . . If I let you go, you'll destroy me just the same –'

'Hush!' she said wearily. 'I don't wish you harm, I want no revenge, only to be free of you on the best terms I may.'

'How does that help me? Do you think they'll let you reappear, and ask no questions? Even if you hold your peace, how am I helped? There'll be no respite until you tell them all, and that's my undoing. Oh, if I knew which way to turn!'

'It would suit me no less than you,' said Judith, 'if we could smooth away this scandal peaceably, but it needs a miracle to account for these two lost days. And I must protect myself, if that's possible. You must fend for yourself, but I'd as lief you went unharmed, too, if that may be. What now? What ails you?'

He had started and stiffened, quick to alarm, and was listening with stretched sinews. 'Someone outside,' he said in a whisper. 'Again – didn't you hear? Someone is spying . . . Listen!'

She fell silent, though she was not convinced. He was so tense and frightened by this time that he could have conjured enemies out of the air. Through a long, hushed moment she heard no sound at all, even the very slight sigh of the breeze in the shutters had ceased.

'There's no one; you imagined it. Nothing!' She gripped his hands suddenly, asserting her mastery, where hitherto she had merely suffered his touch without response. 'Listen to me! There might be a way! When Sister Magdalen visited me, she offered me a place of retreat at Godric's Ford with her, if ever I reached the end of my tether and needed a refuge and a pause for breath. As God knows I have needed both, and still do. If you will take me there by night, secretly, then I can return later and say where I have been, and why, and how this turmoil and hunt for me never came to our ears there. As I hope may be true. I will say that I fled from my life for a while, to get courage to take it up again to better purpose. And I hope to God that may also be true. I will not name you, nor betray what you have done to me.'

He was staring up at her wide-eyed, hesitant to hope but unable to resist, glowing only to doubt again the possibility of salvation. 'They'll press you hard, they'll ask why did you say no word, why go away and leave everyone to fear for you. And the boat – they know about the boat, they must know –'

'When they ask,' she said starkly. 'I'll answer, or refuse them an answer. Fret as you may, you must needs leave all that to me. I am offering you a way of escape. Take it or leave it.'

'I daren't go all the way with you,' he said, writhing. 'If I were seen it would all come out in spite of you.'

'You need not come all the way. You may leave me to go the last piece of the way alone, I am not afraid. No one need see you.'

He was flushing into hope with every word. 'My father is gone back to his flocks today, he'll stay two nights or more up there with the shepherds, and there's one good horse still in the stable, stout enough to carry two, if you'll ride pillion with me. I could bring him out of the town before the gate's closed. Best not pass through the town together, but set out this way. There's a ford a little way downstream from here, we can make our way south on the other side and get to the road to Beistan. At dusk – if we start at dusk tomorrow . . . Oh, Judith, and I've done you such wrong, and can you so far forgive me? I have not deserved!'

It was something new, she thought wryly, for Vivian Hynde to suppose that his deserts were small, or that there was anything to which he was not entitled. He might yet be all the better for this one salutary fright which he had brought upon himself. He was no great villain, only a weak and self-indulgent boy. But she did not answer his question. There was one thing at least she found it hard to forgive him, and that was that he had exposed her to the rough handling of Gunnar, who had taken palpable delight in the close embrace of her body and the strength which had held her helpless. She had no fear of Vivian, but of Gunnar, if ever she encountered him without Vivian, she might be very much afraid.

'I do this for myself as much as for you,' she said. 'I've given my word and I'll keep it. Tomorrow at dusk. Agreed, it's too late to move tonight.'

He had recoiled again into doubt and fear, recalling the noises without, and the baying of the mastiff. 'But how if someone has suspicions of this place? How if they come again tomorrow demanding the keys? Judith, come back with me now, come to our house, it's not far from the wicket, no one will see us now. My mother will hide you and help us, and be grateful to you for sparing me. And my father's away in the hills, he'll never know. And there you may have rest and a bed, and water for washing, and all you need for your comfort . . .'

'Your mother knows of what you've done?' she demanded, aghast.

'No, no, nothing! But she'll help us now, for my sake.' He

was at the narrow door which had lain hidden behind the baled fleeces, turning the key, drawing her after him, feverish in his haste to be out of here and safe in his own home. 'I'll send Gunnar to make all innocent here. If they come they must find the place bare and deserted.'

She blew out the wick of the lamp and went with him, backwards down the ladder from the loft, out through the lower door and into the night. The moon was just rising, bathing the slope in pale-green light. The air was sweet and cool on her face after the close, musty smell and dust and the smoke of the lamp in the enclosed space. It was no very long walk to the shadows of the castle towers, and the wicket in the wall.

A darker shadow made its way round the spreading plane of moonlight, by the shortest route from behind the warehouse to the cover of trees, and so roundabout to the river-bank, rapid and silent. The overhang where Bertred had made his leap to evade the mastiff was still in shadow. He lay as he had fallen, still out of his senses, though he was beginning to stir and groan, and draw the laborious breath of one quickening to the consciousness of pain. The deeper shadow that fell across his body just as the edge of the moonlight reached the river did not penetrate his dazed mind or trouble his closed eyes. A hand reached down and took him by the hair, turning his face up to view it closely. He lived, he breathed, a little patching and a few hours to recover, and he would be able to account for himself and confess everything he knew.

The shadow stooping over him straightened and stood a moment looking down at him dispassionately. Then he thrust a booted toe into Bertred's side, levered him towards the edge of the stones on which he lay, and heaved him out into deep water, where the current curled fast, bearing the body out across midstream towards the further shore.

The twentieth of June dawned in a series of sparkling showers, settling by mid-morning into a fine, warm day. There was plenty of work waiting to be done in the orchards of the Gaye, but because of the morning rain it was necessary to wait for the midday heat before tackling them. The sweet cherries were ready for picking, but needed to be gathered dry, and there were also the first strawberries to pick, and there it was equally desirable to let the sun dry off the early moisture. On the open, sunlit expanse of the vegetable plots the ground dried out earlier, and the brothers on duty were busy sowing lettuces for succession, and hoeing and weeding, before noon, but it was after dinner that the orchard party began work at the extreme end of the abbey grounds.

There was no particular need for Brother Cadfael to go out with them, but neither was there anything urgently needing his attention in the herbarium, and the mounting uneasiness of the three-day vain hunt for Judith Perle would not let him rest or settle to any routine occupation. There had been no further word from Hugh, and nothing to tell Niall when he came anxiously enquiring. The entire affair stood still, the very hours of the day held their breath, making time endless.

To fill it at least with some physical movement, Cadfael went out to the orchards with the rest. As so often in a late season, nature had set out to make good the weeks that had been lost to the spring cold, and contrived to bring on, almost at the usual time, both strawberries and the first of the little hard gooseberries on their thorny bushes. But Cadfael's mind was not on fruit-picking. The orchards lay just opposite the level where the young archers shot at the butts on fair-days, under the sweep of the town wall and in the lee of the castle towers. Only a little way beyond, through the first belt of woodland, and he would be gazing straight across the water at the fulling-works, and just downstream at William Hynde's jetty.

Cadfael worked for a while, so distractedly that he collected more than his share of scratches. But after a while he straightened his back, sucked out of his finger the latest of many thorns, and walked on along the riverside into the belt of trees. Through their leaning branches the sweeping coronal of the town wall unrolled beside him across the water, and the steep green slope beneath the wall. Then the first jutting bastion of the castle, with the narrower level of meadow under it. Cadfael walked on, through the trees and out to a broad greensward beyond, dotted with low bushes close to the bank, and here and there a bed of reeds where the shallows ran gently and the fast current sped out into midstream. Now he was opposite the tenterground, where Godfrey Fuller's men were working, and a length of brown cloth was stretched taut between the frames to dry.

He reached a spot directly opposite the overhanging bushes where they had found the stolen boat abandoned. Along the bank beyond, a small boy was pasturing goats. Sunlit and peaceful, the Severn landscape lay somnolent in the afternoon light, denying the existence of murder, malice and abduction in so lovely a world.

Cadfael had gone but a hundred or so paces further, and was about to turn back, when he reached a curve where the bank opposite was undercut and the water beneath it deep, while on his side it shallowed into a sandy shoal, and subsided into soft, innocent ripples, barely moving. One of those places Madog knew well, where whatever had gone into the river upstream might fetch up again on land.

And something had indeed fetched up here in the night just past. It lay almost submerged, at rest on the sand but barely breaking the surface, a mass of darker colour washed over by the silvery shimmer of water, and lodged in the dull gold of the sand beneath. It was the small, languid pallor, which swung lightly with the flow but was no fish, that first caught Cadfael's eye. A man's hand, at the end of a dark sleeve that buoyed it up just enough to set it swaying. A man's brown head, the back of it just dimpling the surface, all its curling locks stretching out with the ripples and stirring like drowsy living things.

Cadfael slid down the shelving bank in haste, and waded into the shallow water to get a double grip on the sodden clothing under the trailing arms, and drag the body ashore. Dead beyond doubt, probably several hours dead. He lay on his face in the sand just clear of the water, and tiny rivulets ran out of him from every fold of clothing and every tangled curl of hair. A young man, very well made and shapely. Far too late to do anything for him but carry him home and provide him a decent burial. It would need more than one man to get him up the bank and bear him back along the Gaye, and Cadfael had better be about getting help as fast as possible.

The build, the common dun-coloured coat and chausses, might have belonged to a hundred young fellows from Shrewsbury, being the common working wear, and the body was not immediately recognisable to Cadfael. He stooped to resume a careful hold under the lax arms, and turned the dead man over to lie on his back, revealing to the indifferent sunlight the smeared, pallid but still comely face of Bertred, Judith Perle's foreman weaver.

Chapter Nine

THEY CAME in haste at his call, fluttered and dismayed, though a drowned man cast up by the Severn was no such rare matter, and these young brothers knew no more of the affair than that. No doubt whispers of the outer world's crises made their way in among the elders, but by and large the novices lived in innocence. Cadfael chose the strongest and the least likely to be distressed by the contemplation of death, and sent the others back to their work. With their hoes and rope girdles and scapulars they rigged a makeshift litter, and carried it down the riverside path to where the dead man lay.

In awed silence they took up their sodden burden, and bore him back in dripping procession through the belt of woodland and all along the lush level of the Gaye, to the path that climbed to the Foregate.

'We'd best take him to the abbey,' said Cadfael, halting a moment to consider. 'That's the quickest means of getting him decently out of the public view, and we can send for his master or his kin from there.' There were other reasons for the decision, too, but he did not think fit to mention them at this point. The dead man came from Judith Perle's household, and what had befallen him surely could not be entirely disconnected from all the other disasters which seemed to be haunting the house and the heiress of the Vestier business. In which case Abbot Radulfus had a direct interest and a right to be informed, and even more surely, so had Hugh Beringar.

Not only a right, but a need. Two deaths and a disappearance, all circling round the same lady and her dealings with the abbey, demanded very close attention. Even young, strong men in the most exuberant of health can drown. But Cadfael had already seen the broken bruise on the dead man's right temple, washed white and bleached of blood by the water of the river. 'Run on ahead, lad,' he said to Brother Rhun, the youngest of the novices, 'and let Father Prior know what manner of guest we're bringing.'

The boy bowed his flaxen head in the small gesture of respect with which he received any order from an elder, and was off in an instant, willing and eager. To bid Rhun run was a kindness rather than an imposition, for there was nothing in which he took greater delight than making use of the fleetness and grace he had possessed for barely a year, after coming to Saint Winifred's festival a cripple and in pain. His year's novitiate was almost over, and soon he would be admitted as a full brother. No power or persuasion could have induced him to depart from the service of the saint who had healed him. What to Cadfael was still the serious burden and stumbling-block of obedience, Rhun embraced as a privilege, as happily as he accepted the sunlight on his face.

Cadfael turned from watching the bright head and flashing feet ascend the path, and covered the dead man's face with the corner of a scapular. Water dripped through the saturated cloth as they carried Bertred up to the road, and along the Foregate to the abbey gatehouse. Inevitably there were people abroad to halt at sight of the mournful procession, and nudge and whisper and stare as they passed. It was always a mystery where the urchins of the Foregate sprang from, as soon as there was something unusual to stare at, and how they multiplied at every step, and how the dogs, their inseparable playmates, also halted and dawdled alongside them with much the same expression of alerted curiosity on their faces. Soon guess and counter-guess would be running through the streets, but none of them would yet be able to name the drowned man. The little time before it was common knowledge who he was could be useful to Hugh Beringar, and merciful to the dead man's mother. One more widow, Cadfael recalled, as they turned in at the gatehouse and left a ring of watchers gathered at a respectable distance outside.

Prior Robert came hastening to meet the procession, with Brother Jerome scurrying at his heels, and Brother Edmund from the infirmary and Brother Denis from the guest-hall converged at the same time upon the bearers and the bier. Half a dozen brothers who had been crossing the great court variously about their own proper business lingered to watch, and to draw closer by degrees to hear and see the better.

'I have sent Brother Rhun to notify the lord abbot,' said Robert, stooping his lofty silver head over the still body on the improvised litter. 'This is a very bad business. Where did you find the man? Was it on our ground you took him ashore?'

'No, some way beyond,' said Cadfael, 'cast up on the sand. Dead some hours, I judge. There was nothing to be done for him.'

'Was it necessary, then, to bring him here? If he is known, and has family in the town or the Foregate, they will take charge of his burial rites.'

'If not necessary,' said Cadfael, 'I thought it advisable he should be brought here. I believe the lord abbot will also think so. There are reasons. The sheriff may have an interest in this matter.'

'Indeed? Why should that be so, if the man died by drowning? Surely an accident not unknown here.' He reached a fastidious hand to turn back the scapular from the bleached and bluish face which in life had glowed with such self-conscious health. But these features meant nothing to him. If he had ever seen the man, it could have been only casually, passing the gates. The house at Maerdol-head lay in the town parish of Saint Chad; neither worship nor commerce would bring Bertred into frequent contact with the Foregate. 'Do you know this man?'

'By sight, yes, though little more than that. But he is one of Mistress Perle's weavers, and lives in her household.'

Even Prior Robert, who held himself aloof from those uncomfortable worldly concerns which sometimes infiltrated into the abbey's well-ordered enclave and bred disruption there, opened his eyes wide at that. He could not choose but know what untoward things had happened connected with that household, nor quite resist the conviction that any new disaster similarly connected must be a part of the whole deplorable pattern. Coincidences do occur, but they seldom cluster by the dozen round one dwelling and one name.

'Well!' he said on a long breath, cautiously noncommittal. 'Yes, the lord abbot should certainly know of this.' And with due relief he added: 'He is coming now.'

Abbot Radulfus had emerged from his garden and was approaching briskly, with Rhun attendant at his elbow. He said nothing until he had drawn back the covering from Bertred's head and shoulders and surveyed him in sombre and thoughtful silence for a long moment. Then he again covered the dead face, and turned to Cadfael.

'Brother Rhun has told me where he was found, and how, but he does not know who the man is. Do you?'

'Yes, Father. His name is Bertred, he is Mistress Perle's foreman weaver. I saw him yesterday out with the sheriff's men, helping in the hunt for the lady.'

'Who has not been found,' said Radulfus.

'No. This is the third day of searching for her, but she has not been found.'

'And her man is found dead.' There was no need to point out to him implications which were already plain. 'Are you satisfied that he drowned?'

'Father, I need to consider that, I think he did, but also he has suffered a blow to the head. I would like to examine his body further.'

'So, I suppose, would the lord sheriff,' said the abbot briskly. 'I'll send to him at once, and keep the body here for the present. Do you know if he could swim?'

'No, Father, but there are few born here who can't. His kin or his master will tell us.'

'Yes, we must also send to them. But perhaps later, after Hugh has seen him, and made what you and he between you can of the matter.' And to the bearers of the litter, who had laid it down meanwhile and stood waiting silently, a little apart, he said: 'Take him to the mortuary chapel. You had best strip him and lay him decently. Light candles for him. However and for whatever cause he died, he is our mortal brother. I'll send a groom to look for Hugh Beringar. Wait with me, Cadfael, until he comes. I want to know everything you have gathered concerning this poor girl who is lost.'

In the mortuary chapel they had laid Bertred's naked body on the stone bier, and covered him with a linen cloth. His sodden clothes lay loosely folded aside, with the boots they had drawn from his feet. The light being dim in there, they had also provided candles on tall holders, so that they could be placed wherever they gave the best light. They stood close about the slab, Abbot Radulfus, Brother Cadfael and Hugh Beringar. It was the abbot who drew down the linen and uncovered the dead, who lay with his hands duly crossed on his breast, drawn out very straight and dignified. Someone had reverently closed the eyes Cadfael remembered as half-open, like someone just waking, too late ever to complete the awakening.

A youthful body and a handsome, perhaps slightly over-muscled for perfection. Not much past twenty, surely, and blessed with features regular and shapely, again perhaps a shade over-abundant in flesh or under-provided with bone. The Welsh are accustomed to seeing in the faces of their neighbours the strong solidity and permanence of bone, and are sensitive to loss where they see it pared down and over-cushioned in others. Nevertheless, a very comely young man. Face and neck and shoulders, and from elbow to fingertips, he was tanned by outdoor sun and wind, though the brown was dulled and sad now.

'Not a mark on him,' said Hugh, looking him over from head to feet, 'barring that knock on his forehead. And that surely caused him nothing worse than a headache.'

High near the hairline the skin was certainly broken, but it seemed no more than a glancing blow. Cadfael took up the head, with its thick thatch of brown hair plastered to the broad forehead, between his hands, and felt about the skull with probing fingers. 'He has another dunt, here, on the left side, here in his hair, above the ear. Something with a long, sharp edge – through all this thickness of hair it made a scalp wound. That could have knocked the wits out of him for some time, perhaps, but not killed. No, he certainly drowned.'

'What could the man have been doing?' asked the abbot, pondering. 'At that spot on that shore, in the night? There is nothing there, no path that leads anywhere, no house to be visited. Hard to see what business a man could possibly have there in the dark.'

'The business he'd been on all yesterday,' said Hugh, 'Is the hunt for his mistress. He was in Mistress Perle's service, of her household, he offered his help, and so far as I saw he gave it, unsparingly, and in good earnest. How if he was still bent on continuing the search?'

'By night? And there? There is nothing there but open meadow and a few groves of trees,' said Radulfus, 'not one cottage for some distance, once past our border, nowhere that a stolen woman could be hidden. Even if he had been found on the opposite bank it would have been more believable, at least that gives access to the town and the houses of the Castle Foregate. But even so – by night, and a dark night until late . . .'

'And even so, how did he come by two blows on the head and end in the river? A man might go too near on a shelving bank, and miss his footing in the dark,' said Hugh, shaking his head, 'but of a native Shrewsbury lad I doubt it. They know their river. We must find out if he was a swimmer, but the most of them learn early. Cadfael, we know where he was cast up. Is it possible he went into the water on the other side? If he tried to swim across, half-stunned after he got these injuries, might he fetch up about where you found him?'

'That we should ask of Madog,' said Cadfael. 'He'll know. The currents are certainly very strong and contrary in places, it would be possible.' He straightened the wet hair almost absently on the dead man's forehead, and drew up the linen over his face. 'There's nothing more he can tell us. It remains to tell his kin. At least they may be able to say when last they saw him, and whether he owned to having any plans for the night.'

'I've sent for Miles Coliar, but said nothing to him yet of the reason. Better he should break it to the mother, it will come easier for her there, in her own home – for I'm told she belongs there, in the kitchen. And Coliar will need to have the body taken back there to make ready for burial, if you see no need to keep it longer.'

'None,' said Cadfael, turning away from the bier with a sigh. 'At your discretion, both! I have done.' But at the door, last to leave the chapel, he cast one long glance back at the still white shape on the slab of stone. One more young man dead untimely, sad waste of the stuff of life. 'Poor lad!' said Cadfael, and closed the door gently after him.

Miles Coliar came from the town in haste and alone, uninformed of the occasion for the summons, but certainly aware that there must be a grave reason, and by the look of his face speculating anxiously and fearfully as to what that might be. They awaited him in the ante-room of the gatehouse. Miles made his reverence to abbot and sheriff, and raised a worried countenance to look rapidly from face to face, questioning their solemnity.

'My lord, is there news? My cousin . . .? Have you got word of her, that you sent for me here?' His pallor blanched still more, and his face stiffened into a mask of dread, misreading, it seemed, their mute and sombre looks. 'Oh, God, no! Not . . . no, she cannot be . . . You have not found her . . .?' His voice foundered on the word 'dead', but his lips shaped it.

'No, no!' said Hugh in haste. 'Not that! No, there's nothing new, no word of her yet, no need to think the worst. This is quite another matter, though grim enough. The hunt for your cousin goes on, and will go on until we find her.'

Miles said: 'Thank God!' just audibly, and drew deep breath, the tense lines of his face relaxing. 'Pardon if I am slow to think and speak and understand, and too hasty to fear extremes. These few days I have hardly slept or rested at all.'

'I am sorry to add more to your troubles,' said Hugh, 'but needs must. It's not Mistress Perle we're concerned with here. Have you missed any man from your looms today?'

Miles stared, and scratched his bushy brown head, at once relieved and puzzled. 'None of the weavers are working today, the looms have been neglected since yesterday morning, we've all or most been out on the hunt. I've kept the women spinning, it's no work for them to go stravaging about with the sergeants and the men of the garrison. Why do you ask, my lord?'

'Then have you seen your man Bertred at all since last night? He lives in your household, I'm told.'

'He does,' agreed Miles, frowning. 'No, I've not seen him today, with the looms quiet there's no reason I should. He eats in the kitchen. I suppose he's out again on the hunt, though God knows we've knocked on every door and probed round every yard in the town, and not a housewife or good man who hasn't been alerted to watch for any sign and listen for any word that could lead us to her. Yet what can we do but search and ask all over again? They're out on all the roads and asking at the hamlets for a mile round, now, as you best know, my lord. Bertred will be out raking the countryside with them, no question. He's been tireless for her, that I grant him.'

'And his mother – she's in no anxiety about him? Nothing has been said of things he may have had on his mind? She has not spoken of him to you?'

'No!' Miles was again looking bewilderedly from face to face. 'You'll hardly find a soul in our house who is not anxious, and they show it, but I've noticed nothing amiss with her more than with all the rest of us. Why? What is this, my lord? Do you know something of Bertred that I do not know? Not guilt!

Impossible! He's run himself raw scouring the town for my cousin . . . a decent man . . . You cannot have taken *him* in any wickedness . . .?'

It was a reasonable supposition, when the lord sheriff began asking such close questions about any man. Hugh put him out of his defensive agitation, but without over-haste.

'I know no wrong of your man, no. He is the victim of harm, not the cause. This is bad news we have for you, Master Coliar.' Its purport was already implicit in his tone, but he put it into words bleak and blunt enough. 'An hour ago the brothers working on the Gaye plucked Bertred out of the river and brought him here, dead. Drowned.'

In the profound silence that followed Miles stood motionless, until finally he stirred and moistened his lips.

'Where is he?'

'Laid decently in the mortuary chapel here,' said the abbot. 'The lord sheriff will take you to him.'

In the dim chapel Miles stared down at the known face now so strangely unfamiliar, and shook his head repeatedly and vigorously, as though he could shake away, if not the fact of death, his own shock at its suddenness. He had recovered his down-to-earth calmness and acceptance. One of his weavers was dead, the task of getting him out of here and into his grave with proper rites fell to Miles as his master. What was due from him he would do.

'How could this be?' he said. 'Yesterday he came late in the evening for his meal, but there was nothing in that, all day he'd been out abroad with your men, my lord. He went to his bed soon after. He said good night to me, it must have been about the hour of Compline. The house was already quiet, but some of us were still up. I never saw him again.'

'So you don't know whether he went out again by night?'

Miles looked up sharply, the blue of his eyes at their widest startlingly bright. 'It seems that he must have done. But in God's name, why should he? He was tired out after a long day. I know no reason why he should have stirred again till morning. You said it was but an hour since you took him out of the Severn . . .'

'*I* took him out,' said Cadfael, unobtrusive in a dark corner of the chapel. 'But he had been there more hours than one. In my judgement, since the small hours of the morning. It is not easy to say how long.'

'And, look, his brow is broken!' The wide, low forehead was dry now, but for the damp fringe of hair. The skin had shrunk apart, leaving the moist wound bared. 'Are you sure, Brother, that he drowned?'

'Quite sure. How he came by that knock there's no knowing, but he surely had it before he went into the water. You can't tell us anything that may help us, then?'

'I wish I could,' said Miles earnestly. 'I've seen no change in him, he's said nothing to me that could shed any light. This comes out of the dark to me. I cannot account for it.' He looked doubtfully at Hugh across the body. 'May I take him home? I'll need to speak with his mother first, but she'll want him home.'

'Naturally,' agreed Hugh resignedly. 'Yes, you may fetch him away when you will. Do you need help with the means?'

'No, my lord, we'll do all ourselves. I'll bring down a handcart and decent covering. And I do thank you and this house for the care you've had of him.'

He came again about an hour later, looking strained from the ordeal of breaking bad news to a widow now childless. Two of his men from the looms followed him with a simple, high-sided handcart used for wheeling goods, and waited mute and sombre in the great court until Brother Cadfael came to lead them to the mortuary chapel. Between them they carried Bertred's body out into the early evening light, and laid him on a spread brychan in the cart, and covered him tidily from view. They were still about it when Miles turned to Cadfael, and asked simply: 'And his clothes? She should have back with him all that was his. Small comfort for a woman, but she'll want them. And she'll need what they'll fetch, too, poor soul, though I'll see she's taken care of still, and so will Judith . . . when she's found. If . . .' His mind seemed to be drifting back into expectations of the worst, and fiercely rejecting them.

'I had forgot,' Cadfael owned, never having handled the clothes stripped from Bertred's body. 'Wait, I'll bring them.'

The forlorn little bundle of clothes laid aside in the chapel had been folded together as tidily as haste and their sodden condition permitted, and had drained gradually where they lay. The folds of coat and shirt and homespun hose were beginning to dry. Cadfael took the pile in one arm, and picked up in the other hand the boots that stood beside it. He carried them out into the court as Miles was smoothing the blanket neatly over Bertred's feet. The young man turned to meet him and take the bundle from him, and in the exchange, as Miles leaned to stow the clothes under the blanket, the cart tilted, and the boots, just balanced at the tail, fell to the cobbled paving.

Cadfael stooped to pick them up and restore them to their place. It was the first time he had really looked at them, and the light here in the court was clear and bright. He stood arrested in mid-movement, a boot in either hand, and slowly he turned up the left one to look attentively at the sole. For so long a time that when he did look up he found Miles standing just as still in wonder, gazing at him with open mouth, his head on one side like a puzzled hound on a lost scent.

'I think,' said Cadfael with deliberation, 'I had better get leave from the lord abott, and come up into the town with you. I need to speak once again with the lord sheriff.'

It was but a short walk from the castle to the house at Maerdol-head, and the boy sent in haste to find Hugh brought him within the quarter-hour, cursing mildly at being side-tracked on the point of further action he had intended, but reconciled by sharp curiosity, for Cadfael would not have sent for him again so soon without good reason.

In the hall Dame Agatha, attended by a tearful Branwen, volubly lamented the rockfall of disasters which had befallen the Vestier household. In the kitchen the bereaved Alison mourned with more bitter reason the loss of her son, while all the spinning-girls formed a chorus to her threnody. But in the loom-shed, where Bertred's body had been laid out decorously on a trestle table to await the visit of Martin Bellecote, the master-carpenter from the Wyle, it was quiet to the point of oppression, even though there were three of them there conversing in low voices and few words.

'There is no shadow of doubt,' said Cadfael, holding the boot sole-up to the light of a small lamp one of the girls had set at the head of the table. The light outside was still hardly less bright than in the afternoon, but half the shed was shuttered because the looms were at rest. 'This is the boot that made the print I took from the soil under Niall's vine, and the man who wore it is the man who tried to hack down the rose-bush, the same who also killed Brother Eluric. I made the mould, I know I am not mistaken. But here is the mould itself, for I brought it with me. You will find it matches exactly.'

'I take your word for it,' said Hugh. But as one who must verify for himself every morsel of evidence, he took the boot and the waxen mould, and carried them out to the doorway to match the two together. 'There is no doubt.' The two fitted like seal and matrix. There was the oblique tread that had worn down outer heel and inner toe, and the crack reaching half across the sole at the ball of the foot. 'It seems,' said Hugh, 'the Severn has saved us the cost of a trial, and him a worse fate than drowning.'

Miles had remained standing somewhat apart, looking from face to face with the same baffled wonder with which he had brooded over Bertred's body in the mortuary chapel. 'I don't understand,' he said dubiously at last. 'Are you saying that it was *Bertred* who got into the smith's garden to spoil Judith's rose-bush? And *killed . . .'* The same vigorous, even violent, shaking of his head, trying to toss the unwelcome belief from him, like a bull trying to throw off a dog that had him by the soft nose. And with as little success, for slowly the conviction began to penetrate his mind, to judge by the slacking of the lines of his face, and his final resigned calm and glint of rising interest. A very eloquent face, had Miles; Cadfael could follow every change. 'Why should *he* do such a thing?' he said slowly, but rather as if his own wit was already beginning to supply answers.

'The killing he never meant, as like as not,' said Hugh reasonably. 'But as for hacking down the bush – it was you yourself gave us a good reason why a man might do so.'

'But what did it benefit Bertred? All it would have done was to prevent my cousin getting her rent paid. What was that to him? *He* had no rights in it.' But there Miles halted to reflect again. 'I don't know – it seems reaching far. I know I said he fancied he had some small chance with her. He did presume, sometimes, he had a good conceit of himself. He may even have believed he might win her favour, such things have been known. Well . . . there's no denying, if he had such vaulting ideas, the Foregate house was a good half of her property, worth a man's while trying to regain.'

'As all her suitors may have reasoned,' said Hugh, 'not merely Bertred. He slept in here?'

'He did.'

'And therefore could go in and out at will, by night or day, without disturbing any other creature.'

'Well, so he could. It seems so he did, last night, for none of us within heard a sound.'

'But granted we have the proof now that links him to the

death of Brother Eluric,' said Hugh, frowning, 'we are still floundering when it comes to the vanishing of Mistress Perle. There's nothing whatever to connect him with that, and we have still a second malefactor to find. Bertred has been among the most assiduous of our helpers in the search for her. I don't think he would have spent quite so much energy if he had had any knowledge of where she was, however desirable it might be to make a show of zeal.'

'My lord,' said Miles slowly, 'I never would have believed such devious work of Bertred, but now you have shown me so far into his guilt I cannot help following further. It's a strange thing, his own mother has been pouring out to us all, since we brought him home, what he said to her last night. You may ask her yourself, my lord, she will surely repeat it to you as she has to us. I would rather not be the bearer, nor risk being suspect of mangling the purport. If it means anything, let her deliver, not I.'

The widow, bloated with tears and surrounded by her would-be comforters, was indeed still spouting words between her bouts of weeping, and had no objection to continuing her threnody for the benefit of the sheriff, when he drove her companions away for a short while, to have the bereaved woman to himself.

'A good son he was always to me, a good worker to his mistress, and deserved well of her, and well she thought of him. But great notions he had, like his father before him, and where have they got him now? How would I like, says he to me last night, how would I like to be better than a servant in this house – a gentlewoman, fit for the hall instead of the kitchen? Only wait a day or so, says he, and you'll see. I mean to make your fortune and my own. There's not one, he says, knows what I know. If there's ought you know to the purpose, I said, why haven't you told? But would he? And spend the credit along with my breath? he says. No, you leave all to me.'

'And did he say anything about what he intended in the night?' asked Hugh, slipping his question quietly and unobtrusively into the first chink in her outpourings, while she drew breath.

'He said he must go out again when it was full dark, but he wouldn't tell me where, or why, not what he was about at all. Wait till tomorrow, he says, and not a word to any tonight. But what does it matter now? Speak or keep silent, it does him no good now. Don't you go running your head into trouble, I told him. There may be more than you out about risky business in the night.'

Her flow of words was by no means exhausted, but its matter became repetitive, for she had told everything she knew. They left her to the ministrations of the women and the diminishing bitterness of her grief as it drained away into exhaustion. The house of Vestier, Miles assured them earnestly as they left the premises, would not let any of its old servants go short of the means of a decent life. Alison was safe enough.

Chapter Ten

COME WITH me,' said Hugh, setting off briskly up the hill towards the high cross, and turning his back with some relief on the troubled household at the clothiers' shop. 'Since you have honest leave to be out, you may as well join me on the errand you delayed for me a while ago. I was all but out of the town gate when your messenger came and Will came running after me to say I was wanted at the Vestiers'. I sent him on ahead with a couple of men, he's down there and at it by now, but I'd as lief see to it for myself.'

'Where are we going?' asked Cadfael, falling in willingly beside his friend up the steep street.

'To talk to Fuller's watchman. That's the one place outside the town walls where there'd be a waking witness even in the night, and a watchdog to alert him if anyone came prowling close by. If the fellow did by any chance go into the water this side of the river, works and warehouse are only a little way upstream from where you found him. Fuller's man has both places in charge. He may have heard something. And as we go, tell me what you make of all that – Bertred's night affairs, and the fortune he was going to make.'

'By reason of knowing something no one else knew – hmm! For that matter, I noticed he stayed behind when your men left the jetty yesterday afternoon. He let you all go on well before, and then slipped back alone into the trees. And he came late for his supper, told his mother she should be a gentlewoman in the house instead of a cook, and went off again in the night to set about making his word good. And according to Miles he not only fancied his mistress, but had the assurance to feel there was no reason he should not bring her to fancy him.'

'And how persuade her?' asked Hugh, wryly smiling. 'By abduction and force? Or by a gallant rescue?'

'Or both,' said Cadfael.

'Now truly you interest me! Those who hide can find! If by any chance the lady is where he put her, but doesn't know who put her there – for a Bertred can as easily find rogues to do his work for him as any wealthier man, it is but a matter of degrees of greed! – then who could better come to her rescue? Even if gratitude did not go so far as to make her marry him, he certainly would not be the loser.'

'It offers one way of accounting,' Cadfael acknowledged. 'And in its favour, the maid Branwen blabbed out what her mistress intended in the kitchen, so we are told. And Bertred ate in the kitchen, and was probably there to hear it. The kitchen knew of it, the hall knew nothing until next day, after she was lost. But there are other possibilities. That someone else took her, and Bertred had found out where she was. And said no word to you or your men, but kept the rescue for himself. It seems a simpler and a smaller villainy, for one surely not so subtle as to make tortuous plans.'

'You forget,' Hugh pointed out grimly, 'that by all the signs he had already committed murder, whether with intent beforehand or not, still murder. He might be forced into plans far beyond his ordinary scope after that, to cover his tracks and secure at least some of his desired gains.'

'I forget nothing,' said Cadfael sturdily. 'One point in favour of your story I've given you. Here is one against: If he had her hidden away somewhere, securely enough to baffle all your efforts to find her, why should it not be a safe and simple matter for him to effect that rescue of his without a single stumble? And the man is dead! Far more likely to come to grief in spite of all his planning, if he crossed the plans of some other man.'

'True again! Though for all we yet know, his death could have been pure mischance. True, it could be either way. If he is the abductor as well as the murderer, then we have no second villain to find, but alas, we still lack the lady, and the only man who could lead us to her is dead. If murderer and abductor are two different people, then we have still to find both the captor and his captive. And since it seems the most likely object of taking her is to inveigle her into marriage, we may hope and believe both that she is living, and that in the end he must release her. Though I own I'd rather forestall that by plucking her out of his hold myself.'

They were over the crest by the high cross, and striding downhill now, past the ramp that led up to the castle gatehouse, and still downhill alongside the towering walls, until town wall on their left and castle wall on their right met in a low tower, under which the highway passed. Once through that gateway, the level of the road opened before them, fringed for only a short way by small houses and gardens. Hugh turned right on the outer side of the deep, dry castle ditch, before the houses began, and started down towards the riverside, and Cadfael followed more sedately.

Godfrey Fuller's tenterground stood empty, the drying cloth just unhooked and rolled up for the finishing. Most of his men had already stopped work for the day, and the last few had lingered to watch and listen at the arrival of the sheriff's men, before making for their homes in the town. A close little knot of men had gathered at the edge of the tenterground, between dye-works and wool warehouse: Godfrey Fuller himself, his finery shed in favour of stout working clothes, for he was by no means ashamed to soil his hands alongside his workmen, and prided himself on being able to do whatever he asked of them, and possibly as well or better than they could; the watchman, a thickset, burly fellow of fifty, with his mastiff on a leash; Hugh's oldest sergeant, Will Warden, bushy-bearded and massive; and two men from the garrison in watchful attendance at a few yards distance. At sight of Hugh dropping with long strides down the slope of the meadow, Warden swung away from the colloquy to meet him.

'My lord, the watchman here says there was an alarm in the night, the dog gave tongue.'

The watchman spoke up freely for himself, aware of duty properly done. 'My lord, some sneak thief was here in the night, well past midnight, climbing to the hatch behind Master Hynde's storehouse. Not that I knew then that he'd got so far, but the hound here gave warning, and out we went, and heard him running for the river, I made to cut him off, but he was past me too fast, all I got was one clout at him as he rushed by. I hit him, but did him precious little harm, surely, by the speed he made down to the bank and into the water, I heard the splash as he went in, and called off the dog, and went to look had he got into the store. But there was no sign, not to be seen in the night, and I took it he was well across and off by then, no call to make any more stir about him. I never knew till now it was a dead man came ashore on the other side. That I never meant.'

'It was not your doing,' said Hugh. 'The blow you got in did him no great damage. He drowned, trying to swim across.'

'But, my lord, there's more! When I looked round the warehouse by daylight this morning, see what I found lying in the grass under the hatch. I've just handed them over to your sergeant here.' Will Warden had them in his hands, displayed in meaning silence, a long chisel and a small clawed hammer. 'And the sill beam under the hatch broken from its nails at one end, and dangling. I reckon surely he was up there trying to break through the shutter and get in at the fleeces. A year ago when the clip was in there thieves got in and stole a couple of bales. Old William Hynde near went out of his wits with rage. Come and see, my lord.'

Cadfael followed slowly and thoughtfully as they set off round the bulk of the warehouse to the rear slope, where the shuttered hatch showed still securely fastened, though the stout beam under it hung vertically against the planks on the wall, the splintered gaps where it had broken free from its anchoring nails rotten and soft to the touch.

'Gave under his weight,' said the watchman, peering upward. 'It was his fall the dog heard. And these tools came down with him, and he had no time to pick them up. If he'd delayed a moment we should have had him. But here's good proof he was trying to break in and steal. And the best is,' said the watchman, shaking his head over the folly of the too-clever, 'if he'd got in through the hatch he couldn't have got at the fleeces.'

'No?' said Hugh sharply, turning a startled glance on him. 'Why? What would have prevented?'

'There's another locked door beyond, my lord, between him and what he came for. No, belike you wouldn't know of it, why should you? William Hynde's clerk used to work in the little back room up there, it was used as a counting-house until that time thieves broke in by this back way. By then the woolman was buying here for the foreign trade, and old Hynde thought better to bid him up to his own house and make much of him. And what with their business being all transacted there, the old counting-house was out of use. He had the door locked and barred, for an extra barrier against thieves. If this rogue had got in, it would have done him no good.'

Hugh gazed and pondered, and gnawed a dubious lip. 'This rogue, my friend, was in the wool trade himself, and knew this place very well. He fetched the fleeces for the Vestiers from here, he'd been in and out more than once. How comes it that he would not know of this closed counting-house? And my deputy had them open up here two days ago, and saw the upper floor full almost to the ladder with bales. If there's a door there, it was buried behind the wool.'

'So it would be, my lord. 'Why not? I doubt if a soul had gone through that door since it was first shut up. There's nothing within there.'

Nothing now, Cadfael was thinking. But was there something – someone – there only yesterday? It would seem that Bertred thought so, though of course Bertred could be wrong. He must have known of the abandoned room, he may well have though it worth putting to the test at a venture, without special cause. If so, it cost him dear. All those dreams of bettering his fortune by a gallant rescue, of exploiting a woman's gratitude to the limit and advancing his own cause step by step with insinuating care, all shattered, swept away down the currents of the Severn. Did he really know something no one else among the searchers knew, or was he speaking only of this hidden room as a possibility?

'Will,' said Hugh, 'send a man up to Hynde's house, and ask him, or his son, to come down here and bring the keys. All his keys! It's time I took a look within here myself. I should have done it earlier.'

But it was neither William Hynde nor his son Vivian who came striding down the field with the sergeant after a wait of some ten or fifteen minutes. It was a serving-man in homespun and leather, a tall, bold-faced, muscular fellow in his thirties, sporting a close-trimmed beard that outlined a wide mouth and a jaunty jaw with all the dandified elegance of a Norman lordling, though his build was Saxon and his colouring, reddish-fair. He made a careless obeisance to Hugh, and straightened up to measure eyes with him, ice-pale eyes with only the glittering Norse-tinge of blue in them.

'My lord, my mistress sends you these, and my services.' He had the keys in his hand on a great ring, a rich bunch of them.

His voice was loud, with a brazen ring to it, though his manner was civil enough. 'My master's away at his sheepfolds by Forton, has been since yesterday, and the young master's gone up there to help them today, but he'll be back tomorrow if you need him. Will it please you command me? I'm here to serve.'

'I've seen you about the town,' said Hugh, eyeing him with detached interest. 'So you're in Hynde's service, are you? What's your name?'

'Gunnar, my lord.'

'And he trusts you with his keys. Well, Gunnar, open these doors for us. I want to see what's within.' And he added, as the man turned willingly to obey: 'When is the barge expected, if Master Hynde can spare time to go in person to his flocks?'

'Before the end of the month, my lord, but the merchant sends word ahead from Worcester. They take the clip by water to Bristol, and then overland to Southampton for shipping, it cuts off the long voyage round. A rough passage they say it is, all round the south-west.' He was busy as he talked, unfastening two massive padlocks from the bar of the warehouse doors, and drawing both leaves wide open to let in the light upon a clean-swept, slightly raised floor of boards, on which the lower-grade fleeces had been stacked. This level was empty now. From the left-hand corner within the door a wooden ladder led up through a wide, open trap to the floor above.

'You're well informed concerning Master Hynde's business affairs, Gunnar,' said Hugh mildly, stepping over the threshold.

'He trusts me. I made the journey down to Bristol with the barge once, when they had a man injured, and were short-handed. Will it please you go up, sir? Shall I lead the way?'

A very self-assured and articulate person, this Gunnar, Cadfael reflected, the very image of the intelligent and trusted servant of a commercial house, capable of adapting to travel, and learning from every experience. By his stature, bearing and colouring he proclaimed his northern ancestry. The Danes had reached no further south than Brigge in this shire, but they had left a few of their getting behind when they retreated. Cadfael followed without haste as they mounted the ladder and stepped on to the upper floor. Here the light was dim, reflected up from the wide doors below, but enough to show the stacked bales, stretching the full length of the storehouse.

'We could do with more light,' said Hugh.

'Wait, my lord, and I'll open.' And Gunnar made no more ado, but seized one of the bales in the centre of the array and hauled it down to set aside, and after it several more, until the stout wooden planks of a narrow door were laid bare. He flourished his ring of keys with a flurry of sound, selected one, and thrust it into the lock. There were two iron bars slotted across the door in addition, and they grated rustily as he drew them from the sockets. The key creaked as it turned. 'There's been no use made of this for a while now,' said Gunnar cheerfully. 'We'll do no harm by letting in the air for once.'

The door opened inward. He thrust it wide and made straight across to the shuttered hatch, and with a lusty banging of latches and beams released the shutters and pushed them wide to let in the slanting sunlight. 'Mind the dust, my lord,' he warned helpfully, and stood back to let them examine the whole narrow room. A rising breeze blew in, fluttering trailers of cobweb from the rough wood of the hatch.

A small, barren space, an old bench against the wall, a heap of discarded fragments of vellum and cloth and wool and wood, and indistinguishable rubbish drifted into one corner, a large ewer with a broken lip, the ancient desk leaning askew, and over all the grime and dust of abandonment, of a place two years disused, and a year sealed and forgotten.

'There was a thief got in this way once,' said Gunnar airily. 'They'd have much ado to manage it a second time. But I must make all secure again before I leave it, my master'd have my head if I forgot to shoot every bolt and turn every key.'

'There was a thief tried to get in this way only last night,' said Hugh casually. 'Have they not told you?'

Gunnar had turned to him a face fallen open in sheer astonishment. 'A thief? Last night? Not the word of this have I heard, or the mistress, either. Who says it's so?'

'Ask the watchman below, he'll tell you. One Bertred, a weaver who works for Mistress Perle. Take a look at the sill outside the hatch, Gunnar, you'll see how it came down with his weight. The hound hunted him into the river,' said Hugh, offhand, gazing musingly all round the neglected room, but well aware of the look on Gunnar's face. 'He drowned.'

The silence that followed was brief but profound. Gunnar stood mute, staring, and all his light assuranced had frozen into a steely gravity.

'You'd heard nothing?' marvelled Hugh, his eyes on the dusty floor, on which Gunnar's vigorous passage had printed the only pattern of footmarks perceptible between door and hatch.

'No, my lord – nothing.' The loud, confident voice had become taut, intent and quiet. 'I know the man. Why should he want to steal fleeces? He is very well settled as he is – he was . . . *Dead*?'

'Drowned, Gunnar. Yes.'

'Sweet Christ have his soul!' said Gunnar, slowly and quietly, to himself rather than to them. 'I knew him. I've diced with him. God knows neither I nor any that I know of bore Bertred any ill will, or ever wished him harm.'

There was another silence. It was as if Gunnar had left them, and was withdrawn into another place. The ice-blue eyes looked opaque, as if he had drawn a shutter down over them, or turned their gaze within rather than without. In a few moments he stirred, and asked levelly: 'Have you done here, my lord? May I close these again?'

'You may,' said Hugh as shortly. 'I have done.'

On the way back into the town through the castle gate they were both silent and thoughtful, until Hugh said suddenly: 'If ever she was there in that dusty hole, someone has done excellent work wiping out every trace.'

'Bertred thought she was,' said Cadfael. 'Though Bertred may have been wrong. Surely he was there to try and set her free, but he may have been guessing, and guessing wrongly. He knew of the room, and knew it was not common knowledge and therefore, with care, might be used for such a purpose. And he knew that young Hynde made a very possible abductor, being vain, persistent and in urgent need of money to maintain his easy life. But was it more than a guess? Did he really discover something that made it a certainty?'

'The very dust!' said Hugh. 'No mark of any foot but Gunnar's, or none that I could see. And the young fellow, the son, this Vivian – he did ride off this morning, out of the town, that I knew already. Will reported it to me. So there's no one there but the mother now. And would *she* be lying? Hardly likely he'd tell *her* if he had a woman hidden away. If he's taken the girl elsewhere after the night alarm, it would hardly be to his mother. But I'll pay the house another visit, all the same. I fancy Bertred must have been trying his luck – but that poor wretch had no luck! No luck with the roses, no luck with the rescue. No luck in any of his schemes.'

Another long silence, while they climbed the gradual slope within the gate, and approached the ramp to the castle entrance. 'And he did not know!' said Hugh. 'He really did not know!'

'He? And know what?'

'This man Gunnar. I had my doubts about him until then. So confident and assured, light as air, until mention was made of a man's death. That I am sure came new to him. There was no pretence there. What say you, Cadfael?'

'I say there is a man who could lie and lie, whenever the occasion needed it. But who was not lying then. His very voice changed, no less than his face. No, he did not know. He was shaken to the heart. Whatever mischief he might have a part in, he had not contemplated a death. Let alone Bertred's death!' They had reached the ramp and halted. 'I must get back,' said Cadfael, looking up into a sky just veiled and softened with the approach of twilight. 'What more can we do tonight? And what will you do tomorrow?'

'Tomorrow,' said Hugh with deliberation. 'I'll have Vivian Hynde brought to me as soon as he shows his face in the town gate, and see what's to be got out of him concerning his father's old counting-house. From all I've heard of him, he should be easier to frighten than his man shows any sign of being. And even if he's a snow-white innocent, from all accounts a fright will do him no harm.'

'And will you make it public.' Cadfael asked, 'that at least Brother Eluric's murderer is known? And is dead?'

'No, not yet. Perhaps not at all, but at least let the poor woman have what peace she can find until her son's buried. What point in blazoning forth guilt where there can never be a trial?' Hugh was looking back with a frown, and somewhat regretting that Miles had been present to witness that manifestation in the loom-shed. 'If I know the sharp ears and long tongues of Shrewsbury it may yet be common talk by morning without any word from me. Perhaps not, perhaps Coliar will hold his tongue for the mother's sake. But at any rate they shall have no official declaration to grit their teeth in until we find Judith Perle. As we will, as we must. Let them gossip and speculate. Someone may take fright and make the blunder I'm waiting for.'

'The lord abbot will have to know all that I know,' said Cadfael.

'So he will, but he's another matter. He has the right and you have the duty. So you'd best be about getting back to him,' said Hugh, sighing, 'and I'd best go in and see if any of those men of mine who've been out raking the countryside has done any better than I have.'

Upon which impeccably conscientious but none too hopeful note they parted.

Cadfael arrived back at the gatehouse too late for Vespers. The brothers were in the choir, and the office almost over. A great deal had happened in one short afternoon.

'There's one here been waiting for you,' said the porter, looking out from his lodge as Cadfael stepped through the wicket. 'Master Niall the bronzesmith. Come in to him here, we've been passing the time of evening together, but he wants to be on his way as soon as may be.'

Niall had heard enough to know who came, and emerged from the gatehouse with a coarse linen bag under his arm. It needed but one glance at Cadfael's face to show that there was nothing to tell, but he asked, all the same. 'No word of her?'

'None that's new. No, sorry I am to say it. I'm just back from the sheriff himself, but without comfort.'

'I waited,' said Niall, 'in case you might bring at least some news. The least trace would be welcome. And I can do nothing! Well, I must be on my way, then.'

'Where are you bound tonight?'

'To my sister and her man at Pulley, to see my little girl. I have a set of harness ornaments to deliver for one of Mortimer's horses, though that could have waited a few days yet. But the child will be looking for me. This is the evening I usually go to her, else I wouldn't stir. But I shall not stay overnight. I'll walk back in the dark. At least to be there with the roses, if I can do nothing better for her.'

'You've done more than the rest of us,' said Cadfael ruefully, 'for you've kept the bush alive. And she'll be back yet to take the pick of its flowers from your hand, the day after tomorrow.'

'Should I read that as a promise?' asked Niall, with a wry and grudging smile.

'No, as a prayer. The best I can do. With three miles or more to walk to Pulley, and three miles back,' said Cadfael, 'you'll have time for a whole litany. And bear in mind whose festival it will be in two days' time! Saint Winifred will be listening. Who more likely? She herself stood off an unwanted suitor and kept her virtue, she'll not forsake a sister.'

'Well ... I'd best be off. God with you, Brother.' Niall

shouldered his bag of ornamental bronze rosettes and harness buckles for Mortimer's horse, and strode away along the Foregate, towards the track that led south-west from the bridge, a square, erect figure thrusting briskly into the pearly evening air cooling towards twilight. Cadfael stood looking after him until he turned the corner beyond the mill-pond and vanished from sight.

Not a man for grand gestures or many words, Niall Bronzesmith, but Cadfael was bitterly and painfully aware of the gnawing frustration that eats away at the heart from within, when there is nothing to be done about the one thing in the world of any importance.

Chapter Eleven

NIALL SET out from Pulley on his return walk to Shrewsbury a little before midnight. Cecily would have had him stay, urging truly enough that if he did go back it would change nothing, and stating bluntly what Cadfael had refrained from stating, that while the woman herself was still safely out of reach there was hardly likely to be any further attack on the rose-bush, for any such attack was unnecessary. No one could deliver a rose into the hand of a woman who was missing. If someone was plotting to break the bargain and recover the house in the Foregate, as by now everyone seemed to be agreed, the thing was already done, without taking any further risk.

Niall had said very little about the affair to his sister, and nothing at all about his own deep feelings, but she seemed to know by instinct. The talk of Shrewsbury found its way out here softened and distanced into a kind of folk-tale, hardly bearing at all on real life. The reality here was the demesne, its fields, its few labourers, the ditched coppice from which the children fended off the goats at pasture, the plough-oxen, and the enshrouding forest. The two little girls, listening round-eyed to the grown-ups' talk, must have thought of Judith Perle as of one of the enchanted ladies bewitched by evil magic in old nursery tales. Cecily's two shock-headed, berry-brown boys, at home in all the woodland skills, had only two or three times in their lives, thus far, set eyes on the distant towers of Shrewsbury castle. Three miles is not so far, but far enough when you have no need to cross it. John Stury came into the town perhaps twice a year to buy, and for the rest the little manor was self-supporting. Sometimes Niall was moved to feel that he must soon remove his daughter and take her back with him to the town, for fear he might lose her for ever. To a happy household, a peaceful, simple life and good company, truly, but to his own irrevocable loss and bereavement.

She was asleep long before this hour, in her nest with the other three in the loft. He had laid her there himself, already drowsy. A fair creature, with a bright sheen of gold in her cloud of hair, like her mother before her, and a skin like creamy milk, that glowed in sunny weather with the same gilded gloss. Cecily's brood were reddish-dark, after their father, with lithe, lean bodies and black eyes. She was rounded and smooth and soft. Almost from birth she had been here with her cousins, it would be hard to take her away.

'You'll have a dark walk home,' said John, peering out from the doorway. In the summer night the smell of the forest was spicy and strong, heavy in the windless dark. 'The moon won't be up for hours yet.'

'I don't mind it. I should know the way well enough by now.'

'I'll come out with you as far as the track,' said Cecily, 'and set you on your road. It's fine and warm still, and I'm wakeful.'

She walked beside him in silence as far as the gate in John's stockade, and out across the clearing of open grass to the edge of the trees, and there they halted.

'One of these days,' she said, as though she had been listening to all that he had been thinking, 'you'll be taking the little one away from us. It's only right you should, though we shall grudge her to you. As well we're not so far away that we can't borrow her back now and then. It wouldn't do to leave it too long, Niall. I've had the gift of her, and been glad of it, but yours she is, yours and Avota's, when all's said, and best she should grow up knowing it and content with it.'

'She's young yet,' said Niall defensively. 'I dread to confuse her too soon.'

'She's young, but she's knowing. She begins to ask why you always leave her, and to wonder how you do, alone, and who cooks and washes for you. I reckon you could as well take her on a visit, show her how you live and what you make. She's hungry to know, you'll find she'll drink it in. And much as she joys in playing with my brood, she never likes sharing you with them. That's a true woman you'll find there,' said Cecily with conviction. 'But for all that, it might be the best thing of all you could do for her, Niall, just now is to give her another mother. One of her own, with no rival childer by. For she's sharp enough, my dear, to know that I'm none of hers, love her as I may.'

Niall said his good night to her without comment on that, and went off with a rapid stride into the trees. She knew him well enough to expect nothing more, and turned back to the house, when he had vanished from sight, aware that he had listened and been torn. It was time he should give thought to it. The life of a respected town craftsman's daughter, with property to inherit and social skills to learn, must necessarily be different from that of a country steward's girl; her betrothal prospects must be sought among a different group of people, her upbringing be aimed at a somewhat different kind of household with a different round of duties. Sharp beyond her years, the child might begin to think that a father who leaves her too long apart from him does not really want her, but visits only out of duty. Yet she was very young, very young to be taken where there was no woman to care for her. Now if only there should be some real hope in this widow woman of whom he had nothing to say! Or, for that matter, any other decent woman with a warm heart and a cool head, and patience enough for two!

Niall walked on along the narrow path between the trees, in dark-green night, full-leaved and heady with scents, with his sister's voice still in his ears. The woods were thick and well grown here, the ground so shadowed that herbal cover was scant, but the interlacing of boughs above shut out the sky. Sometimes the path emerged for a short way into more open upland where the trees thinned and clearings of heath appeared, for all this stretch of country was the northern fringe of the Long Forest, where men had encroached with their little assarts and their legal or illegal cutting of timber and pasturing of pigs on acorns and beech-mast. But even here settlements were very few. He would not see more than a couple of small, precarious holdings before he came to the hamlet of Brace Meole, nearly half his way home.

On that thought he checked to reconsider, for it might be a little quicker to turn aside to the east on a path he knew, and hit the high road, if such a track through forest could be called a high road, well before the village, instead of staying on the forest path. Every variation on this journey was familiar to him. The path of which he was thinking crossed the one on which he was walking diagonally, striking south-west, and where the ways met there was a small open clearing, the only such space in a belt of thicker woodland. Here he halted for a moment, still undecided, and stood to savour the awesome quietness of the night, just as the hush was mysteriously broken by small, persistent sounds. In such windless silence any sound, however soft, came startlingly upon the ear. Instinctively Niall drew back from the open ground, deep into the cover of the trees, and stood with head up and ears stretched to decipher the signs.

There are always some nocturnal creatures about their business in the dark, but their small rustlings keep low to the ground and furtive, and freeze when a man is scented in the night, since every man is an enemy. These sounds proceeded steadily though softly, and were gradually drawing nearer. The dull, solid but muffled thud of hooves in deep turf, drawing near at a brisk walk from the direction of the road, and a light rustling and swish of pliable twigs brushing a passing bulk. The summer growth was at its height, the trees had reached new and tender shoots just far enough to encroach upon the path with their soft tips.

What was a horseman doing, coming this way at this hour, and by the pace and the sounds heavily laden? Niall stayed where he was, well within the trees and hidden, but looking out into the clearing, where by contrast there was light enough to distinguish shapes and degrees of grey and black. No moon, and a high, faint veil of cloud between the earth and stars, a night for dark undertakings. And though masterless men seldom ventured within ten miles of Shrewsbury, and the worst to be encountered should be only a poacher, yet there was always the possibility of worse. And when did poachers go mounted about their business?

Between the dark woodland walls of the right-hand path a vague pallor appeared. The new foliage whispered along a horse's barrel and a rider's arm. A white horse, or a pale dapple-grey or very light roan, for his hide brought with it into the clearing its own lambent gleam. The shape of the man on his back appeared at first squat and monstrously thickset, until some unevenness of the ground set up a swaying movement that showed the mount was carrying not one person, but two. A man before, a woman riding pillion behind. One shadowy bulk, without detail, became clearly two, though still without identity, as horse and riders passed by, crossed the path and continued on their cautious way south-west. The swing of the long skirt showed, there were even points of pallor mysterious in the moving darkness, a hand holding by the horseman's belt, an oval face raised to the sky, free of the hood that had fallen back on to the woman's shoulders.

There was nothing clearer to view than that, and yet he knew her. It might have been the poise of the head with its great sheaf of hair, moving against a sky almost as dark, or the erect carriage and balance of her body, or some overstrung cord within his own being that could not but vibrate to her nearness. This woman of all women could not pass by, even in the dark and unaware of him, and he not know.

And what was Judith Perle doing here in the night, three days after vanishing from her rightful place, riding pillion behind a horseman going south-west, and she under no constraint, but going with him willingly?

He stood for so long motionless and silent that the small creatures of the night seemed to have lost all awe of him, or forgotten he was there. Somewhere across the clearing, where the path by which he had come continued, something rustled hastily from one tangle of undergrowth to another, and made off westward into safety and silence. Niall stirred out of his chilled stillness, and turned to follow the sound of the muffled hooves down the grassy ride until they died into the same profound silence.

He could neither believe in nor understand what he had seen. It was not, it could not be, what it seemed. Where she was going, who was her companion, what she intended, these were mysteries, but they were her mysteries, and in her Niall had so strong and unquestioning a faith that no strange night venture could shake it. The one certainty was that by the grace of God he had found her, and now he must not lose her again, and that was enough. If she had no need of him, if she was in no danger or distress, so be it, and he would never trouble her. But he would, he must, follow and be near to see that no harm came to her, until all this dark interlude was over and done, and she vindicated and restored to the light. The conviction was unbearably strong within him that if he lost her now she would be lost forever.

He emerged from his cover and crossed into the path they had taken. There was no danger of losing them; through the thickening forest ahead a horse must hold to the path, especially by night, and in this darkness could not press beyond a walk. A man afoot could have outrun them, provided he knew the woods as Niall knew them. But for his purpose it was enough to recover the sounds that were his guide, and if possible approach close enough to be with her in a moment if anything untoward threatened. This ground was less familiar to him than the various ways to Pulley, having left that hamlet aside on the left, but it was similar country, and he could thread his way among the trees, aside from the path, at a faster speed than the horseman was making. Soon he recovered the small, regular beat of hooves, and the light ring of the bridle as the horse tossed its head at some sudden nocturnal stir, perhaps, in the undergrowth on the other side of the track. Twice he caught that brief, abrupt peal of bells, like a summons to service, reassuring him that he was near, and could close quickly if there should be need.

They were moving steadily south-west, deeper into the recesses of the Long Forest, and here there were fewer places where the cover became more open, and patches of heath and outcrop rock appeared. Surely more than a mile past now, and still the riders pressed on, keeping the same cautious pace. The veiled sky had grown somewhat darker with thickening cloud cover. Looking up, Niall could barely distinguish the shapes of the upper branches against the heavens. He went with hands spread to touch the trees and weave his way between, but still he kept within earshot of the horse's steady progress, and once he found he had drawn abreast of it, and was aware of movement along the path on his right, by sense rather than by sight. He hung back to let the vague blur of the pale hide draw ahead again, and then took up the patient pursuit with greater care.

He had lost all idea of how long they had been engaged in this nocturnal pilgrimage through the forest, but thought it must be almost an hour, and if the riders had come from the town they must have set out an hour earlier still. As to where they were bound, he had no notion. He knew nothing in this part of the woods, barring perhaps a solitary scratched-out assart hacked recently from the waste. They must be fairly close to the source of the Meole Brook, and riding upstream. From the higher ground on the left two or three tiny tributaries came down and trickled across the path, none of them any barrier, for any one of them could be stepped over dry-shod, at least in summer. The little serpents of water made one more tiny sound, hissing drowsily between the stones. They had gone perhaps three miles, Niall reckoned, since he first began to follow.

Somewhere not too distant on the right the woods rustled and stilled. The rhythm of the horse's gait was broken, hooves shifted, at check on a harder floor where stone came near the surface, then moved more slowly back to turf and halted. Niall crept closer, feeling his way from tree to tree and putting off the hampering branches with careful quietness. It seemed by the slight easing of the darkness that the path he was approaching had widened into a grassy ride where the sky, if clouded, could at least peer in. Then he saw through the lace of leaves the dim pallor which was the body of the horse, standing still. For the first time there was a voice, a man's, in a sibilant whisper that carried clearly through the silence.

'I should take you to the gate.'

The rider was already out of the saddle. In the forest aisle where the darkness became relative there was movement upon the ground, a blacker shape shifting across the pallor of the horse like drifts of cloud across the moon.

'No,' said Judith's voice, chill and clear. 'That was not in the bargain. I do not wish it.'

By the horse's stirring and the susurration of movement Niall knew the moment when the man lifted her down, though still, without conviction, his voice protested: 'I cannot let you go alone.'

'It is not far,' she said. 'I am not afraid.'

And he was accepting his dismissal, for again the horse stirred and trod the turf, and a stirrup rang once. The rider was remounting. Something more he said, but it was lost as his mount turned, not to go back the way he had come, but onward to the left, uphill by another track, to cut through the rough uplands the nearest way to the road. Speed rather than secrecy was his concern now. But after a few hasty paces he did check and turn to offer again what she had refused, knowing she would still refuse it.

'I'm loth to leave you so . . .'

'I know my way now,' she said simply. 'Go, get home before light.'

At that he did turn, shake his bridle, and start along a rising ride that seemed to offer better speed and a more open and smooth surface, for in a little while the receding sound of the hooves became a cautious trot, intent on making good speed away from this mysterious errand. Judith still stood where he had set her down, quite invisible in the edge of the trees, but Niall would know when she moved. He drew nearer still, ready to follow whatever move she made. She knew her way, it was not far, and she was not afraid. But he would go at her back until she reached her chosen haven, wherever that might be.

The rider was gone, the last muted sound had died into silence, before she stirred, and then he heard her turn away to the right, out of the comparative twilight of the open ride, back into the lush, leafy blackness of thick forest, for a twig snapped under her foot. He crossed the ride and followed. There was a narrow but trodden path slanting away downhill, towards some larger tributary of the Meole, for he caught the distant small whispering of water from below.

He had gone no more than twenty paces down the path, and she was perhaps twenty before him, when there was a sudden violent threshing of bushes from the right, out of the thick undergrowth, and then Judith cried out, one wild, brief cry of alarm and dread. Niall sprang forward in a reckless run towards the cry, and felt, rather than heard or saw, the night convulsed before him with the turbulence of an almost silent struggle. His spread arms embraced two bodies, blindly and clumsily, and struggled to pluck them apart. Judith's long hair, torn from its coil, streamed across his face, and he took her about the waist to put her behind him and out of danger. He felt the upward swing of a long arm reaching past him to strike at her, and some strange trick of lambent light flashed for one instant blue along the blade of a knife.

Niall caught the descending arm and wrenched it aside, hooked a knee round the assailant's knee with a wrestler's instinct, and brought them both crashing to the ground. They rolled and strained, twigs crackling under them in the blind dark, bruised shoulders against the boles of trees, wrenched and struggled, the one to free his knife arm, the other to hold the blade away from himself or get possession of it. Their breath mingled as they strained and panted face to face, and each still invisible to the other. The attacker was strong, muscular and determined, and had a fund of vicious tricks to play, using head and teeth and knees freely, but he could not break away or get to his feet again. Niall had him by the right wrist, and with his other arm wound about the man's body, pinning the upper arm so that his opponent could only claw fiercely at neck and face, drawing blood. With a grunting effort he heaved up his body and rolled them both over to make violent impact with the bole of a tree, intent on half-stunning Niall and breaking his grip to free the knife, but he succeeded all too well, and his own knife arm, already weakened with cramps from the grip on his wrist, struck the solid timber hard, jarring from elbow to fingers. His hand started open, the knife flew wide and was lost in the grass.

Niall came dazedly to his knees, to hear his enemy gasping and moaning, groping about in the turf and leaf-mould for his weapon, and muttering curses because he could not find it. And at the first lunge Niall made to grapple with him again he dragged himself to his feet and ran, breaking through the bushes, back the way he had come. The lashing of branches and rustling of leaves marked his path through the thick woods, until the last sound faded away into distance, and he was gone.

Niall clambered to his feet, shaking his ringing head, and groped for a tree to hold by. He was no longer sure which way he was facing on the path, or where to find Judith, until a still voice said, with slow, composed wonder: 'I am here!' and the barely perceptible pallor of an extended hand beckoned him, and closed on the hand he reached out to meet it. Her touch was chill but firm. Whether she knew him or not, of him she had no fear. 'Are you hurt?' she said. They drew together very gently, rather out of a startled and mutual respect than out of any caution, and their human warmth met and mingled.

'Are *you*? He struck at you before I could reach him. Did he wound you?'

'He has slit my sleeve,' she said, feeling at her left shoulder. 'A scratch, perhaps – nothing more. I'm not hurt, I can go. But you . . .'

She laid her hands on his breast, and felt anxiously down from shoulders to forearms, and found blood. 'He has gashed you – this left arm . . .'

'It's nothing,' said Niall. 'We're lightly rid of him.'

'He meant killing,' said Judith gravely. 'I didn't know there could be outlaws prowling so close to the town. Night travellers could be butchered for the clothes they wear, let alone the money they might be carrying.' Only then did she begin to quiver with the laggard disruption of shock, and he drew her into his arms to warm the chill out of her. Then she did know him. His voice had started echoes for her, his touch was certainty. 'Master Bronzesmith? How did you come to be here? So happily for me! But how?'

'No matter for that now,' said Niall. 'First let me bring you wherever you were going. Here in the forest, if there are such scum abroad, we could still come to grief. And you may take cold from the very malice and violence of it. How far have you to go?'

'Not far,' she said. 'Down to the brook here, barely half a mile. All the stranger that footpads should be loose here. I am going to the Benedictine nuns at Godric's Ford.'

He asked her nothing more. Her plans were her own, there was nothing here for him to do but see that they were not impeded. He kept an arm about her as they set off down the path, until presently it widened into a grassy ride, where a faint light came in like mist. Invisibly beyond the trees the moon was rising at last. Somewhere before them there was the elusive gleam of water in motion, in mysterious, vibrant glimpses that shifted and vanished, and emerging from the misty air on their side of it, the sharp black edges of roofs and a fence, and a little bell-turret, the only vertical line.

'This is the place?' asked Niall. He had heard of the cell, but never before questioned where it lay, or been anywhere near it.

'Yes.'

'I'll bring you as far as the gate, and see you within.'

'No, you must come in with me. You must not go back now, alone. Tomorrow, by daylight, we shall be safe enough.'

'There's no place here for me,' he said doubtfully.

'Sister Magdalen will find a place.' And she said with sudden passionate entreaty: 'Don't leave me now!'

They came down together to the high timber fence that enclosed the cell and its gardens. Though the moon was still hidden from their sight beyond the forested uplands, its reflected light was growing with every moment; buildings, trees, bushes, the curve of the brook and cushioned strips of meadow along its banks, all emerged slowly from black obscurity into subtle modulations of grey, soon to be silvered as the moon climbed. Niall hesitated with his hand on the rope of the bell at the closed gate, such a violation it seemed to break the silence. When he did rouse himself to pull, the jangle of sound went echoing along the water, and rang back from the trees of the opposite shore. But there was only a short wait before the portress came grumbling and yawning to open the grille and peer out at them.

'Who is it? Benighted, are you?' She saw a man and a woman, both unknown to her and astray here in the forest at night, and took them for what they seemed, respectable travellers who had lost their way and found themselves in unfrequented solitudes where any shelter was more than welcome. 'You want a night's lodging?'

'My name is Judith Perle,' said Judith. 'Sister Magdalen knows of me, and once offered me a place of refuge when I needed it. Sister, I need it now. And here with me is my good friend who has stood between me and danger and brought me safely here. I pray shelter through the night for him, too.'

'I'll call Sister Magdalen,' said the portress with wise caution, and went away to do so, leaving the grille open. In a very few minutes the two returned together, and Sister Magdalen's bright, shrewd brown eyes looked through the lattice with wide-awake interest, alert even at this hour of the night.

'You may open,' she said cheerfully. 'Here is a friend, and a friend's friend is just as welcome.'

In the tiny parlour, without fuss and without questions, Sister Magdalen did first things first, mulled strong wine to warm the last chill of shock and fright out of them, rolled back Niall's bloody sleeve, bathed and bandaged the long gash in his forearm, anointed the scratch on Judith's shoulder, and briskly repaired the long tear in her bodice and sleeve.

'It is but cobbled,' she said. 'I was never a good hand with a needle. But it will serve until you're home.' And she picked up the bowl of stained water and bore it away, leaving them for the first time alone together by candle-light, gazing earnestly and wonderingly at each other.

'And you have asked me nothing,' said Judith slowly. 'Neither where I have been all these days past, nor how I came to be riding through the night to this place, in company with a man. Neither how I vanished, nor how I got my freedom again. And I owe you so much, and I have not even thanked you. But I do, from my heart! But for you I should be lying dead in the forest. He meant killing!'

'I know well enough,' said Niall steadily, 'that you never would willingly have left us all in distress and dismay for you these three days. And I know that if you choose now to spare the man who put you to such straits, you do it of good intent, and in the kindness of your heart. What more do I need to know?'

'I want it buried for my own sake, too,' she said ruefully.

'What is there to gain by denouncing him? And much to lose. He is no such great villain, only presumptuous and vain and foolish. He has done me no violence, no lasting wrong. Better it should all be put away. You did not recognise him?' she asked, looking at him earnestly with her penetrating grey eyes, a little bruised with tiredness.

'That was he who rode with you? No, I could not tell who he was. But if I could, I would still go with your wish. Provided it was not he,' said Niall sharply, 'who came back afoot to make sure of your silence. For yes, *he* meant killing!'

'No, no, that was not he. He was gone, you heard him go. Besides, he would not. We had agreed, he knew I would keep my word. No, that other was some wretch living wild on the pickings of the roads. And we must warn Hugh Beringar so,' she said, 'when we go back. This place is very lonely. As well he should know there are masterless men abroad here.'

She had left the great waving sheaf of her hair loose on her shoulders, ready for the sleep she sorely needed. The large, high eyelids, iris-veined and translucent, hung heavily over the grey eyes. The sheen of candlelight over her tired pallor made her look like a woman fashioned in mother-of-pearl. He looked at her, and his heart ached.

'How came it,' she asked wonderingly, 'that you were there when I so needed you? I had but to cry out, and you came. I was on my way home from Pulley,' said Niall, shaken and tongue-tied for a moment by the sudden sweet intensity of her voice, 'and I saw – saw, heard, no, felt in my blood – when you passed by. I never thought to trouble you, only to see that you came safely wherever it was you wished to be.'

'You knew me?' she said, marvelling.

'Yes. Yes, I knew you.'

'But not the man?'

'No, not the man.'

'I think,' she said, with abrupt and reviving resolution, 'that you may, you of all people, that you should. I think I want to tell everything to you, you and Sister Magdalen – even what the world must not know, even what I have promised to keep hidden.'

'So you see,' she said starkly, coming to the end of her story, which had taken but a few minutes to tell, 'how shamelessly I am making use of you, Sister, in coming here. I have been lost and sought, hunted high and low, for three days, and tomorrow I must go back and face all those who have laboured and agonised for me, and tell them I have been here with you, that I fled all my troubles because they fell too heavily on me, and I took refuge without a word to any, here in this retreat, where you once offered me shelter from the world. Well, it will not be quite a lie, for I am here, if only for the half of this one night. But it shames me, so to use you. Yet I must go back tomorrow.' Though it was already today, she recalled through a haze of weariness and relief. 'I cannot leave them longer than need be in doubt and anxiety, now I'm free to return. Or God knows I would stay here, and how gladly!'

'I see no need to fret over a scruple,' said Sister Magdalen sensibly. 'If this spares both you and this idiot youth you have forgiven, and shuts the mouths of gossips, then I find it as good a way of serving as any. And the need for quietness and counsel you can declare without ever a blush, for that's no lie. For that matter, you may come back again when you will, and stay as long as you will, as once I told you. But you're right, it is but fair to set their minds at rest and call off the hunt. Later, when you're rested, you shall go back and face them all, and say that you came to me when the world and the stupidity of men – saving present company, that's understood! – bore you down to despair. But creep back afoot, no, that you shan't. Would I let a woman go so poorly provided from a retreat with me? You shall have Mother Mariana's mule – poor soul, she's bedridden now, she'll do no more riding – and I'll ride with you, to give colour and body to all, I have an errand I can do to the lord abbot at the same time.'

'How if they ask how long I have been here?' asked Judith.

'With me beside you? They won't ask. Or if they do, we shall not answer. Questions are as supple as willow wands,' said Sister Magdalen, rising authoritatively to lead them to the beds prepared, 'it's easy to brush by them and slip them aside, and no one the worse for it.'

Chapter Twelve

THE BROTHERS were just issuing from the church after High Mass, and the sun was climbing high into a pale blue sky, when Sister Magdalen's little cavalcade turned in at the abbey gatehouse. This was the eve of the translation of Saint Winifred, and not even for violent deaths, disappearances and disasters can the proper routine of the church be allowed to lapse into disorder. This year there would be no solemn procession from Saint Giles, at the edge of the town, to bring the relics once again to their resting-place on Winifred's altar, but there would be celebratory Masses, and day-long access to her shrine for the pilgrims who had special pleas to make for her intercession. Not so many of them this year, yet the guest-hall was well filled, and Brother Denis kept busy with provision for the arrivals, as Brother Anselm was with the new music he had prepared in the saint's honour. The novices and the children hardly realised what mortal preoccupations had convulsed town and Foregate in the recent days. The younger brothers, even those who had been closest to Brother Eluric and deeply shaken by his death, had almost forgotten him now in the cheerful prospect of a festival which brought them extra dishes at meals, and additional privileges.

Brother Cadfael was in no such case. Try as he would to keep his mind firmly on the divine office, it would stray away at every turn to worry at the problem of where Judith Perle could be hidden away now, and whether, after so many sinister happenings, the death of Bertred could really be the random and callous accident it seemed, or whether that, too, had the taint of murder about it. But if so, why murder, and by whom? There seemed no doubt that Bertred himself was the murderer of Brother Eluric, but the signs indicated that so far from being the abductor of his mistress, he had been probing that ill deed for himself, and had intended to be her deliverer, and exploit the favour to the limit afterwards. No question but the watchman was telling the truth as far as he knew it, Bertred had fallen from the hatch, roused the mastiff, and been hunted to the river-bank, with a single clout on the head to speed his flight. Yes, but only one, and the body that was drawn out of the river on the other side showed a second, worse injury, though neither in itself could have been fatal. How if someone had helped him into the water with that second blow, after the watchman had called off his dog?

If that was a possibility, who could it have been but the abductor, alarmed by Bertred's interference and intent on covering up his own crime?

And Vivian Hynde was away helping his father with the flocks at Forton, was he? Well, perhaps! Not for long! If he did not ride into the arms of the watch at the town gates before noon, Hugh would be sending an armed guard to fetch him.

Cadfael had arrived at this precise point as they emerged into the sunlight of the morning, and beheld Sister Magdalen just riding in at the gatehouse on her elderly dun-coloured mule, at its usual leisurely and determined foot-pace. She rode with the same unhurried competence with which she did everything, without fuss or pretence, and looked about her as she entered with a bright, observant eye. Close to her stirrup walked the miller from the Ford, her trusted ally in all things. Sister Magdalen would never be short of a man to do what she wanted.

But there was another mule following, a taller beast, and white, and as he cleared the arch of the gateway they saw that his rider, also, was a woman, and not in the Benedictine habit, but gowned in dark green, and with a scarf over her hair. A tall, slender woman, erect and graceful in the saddle, the carriage and balance of her head arrestingly dignified, and suddenly, startlingly, familiar.

Cadfael checked so suddenly that the brother behind collided with him, and stumbled. At the head of their company the abbot had also halted abruptly, staring in wonder.

So she had come back, of her own will, at her own time, free, composed, not greatly changed, to confound them all. Judith Perle reined her mule alongside Magdalen's, and there halted. She was paler than Cadfael remembered her. By nature her skin was clear and translucent as pearl, but now with a somewhat dulled whiteness, and her eyelids were a little swollen and heavy from want of sleep, and blanched and bluish like snow. But also there was a calm and serenity upon her, though without joy. She had the mastery of herself, she looked back into the astonished and questioning eyes that devoured her, and did not lower her own.

John Miller went to lift her down, and she laid her hands on his shoulders and set foot to the cobbles of the great court with a lightness that did not quite conceal her weariness. Abbot Radulfus had got his breath back, and started forward to meet her as she came towards him, bent the knee to him deeply, and stooped to kiss the hand he extended to her.

'Daughter,' said Radulfus, shaken and glad, 'how I rejoice to see you restored here, whole and well. We have been in great trouble for you.'

'So I have learned, Father,' she said in a low voice, 'and I take it to my blame. God knows it was never my wish that anyone should be in distress of mind for me, and I am sorry to have put you and the lord sheriff and so many good men to such a trouble and expense on my behalf. I will make amends as best I may.'

'Oh, child, pains spent in goodwill require no payment. If you are come back to your place safe and well, what else matters? But how does this come about? Where have you been all this time?'

'Father,' she said, drawing breath in a moment's hesitation, 'you see no harm has come to me. It was rather I who fled from a burden that had become too hard to bear alone. That I never said word to any you must excuse, but my need, my compulsion, was sudden and urgent. I needed a place of quietness and peace, and a time for thought, all that Sister Magdalen once promised me if ever I needed to shut out the world for a little while, until my heart could stand it. I fled to her, and she has not failed me.'

'And you are just come from Godric's Ford?' said Radulfus, marvelling. 'All this while that you have been thought lost, you were safe and quiet there? Well, I thank God for it! And no news of this turmoil we were in here ever came to your ears there at the Ford?'

'Never a word, Father Abbot,' said Sister Magdalen

promptly. She had lighted down and approached without haste, smoothing the skirt of her habit from the creases of riding with plump, shapely, ageing hands. 'We live out of the world there, and seldom feel the want of it. News is slow to reach us. Since I was last here, not a soul has come our way from Shrewsbury until late last night, when a man from the Foregate happened by. So here I have brought Judith home, to put an end to all this doubt, and set all minds at rest.'

'As hers, I hope,' said the abbot, closely studying the pale but calm face, 'is now at rest, after those stresses that drove her into hiding. Three days is not long, to bring about the healing of a heart.'

She looked up steadily into his face with her wide grey eyes, and very faintly smiled. 'I thank you, Father, and I thank God, I have regained my courage.'

'I am well sure,' said the abbot warmly, 'that you could not have placed yourself in better hands, and I, too, thank God that all our fears for you can be so happily put away.'

In the brief, profound silence the long file of brothers, halted perforce at the abbot's back, shifted and craned and peered to get a good look at this woman who had been sought as lost, and even whispered about with sly undertones of scandal, and now returned immaculate in the blameless company of the sub-prioress of a Benedictine cell, effectively silencing comment, if not speculation, and confronting the world with unassailable composure and dignity. Even Prior Robert had so far forgotten himself as to stand and stare, instead of waving the brothers authoritatively away through the cloister to their proper duties.

'Will you not have your beasts cared for here,' the abbot invited, 'and take some rest and refreshment? And I will send at once to the castle and let the lord sheriff know that you are back with us safe and sound. For you should see him as soon as possible, and explain your absence to him as you have here to me.'

'So I intend, Father,' said Judith, 'but I must go home. My aunt and cousin and all my people will still be fretting for me. I must go at once and show myself, and put an end to their anxiety. I'll send to the castle immediately to let Hugh Beringar know, and he may come to me or send for me to come to him, as soon as he pleases. But we could not pass by into the town without first coming to inform you.'

'That was considerate, and I am grateful. But, Sister, I trust you will be my guest while you are here?'

'Today, I think,' said Sister Magdalen, 'I must go with Judith and see her safely restored to her family, and be her advocate with the sheriff, should she need one. Authority may be less indulgent over time and labour wasted than you are, Father. I shall stay with her at least overnight. But tomorrow I hope to have some talk with you. I've brought with me the altar frontal Mother Mariana has been working on since she took to her bed. Her hands still have all their skill, I think you will be pleased with it. But it's packed carefully away in my saddle-roll. I would rather not delay to undo it now. If I might borrow Brother Cadfael, to walk up into the town with us, I think perhaps Hugh Beringar would be glad to have him in council when we meet, and he could bring down the altar-cloth to you afterwards.'

By this time Abbot Radulfus knew her well enough to know that there was always a reason for any request she might make. He looked round for Cadfael, who was already making his way out from the ranks of the brothers.

'Yes, go with our sister. You have leave for as long as you may be needed.'

'With your countenance, Father,' said Cadfael readily, 'and if Sister Magdalen agrees, I could go straight on to the castle and take the message to Hugh Beringar, after we have brought Mistress Perle home. He'll have men still out round the countryside, the sooner he can call them off, the better.'

'Yes, agreed! Go, then!' He led the way back to where the mules stood waiting, with John Miller solid and passive beside them. The file of brothers, released from the porch, went its dutiful way, not without several glances over shoulders to watch the two women mount and depart. While they were about it, Radulfus drew Cadfael aside and said quietly: 'If the news came so laggardly to Godric's Ford, there may still be some things that have happened here that she does not know, and not all will be pleasant hearing. This man of hers who is dead, worse, guilty . . .'

'I had thought of it,' said Cadfael as softly. 'She shall know, before she ever reaches home.'

As soon as they were on the open stretch of the bridge, going at the dogged mule-pace that would not be hurried, Cadfael moved to Judith's bridle, and said mildly: 'Three days you've been absent. Have I to give account, before you face others, of all that has happened during those three days?'

'No need,' she said simply. 'I have had some account already.'

'Perhaps not of all, for not all is generally known. There has been another death. Yesterday, in the afternoon, we found a body washed up on our side the river, beyond where the Gaye ends. A drowned man – one of your weavers, the young man Bertred. I tell you now,' he said gently, hearing the sharp and painful intake of her breath, 'because at home you will find him being coffined and readied for burial. I could not let you walk into the house and come face to face with that, and all unwarned.'

'Bertred drowned?' she said in a shocked whisper. 'But how could such a thing happen? He swims like an eel. How could he drown?'

'He had had a blow on the head, though it would not have done more than make his wits spin for a while. And somehow he came by another such knock before he went into the water. Whatever happened to him happened in the night. The watchman at Fuller's had a tale to tell,' said Cadfael with careful deliberation, and went on to repeat it as nearly word for word as he could recall. She sat on her mule in chill silence throughout the story, almost he felt her freeze as she connected the hour of the night, the place, and surely also the narrow, dusty, half-forgotten room behind the bales of wool. Her silence and her word would be hard to keep. Here was lost a second young man, withered by the touch of some fatal flaw in her, and yet a third she might scarcely be able to save, now they had drawn so near to the truth.

They had reached the gate, and entered under the archway. On the steep climb up the Wyle the mules slowed even more, and no one sought to hurry them.

'There is more,' said Cadfael. 'You will remember the morning we found Brother Eluric, and the mould I made of the boot-print in the soil. The boots we took from Bertred's body, when we carried him to the abbey dead – the left boot . . . fits that print.'

'No!' she said in sharp distress and disbelief. 'That is impossible! There is here some terrible mistake.'

'There is no mistake. No possibility of a mistake. The match is absolute.'

'But why? Why? What reason could Bertred have had to try to cut down my rose-bush? What possible reason to strike at the young brother?' And in a lost and distant voice, almost to herself, she said: 'None of this did he tell me!'

Cadfael said nothing, but she knew he had heard. After a silence she said: 'You shall hear. You shall know. We had better hurry. I must talk to Hugh Beringar.' And she shook her bridle and pressed ahead along the High Street. From open booths and shop doorways heads were beginning to be thrust in excited recognition, neighbour nudging neighbour, and presently, as she drew nearer to home, there were greetings called out to her, but she hardly noticed them. The word would soon be going round that Judith Perle was home again, and riding, and in respectable religious company, after all that talk of her being carried off by some villain with marriage by rape in mind.

Sister Magdalen kept close at her heels, so that there should be no mistaking that they were travelling together. She had said nothing throughout this ride from the abbey, though she had sharp ears and a quick intelligence, and had certainly heard most of what had been said. The miller, perhaps deliberately, had let them go well ahead of him. His sole concern was that whatever Sister Magdalen designed was good and wise, and nothing and no one should be allowed to frustrate it. Of curiosity he had very little. What he needed to know in order to be of use to her she would tell him. He had been her able supporter so long now that there were things between them that could be communicated and understood without words. They had reached Maerdol-head, and halted outside the Vestier house. Cadfael helped Judith down from the saddle, for the passage through the frontage to the yard, though wide enough, was too low for entering mounted. She had barely set foot to the ground when the saddler from the shop next door came peering out from his doorway in round-eyed astonishment, and bolted as suddenly back again to relay the news to some customer within. Cadfael took the white mule's bridle, and followed Judith in through the dim passage and into the yard. From the shed on the right the rhythmic clack of the looms met them, and from the hall the faint sound of muted voices. The women sounded subdued and dispirited at their spinning, and there was no singing in this house of mourning.

Branwen was just crossing the yard to the hall door, and turned at the crisp sound of the small hooves on the beaten earth of the passage. she gave a sharp, high-pitched cry, half started towards her mistress, her face brightening into wonder and pleasure, and then changed her mind and turned and ran for the house, shouting for Dame Agatha, for Miles, for all the household to come quickly and see who was here. And in headlong haste Miles came bursting out from the hall, to stare wildly, burn up like a lighted lamp, and rush with open arms to embrace his cousin.

'Judith . . . Judith, it *is* you! Oh, my dear heart, all this time where were you? Where *were* you? While we've all been sweating and worrying, and hunting every ditch and alley for you? God knows I began to think I might never see you again. Where have you been? What happened to you?'

Before he had finished exclaiming his mother was there, overflowing with tearful endearments and pious thanks to God at seeing her niece home again, alive and well. Judith submitted patiently to all, and was spared having to answer until they had run out of questions, by which time all the spinning-women were out in the yard, and the weavers from their looms, and a dozen voices at once made a babel in which she would not have been heard, even if she had spoken. A wind of joy blew through the house of mourning, and could not be quenched even when Bertred's mother came out to stare with the rest.

'I am sorry,' said Judith, when there was a lull in the gale, 'that you have been concerned about me, that was no intent of mine. But now you see I'm whole and unharmed, no need to trouble further, I shall not be lost again. I have been at Godric's Ford with Sister Magdalen, who has been kind enough to ride back with me. Aunt Agatha, will you prepare a bed for my guest? Sister Magdalen will stay with me overnight.'

Agatha looked from her niece to the nun, and back again, with a soft smile on her lips and a shrewdly hopeful light in her blue eyes. The girl was come home with her patroness from the cloister. Surely she had returned to that former longing for the peace of renunciation, why else should she run away to a Benedictine nunnery?

'I will, with all my heart!' said Agatha fervently. 'Sister, you're warmly welcome. Pray come into the house, and I'll bring you wine and oat-cakes, for you must be tired and hungry after your ride. Use the house and us freely, we are all in your debt.' And she led the way with the conscious grace of a chatelaine. In three days, thought Cadfael, watching apart, she has grown accustomed to thinking of herself as the lady of the house; the habit can't be shaken off in an instant.

Judith moved to follow, but Miles laid a hand earnestly on her arm to detain her for a moment. 'Judith,' he said in her ear, with anxious solicitude, 'have you made her any promises? The nun? You haven't let her persuade you to take the veil?'

'Are you so set against the cloistered life for me?' she asked, studying his face indulgently.

'Not if that's what you want, but – Why did you run to her, unless . . .? You *haven't* promised yourself to her?'

'No,' she said, 'I've made no promises.'

'But you did go to her – well!' he said, and shrugged off his own solemnity. 'It's for you to do whatever you truly want. Come, let's go in!' And he turned from her briskly to call one of the weavers to take charge of the miller and the mules, and see both well cared for, and to shoo the spinners back to their spindles, but with good humour. 'Brother, come in with us and most welcome. Do they know, then, at the abbey? That Judith's home again?'

'Yes,' said Cadfael, 'they know. I'm here to take back some gift Sister Magdalen has brought for our Lady Chapel. And I have an errand to the castle on Mistress Perle's behalf.'

Miles snapped his fingers, abruptly grave again. 'By God, yes! The sheriff can call off this hunt now, the quest's over. But – Judith, I'd forgotten! There must be things here you don't yet know. Martin Bellecote is here, and his boy helping him. Don't go into the small chamber, they are coffining Bertred. He drowned in the Severn, two nights ago. I wish I had not to spoil this day with such ill news!'

'I have already been told,' said Judith levelly. 'Brother Cadfael would not let me return here unprepared. An accident, I hear.' There was that in the sparsity of the words and the bleakness of her voice that caused Cadfael to check and look at her closely. She shared his own trouble. She found it almost impossible to accept that anything that had happened in connection with her person and her affairs during these June days was merely accidental.

'I am going now to find Hugh Beringar,' said Cadfael, and withdrew from them on the threshold to turn back into the street.

In Judith's own private chamber they sat down together in sombre conference, Hugh, Sister Magdalen, Judith and Cadfael, greetings over, in mildly constrained formality. Miles had hovered, unwilling to be parted from the cousin he had regained, but with a respectful eye upon Hugh, half expecting to be dismissed, but with a protective hand on Judith's shoulder, as if she might need defending. But it was Judith who sent him away. She did it with a sudden flush of family tenderness, looking up into his face with a faint, affectionate smile. 'No, leave us, Miles, we shall have time later to talk as much as you wish, and you shall know whatever you need to ask, but now I would rather be without distractions. The lord sheriff's time is of value, and I owe him all my attention, after the great trouble I have caused him.'

Even then he hesitated, frowning, but then he closed his hand warmly on hers. 'Don't vanish again!' he said, and went light-footed out of the room, closing the door firmly behind him.

'The first and most urgent thing I have to tell you,' said Judith then, looking Hugh in the face, 'I didn't want him or my aunt to hear. They have been through enough anxiety for me, no need for them to know that I've been in danger of my life. My lord, there are footpads in the forest not a full mile from Godric's Ford, preying on travellers by night. I was attacked there. One man at least, I cannot answer for more, though commonly they hunt in pairs, I believe. He had a knife. I have only a scratch on my arm to show for it, but he meant to kill. The next wayfarer may not be so lucky. This I had to tell you first.'

Hugh was studying her with an impassive face but intent eyes. In the hall Miles crossed the room, whistling, towards the shop.

'And this was on your way to Godric's Ford?' said Hugh.

'Yes.'

'You were alone? By night in the forest? It was early morning when you vanished from Shrewsbury – on your way to the abbey.' He turned to Sister Magdalen. 'You know of this?'

'I know of it from Judith,' said Magdalen serenely. 'Otherwise, no, there has been no sign of outlawry so close to us. If any of the forest men had heard of such, I should have been told. But if you mean do I believe the story, yes, I believe it. I dressed her arm, and did as much for the man who came to her aid and drove off the outlaw. I know that what she tells you is true.'

'This is the fourth day since you disappeared,' said Hugh, turning his innocent black gaze again on Judith. 'Was it wise to delay so long before giving me warning of masterless men coming so close? And the sisters themselves so exposed to danger? One of Sister Magdalen's forester neighbours would have carried a message. And we should have known, then, that you were safe, and we need not fear for you. I could have sent men at once to sweep the woods clean.'

Judith hesitated only a moment, and even that rather with the effect of clearing her own mind than of considering deceit. Something of Magdalen's confident tranquillity had entered into her. She said slowly, choosing her words. 'My lord, my story for the world is that I fled from a load of troubles to take refuge with Sister Magdalen, that I have been with her all this time, and no man has anything to do with my going or my returning. But my story for you, if you will respect that, can be very different. There are true things I will not tell you, and questions I will not answer, but everything I do tell you, and every answer I give you, shall be the truth.'

'I call that a fair offer,' said Sister Magdalen approvingly, 'and if I were you, Hugh, I would accept. Justice is a very fine thing, but not when it does more harm to the victim than to the wrongdoer. The girl comes well out of it, let it rest at that.'

'And on which night,' asked Hugh, not yet committing himself, 'were you attacked in the forest?'

'Last night. Past midnight it must have been, probably an hour past.'

'A good hour,' said Magdalen helpfully. 'We had just gone back to bed after Lauds.'

'Good! I'll have a patrol go out there and quarter the woods for a mile around. But it's unheard-of for any but occasionally the lads from Powys to give trouble in those parts, and if they move we usually have good warning of it. This must be some lone hand, a misused villein gone wild. Now,' said Hugh, and suddenly smiled at Judith, 'tell me what you see fit, from the time you were dragged into a boat under the bridge by the Gaye, to last night when you reached the Ford. And for what I shall do about it you will have to trust me.'

'I do trust you,' she said, eyeing him long and steadily. 'I believe you will spare me, and not force me to break my word. Yes, I was dragged away, yes, I have been held until two nights ago, and pestered to agree to a marriage. I will not tell you where, or by whom.'

'Shall I tell you?' offered Hugh.

'No,' she said in sharp protest. 'If you know, at least let me be sure it was not from me, neither in word nor look. Within two days he was repenting what he did, bitterly, desperately, he could see no way out, to escape paying for it, and it had gained him nothing, and never would, and he knew it. Very heartily he wished himself safely rid of me, but if he let me go he feared I should denounce him, and if I was found it would equally be his ruin. In the end,' she said simply, 'I was sorry for him. He had done me no violence but the first seizing me, he had tried to win me, he was too fearful, yes, and too well conditioned, to take me by force. He was helpless, and he begged me to help him. Besides,' she reasoned strongly, 'I also wanted the thing ended without scandal, I wanted that far more than I wanted any revenge on him. By the end I didn't want revenge at all, I *was* avenged. I had the mastery of him, I could make him do whatever I ordered. It was I who made the plan. He should take me by night to Godric's Ford, or close, for he was afraid to be seen or known, and I would return home from there as if I had been there all that time. It was too late to set out that night, but the next night, last night, we rode together. He set me down barely half a mile from the Ford. And it was after that, when he was gone, that I was attacked.'

'You could not tell what manner of man? Nothing about him you could recognise or know again, by sight or by touch, scent, anything?'

'In the woods there, before the moon, it was raven-dark. And over so quickly. I have not told you yet who it was who came to my aid. Sister Magdalen knows, he came back with us this morning, we left him at his house in the Foregate. Niall Bronzesmith, who lives in the house that was mine once. How everything I am, and know, and feel, and everyone who draws near me,' she said with sudden passion, 'spins around that house and those roses. I wish I had never left it, I could have given it to the abbey and still been its tenant. It was wrong to abandon the place where love was.'

Where love *is*, Cadfael thought, listening to the controlled voice so abruptly vibrant and fierce, and watching the pale, tired face blaze like a lighted lantern. And it was Niall who was by her when it came to life or death!

The flame burned down a little and steadied, but was not quenched. 'Now I have told you,' she said. 'What will you do? I promised that I would not urge any charge against – him, the man who snatched me away. I bear him no malice. If you take him and charge him, I will not bear witness against him.'

'Shall I tell you,' asked Hugh gently, 'where he is now? He is in a cell in the castle. He rode in at the eastern gate not half an hour before Cadfael came for me, and we whisked him into the wards before he knew what we were about. He has not yet been questioned or charged with anything, and no one in the town knows that we have him. I can let him go, or let him rot there until the assize. Your wish to bury the affair I can understand, your intent to keep your word I respect. But there is still the matter of Bertred. Bertred was abroad that night when you made your plans . . .'

'Cadfael has told me,' she said, erect and watchful again.

'The night of his death, which may or may not be mere accident. He was prowling with intent to break in and – steal, shall we say? And it is possible that he was helped to his death in the river.'

Judith shook her head decidedly. 'Not by the man you say you are holding. I know, for I was with him.' She bit her lips, and considered a moment. There was hardly anything left unsaid but the name she would not name. 'We both were within there, we heard his fall, though we did not know then what was happening. We had heard small sounds outside, or thought we had. So we did again, or so he did, afterwards. But by then he was so fraught, every whisper jarred him from head to heel. But he did not leave me. Whatever happened to Bertred, he had no hand in it.'

'That's proof enough,' agreed Hugh, satisfied. 'Very well, you shall have your way. No one need know more than you care to tell. But, by God, *he* shall know what manner of worm he is, before I kick him out of the wards and send him home with a flea in his ear. That much you won't grudge me, he may still count himself lucky to get off so lightly.'

'He is of no great weight,' she said indifferently, 'for good or ill. Only a foolish boy, but he is not great villain, and young enough to mend. But there is still Bertred. Brother Cadfael tells me it was he who killed the young monk. I understand nothing, neither that nor why Bertred himself should die. Niall told me, last night, how things had been here in the town after I vanished. But he did not tell me about Bertred.'

'I doubt if he knew,' said Cadfael. 'It was only in the afternoon we had found him, and though the word was going round in the town, naturally, after he was brought back here, I doubt if it had reached Niall's end of the Foregate, and certainly I did not mention it to him. How did he come to be there at hand, close by Godric's Ford, when you needed him?'

'He saw us pass,' said Judith, 'before we were into the forest. He was on his way home then, but he knew me, and he followed. Well for me! But Niall Bronzesmith has always been well for me, the few times ever we've met or touched.'

Hugh rose to depart. 'Well, I'll have Alan take a patrol down into the forest, and make a thorough drive there. If we have a nest of wild men in those parts, we'll smoke them out. Madam, there shall be nothing made public of what has been said here. That matter is finished as you would have it. And thank God it ended no worse. Now I trust you may be left in peace.'

'Only I am not easy about Bertred,' Judith said abruptly. 'Neither about his guilt nor his death. So strong a swimmer, born and raised by the river. Why should his skill fail him that night, of all nights?'

Hugh was gone, back to the castle to call off his hunters as fast as they came in to report, and either to deal faithfully with the wretched Vivian Hynde, or, more probably, leave him sweating and worrying overnight or longer in a chilly cell. Cadfael took the carefully rolled altar frontal Sister Magdalen had extracted from her saddle-roll, and set off back to the abbey. But first he looked in at the small bare room where Bertred's coffined body lay on trestles, and the master-carpenter and his son were just fitting the lid, and said a prayer for a young man lost. Sister Magdalen came out with him as far as the street, and there halted, still silent and frowning in intense thought.

'Well?' said Cadfael, finding her so taciturn.

'No, not well. Very ill!' She shook her head dubiously. 'I can make nothing of this pattern. Plain enough what happened to Judith, but the rest I cannot fathom. You heard what she said of Bertred's death. The same doubts I feel about what so nearly might have been her own, but for the smith. Is there anything in all this coil that has happened by pure chance? I doubt it!'

He was still pondering that as he started uphill towards the High Street, and as he neared the corner, for some reason he slowed and turned to look back, and she was still standing in the mouth of the passage, gazing after him, her strong hands folded at her girdle. Nothing by pure chance, no, surely not, even those happenings that seemed wanton carried a false echo. Rather a sequence of events had set off each the following one, and called in motives and interests until then untouched, so that the affair had come about in a circle, and brought up the hapless souls involved in it facing where they had never intended to go. A deal more rapidly and purposefully than he had left her, Cadfael started back towards Sister Magdalen.

'I did wonder,' she said without apparent surprise, 'what was going on in your mind. I've seldom known you sit through such a conference saying so little and scowling so much. What have you thought of now?'

'There's something I should like you to do for me, since you'll be staying in this house,' said Cadfael. 'What with the youngster's burial and Judith's return, it shouldn't be too difficult to filch a couple of things for me, and send them down to me at the abbey. By Martin's boy Edwy, if they're still here, but not a word to anyone else. Borrowing, not stealing. God knows I shan't need them for long, one way or the other.'

'You interest me,' said Magdalen. 'What are these two things?'

'Two left shoes,' said Cadfael.

Chapter Thirteen

NOW THAT his mind was stringing together a thread of abhorrent sense out of details which hitherto had seemed to make none, he could not turn his thoughts to anything else. Throughout Vespers he struggled to concentrate on the office, but the lamentable sequence of disasters connected with the rose marched inexorably through his mind, gradually assembling into a logical order. First there was Judith, still deprived and unhappy after three lonely years, thinking and sometimes speaking of retreating into a nunnery, and vexed by a number of suitors both old and young, who had had an eye on her person and her wealth all this time, and wooed and pleaded without reward, and were now beginning to get desperate in case she carried out her design to become a religious. Then the attempt on the rose-bush, to retrieve at least the possibility of regaining the gift-house, and the resultant death of Brother Eluric, probably, indeed almost certainly, unplanned and committed in panic. After that, however bitterly regretted, one man at least had murder already against him, and would be far more likely afterwards to stick at nothing. But then, to confound and complicate, came the abduction of Judith, another panic measure to prevent her from making her gift unconditional, and try to persuade or threaten her into marriage. Even if he had not been named, the perpetrator of that enormity was known. And the nocturnal death of Bertred might have been logical enough, had the abductor brought it about, but plainly he had not.

Judith vouched for that, and so, probably, could Vivian Hynde's mother, since it seemed clear that once the bargain was made between captive and captor, Judith had been removed to the greater comfort of a house which had already been visited in search of her, and the buried room in the warehouse hurriedly and ingeniously cleared of all traces of her presence. So far, well! But there had been listeners outside in the night, Bertred first and possibly another afterwards, unless Vivian had reached a state in which every stirring of a spider or a mouse in the roof could alarm him. The plan might well have been overheard, and the horse with the double load might have had another follower, besides Niall Bronzesmith. And that would round off the whole disastrous circle, all the more surely if he who began it was also the one who sought to end it.

For consider, thought Cadfael, while his mind should have been on more tranquil and timeless things, what an excellent scapegoat Vivian Hynde makes for whoever attacked Judith in the forest. The man who had snatched her away and tried in vain to force marriage upon her, now riding away with her into the forest by night, and perhaps not trusting to her promise not to betray him, but preferring, once he had set her down, to dismount and hurry back to put an end to her. True, as things were, Judith vindicated him, she was quite certain he had not turned back, but made all haste away home, or up to Forton, to his father's flocks. But how if the attempt had succeeded, and Judith had been left dead in the forest, and there had been no witness to do him justice?

A scapegoat provided for one murder beforehand, Cadfael pursued. How if there had been another provided for the first murder, not beforehand, since that killing was not premeditated, but afterwards? A scapegoat suddenly presented helpless and vulnerable and already trussed for execution, bringing with him in an instant the inspiration of his usefulness, and the certainty of his death? Still not chance, but the bitterly ironic consequence of what had gone before.

And all this complication of logic and guilt depended upon two left shoes, which as yet he had not seen. The older the better, he had said, when Magdalen, intelligent and immune from surprise, questioned him on detail, I want them well worn. Few but the rich own many pairs of shoes, but one of the wearers of those he had in mind had no further use for whatever he did possess, and the other must surely have more than one pair. Not the new, Cadfael had said firmly, for he surely has some that are new. His oldest he'll hardly miss.

Vespers was over, and Cadfael spared time to pay a visit to his workshop in the herb-garden before supper, in case the boy was waiting for him there. The mastercarpenter's son knew his way about very well, from old acquaintance of some years past, and would certainly look for him there. But all was cool and quiet and solitary within, a single wine-jar bubbling contentedly on its bench, in a slow, drowsy rhythm, the dried bunches of herbs rustling softly overhead along the eaves without and the beams within, the brazier quenched and cold. These were the longest days of the year, the light outside was barely subdued from its afternoon brightness, but in another hour it would be mellowing into the level beams of sunset and the greenish glow of twilight.

Nothing yet. He closed the door on his small inner kingdom, and went back to supper in the refectory, and bore with Brother Jerome's unctuous reproof for being a moment late without comment or complaint. Indeed, without even noticing it, though he made appropriately placating answer by instinct. The household at Maerdol-head must be too busily awake and in motion for Sister Magdalen to manage her depredations as easily and quickly as he had hoped. No matter! Whatever she took in hand she would complete successfully.

He evaded Collations, but went dutifully to Compline, and still there was no sign. He retired again to his workshop, always a convenient excuse for not being where according to the horarium he should have been, even thus late in the evening. But it was full dark, and the brothers already in their cells in the dortoir, before Edwy Bellecote came, in haste and full of apologies.

'My father sent me on an errand out to Frankwell, and I had no leave to tell him what I was about for you, Brother Cadfael, so I thought best to hold my tongue and go. It took me longer than I thought for, and I had to pretend I'd left my tools behind as an excuse for going back to the house so late. But the sister was on the watch for me. She's quick, that one! And she had what you asked for.' He produced a bundle rolled in sacking from under his coat, and sat down comfortably, uninvited but sure of his welcome, on the bench by the wall. 'What would you be needing two odd shoes for?'

Cadfael had known him well since the boy, turned eighteen now, was a lively imp of fourteen, tall for his years and lean and venturesome, with a bush of chestnut hair, and light hazel eyes that missed very little of what went on about him. He was using them now to good effect, as Cadfael unwrapped the sacking, and tipped out the shoes on the earth floor.

'For the proper study of two odd feet,' he said, and viewed them for a moment without touching. 'Which of the two is Bertred's?'

'This. This one I purloined for her from where his few things were laid by, but she had to wait for a chance to get at the other, or I should have been here before ever I got sent out to Frankwell.'

'No matter,' said Cadfael absently, and turned the shoe sole-upward in his hands. Very well worn, the whole-cut upper rubbed thin at the toe and patched, the single-thickness sole reinforced with a triangular lift of thick leather at the heel. It was of the common sort that have no fastening, but are simply slipped on the foot. The leather thonging that seamed the instep at the outer side was almost worn through. But after all its probable years of wear, the sole was trodden straight and true from back of heel to tip of toe. No pressure to either side, no down at heel nor oblique wear at the toe.

'I should have known,' said Cadfael. 'I can't recall seeing the man walking more than half a dozen times, but I should have known. Straight as a lance! I doubt if he ever trod a sole sidelong or ground down a heel askew in his life.'

The other shoe was rather a low-cut ankle boot, made on the same one-piece pattern as to the upper, and similarly seamed at the instep, with a slightly pointed toe, a thicker lift of leather at the heel, and a thong that encircled the ankle and was fastened with a bronze buckle. The outer side of the back of the heel was trodden down in a deep segment, and the same wear showed at the inner side of the toe. The light of Cadfael's small lamp, falling close but sidelong over it, accentuated the lights and shadows. Here there was only the faint beginning of a crack under the big toe, but it showed in the same spot as on the boot that had been taken from Bertred's dead foot, and it was enough.

'What does it prove?' wondered Edwy, his bright shock-head bent curiously over the shoe.

'It proves that I am a fool,' said Cadfael ruefully, 'though I have sometimes suspected as much myself. It proves that the man who wears a certain shoe this week may not be the man who wore it last week. Hush, now, let me think!' He was in two minds whether there was any need to take further action immediately, but recalling all that had been said that afternoon, he reasoned that action could wait until morning. What could have been more reassuring than Judith's simple assumption that the attack on her had been a mere matter of the hazards of forest travel, an opportunist blow at a woman benighted, any woman, simply for the clothes she wore if she proved to have nothing else of value about her? No, no need to start an alarm and rouse Hugh again before morning, the murderer had every cause to believe himself safe.

'Son,' said Cadfael, sighing, 'I am getting old, I miss my bed. And you had better be off to yours, or your mother will be blaming me for getting you into bad ways.'

When the boy had gone, with his curiosity still unsatisified, Cadfael sat still and silent, at last admitting into his thoughts the realisation of which even his mind had been fighting shy. For the murderer, so well persuaded now of his own skill, feeling himself invulnerable, would not give up now. Having come so far, he would not turn back. Well, his time was short. He had only this one night left, though he did not know it, and he neither would nor could attempt anything against Judith now, in her own home, with Sister Magdalen keeping her formidable company. He would prefer to bide his time, unaware that tomorrow was to see an ending.

Cadfael started erect, causing the lamp to flicker. No, not against Judith! But if he was so sure of himself, then he had still this one night to try again to conserve the house in the Foregate, for tomorrow the rose rent would be paid, and for another year the abbey's title would be unassailable. If Judith was not vulnerable, the rose-bush still was.

He told himself that he was being a superstitious fool, that no one, not even a criminal at once lulled and exhilarated by success, would dare venture anything again so soon, but by the time he had completed even the thought he found himself halfway across the garden, heading at a hasty walk out into the great court, and making for the gatehouse, and tonight the sky was clear, and there were stars, though fine as pinpricks in the midnight blackness. Along the Foregate it was very quiet, nothing moving but the occasional prowling cat among the alleys. But somewhere ahead, near the corner of the abbey wall at the horse-fair ground, there was a small, vibrating glow in the sky, low down behind the house-roofs, and its quivering alternately lit them into black silhouette and quenched them again in the common darkness. Cadfael began to run. Then he heard, distant and muted, the flurry of many voices in half-unbelieving alarm, and suddenly the glow was swallowed up in a great burst of flame, that fountained into the sky with a crackling of wood and thorn. The babble of voices became an uproar of men shouting and women shrilling, and all the Foregate dogs baying echoes from wall to wall along the highway.

Doors were opening, men running out into the roadway, pulling on hose and coats as they came and breaking into shuffling, entangled motion towards the fire. Questions flew at random, and were not answered because no one as yet knew the answers. Cadfael arrived among the rest at the gate of Niall's yard, which already stood wide. Through the wicket into the garden the poppy-red glow glared, quivering, and above the crest of the wall the column of fire soared, breathing upward a whirlwind of burning air and spinning flakes of ash, double a tall man's height, to dissolve into the darkness. Thank God, thought Cadfael at sight of its vertical ascent, there's no wind, it won't reach either the house or the farrier's toft on the other side. And by the fury and noise of it, it may burn out quickly. But he knew already what he would see as he stepped through the wicket.

In the middle of the rear wall the rose-bush was a great globe of flames, roaring like a furnace and crackling like the breaking of bones as the thorns spat and writhed in the heat. The fire had reached the old, crabbed vine, but beyond that there was nothing but the stone wall to feed it. The fruit trees were far enough removed to survive, though their nearer branches might be scorched. But nothing, nothing but blackened, outspread arms and white wood-ash, would be left of the rose-bush. Against the blinding brightness of the flames, a few helpless figures circled and flinched away, unable to approach. Water thrown from a safe distance exploded into steam and vanished in a frantic hissing, but did no good. They had given up the attempt to fight it, and stood back dangling buckets, to watch the old, gnarled bole, so many years fruitful, twist and split and groan in its death-agony.

Niall had drawn back to the wall opposite, and stood watching with a soiled, discouraged face and drawn brows. Cadfael came to his side, and the brown head turned to acknowledge his coming, and nodded brief recognition before turning back again to resume his interrupted watch.

'How did he get this furnace going?' asked Cadfael. 'Not with simple flint and steel and tinder, that's certain, and you in the house. It would have taken him a good quarter-hour to get beyond the first smoulder.'

'He came the same way,' said Niall, without removing his bleak gaze from the tower of smoke and spinning ash surging up into the sky. 'Through the paddock at the back, where the ground's higher. He never even entered the garden this time. He must have poured oil over the wall on to the bush and the vine – drenched them in oil. And then he dropped a torch over. Well alight . . . And he away in the dark. And there's nothing we can do, nothing!'

Nothing any man could do, except stand back from the heat and watch, as very gradually the first fury began to slacken, and the blackened branches to sag from the wall and collapse into the blazing heart of the fire, sending up drifts of fine grey ash that soared upwards like a flight of moths. Nothing except be thankful that the wall behind was of solid stone, and would not carry the fire towards either human habitation.

'It was dear to her,' said Niall bitterly.

'It was. But at least she has her life still,' said Cadfael, 'and has rediscovered its value. And she knows who to thank for the gift, next after God.'

Niall said nothing to that, but continued grimly to watch as the fire, appeased, began to settle into a bed of crimson, and the flying moths of ash to drift about the garden, no longer torn headlong upward by the draught. The neighbours stood back, satisfied that the worst was over, and began gradually to drift away, back to their beds. Niall heaved a great breath, and shook himself out of his daze.

'I had been thinking,' he said slowly, 'of bringing my little girl home here today. We were talking of it only the other night, that I should do well to have her with me, now she's no longer a babe. But now I wonder! With such a madman haunting this house, she's safer where she is.'

'Yes,' said Cadfael, rousing, 'yes, do that, bring her home! You need not fear. After tomorrow, Niall, this madman will haunt you no more. I promise it!'

The day of Saint Winifred's translation dawned fine and sunny, with a fresh breeze that sprang up only with the light, and drifted the stench of burning across the roofs of the Foregate as inevitably as the first labourer to cross the bridge brought the news of the fire into the town. It reached the Vestier shop as soon as the shutters were taken down and the first customer entered. Miles came bursting into the solar with a face of consternation, like someone charged with bad news and uncertain how to convey it delicately.

'Judith, it seems we're not done yet with the ill luck that hangs around your rose-bush. There's yet one more strange thing happened, I heard it just this moment. No need for you to trouble too much, no one is dead or hurt this time, it's not so terribly grave. But I know it will distress you, all the same.'

So long and deprecating a preamble was not calculated to reassure her, in spite of its soothing tone. She rose from the window-bench where she was sitting with Sister Magdalen. 'What is it now? What was there left that could happen?'

'There's been a fire in the night – someone set fire to the rose-bush. It's burned, every leaf, burned down to the bole, so they're saying. There can't be a bud or a twig left, let alone a flower to pay your rent.'

'The house?' she demanded, aghast. 'Did that take fire? Was there damage? No harm to Niall? Only the bush?'

'No, no, nothing else touched, never fret for the smith, nor for the house, they're safe enough. They'd have said if anyone had been harmed. Now, be easy, it's over!' He took her by the shoulders, very gently and brotherly, smiling into her face. 'Over now, and no one the worse. Only that plaguey bush gone, and I say just as well, considering all the mischief it's caused. Such a queer bargain to make, you're well rid of it.'

'It need never have brought harm to anyone,' she said wretchedly, and slowly sat down again, drawing herself out of his hands quite gently. 'The house was mine to give. I had been happy in it. I wanted to give it to God, I wanted it blessed.'

'It's yours again to give or keep, now,' said Miles, 'for you'll get no rose for your rent this year, my dear. You could take your house back for the default. You could give it as your dowry if you do go so far as to join the Benedictines.' He looked sidelong at Sister Magdalen with his blue, clear eyes, smiling. 'Or you could live in it again if you're so minded – or let Isabel and me live in it when we marry. Whatever you decide, the old bargain's broken. If I were you, I would be in no hurry to make such another, after all that's happened in consequence.'

'I don't take back gifts,' she said, 'especially from God,' Miles had left the door of the solar open behind him; she could hear the murmur of the women's voices from the far end of the long room beyond, suddenly and sharply cut across by other voices at the hall door, a man's first courteous and low, then her aunt's, with the sweet social note in it. There might be a number of neighbourly visits this day, as Bertred went to his burial. At mid-morning he would be carried to Saint Chad's churchyard. 'Let it rest,' said Judith, turning away to the window. 'Why should we be talking of this now? If the bush is burned . . .' That had an ominous biblical ring about it, the burning bush of revelation. But that one, surely, was not consumed.

'Judith, my dear,' said Agatha, appearing in the doorway, 'here is the lord sheriff to visit you again, and Brother Cadfael is come with him.'

They came in quietly, with nothing ominous about them, but for the fact that two sergeants of the garrison followed them into the room and stood well withdrawn, one on either side the doorway. Judith had turned to meet the visitors, anticipating news already known.

'My lord, I and my affairs are causing you trouble still. My cousin has already told me what happened in the night. With all my heart I hope this may be the last ripple of this whirlpool. I'm sorry to have put you to such shifts, it shall end here.'

'That is my intent,' said Hugh, making a brief formal reverence to Magdalen, who sat magisterial and composed by the window, an admirably silent woman when the occasion demanded. 'My business here this morning is rather with Master Coliar. A very simple question, if you can help us.' He turned to Miles with the most amiable and inviting of countenances, and asked, on a silken, rapid level that gave no warning: 'The boots we found on Bertred, when he was taken out of the river – *when did you give them to him*?'

Miles was quick in the wits, but not quick enough. He had caught his breath momentarily, and before he could release it again his mother had spoken up with her usual ready loquacity, and her pride in every detail that touched her son. 'It was the day that poor young man from the abbey was found dead. You remember, Miles, you went down to bring Judith home, as soon as we heard. She'd gone to collect her girdle –'

He had himself in hand by then, but it was never an easy matter to stop Agatha, once launched. 'You're mistaken, Mother,' he said, and even laughed, with the light note of an indulgent son used to tolerating a woolly-witted parent. 'It was weeks ago, when I saw his shoes were worn through into holes. I've given him my cast-offs before,' he said turning to confront Hugh's levelled black eyes boldly. 'Shoes are costly items.'

'No, my dear,' Agatha pursued with impervious certainty. 'I recollect very well; after such a day how could I forget? It was that same evening, you remarked that Bertred was going almost barefoot, and it showed very ill for our house to let him run abroad so ill-shod on our errands . . .'

She had run on as she always ran on, hardly paying heed to anyone else, but gradually she became aware of the way her son was standing stiff as ice, and his face blanched almost to the burningly cold blue-white of his eyes, that were fixed on her without love, without warmth, with the cold, ferocious burning of death. Her amiable, silly voice faltered away into small, broken sounds, and fell silent. If she had done nothing to help him, she had delivered herself in her blind, self-centred innocence.

'Perhaps, after all,' she faltered, her lips shaking, fumbling for words better calculated to please, and to wipe away that look from his face. 'Now I'm not sure – I may be mistaken . . .'

It was far too late to undo what she had done. Tears started into her eyes, blinding her to the aquamarine glare of hatred Miles had fixed upon her. Judith stirred out of her puzzled, shocked stillness and went quickly to her aunt's side, folding an arm about her trembling shoulders.

'My lord, is this of so great importance? What does it mean? I understand nothing of all this. Please be plain!' And indeed it had happened so suddenly that she had not followed what was said, nor grasped its significance, but as soon as she had spoken understanding came, sharp as a stab-wound. She paled and stiffened, looking from Miles, frozen in his bitter, useless silence, to Brother Cadfael standing apart, from Cadfael to Sister Magdalen, from Magdalen to Hugh. Her lips moved, saying silently: 'No! No! No . . .' but she did not utter it aloud.

They were in her house, and she had her own authority here. She confronted Hugh, unsmiling but calm. 'I think, my lord, there is no need for my aunt to distress herself, this is some matter that can be discussed and settled between us quietly. Aunt, you had much better go and help poor Alison in the kitchen. She has everything on her hands, and this is a most unhappy day for her, you should not leave her to carry all alone. I will tell you, later, all that you need to know,' she promised, and if the words had a chill of foreboding about them, Agatha did not hear it. She went from the room docilely in Judith's arm, half-reassured, half-daunted, and Judith returned and closed the door at her back.

'Now we may speak freely. I know now, all too well, what this is about. I know that two people may look back on events no more than a week past, and recall them differently. And I know, for Brother Cadfael told me, that the boots Bertred was wearing when he drowned made the print left behind by Brother Eluric's murderer in the soil under the vine, when he climbed back over the wall. So it matters indeed, it matters bitterly, Miles, who was wearing those boots that night, you or Bertred.'

Miles had begun to sweat profusely, his own body betraying him. On the wax-white, icy forehead great globules of moisture formed and stood, quivering. 'I've told you, I gave them to Bertred long ago . . .'

'Not long enough,' said Brother Cadfael, 'for him to stamp his own mark on them. They bear your tread, not his. You'll remember, very well, the mould I made in wax. You saw it when you came to fetch Mistress Perle home from the bronzesmith's. You guessed then what it was and what it meant. And that same night, your mother bears witness, you passed on those boots to Bertred. Who had nothing to do with the matter, and who was never likely to be called in question, neither he nor his possessions.'

'No!' cried Miles, shaking his head violently. The heavy drops flew from his forehead. 'It was not then! No! Long before! Not that night!'

'Your mother gives you the lie,' said Hugh quite gently. 'His mother will do no less. You would do well to make full confession, it would stand to your credit when you come to trial. For come to trial you will, Miles! For the murder of Brother Eluric . . .'

Miles broke then, crumpling into himself and clutching his head between spread hands, at once to hide it and hold it together. 'No!' he protested hoarsely between rigid fingers. 'Not murder . . . no . . . He came at me like a madman, I never meant him harm, only to get away . . .'

And it was done, so simply, at so little cost in the end. After that admission he had no defence; whatever else he had to tell would be poured out freely at last, in the hope of mitigation. He had trapped himself into a situation and a character he could not sustain. And all for ambition and greed!

'. . . perhaps also for the murder of Bertred,' went on Hugh mercilessly, but in the same disapassionate tone.

There was no outcry this time. He had caught his breath in chilling and sobering astonishment, for this he had never foreseen.

'. . . and thirdly, for the attempt to murder your cousin, in the forest close by Godric's Ford. Much play has been made, Miles Coliar, and reasonably enough, seeing what happened, with the many suitors who have plagued Mistress Perle, and the motive they had for desiring marriage, and marriage to her whole estate, not the half only. But when it came to murder, there was only one person who had anything to gain by that, and that was you, her nearest kin.'

Judith turned from her cousin lamely, and slowly sat down again beside Sister Magdalen, folding her arms about her body as if she felt the cold, but making no sound at all, neither of revulsion nor fear nor anger. Her face looked pinched and still, the flesh hollowed and taut under her white cheekbones, and the stare of her grey eyes turned within rather than without. And so she sat, silent and apart, while Miles stood helplessly dangling the hands he had lowered from a face now dulled and slack, and repeating over and over, with strenuous effort: 'Not murder! Not murder! He came at me like a madman – I never meant to kill. And Bertred drowned; he drowned! It was not my doing. Not murder . . .' But he said no word of Judith, and kept his face turned away from her to the last, in a kind of horror, until Hugh stirred and shook himself in wondering detestation, and made a motion of his hand towards the two sergeants at the door.

'Take him away!'

Chapter Fourteen

WHEN HE was gone, and the last receding footstep had sunk into silence, she stirred and breathed deeply, and said rather to herself than to any other: 'This I never thought to see!' And to the room in general, with reviving force: 'Is it true?'

'As to Bertred,' said Cadfael honestly, 'I cannot be sure, and we never shall be quite sure unless he tells us himself, as I believe he may. As to Eluric – yes, it is true. You heard your aunt – as soon as he realised what witness he had left behind against himself, he got rid of the boots that left it. Simply to be rid of them, not then, I think, with any notion of sloughing off his guilt upon Bertred. I think he had come to believe that you really would take the veil, and leave the shop and the trade in his hands, and therefore it seemed worth his while to try and break the abbey's hold on the Foregate house, and have all.'

'He never urged me to take vows,' she said wonderingly, 'rather opposed it. But he did somehow touch on it now and then – keeping it in mind.'

'But that night made him a murderer, a thing he never intended. That I am sure is truth. But it was done, and could not be undone, and then there was no turning back. What he would have done if he had heard in time of your resolve to go to the abbot and make your gift absolute, there's no knowing, but he did not hear of it until too late, and it was someone else who took action to prevent. There was no question but his desperation then was real enough, he was frantic to recover you, fearing you might give way and commit your person and estate to your abductor, and he be left out in the cold, with a new master, and no hope of the power and wealth he had killed to gain.'

'And Bertred?' she asked. 'How did Bertred come into it?'

'He joined my men in the hunt for you,' said Hugh, 'and by the look of things he had found you, or had a shrewd notion where you were hidden, and said never a word to me or any, but set out by night to free you himself, and have the credit for it. But he took a fall, and roused the dog – you'll have heard. The next of him was being fished out of the Severn on the other bank, next day. What happened between, and just how he came by his death, is still conjecture. But you'll recall you heard, or thought you heard, sounds as of someone else abroad in the night, after Bertred was gone. While you were making your plans to ride to Godric's Ford the next night.'

'And you think that must have been Miles?' She spoke her cousin's name with a strange, lingering regret. She had never dreamed that the man who was her right hand could strike at her with mortal intent.

'It makes sense of all,' said Cadfael sadly. 'Who else had such close opportunity to note some suspect complacency about Bertred, who else could so easily watch and follow him, when he slipped out in the night? And if your cousin then crept close, after Bertred was hunted away, and overheard what you intended, see how all things played into his hands! In the forest, well away from the town, once the other man parted from you, how simple a matter it was to leave you dead and plundered, and the blame would fall first on outlaws, and if ever that was brought in question, on the man who had held you prisoner and brought you there into remote forest, to make sure you should never betray him. I do not think,' said Cadfael with careful consideration, 'that the idea of murder had ever occurred to him until then, when chance so presented it that it must have seemed to him the perfect solution. Better than persuading you into a nunnery. For he would have been your heir. Everything would have fallen into his hands. And how if then, with this intent already filling his mind, he came upon Bertred, already half-stunned from one blow, and was visited by yet another fearful inspiration – for Bertred alive could possibly meddle with his plans, but Bertred dead could tell nothing, and Bertred dead would be found to be wearing the boots of Eluric's murderer. Thus he was provided with a scapegoat even for that.'

'But this *is* conjecture,' said Judith, wringing at disbelief. 'There is nothing, nothing to bear witness to it.'

'Yes,' said Cadfael heavily, 'I fear there is. For it so happened that when your cousin came down to the abbey with a cart, to bring home Bertred's body, he found that those who had stripped off the boy's sodden clothes had paid no heed to his boots, and neither did I pay any heed, or give a thought to them, when I brought out the bundle of clothing to the cart. Miles had to tilt the cart and spill the boots at my feet for me to pick up, before I looked at them, and knew what I was seeing. He did not intend that that infallible proof should be overlooked.'

'It was not so clever a move,' she said doubtfully, 'for Alison would have been able to tell you that her son had the boots from Miles.'

'True, if ever she was asked. But bear in mind, this was a dead murderer discovered – no trial to come, no mystery, no point in asking questions, and none in hounding a dead body, let alone a wretched, bereaved woman. Even if I had had no doubts,' said Hugh, 'and somehow a crumb of doubt there always was, I should not have kept his body from peaceable burial, or put her to any more grief than she already bore. Nevertheless, it was a risk, he might have had to brazen it out. But not even the shrewdest schemer can think of everything. And he,' said Hugh, 'was new to such roguery.'

'He must have gone in torment,' said Judith, marvelling, 'all night long since I escaped him, knowing I should return, not knowing how much I might be able to tell. And then I made it plain enough I had no notion who it was who had struck at me, and he felt himself safe . . . Strange!' she said, frowning over things now beyond help or remedy. 'When he went out, he did not seem to me evil, or malicious, or aware of guilt. Only bewildered! As though he found himself where he had never thought or meant to be, in some place he could not even recognise, and not knowing how he made his way there.'

'In some sort,' said Cadfael soberly, 'I think that is truth. He was like a man who has taken the first slippery step into a marsh, and then cannot draw back, and at every step forward sinks the deeper. From the assault on the rose-bush to the attempt on your life, he went where he was driven. No wonder if the place where he arrived was utterly alien to him, and the face that waited for him in a mirror there was one he did not even know, a terrible stranger.'

*

They were all gone, Hugh Beringar back to the castle, to confront and question his prisoner now, while the shock of self-knowledge endured and the cold cunning of self-interest had not yet closed in to reseal a mind and conscience for a while torn open to truth; Sister Magdalen and Brother Cadfael back to the abbey, she to dine with Radulfus, having assured herself affairs in this house were in no need of her presence for a few hours, he back to his duties within the enclave, now that all was done and said that had to be done and said, and silence and time would have to be left to take their course, where clamour and haste were of no help. They were all gone, even the body of poor Bertred, gone to a grave in Saint Chad's churchyard. The house was emptier than ever, half-depeopled by death and guilt, and the burden that fell back upon Judith's shoulders was the heavier by two childless widows for whom she must make provision. Must and would. She had promised that she would tell her aunt all that she needed to know, and she had kept her promise. The first wild lamentation was over, the quiet of exhaustion came after. Even the spinning-women had deserted the house for today. The looms were still. There were no voices.

Judith shut herself up alone in the solar, and sat down to contemplate the wreckage, but it seemed rather that what she regarded was an emptiness, ground cleared to make room for something new. There was no one now on whom she could lean, where the clothiers' trade was concerned, it was again in her own hands, and she must take charge of it. She would need another head weaver, one she could trust, and a clerk to keep the accounts, able to fill the place Miles had held. She had never shirked her responsibilities, but never made a martyrdom out of them, either. She would not do so now.

She had almost forgotten what day this was. There neither would nor could be any rose rent paid, that was certain. The bush was burned to the ground, it would never again bear the little, sweet-scented white roses that brought the years of her marriage back to mind. It did not matter now. She was free and safe and mistress of what she gave and what she retained; she could go to Abbot Radulfus and have a new charter drawn up and witnessed, giving the house and grounds free of all conditions. All the greed and calculation that had surrounded her was surely spent now, but she would put an end to it once for all. What did linger on after the roses was a faint bitter-sweetness of regret for the few short years of happiness, of which the one rose every year had been a reminder and a pledge. Now there would be none, never again.

In mid-afternoon Branwen put her head in timidly at the door to say that there was a visitor waiting in the hall. Indifferently Judith bade her admit him.

Niall came in hesitantly, with a rose in one hand, and a child by the other, and stood for a moment just within the doorway to get his bearings in a room he had never before entered. From the open window a broad band of bright sunlight crossed the room between them, leaving Judith in shadow on one side, and the visitors upon the other. Judith had risen, astonished at his coming, and stood with parted lips and wide eyes, suddenly lighter of heart, as though a fresh breeze from a garden had blown through a dark and gloomy place, filling it with the summer and sanctity of a saint's festival day. Here without being summoned, without warning, was the one creature about her who had never asked or expected anything, made no demands, sought no advantages, was utterly without greed or vanity, and to him she owed more than merely her life. He had brought her a rose, the last from the old stem, a small miracle.

'Niall . . .' she said on a slow, hesitant breath, and that was the first time she had ever called him by his name.

'I've brought you your rent,' he said simply, and took a few paces towards her and held out the rose, half-open, fresh and white without a stain.

'They told me,' she said, marvelling, 'there was nothing left, that all was burned. How is this possible?' And in her turn she went to meet him, almost warily, as though if she touched the rose it might crumble into ash.

Niall detached his hand very gently from the child's grasp, as she hung back shyly. 'I picked it yesterday, for myself, when we came home.'

The two extended hands reached out and met in the band of brightness, and the opened petals turned to the rosy sheen of mother-of-pearl. Their fingers touched and clasped on the stem, and it was smooth, stripped of thorns.

'You've taken no harm?' she said. 'Your wound will heal clean?'

'It's nothing but a scratch. I dread,' said Niall, 'that you have come by worse grief.'

'It's over now. I shall do well enough.' But she felt that to him she seemed beyond measure solitary and forsaken. They were looking steadily into each other's eyes, with an intensity that was hard to sustain and harder to break. The little girl took a shy step or two and again hesitated to venture nearer.

'Your daughter?' said Judith.

'Yes.' He turned to hold out his hand to her. 'There was no one with whom I could leave her.'

'I'm glad. Why should you leave her behind when you come to me? No one could be more welcome.'

The child came to her father in a sudden rush of confidence, seeing this strange but soft-voiced woman smile at her. Five years old and tall for her age, with a solemn oval face of creamy whiteness with the gloss of the sun on it, she stepped into the bar of brilliance, and lit up like a candle-flame, for the hair that clustered about her temples and hung on her shoulders was a true dark gold, and long gold lashes fringed her dark-blue eyes. She made a brief dip of the knee by way of reverence, without taking those eyes or their bright, consuming curiosity from Judith's face. And in a moment, having made up her mind, she smiled, and unmistakably held up her face for the acceptable kiss from an accepted elder.

She could as well have put her small hand into Judith's breast and wrung the heart that had starved so many years for just such fruit. Judith stooped to the embrace with tears starting to her eyes. The child's mouth was soft and cool and sweet. On the way through the town she had carried the rose, and the scent of it was still about her. She had nothing to say, not yet, she was too busy taking in and appraising the room and the woman. She would be voluble enough later, when both became less strange.

'It was Father Adam gave her her name,' said Niall, looking down at her with a grave smile. 'An unusual name – she's called Rosalba.'

'I envy you!' said Judith, as she had said once before.

A slight constraint had settled upon them again, it was difficult to find anything to say. So few words, and so niggardly, had been spent here throughout. He took his daughter's hand again, and drew back out of the bar of light towards the door, leaving Judith with the white rose still sunlit on her breast. The other white rose gave a skipping step back, willing to go, but looked back over her shoulder to smile by way of leave-taking.

'Well, chick, we'll be making for home. We've done our errand.'

And they would go, both of them, and there would be no

more roses to bring, no more rents to pay on the day of Saint Winifred's translation. And if they went away thus, there might never again be such a moment, never these three in one room together again.

He had reached the door when she said suddenly: 'Niall . . .'

He turned, abruptly glowing, to see her standing full in the sunlight, her face as white and open as the rose.

'Niall, don't go!' She had found words at last, the right words, and in time. She said to him what she had said in the dead of night, at the gate of Godric's Ford:

'Don't leave me now!'

The Hermit of Eyton Forest

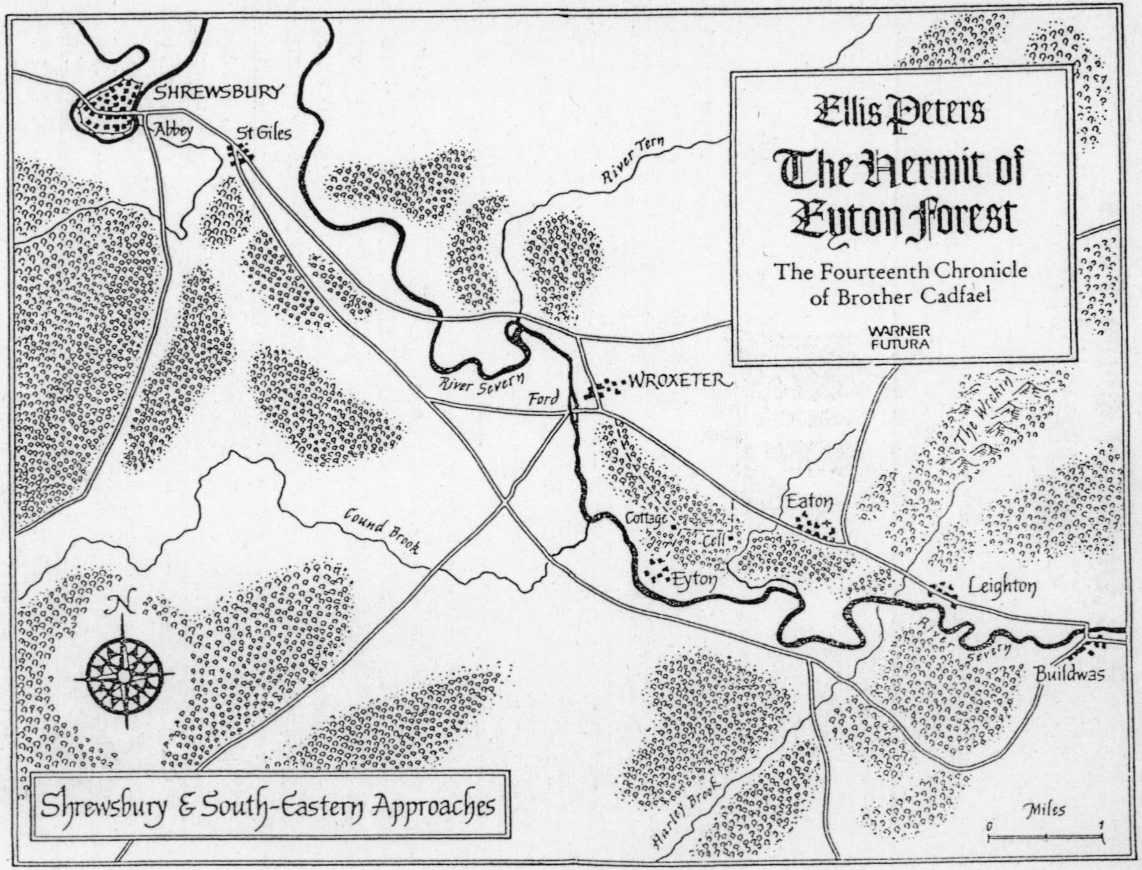
Ellis Peters
The Hermit of Eyton Forest
The Fourteenth Chronicle of Brother Cadfael
WARNER FUTURA
SHREWSBURY
Abbey
St Giles
River Tern
River Severn
Ford
WROXETER
Cound Brook
Cottage
Cell
Eyton
Eaton
The Wrekin
Leighton
River Severn
Buildwas
Harley Brook
N
Miles
0
1
Shrewsbury & South-Eastern Approaches

Chapter One

IT WAS on the eighteenth day of October of that year 1142 that Richard Ludel, hereditary tenant of the manor of Eaton, died of a debilitating weakness, left after wounds received at the battle of Lincoln, in the service of King Stephen.

The news was duly brought to Hugh Beringar in Shrewsbury castle, since Eaton was one of the many manors in the shire which had been expropriated from William FitzAlan, after that powerful nobleman took arms on the wrong side in the struggle for the throne, held Shrewsbury for the Empress Maud, and took to flight when Stephen besieged and captured the town. His wide lands, forfeited to the crown, had been placed in the sheriff's care as overlord, but their tenants of long standing had been left undisturbed, once it was clear that they had wisely accepted the judgement of battle, and pledged their allegiance to the king. Ludel, indeed, had done more than declare his loyalty, he had proved it in arms at Lincoln, and now, it seemed, paid a high price for his fealty, for he was no more than thirty-five years old at his death.

Hugh received the news with the mild regret natural to one who had barely known the man, and whose duties were unlikely to be complicated by any closer contact with the death. There was an heir, and no second son to cloud the issue of inheritance, certainly no need to interfere with the smooth succession. The Ludels were Stephen's men, and loyal, even if the new incumbent was hardly likely to take arms for his king for many years to come, being, Hugh recalled, about ten years old. The boy was in school at the abbey, placed there by his father when the mother died, most likely, so rumour said, to get him out of the hands of a domineering grandmother, rather than simply to ensure that he learned his letters.

It seemed, therefore, that the abbey, if not the castle, had some unenviable responsibility in the matter, for someone would have to tell young Richard that his father was dead. The funeral rites would not fall to the abbey, Eaton having its own church and parish priest, but the custody of the heir was a matter of importance. And as for me, thought Hugh, I had better make certain how competent a steward Ludel has left to manage the boy's estate, while he's not yet of age to manage it himself.

'You have not taken this word to the lord abbot yet?' he asked the groom who had brought the message.

'No, my lord, I came first to you.'

'And have you orders from the lady to speak with the heir himself?'

'No, my lord, and would as soon leave that to those who have the daily care of him.'

'You may well be right there,' Hugh agreed. 'I'll go myself and speak with Abbot Radulfus. He'll know best how to deal. As to the succession, Dame Dionisia need have no concern, the boy's title is secure enough.'

In times full of trouble, with cousins contending bitterly for the throne, and opportunist lords changing their coats according to the pendulum fortunes of this desultory war, Hugh was only too glad to be guardian of a shire which had changed hands but once, and settled down doggedly thereafter to keep King Stephen's title unchallenged and the tide of unrest at bay from its borders, whether the threat came from the empress's forces, the unpredictable cantrips of the wild Welshmen of Powys to the west, or the calculating ambition of the earl of Chester in the north. Hugh had balanced his relationships with all these perilous neighbours for some years now with fair success, it would have been folly to consider handing over Eaton to another tenant, whatever the possible drawbacks of allowing the succession to pass unbroken to a child. Why upset a family which had remained submissive and loyal, and dug in its heels sturdily to await events when its overlord fled to France? Recent rumour had it that William FitzAlan was back in England, and had joined the empress in

Oxford, and the sense of his presence, even at that distance, might stir older loyalties among his former tenants, but that was a risk to be met when it showed signs of arising. To give Eaton to another tenant might well be to rouse the old allegiance needlessly from its prudent slumber. No, Ludel's son should have his rights. But it would be well to have a look at the steward, and make sure he could be trusted, both to keep to his late lord's policies and to take good care of his new lord's interests and lands.

Hugh rode out unhurriedly through the town, in the fine mid-morning after the early mist had lifted, gently uphill to the High Cross, steeply downhill again by the winding Wyle to the eastward gate, and across the stone bridge towards the Foregate, where the crossing tower of the abbey church loomed solidly against a pale blue sky. The Severn ran rapid but tranquil under the arches of the bridge, still at its mild summer level, its two small, grassy islands rimmed with a narrow edging of bleached brown which would be covered again when the first heavy rain brought storm-water down from Wales. To the left, where the highroad opened before him, the clustering bushes and trees rising from the riverside just touched the dusty rim of the road, before the small houses and yards and gardens of the Foregate began. To the right the mill-pool stretched away between its grassy banks, a faint bloom of lingering mist blurring its silver surface, and beyond, the wall of the abbey enclave arose, and the arch of the gatehouse.

Hugh dismounted as the porter came out to take his bridle. He was as well known here as any who wore the Benedictine habit and belonged within the walls.

'If you're wanting Brother Cadfael, my lord,' offered the porter helpfully, 'he's away to Saint Giles to replenish their medicine cupboard. But he's been gone an hour or so now, he left after chapter. He'll be back soon, surely, if you're minded to wait for him.'

'My business is with the lord abbot first,' said Hugh, acknowledging without protest the assumption that his every visit here must inevitably be in search of one close crony. 'Through no doubt Cadfael will hear the same word afterwards, if he hasn't heard it in advance! The winds always seem to blow news his way before they trouble about the rest of us.'

'His duties take him forth, more than most of us ever get the chance,' said the porter good-humouredly. 'Come to that, how do the poor afflicted souls at Saint Giles ever come to hear so much of what goes on in the wide world? For he seldom comes back without some piece of gossip that's amazement to everybody this end of the Foregate. Father Abbot's down in his own garden. He's been closeted over accounts with the sacristan for an hour or more, but I saw Brother Benedict leave him a little while ago.' He reached a veined brown hand to caress the horse's neck, very respectfully, for Hugh's big, raw-boned grey, as cross-grained as he was strong, had little but contempt for all things human except his master, and even he was regarded rather as an equal, to be respected but kept in his place. 'There's no news from Oxford yet?'

Even within the cloister they could not choose but keep one ear cocked for news of the siege. Success there now might well see the empress a prisoner, and force an end at last to this dissension that tore the land apart.

'Not since the king got his armies through the ford and into the town. We may hear something soon, if some who had time to get out the city drift up this way. But the garrison will have made sure the castle larders were well filled. I doubt it will drag on for many weeks yet.'

Siege is slow strangulation, and King Stephen had never been noted for patience and tenacity, and might yet find it tedious to sit waiting for his enemies to reach starvation, and take himself off to find brisker action elsewhere. It had happened before, and could happen again.

Hugh shrugged off his liege lord's shortcomings, and set off down the great court to the abbot's lodging, to distract Father Radulfus from his cherished if slightly jaded roses.

Brother Cadfael was back from the hospital of Saint Giles and busy in his workshop, sorting beans for next year's seed, when Hugh came back from the abbot's lodging and made his way to the herbarium. Recognising the swift, light tread on the gravel, Cadfael greeted him without turning his head.

'Brother Porter told me you'd be here. Business with Father Abbot, he says. What's in the wind? Nothing new from Oxford?'

'No,' said Hugh, seating himself comfortably on the bench against the timber wall, 'nearer home. This is from no farther off than Eaton. Richard Ludel is dead. The dowager sent a groom with the news this morning. You've got the boy here at school.'

Cadfael turned then, with one of the clay saucers, full of seed dried on the vine, in his hand. 'So we have. Well, so his sire's gone, is he? We heard he was dwindling. The youngster was no more than five when he was sent here, and they fetch him home very seldom. I think his father thought the child was better here with a few fellows near his own age than kept around a sick man's bed.'

'And under the rule of a strong-willed grandmother, from all I hear. I don't know the lady,' said Hugh thoughtfully, 'except by reputation. I did know the man, though I've seen nothing of him since we got our wounded back from Lincoln. A good fighter and a decent soul, but dour, no talker. What's the boy like?'

'Sharp – venturesome . . . A very fetching imp, truth to tell, but as often in trouble as out of it. Bright at his letters, but he'd rather be out at play. Paul will have the task of telling him his father's dead, and himself master of a manor. It may trouble Paul more than it does the boy. He hardly knows his sire. I suppose there's no question about his tenure?'

'None in the world! I'm all for letting well alone, and Ludel earned his immunity. It's a good property, too, fat land, and much of it under the plough. Good grazing, water-meadows and woodland, and it's been well tended, seemingly, for it's valued higher now than ten years since. But I must get to know the steward, and make sure he'll do the boy right.'

'John of Longwood,' said Cadfael promptly. 'He's a good man and a good husbandman. We know him well, we've had dealings with him, and always found him reasonable and fair. That land falls between the abbey holdings of Eyton-by-Severn on the one side, and Aston-under-Wrekin on the other, and John has always given our forester free access between the two woodlands whenever needed, to save him time and labour. We bring wood out from our part of the Wrekin forest that way. It suits us both very well. Ludel's part of Eyton forest bites into ours there, it would be folly to fall out. Ludel had left everything to John these last two years, you'll have no trouble there.'

'The abbot tells me,' said Hugh, nodding satisfaction with this good-neighbourliness, 'that Ludel gave the boy as ward into his hands, four years ago, should he himself not live to see his son grown to manhood. It seems he made all possible provision for the future, as if he saw his own death coming towards him.' And he added, somewhat grimly: 'As well most of us have no such clear sight, or there'd be some hundreds in Oxford now hurrying to buy Masses for their souls. By this time the king must hold the town. It would fall into his hands of itself once he was over the ford. But the castle could hold out to the year's end, at a pinch, and there's no cheap way in there, it's a matter of starving them out. And if Robert of Gloucester in Normandy has not had word of all this by now, then his intelligencers are less able than I gave them credit for. If he knows how his sister's pressed, he'll be on his way home in haste. I've known the besiegers become the besieged before now, it could as well happen again.'

'It will take him some time to get back,' Cadfael pointed out comfortably. 'And by all accounts no better provided than when we went.'

The empress's half-brother and best soldier had been sent overseas, much against his inclination, to ask help for the lady from her less than loving husband, but Count Geoffrey of Anjou was credibly reported to be much more interested in his own ambitions in Normandy than in his wife's in England, and had been astute enough to inveigle Earl Robert into helping him pick off castle after castle in the duchy, instead of rushing to his wife's side to assist her to the crown of England. As early as June Robert had sailed from Wareham, against his own best judgement but at his sister's urgent entreaty, and Geoffrey's insistence, if he was to entertain any ambassador from her at all. And here was September ended, Wareham back in King Stephen's hands, and Robert still detained in Geoffrey's thankless service in Normandy. No, it would not be any quick or easy matter for him to come to his sister's rescue. The iron grip of siege tightened steadily round Oxford castle, and for once Stephen showed no sign of abandoning his purpose. Never yet had he come so close to making his cousin and rival his prisoner, and forcing her acceptance of his sovereignty.

'Does he realise,' wondered Cadfael, closing the lid of a stone jar on his selected seed, 'how near he's come to getting her into his power at last? How would you feel, Hugh, if you were in his shoes, and truly got your hands on her?'

'Heaven forefend!' said Hugh fervently, and grinned at the very thought. 'For I shouldn't know what to do with her! And the devil of it is, neither will Stephen, if ever it comes to that. He could have kept her tight shut into Arundel the day she landed, if he'd had the sense. And what did he do? Gave her an escort, and sent her off to Bristol to join her brother! But if the queen ever gets the lady into her power, that will be another story. If he's a grand fighter, she's the better general, and knows how to hold on to her advantages.'

Hugh rose and stretched, and a rising breeze from the open door ruffled his smooth black hair, and rustled the dangling bunches of dried herbs hanging from the roof beams. 'Well, there's no hurrying the siege to an end, we must wait and see. I hear they've finally given you a lad to help you in the herb garden, is it true? I noticed your hedge has had a second clipping, was that his work?'

'It was.' Cadfael went out with him along the gravel path between the patterned beds of herbs, grown a little wiry at this end of the growing season. The box hedge at one side had indeed been neatly trimmed of the straggling shoots that come late in the summer. 'Brother Winfrid – you'll see him busy in the patch where we've cleared the bean vines, digging in the holms. A big, gangling lad all elbows and knees. Not long out of his novitiate. Willing, but slow. But he'll do. They sent him to me, I fancy, because he turned out fumble-fisted with either pen or brush, but give him a spade, and that's more his measure. He'll do!'

Outside the walled herb garden the vegetable plots extended, and beyond the slight rise on their right the harvested pease fields ran down to the Meole Brook, which was the rear border of the abby enclave. And there was Brother Winfrid in full vigorous action, a big, loose-jointed youth with a shock-head of wiry hair hedging in his shaven crown, his habit kilted to brawny knees, and a broad foot shod in a wooden clog driving the steel-edged spade through blades of grass. He gave them one beaming glance as they passed, and returned to his work without breaking the rhythm. Hugh had one glimpse of a weather-browned country face and round, guileless blue eyes.

'Yes, I should think he might do very well,' he said, impressed and amused, 'whether with a spade or a battle-axe. I could do with a dozen such at the castle whenever they care to offer their services.'

'He'd be no use to you,' said Cadfael with certainty. 'Like most big men, the gentlest soul breathing. He'd throw his sword away to pick up the man he'd flattened. It's the little, shrill terriers that bare their teeth.'

They emerged into the band of flowerbeds beyond the kitchen garden, where the rose bushes had grown leggy and begun to shed their leaves. Rounding the corner of the box hedge, they came out into the great court, at this working hour of the morning almost deserted but for one or two travellers coming and going about the guest hall, and a stir of movement down in the stables. Just as they rounded the tall hedge to step into the court, a small figure shot out of the gate of the grange court, where the barns and storage lofts lined three sides of a compact yard, and made off at a run across the narrows of the court into the cloister, to emerge a minute later at the other end at a decorous walk, with eyes lowered in seemly fashion, and plump, childish hands devoutly linked at his belt, the image of innocence. Cadfael halted considerately, with a hand on Hugh's arm, to avoid confronting the boy too obviously.

The child reached the corner of the infirmary, rounded it, and vanished. There was a distinct impression that as he quit the sight of any watchers in the great court he broke into a run again, for a bare heel flashed suddenly and was gone. Hugh was grinning. Cadfael caught his friend's eye, and said nothing.

'Let me hazard!' said Hugh, twinkling. 'You picked your apples yesterday, and they're not yet laid up in the trays in the loft. Lucky it was not Prior Robert who saw him at it, and he with the breast of his cotte bulging like a portly dame!'

'Oh, there are some of us have a sort of silent understanding. He'll have taken the biggest, but only four. He thieves in moderation. Partly from decent obligation, partly because half the sport is to tempt providence again and again.'

Hugh's agile black eyebrow signalled amused enquiry. 'Why four?'

'Because we have but four boys still in school, and if he thieves at all, he thieves *for* all. There are several novices not very much older, but to them he has no obligation. They must do their own thieving, or go without. And do you know,' asked Cadfael complacently, 'who that young limb is?'

'I do not, but you are about to astonish me.'

'I doubt if I am. That is Master Richard Ludel, the new lord of Eaton. Though plainly,' said Cadfael, wryly contemplating shadowed innocence, 'he does not yet know it.'

Richard was sitting cross-legged on the grassy bank above the mill-pond, thoughtfully nibbling out the last shreds of white flesh round his apple core, when one of the novices came looking for him.

'Brother Paul wants you,' announced the messenger, with

the austerely complacent face of one aware of his own virtue, and delivering a probably ominous summons to another. 'He's in the parlour. You'd best hurry.'

'Me?' said Richard, round-eyed, looking up from his enjoyment of the stolen apple. No one had any great cause to be afraid of Brother Paul, the master of the novices and the children, who was the gentlest and most patient of men, but even a reproof from him was to be evaded if possible. 'What does he want me for?'

'You should best know that,' said the novice, with mildly malicious intent. 'It was not likely he'd tell me. Go and find out for yourself, if you truly have no notion.'

Richard committed his denuded core to the pond, and rose slowly from the grass. 'In the parlour, you say?' The use of so private and ceremonial a place argued something grave, and though he was unaware of any but the most venial of misdeeds that could be laid to his account during the past weeks, it behoved him to be wary. He went off slowly and thoughtfully, trailing his bare feet in the coolness of the grass, deliberately scuffing hard little soles along the cobbles of the court, and duly presented himself in the small, dim parlour, where visitors from the outside world might occasionally talk in private with their cloistered sons.

Brother Paul was standing with his back to the single window, rendering the small room even dimmer than it need have been. The straight, close-shorn ring of hair round his polished crown was still black and thick at fifty, and he habitually stood, as indeed he also sat, stooped a little forward, from so many years of dealing with creatures half his size, and desiring to reassure them rather than awe them with his stature and bearing. A kindly, scholarly, indulgent man, but a good teacher for all that, and one who could keep his chicks in order without having to keep them in terror. The oldest remaining *oblatus*, given to God when he was five years old, and now approaching fifteen and his novitiate, told awful stories of Brother Paul's predecessor, who had ruled with the rod, and been possessed of an eye that could freeze the blood.

Richard made his small obligatory obeisance, and stood squarely before his master, lifting to the light an impenetrable countenance, lit by two blue-green eyes of radiant innocence. A thin, active child, small for his years but agile and supple as a cat, with a thick, curly crest of light brown hair, and a band of golden freckles over both cheekbones and the bridge of his neat, straight nose. He stood with feet braced sturdily apart, toes gripping the floorboards, and stared up into Brother Paul's face, dutiful and guileless. Paul was well acquainted with that unblinking gaze.

'Richard,' he said gently, 'come, sit down with me. I have something I must tell you.'

That in itself was enough to discount one slight childish unease, only to replace it with another and graver, for the tone was so considerate and indulgent as to prophesy the need for comfort. But what Richard's sudden flickering frown expressed was simple bewilderment. He allowed himself to be drawn to the bench and seated there within the circle of Brother Paul's arm, bare toes just touching the floor, and braced there hard. He could be prepared for scolding, but here was surely something for which he was not prepared, and had no idea how to confront.

'You know that your father fought at Lincoln for the king, and was wounded? And that he has since been in poor health.' Secure in robust, well-fed and well-tended youth, Richard hardly knew what poor health might be, except that it was something that happened to the old. But he said: 'Yes, Brother Paul!' in a small, accommodating voice, since it was expected of him.

'Your grandmother sent a groom to the lord sheriff this morning. He has brought a sad message, Richard. Your father has made his last confession and received his Saviour. He is dead, my child. You are his heir, and you must be worthy of him. In life and in death,' said Brother Paul, 'he is in the hand of God. So are we all.'

The look of thoughtful bewilderment had not changed. Richard's toes shoved hard against the floor, and his hands gripped the edge of the bench on which he was perched.

'My father is dead?' he repeated carefully.

'Yes, Richard. Soon or late, it touches us all. Every son must one day step into his father's place and take up his father's duties.'

'Then I shall be the lord of Eaton now?'

Brother Paul did not make the mistake of taking this for a simple expression of self-congratulation on a personal gain, rather as an intelligent acceptance of what he himself had just said. The heir must take up the burden and the privilege his sire had laid down.

'Yes, you are the lord of Eaton, or you will be as soon as you are of fit age. You must study to get wisdom, and manage your lands and people well. Your father would expect that of you.'

Still struggling with the practicalities of his new situation, Richard probed back into his memory for a clear vision of this father who was now challenging him to be worthy. In his rare recent visits home at Christmas and Easter he had been admitted on arrival and departure to a sick-room that smelled of herbs and premature aging, and allowed to kiss a grey, austere face and listen to a deep voice, indifferent with weakness, calling him son and exhorting him to study and be virtuous. But there was little more, and even the face had grown dim in his memory. Of what he did remember he went in awe. They had never been close enough for anything more intimate.

'You loved your father, and did your best to please him, did you not, Richard?' Brother Paul prompted gently. 'You must still do what is pleasing to him. And you may say prayers for his soul, which will be a comfort also to you.'

'Shall I have to go home now?' asked Richard, whose mind was on the need for information rather than comfort.

'To your father's burial, certainly. But not to remain there, not yet. It was your father's wish that you should learn to read and write, and be properly instructed in figures. And you're young yet, your steward will take good care of your manor until you come to manhood.'

'My grandmother,' said Richard by way of explanation, 'sees no sense in my learning my letters. She was angry when my father sent me here. She says a lettered clerk is all any manor needs, and books are no fit employment for a nobleman.'

'Surely she will comply with your father's wishes. All the more is that a sacred trust, now that he is dead.'

Richard jutted a doubtful lip. 'But my grandmother has other plans for me. She wants to marry me to our neighbour's daughter, because Hiltrude has no brother, and will be the heiress to both Leighton and Wroxeter. Grandmother will want that more than ever now,' said Richard simply, and looked up ingenuously into Brother Paul's slightly startled face.

It took a few moments to assimilate this news, and relate it to the boy's entry into the abbey school when he was barely five years old. The manors of Leighton and Wroxeter lay one on either side of Eaton, and might well be a tempting prospect, but plainly Richard Ludel had not concurred in his mother's ambitious plans for her grandson, since he had taken steps to place the boy out of the lady's reach, and a year later had made Abbot Radulfus Richard's guardian, should he himself have to relinquish the charge too soon. Father Abbot had better know what's in the wind, thought Brother Paul. For of such a misuse of his ward, thus almost in infancy, he would certainly not approve.

Very warily he said, fronting the boy's unwavering stare with a grave face: 'Your father said nothing of what his plans for you might be, some day when you are fully grown. Such matters must wait their proper time, and that is not yet. You need not trouble your head about any such match for years yet. You are in Father Abbot's charge, and he will do what is best for you.' And he added cautiously, giving way to natural human curiosity: 'Do you know this child – this neighbour's daughter?'

'She isn't a child,' Richard stated scornfully. 'She's quite old. She was betrothed once, but her bridegroom died. My grandmother was pleased, because after waiting some years for him, Hiltrude wouldn't have many suitors, not being even pretty, so she would be left for me.'

Brother Paul's blood chilled at the implications. 'Quite old' probably meant no more than a few years past twenty, but even that was an acceptable difference. Such marriages, of course, were a commonplace, where there was property and land to be won, but they were certainly not to be encouraged. Abbot Radulfus had long had qualms of conscience about accepting infants committed by their fathers to the cloister, and had resolved to admit no more boys until they were of an age to make the choice for themselves. He would certainly look no more favourably on committing a child to the equally grave and binding discipline of matrimony.

'Well, you may put all such matters out of your mind,' he said very firmly. 'Your only concern now and for some years to come must be with your lessons and the pastimes proper to your years. Now you may go back to your fellows, if you wish, or stay here quietly for a while, as you prefer.'

Richard slid out of the supporting arm readily and stood up sturdily from the bench, willing to face the world and his curious fellow pupils at once, and seeing no reason why he would shun the meeting even for a moment. He had yet to comprehend the thing that had happened to him. The fact he could grasp, the implications were slow to reach beyond his intelligence into his heart.

'If there is anything more you wish to ask,' said Brother Paul, eyeing him anxiously, 'or if you feel the need for comfort or counsel, come back to me, and we'll go to Father Abbot. He is wiser than I, and abler to help you through this time.'

So he might be, but a boy in school was hardly likely to submit himself voluntarily to an interview with so awesome a personage. Richard's solemn face had settled into the brooding frown of one making his way through unfamiliar and thorny paths. He made his parting reverence and went out briskly enough, and Brother Paul, having watched him out of sight from the window, and seen no signs of imminent distress, went to report to the abbot what Dame Dionisia Ludel was said to be planning for her grandson.

Radulfus heard him out with alert attention and a thoughtful frown. To unite Eaton with both its neighbouring manors was an understandable ambition. The resulting property would be a power in the shire, and no doubt the formidable lady considered herself more than capable of ruling it, over the heads of bride, bride's father and infant bridegroom. Land greed was a strong driving force, and children were possessions expendable for so desirable a profit.

'But we trouble needlessly,' said Radulfus, shaking the matter resolutely from his shoulders. 'The boy is in my care, and here he stays. Whatever she may intend, she will not be able to touch him. We can forget the matter. She is no threat to Richard or to us.'

Wise as he might be, this was one occasion when Abbot Radulfus was to find his predictions going far astray.

Chapter Two

THEY WERE all at chapter, on the twentieth morning of October, when the steward of the manor of Eaton presented himself, requesting a hearing with a message from his mistress. John of Longwood was a burly, bearded man of fifty, with a balding crown and neat, deliberate movements. He made a respectful obeisance to the abbot, and delivered his errand bluntly and practically, as one performing a duty but without committing himself to approval or disapproval.

'My lord, Dame Dionisia Ludel sends me to you with her devout greetings, and asks that you will send back to her, in my charge, her grandson Richard, to take up his rightful place as lord of the manor of Eaton in his father's room.'

Abbot Radulfus leaned back in his stall and regarded the messenger with an impassive face. 'Certainly Richard shall attend his father's funeral. When is that to be?'

'Tomorrow, my lord, before High Mass. But that is not my mistress's meaning. She wants the young lord to leave his studies here and come to take his proper place as lord of Eaton. I'm to say that Dame Dionisia feels herself to be the proper person to have charge of him, now that he's come into his inheritance, as she's assured he shall do, without delay or hindrance. I have orders to bring him back with me.'

'I fear, master steward,' said the abbot with deliberation, 'that you may not be able to carry out your orders. Richard Ludel committed the care of his son to me, should he himself die before the boy came to manhood. It was his wish that his son should be properly educated, the better to manage his estate when he came to inherit. I intend to fulfil what I undertook. Richard remains in my care until he comes of age and takes control of his own affairs. Until which time, I am sure, you will serve him as well as you have served his father, and keep his lands in good heart.'

'Very surely I will, my lord,' said John of Longwood, with more warmth than he had shown in delivering his mistress's message. 'My lord Richard has left all to me since Lincoln, and he never had cause to find fault, and neither shall his son ever be the loser by me. On that you may rely.'

'So I do. And therefore we may continue here with easy minds, and take as good care of Richard's schooling and wellbeing as you do of his estates.'

'And what reply am I to take back to Dame Dionisia?' asked John, without any apparent disappointment or reluctance.

'Say to your lady that I greet her reverently in Christ, and that Richard shall come tomorrow, as is due, properly escorted,' said the abbot with a slightly admonitory emphasis, 'but that I have his father's sacred charge to hold him in wardship myself until he is a man, and by his father's wishes I shall abide.'

'I will say so, my lord,' said John with a straight, wide stare and a deep reverence, and walked jauntily out of the chapterhouse.

Brother Cadfael and Brother Edmund the infirmarer emerged into the great court just in time to see the messenger from Eaton mount his stocky Welsh cob at the gatehouse and ride unhurriedly out into the Foregate.

'There goes a man, unless I'm much mistaken,' remarked Brother Cadfael sagely, 'no way seriously displeased at taking back a flat refusal. Nor at all afraid of delivering it. A man might almost think he'll savour the moment.'

'He is not dependent on the dame's good will,' said Brother Edmund. 'Only the sheriff as overlord can threaten his tenure, until the boy is his own master, and John knows his worth. And so does she, for that matter, having a shrewd head and proper appreciation of good management. For the sake of peace he'll do her bidding, he does not have to relish the task, only to keep his mouth shut.'

And John of Longwood was a man of few words at the best of times, it would probably be no hardship to him to contain his dissent and keep a wooden face.

'But this will not be the end of it,' Cadfael warned. 'If she has a greedy eye on Wroxeter and Leighton she'll not give up so easily, and the boy's her only means of getting her hands on them. We shall yet hear more from Dame Dionisia Ludel.'

Abbot Radulfus had taken the warning seriously. Young Richard was accompanied to Eaton by Brother Paul, Brother Anselm and Brother Cadfael, a bodyguard stout enough to fend off even an attempt at abduction by force, which was unlikely in the extreme. Far more probable that the lady would try using the fond persuasions of affection and the ties of blood to work upon the boy with tears and blandishments, and turn him into a homesick ally in the enemy camp. If she had any such ideas, Cadfael reflected, studying Richard's face along the way, she was underestimating the innocent shrewdness of children. The boy was quite capable of weighing up his own interests and making the most of what advantages he had. He was happy enough at school, he had companions of his own age, he would not lightly abandon a known and pleasant life for one as yet strange, devoid of brothers, and threatened with a bride already old in his eyes. No doubt he valued and longed for his inheritance, but his it was, and safe, and whether he stayed at school or came home, he would not yet be allowed to rule it as he wished. No, it would take more than grandmotherly tears and embraces to secure Richard's alliance, especially tears and embraces from a source never before known to be demonstratively fond.

It was a matter of seven miles or more from the abbey to the manor of Eaton, and for the honour and dignity of the monastery of Saint Peter and Saint Paul, in attendance on so solemn an occasion, they were sent forth mounted. Dame Dionisia had sent a groom with a stout Welsh pony for her grandson, perhaps as a first move in a campaign to enlist him as her ally, and the gift had been received with greedy pleasure, but it would not therefore necessarily produce a return in kind. A gift is a gift, and children are shrewd enough, and have a sharp enough perception of the motives of their elders, to take what is offered unsolicited, without the least intention of paying for it in the fashion expected of them. Richard sat his new pony proudly and happily, and in the fine, dewy autumn morning and the pleasure of being loosed from school for the day, almost forgot the sombre reason for the ride. The groom, a long-legged boy of sixteen, loped cheerfully beside him, and led the pony as they splashed through the ford at Wroxeter, where centuries back the Romans had crossed the Severn before them. Nothing remained of their sojourn now but a gaunt, broken wall standing russet against the green fields, and a scattering of stones long ago plundered by the villagers for their own building purposes. In the place of what some said had been a city and a fortress there was now a flourishing manor blessed with fat, productive land, and a prosperous church that maintained four canons.

Cadfael viewed it with some interest as they passed, for this was one of the two manors which Dame Dionisia hoped to secure to the Ludel estate by marrying off Richard to the girl Hiltrude Astley. So fine a property was certainly tempting. All this stretch of country on the northern side of the river extended before them in rich water meadows and undulating fields, rising here and there into a gentle hill, and starred with clusters of trees just melting into the first gold of their autumn foliage. The land rose on the skyline into the forested ridge of the Wrekin, a great heaving fleece of woodland that spread downhill to the Severn, and cast a great tress of its dark mane across Ludel land and into the abbey's woods of Eyton-by-Severn. There was barely a mile between the grange of Eyton, close beside the river, and Richard Ludel's manor house at Eaton. The very names sprang from the same root, though time had prised them apart, and the Norman passion for order and formulation had fixed and ratified the differences.

As they rode nearer, their view of the long hog-back of forest changed and foreshortened. By the time they reached the manor they were viewing it from its end, and the hill had grown into an abrupt mountain, with a few sheer faces of rock just breaking the dark fell of the trees near the summit. The village sat serenely in the meadows, just short of the foothills, the manor within its long stockade raised over an undercroft, and the small church close beside it. Originally it had been a dependent chapel of the church at its neighbour Leighton, downriver by a couple of miles.

They dismounted within the stockade, and Brother Paul took Richard firmly by the hand as soon as the boy's foot touched ground, as Dame Dionisia came sweeping down the steps from the hall to meet them, advanced with authority upon her grandson, and stooped to kiss him. Richard lifted his face somewhat warily, and submitted to the salute, but he kept fast hold of Paul's hand. With one power bidding for his custody he knew where he stood, with the other he could not be sure of his standing.

Cadfael eyed the lady with interest, for though her reputation was known to him, he had never before been in her presence. Dionisia was tall and erect, certainly no more than fifty-five years old, and in vigorous health. She was, moreover, a handsome woman, if in a somewhat daunting fashion, with sharp, clear features and cool grey eyes. But their coolness showed one warning flash of fire as they swept over Richard's escort, recording the strength of the enemy. The household had come out at her back, the parish priest was at her side. There would be no engagement here. Later, perhaps, when Richard Ludel was safely entombed, and she could open the house in funeral hospitality, she might make a first move. The heir could hardly be kept from his grandmother's society on this day of all days.

The solemn rites for Richard Ludel took their appointed course. Brother Cadfael made good use of the time to survey the dead man's household, from John of Longwood to the youngest villein herdsman. There was every indication that the place had thrived well under John's stewardship, and his men were well content with their lot. Hugh would have good reason to let well alone. There were neighbours present, too, Fulke Astley among them, keeping a weather eye on what he himself might have to gain if the proposed match ever took place. Cadfael had seen him once or twice in Shrewsbury, a gross, self-important man in his late forties, running to fat, ponderous of movement, and surely no match for that restless, active, high-tempered woman standing grim-faced over her son's bier. She had Richard beside her, a hand possessively rather than protectively on his shoulder. The boy's eyes had dilated to engulf half his face, solemn as the grave that had been opened for his father, and was now about to be sealed. Distant death is one thing, its actual presence quite another. Not until this minute had Richard fully realised the finality of this deprivation and severance.

The grandmotherly hand did not leave his shoulder as the cortège of mourners wound its way back to the manor, and the funeral meats spread for them in the hall. The long, lean, aging fingers had a firm grip on the cloth of the boy's best coat, and she guided him with her among guests and neighbours, properly but with notable emphasis making him the man of the house, and presiding figure at his father's obsequies. That did no harm at all. Richard was fully aware of his position, and well able to resent any infringement of his privilege. Brother Paul watched with some anxiety, and whispered to Cadfael that they had best get the boy away before all the guests departed, or they might fail to get him away at all, for want of witnesses. While the priest was still present, and those few others not of the household, he could hardly be retained by force.

Cadfael had been observing those of the company not well known to him. There were two grey-habited monks from the Savigniac house of Buildwas, a few miles away down-river, to which Ludel had been a generous patron on occasion, and with them, though withdrawn modestly throughout into the background, was a personage less easily identifiable. He wore a monastic gown, rusty black and well worn at the hems, but a head of unshorn dark hair showed within his cowl, and a gleam of reflected light picked out two or three metallic gleams from his shoulder that looked like the medals of more than one pilgrimage. Perhaps a wandering religious about to settle for the cloister. Savigny had been at Buildwas now for some forty years, a foundation of Roger de Clinton, bishop of Lichfield. Good, detached observers surely, these three. Before such reverend guests no violence could be attempted.

Brother Paul approached Dionisia courteously to take a discreet leave and reclaim his charge, but the lady took the wind from his sails with a brief, steely flash of her eyes and a voice deceptively sweet: 'Brother, let me plead with you to let me keep Richard overnight. He has had a tiring day and begins to be weary now. He should not leave until tomorrow.' But she did not say that she would send him back on the morrow, and her hand retained its grip on his shoulders. She had spoken loudly enough to be heard by all, a solicitous matron anxious for her young.

'Madam,' said Brother Paul, making the best of a disadvantaged position, 'I was about to tell you, sadly, that we must be going. I have no authority to let Richard stay here with you, we are expected back for Vespers. I pray you pardon us.'

The lady's smile was honey, but her eyes were sharp and cold as knives. She made one more assay, perhaps to establish her own case with those who overheard, rather than with any hope of achieving anything immediately, for she knew the occasion rendered her helpless.

'Surely Abbot Radulfus would understand my desire to have

the child to myself one day. My own flesh and blood, the only one left to me, and I have seen so little of him these last years. You leave me uncomforted if you take him from me so soon.'

'Madam,' said Brother Paul, firm but uneasy, 'I grieve to withstand your wish, but I have no choice. I am bound in obedience to my abbot to bring Richard back with me before evening. Come, Richard, we must be going.'

There was an instant while she kept and tightened her hold, tempted to act even thus publicly, but she thought better of it. This was no time to put herself in the wrong, rather to recruit sympathy. She opened her hand, and Richard crept doubtfully away from her to Paul's side.

'Tell the lord abbot,' said Dionisia, her eyes daggers, but her voice still mellow and sweet, 'that I shall seek a meeting with him very soon.'

'Madam, I will tell him so,' said Brother Paul.

She was as good as her word. She rode into the abbey enclave the next day, well attended, bravely mounted, and in her impressive best, to ask audience of the abbot. She was closeted with him for almost an hour, but came forth in a cold blaze of resentment and rage, stormed across the great court like a sudden gale, scattering unoffending novices like blown leaves, and rode away again for home at a pace her staid jennet did not relish, with her grooms trailing mute and awed well in the rear.

'There goes a lady who is used to getting her own way,' remarked Brother Anselm, 'but for once, I fancy, she's met her match.'

'We have not heard the last of it, however,' said Brother Cadfael drily, watching the dust settle after her going.

'I don't doubt her will,' agreed Anselm, 'but what can she do?'

'That,' said Cadfael, not without quickening interest, 'no doubt we shall see, all in good time.'

They had but two days to wait. Dame Dionisia's man of law announced himself ceremoniously at chapter, requesting a hearing. An elderly clerk, meagre of person but brisk of bearing and irascible of feature, bustled into the chapterhouse with a bundle of parchments under his arm, and addressed the assembly with chill, reproachful dignity, in sorrow rather than in anger. He marvelled that a cleric and scholar of the abbot's known uprightness and benevolence should deny the ties of blood, and refuse to return Richard Ludel to the custody and loving care of his only surviving close kinswoman, now left quite bereft of all her other menfolk, and anxious to help, guide and advise her grandson in his new lordship. A great wrong was being done to both grandmother and child, in the denial of their natural need and the frustration of their mutual affection. And yet once more the clerk put forth the solemn request that the wrong should be set right, and Richard Ludel sent back with him to his manor of Eaton.

Abbot Radulfus sat with a patient and unmoved face and listened to the end of this studied speech very courteously. 'I thank you for your errand,' he said then mildly, 'it was well done. I cannot well change the answer I gave to your lady. Richard Ludel who is dead committed the care of his son to me, by letter properly drawn and witnessed. I accepted that charge, and I cannot renounce it now. It was the father's wish that the son should be educated here until he comes to manhood, and takes command of his own life and affairs. That I promised, and that I shall fulfil. The death of the father only makes my obligation the more sacred and binding. Tell your mistress so.'

'My lord,' said the clerk, plainly having expected no other answer, and ready with the next step in his embassage, 'in changed circumstances such a private legal document need not be the only argument valid in a court of law. The king's justices would listen no less to the plea of a matron of rank, widowed and now bereaved of her son, and fully able to provide all her grandson's needs, besides the natural need she has of the comfort of his presence. My mistress desires to inform you that if you do not give up the boy, she intends to bring suit at law to regain him.'

'Then I can but approve her attention,' said the abbot serenely. 'A judicial decision in the king's court must be satisfying to us both, since it lifts the burden of choice from us. Tell her so, and say that I await the hearing with due submission. But until such a judgement is made, I must hold to my own sworn undertaking. I am glad,' he said with a dry and private smile, 'that we are thus agreed.'

There was nothing left for the clerk to do but accept this unexpectedly pliant response at its face value, and bow himself out as gracefully as he could. A slight rustle and stir of curiosity and wonder had rippled round the chapterhouse stalls, but Abbot Radulfus suppressed it with a look, and it was not until the brothers emerged into the great court and dispersed to their work that comment and speculation could break out openly.

'Was he wise to encourage her?' marvelled Brother Edmund, crossing towards the infirmary with Cadfael at his side. 'How if she does indeed take us to law? A judge might very well take the part of a lone lady who wants her grandchild home.'

'Be easy,' said Cadfael placidly. 'It's but an empty threat. She knows as well as any that the law is slow and costs dear, at the best of times, and this is none of the best, with the king far away and busy with more urgent matters, and half his kingdom cut off from any manner of justice at all. No, she hoped to make the lord abbot think again and yield ground for fear of long vexation. She had the wrong man. He knows she has no intention of going to law. Far more likely to take law into her own hands and try to steal the boy away. It would take slow law or swift action to snatch him back again, once she had him, and force is further out of the abbot's reach than it is out of hers.'

'It is to be hoped,' said Brother Edmund, aghast at the suggestion, 'that she was not yet used up all her persuasions, if the last resort is to be violence.'

No one could quite determine exactly how young Richard came to know every twist and turn of the contention over his future. He could not have overheard anything of what went on at chapter, nor were the novices present at the daily gatherings, and there was none among the brothers likely to gossip about the matter to the child at the centre of the conflict. Yet it was clear that Richard did know all that went on, and took perverse pleasure in it. Mischief made life more interesting, and here within the enclave he felt quite safe from any real danger, while he could enjoy being fought over.

'He watches the comings and goings from Eaton,' said Brother Paul, confiding his mild anxiety to Cadfael in the peace of the herb garden, 'and is sharp enough to be very well aware what they mean. And he understood all too well what went on at his father's funeral. I could wish him less acute, for his own sake.'

'As well he should have his wits about him,' said Cadfael comfortably. 'It's the knowing innocents that avoid the snares. And the lady's made no move now for ten days. Maybe she's grown resigned, and given up the struggle.' But he was by no means convinced of that. Dame Dionisia was not used to being thwarted.

'It may be so,' agreed Paul hopefully, 'for I hear she's taken in some reverend pilgrim, and refurbished the old hermitage in her woodland for his use. She wants his prayers daily for her son's soul. Eilmund was telling us about it when he brought our allowance of venison. We saw the man, Cadfael, at the funeral. He was there with the two brothers from Buildwas. He'd been lodged with them a week, they give him a very saintly report.'

Cadfael straightened up with a grunt from his bed of mint, grown wiry and thin of leaf now in late October. 'The fellow who wore the scallop shell? And the medal of Saint James? Yes, I remember noticing him. So he's settling among us, is he? And chooses a cell and a little square of garden in the woods rather than a grey habit at Buildwas! I never was drawn to the solitary life myself, but I've known those who can think and pray the better that way. It's a long time since that cell was lived in.'

He knew the place, though he seldom passed that way, the abbey's forester having excellent health, and very little need of herbal remedies. The hermitage, disused now for many years, lay in a thickly wooded dell, a stone-built hut with a square of ground once fenced and cultivated, now overgrown and wild. Here the belt of forest embraced both Eaton ground and the abbey's woodland of Eyton, and the hermitage occupied a spot where the Ludel border jutted into neighbour territory, close to the forester's cherished coppice. 'He'll be quiet enough there,' said Cadfael, 'if he means to stay. By what name are we to know him?'

'They call him Cuthred. A neighbour saint is a fine thing to have, and it seems they're already beginning to bring their troubles to him to sort. It may be,' ventured Brother Paul optimistically, 'that it's he who has tamed the lady. He must have a strong influence over her, or she'd never have entreated him to stay. And there's been no move from her these ten days. It may be we're all in his debt.'

And indeed, as the soft October days slid away tranquilly one after another, in dim, misty dawns, noondays bright but veiled, and moist green twilights magically still, it seemed that there was to be no further combat over young Richard, that Dame Dionisia had thought better of the threat of law, and resigned herself to submission. She even sent, by her parish priest, a gift of money to pay for Masses in the Lady Chapel for her son's soul, a gesture which could only be interpreted as a move towards reconciliation. So, at least, Brother Francis, the new custodian of Saint Mary's altar, considered it.

'Father Andrew tells me,' he reported after the visitor had departed, 'that since the Savigniac brothers from Buildwas brought this Cuthred into her house she sets great store by his counsel, and rules herself by his advice and example. The man has won a great report for holiness already. They say he's taken strict vows in the old way, and never leaves his cell and garden now. But he never refuses help or prayers to any who ask. Father Andrew thinks very highly of him. The anchorite way is not our way,' said Brother Francis with great earnestness, 'but it's no bad thing to have such a holy man living so close, on a neighbouring manor. It cannot but bring a blessing.'

So thought all the countryside, for the possession of so devout a hermit brought great lustre to the manor of Eaton, and the one criticism that ever came to Cadfael's ears concerning Cuthred was that he was too modest, and at first deprecated, and later forbade, the too lavish sounding of his praises abroad. No matter what minor prodigy he brought about, averting by his prayers a threatened cattle murrain, after one of Dionisia's herd sickened, sending out his boy to give warning of a coming storm, which by favour of his intercessions passed off without damage, whatever the act of grace, he would not allow any of the merit for it to be ascribed to him, and grew stern and awesomely angry if the attempt was made, threatening the wrath of God on any who disobeyed his ban. Within a month of his coming his discipline counted for more in the manor of Eaton than did either Dionisia's or Father Andrew's, and his fame, banned from being spread openly, went about by neighbourly whispers, like a prized secret to be exulted in privately but hidden from the world.

Chapter Three

EILMUND, THE forester of Eyton, came now and then to chapter at the abbey to report on work done, or on any difficulties he might have encountered, and extra help he might need. It was not often he had anything but placid progress to report, but in the second week of November he came one morning with a puzzled frown fixed on his brow, and a glum face. It seemed that a curious blight of misfortune had settled upon his woodland.

Eilmund was a thickset, dark, shaggy man past forty, very powerful of body, and sharp enough of mind. He stood squarely in the midst at chapter, solidly braced on his sturdy legs like a wrestler confronting his opponent, and made few words of what he had to tell.

'My lord abbot, there are things happening in my charge that I cannot fathom. A week ago, in that great rainstorm we had, the brook that runs between our copice and the open forest washed down some loose bushes, and built up such a dam that it overflowed and changed its course, and flooded my newest planting. And no sooner had I cleared the block than I found the floodwater had undercut part of the bank of my ditch, a small way upstream, and the fall of soil had bridged the ditch. By the time I found it the deer had got into the coppice. They've eaten off all the young growth from the plot we cropped two years ago. I doubt some of my trees may die, and all will be held back a couple more years at least before they get their growth. It spoils my planning,' complained Eilmund, outraged for the ruin of his cycle of culling, 'besides the present loss.'

Cadfael knew the place, Eilmund's pride, the farmed part of Eyton forest, as neat and well-ditched a coppice as any in the shire, where the regular cutting of six- or seven-year-old wood let in the light at every cropping, so that the wealth of ground cover and wild flowers was always rich and varied. Some trees, like ash, spring anew from the stool of the original trunk, just below the cut. Some, like elm or aspen, from below the ground all round the stump. Some of the stools in Eilmund's care, several times cropped afresh, had grown into groves of their own, their open centres two good paces across. No grave natural disaster had ever before upset his pride in his skills. No wonder he was so deeply aggrieved. And the loss to the abbey was itself serious, for coppice wood for fuel, charcoal, hafts of tools, carpentry and all manner of uses brought in good income.

'Nor is that the end of it,' went on Eilmund grimly, 'for yesterday when I made my rounds on the other side of the copse, where the ditch is dry but deep enough and the bank steep, what should have happened but the sheep from Eaton had broke out of their field by a loose pale, just where Eaton ground touches ours, and sheep, as you know, my lord, make nothing of a bank that will keep out deer, and there's nothing they like better for grazing than the first tender seedlings of ash. They've made short work of much of the new growth before I could get them out. And neither I nor John of Longwood can tell how they got through so narrow a gap, but you know if the matron ewe takes a notion into her head there's no stopping her, and the others will follow. It seems to me my forest is bewitched.'

'Far more like,' suggested Prior Robert, looking severely down his long nose, 'that there has been plain human negligence, either on your part or your neighbour's.'

'Father Prior,' said Eilmund, with the bluntness of one who knows his value, and knows that it is equally well known to the only superior he needs to satisfy here, 'in all my years in the abbey's service there has never yet been complaint of my work. I have made my rounds daily, yes, and often nightly, too, but I cannot command the rain not to fall, nor can I be everwhere at once. Such a spate of misfortunes in so short a time I've never before known. Nor can I blame John of Longwood, who has always been as good a neighbour as any man needs.'

'That is the truth,' said Abbot Radulfus with authority. 'We have had cause to be thankful for his good will, and do not doubt it now. Nor do I question your skill and devotion. There has never been before, and I see none now. Reverses are sent to us so that we may overcome them, and no man can presume to escape such testings for ever. The loss can be borne. Do what you can, Master Eilmund, and if you should feel in need of another helper, you shall have one.'

Eilmund, who had always been equal to his tasks and was proud of his self-sufficiency, said thanks for that somewhat grudgingly, but declined the offer for the time being, and promised to send word if anything further should happen to change his mind. And off he went as briskly as he had come, back to his cottage in the forest, his daughter, and his grievance against fate, since he could not honestly find a human agency to blame.

By some mysterious means young Richard got to know of the unusual purport of Eilmund's visit, and anything to do with his grandmother, and all those people who had their labour and living about the manor of Eaton, was of absorbing interest to him. However wise and watchful his guardian the abbot might be, however competent his steward, it behoved him to keep an eye on his estate for himself. If there was mischief afoot near Eaton, he itched to know the reason, and he was far more likely than was the Abbot Radulfus to attribute mischief, however incomprehensibly procured, to the perversity or malice of humanity, having so often found himself arraigned as the half-innocent agent of misrule.

If the sheep of Eaton had made their way into the ash coppice of Eyton not by some obscure act of God, but because someone had opened the way for them and started them towards their welcome feast, then Richard wanted to know who, and why. They were, after all, his sheep.

Accordingly, he kept a sharp eye open for any new comings and goings about the hour of chapter each morning, and was curious when he observed, two days after Eilmund's visit, the arrival at the gatehouse of a young man he had seen but once before, who asked very civilly for permission to appear at chapter with an embassage from his master, Cuthred. He was early, and had to wait, which he did serenely. That suited Richard very well, for he could not play truant from school, but by the time the chapter ended he would be at liberty, and could ambush the visitor and satisfy his curiosity.

Every hermit worth his salt, having taken vows of stability which enjoin him to remain thenceforth within his own cell and closed garden, and having gifts of foresight and a sacred duty to use them for his neighbours' good, must have a resident boy to run his errands and deliver his admonitions and reproofs. Cuthred's boy, it seemed, had arrived already in his service, accompanying him in his recent wanderings in search of the place of retirement appointed for him by God. He came into the chapterhouse of the abbey with demure assurance, and stood to be examined by all the curious brothers, not at all discomposed by such an assault of bright, inquisitive eyes.

From the retired stall which he preferred, Cadfael studied the messenger with interest. A more unlikely servitor to an anchorite and popular saint, in the old Celtic sense that took no account of canonisation, he could not well have imagined, though he could not have said on the instant where the incongruity lay. A young fellow of about twenty years, in a rough tunic and hose of brown cloth, patched and faded – nothing exceptional there. He was built on the same light, wiry lines as Hugh Beringar, but stood a hand's breadth taller, and he was lean and brown and graceful as a fawn, managing his long limbs with the same angular, animal beauty. Even his composed stillness held implications of sudden, fierce movement, like a wild creature motionless in ambush. His running would be swift and silent, his leaping long and lofty as that of a hare. And his face had a similar slightly ominous composure and awareness, under a thick, close-fitted cap of waving hair the colour of copper beeches. A long oval of a face, tall-browed, with a long, straight nose flared at the nostrils, again like a wild thing sensitive to every scent the breeze brought him, a supple, crooked mouth that almost smiled even in repose, as if in secret and slightly disturbing amusement, and long amber eyes that tilted upwards at the outer corners, under oblique copper brows. The burning glow of those eyes he shaded, but did not dim or conceal, beneath round-arched lids and copper lashes long and rich as a woman's.

What was an antique saint doing with an unnerving fairy thing in his employ?

But the boy, having waited a long moment to be inspected thoroughly, lifted his eyelids and showed to Abott Radulfus a face of candid and childlike innocence, and made him a very charming and respectful reverence.

He would not speak until he was spoken to, but waited to be questioned.

'You come from the hermit of Eyton?' asked the abbot mildly, studying the young, calm, almost smiling face attentively.

'Yes, my lord. The holy Cuthred sends a message by me.' His voice was quiet and clear, pitched a little high, so that it rang bell-like under the vault.

'What is your name?' Radulfus questioned.

'Hyacinth, my lord.'

'I have known a bishop of that name,' said the abbot, and briefly smiled, for the sleek brown creature before him had certainly nothing of the bishop about him. 'Were you named for him?'

'No, my lord. I have never heard of him. I was told, once, that there was a youth of that name in an old story, and two gods fell out over him, and the loser killed him. They say flowers grew from his blood. It was a priest who told me,' said the boy innocently, and slanted a sudden brief smile round the chapterhouse, well aware of the slight stir of disquiet he had aroused in these cloistered breasts, though the abbot continued unruffled.

Into that old story, thought Cadfael, studying him with pleasure and interest, you, my lad, fit far better than into the ambit of bishops, and well you know it. Or hermits either, for that matter. Now where in the world did he discover you, and how did he tame you?

'May I speak my message?' asked the boy ingenuously, golden eyes wide and clear and fixed upon the abbot.

'You have learned it by heart?' enquired Radulfus, smiling.

'I must, my lord. There must be no word out of place.'

'A very faithful messenger! Yes, you may speak.'

'I must be my master's voice, not my own,' said the boy by way of introduction, and forthwith sank his voice several tones below its normal ringing lightness, in a startling piece of mimicry that made Cadfael, at least, look at him more warily and searchingly than ever. 'I have heard with much distress,' said the proxy hermit gravely, 'both from the steward of Eaton and the forester of Eyton, of the misfortunes suddenly troubling the woodland. I have prayed and meditated, and greatly dread that these are but the warnings of worse to come, unless some false balance or jarring discord between right and wrong can be amended . I know of no such offence hanging over us, unless it be the denial of right to Dame Dionisia Ludel, in witholding her grandchild from her. The father's wish must indeed be regarded, but the grief of the widow for her young cannot be put away out of mind, and she bereaved and alone. I pray you, my lord abbot, for the love of God, consider whether what you do is well done, for I feel the shadow of evil heavy over us all.'

All this the surprising young man delivered in the sombre and weighty voice which was not his own, and undeniably the trick was impressive, and caused some of the more superstitious young brothers to shift and gape and mutter in awed concern. And having ended his recital, the messenger again raised his amber eyes and smiled, as if the purport of his embassage concerned him not at all.

Abbot Radulfus sat in silence for a long moment, closely eyeing the young man, who gazed back at him unwinking and serene, satisfied at having completed his errand.

'Your master's own words?'

'Every one, my lord, just as he taught them to me.'

'And he did not commission you to argue further in the matter on his behalf? You do not want to add anything?'

The eyes opened still wider in astonishment. 'I, my lord? How could I? I only run his errands.'

Prior Robert said superciliously into the abbot's ear: 'It is not unknown for an anchorite to give shelter and employment to a simpleton. It is an act of charity. This is clearly one such.' His voice was low, but not low enough to escape ears as sharp, and almost as pointed, as those of a fox, for the boy Hyacinth gleamed, and flashed a crooked smile. Cadfael, who had also caught the drift of this comment, doubted very much whether the abbot would agree with it. There seemed to him to be a very sharp intelligence behind the brown faun's face, even if it suited him to play the fool with it.

'Well,' said Radulfus, 'you may go back to your master, Hyacinth, and carry him my thanks for his concern and care, and for his prayers, which I hope he will continue on behalf of us all. Say that I have considered and do consider every side of Dame Dionisia's complaint against me, and have done and will continue to do what I see to be right. And for the natural misfortunes that give him so much anxiety, mere men cannot control or command them, though faith may overcome them.

What we cannot change we must abide. That is all.'

Without another word the boy made him a deep and graceful obeisance, turned, and walked without haste from the chapterhouse, lean and light-footed, and moving with a cat's almost insolent elegance.

In the great court, almost empty at this hour when all the brothers were at chapter, the visitor was in no hurry to set out back to his master, but lingered to look about him curiously, from the abbot's lodging in its small rose garden to the guest halls and the infirmary, and so round the circle of buildings to the gatehouse and the long expanse of the south range of the cloister. Richard, who had been lying in wait for him for some minutes, emerged confidently from the arched southern doorway, and advanced into the stranger's path.

Since the intent was clearly to halt him, Hyacinth obligingly halted, looking down with interest at the solemn, freckled face that studied him just as ardently. 'Good morrow, young sir!' he said civilly. 'And what might you want with me?'

'I know who you are,' said Richard. 'You are the serving-man the hermit brought with him. I heard you say you came with a message from him. Was it about me?'

'That I might better answer,' said Hyacinth reasonably, 'if I knew who your lordship might be, and why my master should be concerning himself with such small fry.'

'I am not small fry,' said Richard with dignity. 'I am Richard Ludel, the lord of Eaton, and your master's hermitage is on my land. And you know very well who I am, for you were there among the servants at my father's funeral. And if you did bring some message that concerns me, I think I have a right to know about it. That's only fair.' And Richard jutted his small, square chin and stood his ground with bare feet spread apart, challenging justice with unblinking blue-green eyes.

For a long moment Hyacinth returned his gaze with a bright, speculative stare. Then he said in a brisk, matter-of-fact tone, as man to man and quite without mockery: 'That's a true word, and I'm with you, Richard. Now, where can we two talk at ease?'

The middle of the great court was, perhaps, a little too conspicuous for lengthy confidences, and Richard was sufficiently taken with the unmistakably secular stranger to find him a pleasing novelty among these monastic surroundings, and meant to get to know all about him now that he had the opportunity. Moreover, very shortly chapter would be ending, and it would not do to invite Prior Robert's too close attention in such circumstances, or court Brother Jerome's busybody interference. With hasty confidence he caught Hyacinth by the hand, and towed him away up the court to the retired wicket that led through the enclave to the mill. There on the grass above the pool they were private, with the wall at their backs and the thick, springy turf under them, and the midday sun still faintly warm on them through the diaphanous veil of haze.

'Now!' said Richard, getting down sternly to the matter in hand. 'I need to have a friend who'll tell me truth, there are so many people ordering my life for me, and can't agree about it, and how can I take care of myself and be ready for them if there's no one to warn me what's in their minds? If you'll be on my side I shall know how to deal. Will you?'

Hyacinth leaned his back comfortably against the abbey wall, stretched out before him shapely, sinewy legs, and half-closed his sunlit eyes. 'I tell you what, Richard, as you can best deal if you know all that's afoot, so can I be most helpful to you if I know the why and wherefore of it. Now I know the end of this story thus far, and you know the beginning. How if we put the two together, and see what's to be made of them?'

Richard clapped his hands. 'Agreed! So first tell me what was the message you brought from Cuthred today!'

Word for word as he had delivered it in chapter, but without the mimicry, Hyacinth told him.

'I knew it!' said the child, thumping a small fist into the thick grass. 'I knew it must be some way about me. So my grandmother has cozened or persuaded even her holy man into arguing her cause for her. I heard about these things that have been happening in the coppice, but such things do happen now and then, who can prevent? You'll need to warn your master not to be over-persuaded, even if she has made herself his patroness. Tell him the whole tale, for *she* won't.'

'So I will,' agreed Hyacinth heartily, 'when I know it myself.'

'No one has told you why she wants me home? Not a word from your master?'

'Lad, I just run his errands, he doesn't confide in me.' And it seemed that the unquestioning servitor was in no hurry about returning from this errand, for he settled his back more easily against the mosses of the wall, and crossed his slim ankles. Richard wriggled a little nearer, and Hyacinth shifted good-naturedly to accommodate the sharp young bones that leaned into his side.

'She wants to marry me off,' said Richard, 'to get hold of the manors either side of mine. And not even to a proper bride. Hiltrude is old – at least twenty-two . . .'

'A venerable age,' agreed Hyacinth gravely.

'But even if she was young and pretty I don't want her. I don't want any woman. I don't *like* women. I don't see any need for them.'

'You're in the right place to escape them, then,' suggested Hyacinth helpfully, and under his long copper lashes his amber eyes flashed a gleam of laughter. 'Become a novice, and be done with the world, you'll be safe enough here.'

'No, that's no sport, neither. Listen, I'll tell you all about it.' And the tale of his threatened marriage, and his grandmother's plans to enlarge her little palatine came tripping volubly from his tongue. 'So will you keep an eye open for me, and let me know what I must be ware of? I need someone who'll be honest with me, and not keep everything from me, as if I were still a child.'

'I will!' promised Hyacinth contentedly, smiling. 'I'll be your lordship's liege man in the camp at Eaton, and be eyes and ears for you.'

'And make plain my side of it to Cuthred? I shouldn't like him to think evil of Father Abbot, he's only doing what my father wanted for me. And you haven't told me your name. I must have a name for you.'

'My name is Hyacinth. I'm told there was a bishop so named, but I'm none. Your secrets are safer with a sinner than with a saint, and I'm closer than the confessional, never fear me.'

They had somehow become so content and familiar with each other that only the timely reminder of Richard's stomach, nudging him that it was time for his dinner, finally roused them to separate. Richard trotted beside his new friend along the path that skirted the enclave wall as far as the Foregate, and there parted from him, and watched the light, erect figure as it swung away along the highroad, before he turned and went dancing gleefully back to the wicket in the enclave wall.

Hyacinth covered the first miles of his return journey at a springy, long-stepping lope, less out of any sense of haste or duty than for pure pleasure in the ease of his own gait, and the power and precision of his body. He crossed the river by the bridge at Attingham, waded the watery meadows of its tributary the Tern, and turned south from Wroxeter towards Eyton. When he came into the fringes of the forest land he slowed to a loitering walk, reluctant to arrive when the way was so pleasant. He had to cross abbey land to reach the hermitage which lay in the narrow, thrusting finger of Ludel land probing into its neighbour woods. He went merrily whistling along the track that skirted the brook, close round the northern rim of Eilmund's coppice. The bank that rose beyond, protecting the farmed woodland, was high and steep, but well kept and well turfed, never before had it subsided at any point, nor was the brook so large or rapid that it should have undercut the seasoned slope. But so it had, the raw soil showed in a steep dark scar well before he reached the place. He eyed it as he approached, gnawing a thoughtful lip, and then as suddenly shrugged and laughed. 'The more mischief the more sport!' he said half-aloud, and passed on to where the bank had been deeply undercut.

He was still some yards back from the worst, when he heard a muted cry that seemed to come from within the earth, and then an indrawn howl of struggle and pain, and a volley of muffled curses. Startled but quick in reaction, he broke into a leaping run, and pulled up as abruptly on the edge of the ditch, no more than placidly filled now with the still muddied stream, but visibly rising. On the other side of the water there had been a fresh fall, and a solitary old willow, its roots partially stripped by the first slip, had heeled over and fallen athwart the brook. Its branches heaved and rustled with the struggles of someone pinned beneath, half in, half out of the water. An arm groped for a hold through the leaves, heaving to shift the incubus, and the effort fetched a great groan. Through the threshing leaves Hyacinth caught a glimpse of Eilmund's soiled and contorted face.

'Hold still!' he shouted. 'I'm coming down!'

And down he went, thigh-deep, weaving under the first boughs to get his back beneath their weight and try to lift them enough for the imprisoned forester to drag himself clear. Eilmund, groaning and gasping, doubled both fists grimly into the soil at his back and hauled himself partially free of the bough that held him by the legs. The effort cost him a half-swallowed scream of pain.

'You're hurt!' Hyacinth took him under the armpits with both hands, arching his supple back strongly beneath the thickest bough, and the tree rocked ponderously. 'Now! Heave!'

Eilmund braced himself yet again, Hyacinth hauled with him,

fresh slithers of soil rolled down on them both, but the willow shifted and rolled over with a splash, and the forester lay in the raw earth, gasping, his feet just washed by the rim of the brook. Hyacinth, muddy and streaked with green, went on his knees beside him.

'I'll need to go for help, I can't get you from here alone. And you'll not be going on your own two feet for a while. Can you rest so, till I fetch John of Longwood's men up from the fields? We'll need more than one, and a hurdle or a shutter to carry you. Is there worse than I can see?' But what he could see was enough, and his brown face was shaken and appalled under the mud stains.

'My leg's broke.' Eilmund let his great shoulders sink cautiously back into the soft earth, and drew long, deep breaths. 'Main lucky for me you came this way, I was pinned fast, and the brook's building again. I was trying to shore up the bank. Lad,' he said, and grinned ruefully round a groan, 'there's more strength in those shoulders of yours than anyone would think to look at you.'

'Can you bide like that for a little while?' Hyacinth looked up anxiously at the bank above, but only small clods shifted and slid harmlessly, and the rim of impacted turf, herbage and roots at the top looked secure enough. 'I'll run. I'll not be long.'

And run he did, fast and straight for the Eaton fields, and hailed the first Eaton men he sighted. They came in haste, with a hurdle borrowed from the sheep fold, and between them with care and with some suppressed and understandable cursing from the victim, lifted Eilmund on to it, and bore him the half-mile to his forest cottage. Mindful that the man had a daughter at home, Hyacinth took it upon himself to run on before to give her warning and reassurance, and time to prepare the injured man's couch.

The cottage lay in a cleared assart in the forest, with a neat garden about it, and when Hyacinth reached it the door was standing open, and within the house a girl was singing softly to herself as she worked. Strangely, having run his fastest to get to her, Hyacinth seemed almost reluctant to knock at the door, or enter without knocking, and while he was hesitating on the doorstone her singing ceased, and she came out to see whose fleet footsteps had stirred the small stones of the pathway.

She was small but sturdy, and very trimly made, with a straight blue gaze, the fresh colouring of a wild rose, and smoothly-braided hair of a light brown sheen like the grain of polished oak, and she looked him over with a candid curiosity and friendliness that for once silenced his ready silver tongue. It was she who had to speak first, for all the urgency of his errand.

'You're looking for my father? He's away to the coppice, you'll find him where the bank slid.' And the blue eyes quickened with interest and approval, liking what they saw. 'You're the boy who came with the old dame's hermit, aren't you? I saw you working in his garden.'

Hyacinth owned to it, and recalled with a lurch of the heart what he had to tell. 'I am, mistress, and my name's Hyacinth. Your father's on his way back to you now, sorry I am to say it, after a mishap that will keep him to the house for a while, I fear. I came to let you know before they bring him. Oh, never fret, he's live and sound, he'll be his own man again, give him time. But his leg's broken. There was another slip, it brought down a tree on him in the ditch. He'll mend, though, no question.'

The quick alarm and blanching of her face had brought no outcry. She took in what he said, shook herself abruptly, and went to work at once setting wide the inner and outer doors to open the way for the hurdle and its burden, and making ready the couch on which to lay him, and from that to setting on a pot of water at the fire. And as she went she talked to Hyacinth over her shoulder, very practically and calmly.

'Not the first time he's come by injuries, but never a broken leg before. A tree came down, you say? That old willow – I knew it leaned, but I never thought it could fall. It was you found him? And fetched help for him?' The blue eyes looked round and smiled on him.

'Some of the Eaton men were close, clearing a drainage ditch. They're carrying him in.' They were approaching the door by then, coming as fast as they could. She went out to meet them, with Hyacinth at her elbow. It seemed that he had something more, something different to say to her, and for the moment had lost his opportunity, for he hovered silently but purposefully on the edge of the scurry of activity, as Eilmund was carried into the house and laid on the couch, and stripped of his wet boots and hose, very carefully but to a muffled accompaniment of groans and curses. His left leg was misshapen below the knee, but not so grossly that the bone had torn through the flesh.

'Above an hour lying there in the brook,' he got out, between gritting his teeth on the pain as they handled him, 'and if it hadn't been for this young fellow I should have been there yet, for I couldn't shift the weight, and there was no one within call. God's truth, there's more muscle in the lad than you'd believe. You should have seen him heft that tree off me.'

Very strangely, Hyacinth's spare, smooth cheeks flushed red beneath their dark gold sheen. It was a face certainly not given to blushing, but it had not lost the ability. He said with some constraint: 'Is there anything more I could be doing for you? I would, gladly! You'll be needing a skilled hand to set that bone. I'm no use there, but make use of me if you need an errand run. That's my calling, that I can do.'

The girl turned for an instant from the bed, her blue eyes wide and shining on her face. 'Why, so you can, if you'll be so good and add to our debt. Will you send to the abbey, and ask for Brother Cadfael to come?'

'I will well!' said Hyacinth, as heartily as if she had made him a most acceptable gift. But as she turned back from him he hesitated, and caught her by the sleeve for an instant, and breathed into her ear urgently: 'I must talk to you – alone, later, when he's cared for and resting easy.' And before she could say yes or no, though her eyes certainly were not refusing him, he was off and away through the trees, on the long run back to Shrewsbury.

Chapter Four

HUGH CAME looking for Brother Cadfael in mid-afternoon, with the first glimmers of news that had found their way out of Oxford since the siege began.

'Robert of Gloucester is back in England,' he said. 'I have it from an armourer who took thought in time to get out of the city. A few were lucky and took warning. He says Robert has landed at Wareham in spite of the king's garrison, brought in all his ships safely and taken the town. Not the castle, though, not yet, but he's settled down to siege. He got precious little out of Geoffrey, maybe a handful of knights, no more.'

'If he's safe ashore and holds the town,' said Cadfael reasonably, 'what does he want with the castle? I should have thought he'd be hotfoot for Oxford to hale his sister out of the trap.'

'He'd rather lure Stephen to come to him, and draw him off from his own siege. My man says the castle at Wareham's none too well garrisoned, and they've come to a truce agreement, and sent to the king to relieve them by a fixed date – a know-all, but truly well informed, though even he doesn't know the day appointed – or if he fails them they'll surrender. That suits Robert. He knows it's seldom any great feat to lure Stephen off a scent, but I fancy he'll hold fast this time. When will he get such a chance again? Even he can't throw it away, surely.'

'There's no end to the follies any man can commit,' said

Cadfael tolerantly. 'To give him his due, most of his idiocies are generous, which is more than can be said for the lady. But I could wish this siege at Oxford might be the end of it. If he does take castle and empress and all, she'll be safe enough of life and limb with him, it's rather he who may be in danger. What else is new from the south?'

'There's a tale he tells of a horse found straying not far from the city, in the woods close to the road to Wallingford. Some time ago, this was, about the time all roads out of Oxford were closed, and the town on fire. A horse dragging a blood-stained saddle, and saddlebags slit open and emptied. A groom who'd slipped out of the town before the ring closed recognised horse and harness as belonging to one Renaud Bourchier, a knight in the empress's service, and close in her confidence, too. My man says it's known she sent him out of the garrison to try and break through the king's lines and carry a message to Wallingford for her.'

Cadfael ceased to ply the hoe he was drawing leisurely between his herb beds, and turned his whole attention upon his friend. 'To Brian FitzCount, you mean?'

The lord of Wallingford was the empress's most faithful adherent and companion, next only to the earl, her brother, and had held his castle for her, the most easterly and exposed outpost of her territory, through campaign after campaign and through good fortune and bad, indomitably loyal.

'How comes it he's not with her in Oxford? He hardly ever leaves her side, or so they say.'

'The king moved so much faster than anyone thought for. And now he's cut off from her. Moreover, she needs him in Wallingford, for if that's ever lost she has nothing left but an isolated holding in the west country, and no way out towards London. She may well have sent out to him at the last moment, in so desperate a situation as she's in now. And rumour down there says, it seems, that Bouchier was carrying treasure to him, less in coin than in jewels. It may well be so, for he needs to pay his men. Loyal for love though they may be, they still have to live and eat, and he's beggared himself already in her service.'

'There's been talk, this autumn,' said Cadfael, thoughtfully frowning, 'that Bishop Henry of Winchester has been busy trying to lure away Brian to the king's side. Bishop Henry has money enough to buy whoever's for sale, but I doubt if even he could bid high enough to move FitzCount. All this time the man has shown as incorruptible. She had no need to try and outbid her enemies for Brian.'

'None. But she may well have thought, when the king's host closed round her, to send him an earnest of the value she sets on him, while the way was still open, or might at least be attempted by a single brave man. At such a pass, it may even have seemed to her the last chance for such a word ever to pass between them.'

Cadfael thought on that, and acknowledged its truth. King Stephen would never be a threat to his cousin's life, however bitter their rivalry had been, but if once she was made captive he would be forced to hold her in close ward for his crown's sake. Nor was she likely ever to relinquish her claim, even in prison, and agree to terms that would lightly release her. Friends and allies thus parted might, in very truth, never see each other again.

'And a single brave man did attempt it,' reflected Cadfael soberly. 'And his horse found straying, his harness awry, his saddlebags emptied, and blood on saddle and saddlecloth. So where is Renaud Bourchier? Murdered for what he carried, and buried somewhere in the woods or slung into the river?'

'What else can a man think? They have not found his body yet. Round Oxford men have other things to do this autumn besides scour the woods for a dead man. There are dead men enough to bury after the looting and burning of Oxford town,' said Hugh with dry bitterness, almost resigned to the random slaughters of this capricious civil war.

'I wonder how many within the castle knew of his errand? She would hardly blazon abroad her intent, but someone surely got wind of it.'

'So it seems, and made very ill use of what he knew.' Hugh shook himself, heaving off from his shoulders the distant evils that were out of his writ. 'Thanks be to God, I am not sheriff of Oxfordshire! Our troubles here are mild enough, a little family bickering that leads to blows now and then, a bit of thieving, the customary poaching in season. Oh, and of course the bewitchment that seems to have fallen on your woodland of Eyton.' Cadfael had told him what the abbot, perhaps, had not thought important enough to tell, that Dionisia had somehow coaxed her hermit into her quarrel, and that good man had surely taken very seriously her impersonation of a grieving grandam cruelly deprived of the society of her only grandchild. 'And he fears worse to come, does he? I wonder what the next news from Eyton will be?'

As it so happened the next news from Eyton was just hurrying towards them round the corner of the tall box hedge, borne by a novice despatched in haste by Prior Robert from the gatehouse. He came at a run, the skirts of his habit billowing, and pulled up with just enough breath to get out his message without waiting to be asked.

'Brother Cadfael, you're wanted urgently. The hermit's boy's come back to say you're needed at Eilmund's assart, and Father Abbot says take a horse and go quickly, and bring him back word how the forester does. There's been another landslip, and a tree came down on him. His leg's broken.'

They offered Hyacinth rest and a good meal for his trouble, but he would not stay. As long as he could hold the pace he clung by Cadfael's stirrup leather and ran with him, and even when he was forced to slacken and let Cadfael ride on before at his best speed, the youth trotted doggedly and steadily behind, bent on getting back to the woodland cottage, it seemed, rather than to his master's cell. He had been a good friend to Eilmund, Cadfael reflected, but he might come in for a lashing with tongue or rod when he at last returned to his sworn duty. Though Cadfael could not, on consideration, picture that wild, unchancy creature submitting tamely to reproof, much less to punishment.

It was about the hour for Vespers when Cadfael dismounted within the low pale of Eilmund's garden, and the girl flung open the door and came out eagerly to meet him.

'Brother, I hardly expected you for a while yet. Cuthred's boy must have run like the wind, and all that way! And after he'd soaked himself in the brook getting my father clear! We've had good cause to be glad of him and his master this day, there might have been no one else by for hours.'

'How is he?' asked Cadfael, unslinging his scrip and making for the house.

'His leg's broken below the knee. I've made him lie still, and packed it round as well as I could, but it needs your hand to set it. And he lay half in the brook a long time before the young man found him, I fear he's taken a chill.'

Eilmund lay well covered, and by now grimly reconciled to his helplessness. He submitted stoically to Cadfael's handling, and gritted his teeth and made no other sound as his leg was straightened and the fractured ends of bone brought into line.

'You might have come off worse,' said Cadfael, relieved. 'A good clean break, and small damage to the flesh, though it's a pity they had to move you.'

'I might have drowned else,' growled Eilmund, 'the brook was building. And you'd best tell the lord abbot to get men out here and shift the tree, before we have a lake there again.'

'I will, I will! Now, hold fast! I don't want to leave you with one leg shorter than the other.' By heel and instep he drew out the broken leg steadily to match its fellow. 'Now, Annet, your hands where mine are, and hold it so.'

She had not wasted her time while waiting, but had hunted out straight spars of wood from Eilmund's store, and had ready sheep's wool for padding, and rolled linen for bindings. Between them they completed the work neatly, and Eilmund lay back on his brychan and heaved a great breath. His face, weatherbeaten always, nonetheless had a fierce flush over the cheekbones. Cadfael was not quite easy about it.

'Now if you can rest and sleep, so much the better. Leave the lord abbot, and the tree, and everything else that needs to be dealt with here, to me, I'll see it cared for. I'll make you a draught that will ease the pain and help you to sleep.' He mixed it and administered it to Eilmund's scornful denial of the need, but it went down without protest nonetheless.

'And sleep he will,' said Cadfael to the girl, as they withdrew into the outer room. 'But make sure he keeps warm and covered through the night, for there may be a slight fever if he's taken cold. I'll make certain I get leave to go back and forth for a day or two, till I see all's well. If he gives you a hard time, bear with him, it will mean he's taken no great harm.'

She laughed softly, undisturbed. 'Oh, he's mild as milk for me. He growls, but never bites. I know how to manage him.'

It was already beginning to be twilight when she opened the house door. The sky above was still faintly golden with the moist, mysterious afterglow, dripping light between the dark branches of the trees that surrounded the garden. And there in the turf by the gate Hyacinth was sitting motionless, waiting with the timeless patience of the tree against which his straight, supple back was braced. Even so his stillness had the suggestion of a wild thing in ambush. Or perhaps, thought Cadfael, changing his mind, of a hunted wild thing trusting to silence and stillness to be invisible to the hunter.

As soon as he saw the door open he was on his feet in a single lissome movement, though he did not come within the pale.

Twilight or no, Cadfael saw the glance that locked and held fast between the youth and the girl. Hyacinth's face was still and mute as bronze, but a gleam of the fading light caught the amber brilliance of his eyes, fierce and secret as a cat's, and a sudden quickening and darkening in their depths that was reflected in the flush and brightness in Annet's startled countenance. It was no great surprise. The girl was pretty, and the boy undoubtedly attractive, all the more because he had been of invaluable service to her father. And it was natural and human, that that circumstance should endear father and daughter to him, no less than him to them. Nothing is more pleasing and engaging than the sense of having conferred benefits. Not even the gratification of receiving them.

'I'll be on my way, then,' said Cadfael to the unregarding air, and mounted softly, not to break the spell that held them still. But from the shelter of the trees he looked back, and saw them standing just as he had left them, and heard the boy's voice clear and solemn in the silence of the dusk, saying: 'I must speak to you!'

Annet did not say anything, but she closed the house door softly behind her, and came forward to meet him at the gate. And Cadfael rode back through the woods mildly aware that he was smiling, though he could not be sure, on more sober reflection, that there was anything to smile about in so unlikely an encounter. For what common ground could there be, for those two to meet on, and hold fast for more than a moment: the abbey forester's daughter, a good match for any lively and promising young man this side the shire, and a beggarly, rootless stranger dependent on charitable patronage, with no land, no craft and no kin?

He went to tend and stable his horse before he sought out Abbot Radulfus to tell him how things stood in Eyton forest. There was a late stir within there, of new guests arrived, and their mounts being accommodated and cared for. Of late there had been little movement about the county; the business of the summer, when so many merchants and tradesmen were constantly on the move, had dwindled gently away into the autumn quiet. Later, as the Christmas feast drew near, the guest halls would again be full with travellers hastening home, and kinsmen visiting kinsmen, but at this easy stage between, there was time to note those who came, and feel the human curiosity that is felt by those who have sworn stability about those who ebb and flow with the tides and seasons.

And here just issuing from the stables and crossing the yard in long, lunging strides, the gait of a confident and choleric man, was someone undoubtedly of consequence in his own domain, richly dressed, elegantly booted, and wearing sword and dagger. He surged past Cadfael in the gateway, a big, burly, thrusting man, his face abruptly lit as he swung past the torch fixed at the gate, and then as abruptly darkened. A massive face, fleshy and yet hard, muscled like a wrestler's arms, handsome in a brutal fashion, the face of a man not in anger at this moment, but always ready to be angry. He was shaven clean, which made the smooth power of his features even more daunting, and the eyes that stared imperiously straight before him looked disproportionately small, though in reality they probably were not, because of the massy flesh in which they were but shallowly set. By the look of him, not a man to cross. He might have been fifty years old, give or take a few years, but time certainly had not softened what must have been granite from the start.

His horse was standing in the stable yard outside an open stall, stripped and gently steaming as if his saddle-cloth had only just been removed, and a groom was rubbing him down and hissing to him gently as he worked. A meagre but wiry fellow, turning grey, in faded homespun of a dull brown, and a rubbed leather coat. He slid one sidelong glance at Cadfael and nodded a silent greeting, so inured to being wary of all men that even a Benedictine brother was to be avoided rather than welcomed.

Cadfael gave him good-even cheerfully, and began his own unsaddling. 'You've ridden far? Was that your lord I met at the gate?'

'It was,' said the man without looking up, and spared no more words.

'A stranger to me. Where are you from? Guests are thin this time of year.'

'From Bosiet – it's a manor the far side of Northampton, some miles south-east of the town. He *is* Bosiet – Drogo Bosiet. He holds that and a fair bit of the county besides.'

'He's well away from his home ground,' said Cadfael with interest. 'Where's he bound? We see very few travellers from Northamptonshire in these parts.'

The groom straightened up to take a longer and narrower look at this inquisitive questioner, and visibly his manner eased a little, finding Cadfael amiable and harmless. But he did not on that account grow less morose, nor more voluble.

'He's hunting,' he said with a grim and private smile.

'But not for deer,' hazarded Cadfael, returning the inspection and caught by the wryness of the smile. 'Nor, I dare say, for the beasts of the warren.'

'You dare say well. It's a man he's after.'

'A runaway?' Cadfael found it hard to believe. 'So far from home? Was a runaway villein worth so much time and expense to him?'

'This one is. He's valuable and skilled, but that's not the whole of it,' confided the groom, discarding his suspicion and reticence. 'He has a score to settle with this one. One report we got of him, setting out westwards and north, and *he's* combed every village and town along all this way, dragging me one road while his son with another groom goes another, and he won't stop short of the Welsh border. Me? If I did clap eyes on the lad he's after, I'd be blind. I wouldn't give him back a dog that ran from him, let alone a man.' His dry voice had gathered sap and passion as he talked, and he turned fully for the first time, so that the torchlight fell on his face. One cheek was marked with a blackening bruise, the corner of his mouth torn and swollen, with the look of a festering infection about it.

'His mark?' asked Cadfael, eyeing the wound.

'His seal, sure enough, and done with a seal ring. I was not quick enough at his stirrup when he mounted, yesterday morning.'

'I can dress that for you,' said Cadfael, 'if you'll wait while I go and make report to my abbot about another matter. You'd best let me, it could take bad ways. By the same token,' he said quietly, 'you're far enough out of his country, and near enough to the border, to do some running of your own, if you're so minded.'

'Brother,' said the groom with the briefest and harshest of laughs, 'I have a wife and children in Bosiet, I'm manacled. But Brand was young and unwed, his heels are lighter than mine. And I'd best get this beast stalled, and be off to wait on my lord, or he'll be laying the other cheek open for me.'

'Then come out to the guest hall steps,' said Cadfael, recalled as sharply to his own duty, 'when he's in bed and snoring, and I'll clean that sore for you.'

Abbot Radulfus listened with concern, but also with relief, to

Cadfael's report, promised to send at first light enough helpers to clear away the willow tree, clean out the brook and shore up the bank above, and nodded gravely at the suggestion that Eilmund's long wait in the water might complicate his recovery, even though the fracture itself was simple and clean.

'I should like,' said Cadfael, 'to visit him again tomorrow and make sure he stays in his bed, for there may be a degree of fever, and you know him, Father, it will take more than his daughter's scolding to keep him tamed. If he has your orders he may take heed. I'll take his measure for crutches, but not let them near him till I'm sure he's fit to rise.'

'You have my leave to go and come as you see fit,' said Radulfus, 'for as long as he needs your care. Best keep that horse for your use until then. The journey would be too slow on foot, and we shall need you here some part of the day, Brother Winfrid being new to the discipline.'

Cadfael smiled, remembering. 'It was no slow journey the young man Hyacinth made of it. Four times today he's run those miles, back and forth on his master's errand, and back and forth again for Eilmund. I only hope the hermit did not take it ill that his boy was gone so long.'

It was in Cadfael's mind that the groom from Bosiet might be too much in fear of his master to venture out by night, even when his lord was sleeping. But come he did, slipping out furtively just as the brothers came out from Compline. Cadfael led him out through the gardens to the workshop in the herbarium, and there kindled a lamp to examine the lacerated wound that marred the man's face.

The little brazier was turfed down for the night, but not exinguished, evidently Brother Winfrid had been careful to keep it alive in case of need. He was learning steadily, and strangely the delicacy of touch that eluded him with pen or brush showed signs of developing now that he came to deal with herbs and medicines. Cadfael uncovered the fire and blew it into a glow, and put on water to heat.

'He's safe asleep, is he, your lord? Not likely to wake? Though if he did, he should have no need of you at this hour. But I'll be as quick as I may.'

The groom sat docile and easy under the ministering hands, turning his face obediently to the light of the lamp. The bruised cheek was fading at the edges from black to yellow, but the tear at the corner of his mouth oozed blood and pus. Cadfael bathed away the encrusted exudations and cleaned the gash with a lotion of water betony and sanicle.

'He's free with his fists, your lord,' he said ruefully. 'I see two blows here.'

'He seldom stops at one,' said the groom grimly. 'He does after his kind. There are some worse than him, God help all those who serve them. His son's another made to the same pattern. What else could we look for, when he's lived so from birth? In a day or so he's to join us here, and if he has not got his hands on Brand by then – God forbid! – the hunt will go on.'

'Well, at least if you stay a day or so I can get this gash healed for you. What's your name, friend?'

'Warin. Yours I know, Brother, from the hospitaller. That feels cool and kind.'

'I should have thought,' said Cadfael, 'that your lord would have gone first to the sheriff, if he had real complaint against this runaway of his. The guildsmen of the town would likely keep their mouths shut, even if they knew anything, a town stands to gain by taking in a good craftsman. But the king's officers are bound, willing or no, to help a man to his own property.'

'We got here too late, as you saw, to do much in that kind until the morrow. He knows, none so well, that Shrewsbury is a charter borough, and may cheat him of his prey if the lad has got this far. He does intend going to the sheriff. But since he's lodged here, and reckons the church as well as the law ought to help him to his own, he's asked to put his case at chapter tomorrow, and after that he'll be off into the town to seek out the sheriff. There's no stone he won't up-end to get at Brand's hide.'

Cadfael was thinking, though he did not say it, that there might be time in between to send word to Hugh to make himself very hard to find. 'What in the world,' he asked, 'has the man done, to make your master so vindictive against him?'

'Why, he was for ever on the edge of trouble, being a lad that would stand up for himself, yes, and for others, too, and that's crime enough for Drogo. I don't know the rights of what happened that last day, but however it was, I saw Bosiet's steward, who takes his style from his master, carried into the manor on a shutter, and he was laid up for days. Seemingly something had happened between them, and Brand had laid him flat, for the next we knew, Brand was nowhere, and they were hunting him along all the roads out of Northampton. But they never caught up with him, and here we are still hot on his trail. If ever Drogo lays hands on him he'll flay him, but he won't cripple him, he's too valuable to waste. But he'll have every morsel of his grudge out of the lad's skin, and then wring every penny of profit out of his skills lifelong, and make good sure he never gets the chance to run again.'

'Then he had better make a good job of it now,' agreed Cadfael wryly. 'If well-wishing can help him, he has it. Now hold still a moment – there! And this ointment you can take with you and use as often as you choose. It helps take out the sting and lower the swelling.'

Warin turned the little jar curiously in his hand, and touched a finger to his cheek. 'What's in it, to work such healing?'

'Saint John's wort and the small daisy, both good for wounds. And if chance offers tomorrow, let me see you again and hear how you do. And keep out of his reach!' said Cadfael warmly, and turned to bed down his brazier again with fresh turves, to smoulder quietly and safely until morning.

Drogo Bosiet duly appeared at chapter next morning, large, loud and authoritative in an assembly where a wiser man would have realised that authority lay with the abbot, and the abbot's grip on it was absolute, however calm and measured his voice and austere his face. So much the better, thought Cadfael, watching narrowly and somewhat anxiously from his retired stall, Radulfus will know how to weigh the man, and let nothing slip too soon.

'My lord abbot,' said Drogo, straddling the flags of the floor like a bull before the charge, 'I am here in search of a malefactor who attacked and injured my steward and fled my lands. He is known to have made for Northampton, my manor, to which he is tied, being several miles south-east of the town, and I have it in mind that he would make for the Welsh border. We have hunted for him all this way, and from Warwick I have taken this road from Shrewsbury, while my son goes on to Stafford, and will join me here from that place. All I ask here is whether any stranger of his years has lately come into these parts.'

'I take it,' said the abbot after a long and thoughtful pause, and steadily eyeing the powerful face and arrogant stance of his visitor, 'that this man is your villein.'

'He is.'

'And you do know,' pursued Radulfus mildly, 'that since it would seem you have failed to reclaim him within four days, it will be necessary to apply to the courts to regain possession of him legally?'

'My lord,' said Drogo with impatient scorn, 'so I can well do, if I can but find him. The man is mine, and I mean to have him. He has been a cause of trouble to me, but he has skills which are valuable, and I do not mean to be robbed of what is mine. The law will give me my rights in the lands where the offence arose.' And so, no doubt, such a law as survived in his own shire would certainly do, at the mere nod of his head.

'If you will tell us what your fugitive is like,' said the abbot reasonably, 'Brother Denis can tell you at once whether we have had such a one as guest in our halls.'

'He goes by the name of Brand – twenty years old, dark of hair but reddish, lean and strong, beardless—'

'No,' said Brother Denis the hospitaller without hesitation, 'I have had no such young man lodged here, not for five or six weeks back certainly. If he had found work along the way with some trader or merchant carrying goods, such as come with three or four servants, then he might have passed this way. But a young man alone – no, none.'

'As to that,' said the abbot with authority, forestalling reply from any other, though indeed no one but Prior Robert would have ventured to speak before him, 'you would do well to take your question to the sheriff at the castle, for his officers are far more likely than we here within the enclave to know of any newcomers entering the town. The pursuit of criminals and offenders such as you describe is their business, and they are thorough and careful about it. The guildsmen of the town are also wary and jealous of their rights, and have good reason to keep their eyes open, and their wits about them. I recommend you to apply to them.'

'So I intend, my lord. But you will bear in mind what I have asked, and if any here should recall anything to the purpose, let me hear of it.'

'This house will do whatever is incumbent upon it in good conscience,' said the abbot with chilly emphasis, and watched with an unrevealing face as Drogo Bosiet, with only the curtest of nods by way of leavetaking, turned on his booted heel and strode out of the chapterhouse. Nor did Radulfus see fit to make any comment or signify any conclusion when the petitioner was gone, as if he felt no need to give any further instruction than he had given by the tone of his replies. And by the time they emerged from chapter, some time later, both Drogo and his groom had saddled and ridden forth, no doubt over the bridge and into the town, to seek out Hugh Beringar at the castle.

Brother Cadfael had intended to pay a quick visit to the herbarium and his workshop, to see all was in order there and set Brother Winfrid to work on what was safest and most suitable for his unsupervised attentions, and then set off at once for Eilmund's cottage, but events prevented. For there was a death that day among the old, retired brothers in the infirmary, and Brother Edmund, in need of a companion to watch out the time with him after the tired old man had whispered the few almost inaudible words of his last confession and received the final rites, turned first and confidently to his closest friend and associate among the sick. They had done the same service together many times in forty years of a vocation imposed from birth in Edmund's case, though willingly embraced later, but chosen after half a lifetime in the outer world by Cadfael. They stood at the opposite poles of *oblatus* and *conversus*, and they understood each other so well that few words ever needed to pass between them.

The old man's dying was painless and feather-light, all the substance of his once sharp and vigorous mind gone on before; but it was slow. The fading candle flame did not flicker, only dimmed in perfect stillness second by second, so mysteriously that they missed the moment when the last spark withdrew, and only knew he was gone when they began to realise that the prints of age were smoothing themselves out gently from his face.

'So pass all good men!' said Edmund fervently. 'A blessed death as ever I saw! I wonder will God deal as gently with me, when my time comes!'

They cared for the dead man together, and together emerged into the great court to arrange for his body to be carried to the mortuary chapel. And then there was a small matter of Brothers Paul's youngest schoolboy, who had missed his footing in haste on the day stairs and rolled down half the flight, bloodying his knees on the cobbles of the court, and had to be picked up and bathed and bandaged, and despatched to his play with an apple by way of reward for his bravery in denying stoutly that he was hurt. Only then could Cadfael repair to the stable and saddle the horse assigned to him, and by then it was almost time for Vespers.

He was leading his horse across the court to the gatehouse when Drogo Bosiet rode in under the archway, his finery a little jaded and dusty from a day's frustration and exertion, his face blackly set, and the groom Warin a few yards behind him, warily attentive, alert to obey the least gesture, but anxious meantime to stay out of sight and out of mind. Clearly the hunt had drawn no quarry anywhere, and the hunters came back with the approach of evening empty-handed. Warin would have to stand clear of the length of that powerful arm tonight.

Cadfael went forth through the gate reassured and content, and made good speed towards his patient at Eyton.

Chapter Five

RICHARD HAD been out all afternoon with the other boys in the main abbey gardens beside the river, where the last pears were just being harvested. The children were allowed to help, and within reason to sample, though the fruit had still to ripen after gathering. But these, the last, had hung so long on the tree that they were already eatable. It had been a good day, with sun, and freedom, and some dabbling in the river where there were safe shallows, and he was reluctant to go indoors to Vespers at the end of it, and then to supper and bed. He loitered at the end of the procession winding its way along the riverside path, and up the green, bushy slope to the Foregate. In the stillness of late afternoon there were still clouds of midges dancing over the water, and fish rising to them lazily. Under the bridge the flow looked almost motionless though he knew it was fast and deep. There had been a boatmill moored there once, powered by the stream.

Nine-year-old Edwin, his devoted ally, loitered with him, but a little anxiously, casting a glance over his shoulder to see how the distance between them and the tailend of the procession lengthened. He had been praised for his stoicism after his fall, and was in no mind to lose the warm sense of virtue the incident had left with him by being late for Vespers. But neither could he lightly desert his bosom friend. He hovered, rubbing at a bandaged knee that still smarted a little.

'Richard, come on, we mustn't dawdle. Look, they're nearly

at the highroad.'

'We can easily catch up with them,' said Richard, dabbling his toes in the shallows. 'But you go on, if you want to.'

'No, not without you. But I can't run as fast as you, my knee's stiff. Do come on, we shall be late.'

'*I* shan't, I can be there long before the bell goes, but I forgot you couldn't run as well as usual. You go on, I'll overtake you before you reach the gatehouse. I just want to see whose boat this is, coming down towards the bridge.'

Edwin hesitated, weighing his own virtuous peace of mind against desertion, and for once decided in accordance with his own wishes. The last black habit at the end of the procession was just climbing to the level of the highroad, to vanish from sight. No one had looked back to call the loiterers, or scold, they were left to their own consciences. Edwin turned and ran after his fellows as fast as he could for his stiffening knee. From the top of the slope he looked back, but Richard was ankle-deep in his tiny cove, skimming stones expertly across the surface of the water in a dotted line of silvery spray. Edwin decided on virtue, and abandoned him.

It had never been in Richard's mind to play truant, but his game seduced him as each cast bettered the previous one, and he began to hunt for smoother and flatter pebbles under the bank, ambitious to reach the opposite shore. And then one of the town boys who had been swimming under the green sweep of turf that climbed to the town wall took up the challenge, and began to return the shower of dancing stones, splashing naked in the shallows. So absorbed was Richard in the contest that he forgot all about Vespers, and only the small, distant chime of the bell startled him back to his duty. Then he did drop his stone, abandon the field to his rival, and scramble hastily ashore to snatch up his discarded shoes and run like a hare for the Foregate and the abbey. He had left it too late. The moment he arrived breathless at the gatehouse, and sidled in cautiously by the wicket to avoid notice, he heard the chanting of the first psalm from within the church.

Well, it was not so great a sin to miss a service, but for all that, he did not wish to add it to his score at this time, when he was preoccupied with grave family matters outside the cloister. By good fortune the children of the stewards and the lay servants were also accustomed to attend Vespers, which so conveniently augmented the numbers of the schoolboys that one small truant might not be missed, and if he could slip back into their enveloping ranks as they left the church afterwards it might be assumed that he had been among them all along. It was the best course he could think of. Accordingly he slipped into the cloister, and installed himself in the first carrel of the south walk, curled up in the corner, where he could see the south door of the church, by which brothers, guests and boys would all emerge when the service ended. Once the obedientiaries and choir monks had passed, it should not be difficult to worm his way in among the boys without being noticed.

And here they came at last, Abbot Radulfus, Prior Robert and all the brothers, passing decorously by, and out into the evening on their way to supper; and then the less orderly throng of the abbey young. Richard was sidling along the wall that concealed him, ready to slip out and mingle with them as they passed, when a familiar and censorious voice made itself heard just on the other side of the wall, in the very archway through which the children must pass.

'Silence, there! Let me hear no chattering so soon after divine worship! Is this how you were taught to leave the holy place? Get into line, two and two, and behave with due reverence.'

Richard froze, his back pressed against the chill stone of the wall, and drew back stealthily into the darkest corner of the carrel. Now what had possessed Brother Jerome to let the procession of the choir monks pass by without him, and wait here to hector and scold the unoffending children? For there he stood immovable, harrying them into tidy ranks, and Richard was forced to crouch in hiding and let his best hope of escape dwindle away into the evening air in the great court, leaving him trapped. For of all the brothers, Jerome was the one before whom he would least willingly creep forth ignominiously to be arraigned and lectured. And now the boys were gone, a few abbey guests emerging at leisure from the church, and still Jerome stood there waiting, for Richard could see his meagre shadow on the flags of the floor.

And suddenly it appeared that he had been waiting for one of the guests, for the shadow intercepted and melted into a more substantial shadow. Richard had seen the substance pass, a big, muscular striding man with a face as solid and russet as a sandstone wall, and the rich gown of the middle nobility, short of the baronage or even their chief tenants, but still to be reckoned with.

'I have been waiting, sir,' said Brother Jerome, self-important but respectful, 'to speak a word to you. I have been thinking of what you told us at chapter this morning. Will you sit down with me in private for a few moments?'

Richard's young heart seemed to turn over within him, for there was he crouched on the stone bench by one of Brother Anselm's aumbries in the carrel right beside them, and he was in terror that they would immediately walk in upon him. But for his own reasons, it seemed, Brother Jerome preferred to be a little more retired, as if he did not want anyone still within the church, perhaps the sacristan, to observe this meeting as he left, for he drew his companion deep into the third carrel, and there sat down with him. Richard could easily have slid round the corner and out of the cloister now that the way was free, but he did not do so. Pure human curiosity kept him mute and still where he was, almost holding his breath, a little pitcher with very long ears.

'This malefactor of whom you spoke,' began Jerome, 'he who assaulted your steward and has run from you – how did you say he was called?'

'His name is Brand. Why, have you any word of him?'

'No, certainly none by that name. I do firmly believe,' said Jerome virtuously, 'that it is every man's duty to help you to reclaim your villein if he can. Even more it is the duty of the church, which should always uphold justice and law, and condemn the criminal and lawbreaker. You did tell us this fellow is young, about twenty years? Beardless, reddish dark as to his hair?'

'All that, yes. You know of such a one?' demanded Drogo sharply.

'It *may* not be the same man, but there is one young man who would answer to such a description, only one to my knowledge who is lately come into these parts. It would be worth asking. He came here with a pilgrim, a holy man who has settled down in a hermitage only a few miles from us, on the manor of Eaton. He serves the hermit. If he is indeed your rogue, he must have imposed on that good soul, who in the kindness of his heart has given him work and shelter. If it is so, then it is only right that his eyes should be opened to the kind of servitor he is harbouring. And if he proves not to be the man, there is no harm done. But indeed I did have my doubts about him, the one time he came here with a message. He has a sort of civil insolence about him that sorts ill with a saint's service.'

Richard crouched motionless, hugging his knees, his ears stretched to catch every word that passed.

'Where is this hermitage to be found?' demanded Drogo, with the hunger of the manhunt in his voice. 'And what is the fellow calling himself?'

'He goes by the name of Hyacinth. The hermit's name is Cuthred, anyone in Wroxeter or Eaton can show you where he dwells.' And Jerome launched willingly into exact instructions as to the road, which occupied him so happily that even if there had been any small sounds from the neighbouring carrel he probably would not have heard them. But Richard's small bare feet made no sound on the flags as he slid hastily round into the archway, and fled down the court to the stables, still carrying his shoes. His hard little soles pattered like pebbles on the cobbles of the stableyard, careless of being overheard now that he was safely out of that narrow, darkening carrel, echoing hollowly to the sound of one self-righteous voice and one wolfish one plotting the capture and ruin of Hyacinth, who was young and lively and ranked as a friend. But they should not have him, not if Richard could prevent. No matter how detailed Brother Jerome's directions, that man who wanted his villein back, and certainly meant him no good if ever he got him, would still have to find his way and sort out the woodland paths as he came to them, but Richard knew every track, and could ride by the shortest way, and fast, if only he could get his pony saddled and smuggled quietly out at the gatehouse before the enemy sent a groom to saddle his own tall horse. For he was hardly likely to do it for himself if he had a servant to do it for him. The thought of the twilit woods did not daunt Richard, his heart rose excitedly to the adventure.

Luck or heaven favoured him, for it was the hour when everyone was at supper, and even the porter at the gatehouse was taking his meal within, and left the gate unwatched while he ate. If he did hear hooves, and come out to see who the rider might be, he came too late to see Richard scramble into the saddle and set off at a round trot along the Foregate towards Saint Giles. He had even forgotten that he was hungry, and felt no pang at going supperless. Besides, he was a favourite with Brother Petrus, the abbot's cook, and might be able to wheedle something out of him later. As for what was to happen when his absence was discovered, as it surely must be at bedtime even if it passed unremarked at supper, there was no point in giving any thought to that. What mattered was to find Hyacinth, and warn him, if he was indeed this Brand, that he had better get away into hiding as fast as he could, for the hunt was out after him, and close on his heels. After that, let what was bound to happen, happen!

He turned into the forest beyond Wroxeter, on a broad ride which Eilmund had cleared for the passage of his coppice wood and trimmed poles. It led directly to the forester's cottage, but also provided the quickest way to a side-path which continued to the hermitage, the obvious place to look first for Cuthred's servant. The forest here was chiefly oak, and old, the ground cover light and low, and the deep layers of the leaves of many autumns made riding silent. Richard had slackened speed among the old trees, and the pony stepped with delicate pleasure in the cushioned mould. But for the hush, the boy would never have heard the voices, for they were low and intent, and manifestly the one was a man's, the other a girl's, though their words were too soft to be distinguished, meant only for each other. Then he saw them, aside from the path, very still and very close beside the broad bole of an oak tree. They were not touching, though they had eyes only for each other, and whatever they had to say was earnest and of high importance. The shout Richard launched at sight of them startled them apart like fluttered birds.

'Hyacinth! Hyacinth!'

He rolled and fell from his pony, rather than dismounted, and flew to meet them as they started towards him.

'Hyacinth, you must hide – you must get away quickly! They're after you, if you're Brand – *are* you Brand? There's a man has come looking for you, he says he's hunting a runaway villein named Brand . . .'

Hyacinth, alert and quivering, held him by the shoulders, and dropped to his knees to have him eye to eye. 'What like of man? A servant? Or the man himself? And when was this?'

'After Vespers. I heard them talking – Brother Jerome told him there was a young man newly come into this country, who might be the one he's looking for. He told him where to find you, and he's coming to look for you at the hermitage now, this very night. An awful man, big and loud-mouthed. I ran to get my pony while they were still talking, I got away before him. But you mustn't go back to Cuthred, you must get away quickly and hide.'

Hyacinth caught the boy in his arms in a brief, boisterous embrace. 'You're a true and gallant friend as any man could have, and never fear for me, now I'm warned what can harm me? That's the man himself, no question! Drogo Bosiet thinks highly enough of me to waste time and men and money on hunting me down, and in the end he'll get nothing for his pains.'

'Then you *are* Brand? You *were* his villein?'

'I love you all the more,' said Hyacinth, 'for viewing my villeinage as past. Yes, the name they gave me long ago was Brand, I chose Hyacinth for myself. You and I will keep to that name. And now you and I, my friend, must part, for what you must do now is ride back to the abbey quickly, before the light's gone, and before you're missed. Come, I'll see you safe to the edge of the wood.'

'No!' said Richard, outraged. 'I'll go alone, I'm not afraid. You must vanish – now, at once!'

The girl had laid her hand on Hyacinth's shoulder. Richard saw her eyes wide and bright with resolution rather than alarm in the encroaching twilight. 'He shall, Richard! I know a place where he'll be safe.'

'You ought to try to get into Wales,' said Richard anxiously, even somewhat jealously, for this was his friend, and he was the rescuer, and almost he resented it that Hyacinth should owe any part of his salvation to someone else, and a woman, at that.

Hyacinth and Annet looked briefly at each other, and smiled, and the quality of their smiles lit up the woodland. 'No, not that,' said Hyacinth gently. 'If run I must, I'll not run far. But you need not fear for me, I shall be safe enough. Now mount, my lord, and be off with you, back where *you'll* be safe, or I won't stir a step.'

That set him in motion briskly enough. Once he looked back to wave, and saw them standing as he had left them, gazing after him. A second time he looked back, before the spot where they stood was quite hidden from him among the trees, but they were gone, vanished, and the forest was silent and still. Richard remembered his own problems ahead, and took the road homeward at an anxious trot.

Drogo Bosiet rode through the early twilight by the ways Brother Jerome had indicated to him, asking peremptorily of the villagers in Wroxeter for confirmation that he was on the best road to the cell of the hermit Cuthred. It seemed that the holy man was held in the kind of unofficial reverence common to the old Celtic eremites, for more than one of those questioned spoke of him as Saint Cuthred.

Drogo entered the forest close to where Eaton land, as the shepherd in the field informed him, bordered Eyton land, and a narrow ride brought him after almost a mile of forest to a small, level clearing ringed round with thick woodland. The stone hut in the centre was stoutly built but small and low-roofed, and showed signs of recent repair after being neglected for years. There was a little square garden enclosure round it, fenced in with a low pale, and part of the ground within had been cleared and planted. Drogo dismounted at the edge of the clearing and advanced to the fence, leading his horse by the bridle. The evening silence was profound, there might have been no living being within a mile of the place.

But the door of the hut stood open, and from deep within a steady gleam of light showed. Drogo tethered his horse, and strode in through the garden and up to the door, and still hearing no sound, went in. The room into which he stepped was small and dim, and contained little but a pallet bed against the wall, a small table and a bench. The light burned within, in a second room, and through the open doorway, for there was no door between, he saw that this was a chapel. The lamp burned upon a stone altar, before a small silver cross set up on a carved wooden casket reliquary, and on the altar before the cross lay a slender and elegant breviary in a gilded binding. Two silver candlesticks, surely the gifts of the hermit's patroness, flanked the cross, one on either side.

Before this altar a man was kneeling motionless, a tall man in a rough black habit, with the cowl raised to cover his head. Against the small, steady light the dark figure was impressive, the long, erect back straight as a lance, the head not bowed but raised, the very image of sanctity. Even Drogo held his tongue for a moment, but no longer. His own needs and desires were paramount, a hermit's prayers could and must yield to them. Evening was rapidly deepening into night, and he had no time to waste.

'You are Cuthred?' he demanded firmly. 'They told me at the abbey how to find you.'

The dignified figure did not move, unless he unfolded his unseen hands. But he said in a measured and unstartled voice: 'Yes, I am Cuthred. What do you need from me? Come in and speak freely.'

'You have a boy who runs your errands. Where is he? I want

to see him. You may well have been cozened into keeping a rogue about you unawares.'

And at that the habited figure did turn, the cowled head reared to face the stranger, and the sidelong light from the altar lamp showed a lean, deep-eyed, bearded face, a long, straight, aristocratic nose, a fell of dark hair within the hood, as Drogo Bosiet and the hermit of Eyton forest looked long and steadily at each other.

Brother Cadfael was sitting by Eilmund's couch, supping on bread and cheese and apples, since like Richard he had missed his usual supper, and was well content with a very discontented patient, when Annet came back from feeding the hens and shutting them in, and milking the one cow she kept for their own use. She had been an unconscionable time about it, and so her disgruntled father told her. All trace of fever had left him, his colour was good, and he was in no great discomfort, but he was in a glum fury with his own helplessness, and impatient to be out and about his business again, distrusting the abbot's willing but untutored substitutes to take proper care of his forest. The very shortness of his temper was testimony to his sound health. And the offending leg was straight and gave no great pain. Cadfael was well satisfied.

Annet came in demurely, and laughed at her father's grumbling, no way in awe of him. 'I left you in the best of company, and I knew you'd be the better for an hour or so without me, and so would I for an hour without you, such an old bear as you're become! Why should I hurry back, on such a fine evening? You know Brother Cadfael has taken good care of you, don't grudge me a breath of air.'

But by the look of her she had enjoyed something more potent than a mere breath of air. There was a brightness and a quivering aliveness about her, as if after strong wine. Her brown hair, always so smoothly banded, had shaken loose a few strands on her shoulders, Cadfael noted, as though she had wound her way through low branches that caught at the braids, and the colour in her cheeks was rosy and roused, to match the brilliance of her eyes. She had brought in a few of the month's lost leaves on her shoes. True, the byre lay just within the trees at the edge of the clearing, but there were no well-grown oaks there.

'Well, now that you're back, and I shan't be leaving him to complain without a listener,' said Cadfael, 'I'd best be getting back before it's full dark. Keep him off his feet for a few days yet, lass, and I'll let him up on crutches soon if he behaves himself. At least he's taken no harm from lying fast in the water, that's a mercy.'

'Thanks to Cuthred's boy Hyacinth,' Annet reminded them.

She flicked a swift glance at her father, and was pleased when he responded heartily: 'And that's truth if ever there was! He was as good as a son to me that day, and I don't forget it.'

And was it fancy, or did Annet cheeks warm into a deeper rose? As good as a son to a man who had no son to be his right hand, but only this bright, confident, discreet and loving daughter?

'Possess your soul in patience,' advised Cadfael, rising, 'and we'll have you as sound as before. It's worth waiting for. And don't fret about the coppice, for Annet here will tell you they've made a good job of clearing the brook and shaved off the overhang of the bank. It will hold.' He made fast his scrip to his girdle, and turned to the door.

'I'll see you to the gate,' said Annet, and came out with him into the deep twilight of the clearing, where his horse was placidly pulling at the turf.

'Girl,' said Cadfael with his foot in the stirrup, 'you blossom like a rose tonight.'

She was just taking up the loose tresses in her hands, and smoothing them back into neatness with the rest. She turned and smiled at him. 'But I seem to have been through a thorn bush,' she said.

Cadfael leaned from the saddle and delicately picked a sear oak leaf out of her hair. She looked up to see him twirling it gently between his fingers by the stem, and wonderfully she smiled. That was how he left her, roused and braced, and surely having made up her mind to go, undaunted, through all the thorny thickets that might be in the path between her and what she wanted. She was not ready yet to confide even in her father, but it troubled her not at all that Cadfael should guess at what was in the wind, nor had she any fear of a twisted ending. Which did not preclude the possibility that others might have good reason to fear on her account.

Cadfael rode without haste through the darkening wood. The moon was already up, and bright where it could penetrate the thickness of the trees. Compline must be long over by now, and the brothers making ready for sleep. The boys would be in their beds long ago. It was cool and fresh in the green-scented forest, pleasant to ride alone and at leisure, and have time to think of timeless things that could not be accommodated in the bustle of the day, sometimes not even during the holy office or the quiet times of prayer, where by rights they belonged. There was more room for them here under this night sky still faintly luminous round the rims of vision. Cadfael rode in a deep content of mind through the thickest part of the woodland growth, with a glimmer of light from the open fields ahead before him.

It was the rustling movement on his left, among the trees, that startled him out of his muse. Something vaguely pale in the gloom moved alongside him, and he heard the slight jingling of a horse's bit and bridle. A riderless horse, wandering astray but saddled and bridled, for the small metallic sounds rang clear. He had not been riderless when he set out from his stable. In glimpses of moonlight between the branches the pale shape shone elusively, drawing nearer to the path. Cadfael had seen that light roan hide before, that same afternoon in the great court of the abbey.

He dismounted in haste, and called, advancing to take the slack bridle and run a hand over the dappled forehead. The saddle was still in place, but the straps that had held a small saddle-roll behind it had been sliced through. And where was the rider? And why, indeed, had he set out yet again, after returning empty-handed from a day's hunting? Had someone provided him with a clue to start him off again after his prey, even thus late at night?

Cadfael parted the bushes and turned in from the path, where he had first glimpsed the pale form moving. Here nothing seemed disturbed, the tangle of branches showed no disrupting passage. He worked back a little to emerge again on the path, and there, aside under the bushes in long grass, so hidden that he had ridden past it and seen no sign, he found what he had feared to find.

Drogo Bosiet lay sprawled on his face, sunk deep in the ripe autumnal herbage, and even against the dark colouring of his gown, Cadfael could just distinguish the darker blot that was his blood, welling out under his left shoulder blade, where the dagger that killed him had plunged and been withdrawn.

Chapter Six

AT SO late an hour there was small chance of reaching immediate help at either abbey or castle, and none of deriving any knowledge from the darkening scene here in the forest. All Cadfael could do, thus alone, was to kneel beside the mute body and feel for a heartbeat or pulse, and listen for any faint sign of breathing. But though Drogo's flesh was warm, and yielded pliably to handling, there was no breath in him, and the heart in his great chest, almost certainly pierced by the thrust from behind, was stonily still. He could not have been dead very long, but the gush of blood that had sprung out with the blade had ceased to flow, and was beginning to dry at its edges into a dark crust. More than an hour ago, Cadfael thought, judging by what signs he had, perhaps as much as two hours. And his saddle-roll cut loose and taken. Here, in our woods! When did any man ever hear of footpads so close? Or has some cutthroat from the town heard of Eilmund being laid up at home, and ventured to try his luck here for a chance traveller riding alone?

Delay could not harm Drogo now, and daylight might show at least some trace to lead to his murderer. Best leave him so, and take word to the castle, where there was always a guard waking, and leave a message for Hugh, to be delivered as soon as there was light. At midnight the brothers would rise for Matins, and the same grim news could and should be delivered then to Abbot Radulfus. The dead man was the abbey's guest, and his son expected within a few days, and to the abbey he must be taken for proper and reverent care.

No, there was nothing more to be done for Drogo Bosiet, but least he could get the horse back to his stable. Cadfael mounted, and gathered the loose bridle in his left hand, and the horse came with him docilely. There was no haste. He had until midnight. No need to save time, since even if he reached his bed before Matins, sleep would be impossible. Better take care of the horses and then wait for the bell.

Abbot Radulfus came early to the church for Matins, to find Cadfael waiting for him in the south porch as he crossed from his lodging. The bell in the dortoir was only just sounding. It takes but a few moments to say bluntly that a man is dead, and by an act of man, not of God.

Radulfus was never known to waste words in exclamation, and did not do so now at the news that a guest of his house had come to an unlawful end in the abbey's own forest. The gross affront and grosser wrong he accepted in sombre silence, and the right and duty of retribution, as incumbent now upon the church as on the secular authority, he took up with a deep assenting nod of his head, and a grim tightening of his long, firm lips. In the hush while he thought, they heard the soft, sandalled steps of the brothers descending the night stairs.

'And you have left word for Hugh Beringar?' asked the abbot.

'At his house and at the castle.'

'No man can do more, then, until first light. He must be brought here, for here his son will come. But you – you will be needed, you can lead straight to where he lies. Go now, I excuse you from the office, go and take some rest, and at dawn ride to join the sheriff. Say to him that I will send a party after, to bring the body home.'

In the first hesitant light of a chill morning they stood over Drogo Bosiet's body, Hugh Beringar and Cadfael, a sergeant of Hugh's garrison and two men-at-arms, all silent, all with eyes fixed on the great patch of encrusted blood that soaked the back of the rich riding coat. The grass hung as heavy and flattened with dew as if after rain, and the moisture had gathered in great pearls in the woollen pile of the dead man's clothing, and starred the bushes in a treasury of cobwebs.

'Since he plucked out the dagger from the wound,' said Hugh, 'most likely he took it away with him. But we'll look about for it, in case he discarded it. And you say the straps of the saddle-roll were sliced through? After the slaying – he needed the knife for that. Quicker and easier in the dark to cut it loose than unbuckle it, and whoever he was, he wouldn't want to linger. Strange, though, that a mounted man should fall victim to such an attack. At the least sound he had only to spur and draw clear, surely.'

'But I think,' said Cadfael, studying how the body lay, 'that he was on foot here, and leading the horse. He was a stranger, and the path here is very narrow and the trees crowd close, and it was dark or getting dark. See the leaves that have clung to his boot soles. He never had time to turn, the one stroke was enough. Where he had been I don't know, but he was on his way back to his lodging in our guest hall when he was struck down. With no struggle and little noise. The horse had taken no great alarm, he strayed only a few yards.'

'Which argues an expert footpad and thief,' said Hugh. 'But do you believe in that? In my writ and so close to the town?'

'No. But some secret rogue, perhaps even a sneak thief out of the town, might risk one exploit, knowing Eilmund is laid up at home. But this is guessing,' said Cadfael, shaking his head. 'Now and then even a poacher might be tempted to try murder, if he came on a man of substance, alone and at night. But guessing is small use.'

The party sent by Abbot Radulfus to carry Drogo back to the abbey were already winding their way along the path with their litter. Cadfael knelt in the grass, soaking his habit at the knees in the plenteous dew, and carefully turned the stiffening body face upward. The heavy muscling of the cheeks had fallen slack, the eyes, so disproportionately small for the massive countenance, were half open. He looked older and less arrogantly brutal in death, a mortal man like other men, almost piteous. The hand that had lain hidden under his body wore a heavy silver ring.

'Something the thief missed,' said Hugh, looking down with something of startled regret in his face for so much power now powerless.

'Another sign of haste. Or he would have ransacked every garment. And proof enough that the body was not moved. He lies as he fell, facing towards Shrewsbury. It's as I said, he was on his way home.'

'There's a son expected, you said? Come,' said Hugh, 'we can leave him to your men now, and my fellows will comb the woods all round in case there's sign or trace to be found, though I doubt it. You and I will be off back to the abbey, and see what the abbot has brought to light at chapter. For someone must surely have put some notion into his mind, to send him out again so late.'

The sun was above the rim of the world, but veiled and pale, as they mounted and turned back along the narrow ride. The spider-draped bushes caught the first gleams that pierced the mist, and flashed in coruscations of diamonds. When they emerged into the open, low-lying fields the horses waded through a shallow lilac-tinted sea of vapour.

'What do you know of this man Bosiet,' asked Hugh, 'more than he has told me, or I have gleaned without his telling?'

'Little enough, I expect. He's lord of several manors in Northamptonshire, and some little while since a villein of his, as like as not for a very good reason, laid his steward flat and put him to bed for some days, and then very wisely took to his heels before they could lay hands on him. Bosiet and his men have been hunting for the fellow ever since. They must have wasted a good while searching the rest of the shire, I fancy, before they got word from someone that he'd made for Northampton and seemed to be heading north and west. And between them they've followed this far, making drives in both directions from every halt. He must have cost them far above his value, valuable though they say he is, but it's his blood they're after first and foremost, and seemingly they set a higher price on that than on his craft, whatever that may be. There was a very vigorous hate there,' said Cadfael feelingly. 'He brought it to chapter with him. Father Abbot was not greatly taken with the notion of helping him to the sort of revenge he'd be likely to take.'

'And shrugged him off on to me,' said Hugh, briefly grinning. 'Well, small blame to him. I took your word for it, and stayed out of his way as long as I could. In any case I could give him no help. What else do you know of him?'

'That he has a groom named Warin, the one that rode with him, though not, it seems, on his last ride. Maybe he'd sent his man on some other errand, and couldn't wait once he got the word, but set off alone. He's – he *was* – a man who liked to use his fists freely on his servants, for any offence or none. At least he'd laid Warin's face open for him, and according to the groom that was no rarity. As for the son, according to Warin he's much like his father, and just as surely to be avoided. And he'll be coming from Stafford any day now.'

‘To find he has to coffin his father’s body and take it home for burial,’ said Hugh ruefully.

‘To find he’s now lord of Bosiet,’ said Cadfael. ‘That’s the reverse of the coin. Who knows which side up it will look to him?’

‘You’re grown very cynical, old friend,’ remarked Hugh, wryly smiling.

‘I’m thinking,’ Cadfael owned, ‘of reasons why men do murder. Greed is one, and might be spawned in a son, waiting impatiently for his inheritance. Hate is another, and a misused servant might entertain it willingly if chance offered. But there are other and stranger reasons, no doubt, like a simple taste for thieving, and a disposition to make sure the victim never blabs. A pity, Hugh, a great pity there should be so much hurrying on of death, when it’s bound to reach every man in its own good time.’

By the time they emerged on to the highroad at Wroxeter the sun was well up, and the mist clearing from its face, though the fields still swam in pearly vapour. They made good speed from there along the road to Shrewsbury, and rode in at the gatehouse after the end of High Mass, when the brothers were dispersing to their work until the hour of the midday meal.

‘The lord abbot’s been asking after you,’ said the porter, coming out from his lodge at sight of them. ‘He’s in his parlour, and the prior with him, and asks that you’ll join him there.’

They left their horses to the grooms, and went at once to the abbot’s lodging. In the panelled parlour Radulfus looked up from his desk, and Prior Robert, very erect and austere on a bench beside the window, looked down his nose with a marked suggestion of disapproval and withdrawal. The complexities of law and murder and manhunt had no business to intrude into the monastic domain, and he deplored the necessity to recognise their existence, and the very processes of dealing with them when they did force a breach in the wall. Close to his elbow, unobtrusive in his shadow, stood Brother Jerome, his narrow shoulders hunched, thin lips drawn tight, pale hands folded in his sleeves, the image of virtue assailed and bearing the cross with humility. There was always a strong element of complacency in Jerome’s humility, but this time there was also a faintly defensive quality, as though his rightness had somehow, if only by implication, been questioned.

‘Ah, you are back!’ said Radulfus. ‘You have not brought back the body of our guest so quickly?’

'No, Father, not yet, they will be following us, but on foot it will take some time. It is just as Brother Cadfael reported it to you in the night. The man was stabbed in the back, probably as he was leading his horse, the path there being narrow and overgrown. You will know already that his saddle-roll was cut loose and stolen. By what Brother Cadfael observed of the body when he found it, the thing must have been done about the time of Compline, perhaps a little before. There's nothing to show by whom. By the hour, he must have been on his way back here to your guest hall. By the way he faced as he fell, also, for the body was not moved, or his ring would have been taken, and he still wears it. But as to where he had been in those parts, there's no knowing.'

'I think,' said the abbot, 'we have something to show on that head. Brother Jerome here will tell you what he has now told to Prior Robert and me.'

Jerome was usually only too ready to hear his own voice, whether in sermon, homily or reproof, but it was noticeable that this time he was assembling his words with more than normal care.

'The man was a guest and an upright citizen,' he said, 'and had told us at chapter that he was pursuing an offender against the law, one who had committed assault against the person of his steward and done him grievous harm, and then absconded from his master. I took thought afterwards that there was indeed one newcomer in these parts who might well be the man he sought, and I considered it the duty of every one of us to help the cause of justice and law. So I spoke to the lord of Bosiet. I told him that the young man who serves the hermit Cuthred, and who came here with him only a few weeks ago, does answer to the description he gave of his runaway villein Brand, though he calls himself Hyacinth. He is of the right age, his colouring as his master described it. And no one here knows anything about him. I thought it only right to tell him the truth. If the young man proved not to be Brand, there was no harm to him.'

'And you told him, I believe,' said the abbot neutrally, 'how to get to the hermit's cell, where he could find this young man?'

'I did, Father, as was my duty.'

'And he at once set off to ride to that place.'

'Yes, Father. He had sent his groom on an errand into the town, he was obliged to saddle up for himself, but he did not wish to wait, since most of the day was gone.'

'I have spoken to the groom Warin, since we learned of his master's death,' said the abbot, looking up at Hugh. 'He was sent to enquire after any craftsman in fine leather-work in Shrewsbury, for it seems that was the young man's craft also, and Bosiet thought he might have tried to get work within the borough among those who could use his skills. There is no blame can attach to the servant, by the time he returned his master was long gone. His errand could not wait, it seems, until morning.' His voice was measured and considered, with no inflection of approval or disapproval. 'That solves, I think, the problem of where he had been.'

'And where I must follow him,' said Hugh, enlightened. 'I'm obliged to you, Father, for pointing me the next step of the road. If he did indeed talk to Cuthred, at least we may learn what passed, and whether he got the answer he wanted – though plainly he was returning alone. Had he been bringing a captive villein with him, he would hardly have left him with free hands and a dagger about him. With your permission, Father, I'll keep Brother Cadfael with me as witness, rather than take men-at-arms to a hermitage.'

'Do so,' said the abbot willingly. 'This unfortunate man was a guest of our house, and we owe him every effort which may lead to the capture of his murderer. And every proper rite and service that can still be paid to his corpse. Robert, will you see to it that the body is reverently received when it comes? And Brother Jerome, you may assist. Your zeal to be of help to him should not be frustrated. You shall keep a night vigil with him in prayers for his soul.'

So there would be two lying side by side in the mortuary chapel tonight, Cadfael thought as they went out together from the parlour: the old man who had closed a long life as gently as a spent flower sheds its petals, and the lord of lands taken abruptly in his malice and hatred, with no warning, and no time to make his peace with man or God. Drogo Bosiet's soul would be in need of all the prayers it could get.

'And has it yet entered your mind,' asked Hugh abruptly, as they rode out along the Foregate for the second time, 'that Brother Jerome in his zeal for justice may have helped Bosiet to his death?'

If it had, Cadfael was not yet minded to entertain the thought. 'He was on his way back,' he said cautiously, 'and empty-handed. It argues that he was disappointed. The boy is not his lost villein.'

'It could as well argue that he is, and saw his doom bearing down on him in time to vanish. How then? He's been in the woods there now long enough to know his way about. How if he was the hand that held the dagger?'

No denying that it was a possibility. Who could have better reason for slipping a knife into Drogo Bosiet's back than the lad he meant to drag back to his own manor court, flay first, and exploit afterwards lifelong? 'It's what will be said,' agreed Cadfael sombrely. 'Unless we find Cuthred and his boy sitting peacefully at home minding their own business and meddling with no one else's. Small use guessing until we hear what happened there.'

They approached the projecting tongue of Eaton land by the same path Drogo had used, and saw the small clearing in thick woodland open before them almost suddenly, as he had seen it, but in full daylight, while he had come in early dusk. Muted sunlight filtering through the branches turned the sombre grey of the stone hut to dull gold. The low pales of the fence that marked out the garden were set far apart, a mere sketched boundary, no bar to beast or man, and the door of the hut stood wide open, so that they saw through into the inner room where the constant lamp on the stone altar showed tiny and dim as a single spark, almost quenched by the light falling from the tiny shutterless window above. Saint Cuthred's cell, it seemed, stood wide open to all who came.

A part of the enclosed garden was still wild, though the grass and herbage had been cut, and there the hermit himself was at work with mattock and spade, heaving up the matted clods and turning the soil below as he cleared it. They watched him at it as they approached, inexpert but dogged and patient, plainly unused to handling such tools or stooping to such labours as should have fallen to Hyacinth. Who, by the same token, was nowhere to be seen.

A tall man, the hermit, long-legged, long-bodied, lean and straight, his coarse dark habit kilted to his knees, and the cowl flung back on his shoulders. He saw them coming and straightened up from his labours with the mattock still in his hands, and showed them a strong, fleshless face, olive-skinned and deep-eyed, framed in a thick bush of dark hair and beard. He looked from one to the other of them, and acknowledged Hugh's reverence with a deep inclination of his head, without lowering his eyes.

'If you errand is to Cuthred the hermit,' he said in a deep

and resonant voice and with assured authority, 'come in and welcome. I am he.' And to Cadfael, after studying his face for a moment: 'I think I saw you at Eaton when the lord Richard was buried. You are a brother of Shrewsbury.'

'I am,' said Cadfael. 'I was there in the boy's escort. And this is Hugh Beringar, sheriff of this shire.'

'The lord sheriff does me honour,' said Cuthred. 'Will you enter my cell?' And he loosed his frayed rope girdle and shook down the skirt of his habit to his feet, and led the way within. The thick tangle of his hair brushed the stone above the doorway as he entered. He stood a good head taller than either of his visitors.

In the dim living room there was one narrow window that let in the afternoon light, and a small stir of breeze that brought in the scent of mown herbage and moist autumn leaves. Through the doorless opening into the chapel within they saw all that Drogo had seen, the stone slab of the altar with its carved casket, the silver cross and candlesticks, and the open breviary lying before the small spark of the lamp. The hermit followed Hugh's glance to the open book and, entering, closed it reverently, and laid it with loving care in accurate alignment with the forward edge of the reliquary. The fine gilt ornament and delicate tooling of the leather binding gleamed in the small light of the lamp.

'And how may I be of service to the lord sheriff?' asked Cuthred, his face still turned towards the altar.

'I need to ask you some few questions,' said Hugh with deliberation, 'in the matter of a murdered man.'

That brought the lofty head round in haste, staring aghast and astonished. 'Murdered? Here and now? I know of none. Say plainly what you mean, my lord.'

'Last night a certain Drogo Bosiet, a guest at the abbey, set out to visit you, at the prompting of one of the brothers. He came here in search of a runaway villein, a young man of about twenty years, and his intent was to view your boy Hyacinth, being a stranger and of the right age and kind, and see whether he is or is not the bondman who ran away from Bosiet. Did he ever reach you? By the time he had ridden this far it would already be evening.'

'Why, yes, such a man did come,' said Cuthred at once, 'though I did not ask his name. But what has this to do with murder? A murdered man, you said.'

'This same Drogo Bosiet, on his way back towards the town

and the abbey, was stabbed in the back and left beside the track, a mile or more from here. Brother Cadfael found him dead and his horse wandering loose, last night in the full dark.'

The hermit's deep-set eyes, flaring reddish in their gaunt sockets, flashed from one face to the other in incredulous questioning. 'Hard to believe, that there could be cutthroats and masterless men here, in this well-farmed, well-managed country – within your writ, my lord, and so near the town. Can this be what it seems, or is there worse behind it? Was the man robbed?'

'He was, of his saddle-roll, whatever that may have held. But not of his ring, not of his gown. What was done was done in haste.'

'Masterless men would have stripped him naked,' said Cuthred with certainty. 'I do not believe this forest is shelter for outlaws. This is some very different matter.'

'When he came to you,' said Hugh, 'what did he have to say? And what followed?'

'He came when I was saying Vespers, here in the chapel. He entered and said that he had come to see the boy who runs my errands, and that I might find I had been deceived into taking a villain into my employ. For he was seeking a runaway serf, and had been told that there was one here of the right age, newly come and a stranger to all, who might well be his man. He told me whence he came, and in what direction he had reason to believe his fugitive had fled. These things, and the time, fitted all too well for my peace of mind with the time and place where first I met and pitied Hyacinth. But it was not put to the test,' said Cuthred simply. 'The boy was not here. A good hour earlier I had sent him on an errand to Eaton. He did not come back. He has not come back even today. Now I doubt much if he ever will.'

'You do believe,' said Hugh, 'that he is this Brand.'

'I cannot judge. But I saw that he well might be. And when he failed to come back to me last night, then I felt it must be so. It is no part of my duty to give up any man to retribution, that is God's business. I was glad I could not say yes or no, and glad he was not here to be seen.'

'But if he had simply got wind of the search for him, and kept out of the way,' said Cadfael, 'he would have come back to you by now. The man who hunted him had gone away empty-handed, and if another visit threatened, he could do as much again, provided you did not betray him. Where else would he be so safe as with a holy hermit? But still he has not come.'

'But now you tell me,' said Cuthred gravely, 'that his master is dead – if this man was indeed his lord. Dead and murdered! Say that my servant Hyacinth had got wind of Bosiet's coming, and did more than absent himself. Say that he thought it better to lie in ambush and end the search for him once for all! No, I do not think now that I shall ever see Hyacinth again. Wales is not far, and even an incomer without a kinship can find service there, though upon hard terms. No, he will not come back. He will never come back.'

It was a strange moment for Cadfael's mind to wander, as though some corner of his consciousness had made even more of one remembered moment than he had realised, for he found himself thinking suddenly of Annet coming into her father's house radiant and roused and mysterious, with an oak leaf in her disordered hair. A little flushed and breathing as though she had been running. And past the hour of Compline, at a time when surely Drogo of Bosiet already lay dead more than a mile away on the track to Shrewsbury. True, Annet had gone out dutifully to shut up the hens and the cow for the night, but she had been a very long time about it, and come back with the high colour and triumphant eyes of a girl returning from her lover. And had she not made occasion to say a good word for Hyacinth, and taken pleasure in hearing her father praise him?

'How did you come upon this young man in the first place?' Hugh was asking. 'And why did you take him into your service?'

'I was on my way from St Edmundsbury, by way of the Augustinian canons at Cambridge, and I lodged two nights over at the Cluniac priory in Northampton. He was among the beggars at the gate. Though he was able-bodied and young he was also shabby and unkempt as if he had been living wild. He told me his father had been dispossessed and was dead, and he had no kin left and no work, and out of compassion I clothed him and took him as my servant. Otherwise he would surely have sunk into thieving and banditry in order to live. And he has been quick and obedient to me, and I thought him grateful, and so perhaps he truly was. But now it may all be in vain.'

'And when was this that you met him there?'

'In the last days of September. I cannot be sure of the exact day.'

Time and place fitted all too well. 'I see I have a manhunt on my hands,' said Hugh wryly, 'and I'd best be getting back to Shrewsbury, and setting on the hounds at once. For whether the lad's a murderer or no, I've no choice now but to find and take him.'

Chapter Seven

IT HAD always been brother Jerome's contention, frequently and vociferously expressed, that Brother Paul exercised far too slack an authority over his young charges, both the novices and the children. It was Paul's way to make his supervision of their days as unobtrusive as possible except when actually teaching, though he was prompt to appear if any of them needed or wanted him. But such routine matters as their ablutions, their orderly behaviour at meals, and their retiring at night and rising in the morning were left to their good consciences and to the sound habits of cleanliness and punctuality they had been taught. Brother Jerome was convinced that no boy under sixteen could be trusted to keep any rule, and that even those who had reached that mature age still had more of the devil in them than of the angels. He would have watched and hounded and corrected their every movement, had he been master of the boys, and made a great deal more use of punishments than ever Paul could be brought to contemplate. It was pleasure to him to be able to say, with truth, that he had always prophesied disaster from such lax stewardship.

Three schoolboys and nine novices, in a range of ages from nine years up to seventeen, are quite enough active youngsters to satisfy the casual eye at breakfast, unless someone has reason to count them, and discover that they fall one short of the right tally. Probably Jerome would have counted them on every occasion, certain that sooner or later there would be defaulters. Brother Paul did not count. And as he was needed at chapter and afterwards that day on specific business concerning his office, he had confided the morning's schooling to the most responsible of the novices, another policy which Jerome deplored as ruinous to discipline. In church the small fry occupied such insignificant places that one more or less would never be noticed. So it was only late in the afternoon, when Paul mustered his flock again into the schoolroom, and separated the class of novices from the younger boys, that the absence of Richard was at last manifest.

Even then Paul was not at first alarmed or disturbed. The child was simply loitering somewhere, forgetful of time, and would appear at a run at any moment. But time slid by and Richard did not come. Questioned, the three boys remaining shuffled their feet uneasily, shifted a little closer together to have the reassurance of shoulder against shoulder, shook their heads wordlessly, and evaded looking Brother Paul in the eye. The youngest in particular looked less than happy, but they volunteered nothing, which merely convinced Paul that Richard was deliberately playing truant, that they were well aware of it and disapproved but would not let out one word to betray him. That he refrained from threatening them with dire penalties for such refractory silence would only have confirmed Jerome in his black disapproval of such an attitude.

Jerome encouraged tale-bearers. Paul had a sneaking sympathy with the sinful solidarity that would invite penalties to fall on its own head rather than betray a companion. He merely stated firmly that Richard should be called to account for his behaviour later and pay the penalty of his foolishness, and proceeded with the lesson. But he was increasingly aware of his pupils' inattention and uneasiness, and the guilty glances they slid sidelong at one another over their letters. By the time they were dismissed he felt that the youngest, at any rate, was on the verge of blurting out whatever he knew, and his very distress argued that there was more behind this defection than the mere capricious cutting of a class.

Paul called the child back as they were leaving, half-gratefully, half-fearfully. 'Edwin, come here to me!'

Understandably, the other two fled, certain now that the sky was about to fall on them, and in haste to avoid the first shock, whatever followed later. Edwin halted, turned, and slowly trailed his way back across the room, his eyes lowered to the small feet he was dragging reluctantly along the boards of the floor. He stood before Brother Paul, and trembled. One knee was still bandaged, and the linen had slipped awry. Without thinking, Paul unwound it and made it neat again.

'Edwin, what is it you know about Richard? Where is he?'

The child gulped out with utter conviction: 'I don't *know*!' and burst into tears. Paul drew him close and let him bury his nose in a long-suffering shoulder.

'Tell me! When did you last see him? When did he go?'

Edwin sobbed inarticulately into the rough woollen folds, until Paul held him off and peered into the smudged and woeful face. 'Come! Tell me everything you know.'

And it came out in a flood, between hectic sniffs and sobs. 'It was yesterday, after Vespers. I saw him, he took his pony and rode out along the Foregate. I thought he'd come back, but he didn't, and we were frightened – We didn't want him to be caught, he'd be in such terrible trouble – We didn't want to tell, we thought he'd come back and no one need know . . .'

'Do you tell me,' demanded Paul, appalled and for once sounding formidable, 'that he did not sleep here in his bed last night? That he's been gone since yesterday and not a word said?'

A fresh burst of despairing tears distorted Edwin's round flushed face, and his violently nodding head admitted the impeachment.

'And all of you knew this? You three? Did you never think that he might be hurt somewhere, or in danger? Would he stay out all night willingly? Oh, child, why did you not tell me? All this time we've lost!' But the boy was frightened enough already, there was nothing to be done with him but hush and reassure and comfort him, where reassurance and comfort were very hard to find. 'Now, tell me – you saw him go, mounted. After Vespers? Did he not say what he intended?'

Edwin, very drearily, gathered what sense he had left and fumbled out the rest of it. 'He came too late for Vespers. We were down on the Gaye, by the river, he didn't want to come in, and when he did run after us it was too late. I think he waited to try and slip in with us when we came out of church, but Brother Jerome was standing talking to – to that man, the one who . . .'

He began to whimper again, recalling what he should not have seen, but of course had, the bearers of the litter coming in at the gatehouse, the bulky body motionless, the powerful face covered. 'I waited at the school door,' whispered the tearful voice, 'and I saw Richard come running out and down to the stables, and then he came back with his pony, and led it out at the gate in a great hurry, and rode away. And that's all I know. I thought he would soon come back,' he wailed hopelessly. 'We didn't want to get him into trouble . . .'

If they had recoiled from doing that, they had certainly given him ample time and scope to get himself into trouble, deeper than any disloyalty of theirs might have plunged him. Brother Paul resignedly shook and patted his penitent into relative calm.

'You have been very wrong and foolish, and if you're in disgrace it's no more than you deserve. But answer everything truthfully now, and we'll find Richard safe and sound. Go now, at once, and find the other two, and the three of you wait here until you are sent for.'

And Paul was off at a shaken run to take the bad news first to Prior Robert and then to the abbot, and then to confirm that the pony Dame Dionisia had sent as bait to her grandson was indeed gone from his stall. And there was great clamour and running about and turning grange court and barns and guest halls inside out, in case the culprit had not, after all deserted the enclave, or for sounder reasons had returned to it furtively, to try and conceal the fact that he had ever left it. The wretched schoolboys, tongue-lashed by Prior Robert and threatened with worse when anyone had time to perform it, cowered shivering and reduced to tears by the enormity of what had seemed to them good intentions, and having survived the first storm of recriminations, settled down stoically to endure the rest supperless and outcast. Not even Brother Paul had time to offer them any further reassuring words, he was too busy searching through the complex recesses of the mill and nearer alleys of the Foregate.

Into this frenzy of alarm and activity Cadfael came riding in the early evening, after parting from Hugh at the gate. This very night there would be sergeants out dragging the woods from Eyton westward for the fugitive who might or might not be Brand, but must at all costs be captured. Hugh was no fonder of manhunts than was Cadfael, and many a misused serf had been driven at last to flight and outlawry, but murder was murder, and the law could not stomach it. Guilty or innocent, the youth Hyacinth would have to be found. Cadfael dismounted at the gatehouse with his mind full of one vanished youngster, to be met by the spectacle of agitated brothers running hither and thither among all the monastic buildings in search of a second one. While he was gaping in amazement at the sight, Brother Paul came bearing down upon him breathless and hopeful.

'Cadfael, you've been in the forest. You haven't seen hide or hair of young Richard, have you? I'm beginning to think he must have run home . . .'

'The last place he'd be likely to go,' said Cadfael reasonably, 'while he's wary of his grandmother's intentions. Why? Do you tell me you've mislaid the imp?'

'He's gone – gone since last night, and we never knew it until an hour ago.' Paul poured out the dismal story in a cascade of guilt and remorse and anxiety. 'I am to blame! I have failed in my duty, been too complacent, trusted them too far . . . But why should he run away? He was happy enough. He never showed signs . . .'

'Doubtless he had his reasons,' said Cadfael, scrubbing thoughtfully at his blunt brown nose. 'But back to the lady? I doubt it! No, if he went off in such haste it was something new and urgent that sent him running. Last night after Vespers, you said?'

'Edwin tells me Richard dawdled too long by the river, and came too late for Vespers, and must have been lurking in the cloister to slip in among the rest of the boys when they came out. But he could not do it because Jerome stood there in the archway, waiting to speak to Bosiet, who had attended among the guests. But when Edwin looked back he saw Richard come running out down to the stables, and then out at the gate in a hurry.'

'Did he so!' said Cadfael, enlightened. 'And where was Jerome, then, and Bosiet, that the boy was able to make off undetected?' But he did not wait for an answer. 'No, never trouble to guess. We already know what they had to talk about, between the two of them – a small matter, and private. Jerome wanted no other audience, but it seems he had one of whom he knew nothing. Paul, I must leave you to your hunt a little while longer, and ride after Hugh Beringar. He's already committed to a search for one vanished lad, he may as well make it for two, and drag the coverts but once.'

Hugh, overtaken under the arch of the town gate, reined in abruptly at the news, and turned to stare meditatively at Cadfael. 'So you think that's the way of it!' he said and whistled. 'Why should he care about a young fellow he's barely seen and never spoken to? Or have you reason to think the two of them have had their heads together?'

'No, none that I know of. Nothing but the timing of it, but that links the pair closely enough. Not much doubt what Richard overheard, and none that it sent him hotfoot on some urgent errand. And before Bosiet can get to the hermitage, Hyacinth vanishes.'

'And so does Richard!' Hugh's black brows drew together, frowning over the implications. 'Do you tell me if I find the one I shall found both?'

'No, that I gravely doubt. The boy surely meant to be back in the fold before bedtime, and all innocence. He's no fool, and he has no reason to want to leave us. But all the more reason we should be anxious about him now. He would be back with us, surely, if something had not prevented. Whether his pony's thrown him somewhere, and he's hurt, or lost – or whether . . . They're wondering if he's run home to Eaton, but that's rankly impossible. He never would.'

Hugh had grasped the unspoken suggestion which Cadfael himself had hardly had time to contemplate. 'No, but he might be taken there! And by God, so he might! If some of Dionisia's people happened on him alone in the woods, they'd know how to please their lady. Oh, I know the household there are Richard's people, not hers, but there must be one or two among them would take the chance of present favours if it offered. Cadfael, old friend,' said Hugh heartily, 'you go back to your workshop and leave Eaton to me. As soon as I've set my men on the hunt, yes, for both, I'll go myself to Eaton and see what the lady has to say for herself. If she baulks at letting me turn her manor inside out for the one lad, I shall know she has the other hidden away somewhere about the place, and I can force her hand. If Richard's there, I'll have him out for you by tomorrow, and back in Brother Paul's arms,' promised Hugh buoyantly. 'Even if it costs the poor imp a whipping,' he reflected with a sympathetic grin, 'he may find that preferable to being married off on his grandmother's terms. At least the sting doesn't last so long.'

Which was a very perverse blasphemy against marriage, Cadfael thought and said, coming from one who had such excellent reason to consider himself blessed in his wife and proud of his son. Hugh had wheeled his horse towards the steep slope of the Wyle, but he slanted a smiling glance back over his shoulder.

'Come up to the house with me now, and complain of me to Aline. Keep her company while I'm off to the castle to start the hunt.'

And the prospect of sitting for an hour or so in Aline's company, and playing with his godson Giles, now approaching three years old, was tempting, but Cadfael shook his head, reluctantly but resignedly. 'No, I'd best be going back. We'll all be busy hunting our own coverts and asking along the Foregate until dark. There's no certainty where he'll be, we dare miss no corner. But God speed your search, Hugh, for it's more likely than ours.'

He walked his horse back over the bridge towards the abbey with a slack rein, suddenly aware he had ridden far enough for one day, and looked forward with positive need to the stillness and soul's quiet of the holy office, and the vast enclosing sanctuary of the church. The thorough search of the forest must be left to Hugh and his officers. No point even in spending time and grief now wondering where the boy would spend the coming night, though an extra prayer for him would not come amiss. And tomorrow, thought Cadfael, I'll go and visit Eilmund, and take him his crutches, and keep my eyes open on the way. Two missing lads to search for. Find one, find both? No, that was too much to hope for. But if he found one, he might also be a long step forward towards finding the other.

There was a newly-arrived guest standing at the foot of the steps that led to up to the door of the guest hall, watching with contained interest the continuing bustle of a search which had now lost its frenetic aspect and settled down grimly into the thorough inspection of every corner of the enclave, besides the parties that were out enquiring along the Foregate. The obsessed activity around him only made his composed stillness the more striking, though his appearance otherwise was ordinary enough. His figure was compact and trim, his bearing modest, and his elderly but well-cared-for boots, dark chausses and good plain cotte cut short below the knee, where the common riding gear of all but the highest and the lowest who travelled the roads. He could as well have been a baron's sub-tenant on his lord's business as a prosperous merchant or a minor nobleman on his own. Cadfael noticed him as soon as he dismounted at the gate. The porter came out from his lodge to plump himself down on the stone bench outside with a gusty sigh, blowing out his russet cheeks in mild exasperation.

'No sign of the boy, then?' said Cadfael though plainly expecting none.

'No, nor likely to be, not within here, seeing he went off pony and all. But make sure first here at home, they say. They're even talking of dragging the mill-pond. Folly! What would he be doing by the pool, when he went off at a trot along the Foregate – that we do know. Besides, he'll never drown, he swims like a fish. No, he's well away out of our reach, whatever trouble he's got himself into. But they must needs turn out all the straw in the lofts and prod through the stable litter. You'd best hurry and keep a sharp eye on your workshop, or they'll be turning that inside out.'

Cadfael was watching the quiet dark figure by the guest hall. 'Who's the newcomer?'

'One Rafe of Coventry. A falconer to the earl of Warwick. He has dealings with Gwynedd for young birds to train, so Brother Denis tells me. He came not a quarter of an hour since.'

'I took him at first to be Bosiet's son,' said Cadfael, 'but I see he's too old – more the father's own generation.'

'So did I take him for the son. I've been keeping a sharp watch for him, for someone has to tell him what's waiting for him here, and I'd rather it was Prior Robert than take it on myself.'

'I like to see a man,' said Cadfael appreciatively, his eyes still on the stranger, 'who can stand stock still in the middle of other people's turmoil, and ask no questions. Ah, well, I'd better get this fellow unsaddled and into his stall, he's had a good day's exercise with all this coming and going. And so have I.'

And tomorrow, he thought, leading the horse at a leisurely walk down the length of the great court towards the stable yard, I must be off again. I may be astray, but at least let's put it to the test.

He passed close to where Rafe of Coventry stood, passively interested in the bustle for which he asked no explanation, and thinking his own thoughts. At the sound of hooves pacing slowly on the cobbles he turned his head, and meeting Cadfael's eyes by chance, gave him the brief thaw of a smile and a nod by way of greeting. A strong but uncommunicative face he showed, broad across brow and cheekbones, with a close-trimmed brown beard and wide-set, steady brown eyes, wrinkled at the corner as if he lived chiefly in the open, and was accustomed to peering across distance.

'You're bound for the stables, Brother? Be my guide there. No reflection on your grooms, but I like to see my own beast cared for.'

'So do I,' said Cadfael warmly, checking to let the stranger fall into step beside him. 'It's a lifetime's habit. If you learn it young you never lose it.' They matched strides neatly, being of the same modest stature. In the stable yard an abbey groom was rubbing down a tall chestnut horse with a white blaze down his forehead, and hissing gently and contentedly to him as he worked.

'Yours?' said Cadfael, eyeing the beast appreciatively.

'Mine,' said Rafe of Coventry briefly, and himself took the cloth from the groom's hand. 'My thanks, friend! I'll take him myself now. Where may I stable him?' And he inspected the stall the groom indicated, with a long, comprehensive glance round and a nod of satisfaction. 'You keep a good stable here, Brother, I see. No offence that I prefer to do my own grooming. Travellers are not always so well provided, and as you said, it's habit.'

'You travel alone?' said Cadfael, busy unsaddling but with a sharp eye on his companion all the same. The belt that circled Rafe's hips was made to carry sword and dagger. No doubt he had shed both in the guest hall with his cloak and gear. A falconer is not easily fitted into a category where travel is concerned. A merchant would have had at least one able-bodied servant with him for protection, probably more. A soldier would be self-sufficient, as this man chose to be, and carry the means of protecting himself.

'I travel fast,' said Rafe simply. 'Numbers drag. If a man depends only on himself, there's no one can let him fall.'

'You've ridden far?'

'From Warwick.' A man of few words and no curiosity, this falconer of the earl's. Or did that quite hold good? Concerning the search for the lost boy he showed no disposition to ask questions, but he was taking a measured interest in the stables and the horses they held. Even after he had satisfied himself of his own beast's welfare, he still stood looking round him at the rest with a keen professional eye. The mules and the working horses he passed by, but halted at the pale roan that had belonged to Drogo Bosiet. That was understandable enough in a lover of good horseflesh, for the roan was a handsome animal and clearly from stock of excellent quality.

'Can your house afford such bloodstock?' He passed a hand approvingly over the glossy shoulder and stroked between the pricked ears. 'Or does this fellow belong to a guest?'

'He did,' said Cadfael, himself sparing of words.

'He *did*? How is that?' Rafe had turned alertly to stare, and in the unrevealing face the eyes were sharp and intent.

'The man who owned him is dead. He's lying in our mortuary chapel this moment.' The old brother had gone to his rest in the cemetery that same morning, Drogo had the chapel to himself now.

'What kind of man was that? And how did he die?' On this head he had questions enough to ask, startled out of his detachment and indifference.

'We found him dead in the forest, a few miles from here, with a knife wound in his back. And robbed.' Cadfael was never quite sure why he himself had become so reticent at this point, and why, for instance, he did not simply name the dead man. And had his companion persisted, as would surely have been natural enough, he would have answered freely. But there the questioning stopped. Rafe shrugged off the implied perils of riding alone in the forests of the border shires, and closed the low door of the stall on his contented horse.

'I'll bear it in mind. Go well armed, I say, or keep to the highroads.'

He dusted his hands and turned towards the gateway of the yard. 'Well, I'll go and make ready for supper.' And he was off at a purposeful walk, but not immediately towards the guest hall. Instead, he crossed to the archway of the cloister, and entered there. Cadfael found something so significant in that arrow-straight progress towards the church that he followed, candidly curious and officiously helpful, and finding Rafe of Coventry standing hesitant by the parish altar, looking round him at the multiplicity of chapels contained in transepts and chevet, directed him with blunt simplicity to the one he was looking for.

'Through here. The arch is low, but you're my build, no need to stoop your head.'

Rafe made no effort to disguise or disclaim his purpose, or to reject Cadfael's company. He gave him one calm, considering look, nodded his acknowledgements, and followed. And in the stony chill and dimming light of the chapel he crossed at once to the bier where Drogo Bosiet's body lay reverently covered, with candles burning at head and feet, and lifted the cloth from the dead face.

Very briefly he studied the fixed and pallid features, and again covered them, and the movements of his hands as they replaced the cloth had lost their urgency and tension. He had time even for simple human awe at the presence of death.

'You don't, by any chance, know him?' asked Cadfael.

'No, I never saw him before. God rest his soul!' And Rafe straightened up from stooping over the bier, and drew a liberating breath. Whatever his interest in the body had been, it was over.

'A man of property, by the name of Drogo Bosiet, from Northamptonshire. His son is expected here any day now.'

'Do you tell me so? A bleak coming that will be for him.' But the words he used now were coming from the surface of his mind only, and answers concerned him scarcely at all. 'Have you many guests at this season? Of my own years and condition, perhaps? I should enjoy a game of chess in the evening, if I can find a partner.'

If he had lost interest in Drogo Bosiet, it seemed he was still concerned to know of any others who might have come here as travellers. Any of his own years and condition!

'Brother Denis could give you a match,' said Cadfael, deliberately obtuse. 'No, it's a quiet time with us. You'll find the hall half-empty.' They were approaching the steps of the guest hall, side by side and easy together, and the late afternoon light, overcast and still, was beginning to dim into the dove grey of evening.

'This man who was struck down in the forest,' said Rafe of Coventry. 'Your sheriff will surely have the hounds out after an outlaw so near the town. Is there suspicion of any man for the deed?'

'There is,' said Cadfael, 'though there's no certainty. A newcomer in these parts, who's missing from his master's service since the attack.' And he added, innocently probing without seeming to probe: 'A young fellow he is, maybe twenty years old . . .'

Not of Rafe's years or condition, no! And of no interest to him, for he merely nodded his acceptance of the information, and by the indifference of his face as promptly discarded it. 'Well, God speed their hunting!' he said, dismissing Hyacinth's guilt or innocence as irrelevant to whatever he had on that closed and armoured mind of his.

At the foot of the guest hall steps he turned in, surely to examine, thought Cadfael, every man of middle years who would come to supper in hall. Looking for one in particular? Whose name, since he did not ask for names, would be unhelpful, because false? One, at any rate, who was not Drogo Bosiet of Northamptonshire!

Chapter Eight

HUGH CAME to the manor of Eaton early in the morning, with six mounted men at his back, and a dozen more deployed behind him between the river and the highroad, to sweep the whole expanse of field and forest from Wroxeter to Eyton and beyond. For a fugitive murderer they might have to turn the hunt westward, but Richard must surely be somewhere here in this region, if he had indeed set out to warn Hyacinth of the vengeance bearing down on him. Hugh's party had followed the direct road from the Abbey Foregate to Wroxeter, an open, fast track, and thence by the most direct path into the forest, to Cuthred's cell, where Richard would have expected to find Hyacinth. By young Edwin's account he had been only a few minutes ahead of Bosiet, he would have made all haste and taken the shortest and fastest way. But he had never reached the hermitage.

'The boy Richard?' said the hermit, astonished. 'You did not ask me of him yesterday, only of the man. No, Richard did not come. I remember the young lord well, God grant no harm has come to him! I did not know he was lost.'

'And you've seen nothing of him since? It's two nights now he's been gone.'

'No, I have not seen him. My doors are always open, even by night,' said Cuthred, 'and I am always here if any man needs me. Had the child been in any peril or distress within reach of me, he would surely have come running here. But I have not seen him.'

It was simple truth that both doors stood wide, and the sparse furnishings of both living room and chapel were clear to view.

'If you should get any word of him,' said Hugh, 'send to me, or to the abbey, or if you should see my men drawing these coverts round you – as you will – give them the message.'

'I will do so,' said Cuthred gravely, and stood at the open gateway of his little garden to watch them ride away towards Eaton.

John of Longwood came striding out from one of the long barns lining the stockade, as soon as he heard the dull drumming of many hooves on the beaten earth of the yard. His bare arms and balding crown were the glossy brown of oak timber, for he spent most of his time out and active in all weathers, and there was no task about the holding to which he could not turn his hand. He stared at the sight of Hugh's men riding in purposefully at the gate, but in wonder and curiosity rather than consternation, and came readily to meet them.

'Well, my lord, what's afoot with you so early?' He had already taken in the significance of their array. No hounds, no hawks, but steel by their sides, and two of them archers shouldering bows. This was another kind of hunt. 'We've had no trouble hereabouts. What's the word from Shrewsbury?'

'We're looking for two defaulters,' said Hugh briskly. 'Don't tell me you haven't heard we have a man murdered between here and the town, two nights ago. And the hermit's boy is fled, and suspect of being the man's runaway villein, with good reason to make away with him and run for the second time. That's the one quarry we're after.'

'Oh, ay, we'd heard about him,' said John readily, 'but I doubt he's a good few miles from here by this time. We've not seen hide or hair of him since late that afternoon, when he was here to fetch some honey cakes our dame had for Cuthred. She was not best pleased with him, neither, I heard her scolding. And for sure he was an impudent rogue. But the start he's had, I fancy you won't see him again. I never saw him carry steel, though,' said John by way of a fair-minded afterthought, and frowned over the resultant doubt. 'There's a chance at least that some other put an end to his master. The threat to haul him back to villeinage would be enough to make the lad take to his heels, the faster the better. In unknown country his lord would be hard put to it to track him down. No need, surely, to kill him. Small inducement to stay and take the risk.'

'The fellow's neither convicted nor charged yet,' said Hugh, 'nor can be until he's taken. But neither can he be cleared until then. And either way I want him. But we're after another runaway, too, John. Your lady's grandson, Richard, rode out of the abbey precinct that same evening, and hasn't come back.'

'The young lord!' echoed John, stricken open-mouthed with astonishment and consternation. 'Two nights gone, and only now we get to hear of it? God help us, she'll run mad! What happened? Who fetched the lad away?'

'No one fetched him. He up and saddled his pony and off he went, alone, of his own will. And what's befallen him since nobody knows. And since one of the pair I'm seeking may be a murderer, I'm leaving no barn unransacked and no house unvisited, and with orders to every man to keep a sharp lookout for Richard, too. Granted you're a good steward, John, not even you can know what mouse has crept into every byre and sheep fold and storehouse on the manor of Eaton. And that's what I mean to know, here and everywhere between here and Shrewsbury. Go in and tell Dame Dionisia I'm asking to speak with her.'

John shook his head helplessly, and went. Hugh dismounted, and advanced to the foot of the stairs that led up to the hall door, above the low undercroft, waiting to see how Dionisia would bear herself when she emerged from the broad doorway above. If she really had not heard of the boy's disappearance until this moment, when her steward would certainly tell her, he could expect a fury, fuelled all the more by genuine dismay and grief. If she had, then she had had time to prepare herself to present a fury, but even so she might let slip something that would betray her. As for John, his honesty was patent. If she had the boy hidden away, John had had no part in it. He was not an instrument she would have used for such a purpose, for he was stubbornly determined to be Richard's steward rather than hers.

She came surging out from the shadow of the doorway, blue skirts billowing, imperious eyes smouldering.

'What's this I hear, my lord? It surely cannot be true! Richard missing?'

'It is true, madam,' said Hugh watching her intently, and undisturbed by the fact of having to look up to do it, as indeed he would have had to do even if she had come darting down the steps to his level, for she was taller than he. 'Since the night before last he's been gone from the abbey school.'

She flung up her clenched hands with an indignant cry. 'And only now am I told of it! Two nights gone! Is that the care they take of their children? And these are the people who deny me the charge of my own flesh and blood! I hold the abbot responsible for whatever distress or harm has come to my grandson. The guilt is on his head. And what are you doing, my lord, to recover the child? Two days you tell me he's been lost, and late and laggard you come to let me know of it . . .'

The momentary hush fell only because she had to stop to draw breath, standing with flashing eyes at the head of the steps, tall and greying fair and formidable, her long patrician face suffused with angry blood. Hugh took ruthless advantage of the lull, while it lasted, for it would not last long.

'Has Richard been here?' he demanded bluntly, challenging her show of furious deprivation and loss.

She caught her breath, standing open-mouthed. '*Here*? No, he did not come here. Should I be thus distraught if he had?'

'You would have sent word to the abbot, no doubt,' said Hugh guilelessly, 'if he had come running home? They are no less anxious about him at the abbey. And he rode away alone, of his own will. Where should we first look for him but here? But you tell me he is not here, has not been here. And his pony has not come wandering home to his old stable?'

'He has not, or I should have been told at once. If he'd come home riderless,' she said, her nostrils flaring, 'I would have had every man who is mine scouring the woods for Richard.'

'My men are busy this minute doing that very thing,' said Hugh. 'But by all means turn out Richard's people to add to the number, and welcome. The more the better. Since it seems we've drawn blank,' he said, still thoughtfully studying her face, 'and after all, he is not here.'

'No,' she blazed, 'he is not here! No, he has not been here! Though if he left of his own will, as you claim, perhaps he meant to come home to me. And for whatever has befallen him on the way I hold Radulfus to blame. He is not fit to have charge of a noble child, if he cannot take better care of him.'

'I will tell him so,' said Hugh obligingly, and went on with aggravating mildness: 'My present duty is to continue the search, then, both for Richard and for the thief who killed an abbey guest in Eyton forest. You need not fear, madam, that my search will not be thorough. Since I cannot expect you to make daily rounds of every corner of your grandson's manor, no doubt you'll be glad to allow me free access everywhere, to do that service for you. You'll wish to set example to your tenants and neighbours.'

She gave him a long, long, hostile look, and as suddenly whirled on John of Longwood, who stood impassive and neutral at her elbow. In the gale of her movements her long skirt lashed like the tail of an angry cat.

'Open my doors to these officers. All my doors! Let them satisfy themselves I'm neither harbouring a murderer nor hiding my own flesh and blood here. Let all our tenants know it's my will they should submit to search as freely as I do. My lord sheriff,' she said, looking down with immense dignity upon Hugh, 'enter and search wherever you wish.'

He thanked her with unabashed civility, and if she saw the glint in his eye, that just fell short of becoming an open smile, she scorned to acknowledge it, but turned her straight back and withdrew with a rapid and angry gait into the hall, leaving him to a search he already felt must prove fruitless. But there was no certainty, and if she had calculated that such a rash and sweeping invitation would be taken as proof, and send them away satisfied, even shamefaced, she was much deceived. Hugh set to work to probe every corner of Dionisia's hall and solar, kitchens and stores, examined every cask and handcart and barrel in the undercroft, every byre and barn and stable that lined the stockade, the smith's workshop, every loft and larder, and moved outward into the fields and sheep folds, and thence to the huts of every tenant and cotter and villein on Richard's land. But they did not find Richard.

Brother Cadfael rode for Eilmund's assart in the middle of the afternoon, with the new crutches Brother Simon had cut to the forester's measure slung alongside, good, sturdy props to bear a solid weight. The fracture appeared to be knitting well, the leg was straight and not shortened. Eilmund was not accustomed to lying by inactive, and was jealous of any other hands tending his woodlands. Once he got hold of these aids Annet would have trouble keeping him in. It was in Cadfael's mind that her father's helplessness had afforded her an unusual measure of freedom to pursue her own feminine ploys, no doubt innocent enough, but what Eilmund would make of them when he found out was another matter.

Approaching the village of Wroxeter, Cadfael met with Hugh riding back towards the town, after a long day in the saddle. Beyond, in fields and woodlands, his officers were still methodically combing every grove and every headland, but Hugh was bound back to the castle alone, to collect together whatever reports had been brought in, and consider how best to cover the remaining ground, and how far the search must be extended if it had not yet borne fruit.

'No,' said Hugh, answering the unasked question almost as soon as they were within hail of each other, 'she has not got him. By all the signs she did not even know you'd lost him until I brought the word, though it's no great trick, I know, for any woman to put on such an exclaiming show. But we've parted every stalk of straw in her barns, and what we've missed must be too small ever to be found. No black pony in the stables. Not a soul but tells the same story, from John of Longwood down to the smith's boy. Richard is not there. Not in any cottage or byre in this village. The priest turned out his house for us, and went with us round the manor, and he's an honest man.'

Cadfael nodded sombre confirmation of his own doubts. 'I had a feeling there might be more to it than that. It would be worth trying yonder at Wroxeter, I suppose. Not that I see Fulke Astley as a likely villain – he's too fat and too cautious.'

'I'm just come from there,' said Hugh. 'Three of my men are still prodding into the last corners, but I'm satisfied he's not there, either. We'll miss no one – manor, cottage, assart, all. Of what falls alike on them all none of them can well complain. Though Astley did bristle at letting us in. A matter of his seigneurial dignity, for there was nothing there to find.'

'The pony,' said Cadfael, gnawing a considering lip, 'must be shut away somewhere.'

'Unless,' said Hugh sombrely, 'the other fugitive has ridden him hard out of the shire, and left the boy in such case that he cannot bear witness – even when we find him.'

They stared steadily upon each other, mutely admitting that it was a black and bitter possibility, but one that could not be altogether banished.

'The child ran off to him, if that is indeed what he did,' Hugh pursued doggedly, 'without saying a word to any other. How if it was indeed to a rogue and murderer he went, in all innocence? The cob is a sturdy little beast, big for Richard, the hermit's boy a light weight, and Richard the only witness. I don't say it is so. I do say such things have happened, and could happen again.'

'True, I would not dispute it,' admitted Cadfael.

There was that in his tone that caused Hugh to say with

certainty: 'But you do not believe it.' It was something of which Cadfael himself had been less certain until that moment. 'Do you feel your thumbs pricking? I know better than to ignore the omen if you do,' said Hugh with a half-reluctant smile.

'No, Hugh.' Cadfael shook his head. 'I know nothing that isn't known to you, I am nobody's advocate in this matter – except Richard's – I've barely exchanged a word with this boy Hyacinth, never seen him but twice, when he brought Cuthred's message to chapter and when he came to fetch me to the forester. All I can do is keep my eyes open between here and Eilmund's house, and that you may be sure I shall do – perhaps even do a little beating of the bushes myself along the way. If I have anything to tell, be sure you'll hear it before any other. Be it good or ill, but God and Saint Winifred grant us good news!'

On that promise they parted, Hugh riding on to the castle to receive whatever news the watch might have for him thus late in the afternoon, Cadfael moving on through the village towards the edge of the woodland. He was in no hurry. He had much to think about. Strange how the very act of admitting that the worst was possible had so instantly strengthened his conviction that it had not happened and would not happen. Stranger still that as soon as he had stated truthfully that he knew nothing of Hyacinth, and had barely spoken a word to him, he should find himself so strongly persuaded that very soon that lack might be supplied, and he would learn, if not everything, all that he needed to know.

Eilmund had regained his healthy colour, welcomed company eagerly, and could not be restrained from trying out his crutches at once. Four or five days cooped up indoors was a sore test of his temper, but the relief of being able to hurdle vigorously out into the garden, and finding himself a fast learner in the art of using his new legs, brought immediate sunny weather with him. When he had satisfied himself of his competence, he sat down willingly, at Annet's orders, to share a supper with Cadfael.

'Though by rights I ought to be getting back,' said Cadfael, 'now I know how well you're doing. The bone seems to be knitting straight and true as a lance, and you'll not need me here harrying you every day. And speaking of inconvenient visitors, have you had Hugh Beringar or his men here today searching the woods around? You'll have heard before now they're hunting Cuthred's boy Hyacinth for suspicion of killing his master? And there's young Richard missing, too.'

'We heard of the both only last night,' said Eilmund. 'Yes, they were here this morning, a long line of the garrison men working their way along every yard of the forest between road and river. They even looked in my byre and henhouse. Will Warden grumbled himself it was needless folly, but he had his orders. Why waste time, he says, aggravating a good fellow we all know to be honest, but it's as much as my skin's worth to leave out a single hut or let my beaters pass by a solitary bush, with his lordship's sharp eye on us all. Do you know, have they found the child?'

'No, not yet. He's not at Eaton, that's certain. If it's any comfort, Eilmund, Dame Dionisia had to open her doors to the search, too. Noble and simple, they'll all fare alike.'

Annet waited upon them in silence, bringing cheese and bread to the table. Her step was as light as always, her face as calm, only at the mention of Richard did her face cloud over in anxious sympathy. There was no knowing what went on behind her composed face, but Cadfael hazarded his own guesses. He took his leave in good time, against Eilmund's hospitable urgings.

'I've been missing too many services, these last days, I'd best get back to my duty, and at least put in an appearance for Compline tonight. I'll come in and see you the day after tomorrow. You take care how you go. And, Annet, don't let him stay on his feet too long. If he gives you trouble, take his props away from him.'

She laughed and said that she would, but her mind, Cadfael thought, was only half on what she said, and she had not made any move to second her father's protest at such an early departure. Nor did she come out to the gate with him this time, but only as far as the door, and there stood to watch him mount, and waved when he looked back before beginning to thread the narrow path between the trees. Only when he had vanished did she turn and go back into the cottage.

Cadfael did not go far. A few hundred yards into the woods there was a hollow of green surrounded by a deep thicket, and there he dismounted and tethered his horse, and made his way back very quietly and circumspectly to a place from which he could see the house door without himself being seen. The light was dimming gently into the soft green of dusk, and the hush was profound, only the last birdsong broke the forest silence.

In a few minutes Annet came out to the door again, and stood for a little while braced and still, her head alertly reared, looking all round the clearing and listening intently. Then, satisfied, she set off briskly out of the fenced garden and round to the rear of the cottage. Cadfael circled with her in the cover of the trees. Her hens were already securely shut in for the night, the cow was in the byre; from these customary evening tasks Annet had come back a good hour ago, while her father was trying out his crutches in the grassy levels of the clearing. It seemed there was one more errand she had to do before the full night came down and the door was closed and barred. And she went to it at a light and joyous run, her hands spread to part the bushes on either side as she reached the edge of the clearing, her light brown hair shaking loose from its coil and dancing on her shoulders, her head tilted back as though she looked up into the trees, darkening now over her head and dropping, silently and moistly, the occasional withered leaf, the tears of the aging year.

She was not going far. No more than a hundred paces into the woods she halted, poised still in the same joyous attitude of flight, under the branches of the first of the ancient oaks, still in full but tarnished leafage. Cadfael, not far behind her in the shelter of the trees, saw her throw back her head and send a high, melodious whistle up into the crown of the tree. From somewhere high above a soft shimmering of leaves answered, dropping through the branches as an acorn might fall, and in a moment the descending shiver of movement reached the ground in the shape of a young man sudden and silent as a cat, who swung by his hands from the lowest bough and dropped lightly on his feet at Annet's side. As soon as he touched ground they were in each other's arms.

So he had not been mistaken. The two of them had barely set eyes on each other when they fell to liking, blessed as they were with the good ground of his services to her father. With Eilmund laid up helpless in the house she could go freely about her own secret business of hiding and feeding a fugitive, but what would they do now that the forester was likely to be up and about, however limited his range must remain? Was it fair to present her father with such a problem in loyalties, and he an official involved with law, if only forest law? But there they stood linked, as candidly as children, with such a suggestion of permanence about their embrace that it surely would take more than father or lord or law or king to disentangle them. With her long mane of hair loosed, and her feet bare, and Hyacinth's classic elegance of shape and movement, and fierce, disquieting beauty, they might have been two creatures bred out of the ancient forest, faun and nymph out of a profane but lovely fable. Not even the gathering twilight could dim their brightness.

Well, thought Cadfael, surrendering to the vision, if this is what we have to deal with, from this we must go on, for there's no going back. And he stepped rustling out of the bushes, and walked towards them without conceal.

They heard him and sprang round instantly with heads reared, cheek to cheek, like deer scenting danger. They saw him, and Annet flung out her arms and shut Hyacinth behind her against the bole of the tree, her face blanched and sharp as a sword, and as decisively Hyacinth laughed, lifted her bodily aside, and stepped before her.

'As if I needed proof!' said Cadfael, to afford them whatever reassurance his voice might convey, and he halted without coming too close, though they knew already there was no point in running. 'I'm not the law. If you've done no wrong you've nothing to fear from me.'

'It takes a bolder man than I am,' said Hyacinth's clear voice softly, 'to claim he's done no wrong.' Even in the dimming light his sudden, unnerving smile shone perceptibly for a moment. 'But I've done no murder, if that's what you mean. Brother Cadfael, is it?'

'It is.' He looked from one roused and wary face to the other, and saw that they were breathing a little more easily and every moment less tensed for flight or attack. 'Lucky for you they brought no hounds with them this morning. Hugh never likes to hunt a man with hounds. I'm sorry, lad, if my visit tonight kept you fretting longer than you need have done in your nest up there. I hope you spend your nights in better comfort.'

At that they both smiled, still somewhat cautiously and with eyes alert and wild, but they said nothing.

'And where did you hide through the sergeant's search, that they never got wind of you at all?'

Annet made up her mind, with the same thorough practical resolution with which she did everything. She stirred and shook herself, the glossy cloak of her hair billowing into a pale cloud about her head. She drew breath deeply, and laughed.

'If you must know, he was under the brychans of Father's bed, while Will Warden sat on the bench opposite drinking ale with us, and his men peered in among my hens and forked through the hay in the loft, outside. You thought, I believe,' she said, coming close to Cadfael and drawing Hyacinth after her by the hand, 'that Father was in ignorance of what I was doing. Did you hold that against me, even a little? No need, he knows all, has known it from the beginning, or at least from the moment this manhunt began. And now that you've found us out, had we not better all go into the house, and see what our four heads can come up with for the future, to get us all out of this tangle?'

'They'll not come here again,' said Eilmund comfortably, presiding over this meeting in his house from the throne of his bed, the same bed under which Hyacinth had couched secure in the presence of the hunters. 'But if they do, we'll know of it in time. Never twice the same hiding place.'

'And never once any qualms that you might be hiding a murderer?' asked Cadfael, hopeful of being convinced.

'No need for any! From the start of it I knew I was not. And you shall know it, too. I'm talking of proof positive, Cadfael, not a mere matter of faith, though faith's no mere matter, come to that. You were here last night, it was on your way back you found the man dead, and dead no more than an hour when you found him. Do you say aye to that?'

'More than willingly, if it helps your proof along.'

'And you left me when Annet here came back from doing the work that keeps her busy in the evening. You'll call to mind I said she'd been long enough about it, and so she had, well above an hour. For good reason, she'd been meeting with this youngster here, and whatever they were about, they were in no hurry about it, which won't surprise you greatly, I daresay. In short, these two were together in the woods a mile or so from here from the time she left you and me together, until she came back nigh on two hours later. And there young Richard found them, and this lad she brought back with her here, and ten minutes after you were gone she brought him in to me. No murderer, for all that while he was with her, or me, or the both of us, and in this house he slept that night. He never was near the man who was killed, and we can swear to it.'

'Then why have you not . . .' Cadfael began, and as hastily caught himself back from the needless question, and held up a hand to ward off the obvious answer. 'No, say no word! I see very well why. My wits are grown dull tonight. If you came forward to tell Hugh Beringar he's after a man proven innocent, true enough you could put that danger away from him. But if one Bosiet is dead, there's another expected at the abbey any day now – he may be there this minute, for all I know. As bad as his sire, so says the groom, and he has good reason to know, he bears the marks of it. No, I see how you're bound.'

Hyacinth sat in the rushes on the floor at Annet's feet, hugging his drawn up knees. He said without passion or emphasis, but with the calm finality of absolute resolution: 'I am not going back there.'

'No, no more you shall!' said Eilmund heartily. 'You'll understand, Cadfael, that when I took the lad in, there was no question of murder at all. It was a runaway villein I chose to shelter, one with good reason to run, and one that had done me the best of turns any man could do for another. I liked him well, I would not for any cause have sent him back to be misused. And then, when the cry of murder did arise, I had no call to feel any differently, for I knew he had no part in it. It went against the grain not to be able to go out and say so to sheriff and abbot and all, but you see it was impossible. And the upshot of it is, here we are with the lad on our hands, and how are we best to make sure of his safety?'

Chapter Nine

IT WAS already taken for granted by all of them, it seemed, that Cadfael was on their side, and wholeheartedly a party to their conspiracy. How could it be otherwise? Here was absolute proof that the boy was no murderer, proof that could be laid in Hugh Beringar's hands with confidence in his justice, no question of that. But it could not be done without exposing Hyacinth to the very danger from which he had escaped once, and could hardly hope to escape a second time. Hugh was bound by law as fast as any man, even his gift for turning a blind eye and a deaf ear would not help Hyacinth if once Bosiet got wind of where he was and who was sheltering him.

'Between us,' said Cadfael, though somewhat dubiously, 'we might be able to get you away out of the country and into Wales, clean away from pursuit . . .'

'No,' said Hyacinth firmly, 'I won't. I'll hide for as long as I must, but I won't run any further. It's what I meant to do, when I set off this way, but I've changed my mind.'

'Why?' demanded Cadfael simply.

'For two good reasons. One, because Richard's lost, and Richard saved my skin for me by bringing warning, and I'm his debtor until I know he's safe, and back where he should be. And two, because I want my freedom here in England, here in Shrewsbury, and I mean to get work in the town when I can with safety, and earn my living, and take a wife.' He looked up with a bright, challenging flash of his amber eyes at Eilmund, and smiled. 'If Annet will have me!'

'You'd best ask my leave about that,' said Eilmund, but with such good humour that it was plain the idea was not entirely new to him, nor necessarily unwelcome.

'So I will, when the time comes, but I would not offer you or her what I am and have now. So let that wait, but don't forget it,' warned the faun, gleaming. 'But Richard I must find, I will find! That's first!'

'What can you do,' said Eilmund practically, 'more than Hugh Beringar and all his men are doing? And you a hunted man yourself, with the hounds close on your tail! You stay quiet like a sensible lad, and hide your head until Bosiet's hunt for you starts costing him more even than his hatred's worth. As it will, in the end. He has manors at home now to think about.'

But whether Hyacinth was, by ordinary standards, a sensible lad was a matter for conjecture. He sat very still, in that taut, suggestive way he had, that promised imminent action, the soft glow of Annet's fire glowing in the subtle planes of his cheeks and brow, turning his bronze to gold. And Annet, beside him on the cushioned bench by the wall, had something of the same quality. Her face was still, but her eyes were sapphire bright. She let them talk about her in her presence, and felt no need to add a word on her own account, nor did she so much as touch Hyacinth's slender shoulder to confirm her secure tenure. Whoever had doubts about Annet's claims on the future, Annet had none.

'Richard left you as soon as he'd delivered his warning?' asked Cadfael.

'He did. Hyacinth wanted to go with him to the edge of the wood,' said Annet, 'but he wouldn't have it. He wouldn't stir unless Hyacinth went into hiding at once, so we promised. And he set off back along the track. And we came back here to Father, as he's told you, and saw no one else along the way. Richard would not have gone anywhere near Eaton, or I'd have thought his grandmother might have taken him. But he was bent on getting back to bed.'

'It was what we all thought,' owned Cadfael, 'not least Hugh Beringar. But he was there early and turned the place wrong side out, and the boy is not there. I think John of Longwood and half the household beside would have told if he'd been seen there. Dame Dionisia is a formidable lady, but Richard is the lord of Eaton, it's his bidding they'll have to do in the future, not hers. If they dared not speak out before her face, they'd have done it softly behind her back. No, he is not there.'

It was long past time for Vespers. Even if he started back now he would be too late for Compline, but still he sat stubbornly going over this whole new situation in his mind, looking for the best way forward, where there seemed to be nothing to be done but wait, and continue to evade the hunt. He was grateful that Hyacinth was no murderer, that at least was a gain. But how to keep him out of the hands of Bosiet was another matter.

'For God's sake, boy,' he said, sighing, 'what was it you did to your overlord, there in Northamptonshire, to get yourself so bitterly hated? Did you indeed assault his steward?'

'I did,' acknowledged Hyacinth with satisfaction, and a red reminiscent spark kindled in his eyes. 'It was after the last of the harvest, and there was a girl gleaning in the poor leavings in one of the demesne fields. There never was a girl safe from him if he came on her alone. It was only by chance I was near. He had a staff, and dropped her to swing at my head with it when I came at him. I got a few bruises, but I laid him flat against the stones under the headland, clean out of his wits. So there was nothing I could do but run for it. I'd nothing to leave, no land – Drogo distrained on my father two years before, when he was in his last illness and I had all to do, our fields and Bosiet's harvest labour, and we ended in debt. He'd been after us a long while, he said I was for ever rousing his villeins against him . . . Well, if I was it was for their rights. There are laws to defend life and limb even for villeins, but they meant precious little in Bosiet's manors. He'd have had me half-killed for attacking the steward – He'd have had me hanged if I hadn't been profitable to him. It was the chance he'd been waiting for.'

'How were you profitable to him?' asked Cadfael.

'I had a turn for fine leather-work – belts, harness, pouches, and the like. When he'd made me landless he offered to leave me the toft if I'd bind myself to turn over all my work to him for my keep. I'd no choice, I was still his villein. But I began to do finer tooling and gilding. He wanted to get some favour out of the earl once, and he had me make a book cover to give him as a present. And then the prior of the Augustinian canons at Huntingdon saw it, and ordered a special binding for their great codex, and the sub-prior of Cluny at Northampton wanted his best missal rebound, and so it grew. And they paid well, but I got nothing out of it. Drogo's done well out of me. That's the other reason he wanted me back alive. And so will his son Aymer want me.'

'If you have a trade the like of that at your finger-ends,' said Eilmund approvingly, 'you can make your way anywhere, once you're free of these Bosiets. Our abbot might very well put some work your way, and some town merchant would be glad to have you in his employ.'

'Where and how did you meet with Cuthred?' asked Cadfael, curiously.

'That was at the Cluniac priory in Northampton. I lay up for the night there, but I dared not go into the enclave, there were one or two there who knew me. I got food by sitting with the beggars at the gate, and when I was making off before dawn, Cuthred was for starting too, having spent the night in the guest hall.' An abrupt dark smile plucked at the corners of Hyacinth's eloquent lips. He kept his startling eyes veiled under their high-arched golden lids. 'He proposed we should travel together. Out of charity, surely. Or so that I should not have to thieve for my food, and sink into a worse condition even than before.' As abruptly he looked up, unveiling the full brilliance of wide eyes fixed full and solemnly on Eilmund's face. The smile had vanished.

'It's time you knew the worst of me, I want no lies among this company. I came this way owing the world nothing, and ripe for any mischief, and a rogue and a vagabond I could be, and a thief I have been at need. Before you shelter me another hour, you should know what cause you have to think better of it. Annet,' he said, his voice soft and assuaged on her name, 'already knows what you must know too. You have that right. I told her the truth the night Brother Cadfael was here to set your bone.'

Cadfael remembered the motionless figure sitting patiently outside the cottage, the urgent whisper: 'I must speak to you!' And Annet coming out into the dark, and closing the door after her.

'It was I,' said Hyacinth with steely deliberation, 'who dammed the brook with bushes so that your seedlings were flooded. It was I who undercut the bank and bridged the ditch so that the deer got into the coppice. It was I who shifted a pale of the Eaton fence to let out the sheep to the ash saplings. I had my orders from Dame Dionisia to be a thorn in the flesh of the abbey until they gave her her grandson back. That was why she set up Cuthred in his hermitage, to put me there as his servant. And I knew nothing then of any of you, and cared less, and I was not going to quarrel with what provided me a comfortable living and a safe refuge until I could do better. It's my doing, more's the pity, that the worse thing happened, and the tree came down on you and pinned you in the brook, my doing that you're lamed and housebound here – thought that slip came of itself, I didn't touch it again. So now you know,' said Hyacinth, 'and if you see fit to take the skin off my back for it, I won't lift a hand to prevent, and if you throw me out afterwards, I'll go.' He reached up a hand to Annet's hand and added flatly: 'But not far!'

There was a long pause while two of them sat staring at him, intently and silently, and Annet watched them no less warily, all of them withholding judgement. No one had exclaimed against him, no one had interrupted this half-defiant confession. Hyacinth's truth was used like a dagger, and his humility came very close to arrogance. If he was ashamed, it did not show in his face. Yet it could not have been easy to strip himself thus of the consideration and kindness father and daughter had shown him. If he had not spoken, clearly Annet would have said no word. And he had not pleaded, nor attempted any extenuation. He was ready to take what was due without complaint. Doubtful if anyone, however eloquent or terrible a confessor, would ever get this elusive creature nearer to penitence than this.

Eilmund stirred, settling his broad shoulders more easily against the wall, and blew out a great, gusty breath. 'Well, if you brought the tree down on me, you also hoisted it off me. And if you think I'd give up a runaway villein to slavery again because he'd played a few foul tricks on me, you're not well acquainted with my simple sort. I fancy the fright I gave you that day was all the thrashing you needed. And since then you've done me no more injury, for from all I hear there's been quiet in the woods from that day. I doubt if the lady's satisfied with her bargain. You show sense, and stay where you are.'

'I told him,' said Annet, confidently smiling, 'you would not pay back injury for injury. I never said a word, I knew he would out with it himself. And Brother Cadfael knows now Hyacinth's no murderer, and has owned to the worst he knows about himself. There's not one of us here will betray him.'

No, not one! But Cadfael sat somewhat anxiously pondering what could best be done now. Betrayal was impossible, certainly, but the hunt would go on, and might well drag all these woods over again, and in the meantime Hugh, in his natural concentration on this most likely quarry, might be losing all likelihood of finding the real murderer. Even Drogo Bosiet was entitled to justice, however he infringed the rights of others. Withholding from Hugh the certainty and proof of Hyacinth's innocence might be delaying the reassessment that would set in motion the pursuit of the guilty.

'Will you trust me, and let me tell Hugh Beringar what you have told me? Give me leave,' urged Cadfael hastily, seeing their faces stiffen in consternation, 'to deal with him privately—'

'No!' Annet laid her hand possessively on Hyacinth's shoulder, burning up like a stirred fire. 'No, you can't give him up! We have trusted you, you can't fail us.'

'No, no, no, not that! I know Hugh well, he would not willingly give up a villein to mistreatment, he is for justice even before law. Let me tell him only that Hyacinth is innocent, and show him the proof. I need say nothing as to how I know or where he is, Hugh will take my word. Then he can hold off this search and leave you alone until it's safe for you to come forth and speak openly.'

'No!' cried Hyacinth, on his feet in one wild, smooth movement, his eyes two yellow flames of alarm and rejection. 'Not a word to him, never a word! If we'd thought you'd go to him we'd never have let you in to us. He's the sheriff, he must take Bosiet's part – he has manors, he has villeins of his own, do you think he'd ever side with me against my legal lord? I should be dragged back at Aymer's heels, and buried alive in his prison.'

Cadfael turned to Eilmund for help. 'I swear to you I can lift this suspicion from the lad by speaking with Hugh. He'll take my word and hold off from the hunt – withdraw his men, or send them elsewhere. He has still Richard to find. Eilmund, you know Hugh Beringar better than to doubt his fairness.'

But no, Eilmund did not know him, not as Cadfael knew him. The forester was shaking his head doubtfully. A sheriff is a sheriff, pledged to law, and law is rigid and weighted, all in all, against the peasant and the serf and the landless man. 'He's a decent, fair-minded man, sure enough,' said Eilmund, 'but I dare not stake this boy's life on any king's officer. No, leave us keep as we are, Cadfael. Say nothing to any man, not until Bosiet's come and gone.'

They were all linked against him. He did his best, arguing quietly what ease it would be to know that the hunt would not be pressed home against Hyacinth, that his innocence, once communicated privily to Hugh, would set free the forces of law to look elsewhere for Drogo's murderer, and also allow them to press their search for Richard more thoroughly, and with more resources, through these forests where the child had vanished. But they had their arguments, too, and there was matter in them.

'If you told the sheriff, even secretly,' urged Annet, 'and if he did believe you, he would still have Bosiet to deal with. His father's man will tell him it's as good as certain his runaway is somewhere here in hiding, murderer or no. He'll go the length of using hounds, if the sheriff draws his men off. No, say nothing to anyone, not yet. Wait until they give up and go home. Then we'll come forth. Promise! Promise us silence until then!'

There was nothing to be done about it. He promised. They had trusted him, and against their absolute prohibition he could not hold out. He sighed and promised.

It was very late when he rose at last, his word given, to begin the night ride back to the abbey. He had given a promise also to Hugh, never thinking how hard it might be to keep. He had said that if he had anything to tell, Hugh should hear it before any other. A subtle, if guileless, arrangement of words, through which a devious mind could find several loopholes, but what he meant had been as clear to Hugh as it was to Cadfael. And now he could not make it good. Not yet, not until Aymer Bosiet should grow restive, count the costs of his vengeance, and think it better to go home and enjoy his new inheritance instead.

In the doorway he turned back to ask of Hyacinth one last question, a sudden afterthought. 'What of Cuthred? With you two living so close – did he have any part in all this mischief of yours in Eilmund's forest?'

Hyacinth stared at him gravely, in mild surprise, his amber eyes wide and candid. 'How could he?' he said simply. 'He never leaves his own pale.'

Aymer Bosiet rode into the great court of the abbey about noon of the next day, with a young groom at his back. Brother Denis the hospitaller had orders to bring him to Abbot Radulfus as soon as he arrived, for the abbot was unwilling to delegate to anyone else the task of breaking to him the news of his father's death. It was achieved with a delicacy for which, it seemed, there was little need. The bereaved son sat silently revolving the news and all its implications at length, and having apparently digested and come to terms with it, expressed his filial grief very suitably, but with his mind still engaged on side issues, a shrewdly calculating mind behind a face less powerful and brutal than his father's, but showing little evidence of sorrow. He did frown over the event, for it involved troublesome duties, such as commissioning coffin and cart and extra help for the journey home, and making the best possible use of such time as he could afford here. Radulfus had already had Martin Bellecote, the master carpenter in the town, make a plain inner coffin for the body, which was not yet covered, since doubtless Aymer would want to look upon his father's face for a last time and take his farewells.

The bereaved son revolved the matter in his mind, and asked point-blank and with sharp intent: 'He had not found our runaway villein?'

'No,' said Radulfus, and if he was shaken he contrived to contain the shock. 'There was a suggestion that the young man was in the neighbourhood, but no certainty that the youth in question was really the one sought. And I believe no one knows where he is gone.'

'My father's murderer is being sought?'

'Very assiduously, with all the sheriff's men.'

'My villein also, I trust. Whether or not,' said Aymer grimly, 'the two turn out to be the same. The law is bound to do all it can to recover my property for me. The rogue is a nuisance, but valuable. For no price would I be willing to let him go free.' He bit off the words with a vicious snap of large, strong teeth. He was as tall and long-boned as his father, but carried less flesh, and was leaner in the face; but he had the same shallowly-set eyes of an indeterminate, opaque colour, that seemed all surface and no depth. Thirty years old, perhaps, and pleasurably aware of his new status. Proprietorial satisfaction had begun to vibrate beneath the hard level of his voice. Already he spoke of 'my property'. That was one aspect of his bereavement which certainly had not escaped him.

'I shall want to see the sheriff concerning this fellow who calls himself Hyacinth. If he has run, does not that make it more likely he is indeed Brand? And that he had a hand in my father's death? There's a heavy score against him already. I don't intend to let such a debt go unpaid.'

'That is a matter for the secular law, not for me,' said Radulfus with chill civility. 'There is no proof of who killed the lord Drogo, the thing is quite open. But the man is being sought. If you will come with me, I'll take you to the chapel where your father lies.'

Aymer stood beside the open coffin on its draped bier, and the light of the tall candles burning at Drogo's head and feet showed no great change in his son's face. He gazed down with drawn brows, but it was the frown of busy thought rather than grief or anger at such a death.

'I feel it bitterly,' said the abbot, 'that a guest in our house should come to so evil an end. We have said Masses for his soul, but other amends are out of my scope. I trust we may yet see justice done.'

'Indeed!' agreed Aymer, but so absently that it was plain his mind was on other things. 'I have no choice but to take him home for burial. But I cannot go yet. This search cannot be so soon abandoned. I must ride into the town this afternoon and see this master carpenter of yours, and have him make an outer coffin and line it with lead, and seal it. A pity, he could have lain just as properly here, but the men of our house are all buried at Bosiet. My mother would not be content else.'

He said it with a note of vexation in his musings. But for the necessity of taking home a corpse he could have lingered here for days to pursue his hunt for the escaped villein. Even as things stood he meant to make the fullest use of his time, and Radulfus could not help feeling that it was the villein he wanted most vindictively, not his father's murderer.

By chance Cadfael happened to be crossing the court when the newcomer took horse again, early in the afternoon. It was his first glimpse of Drogo's son, and he stopped and drew aside to study him with interest. His identity was never in doubt, for the likeness was there, though somewehat tempered in this younger man. The curiously shallow eyes, so meanly diminished by their lack of the shadow and form deep sockets provide, had the same flat malevolence, and his handling of horseflesh as he mounted was more considerate by far than his manner towards his groom. The hand that held his stirrup was clouted aside by the butt of his whip as soon as he was in the saddle, and when Warin started back from the blow so sharply that the horse took fright and clattered backwards on the cobbles, tossing up his head and snorting, the rider swung the whip at the groom's shoulders so readily and with so little apparent anger or exasperation that it was plain this was the common currency of his dealings with his underlings. He took only the younger groom with him into the town, himself riding his father's horse, which was fresh and spoiling for exercise. No doubt Warin was only too glad to be left behind here in peace for a few hours.

Cadfael overtook the groom and fell into step beside him as he turned back towards the stables. Warin looked round to show him a bruise rapidly fading, but still yellow as old parchment, and a mouth still elongated by the healing scar at one corner.

'I've not seen you these two days,' said Cadfael, eyeing the traces of old violence and alert for new. 'Come round with me into the herb garden, and let me dress that gash again for you. He's safely away for an hour or two, I take it, you can breathe easily. And it would do with another treatment, though I see it's clean now.'

Warin hesitated only for a moment. 'They've taken the two fresh horses, and left me the others to groom. But they can wait a while.' And he went willingly at Cadfael's side, his lean person, a little withered before its time, seeming to expand in his lord's absence. In the pleasant aromatic coolness of the workshop, under the faintly stirring herbs that rustled overhead, he sat eased and content to let his injury be bathed and anointed, and was in no hurry to get back to his horses even when Cadfael had done with him.

'He's hotter even than the old one was on Brand's heels,' he said, shaking a helpless but sympathetic head over his former neighbour's fortunes. 'Torn two ways, between wanting to hang him and wanting to work him to death for greed, and it isn't whether or not Brand killed the old lord that will determine which way the cat jumps, for there was no great love lost there, neither. Not much love in all that household to be gained or lost. But good haters, every one.'

'There are more of them?' Cadfael asked with interest. 'Drogo has left a widow?'

'A poor pale lady, all the juice crushed out of her,' answered Warin, 'But better born than the Bosiets, and has powerful kin, so they have to use her better than they use anyone else. And Aymer has a younger brother. Not so loud nor so violent, but sharper witted and better able to twist and turn. That's all of them, but it's enough.'

'Neither one of them married?'

'Aymer's had one wife, but she was a sickly thing and died young. There's an heiress not far from Bosiet they both fancy now – though by rights it's her lands they fancy. And if Aymer is the heir, Roger's far the better at making himself agreeable. Not that it lasts beyond when he gets his way.'

It sounded a poor outlook for the girl, whichever of the two got the better of the contest, but it also sounded one possible reason why Aymer should not loiter here too long, or he might lose his advantages at home. Cadfael felt encouraged. Absence from a newly-inherited honour might even be dangerous, if there was a clever and treacherous younger brother left behind there to make calculated use of his opportunities. Aymer would be bearing that in mind, even while he grudged giving up his vindictive pursuit of Hyacinth, Cadfael still could not think of the boy as Brand, the name he had chosen for himself fitted him so much better.

'I wonder,' said Warin, unexpectedly harking back to the same elusive person, 'where Brand really got to? Lucky for him we did give him some grace – not that my lord intended it so! – for at first they thought that a man with the skill he had at his finger-ends would surely make for London, and we wasted a week or more searching all the roads south. We got beyond Thame before one of his men came riding after us, saying Brand had been seen in Northampton. If he'd started off northwards, Drogo reckoned he'd continue so, and likely to bear west as he went, and make for Wales. I wonder has he reached it. Even Aymer won't follow him over the border.'

'And you picked up no more sightings of him along the way?' asked Cadfael.

'No, never a trace. But we're far out of the country where anyone would know him, and not everybody wants to get tangled into such a business. And he'll have taken another name, for sure.' Warin rose, refreshed but reluctant, to go back to his duties. 'I hope it may stand him in good stead. No matter what the Bosiets say, he was a decent lad.'

Brother Winfrid was busy sweeping up leaves under the orchard trees, for the moist autumn had caused them to fall before they took their bright seasonal colouring, in a soft green rain that rotted gently into the turf. Cadfael found himself alone and without occupation after Warin had left him. The more reason to sit down quietly and think, and a prayer or two wouldn't come amiss, either, for the boy who had gone rushing off on his black pony, on his self-appointed, mad and generous mission, for the rash young man he had set out to save, even for the hard, malignant lordling cut off without time for penitence or absolution and bitterly in need of grace.

The bell for Vespers called him out of his musings, and he went gladly to answer it, out through the gardens and across the court to the cloister and the south door of the church, to be early in his place. In the past few days he had missed all too many services, he was in need of the reassurance of brotherhood.

There were always a few of the people of the Foregate at Vespers, the devout old women who inhabited some of the abbey's grace houses, elderly couples retired and happy to fill up their leisure and meet their friends at church, and often guests of the house coming back from the activities of the day. Cadfael heard them stirring beyond the parish altar, in the vast spaces of the nave. Rafe of Coventry, he noted, had come in from the cloister and chosen a place from which he could see within, past the parish altar and into the choir. Kneeling at prayer, he had still that quiet composure about him, a man secure and at peace with his own body, and wearing his inscrutable face rather as a shield than as a mask. So he had not yet moved on to contact those suppliers of his in Wales. He was the only worshipper from the guest hall. Aymer Bosiet must be still about his funereal business in the town, or else beating the coverts in field and forest somewhere after his runaway.

The brothers came in and took their places, the novices and schoolboys followed. There was a bitter reminder there, for their numbers were still one short. There was no forgetting about Richard. Until he was recovered there would be no peace of mind, no lightness of heart, for any of those children.

At the end of Vespers Cadfael lingered in his stall, letting the procession of brothers and novices file out into the cloister without him. The office had its beauty and consolation, but the solitude afterwards was also salutary in its silence, after the echoes of the music had all died away, and to be here alone in this evening hour had a special beneficence, whether because of the soft, dove-coloured light or the sense of enlargement that seemed to swell the soul to inhabit and fill the last arches of the vault, as a single drop of water becomes the ocean into which it falls. There was no better time for profound prayer, and Cadfael felt the need of it. For the boy in particular, equally solitary somewhere, perhaps afraid. It was to Saint

Winifred Cadfael addressed his plea, a Welshman invoking a Welsh saint, and one to whom he felt very close, and for whom he had an almost family affection. Herself hardly more than a child at her martyrdom, she would not let harm come to another threatened child.

Brother Rhun, whom she had healed, was carefully trimming the scented candles he made for her shrine when Cadfael approached, but he turned his fair young head towards the petitioner, gave him one glance of his aquamarine eyes, that seemed to have their own innate light, and smiled and went away. Not to linger and complete his work when the prayers ended, not to hide in the shadows and watch, but clean away out of knowledge, on swift, agile, silent feet that had once gone lamely and in pain, to leave the whole listening vault ready to receive the appeal in its folded hands, and channel it aloft.

Cadfael arose from his knees comforted, without knowing or asking why. Outside, the light was fading rapidly, and here within, the altar lamp and Saint Winifred's perfumed candles made small islands of pure radiance in a great enfolding gloom, like a warm cloak against the frost of the outside world. The grace that had just touched Cadfael had a long enough reach to find Richard, wherever he was, deliver him if he was a prisoner, console him if he was frightened, heal him if he was hurt. Cadfael went out from the choir, round the parish altar and into the nave, sensible of having done what was most needful, and content to wait patiently and passively until grace should be manifested.

It seemed that Rafe of Coventry had also had solemn and personal prayers to offer, for he was just rising from his knees in the empty and silent nave as Cadfael came through. He recognised his acquaintance of the stable yard with a shadowed but friendly smile, that came and went briefly on his lips but lingered amiably in his eyes.

'Good even, Brother!' Matched in height and pace, they fell naturally into step together as they turned towards the south porch. 'I hope to be held excused,' said Rafe, 'for coming to church booted and spurred and dusty from riding, but I came late, and had no time to make myself seemly.'

'Most welcome, however you come,' said Cadfael. 'Not everyone who lodges with us shows his face in the church. I've had small chance to see you these two days, I've been out and about myself. Have you had successful dealing in these parts?'

'Better, at least, than one of yours guests,' said Rafe, casting a side glance at the narrow door that led towards the mortuary chapel. 'But no, I would not say I've found quite what I needed. Not yet!'

'His son is here now,' said Cadfael, following the glance. 'This morning he came.'

'I have seen him,' said Rafe. 'He came back from the town just before Vespers. By the look and the sound of him he's done none too well, either, with whatever he's about. I suppose it's a man he's after?'

'It is. The young man I told you of,' said Cadfael drily, and studied his companion sidelong as they crossed the lighted parish altar.

'Yes, I remember. Then he's come back empty-handed, no poor wretch tethered to his stirrup leather.' But Rafe remained tolerantly indifferent to young men, and indeed to the Bosiet clan. His thoughts were somewhere else. At the alms box beside the altar he stopped, on impulse, and dug a hand into the pouch slung at his waist, to draw out a handful of coins. One of them slipped through his fingers, but he did not immediately stoop to pick it up, but dropped three of its fellows into the box before he turned to look for the stray. By which time Cadfael had lifted it from the tiled floor, and had it in his open palm.

If they had not been standing where the altar candles gave a clear light he would have noticed nothing strange about it. A silver penny like other silver pennies, the universal coin. Yet not quite like any he had seen before in the alms boxes. It was bright and untarnished, but indifferently struck, and it felt light in the hand. Clumsily arrayed round the short cross on the reverse, the moneyer's name appeared to be Sigebert, a minter Cadfael never remembered to have heard of in the midlands. And when he turned it, the crude head was not Stephen's familiar profile, nor dead King Henry's, but unmistakably a woman's, coiled and coroneted. It hardly needed the name sprawled round the rim: 'Matilda Dom. Ang.' The empress's formal name and title. It seemed her mintage was short-weight.

He looked up to find Rafe watching him steadily, and with a small private smile that held more irony than simple amusement. There was a moment of silence while they eyed each other. Then: 'Yes,' said Rafe, 'you are right. It would have been noted after I was gone. But it has a value, even here.

Your beggars will not reject it because it was struck in Oxford.'

'And no long time ago,' said Cadfael.

'No long time ago.'

'My besetting sin,' said Cadfael ruefully, 'is curiosity.' He held out the coin, and Rafe took it as gravely, and with deliberation dropped it after its fellows into the alms box. 'But I am not loose-mouthed. Nor do I hold any honest man's allegiance against him. A pity there should have to be factions, and decent men fighting one another, and all of them convinced they have the right of it. Come and go freely for me.'

'And does your curiosity not extend,' wondered Rafe softly, the wry smile perceptible in his voice, 'to wondering what such a man is doing here, so far from the battle? Come, I am sure you have guessed at what I am. Perhaps you think I felt it the wiser part to get out of Oxford before it was too late?'

'No,' said Cadfael positively, 'that never did and never would enter my mind. Not of you! And why should so discreet a man as that venture north into king's country?'

'No, granted that argues very little wisdom,' agreed Rafe. 'What would you guess then?'

'I can think of one possibility,' said Cadfael gravely and quietly. 'We heard here of one man who did not take flight of his own will out of Oxford, while there was time, but was sent. On his lady's business, and with that about him well worth stealing. And that he did not get far, for his horse was found straying and blood-stained, all that he had carried gone, and the man himself vanished from the face of the earth.' Rafe was watching him attentively, his face unreadable as ever, the lingering smile sombre but untroubled. 'Such a man as you seem to me,' said Cadfael, 'might well have come so far north from Oxford looking for Renaud Bourchier's murderer.'

Their eyes held, mutually accepting, even approving, what they saw. Slowly and with absolute finality Rafe of Coventry said: 'No.'

He stirred and sighed, breaking the spell of the brief but profound silence that followed. 'I am sorry, Brother, but no, you have not read me right. I am not looking for Bourchier's murderer. It was a good thought, almost I wish it had been true. But it is not.'

And with that he moved on towards the south door, and out into the early twilight in the cloister, and Brother Cadfael followed in silence, asking and offering nothing more. He knew truth when he heard it.

Chapter Ten

IT WAS about the same hour that Cadfael and Rafe of Coventry emerged from the church after Vespers, when Hyacinth stole out from Eilmund's cottage, and made his way through the deepest cover towards the river. He had been all that day pinned close within doors, for there had again been men of the garrison sweeping through the forest, and though their passage was rapid and cursory, for the aim was to carry the search further afield, and though they knew Eilmund, and felt no compulsion to investigate his holding a second time, they were still liable to look in on him in neighbourly fashion as they passed, and ask him casually if anything of note had come to his attention. Hyacinth did not take kindly to being shut within doors, nor, indeed, to hiding. By the evening he was chafing at his confinement, but by then the hunters were on their way back, abandoning the chase until the morrow, and he was free to do a little hunting of his own.

For all the wariness and fear he felt on his own account, and admitted with his infallible and fiery honesty, he could not rest for thinking of Richard, who had come running to warn him, so gallantly and thoughtlessly. But for that the boy would never have placed himself in danger. But why should there be danger to him in his own woods, among his own people? In a troubled England there were lawless men living wild, no doubt of that, but this shire had gone almost untouched by the war for more than four years now, and seemed to enjoy a degree of peace and order unmatched further south, and the town was barely seven miles distant, and the sheriff active and young, and even, so far as a sheriff can be, popular with his people. And the more Hyacinth thought about it, the more clear did it seem to him that the only threat to Richard that he had ever heard of was Dame Dionisia's threat to marry him off to the two manors she coveted. For that she had persisted in every device she could think of. Hyacinth had been her instrument once, and could not forget it. She *must* be the force behind the boy's disappearance.

True, the sheriff had descended on Eaton, searched every corner, and found no trace, and no one, in a household devoted to the boy, able to cast the least suspicion on Dionisia's indignant innocence. She had no other property where she could hide either boy or pony. And though Fulke Astley might be willing to connive, feeling that he had as good a chance of securing Eaton as she had of getting her hands on his daughter's inheritance, yet Wroxeter also had been searched thoroughly, and without success.

Today the hunt had moved on, and according to all that Annet had gathered from the returning sergeants it would continue as doggedly on the morrow, but it had not yet reached Leighton, two miles down-river. And though Astley and his household preferred to live at Wroxeter, the more remote manor of Leighton was also in his hold.

It was the only starting point Hyacinth could find, and it was worth a venture. If Richard had been caught in the woods by some of Astley's men, or those from Eaton who were willing to serve Dionisia's turn, it might well have been thought wisest to remove him as far as Leighton, rather than try to hide him nearer home. Moreover, if she still intended to force this marriage on the boy – there were ways of getting the right answers out of even the most stubborn children, more by guile than by terror – she needed a priest, and Hyacinth had been about the village of Eaton long enough to know that Father Andrew was an honest man, by no means a good tool for such a purpose. The priest at Leighton, less well acquainted with the ins and outs of the affair, might be more amenable.

At least it was one thing which could be tested. It was no use Eilmund counselling him sensibly and good-naturedly to stay where he was and not risk capture; even Eilmund understood and approved what he called folly. Annet had not tried to dissuade Hyacinth, only sensibly provided him a black, much worn coat of Eilmund's too wide for him but excellent for moving invisibly by night, and a dark capuchon to shadow his face.

Between the forest and the meanderings of the river, downstream from the mill and the fisheries and the few cottages that served them, the open water meadows extended, and there the light still hung, and a faint ground mist lay veiling the green, and twined like a silver serpent along the river. But along the northern rim the forest continued, halfway to Leighton, and beyond that point the ground rose towards the last low foothills of the Wrekin, and he would have to make use of what scattered cover remained. But here where trees and grassland met he could move fast, keeping within the edge of the woods but benefiting by the light of the open fields, and the stillness and silence and the careful stealth of his own movements would ensure that he should get due warning of any other creature stirring in the night.

He had covered more than a mile when the first small sounds reached him, and he froze, and stood with pricked ears, listening intently. A single metallic note, somewhere behind him, harness briefly shaken. Then a soft brushing of bushes as something passed, and then, unmistakable though quiet, and still some distance away, a subdued voice ventured briefly what sounded like a question, and as meekly subsided. Not one person abroad in the dusk, but two, or why speak at all? And mounted, and keeping to the rim of the woodland like himself, when it would have been simpler by far to take to the meadows. Riders by night, no more anxious to be observed than he was, and going in the same direction. Hyacinth strained his ears to pick up the muted, leaf-cushioned tread of hooves, and try to determine the line they were taking through the trees. Close to the rim, for the sake of what light remained, but more concerned with secrecy than with haste.

Cautiously Hyacinth withdrew further into the forest and stood motionless in cover to let them pass by. There was still enough light left to make them a little more than shadowy outlines as they came and passed in single file, first a tall horse that showed as a moving pallor, probably a light grey, with a big, gross man on his back, bearded, bare-headed, the folds of his capuchon draped on his shoulders. Hyacinth knew the shape and the bearing, had seen this very man mount and ride, thus sack-like but solid in the saddle, from Richard Ludel's funeral. What was Fulke Astley doing here in the night, making his way thus furtively, not by the roads but through the forest, from one to the other of his own manors? For where else could he be bound?

And the figure that followed him, on a thickset cob, was certainly a woman, and could be nobody else but his daughter, surely, that unknown Hiltrude who seemed so old and unpleasing to young Richard.

So their errand, after all, was not so mysterious. Of course they would want the marriage achieved as soon as possible, if they had Richard in their hands. They had waited these few days until both Eaton and Wroxeter had been searched, but with the hunt being spread more widely they would wait no longer. Whatever risk they might be taking, once the match was a reality they could weather whatever storms followed. They could even afford to set Richard free to return to the abbey, for nothing and no one but the authority of the church could set him free from a wife.

And that being so, what could be done to prevent? There was no time to run back either to Eilmund's house, and have Annet carry words to castle or abbey, or direct to the town, and Hyacinth still found himself humanly reluctant to throw his own chance of liberty to the winds. But it did not arise, there was no time left at all. If he went back, by the time rescue could arrive for Richard he would be married. Perhaps there might yet be time to find where they had hidden him, and whisk him away from under their noses. These two were in no hurry, and Dame Dionisia had still to make the short journey from Eaton without detection. And the priest – where would they have found a willing priest? Nothing could be done until a priest was there.

Hyacinth forsook the thick cover, and made his way deeper into the belt of forest, no longer intent on secrecy, only on speed. At the pace the riders were making he could outrun them on a path, and in this extremity he would venture even the highroad, if need be, and risk meeting others still out on their own lawful occasions. But there was a path, too near the open road for the Astleys to favour it, and merging into the road itself once it had crossed the upland ridge. Hyacinth reached it and ran, fleet and silent on the thick carpet of leaves too moist and limp to rustle under his feet.

Once out on to the open track and plunging downhill towards the village, still almost a mile distant, he drew off again into the fields dipping to the river, and ran from one scattered covert to another, assured now that he was ahead of

Astley. He waded the little stream that came down from the foot of the Wrekin to reach the Severn here, and went on along the river bank. One isolated tongue of woodland came down almost to the water, and from its shelter he could see for the first time the low stockade of the manor, and the long level of the roof within, sharp and clear against the glimmer of the water and the pallor of the sky.

It was good fortune that the trees approached so closely to the stockade on the side nearest to the river bank. From tree to tree Hyacinth darted, and reaching an oak that spread branches across the barrier, climbed nimbly up into the crotch to peer cautiously within the enclosure. He was looking at the long rear face of the house, across the roofs of barn and byre and stable lining the containing fence. The same pattern of a low undercroft, with hall and chamber and kitchen above on the living floor, and the steps to the only door must be on the opposite side. Here there was no entrance except to the undercroft, and only one small window, and that was shuttered. Under it a small wing had been built out, extending the undercroft. The shingled roof was steep, the eaves dipped fairly low. Hyacinth eyed it speculatively, and debated how securely fastened those shutters might be. To reach them would be easily possible, to find a way in by that road might be more of a problem. But this rear face of the house was the only one sheltered from observation. All this nefarious activity of Astleys and Ludels would be centred round the single great doorway into the hall, on the other side.

He swung himself down to hang by his hands within the pale, and dropped into a shadowy corner between barn and stable. At least stumbling on this nocturnal journey eased him of one fear. Richard was surely here, was alive and well and presentable as they wanted him, well fed, well cared for, probably even indulged beyond normal in the hope of cajoling him into willing consent. Indulged, in fact, with everything he could desire and they furnish, except his freedom. And that was the first profound relief. Now to get him out!

Here in the darkening yard there was no one stirring. Hyacinth slid softly out of his shelter and moved round the pale from shadow to shadow, until he slipped round the corner to the eastern end of the house. There were unshuttered windows above him here, subdued light shining through. He refuged in the deep doorway to the undercroft, and stretched his ears for voices from above, and thought that he caught wordless murmurings, as though the aim was to keep everything of this night's activities secret. Round the next corner, where the steep stairway to the hall door ascended, there was a torch fixed, he knew it by the flickering light spilled on the beaten earth before him by fitful glimpses. There were servants moving there, too, soft-stepping and low-voiced. And the dull sound of hooves, coming at a walk into the court. The bride and her father arriving, thought Hyacinth, and wondered for a fleeting moment how the girl felt about the match, and whether she was not as wronged and slighted as Richard, and even more helpless.

He drew back in some haste, for the grooms would be leading the horses to the stables, which were in the near corner of the yard, for he had heard the beasts stirring in their stalls as he hung listening in the tree. The jutting wing of the undercroft provided cover from that corner. He rounded it and flattened himself into the dark angle of the walls behind the obstruction, and heard a single groom come leading both mounts.

He could not move until the man had gone, and time was snapping at his heels like a herdsman's dog. But the groom was brisk, and wasted no time on his charges, perhaps wanting his bed, for it must be getting late. Hyacinth heard the stable door slammed to, and the rapid footsteps scurrying away round the corner of the house. Only then, when he was able to draw off and take another look at this almost blind face of the manor, did Hyacinth observe what he had missed before. Through the join in the massive shutters on this, the only shuttered window in the house in these mild nights, a hair-line of light showed. More noticeable still, in one of the boards, close to the join, there was a small round eye of light, where a slanting knot in the wood had fallen out and left a hole. Why should this rear room be shuttered and lighted, unless it had a guest, and one who must be kept safe and secret? Hyacinth doubted if the space between the stone mullions would be large enough to let a man through, but it might be wide enough for a ten-year-old boy, and one rather small for his years. With that low roof beneath the window, they would not want him to make his escape, nor would they want any inquisitive person to see him there within.

It could at least be tried. Hyacinth leaped to get a hold of the overhanging eaves, and hauled himself up on to the shingles, to lie flat there against the stone wall, listening, though he had made little noise about it, and no one stirred to take note or investigate. He drew himself cautiously up the slope of the roof to the shuttered window. The timbers were heavy and solid, and secured somehow within the room, for when he laid a hand under the centre, where they joined, and essayed to pull them apart, they held fast as iron, and he had no tools to try and force them apart, and doubted if he could have done it even if he had had a whole armoury of implements. The hinges were strong and immovable. Neither top nor bottom of the shutters yielded to force even by a hair. There must be iron bolts that could be shot from within, and securely locked. And time was running out. Richard was strong-willed, obstinate and ingenious. If it had been possible for him to break out from his prison, he would have done it long ago.

Hyacinth laid his ear to the hair-line crack, but could hear nothing moving within. He must now make sure whether he was wasting the time which was so precious and running out so fast. At the risk of being detected, he rapped with his knuckles against the shutter, and setting his lips to the tiny eye of light, sent a shrill whistle through the hole.

This time there was an audible gasp somewhere in the room, then a rapid scrambling, as if someone had uncurled from being coiled defensively into a corner, set foot to floor, and taken a couple of startled steps across the room, only to halt again in doubt and alarm. Hyacinth rapped again, and called softly through the hole: 'Richard, is that you?'

Light footsteps came in a rush, a small body crowded against the inner side of the shutters. 'Who is it?' whispered Richard's voice urgently, close to the crack of light. 'Who's there?'

'Hyacinth! Richard, are you alone? I can't get in to you. Is all well with you?'

'No!' breathed the voice in indignant complaint, and proving by its spirit and anger that in fact he was in very good heart and excellent condition. 'They won't let me out, they keep hammering and hammering at me to do what they want, and agree to be married. They're bringing her tonight, they're going to *make* me . . .'

'I know,' groaned Hyacinth, 'but I can't get you out. And there's no time to get word to the sheriff. Tomorrow I could, but I saw them coming here tonight.'

'They won't let me out until I do what they want,' Richard hissed grievously into the crack. 'I almost said I would. They go on and on at me, and I don't know what to do, and I'm frightened they'll only take me and hide me somewhere else if I refuse, because they know every house is being searched.' His voice was losing its bold, belligerent tone and faltering into distress. It's hard for a boy of ten to stand off for long the implacable adults who hold the upper hand. 'My grandmother promised I should have whatever I liked, whatever I wanted, if I'd say the words she wants me to say. But I *don't want* a wife . . .'

'Richard . . . Richard . . .' Hyacinth was repeating persistently into this lament, and for a while unheard. 'Listen, Richard! They'll have to bring a priest to marry you – not Father Andrew, surely, he'd have scruples – but someone. Speak to him, tell him it's against your will, tell him – Richard, have you heard who it's to be?' A new and arresting thought had entered his mind. '*Who* is to marry you?'

'I heard them,' whispered Richard, grown calm again, 'saying they couldn't trust Father Andrew. My grandmother is bringing the hermit with her to do it.'

'Cuthred? You're sure?' Hyacinth had almost forgotten to keep his voice down in his astonishment.

'Yes, Cuthred. Yes, I'm sure, I heard her say so.'

'Richard, listen, then!' Hyacinth leaned close, his lips to the crack. 'If you refuse, they'll only visit it on you, and take you away somewhere else. Better for you to do what they want. No, trust me, do what I say, it's the only way we can foil them. Believe me, you won't have anything to fear, you won't be burdened with a wife, you're safe as in sanctuary. Just do as I say, be meek and obedient, and let them think you tamed, and they may even let you take your pony and ride back to the abbey, for they'll have what they wanted, and think it can't be undone. But it can! Oh, never fret, they won't want anything more of you, not for years yet! Trust me, and do it! Will you? Quickly, before they come! Will you do it?'

Bemused and doubtful, Richard faltered: 'Yes!' but could not help protesting the next moment: 'But how can that be? *Why* do you say it's safe?'

Hyacinth pressed close and whispered the answer. He knew by the sudden shaken spurt of laughter, exuberant and brief, that Richard had caught it and understood. And just in time, for he heard from across the room the sharp clash of a door being unbolted and flung open, and the voice of Dame Dionisia, honey and gall, half cajoling and half menacing, saying firmly and loudly: 'Your bride is come, Richard. Here is Hiltrude. And you will be gracious and courteous to her, will you not, and please us all?'

Richard must have darted away from the window at the first touch of a hand on the bolt, for his small, cautious voice said just audibly, and from some yards distant: 'Yes, grandmother!' Unwillingly dutiful, reluctantly obedient, a will only half-broken, but half would do! Her gratified but still wary: 'That's my good child!' was the last thing Hyacinth heard as he edged his way carefully down the slope of the roof and dropped to the ground.

He went on his homeward way without haste, content with his night's work. There was now no urgency, he could afford to go slowly, mindful that he himself was still hunted. For the boy was alive, well fed, well cared for, and in good spirits. No actual harm had come to him, none would come, however he chafed at being a prisoner. And in the end he would have the laugh of his captors. Hyacinth made his way blithely through the soft, chilly night scented with the rising mist of the water meadows, and the deep, dank leaf mould of the woods. The moon rose, but so veiled that it gave only a dim grey light. By midnight he would be safely back in his sanctuary in Eyton forest. And in the morning, by some means Annet would contrive for the purpose, Hugh Beringar should learn exactly where to look for Brother Paul's lost schoolboy.

When it was all over, and he had done what they wanted, however grudgingly, Richard had expected to be made much of by way of gratitude, perhaps even let out from this small room which was his prison, however comfortable it might be. He was not so foolish as to suppose that they would set him free to do as he pleased. He would have to keep up this meek front for a while, and suppress the inward glee he felt at having the laugh of them in secret, before they would dare to produce him before the world, with what manner of story to account for his loss and recovery he could not guess, but they would have it all off by heart. Certainly they would say he had consented of his own will to the ceremony just completed, and to the best of their knowledge it would then be far too late for him to say anything to the contrary, since what was done could not be undone. Only Richard knew that in fact nothing had been done to need undoing. He had absolute faith in Hyacinth. Whatever Hyacinth said was sooth.

But he had considered that they would owe him thanks and indulgence for his compliance. He had preserved his sullen but subdued face, because it would have been too betraying to let even a gleam of laughter show through, but he had repeated all the words they dictated to him, had even brought himself to take Hiltrude's hand when he was told to do so, though he had never once looked at her until the sound of her soft, dull voice, repeating the vows as resignedly as his own, had jolted him into wondering for a moment if she was being forced as he was. That possibility had never occurred to him until then, and he did lift a furtive glance to her face. She was not so very old, after all, and not very tall, and did not look like a threat so much as a victim. She might not even be really plain if only she did not look so subdued and glum. His startled impulse of sympathy for her was complicated by a grain of equally surprised resentment that she should seem as depressed at marrying him as he had good cause to be at marrying her.

But after all his compliance, not a word of thanks, rather this grandmother studied him ominously and at length, and he was afraid with some lingering suspicion in her eye, and then admonished him grimly: 'You have done well to come to your duty at last, and behave yourself fittingly towards those who know best for you. See that you keep to that mind, sir! Now say your goodnight to your wife. Tomorrow you shall get to know her better.'

And he had done as he was told, and they had all left him there, still bolted in alone, though they had sent a servant with food from the supper they were no doubt enjoying in the hall. He sat brooding on his bed, thinking over all that had happened in one late evening, and all that might follow next day. Hiltrude he forgot as soon as she was out of sight. He knew about these affairs. If you were only ten years old they didn't, for some reason, make you live with your wife, not until you were grown up. While she remained under the same roof with you, you would be expected to be civil to her, perhaps even attentive, but then she would go back with her father to her own home until you were thought to be old enough to share your bed and household with her. Now that he began to think seriously about it, it seemed to Richard that there were no privileges at all attached to being married, his grandmother would go on treating him just as before, as a child of no account, ordering him about, scolding him, cuffing him if he annoyed her, even beating him if he defied her. In short, it behoved the lord of Eaton to regain his liberty by whatever means offered, and escape out of her hold. He could not be very important to her now, he had served his purpose, what mattered was the land settlement. If she felt she had secured that, she might soon be willing to let go of the instrument.

Richard rolled himself warmly in his brychans and went to sleep. If they were discussing him in hall, and debating what to do about him, that did not trouble his dreams. He was too young and too innocently hopeful to take his problems to bed with him.

His door was still bolted next morning, and the servant who brought his breakfast gave him no chance to slip past, though indeed he had no intention of trying it, since he knew he would not get far, and his role now was to continue to be docile and disarm suspicion. When his grandmother drew the bolt and came in to him it was old familiar habit, rather than guile, that caused him to rise at her entrance, as he had been taught, and lift up his face for her kiss. And the kiss was no chillier than it had always been, and for a moment he felt the inescapable kindness of the blood warm them both, something he had never questioned, though she had very seldom expressed it. The contact caused him to shake, and brought the sudden astonished sting of tears into his eyes just as inevitably as the surge of obstinate recoil into his mind. It did him no harm with her. She looked down at him from her erect and formidable height with a somewhat softened gaze.

'Well, sir, and how do you find yourself this morning? Are you minded to be a good, obedient boy, and do all you can to please me? If so, you shall find you and I will get on very well together. You have made a beginning, now go on as you began. And think shame that you defied and denied me so long.'

Richard drooped his long lashes and looked down at his feet. 'Yes, grandmother.' And then, in meek assay: 'May I go out today? I don't like being shut in here, as if it was night all the time.'

'We'll see,' she said, but to Richard the tone clearly meant: 'No!' She would not reason nor bargain, only lay down the law to him. 'But not yet, you have not deserved it. First prove that you've learned where your duty lies, and then you shall have your freedom again. You are not ill done to, you have everything you need here, be content until you have earned more and better.'

'But I *have*!' he flashed. 'I did what you wanted, you ought to do what I want. It's unfair to shut me up here, unfair and unkind. I don't even know what you've done with my pony.'

'Your pony is safe in the stable,' said Dionisia sharply, 'and well cared for, as you are. And you had best mind your manners with me, sir, or you'll have to cause to regret it. They've taught you at that abbey school to be saucy to your elders, but it's a lesson you had better unlearn as quickly as you can, for your own sake.'

'I'm not being saucy,' he pleaded, relapsing into sullenness. 'I only want to be in daylight, I want to go out, not sit here without even being able to see the trees and the grass. It's wretched in here, without any company . . .'

'You shall have company,' she promised, seizing on one complaint to which she could provide a complaisant answer. 'I'll send your bride to keep you company. I want you to get to know her better now, for after today she'll return to Wroxeter with her father, and you, Richard,' she said warningly and with a sharpening eye on him, 'will return with me to your own manor, to take your proper place. And I shall expect you to conduct yourself properly there, and not go hankering after that school, now that you're married and a man of substance. Eaton is yours, and that is where you should be, and I expect you to maintain that, if anyone – *anyone* – should call it in question. Do you understand me, sir?'

He understood her very well. He was to be cajoled, intimidated, bullied into declaring, even to Brother Paul and Father Abbot if need be, that he had run home to his grandmother of his own will, and of his own will submitted to the marriage they had planned for him. He hugged his secret knowledge gleefully to his heart as he said submissively: 'Yes, madam!'

'Good! And now I'll send in Hiltrude to you, and see that you behave well to her. You will have to get used to her, and she to you, so you may as well begin now.' And she relented so far as to kiss him again on leaving him, though it resembled a slap as much as a kiss. She went out in a dusty swirl of long green skirts, and he heard the bolt shot again after her.

And what had he got out of all that, except the fact that his pony was in the stable here, and if only he could get to it he might make his escape even now. But presently in came Hiltrude, as his grandmother had threatened, and all his resentment and dislike of the girl, undeserved though it was, boiled up within him into childish anger.

She still seemed to him to belong at least to the generation of the mother he could hardly remember, but she was not really utterly plain, she had a clear, pale skin and large, guarded brown eyes, and if her hair was straight and of a mousey brown colour, she had a great mass of it, plaited in a thick braid that hung to her waist. She did not look ill-natured, but she did look bitterly resigned and wretched. She stood for a moment with her back to the door, staring thoughtfully at the boy curled up glumly on his bed.

'So they've sent you to be my guard dog,' said Richard unpleasantly.

Hiltrude crossed the room and sat down on the sill of the shuttered window, and looked at him without favour. 'I know you don't like me,' she said, not sadly but with quite unexpected vigour. 'Small reason why you should, and for that matter, I don't like you. But it seems we're both bound, no help for it now. Why, *why* did you ever give way? I only said I would, at last, because I was so sure *you* were safe enough there at the abbey, and they'd never let it come to this. And then you have to fall into their hands like a fool, and let them break you down. And here we both are, and may God help us!' She relented of the note of exasperation in her own voice, and ended with weary kindness: 'It's not your fault, you're only a child, what could you do? And it is isn't that I dislike you, I don't even know you, it's just that I didn't want you, I don't want you, any more than you want me.'

Richard was staring at her, by this time, with mouth and eyes wide open, struck dumb with astonishment at finding her, as it were, not a token embarrassment, a millstone round his neck, but a real person with a great deal to say for herself, and by no means a fool. Slowly he uncoiled his slim legs and set his feet to the floor, to feel solid substance under him. Slowly he repeated, in a small, shocked voice: 'You never wanted to marry me?'

'A baby like you?' she said, careless of offence. 'No, I never did.'

'Then why did you ever agree to do it?' He was too indignant over her capitulation to resent the reflection on his years. 'If you'd said no, and kept saying it, we should both have been saved.'

'Because my father is a man very hard to say no to, and had begun to tell me that I was getting too old to have another suitor, and if I didn't take you I should be forced to enter a sisterhood and stay a maid until I died. And that I wanted even less. And I thought the abbot would keep fast hold of you, and nothing would ever be allowed to come of it. And now here we are, and what are we to do about it?'

Himself surprised at feeling an almost sympathetic curiosity about this woman who had sloughed a skin before his eyes, and emerged as vivid and real as himself, Richard asked almost shyly: 'What *do* you want? If you could have your way, what would you like to have?'

'I would like,' said Hiltrude, her brown eyes suddenly burning with anger and loss, 'a young man named Evrard, who keeps my father's manor roll and is his steward at Wroxeter, and who likes me, too, whether you think that likely or not. But he's a younger son and has no land, and where there's no land to marry to his own my father has no interest. There's an uncle who may well leave his manor to Evrard, being fond of him and childless, but land now is what my father wants, not someday and maybe land.' The fire burned down. She turned her head aside. 'Why do I tell you this? You can't understand, and it's not your fault. There's nothing you can do to better it.'

Richard was beginning to think that there might be something very pertinent he could do for her, if she in her turn would do something for him. Cautiously he asked: 'What are they doing now, your father and my grandmother? She said you'd be going back to Wroxeter after today. What are they planning? And has Father Abbot been looking for me all this time since I left?'

'You didn't know? Not only the abbot, but the sheriff and all his men are looking for you. They've searched Eaton and Wroxeter, and are beating every bush in the forest. My father was afraid they might reach here by today, but she thought not. They were wondering whether to move you back to Eaton in the night, since it's been searched already, but Dame Dionisia felt sure the officers had several days' work left before they'd reach Leighton, and in any case, she said, if a proper watch was set there'd be ample time to put you over the river with an escort and send you down to shelter at Buildwas. Better, she said, than moving you back towards Shrewsbury yet.'

'Where are they now?' asked Richard intently. 'My grandmother?'

'She's ridden back to Eaton to have everything there looking just as it should. Her hermit went back to his cell in the night. It wouldn't do if anyone knew he'd been away.'

'And your father?'

'He's out and about among his tenants here, but he'll not be far away. He took his clerk with him. There'll be dues unpaid that he wants collected, I daresay.' She was indifferent to her father's movements, but she did feel some curiosity as to what was going on in this child's head, to sharpen his voice into such hopeful purpose, and brighten his disconsolate eye. 'Why? What is there in that for you? Or for me!' she added bitterly.

'There might,' said Richard, beginning to glitter, 'be something I can do for you, something good, if you'll do something for me in return. If they're both out of the house, help me to get away while they're gone. My pony's there in the stable, she told me as much. If I could get to him and slip away, you could bolt the door again, and no one would know I was gone until evening.'

She shook her head decisively. 'And who would get the blame? I wouldn't put it off on to one of the servants, and I've no great appetite for it myself. The troubles I already have are enough for me, I thank you!' But she added warily, seeing that his hopeful fire was by no means quenched: 'But I would be willing to think out the best means, if I thought it would solve anything for me. But how can it? For a fair deliverance I'd venture anything Father could say or do. But what's the use, when we're tied together as we are, and no way out?'

Richard bounded up from his bed and darted across the room to settle confidingly beside her on the broad sill. Close to her ear he said breathlessly: 'If I tell you a secret, will you swear to keep it until I'm safely away, and help me to get out of here? I promise you, I promise you it will be worth your while.'

'You are dreaming,' she said tolerantly, turning to look at him thus closely, and seeing his secret brightness undimmed by her disbelief. 'There's no way out of marriage unless you're a prince and have the Pope's ear, and who cares about lesser folk like us? True, we're not bedded, nor will be for years yet, but if you think your old dame and my father would ever let it come to an annulment, you waste your hopes. They've got their way, they'll never let go of their gains.'

'No, it's nothing like that,' he persisted, 'we need nothing from Pope or law. You must believe me. At least promise not to tell, and when you hear what it is, you'll be willing to help me, too.'

'Very well,' she said, humouring him, even half convinced now that he knew something she did not know, but still doubting if it would or could deliver them. 'Very well, I promise. What is this precious secret?'

Gleefully he advanced his lips to her ear, his cheek teased by the touch of a lock of her hair that curled loose there, and breathed his secret as though the very boards at their backs had ears. And after one incredulous instant of stillness and silence she began to laugh very softly, to shake with her laughter, and throwing her arms about Richard, hugged him briefly to her heart.

'For that you *shall* go free, whatever it cost me! You deserve it!'

Chapter Eleven

ONCE CONVINCED, it was she who made the plans. She knew the house and the servants, and as long as there was no suspicion of her subservience she had the entry everywhere, and could give orders to grooms and maids as she pleased.

'Best wait until after they've brought your dinner and taken away the dish again. It will be a longer time then before anyone comes in to you again. There's a back gate through the pale, from the stable out into the paddock. I could tell Jehan to turn your pony out to grass, he's been shut in too long to be liking it. There are some bushes in the field there, round behind the stable, close to the wicket. I'll make shift to hide your saddle and harness there before noon. I can get you out of here through the undercroft, while they're all busy in hall and kitchens.'

'But your father will be home then,' protested Richard doubtfully.

'After his dinner my father will be snoring. If he does look in on you at all, it will be before he sits down to table, to make sure you're safe in your cage. Better for me, too, I shall have sat out my morning with you gallantly, who's to think I'll change my tune after that? It might even be good sport,' said Hiltrude, growing animated in contemplating her benevolent mischief, 'when they go to take you your supper, and find the window still shuttered and barred, and the bird flown.'

'But then everyone will be harried and cursed and blamed,'

said Richard, 'because somebody must have drawn the bolt.'

'So then we all deny it, and whoever looks likeliest to be suspected I'll bring off safely, saying he's never been out of my sight and never touched the door since your dinner went in. If it comes to the worst,' said Hiltrude, with uncustomary resolution, 'I'll say I must have forgotten to shoot the bolt after leaving you the last time. What can he do? He'll still be thinking he has you trapped in marriage with me, wherever you run to. Better still,' she cried, clapping her hands, 'I'll be the one who brings you your dinner, and waits with you, and brings out the dish again – then no one else can be blamed for leaving the door unbolted. A wife should begin at once to wait on her husband, it will look well.'

'You're not afraid of your father?' ventured Richard, open-eyed with startled respect, even admiration, but reluctant to leave her to sustain so perilous a part.

'I am – I was! Now, whatever happens, it will be worth the pains. I must go, Richard, while there's no one in the stable. You wait and trust me, and keep up your heart. You've lifted mine!'

She was at the door when Richard, still thoughtfully following her light and buoyant passage, so changed from the subdued, embittered creature whose cold hand he had held in the night, said impulsively after her: 'Hiltrude – I think I might do worse than marry you, after all.' And added, with barely decent haste: 'But not yet!'

Everything that she had promised she performed. She brought his dinner, and sat with him and made desultory, awkward talk while he ate it, such talk as might be expected to a stranger, and a child at that, and one forced upon her and reluctantly accepted, so that however much he might be resented, there was no longer any point in being at odds with him. Less from guile than because he was hungry and busy eating, Richard responded with grunts rather than words. Had anyone been listening, they would certainly have found the exchanges depressingly appropriate.

Hiltrude carried the dish back to the kitchen, and returned to him as soon as she had made certain that everyone else about the house was occupied. The narrow wooden stair down into the undercroft was conveniently screened from the passage that led to the kitchen, they had no trouble in skipping hastily down it, and emerging from below ground by the deep doorway where Hyacinth had sheltered, and from there it was just one dangerous dart across open ground to the wicket in the fence, half hidden by the bulk of the stable. Saddle and bridle and all, she had left his harness concealed behind the bushes, and the sable pony came to him gladly. Close under the rear wall of the stable he saddled up in trembling haste, and led the pony out of the paddock and down towards the river, where the belt of trees offered cover, before he dared to tighten the girth and mount. Now, if all went well, he had until early evening before he would be missed.

Hiltrude went back up the stairs from the undercroft, and took care to spend her afternoon blamelessly among the women of the household, within sight every moment, and occupied with the proper affairs of the lady of the manor. She had bolted Richard's door, since clearly if it had been inadvertently left unfastened, and the prisoner taken advantage of the fact, even a ten-year-old boy would have the sense to shoot the bolt again and preserve the appearances. When the flight was discovered she could very well protest that she had no recollection of forgetting to fasten it, though admitting at last that she must have done so. But by then, if all went well, Richard would be back in the abbey enclave, and taking belated thought how to present himself as the blameless victim, and bury all recollection of the guilty truant who had run off without permission and caused all this turmoil and anxiety. Well, that was Richard's affair. She had done her part.

It was a pity that the groom who had turned Richard's pony into the paddock should have occasion to fetch in one of the other beasts out to graze, about the middle of the afternoon, since he had noticed that it was slightly lame. He could hardly fail to observe that the pony was gone. Seizing on the first and obvious, if none too likely, possibility, he was halfway across the court crying that there had been thieves in the paddock before it occurred to him to go back and look in the stable for the saddle and harness. That put a somewhat different complexion on the loss. And besides, why take the least valuable beast in sight? And why risk theft in daylight? Good dark nights were more favourable.

So he arrived in hall announcing loudly and breathlessly that the young bridegroom's pony was gone, saddle and all, and my lord had better look to see if he still had the boy safe under lock and key. Fulke went himself, in haste, hardly believing the news, and found the door securely bolted as before, but the room within empty. He let out a bellow of rage that made Hiltrude flinch over her embroidery frame, but she kept her eyes lowered to her work, and went on demurely stitching until the storm erupted in the doorway and swelled to fill the hall.

'Which of you was it? Who waited on him last? Which fool among you, fools every one as you are, left the door unbarred? Or has one of you loosed him deliberately, in my despite? I'll have the hide of the traitorous wretch, whoever he may be. Speak up! Who took the slippery imp his dinner?'

The menservants held off out of his immediate reach, every one babbling out his own innocence. The maids fluttered and looked sidelong at one another, but hesitated to say a word against their mistress. But Hiltrude, her courage fast in both hands and bulking encouragingly solid now that it came to the test, laid her work aside and said boldly, not yet sounding defensive: 'But, Father, you know I did that myself. You saw me bring out the dish afterwards. Certainly I bolted the door again – I feel sure I did. No one else has been in to him since, unless you have visited him yourself, sir. Who else would, unless he was sent? And *I*'ve sent nobody.'

'Are you so certain, madam?' roared Fulke. 'You'll tell me next the lad's not gone at all, but sitting there where he should be. If you were the last to go in there, then you're to blame for letting him slip out and take to his heels. You must have left the door unbolted, how else could he get out? How could you be such a fool?'

'I did not leave it unbolted,' she repeated, but with less certainty this time. 'Or even if I may have forgotten,' she conceded defensively, 'though I don't believe I did – but if I did, does it matter so much now? He can't alter what's done, nor can anyone else. I don't see why it should cause such a flurry.'

'You don't see, you don't see – you don't see beyond the end of your nose, madam! And he to go running back to his abbot, with the tales he can tell?'

'But he has to come back into the light sooner or later,' she said meekly. 'You couldn't keep him shut up for ever.'

'So he has, we all know it, but not yet, not until we've got his mark – no, for he can sign his name, which is better! – on the marriage settlements, and made him see he may as well fit his story to ours, and accept what's done. A few days and it could all have been done our way, the proper way. But I'll not let him get away without a race for it,' swore Fulke vengefully, and turned to roar at his petrified grooms: 'Saddle my horse, and make haste about it! I'm going after him. He'll make straight for the abbey, and keep well clear of Eaton, surely. I'll have him back by the ear yet!'

In the full light of afternoon Richard did not dare take to the road, even by skirting the village widely. There he could have made better speed, but might all too easily attract the attention of tenants or retainers who would serve Astley's ends for their own sakes, and drag him back to his captivity. Moreover, the road would take him far too close to Eaton. He kept to the belt of woodland that stretched westward for half a mile or so above the river, thinning as it went until it was no more than a belt of single oaks spaced out beside the water. Beyond that, emerald water meadows filled a great bend in the Severn, open and treeless. There he kept inland far enough to have some cover from the few bushes that grew along the headlands of the Leighton fields. Upstream, where he must go, the valley widened into a great green level of flood meadows, with only a few isolated trees on the higher spots, but the northern bank where he rode rose within another mile into the low ridge of Eyton forest, where he could go in thick cover for more than half the distance to Wroxeter. It would mean going more slowly, but it was not pursuit he feared then, it was being recognised and intercepted on the way. Wroxeter he must avoid at all costs, and the only way he knew was by fording the Severn there, short of the village and out of sight of the manor, to reach the road on the southern side, and then ride full tilt for the town.

He made a little too much haste in the forest, where his familiarity with the land had led him to take a short cut between paths, and paid for it with a fall when his pony stepped in the soft edge of a badger's sett. But he dropped lightly enough into the thick cushioning of leaves, and escaped with a few bruises, and the pony, startled and skittish but docile, came back to him readily once the fright was over. After that he bore in mind that haste was not necessarily another word for speed, and took more care until he came to the more open ways. He had not reasoned about his flight, but set off bent on getting back to the abbey and making his peace there, whatever scoldings and punishments might be waiting for him, once all anxiety on his behalf was banished. He knew enough about grown-up people, however various they might seem in all other ways, to understand that they all shared the same instinct when a child in their charge was recovered out of danger, to hug him first, and clout him immediately afterwards. If, indeed,the clout did not come first! He would not mind that. Now that he had been dragged forcibly away from the schoolroom, and Brother Paul, and his fellow pupils, and even the awesome face of Father Abbot, all he wanted was to get back to them, to have the safe walls and the even safer horarium of the monastic day wrapped round him like a warm cloak. He could, had he even thought of it, have ridden to the mill by the river at Eyton, or the forester's cottage, any dwelling on this soil held by the abbey, and been received into safe shelter, but that possibility never entered his head. He made for the abbey like a bird to its nest. At this moment he had no other home, lord of Eaton though he might be.

Once out of the forest there was a good and open track almost to the ford, which lay on the southern side of Wroxeter village. Over these two miles he went briskly, but not so fast as to call attention to himself, for here there were other people to be met with occasionally, about their daily business in the fields or travelling the path between villages. He saw none that he knew, and answered such casual greetings as they gave him as briefly as they were given, and did not loiter.

The belt of trees on the near side of the ford came into view, the few willows dipping to the water, and the top of the tower of the collegiate church just showed among the branches, with one corner of a roof. The rest of the village and the demesne lay beyond. Richard approached the shelter of the trees cautiously, and dismounted in cover to peer through at the shallow spread of the water round a small island, and the path that came down from the village to the ford. He heard the voices before he reached a clear view, and halted to listen acutely, hoping the speakers would pass towards the village and leave his path clear. Two women, chattering and laughing, and an accompanying light splashing in the edge of the water, and then a man's voice, equally idle and easy, teasing and chaffing the girls. Richard ventured closer, until he could see the speakers clearly, and halted with an indrawn breath of exasperation and dismay.

The women had been washing linen, and had it spread on the low bushes to dry, and since the day was not cold, and since they had been joined by a young and not unattractive companion, they were in no hurry to leave the shore. Richard did not know the women, but the man he knew only too well, though not his name. This big, red-haired, strutting young gamecock was Astley's foreman on the demesne farm, and one of the two who had encountered and recognised Richard in the woods, trotting home to the abbey in haste, and taken advantage of the hour and the solitude to do their lord a favour. Those same muscular arms which were now making free with one of the giggling laundresses had hoisted Richard ignominiously out of the saddle, and held him kicking and raging over a thick shoulder that might have been made of oak for all the effect his belabouring fists had on it, until the other miscreant had stopped the boy's mouth with his own capuchon, and pinioned his arms with his own reins. That same night, when it was fully dark, past midnight and all honest folk in their beds, the same trusted pair had bundled him away to the more distant manor for safekeeping. Richard remembered these indignities bitterly. And now here was this very fellow getting in his way once again, for he could not ride out of cover and make for the ford without passing close and being recognised, and almost certainly recaptured.

There was nothing to be done but draw back into deeper cover and wait for them all to go away, back to the village and the manor. No hope of circling Wroxeter by a wider way and continuing on this north bank of the river, he was already too close to the edge of the village and all the approaches were open to view. And he was losing time, and without reasoning why, he felt that time was vital. He lost an hour there, gnawing his knuckles in desperate frustration and watching for the first move. Even when the women did decide to take up their washing and make for home they were in no hurry about it, but dawdled away up the path still bantering and laughing with the young man who strode between them. Only when their voices had faded into silence, and not other soul stirred about the ford, did Richard venture out from cover and spur his pony splashing down into the shallows.

The ford was smooth going in the first stretch, sandy and shallow, then the path trod dry-shod over the tip of the island, and again plunged into the long passage beyond, a wide archipelago of small, sandy shoals, dimpling and gleaming with the soft, circuitous motion of the water. In mid-passage Richard drew rein for a moment to look back, for the broad, innocent expanse of green meadows oppressed him with a feeling of nakedness and apprehension. Here he could be seen from a mile or more away, a small dark figure on horseback, defenceless and vulnerable, against a landscape all moist, pearly light and pale colours.

And there, riding at a gallop towards the ford, on the same path by which he had come, distant and small still but all too purposefully riding after him, came a single horseman on a big, light-grey horse, Fulke Astley in determined pursuit of his truant son-in-law.

Richard shot through the shallows in a flurry of spray, and was off in a desperate hurry through the wet meadows, heading west for the track that would bring him in somewhat over four miles to Saint Giles, and the last straight run to the abbey gatehouse. Over a mile to go before he could find cover in the undulating ground and the scattered groves of trees, but even then he could not hope to shake off the pursuit now that he had been sighted, as surely he must have been. And his pony was no match for that raking dappled beast behind him. But speed was the only hope he had. He still had a fair start, even if he had lost the best of it waiting to cross the ford. He dug in his heels and set his teeth and made for Shrewsbury as if wolves were at his heels.

The ground rose, folded in low hills, dotted with trees and slopes of bushes, hiding hunted and hunter from each other, but the distance between them must be shortening, and where the track ran level and unsheltered for a while Richard stole an uneasy glance over his shoulder, glimpsed his enemy again, nearer than before, and paid for his momentary inattention with another fall, though this time he clung to the reins and saved himself both the worst of the shock and the effort of catching his pony again. Muddied and bruised and furious with himself, he scrambled headlong back into the saddle and rode wildly on, feeling Astley's fixed stare as a dagger in his back. It was fortunate that the pony was Welsh-bred and sturdy, and had been some days spoiling for exercise, and that the weight he carried was so light, but even so the pace was unkind, and Richard knew it and fretted over it, but could not slacken it. By the time the fence of Saint Giles came in sight, and the track broadened into a road, he could hear the hooves pounding somewhere behind him. But for that he might have turned in there for refuge, since the leper hospice was manned and served by the abbey, and Brother Oswin would not have surrendered him to anyone unless on the abbot's orders. But by then there was no time to halt or turn aside.

Richard crouched low and galloped on along the Foregate, every moment expecting to see Fulke Astley's massive shadow cast across his quarter, and a big hand stretching out to grasp his bridle. Round the corner of the abbey wall now, and pounding along the straight stretch to the gatehouse, scattering the craftsmen and cottagers just ending their day's work and turning homeward, and the children and dogs playing in the highway.

There was barely five yards between them when Richard swung recklessly in at the gatehouse.

At Vespers that evening there were several worshippers from the guest hall, as Cadfael noted from his place in the choir. Rafe of Coventry was present, taciturn and unobtrusive as ever, and even Aymer Bosiet, after his day's activities in pursuit of his elusive property, had put in a morose and grim appearance, possibly to pray for a reliable lead from heaven. By the look of him he had weighty matters on his mind, since he was frowning over them all through Vespers, like a man trying to make up his mind. Perhaps the necessity to remain on good terms with his mother's powerful kin was urging him to hasten home at once with Drogo's body, and show some signs of family piety. Perhaps the thought of a subtle younger brother, there on the spot and fully capable of mischief for his own advancement, might also be arguing for the abandonment of a wild-goose chase in favour of a certain inheritance.

Whatever his preoccupations, he provided one more witness to the scene that confronted brothers and guests when the office was over, and they emerged by the south door and passed along the west range of the cloister into the great court, to disperse there to their various preparation for supper. Abbot Radulfus was just stepping out into the court, with Prior Robert and the whole procession of the brothers following, when the evening quiet was broken by the headlong thud of hooves along the beaten earth of the roadway outside the gatehouse, turning abruptly to a steely clatter on the cobbles within, as a stout black pony hurtled in past the gatehouse without stopping, slithering and stamping on the stones, closely followed by a tall grey horse. The rider on the grey was a big, fleshy, bearded man, crimson-faced with anger or haste, or both together, leaning forward to snatch at the bridle of the boy who rode the pony. The two of them had shot a matter of twenty yards or so into the centre of the court when his outstretched hand reached the rein, and hauled both mounts to a sliding, snorting halt, lathered and trembling. He had secured the pony, but not the boy, who let out a yell of alarm, and abandoning his reins, rather fell than dismounted on the other side, and fled like a homing bird to the abbot's feet, where he stumbled and fell flat on his face, and winding his arms desperately round the abbot's ankles, wailed out an indistinguishable appeal into the skirts of the black habit and hung on tightly, half expecting to be plucked away by force, and certain no one could prevent it, if the attempt was made, except for this erect and stable rock to which he clung.

The quiet which had been so roughly shattered had settled again with startling suddenness on the great court. Radulfus raised his intent and austere stare from the small figure hugging his ankles to the stout and confident man who had left the quivering horses sweating side by side, and advanced some paces to meet him, by no means abashed before the monastic authority.

'My lord, this is somewhat unceremonious. We are not accustomed to such abrupt visitations,' said Radulfus.

'My lord abbot, I regret being forced to disturb you. If our entry was unmannerly, I ask your pardon. For Richard rather than for myself,' said Fulke with conscious and confident challenge. 'His foolishness is the cause. I hoped to spare you this silly upheaval by overtaking him earlier and seeing him safely back home. Where I will take him now, and see that he does not trouble you so again.'

It seemed that he was quite sure of himself, though he did not advance another step or reach out a hand to grasp the boy by the collar. He met the abbot's gaze eye to eye, unblinking. Behind Prior Robert's back the brothers broke ranks to come forth into the open and gather round in a discreet half-circle, to peer in awe at the crouching boy, who had begun to gasp out muffled protests and pleas, still incoherent, since he would not raise his head or relax the frantic grasp of his arms. After the brothers came the guests, no less interested in so unusual a spectacle. Cadfael, moving methodically round to a position from which he had a clear view, caught the detached but attentive eye of Rafe of Coventry, and saw the fleeting passage of a smile brush the falconer's bearded lips.

Instead of answering Astley, the abbot looked down again with a frowning face at the boy at his feet, and said crisply: 'Stop your noise, child, and leave go of me. You are in no danger. Get up!'

Richard slackened his hold reluctantly, and raised a face smudged with mud and the green of leaves from his falls, the sweat of his haste and fear, and a few frantic tears of relief from a terror seen now to be none too reasonable. 'Father, don't let him take me! I don't want to go back, I want to be here, I want to stay with Brother Paul, I want to learn. Don't send me away! I never meant to stay away, never! I was on my way back when they stopped me. I was on my way home, truly I was!'

'It would seem,' said the abbot drily, 'that there is some dispute here as to where your home is, since the lord Fulke is offering you safe-conduct there, whereas you are of the opinion that you are already arrived. What account you have to give of yourself can wait another occasion. Where you belong, it seems, cannot. Get up, Richard, at once, and stand erect as you should.' And he reached down a lean and muscular hand to take Richard by the forearm and hoist him briskly to his feet.

For the first time Richard looked about him, uncomfortably aware of many eyes upon him, and a little galled at having to cut so dishevelled and soiled a figure before all the assembled brothers, let alone the indignant shame he felt at the stiffening snail-trails of tears on his cheeks. He straightened his back, and scrubbed hurriedly with a sleeve at his dirty face. He looked briefly for Brother Paul among the habited circle, and found him, and was a little comforted. And Brother Paul, who had been hard put to it not to run to his strayed lamb, put his trust in Abbot Radulfus, and kept his mouth shut.

'You have heard, sir,' said the abbot, 'what Richard's preference is. No doubt you know that his father placed him here in my care, and wished him to remain here and study until he came of age. I have a claim to the custody of this boy by charter, duly witnessed, and it was from my care he disappeared some days ago. I have not so far heard what substance there may be in your claim on him.'

'Richard changes his mind daily,' said Fulke, confidently loud, 'for only last night he went willingly in quite another direction. Nor do I hold that such a child should be left to choose by his own liking, when his elders are better judges of what's good for him. And as for *my* claim on the charge of him, you shall know it. Richard is my son by law, with his grandmother's full knowledge and consent. Last night he was married to my daughter.'

The shiver of consternation that went round the circle of

awestricken watchers subsided into absolute stillness. Abbot Radulfus was not shaken outwardly, but Cadfael saw the lines of his gaunt face tighten, and knew that the shaft had gone home. Such a consummation had been plotted long since by Dionisia, this self-important neighbour was little more than her instrument in the affair. What he announced could very well be true, if they had had the boy in their hands all this time that he had been missing. And Richard, who had stiffened and jerked up his head, open-mouthed to cry that it was false, met the abbot's stern eyes fixed steadily upon him, and was utterly confounded. He was afraid to lie to that judicial countenance, indeed he admired as much as he feared, and he did not wish to lie, and confronted with this flat declaration he found himself at a loss to know what was truth. For they *had* married him to Hiltrude, and simple denial was not enough. A last bolt of fright went through him and took his breath away, for how if Hyacinth was himself deceived, and the vows he had tamely repeated had bound him for life?

'Is this true, Richard?' asked Radulfus.

His voice was level and quiet, but in the circumstances seemed to Richard terrible. He gulped down words that would not do, and Fulke, impatient, answered for him: 'It is true, and he cannot deny it. Do you doubt my word, my lord?'

'Silence!' said the abbot peremptorily, but still quietly. 'I require Richard's answer. Speak up, boy! Did this marriage indeed take place?'

'Yes, Father,' faltered Richard, 'but it is not—'

'Where? With what other witnesses?'

'At Leighton, Father, last night, that is true, but still I am not—'

He was cut off again, and submitted with a sob, frustrated and growing indignant.

'And you spoke the words of the sacrament freely, of your own will? You were not forced? Beaten? Threatened?'

'No, Father, not beaten, but I was afraid. They did so hammer at me—'

'He has been reasoned with, and he was persuaded,' said Fulke shortly. 'Now he takes back what he granted yesterday. He spoke his part without hand being laid on him. Of his own will!'

'And your priest undertook this marriage willingly? Assured the consent of both was freely given? A good man, of honest repute?'

'A man of known holiness, my lord abbot,' said Fulke triumphantly. 'The country folk call him a saint. The holy hermit Cuthred!'

'But, Father,' Richard cried with the courage of desperation, determined to get out at last the plain, untangled truth of it, 'I did what I did so that they'd let me go free, and I could get back to you. I did say the vows, but only because I knew they could not be binding. I am *not* married! It was *not* a marriage, because—'

Both the abbot and Fulke broke into speech, sternly overriding his outburst and ordering his silence, but Richard's blood was up. If it must out here before everyone, then it must. He clenched his fists, and shouted loudly enough to fetch a stony echo from the walls of the cloister: '—because *Cuthred is not a priest!*'

Chapter Twelve

IN THE general ripple and stir of astonishment, doubt and outrage that passed like a sudden gust of wind through the entire assembly, from Prior Robert's indignant snort to the inquisitive and half-gleeful whisperings and shiftings among the novices, the thing that was clearest of all to Cadfael was that Fulke Astley stood utterly confounded. Never had he had the least notion what was coming, it had taken his breath away. He stood dangling his arms in curious helplessness, as though something of his own being had slipped from his grasp and left him lame and mute. When he had recovered breath enough to speak at all he said what would have been expected of him, but without the confidence of conviction, rather forcibly thrusting the very suggestion away from him in panic.

'My lord abbot, this is madness! The boy is lying. He'll say anything to serve his turn. Of course Father Cuthred is a priest! The brothers of Savigny from Buildwas brought him to us, ask them, they have no doubts. There has never been any question. This is wickedness, so to slander a holy man.'

'Such slander would indeed be wickedness,' agreed Radulfus, fixing his deep-set eyes and lowered brows formidably upon Richard. 'Think well, sir, before you repeat it. If this is a device to get your way and remain here with us, think better of it now and confess it. You shall not be punished for it. Whatever else, it would seem that you have been misused, abducted and intimidated, and that shall excuse you.

I would remind Sir Fulke of these circumstances. But if you do not tell truth now, Richard, then you do incur punishment.'

'I have told truth,' said Richard stoutly, jutting his very respectable chin and meeting the awesome eyes without blinking. 'I am telling truth, I swear it! I did what they demanded of me because I knew then that the hermit is not a priest, and a marriage made by him would be no marriage.'

'How did you know?' cried Fulke furiously, stirring out of his confusion. 'Who told you so? My lord, this is all a childish ruse, and a spiteful one. He *is* lying!'

'Well? You may answer those questions,' said Radulfus, never taking his eyes from Richard's. 'How did you know? Who told you?'

But these were the very questions Richard could not answer without betraying Hyacinth, and bringing the hunt on to his trail with renewed vigour. He said with wincing gallantry: 'Father, I will tell you, but not here, only to you. Please believe me, I am not lying.'

'I do believe you,' said the abbot, abruptly releasing him from the scrutiny which had made him tremble. 'I believe you are saying what you have been told, and what you believe to be true. But this is a more serious matter than you can understand, and it must be cleared up. A man against whom such an accusation has been made has the right to speak up for himself, and prove his good faith. I shall go myself, tomorrow early, and ask the hermit whether he is or is not a priest, and who ordained him, and where, and when. These things can be proven, and should be. You will surely have an equal interest, my lord, in finding out, once for all, whether this was indeed a marriage. Though I must warn you,' he added firmly, 'that even if it is it can be annulled, seeing it cannot have been consummated.'

'Make the attempt,' retorted Astley, somewhat recovering his composure, 'and it will be contested to the limit. But I acknowledge that truth must out. We cannot have such doubts lingering.'

'Then will you not meet with me at the hermitage, as early as may be after Prime? It is fair we should both hear what Cuthred has to say. I am well sure,' he said with truth, having seen the effect of Richard's outburst, 'that you believed implicitly the man was a priest, with full right to marry and bury. That is not in dispute. Richard has cause to hold to the contrary. Let us put it to the test.'

There was nothing Astley could object to in that, nor, thought Cadfael, had he any wish to avoid the issue. He had certainly been profoundly shocked by the suggestion of deceit, and wanted the damaging doubt removed. But he did make one more attempt to regain his hold meantime on the boy. He advanced a hand to Richard's shoulder. 'I will come to that meeting,' he said, 'and see this deluded child proved wrong. But for this night I still hold he stands as my son, and should go with me.'

The hand closed on Richard's arm, and the boy started and tore himself away. Brother Paul could no longer restrain himself, he hurried forward out of the staring ranks and drew the truant close to his side.

'Richard stays here,' said Radulfus firmly. 'His father entrusted him to me, and I set no limit on his stay with us. But whose son by law and whose husband the child is we must and will examine.'

Fulke was growing purple in the face again with suppressed anger. He had come so near to capturing the imp, and now to be thwarted, and the whole structure of his and Dionisia's territorial plans put in jeopardy. He would not give up so easily.

'You take much upon yourself, my lord abbot,' he began, 'in denying rights to his kin, you who have no blood claim upon him. And I think you are not without designs upon his lands and goods in keeping him here. You want no marriage for the boy, but rather to school him here until he knows no other world, and will enter tamely into his novitiate, and your house into his inheritance . . .'

He was so intent on his accusations, and all those about him so stricken into wonder at his daring, that no one had yet observed the new arrival at the gatehouse. All eyes were on Astley, and all mouths agape in amazement, and Hugh had tethered his horse at the gate and entered on foot, making no noise. He had taken but ten paces into the court when his eye fell first on the grey horse and the black pony, crusted with the drying lather of their hasty ride, and held now by a groom, who stood gaping at the group framed in the archway of the cloister. Hugh followed the man's fascinated stare, and took in at a glance the same arresting spectacle, the abbot and Fulke Astley face to face in obvious confrontation, and Brother Paul with an arm protectively about the shoulders of a small, wiry, grubby and dishevelled boy, who lifted to the evening light the wide-eyed face, half-frightened, half-defiant, of Richard Ludel.

Radulfus, standing disdainfully silent under abuse, was the first to notice the new arrival on the scene. Looking clean over his adversary's head, as with his height he could very well do, he said distinctly: 'No doubt the lord sheriff will pay the attention due to your charges. As he may also be interested in how Richard came to be in your care at Leighton as late as last night. You should address your complaints to him.' Fulke span upon one heel so precipitately that he all but lost his balance; and there was Hugh coming briskly down the court to join them, one quirky eyebrow tilted into his black hair, and the eye beneath it bright and sharply knowing, and levelled upon Fulke.

'Well, well, my lord!' said Hugh amiably. 'I see you have made shift to discover and restore the truant I have just failed to find in your manor of Leighton. Here am I newly come from there to report failure to the lord abbot as Richard's guardian, and here I find you have been doing my work for me while I was wild-goose chasing. I take that very kindly of you. I'll bear it in mind when it comes to considering the little matter of abduction and forcible imprisonment. It seems the woodland bird that whispered in my ear Richard was at Leighton told simple truth, for all I found no trace of him when I put it to the proof, and no one to admit he'd ever been there. You can have been out of the house barely half an hour by some other path when I reached it by the road.' His observant eye roved over Richard's taut figure and wary face, and came to rest on the abbot. 'Do you find him in good heart, and none the worse for being caged, my lord? He's come to no harm?'

'None to his body, certainly,' said Radulfus. 'But there is another matter unresolved. It seems a form of marriage took place last night at Leighton betwen Richard and Sir Fulke's daughter. To that Richard agrees, but he says that it was no real marraige, since the hermit Cuthred, who conducted it, is not a priest.'

'Do you tell me so?' Hugh pursed his lips in a soundless whistle, and swung round upon Fulke, who stood mute but watchful, all too aware of the need to step warily, and think now before he spoke. 'And what do you say to that, my lord?'

'I say it is an absurd charge that will never stand. He came to us with the good will of the brothers of Buildwas. I never heard word against him, and do not believe it now. We have dealt with him in good faith.'

'That, I am sure, is true,' said the abbot fairly. 'If there is anything in this charge, those who desired this marriage did not know of it.'

'But Richard, I think, did not desire it,' said Hugh, with a somewhat grim smile. 'This cannot rest so, we must have out the truth.'

'So we are all agreed,' said Radulfus, 'and Sir Fulke has contracted to meet with me tomorrow after Prime at the hermitage, and hear what the man himself has to say. I was about to send to you, my lord sheriff, and tell you how this thing stands, and ask you to ride with me tomorrow. This scene,' he said, casting an authoritative glance round at his all too attentive flock, 'need not be prolonged, I think. If you will sup with me, Hugh, you shall hear all that has happened. Robert, have the brothers proceed. I am sorry our evening should have been so rudely disrupted. And, Paul . . .' He looked down at Richard, who had one fist tightly clenced on a fold of Paul's habit, ready to hold fast had his tenure been threatened. 'Take him away, Paul, clean him up, feed him, and bring him to me after supper. He has a great deal to tell us that has not been told yet. There, you may disperse, all, there is no more here to see.

The brothers edged aside obediently, and moved away somewhat raggedly to resume the interrupted order of the evening, though there would be furtive whispering even in the frater, and a great deal of excited talk afterwards in the leisured hour before Collations. Brother Paul marched his restored lamb away to be washed and made presentable before abbot and sheriff after supper. Aymer Bosiet, who had looked on with a certain malevolent satisfaction at someone else's crisis and confusion as a relief from his own, detached himself moodily and went across the court to the guest hall. But Cadfael, suddenly moved to look back, missed the one figure he was seeking. Rafe of Coventry was nowhere to be seen, and now that Cadfael came to think of it, he must have taken himself off quietly some time before the intriguing scene ended. Because he had no interest in it, and was quite capable of detaching himself from a spectacle which held most men spellbound? Or because he had found something in it that interested him deeply and urgently?

Fulke Astley was left hesitant, eye to eye with Hugh, and unsure whether it would serve him better to attempt explanations and justification, or to withdraw – if he was allowed to withdraw – in dignified silence, or at least with as few words as possible, and no concessions.

'Tomorrow, then, my lord,' he said, settling upon brevity, 'I shall be at Cuthred's hermitage as I have promised.'

'Good! And you might do well,' said Hugh, 'to acquaint the hermit's patroness with what's mooted against him. She may wish to be present herself. As at this time, my lord, I have no more immediate need of you. And should I have need in the future, I know where to find you. You may have good reason to be glad that Richard slipped his collar. Mischief undone is best forgotten. Provided, of course, there's no further mischief in contemplation.'

Of that Fulke made the best he could. With a curt reverence to the abbot he turned to reclaim his horse, mounted, and rode out at the gatehouse at a deliberate and stately walking pace.

Brother Cadfael, summoned to join the colloquy in the abbot's lodging after supper, turned aside on his way, on a sudden impulse, and went into the stable yard. Richard's black pony was contented and easy in his stall after his strenuous ride, groomed and watered and placidly feeding. But the big chestnut with the white blaze down his forehead was gone from his place, saddle and harness and all. Whatever the occasion for his silent departure, Rafe of Coventry had ridden forth on some local errand of his own.

Richard sat on a low stool at the abbot's knee, washed and brushed and meekly grateful to be home, and told his story, or as much of it as he felt justified in telling. He had an interested audience. There were present, besides the abbot, Hugh Beringar, Brother Cadfael at Hugh's accepted request, and Brother Paul, still reluctant to let the returned prodigal out of his sight. Richard had tolerated, even enjoyed, being shaken, slapped, scrubbed and made much of, the whole chaotic process which had produced this neat, shining schoolboy for the abbot's inspection. There were gaps in his story, and he knew they would be questioned, but Radulfus was of noble family, and would understand that a nobleman cannot betray those who have helped him, or even certain underlings who at the instance of their masters have injured him.

'Would you know them again, the two who captured you and took you into Wroxeter?' asked Hugh.

Richard considered the tempting prospect of revenge on the strapping young fellow who had laughed at his struggles and hindered him at the ford, but rejected it reluctantly as unworthy of his nobility.

'I couldn't be sure of them. It was getting dark.'

They did not press him. Instead, the abbot asked: 'Had you help in escaping from Leighton? You could hardly have broken out on your own, or you would have done it earlier.'

Answering that presented something of a problem. If he told the truth it would certainly do Hiltrude no harm here among his friends, but if ever it reached her father it could do her harm enough. Better stick to the story as she must have told it, that the door had been mistakenly left unbolted, and he had made his own way out. Cadfael observed the slight flush that mantled in the boy's well-scrubbed cheeks as he recounted that part of his adventures, with notable brevity and modesty. If it had been true he would have been exulting in it.

'He should have known what a slippery fish he had caught,' said Hugh, smiling. 'But you still have not told us why you rode out from the abbey in the first place, nor who told you that the hermit is not the priest he purports to be.'

This was the crux, and Richard had been thinking about it with unaccustomed labour and pain while he submitted to Brother Paul's affectionate homily on obedience and order, and the evil consequences to be expected from transgressing their rules. He looked up warily into the abbot's face, shot an uneasy glance at Hugh, whose reactions as the secular authority were less calculable, and said earnestly: 'Father, I said I would tell you, but I did not say I would tell any other. There is someone who might be harmed if I told what I know of him, and I know he has not deserved it. I can't bring him into danger.'

'I would not wish to make you break faith with any man,' said Radulfus gravely. 'Tomorrow I'll hear your confession myself, and you shall tell me then, and rest happy that you've done right, and your confidence is sacred. Now you'd best get to your bed, for I fancy you need it. Take him away, Paul!'

Richard made his ceremonial reverences, glad to have got off so lightly; but as he passed where Hugh sat he hesitated and stopped, plainly with something still on his mind.

'My lord, you said everyone at Leighton said I had never been there, of course they'd be afraid to say anything else. But did Hiltrude say so?'

Hugh could make connections perhaps faster than most men, but if he instantly made this one he gave no sign of it. With respectful gravity and a blank countenance he said:

'That's Astley's daughter? I never spoke with her, she was not in the house.'

Not there! So she did not have to lie. She must have slipped out discreetly as soon as her father was gone. Richard said a relieved and grateful goodnight, and went away to his bed with a lightened heart.

'She let him out, of course,' said Hugh as soon as the door had closed after the boy. 'She was a victim no less than he. Now I begin to see a pattern. Richard is seized as he rides back through Eyton forest, and what is there in Eyton forest and along that path but Eilmund's cottage and the hermitage? And to the hermitage we know he did not go. And who should walk into Shrewsbury about noon this day and send me off hotfoot to Leighton, which otherwise I should not have reached before tomorrow, but Eilmund's girl? And where she got the news she never clearly said, but some passing villager had said he'd seen a boy there who might well be Richard. And Richard, more forthrightly, *will not* say why he went off there alone, nor who told him the hermit is no true priest. Father, it seems to me that someone – let's not go so far as to name him! – has very good friends among our acquaintance. I hope they are as good judges! Well, tomorrow, at any rate, there'll be no hunting. Richard is safely home with you. And to tell truth, I doubt the other quarry will ever be flushed out of cover. Tomorrow our morning business is laid down for us. Let's first see that resolved.'

As soon as Prime was over they mounted and rode, Abbot Radulfus, Hugh Beringar and Brother Cadfael, who in any case was bound for Eilmund's cottage that day, to see how the forester was progressing. It was by no means the first time he had adjusted his legitimate visits to accommodate his reasoned curiosity. That he could count on Hugh to abet his plans was an added advantage, and an additional witness with a sharp eye for the infinitesimal changes by which the human countenance betrays itself might be invaluable in this encounter.

The morning was clearer of mist than in recent days, there had arisen a steady, drying wind that was crisping the fallen leaves in the forest rides, and colouring in muted gold those that still hung on the trees. The first frost would set the crowns of the forest blazing in russets and browns and flame. Another week or two, thought Cadfael, and there'd be no shelter for Hyacinth in the trees when inconvenient visitors came to the cottage, even the oaks would be half-naked. But in a few more days, God willing, Aymer would have abandoned his revenge, cut his losses, and made off in haste to secure his gains at home. His father's body was safely coffined, and though he had only two grooms with him, there was also Drogo's good horse as a remount for a new master in a hurry, and he would find no difficulty in hiring litter bearers at every way-stage on his journey. He had already scoured the whole region without success, and showed distinct signs of fretting between two desired ends, of which surely the more profitable would win in the end. Hyacinth's freedom might be nearer than he knew. And he had already served and deserved well, for who else could have got word to Richard that the hermit was not all he claimed to be? Hyacinth had travelled with him, known him well before he ever set foot in Buildwas. Hyacinth might well know things about his reverend master that were known to no one else.

The thick woodland hid the hermitage from them until they were very near. The sudden parting of the trees before them came always as a mild surprise, unveiling in an instant the small green clearing, the low pales that made a mere token fence about the garden, and the squat cell of grey stone, patched with the newer and paler grey of its recent repairs. The door of the house was open, as Cuthred had said it always was, to all who came. There was no one at work in the half-cleared garden, no sound from the interior of the cell, as they dismounted at the gateless gateway and tethered their horses. Cuthred must be within, by the silence perhaps at his prayers.

'Go first, Father,' said Hugh. 'This is more within your writ than mine.'

The abbot had to stoop his head to pass through the stone doorway, and stood motionless for a moment within, until his eyes grew accustomed to the dimness. The single narrow window let in a subdued light at this hour by reason of the overhanging trees, and the shapes within the bare room took on substance only gradually, the narrow pallet against the wall, the small table and bench, the few vessels, plate and cup and pottery bowl. The doorless opening into the chapel revealed the stone block of the altar by the tiny glow of the lamp on it, but left all below in obscurity. The lamp had burned very low, was no more than a spark.

'Cuthred!' called Radulfus into the silence. 'Are you within? The abbot of Shrewsbury greets you in the name and grace of God!'

There was no answer but the small, stony echo. Hugh stepped past and advanced into the chapel doorway, and there halted abruptly, drawing in hissing breath.

Cuthred was indeed within, but not at his prayers. He lay sprawled on his back beneath the altar, head and shoulders propped against the stone, as though he had fallen or been hurled backwards while facing the doorway. His habit billowed in dark folds round him, exposing sinewy feet and ankles, and the breast of the gown was matted and blackened by a long stain, where he had bled from the stab that killed him. His face, between the tangled dark fell of hair and beard, was contorted in a grimace which might have been of agony or of rage, the lips drawn back from strong teeth, the eyes glaring half-open. His arms were flung wide, and beside his right hand, as though released in the moment of falling, a long dagger lay spilled on the stone floor.

Priest or no, Cuthred was never going to testify in his own defence. There was no need to question or touch to see that he was some hours dead, and dead by violence.

'Christ aid!' said the abbot in a harsh whisper, and stood like stone over the body. 'God have mercy on a murdered man! Who can have done this thing?'

Hugh was on his knees beside the dead man, touching flesh already grown chill and waxen in texture. There was nothing to be demanded now of the hermit Cuthred, and nothing to be done for him in this world, short of the final balance of justice. 'Dead some hours at least. A second man struck down within my shire, and no requital yet for the first! For God's sake, what is it let loose in these woods to such devilish effect?'

'Can this possibly have any bearing,' wondered the abbot heavily, 'on what the boy has told us? Has someone struck first to prevent him ever answering in his own defence? To bury the proof with the man? There has been such resolute plotting over this marriage, all for greed of land, but surely it could not be carried so far as murder?'

'If this is murder,' said Brother Cadfael, rather to himself than to any other, but aloud. He had remained still and silent in the doorway all this time, looking round him intently at the room he remembered well from a single visit, a room so sparsely furnished that every detail was memorable. The chapel was larger than the living room of the cell, there was room here for free movement, even for a struggle. Only the eastern wall was built up beneath its tiny square window with the great fashioned stone of the altar, and atop that the small carved reliquary on which stood the silver cross, and on either side a silver candlestick holding a tall candle, unlighted. On the stone before the reliquary, the lamp, and laid neatly in front of it – But there was nothing laid in front of it. Strange to have the man thrown down in disordered and disregarded death, but the altar so trim and undisturbed. And only one thing missing from the picture Cadfael carried in his mind's eye. The breviary in the leather binding fit for a prince, tooled in intricate scrolls and leaves and gilded ornament, was gone.

Hugh rose from his knees and stood back to view the room as Cadfael was viewing it. They had seen it together, by rights their memories should match. He shot a sharp glance at Cadfael. 'You see cause to doubt it?'

'I see that he was armed.' Hugh was already looking down at the long dagger that lay so close to Cuthred's half-open hand. He had not touched it. He stood back and touched nothing, now that he knew the discarded flesh before him was cold. 'He loosed his hold as he fell. That dagger is his. It was used. There is blood on it – not his blood. Whatever happened here, it was no furtive stabbing in the back.'

That was certain. The wound was over his heart, the stiffening patch of blood from it had reached his middle. The dagger that killed this man had been withdrawn and let out his lifeblood. Its fellow here on the floor was stained for only a thumb's length from its tip, and had barely shed one drop upon the stone where it lay.

'You are saying,' said the abbot, stirring out of his horrified stillness, 'that this was a fight? But how should a holy hermit keep sword or dagger about him? Even for his own defence against thieves and vagabonds such a man should not resort to arms, but put his trust in God.'

'And if this was a thief,' said Cadfael, 'he was a most strange one. Here are cross and candlesticks of silver, and they are not taken, not even shaken from their places in the struggle. Or else they were set right afterwards.'

'That is truth,' said the abbot, and shook his head over so inexplicable a mystery. 'This was not done for robbery. But what, then? Why should any man attack a solitary religious, one without possessions by choice, one whose only valuables are the furnishings of his altar? He has lived unmolested and serviceable among us, by all accounts open and accessible to all who came with their needs and troubles. Why should anyone wish to harm him? Can this be the same hand that killed the lord of Bosiet, Hugh? Or must we fear we have two murderers loose among us?'

'There is still this lad of his,' said Hugh, frowning over the thought but unable quite to discard it. 'We have not found him, and I had begun to think that he had made off westward and got clean away into Wales. But it's still possible that he has remained close here. There may well be those who are sheltering him and believe in him. We have grounds for thinking so. If he is indeed the villein who ran from Bosiet, he had some cause to rid himself of his master. And say that Cuthred, who disowned him on hearing he had been deceived in him, found out his hiding place now – yes, then he might also have cause to kill Cuthred. All of which is mere matter for conjecture. And yet cannot be quite rejected.'

No, thought Cadfael, not until Aymer Bosiet has gone his way back to Northamptonshire, and Hyacinth can come out of hiding and speak for himself, and Eilmund and Annet, yes, and Richard, can speak for him. For between the three of them I'm sure it can be proved exactly where Hyacinth has been at all times, and he has not been here. No, we need not trouble about Hyacinth. But I wish, he thought regretfully, I wish they had let me confide in Hugh long ago.

The sun was higher in the sky by now, and found a better angle through the leafage of the trees, to shed more light upon the distorted and lamentable body. The skirts of the rusty black habit were gathered together at one side, as if a large fist had drawn them into its grasp, and there the woollen cloth was clotted with a sticky dark stain. Cadfael kneeled and drew the folds apart, and they separated with a faint, rustling reluctance.

'Here he wiped his dagger,' said Cadfael, 'before sheathing it again.'

'Twice,' said Hugh, peering, for there was a second such smear, barely perceptible. Coolly and efficiently, a methodical man cleaning his tools after finishing his work! 'And see here, this casket on the altar.' He had stepped carefully round the body to look closely at the carved wooden box, and draw a finger along the edge of the lid, above the lock. The flaw was no longer than a thumbnail, but showed where the point of a dagger had been thrust in to prise the box open. He lifted down the cross and raised the lid, which gave readily. The lock was sprung and broken, and the casket was empty. Only the faint aromatic scent of the wood stirred upon the air. There was not even a filming of dust within; the box had been well made.

'So something was taken, after all,' said Cadfael. He did not mention the breviary, though he could not doubt that Hugh had noticed its absence as readily as he.

'But not the silver. What could a hermit have about him of greater value than Dame Dionisia's silver? He came to Buildwas on foot, carrying only a scrip like any other pilgrim, though to be sure his boy Hyacinth also carried a pack for him. Now I wonder,' said Hugh, 'whether this casket was also the lady's gift, or whether he brought it with him?'

They had been so intent on what they were observing within that they had failed to pay attention to what was happening without, and there had been no sound to warn them. And in the shock of what they had discovered they had almost forgotten that at least one more witness was expected at this meeting. But it was a woman's voice, not Fulke's, that suddenly spoke in the doorway behind them, high and confidently, and with arrogant disapproval in its tone.

'No need to wonder, my lord. It would be simple and civil to ask me.'

All three of them swung round in dismayed alarm to stare at Dame Dionisia, tall and erect and defiant between them and the brightening daylight from which she had come, and which left her half-blind at stepping into this relative obscurity. They were between her and the body, and there was nothing else to startle or alarm her but the very fact that Hugh stood with his hand on the open casket, and the cross had been lifted down. This she saw clearly, while the dying lamp lit nothing else so well. And she was outraged.

'My lord, what is this? What are you doing with these sacred things? And where is Cuthred? Have you dared to meddle in his absence?'

The abbot moved to place himself more solidly between her and the dead man, and advanced to persuade her out of the chapel.

'Madam, you shall know all, but I beg you, come out into the other room and be seated, and wait but a moment until we set all in order here. Here is no irreverence, I promise you.'

The light from without was still further darkened by the bulk of Astley looming at her shoulder, blocking the retreat the abbot was urging. She stood her ground, imperious and indignant.

'Where is Cuthred? Does he know you are here? How is it he has left his cell? He never does so—' The lie ended on her lips in a sharp indrawn breath. Beyond the abbot's robe she had seen one small pallor jutting from the huddle of dark skirts, a foot that had shaken loose its sandal. Her vision was clearer now. She evaded the abbot's restraining hand and thrust strongly past him. All her questions were answered in one shattering glance. Cuthred was indeed there, and on this occasion at least had not left his cell.

The long, patrician composure of her face turned waxen grey and seemed to disintegrate, its sharp lines fallen slack. She uttered a great wail, rather of terror than of grief, and half-sprang, half-fell backwards into the arms of Fulke Astley.

Chapter Thirteen

SHE NEITHER swooned nor wept. She was a woman who did not lightly do either. But she sat for a long while bolt upright on Cuthred's bed in the living room, rigid and pale and staring straight before her, clean through the stone wall before her face, and a long way beyond. It was doubtful if she heard any of the abbot's carefully measured words, or the uneasy blusterings of Astley, alternately offering her gallantries of comfort she did not value or need, and recalling feverishly that this crime left all questions unanswered, and in some none too logical way went to prove that the hermit had indeed been a priest, and the marriage he had solemnized still a marriage. At least she paid no attention to either. She had gone far beyond any such considerations. All her old plans had become irrelevant. She had looked closely on sudden death, unconfessed, unshriven, and she wanted no part of it. Cadfael saw it in her eyes as he came out from the chapel, having done what he could to lay Cuthred's body straight and seemly, now that he had read all it had to tell him. Through that death she was confronting her own, and she had no intention of meeting it with all her sins upon her. Or for many years yet, but she had had warning that if she was willing to wait, death might not be.

At last she asked, in a perfectly ordinary voice, perhaps milder than any she normally used to her household or tenants, but without moving, or withdrawing her eyes from her ultimate enemy: 'Where is the lord sheriff?'

'He's gone to get hold of a party to carry the hermit away from here,' said the abbot. 'To Eaton, if you so wish, to be cared for there, since you were his patroness. Or, if it will spare you painful reminders, to the abbey. He shall be properly received there.'

'It would be a kindness,' she said slowly, 'if you would take him. I no longer know what to think. Fulke has told me what my grandson says. The hermit cannot answer for himself now, nor can I for him. I believed without question that he was a priest.'

'That, madam,' said Radulfus, 'I never doubted.'

The focus of her stare had shortened, a little colour had come back into her waxen face. She was on her way back, soon she would stir and brace herself, and turn to look at the real world about her, instead of the bleak distances of judgement day. And she would face whatever she had to face with the same ferocious courage and obstinacy with which she had formerly conducted her battles.

'Father,' she said, turning towards him with abrupt resolution, 'if I come to the abbey tonight, will you yourself hear my confession? I shall sleep the better when I have shed my sins.'

'I will,' said the abbot.

She was ready then to be taken home, and Fulke was all too anxious to escort her. No doubt he, who had very little to say here in company, would be voluble enough in private with her. He had not her intelligence, nor nearly so acute an imagination. If Cuthred's death had cast any shadow on him, it was merely the vexation of not being able to claim proof of his daughter's marriage, not at all a bony hand on his shoulder. So at any rate thought Brother Cadfael, watching him arm Dionisia to where her jennet was tethered, in haste to have her away and be free of the abbot's daunting presence.

At the last moment, with the reins gathered in her hand, she suddenly turned back. Her face had regained all its proud tension and force, she was herself again.

'I have only now remembered,' she said, 'that the lord sheriff was wondering about the casket in there on the altar. That was Cuthred's. He brought it with him.'

When the abbot and the litter-bearers and Hugh were all on their slow and sombre way back to the abbey, Cadfael took a last look round the deserted chapel, the more attentively because he was alone and without distractions. There was not a single stain of blood on the flags of the floor where the body had lain, only the drop or two left by the point of Cuthred's own dagger. He had certainly wounded his adversary, though the wound could not be deep. Cadfael sighted a course from the altar to the doorway, and followed it with a newly lighted candle in his hand. In the chapel he found nothing more, and in the outer room the floor was of beaten earth, and such faint traces would be hard to find after the passage of hours. But on the doorstone he found three drops shaken, dried now but plain to be seen, and on the new and unstained timber with which the left jamb of the doorway had been repaired there was a blurred smear of blood at the level of his own shoulder, where a gashed and bloodied sleeve had brushed past.

A man no taller than himself, then, and Cuthred's dagger had taken him in the shoulder or upper arm on the left side, as a stroke aimed at his heart might well do.

Cadfael had intended to ride on to Eilmund's cottage, but on impulse he changed his mind, for it seemed to him that after all he could not afford to miss whatever might follow when Cuthred's body was brought into the court at the abbey, to the consternation of most, the relief, perhaps, of some, and the possible peril of one in particular. Instead of cutting through the forest tides, he mounted and rode back in haste towards Shrewsbury, to overtake the funeral procession.

They had a curious audience as soon as they entered the Foregate, and the camp-following of inquisitive boys and attendant dogs followed at their heels all along the highroad, and even the respectable citizens came after them at a more discreet distance, wary of abbot and sheriff but avid for information, and breeding rumours as fast as flies breed on summer middens. Even when the cortège turned in at the gatehouse the good folk from market and smithy and tavern gathered outside to peer expectantly within, and continued their speculations with relish.

And there in the great court, as they carried one bier in from the world, was another funeral party busy assembling to leave. Drogo Bosiet's sealed coffin was mounted on a low, light cart, hired in the town with its driver for this first day's travelling, which would be on a good road. Warin stood holding two of the saddled horses, while the younger groom was busy adjusting a full saddle-roll to get the weight properly balanced before loading it. At sight of all this activity Cadfael drew a deep breath of gratitude, sensible that one danger, at least, was being lifted away even earlier than he had dared to hope. Aymer had finally made up his mind. He was bound for home, to make sure of his inheritance.

The attendants on one death could not forbear from stopping what they were doing to stare at the attendants on the other. And Aymer, coming out from the guest hall with Brother Denis beside him to wish the departing train godspeed, halted at the top of the steps to take in the scene with surprise and sharp speculation, his eyes dwelling longest on the covered form and face. He came striding down to cross purposefully to where Hugh was just dismounting.

'What this, my lord? Another death? Has your hunt brought down my quarry at last? But dead?' He hardly knew whether to be glad or sorry if the corpse was that of his lost villein. The money and favour Hyacinth's skills brought in were valuable, but revenge would also be a satisfying gain, and just when he had despaired of winning either, and made up his mind to go home.

Abbot Radulfus, too, had dismounted, and stood looking on with an uncommunicative face, for the two groups carried a curious and disturbing suggestion of a mirror image, gathered about the arriving and departing dead. The abbey grooms who had come to take the bridles of abbot and sheriff hung upon the fringes of the assembly, reluctant to move away.

'No,' said Hugh, 'this is no man of yours. If the boy we've been hunting is yours. Of him we've seen no sign, whether he is or no. You're bound for home, then?'

'I've wasted time and effort enough, I'll waste no more, though I grudge letting him go free. Yes, we're away now. I'm needed at home, there's work waiting for me. Who is this one you've brought back?'

'The hermit who was set up no long time ago in Eyton forest. Your father went to visit him,' said Hugh, 'thinking the servant he kept might be the fellow you were looking for, but the youngster had already taken to his heels, so it's never been put to the test.'

'I remember, so the lord abbot told me. So this is the man! I never went to him again, what use if the lad he kept was gone?' He looked curiously down at the shrouded figure. The bearers had laid down their burden, awaiting orders where to take the dead. Aymer stooped and turned back the brychan from

Cuthred's face. They had drawn back the wild fell of hair from his temples, and brushed down his bushy beard into order, and the full light of noon shone over the lean countenance, the deep-set eyes, the lofty lids a little bruised and bluish now, the long, straight, patrician nose and full lips within the dark beard. The glare of the half-open eyes was now veiled, the snarl on the drawn-back lips carefully smoothed out to restore his harsh comeliness. Aymer leaned closer, startled and disbelieving.

'But I know this man! No, that's to say too much, he never said his name. But I've seen him and talked with him. A hermit – he? I never saw sign of it then! He wore his hair trimmed Norman fashion, and had a short, clipped beard, not this untended bush, and he was well clothed in good riding gear, boots and all, not this drab habit and sandals. And he wore sword and dagger into the bargain,' said Aymer positively, 'and as if he was well accustomed to the use of them, too.'

Until he looked up again he was not fully aware of the significance of what he had said, but Hugh's intent face and instant question made it plain he had touched on something more vital than he knew.

'You are sure?' said Hugh.

'Certain, my lord. It was only one night's lodging, but I diced with him for the dinner, and watched my father play a game of chess with him. I'm certain!'

'Where was this? And when?'

'At Thame, when we were looking towards London for Brand. We lodged overnight with the white monks at the new abbey there. This man was there before us, we came well into the evening, and went on south next day. I can't say the exact date, but it was towards the ends of September.'

'Then if you know him again,' said Hugh, 'changed as his condition is, would your father also have recognised him at sight?'

'Surely he would, my lord. His eyes were sharper than mine. He'd sat over a chessboard with the man, eye to eye. He'd know him again.'

And so he had, thought Cadfael, when he went manhunting to the cell in the forest, and came face to face with the hermit Cuthred who had been no hermit a month or so earlier. And he had not lived to return to the abbey and let out to any man what he knew. And what if he knew no great evil of this transformed being? He might still let fall to other ears the casual word that would mean more to them than ever it had to him, and bring to the cell in Eyton forest someone in search of more than a runaway villein, and worse, surely, than a spurious priest. But he had not lived to get further on his return journey than a close forest thicket, sufficiently far from the hermitage to remove suspicion from a local saint reputed never to leave his cell.

The evidence of circumstances is not positive proof, yet Cadfael had no doubts left. There before them the coffined body and the new corpse rested for a few moments side by side, before Prior Robert directed the bearers to the mortuary chapel, and Aymer Bosiet covered Cuthred's face again, and turned afresh to his own preparations for departure. His mind was on other things, why distract and detain him now? But Cadfael did suddenly take thought to ask one curious question.

'What manner of horse was he riding when he halted overnight at Thame?'

Aymer turned from fastening the straps of his saddle-bags in detached surprise, opened his mouth to answer, and found himself at a loss, frowning thoughtfully over his recollections of that night.

'He was there before us. There were two horses in the prior stables when we came. And he'd left before us next morning. But now you come to ask, when we got to horse, the same two beasts we saw there the night before were still in their stalls. That's strange! What would such a well-found man, knightly by the look of him and his arms – what would he be doing without a horse?'

'Ah, well, he may have stabled it somewhere else,' said Cadfael, abandoning the puzzle as trivial.

But it was not trivial, it was the key to open a very strange door in the mind. There before so many eyes lay the slayer and the slain, side by side, justice already done.

But who, then, had slain the slayer?

They were gone, all of them, Aymer on his father's handsome light roan horse, Warin with the horse Aymer had ridden on the outward journey now on a leading rein, the young groom with the carter and the cart. After the first day-stages Aymer would probably be off at speed, leaving the grooms to bring the coffin after at their slower pace, and most likely sending other retainers back along the way to relieve them, once he reached home. In the mortuary chapel Cadfael had seen Cuthred's body laid out in seemly fashion, hair and beard trimmed, not, perhaps, so closely as the knight at Thame had worn them, but enough to display, in the fixed and austere tranquillity of death, a face appropriate enough to a dignified religious. Unfair that a murderer should look as noble in death as any of the empress's paladins.

Hugh was closeted with the abbot, and as yet had said no word to Cadfael of what he made of Aymer's witness, but by the very questions he had asked it was clear he had made the same connections Cadfael had made, and could not have failed to arrive at the same conclusion. He would speak of it first with Radulfus. My part now, thought Cadfael, is to bring Hyacinth out of hiding, and let him shake himself loose from all suspicion of wrong-doing. Barring, of course, the occasional theft to fill his belly while he lived wild, and a lie or two by way of preserving himself alive at all. And Hugh won't grudge him those. And that should settle the matter of Cuthred's ordination once for all, if there's still any lingering question about it. A sudden conversion can turn a soldier into a hermit, yes, but it takes much longer than that to make a priest.

He waited for Hugh in his workshop in the herb garden, where Hugh would certainly come looking for him as soon as he left the abbot. It was quiet and aromatic and homely within there, and Cadfael had been too much away from it of late. He would have to be thinking of replenishing his stocks of the regular winter needs very soon, before the coughs and colds began, and the elder joints started to creak and groan. Brother Winfrid could be trusted to take excellent care of all the work in the garden, the digging and weeding and planting, but here within he had much to learn. One more ride, thought Cadfael, to see how Eilmund does, and let Hyacinth know he can and should come forward and speak up for himself, and then I shall be glad to settle down to work here at home.

Hugh came in through the gardens and sat down beside his friend with a brief, preoccupied smile, and was silent for some moments. 'What I do not understand,' he said then, 'is why? Whatever he was, whatever he has done, aforetime, here he seems to have lived blameless. What can there have been, perilous enough to make him want to stop Bosiet's mouth? It may be a suspect thing to change one's dress and appearance and way of life, but it is not a crime. What was there, more than that, to justify murder? What is there of that enormity, except murder itself?'

'Ah!' said Cadfael with a relieved sigh. 'Yes, I thought you had seen it all as I saw it. But no, I do not think it was murder he had to hide in the obscurity of a hermit's grown and a forest cell. That was my first thought. But it is not so simple.'

'As so often,' said Hugh with his sudden, crooked smile, 'I think you know something that I do not. And what was that about his horse, down there in Thame? What has his horse to do with it?'

'Not his horse, but the fact that he had none. What's a soldier or a knight doing travelling on foot? But a pilgrim may, and never be noticed. But as to knowing something I would have told you long ago if I had been let – yes, Hugh, I do. I know where Hyacinth is. Against my will I promised to say nothing until Aymer Bosiet had given up the pursuit and taken himself off home. As now he has, and now the boy can come forward and speak for himself, as, trust me, he's well able to do.'

'So that's it,' said Hugh, eyeing his friend without any great surprise. 'Well, who can blame him for being wary, what does he know of me? And for all that I knew, he could well have been Bosiet's murderer, we knew of no other with as good a cause. Now he need say no word on that score, the debt is known and paid. And as for his freedom, he need fear nothing from me on that head. I have enough to do without playing the errand boy for Northamptonshire. Bring him forth whenever you like, he may yet shed light on some things we do not know.'

So Cadfael thought, too, reflecting how little Hyacinth had had to say about his relations with his sometime master. Candid enough, among friends, about his own vagabondage and the mischief done in Eilmund's coppice, he had scrupulously refrained from casting any aspersions against Cuthred. But now that Cuthred was dead and known for a murderer Hyacinth might be willing to extend his candour, though surely he had known no great harm of his fellow traveller, and certainly nothing of murder.

'Where is he?' asked Hugh. 'Not far, I fancy, if it was he who got word to young Richard that he could safely go through that marriage service. Who would be more likely to know Cuthred for an impostor?'

'No further,' said Cadfael, 'than Eilmund's cottage, and welcome there to father and daughter alike. And I'm bound there now to see how Eilmund's faring. Shall I bring the boy back with me?'

'Better than that,' said Hugh heartily, 'I'll ride with you.

Better not hale him out of cover until I've called off the hunt by official order, and made it known he has nothing to answer, and is free to walk the town and look for work like any other man.'

In the stable yard, when he went to saddle up, Cadfael found the bright chestnut horse with the white brow standing like a glossy statue under his master's affectionate hands, content and trusting after easy exercise, and being polished to a rippling copper sheen. Rafe of Coventry turned to see who came, and smiled the guarded, calm smile with which Cadfael was becoming familiar.

'Bound out again, Brother? This must be a wearing day you've had.'

'For all of us,' said Cadfael, hoisting down his saddle, 'but we may hope the worst is over. And you? Have you prospered in your errand?'

'Well, I thank you! Very well! Tomorrow morning, after Prime,' he said, turning to face Cadfael fully, and his voice as always measured and composed, 'I shall be leaving. I have already told Brother Denis so.'

Cadfael went on with his preparations for a minute or two in silence. Converse with Rafe of Coventry found silences acceptable. 'If you'll be riding far the first day,' he said then simply, 'I think you may need my services before you set out. He drew blood,' he said briefly, by way of adequate explanation. And when Rafe was slow to answer: 'A part of my function is to tend illness and injury. There is no seal of confession in my art, but there is a decent reticence.'

'I have bled before,' said Rafe, but he smiled, a degree beyond his common smile.

'As you choose. But I am here. If you need me, come to me. It is not wise to neglect a wound, nor to try it too far in the saddle.' He tested the girth, and gathered the reins to mount. The horse sidled and shifted playfully, eager for action.

'I'll bear it in mind,' said Rafe, 'and I thank you. You will not stop me leaving,' he said in amiable but solemn warning.

'Have I tried?' said Cadfael, and swung himself up into the saddle and rode out into the court.

'I never told all the truth,' said Hyacinth, seated beside the hearth in Eilmund's cottage, with the firelight like a copper gloss on cheekbones and jaw and brow, 'not even here to

Annet. As to myself I did, she knows the worst I could tell. But not of Cuthred. I knew he was a rogue and a vagabond, but so was I, and I knew nothing worse of him than that, so I kept my mouth shut. One rogue in hiding doesn't betray another. But now you tell me he's a murderer. And dead!'

'And out of further harm,' said Hugh reasonably, 'at least in this world. I need to know all you can tell. Where did you join fortunes with him?'

'At Northampton, at the Cluniac priory, as I told Annet and Eilmund, though not quite as I told it. He was no habited pilgrim then, he was in good dark clothes, with cloak and capuchon, and armed, though he kept his sword out of sight. It was almost by chance we got into talk, or I thought so. But I fancy he guessed I was running from something, and he made no secret he was, too, and suggested we might be safer and pass unnoticed together. We were both heading north and west. The pilgrim was his notion, he had the face and bearing for it. Well, you've seen him, you know. I stole the habit for him from the priory store. The scallop shell came easy. The medal of Saint James he had – it may even have been his by right, who knows? By the time we got to Buildwas he had his part by rote, and his hair and beard were well grown. And he came very apt to the dame at Eaton, for her own ends. Oh, she knew no worse of him than that he was willing to earn his keep with her. He said he was a priest, and she believed it. I knew he was none, he owned as much when we were alone. He laughed about it. But he had the gift of tongues, he could carry it off. She gave him the hermitage, so close and handy to the abbey's woods, to do all the mischief he could in the abbot's despite. I said that was my part, and he knew nothing of it, but I lied for him. He'd never blabbed on me, no more would I on him.'

'He abandoned you,' said Hugh flatly, 'as soon as he knew the hunt was up for you. You need not scruple to speak out on his account.'

'Well – I live, and he's dead,' said Hyacinth. 'No call now for me to bear him any grudge. You know about Richard? I'd talked with him only once, but he took me so for a true man he'd hear no wrong of me, nor have me run to earth and dragged back into villeinage. That set me up again in my own respect. I never knew till afterwards that he'd been seized like that on his way back, but I was forced to run or hide, and chose to hide till I could make shift to find him. If it hadn't been for Eilmund's goodness to me, and after I'd been a thorn in his flesh, too, your men might have had me a dozen times over. But now you know I never laid hand on Bosiet. And Eilmund and Annet can tell you I've not been a step away from here since I came back from Leighton. What can have happened to Cuthred I know no more than you.'

'Less, I daresay,' said Hugh mildly, and looked across the fire at Cadfael, smiling. 'Well, after all you may call yourself a lucky lad. From tomorrow you'll be in no peril at the hands of any of my people, you can be off into the town and find yourself a master. And which of your names do you choose to keep for a new life? Best have but one, that we may all know with whom we have to deal.'

'Whichever is pleasing to Annet,' said Hyacinth. 'It's she will be calling me by it from this on lifelong.'

'I might have something to say to that,' grunted Eilmund from his corner on the other side of the hearth. 'You mind your impudence, or I'll make you sweat for my good will.' But he sounded remarkably complacent about it, as though they had already arrived at an understanding to which this admonitory growl was merely a gruff counterpoint.

'It was Hyacinth first pleased me,' said Annet. She had kept herself out of the circle until now, like a dutiful daughter, attentive with cup and pitcher, but wanting and needing no voice in the men's affairs. Not from modesty or submission Cadfael judged, but because she already had what she wanted, and was assured no one, sheriff nor father nor overlord, had either the power or the will to wrest it from her. 'You stay Hyacinth,' she said serenely, 'and let Brand go.'

She was wise, there was no sense in going back, none even in looking back. Brand had been a villein and landless in Northamptonshire, Hyacinth would be a craftsman and free in Shrewsbury.

'In a year and a day,' said Hyacinth, 'from the day I find a master to take me, I'll come and ask for your good will, Master Eilmund. Not before!'

'And if I think you've earned it,' said Eilmund, 'you shall have it.'

They rode home together in the deepening dusk, as they had so often ridden together since first they encountered in wary contention, wit against wit, and came to a gratifying stand at the end of the match, fast friends. The night was still and mild, the morning would be misty again, the lush valley fields a translucent blue sea. The forest smelled of autumn, ripe, moist earth, bursting fungus, the sweet, rich rot of leaves.

'I have transgressed against my vocation,' said Cadfael, at once solaced and saddened by the season and the hour. 'I know it. I undertook the monastic life, but now I am not sure I could support it without you, without these stolen excursions outside the walls. For so they are. True, I am often sent upon legitimate labours here without, but also I steal, I take more than is my due by right. Worse, Hugh, I do not repent me! Do you suppose there is room within the bounds of grace for one who has set his hand to the plough, and every little while abandons his furrow to turn back among the sheep and lambs?'

'I think the sheep and lambs might think so,' said Hugh, gravely smiling. 'He would have their prayers. Even the black sheep and the grey, like some you've argued for against God and me in your time.'

'There are very few all black,' said Cadfael. 'Dappled, perhaps, like this great rangy beast you choose to ride. Most of us have a few mottles about us. As well, maybe, it makes for a more tolerant judgement of the rest of God's creatures. But I have sinned, and most of all in relishing my sin. I shall do penance by biding dutifully within the walls through the winter, unless I'm sent forth, and then I'll make haste with my task, and hurry back.'

'Until the next waif stumbles across your path. And when is this penance to begin?'

'As soon as this matter is fittingly ended.'

'Why, these are oracular utterances!' said Hugh, laughing. 'And when will that be?'

'Tomorrow,' said Cadfael. 'If God wills, tomorrow.'

Chapter Fourteen

ON HIS way down the court to the stables, leading his horse, and with the better part of an hour left before Compline, Cadfael saw Dame Dionisia coming from the abbot's lodging, and walking with sober step and decorously covered head towards the guest hall. Her back was as erect as ever, her gait as firm and proud, but somewhat slower than was her wont, and the draped head was lowered, with eyes on the ground rather than fixed challengingly into the distance before her. Not a word would ever be said concerning her confession, but Cadfael doubted if she had left anything out. She was not one to do things by halves. There would be no more attempts to extract Richard from the abbot's care. Dionisia had suffered too profound a reverse to take any such risks again until time had dimmed the recollection of sudden unshriven death coming to meet her.

It seemed she meant to stay overnight, perhaps to make her peace tomorrow, in her own arbitrary fashion, with a grandson by this time fast asleep in his bed, blessedly unmarried still, and back where he preferred to be. The boys would sleep well tonight, absolved of their sins and with their lost member restored. Matter for devout thanksgiving. And as for the dead man in the mortuary chapel, bearing a name which it seemed could hardly be his name, he cast no shadow on the world of the children.

Cadfael led his horse into the stable yard, lighted by two torches at the gate, unsaddled him and rubbed him down.

There was no sound within there but a small sighing of the breeze that had sprung up with evening, and the occasional easy shift and stir of hooves in the stalls. He stabled his beast and hung up his harness, and turned to depart.

There was someone standing in the gateway, compact and still. 'Good even, Brother!' said Rafe of Coventry.

'Is it you?' said Cadfael. 'And were you looking for me? I'm sorry to have kept you up late, and you with a journey to make in the morning.'

'I saw you come down the court. You made an offer,' said the quiet voice. 'If it is still open I should like to take advantage of it. I find it is not so easy to dress a wound neatly with one hand.'

'Come!' said Cadfael. 'Let's go to my hut in the garden, we can be private there.'

It was deep dusk, but not yet dark. The late roses in the garden loomed spikily on overgrown stems, half their leaves shed, ghostly floating pallors in the dimness. Within the walls of the herb garden, high and sheltering, warmth lingered. 'Wait,' said Cadfael, 'till I make light.'

It took him a few minutes to get a spark he could blow gently into flame, and set to the wick of his lamp. Rafe waited without murmur or movement until the light burned up steadily, and then came into the hut and looked about him with interest at the array of jars and flasks, the scales and mortars, and the rustling bunches of herbs overhead, stirring headily in the draught from the doorway. Silently he stripped off his coat, and drew down his shirt from the shoulder until he could withdraw his arm from the sleeve. Cadfael brought the lamp, and set it where the light would best illuminate the stained and crumpled bandage that covered the wound. Rafe sat patient and attentive on the bench against the wall, steadily eyeing the weathered face that stooped over him.

'Brother,' he said deliberately, 'I think I owe you a name.'

'I have a name for you,' said Cadfael. 'Rafe is enough.'

'For you, perhaps. Not for me. Where I take help, generously given, there I repay with truth. My name is Rafe de Genville . . .'

'Hold still now,' said Cadfael. 'This is stuck fast, and will hurt.'

The soiled dressing came away with a wrench, but if it did indeed hurt, de Genville suffered it as indifferently as he did the foregoing pain. The gash was long, running down from the shoulder into the upper arm, but not deep; but the flesh was so sliced that the lips gaped, and a single hand had not been able to clamp them together. 'Keep still! We can better this, you'll have an ugly scar else. But you'll need help when it's dressed again.'

'Once away from here I can get help, and who's to know how I got the gash? But you do know, Brother. He drew blood, you said. There is not very much you do not know, but perhaps a little I can still tell you. My name is Rafe de Genville, I am a vassal, and God knows a friend to Brian FitzCount, and a liege man to my overlord's lady, the empress. I will not suffer gross wrong to be done to either, while I have my life. Well, he'll draw no more blood, neither from any of the king's party nor oversea, in the service of Geoffrey of Anjou – which I think was his final intent, when the time seemed right.'

Cadfael folded a new dressing closely about the long gash. 'Lend your right hand here, and hold this firmly, it shuts the wound fast. You'll get no more bleeding, or very little, and it should heal closed. But rest it as best you can on the road.'

'I will so.' The bandage rolled firmly over the shoulder and round the arm, flat and neat. 'You have a skilled hand, Brother. If I could I would take you with me as a prize of war.'

'They'll have need of all the surgeons and physicians they can get in Oxford, I fear,' Cadfael acknowledged ruefully.

'Ah, not there, not this tide. There'll be no breaking into Oxford until the earl brings up his army. I doubt it even then. No, I go back to Brian at Wallingford first, to restore him what is his.'

Cadfael secured the bandage above the elbow, and held the sleeve of the shirt carefully as Rafe thrust his arm back into it. It was done. Cadfael sat down beside him, face to face, eye to eye. The silence that came down upon them was like the night, mild, tranquil, gently melancholy.

'It was a fair fight,' said Rafe after a long pause, looking into and through Cadfael's eyes to see again the bare stony chapel in the forest. 'I laid by my sword, seeing he had none. His dagger he'd kept.'

'And used,' said Cadfael, 'on the man who had seen him in his own shape at Thame, and might have called his vocation in question. As the son did, after Cuthred was dead, and never knew he was looking at his father's murderer.'

'Ah, so that was it! I wondered.'

'And did you find what you came for?'

'I came for him,' said Rafe grimly. 'But, yes, I understand you. Yes, I found it, in the reliquary on the altar. Not all in coin. Gems go into a small compass, and are easily carried. Her own jewels, that she valued. And valued even more the man to whom she sent them.'

'They said that there was also a letter.'

'There is a letter. I have it. You saw the breviary?'

'I saw it. A prince's book.'

'An empress's. There is a secret fold in the binding, where a fine, small leaf can be hidden. When they were apart, the breviary went back and forth between them by trusted messenger. God he knows what she may not have written to him now, at the lowest ebb of fortune, separated from him by a few miles that might as well be the width of the world, and with the king's army gripping her and her few to strangulation. In the extreme of despair, who regards wisdom, who puts a guard on tongue or pen? I have not sought to know. He shall have it and read it for whose heart's consolation it was meant. One other has read it, and might have made use of it,' said Rafe harshly, 'but he is of no account now.'

His voice had gathered a great tide of passion that yet could not disrupt its steely control, though it caused his disciplined body to quiver like an arrow in flight, vibrating to the force of his devoted love and implacable hate. The letter he carried, with its broken seal as testimony to a cold and loathsome treachery, he would never unfold, the matter within was sacred as the confessional, between the woman who had written and the man to whom it was written. Cuthred had trespassed even into this holy ground, but Cuthred was dead. It did not seem to Cadfael that the penalty was too great for the wrong committed.

'Tell me, Brother,' said Rafe de Genville, the wave of passion subsiding into his customary calm, 'was this sin?'

'What do you need from me?' said Cadfael. 'Ask your confessor when you come safely to Wallingford. All I know is, time has been when I would have done as you have done.'

Whether de Genville's secret would be preserved inviolate was a question never asked, the answer being already clearly understood between them. 'This is better than by morning,' said Rafe, rising. 'Your order of hours tomorrow need not be broken, and I can be away early, and leave my place cleansed and furbished and ready for another guest, and travel the lighter because I do not go without a fair witness. I'll say my farewell here. God be with you, Brother!'

'And go with you,' said Cadfael.

He was gone, out into the gathering darkness, his step firm and even on the gravel path, silent when he reached the grass beyond. And sharp upon the last slight sound of his going, the bell rang distantly for Compline.

Cadfael went down into the stables before Prime, in a morning dry and sunny but chill, a good day for riding. The bright chestnut with the white brow was gone from his stall. It seemed empty and quiet there, but for the cheerful chirpings of chatter and laughter from the last stall, where Richard had come down early to pet and make much of his pony for carrying him so bravely, with Edwin, happily restored to grace and to the company of his playmate, in loyal attendance. They were making a merry noise like a brood of young swallows, until they heard Cadfael come, and then they fell to a very prim and seemly quietness until they peeped out and saw that he was neither Brother Jerome nor Prior Robert. By way of apology they favoured him with broad and bountiful smiles, and went back to the pony's stall to caress and admire him.

Cadfael could not but wonder if Dame Dionisia had already visited her grandson, and gone as far as such a matriarch could be expected to go to re-establish her standing with him. There would certainly be no self-abasement. Something of a self-justifying homily, rather: 'Richard, I have been considering your future with the abbot, and I have consented to leave you in his care for the present. I was grossly deceived in Cuthred, he was not a priest, as he pretended. That episode is over, we had all better forget it.' And she would surely end with something like: 'If I let you remain here, sir, take care that I get good reports of you. Be obedient to your masters and attend to your books . . .' And on leaving him, a kiss perhaps a little kinder than usual, or at least a little more warily respectful, seeing all he could relate against her if he cared to. But Richard triumphant, released from all anxieties for himself and others who mattered to him, bore no grudge against anyone in the world.

By this hour Rafe de Genville, vassal and friend of Brian FitzCount and loyal servitor of the Empress Maud, must be well away from Shrewsbury on his long ride south. So quiet, unobtrusive and unremarkable a man, he had hardly been noticed even while he remained here, his stay would soon be forgotten.

*

'He is gone,' said Cadfael. 'I would not slough off the burden of choice on to you, though I think I know what you would have done. But I have done it for you. He is gone, and I let him go.'

They were sitting together, as so often they had sat at the last ebb of a crisis, weary but eased, on the seat against the north wall of the herbarium, where the warmth of noonday lingered and the light wind was shut out. In another week or two it would be too cold and bleak for comfort here. This prolonged mild autumn could not last much longer, the weather-wise were beginning to sniff the air and foretell the first hard frost, and plentiful snow to come in December.

'I have not forgotten,' said Hugh, 'that this is the tomorrow when you promised me a fitting ending. So *he* is gone! And you let him go! Another he, not Bosiet. You were aching for him to tire of his vengeance and depart, more likely to urge him away than try to prevent. Say on, I'm listening.'

He was always a good listener, not given to exclamation or needless questions, he could sit gazing meditatively across the dishevelled garden in receptive silence, and never trouble his companion with a glance, and never miss a word, nor need many of them for understanding.

'I am in need of the confessional, if you will be my priest,' said Cadfael.

'And keep your confidences as tightly sealed – I know! My answer is yes. I never yet found you in need of absolution from me. Who is this he who is gone?'

'His name,' said Cadfael, 'is Rafe de Genville, though here he called himself Rafe of Coventry, a falconer to the earl of Warwick.'

'The quiet elder with the chestnut horse? I never saw him but the once, I think,' said Hugh. 'He was one guest here who had nothing to ask of me, and I was grateful for it, having my hands full of Bosiets. And what had Rafe of Coventry done, that either you or I should hesitate to let him go?'

'He had killed Cuthred. In fair fight. He laid his sword by, because Cuthred had none. Dagger against dagger he fought and killed him.' Hugh had said no word, only turned his head towards his friend for a moment, studied with penetrating attention the set of Cadfael's face, and waited. 'For good reason,' said Cadfael. 'You'll not have forgotten the tale we heard of the empress's messenger sent out of Oxford, just as King Stephen shut his iron ring round the castle. Sent forth with money and jewels and a letter for Brian FitzCount, cut off from her in Wallingford. And how they found his horse straying in the woods along the road, with blood-stained harness and empty saddlebags. The body they never found. The Thames runs close. There's room in the woods for a grave. So the lord of Wallingford was robbed of the empress's treasure. He has beggared himself for her long ago, ungrudging, and his garrison must eat. And the letter meant for him was stolen along with all the rest. And Rafe de Genville is vassal and devoted friend to Brian FitzCount, and loyal liegeman to the empress, and was not minded to let that crime go unavenged.

'What traces he found along the way to bring him into these parts I never asked, and he never told me, but bring him they did. The day he came I met with him in the stables, and by chance it came out that we had Drogo Bosiet lying dead in the mortuary chapel. I recall that I had not mentioned the name, but perhaps if I had he would still have done what he did, since names can be changed. He went straightway to look at this dead man, but at a glance he lost all interest in him. He was looking for someone, a guest here, a stranger, a traveller, but it was not Bosiet. In a young fellow of twenty, like Hyacinth, he had no interest at all. It was a man of his own years and estate he was seeking. Dame Dionisia's holy man he must surely have heard about, but dismissed him as priest and pilgrim, vouched for and above suspicion. Until he heard, as we all did, young Richard bellow that the hermit was no priest but a cheat. I looked for Rafe afterwards, and he and his horse were gone. It was an impostor and cheat he was looking for. And he found him, Hugh, that night at the hermitage. Found him, fought him, killed him. And took back all that he had stolen, jewels and coin from the casket on the altar, and the breviary that belonged to the empress, and was used to carry letters between her and FitzCount when they were apart. You'll recall that Cuthred's dagger was bloodied. I have dressed Rafe de Genville's wound, I have received his confidence as I have now delivered you mine, and I have wished him godspeed back to Wallingford.'

Cadfael sat back with a deep and grateful sigh, and leaned his head against the rough stones of the wall, and there was a long but tranquil silence between them. Hugh stirred at last, and asked: 'How did you come to know what he was about? There must have been more than that first encounter, to draw you into his secrets. He said little, he hunted alone. What more happened, to bring you so close to him?'

'I was with him when he dropped some coins into our alms box. One of them fell to the flags, and I picked it up. A silver penny of the empress, minted recently in Oxford. He made no secret of it. Did I not wonder, he said, what the empress's liegeman was doing so far from the battle? And I drew a bow at a very long venture, and said he might well be looking for the murderer who robbed and slew Renaud Bourchier on the road to Wallingford.'

'And he owned it?' said Hugh.

'No. He said no, it was not so. It was a good thought, he said, almost he wished it had been true, but it was not so. And he told truth. Every word he ever said to me was truth, and I knew it. No, Cuthred was not a murderer, not then, never until Drogo Bosiet walked into his cell to enquire after a runaway villein, and came face to face with a man he had seen, talked with, played chess with, at Thame some weeks before, in a very different guise. A man who bore arms and showed knightly, but went the roads on foot, for there was no horse belonging to him in the stable at Thame, none that came with him, none that departed with him. And this was early in October. All this Aymer told us, after his father had been silenced.'

'I begin,' said Hugh slowly, 'to read your riddle.' He narrowed his eyes upon distance, through the half-naked branches of the trees that showed above the southern wall of the garden. 'When did you ever question so far astray without a purpose? I should have known when you asked about the horse. A rider without a horse at Thame and a horse without a rider wandering the woods by the Wallingford road make sense when put together. No!' he said in shocked and outraged protest, staring aghast at the image he had raised. 'Where have you brought me? Is this truth, or have I shot wild? *Bourchier himself*?'

The first tremor of the evening chill shook the harvested and sleepy herbs with a colder wind, and Hugh shook with them in a convulsion of incredulous distaste. 'What could be worth so monstrous a treason? This was fouler than murder.'

'So thought Rafe de Genville. And he has taken vengeance for it in measure accordingly. And he is gone, and I wished him godspeed in his going.'

'So would I have done. So I do!' said Hugh, and stared across the garden with lips curled in fastidious disdain, contemplating the enormity of the chosen and deliberate dishonour. 'There is nothing, there can be nothing, worth purchasing at such a price.'

'Renaud Bourchier thought otherwise, having other values. He gained his life and liberty first,' said Cadfael, checking off the score on his fingers, and shaking his head over every item. 'By sending him out of Oxford before the ring of steel shut fast, she released him to make off into safer pastures. Not that I believe he had even the excuse of being a simple coward. Quite coldly, I fancy, he preferred to remove himself from the risk of death or capture, which have come closer to her armies there in Oxford than ever they came before. Coldly and practically he severed all his ties of fealty, and retired into obscurity to look round for the next opportunity. Second, with the theft of the treasure she entrusted to him he had ample means to live, wherever he might go. And third, and worst of all, he had a powerful weapon, one which could be used to secure him new soldier service, and lands, and favour, a new and profitable career to replace the one he had discarded. The letter the empress had written to Brian FitzCount.'

'In the breviary that vanished,' said Hugh. 'I knew no way of accounting for that, though the book had a value even for itself.'

'It had a greater value for what was in it. Rafe told me. A fine leaf of vellum can be folded into the binding. Only consider, Hugh, her situation when she wrote. The town lost, only the castle left, and the king's armies closing round her. And Brian who had been her right hand, her shield and sword, second only to her brother, separated from her by those few miles that could as well have been an ocean. God knows if those gossips are right,' said Cadfael, 'who declare that those two are lovers, but surely it is truth that they love! And now at this extreme, in peril of starvation, failure, imprisonment, loss, even death, perhaps never to meet again, may she not have cried out to him the last truth, without conceal, things that should not be set down, things no other on earth should ever see? Such a letter might be of immense value to a man without scruples, who had a new career to make, and needed the favour of princes. She has a husband years younger than herself, who has no great love for her, nor she for him, one who would not spare a man to come to her aid this summer.

Suppose that some day it should be convenient to Geoffrey to repudiate his older wife, and make a second profitable marriage? In the hands of such as Bourchier her letter, her own hand, might provide him the pretext, and for princes the means can always be found. The informer might stand to gain place, command, even lands in Normandy. Geoffrey has castles newly conquered there to bestow on those who prove useful to him. I don't say the count of Anjou *is* such a man, but I do say so calculating a traitor as Bourchier would reckon it a possibility, and keep the letter to be used as chance offered. What knowledge, what suspicion, brought Rafe de Genville to doubt that death by the Wallingford road I do not know, I never asked. Certain it is that once the spark was lit, nothing would have prevented him from pursuing and exacting the penalty due, not from some supposed murderer – he told me truth there – but from the thief and traitor, Renaud Bourchier himself.'

The wind was rising now, the sky clearing, the broken fragments of cloud that remained scudding away before the wind. For the first time the prolonged autumn hinted at winter.

'I would have done as Rafe did,' said Hugh with finality, and rose abruptly to shake off the residue of loathing.

'When I bore arms, so would I. It grows chilly,' said Cadfael, rising after him. 'Shall we go in?'

Late November would soon be tearing away with frost and gales the rest of the quivering leaves. The deserted hermitage in the woods of Eyton would provide winter cover for the small beasts of the forest, and the garden, running wild again, would shelter the slumbering urchins in their nests through the winter sleep. Doubtful if Dame Dionisia would ever set up another hermit in that cell. The wild things would occupy it in innocence.

'Well,' said Cadfael, leading the way into his workshop, 'that's over. Late but at last, whatever she may have written to him, her letter is on the way to the man for whose heart's comfort it was intended. And I am glad! Whatever the rights or wrongs of their affection, in the teeth of danger and despair love is entitled to speak its mind, and all others should be blind and deaf. Except God, who can read both the lines and between the lines, and who in the end, in matters of passion as in matters of justice, will have the last word.'

The Confession of Brother Haluin

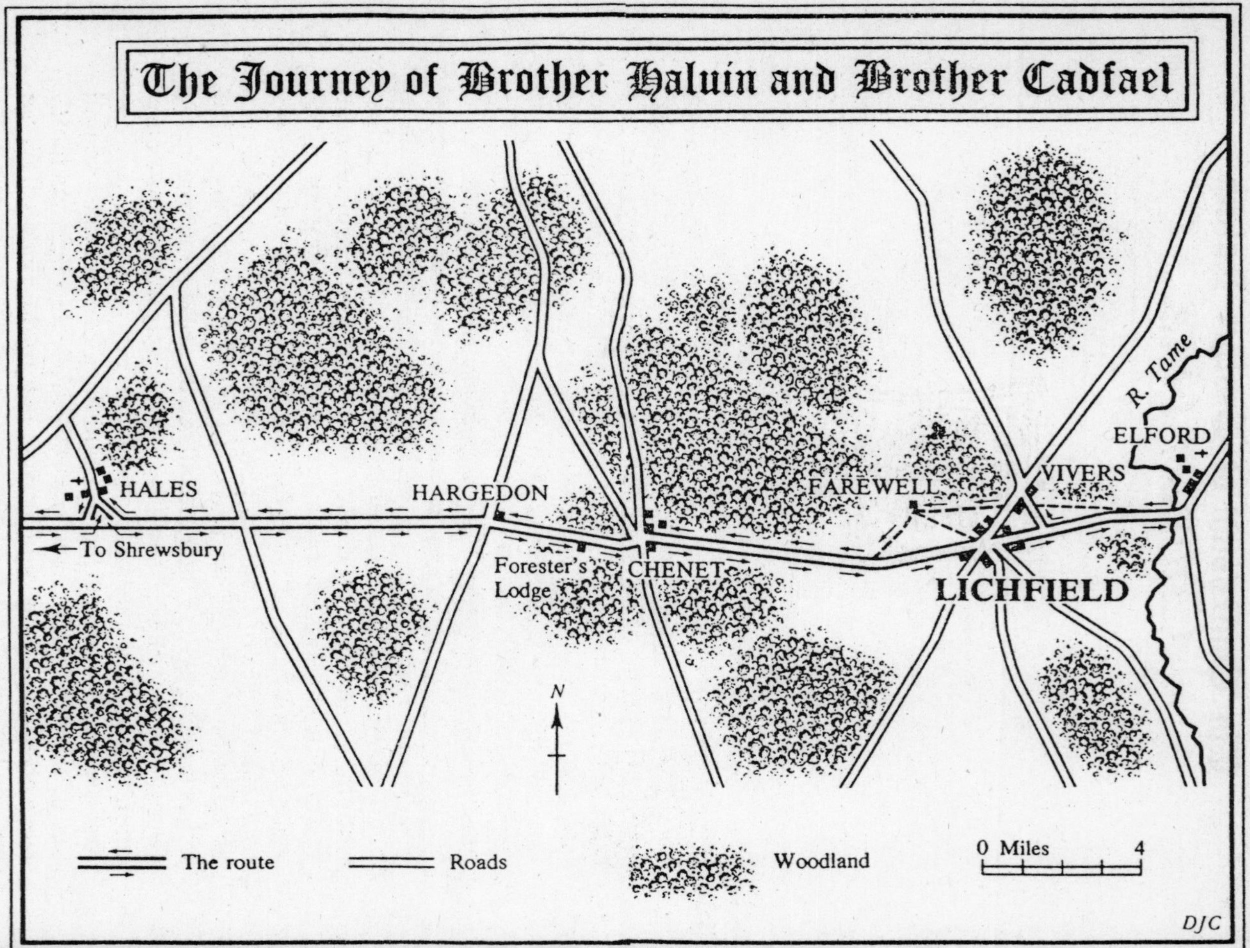
The Journey of Brother Haluin and Brother Cadfael
HALES
To Shrewsbury
HARGEDON
Forester's Lodge
CHENET
FAREWELL
LICHFIELD
VIVERS
ELFORD
R. Tame
N
The route
Roads
Woodland
0 Miles 4
DJC

Chapter One

THE WORST of the winter came early, that year of 1142. After the prolonged autumn of mild, moist, elegiac days, December came in with heavy skies and dark, brief days that sagged upon the rooftrees and lay like oppressive hands upon the heart. In the scriptorium there was barely light enough at noon to form the letters, and the colours could not be used with any certainty, since the unrelenting and untimely dusk sapped all their brightness.

The weather-wise had predicted heavy snows, and in mid-month they came, not with blizzard winds, but in a blinding, silent fall that continued for several days and nights, smoothing out every undulation, blanching all colour out of the world, burying the sheep in the hills and the hovels in the valleys, smothering all sound, climbing every wall, turning roofs into ranges of white, impassable mountains, and the very air between earth and sky into an opaque, drifting whirlpool of flakes large as lilies. When the fall finally ceased, and the heavy swags of cloud lifted, the Foregate lay half buried, so nearly smoothed out into one white level that there were scarcely any shadows except where the tall buildings of the abbey soared out of the pure pallor, and the eerie, reflected light made day even of night, where only a week before the ominous gloom had made night of day.

These December snows, which covered most of the west, did more than disrupt the lives of country people, starve some isolated hamlets, bury not a few hill shepherds with their flocks, and freeze all travel into enforced stillness; they overturned the fortunes of war, made sport of the preoccupations of princes, and sent history spinning off-course into the new year of 1143.

They also brought about a strange cycle of events in the abbey of Saint Peter and Saint Paul, at Shrewsbury.

In the five years that King Stephen and his cousin, the Empress Maud, had fought for the throne of England, fortune had swung between them like a pendulum many times, presenting the cup of victory to each in erratic turn, only to snatch it away again untasted, and offer it tantalisingly to the other contender. Now, in the white disguise of winter, it chose to turn probability topsy-turvy once again, and deliver the empress out of the king's mailed hands as by a miracle, just as his fist seemed closing securely on his prisoner, and his warfare triumphantly ending. Back to the beginning of the five-year struggle, and all to do again. But that was in Oxford, far away beyond the impassable snows, and some time would elapse before the news reached Shrewsbury.

What was happening in the abbey of Saint Peter and Saint Paul was no more than a small annoyance by comparison, or seemed so at first. An envoy from the bishop, lodged in one of the upper chambers of the guest-hall, and already irritated and displeased at being halted here perforce until the roads were passable again, was unpleasantly awakened in the night by the sudden descent of a stream of icy water on to his head, and made very sure that everyone within range of his powerful voice should hear of it without delay. Brother Denis the hospitaller made haste to placate him, and move him to a dry bed elsewhere, but within the hour it became clear that while the first drenching soon slackened, a steady drip continued, and was soon joined by half a dozen more, spanning a circle some yards across. The great weight of snow on the southern roof of the guest-hall had somehow worked a passage through the lead and filtered in between the slates, perhaps even caved in a number of them. Pockets of the driven snow had felt the comparative warmth within, and with the mute malice of inanimate things had chosen to baptise the bishop's emissary. And the leak was rapidly getting worse.

There was urgent conference at chapter that morning over what should and could be done. Perilous and unpleasant work on roofs was certainly to be avoided if possible during such weather, but on the other hand, if repairs were delayed until the thaw came they were in for a flood, and the damage, limited at this point, might be greatly aggravated.

There were several among the brothers who had worked on the building of additions to the enclave, barns and stabling and storehouses, and Brother Conradin, who was still in his fifties and robust as a bull, had been one of the first child oblates, and worked as a boy under the monks of Seez, brought over by the founding earl to supervise the building of his abbey. Where the fabric was concerned, Brother Conradin's advice carried the greatest weight, and having viewed the extent of the leak in the guest-hall, he stated firmly that they could not afford to wait, or they might have to replace half the southern slope of the roof. They had timber, they had slates, they had lead. That southern slope overhung the drainage channel drawn off from the mill leat, frozen hard at present, but there would be no great difficulty in raising a scaffolding. True, it would be bitterly cold work up there, shifting the mountain of snow first, to ease away the deforming weight, and then replacing broken or displaced slates and repairing the lead flashings. But if they worked in short spells, and were allowed a fire in the warming room all day as long as the work lasted, the job could be done.

Abbot Radulfus listened, nodded his formidable head with his usual prompt comprehension and decision, and said: 'Very well, do it!'

As soon as the long snowfall ceased, and the skies lifted, the tough inhabitants of the Foregate sallied forth from their houses, well muffled and armed with shovels and brooms and long-handled rakes, and began to clear their way out to the highroad, and between them dig out a passage to the bridge and the town, where no doubt the stout burgesses within the walls were tackling the same seasonal enemy. The frost still held, and day by day fretted away mysteriously into the air the surface fringes of every drift, by infinitely slow degrees lessening the load. By the time a few of the main highways were again passable, and a few travellers, either foolhardy or having no choice, were laboriously riding them, Brother Conradin had his scaffolding up, his ladders securely braced up the slope of the roof, and all hands taking their turn aloft in the withering cold, cautiously shifting the great burden of snow, to get at the fractured lead and broken slates. A moraine of crumpled, untidy snow hills formed along the frozen drainage channel, and one unwary brother, who had failed to hear or heed the warning shout from above, was briefly buried by a minor avalanche, and had to be dug out hurriedly and despatched to the warming room to thaw out.

By then way was open between town and Foregate, and news, however hampered and slow its passage, could be carried from Winchester even to Shrewsbury in time to reach the castle garrison and the sheriff of the shire some days before Christmas.

Hugh Beringar came down from the town hotfoot to share it with Abbot Radulfus. In a country debilitated by five years of desultory civil war it behoved state and church to work closely together, and where sheriff and abbot were of like mind they could secure for their people a comparatively calm and orderly existence, and fend off the worst excesses of the times. Hugh was King Stephen's man, and held the shire for him loyally enough, but with even greater goodwill he held it for the folk who lived in it. He would welcome, and this autumn and winter had certainly been expecting, the king's triumph at last, but his chief preoccupation was to hand over to his lord a county relatively prosperous, contented and intact when the last battle was over.

He came looking for Brother Cadfael as soon as he had left the abbot's lodging, and found his friend busy stirring a bubbling pot over his brazier, in his workshop in the herb-garden. The inevitable coughs and colds of winter, the chilblained hands and heels, kept him busy replenishing the medicine cupboard in the infirmary, and thanks to the necessary brazier his timber workshop was somewhat warmer to work in than the carrels of the scriptorium.

Hugh came bursting in upon him in a gust of cold air and a wave of what was for him perceptible excitement, though its outward signs would have escaped anyone who knew him less well than Cadfael did. Only the crisp exasperation of his movements and the abruptness of his greeting caused Cadfael to cease his stirring and fix attentively on the young sheriff's face, the pointed brilliance of his black eyes and the little pulse in his cheek.

'It's all overturned!' said Hugh. 'All to do again from the beginning!' And whatever that meant, and Cadfael did not trouble to ask, since he was certainly about to be told, there was no saying whether exasperation and frustration were not outmatched in Hugh's voice and face by amused relief. He flung himself down on the bench against the timber wall, and dangled his hands between his knees in a gesture of helpless resignation.

'A courier got through from the south this morning,' he said, raising his eyes to his friend's attentive face. 'She's gone! Out of the trap, and fled away to join her brother at Wallingford. The king's lost his prize. Even when he has her between his hands he lets her slip through his fingers. I wonder, I wonder,' said Hugh, opening his eyes wide at a new thought, 'whether he did not turn a blind eye and let her go, when it came to the point! It would be like him. God knows he wanted her badly enough, but he may have taken fright when it came to puzzling what he could do with her when he had her. It's one question I'd love to ask him – but never shall!' he concluded with an oblique grin.

'Are you telling me,' asked Cadfael cautiously, eyeing him across the brazier, 'that the empress is escaped out of Oxford, after all? With the king's army all round her, and stores down to starvation level in the castle, from what we last heard? And how did even she contrive it? Tell me next she's grown wings and flown over the king's lines to Wallingford! She could hardly walk through his siege vallations on foot, even if she managed to get out of the castle unseen.'

'Ah, but she did, Cadfael! She did both! She got out of the castle unseen, and passed through some part at least of Stephen's lines. To the best they can guess, she must have been let down by a rope from the rear of the tower towards the river, she and two or three of her men with her. There could not have been more. They muffled themselves all in white to be invisible against the snow. Indeed by all accounts it was snowing then, to hide them the better. They crossed the river on the ice, and walked the six miles or so to Abingdon, for it was there they got horses to take them on to Wallingford. Give her her due, Cadfael, this is a rare woman. From all accounts there's no living with her when she's in high feather, but by God I can see how a man could follow her when she's down.'

'So she's back with FitzCount, after all,' said Cadfael on a long, marvelling breath. Barely a month ago it had seemed certain that the empress and her most faithful and devoted ally were irrevocably cut off from each other, and might never meet again in this world.

Ever since September the lady had been under close siege in Oxford castle, the king's armies drawn tightly round her, the town in his hands, and he content to sit back and starve out her battered garrison. And now, all in one bold bid and one snowy night, she was out of her chains, free to remuster her forces and take up the fight again on equal terms. Surely there never had been such a king as Stephen for conjuring defeat out of victory. But it was a quality they shared, perhaps native to their blood, for the empress too, when she was gloriously installed in Westminster, and her coronation but a few days away, had borne herself so arrogantly and harshly towards the obstinate burgesses of her capital that they had risen in fury and driven her out. It seemed that as often as either of them got within touch of the crown fortune took fright at the prospect of being in the service of either, and hurriedly snatched the prize away.

'So after all,' said Cadfael more placidly, as he lifted his bubbling pot to the grid at the side of the brazier, to simmer in peace, 'at least Stephen has got rid of his problem. He need worry no longer what to do with her.'

'True,' agreed Hugh wryly, 'he'd never have had the iron in him to put her in chains, as she did to him when she had him prisoner after Lincoln, and she's proved it would take more than stone walls to hold her. I fancy he's been blinking the issue all these months, looking no further than the moment when he would force her surrender. He's eased of all the troubles that would have been no more than beginning the day he made her prisoner. Better, perhaps, if he could winnow away her hopes so far that she'd be forced to go back to Normandy. But we've come to know the lady better,' he acknowledged ruefully. 'She never gives up.'

'And how has King Stephen stomached his loss?' asked Cadfael curiously.

'As I've come to expect of him by this time,' said Hugh, with resigned affection. 'As soon as the lady was well out of it, Oxford Castle surrendered to him. Without her, he'd lost interest in the rest of the starved rats within. Most men would have taken out their rage on the garrison. Once, as you'll remember all too well, he let himself be persuaded to take such a revenge, here at Shrewsbury, God knows against his nature. Never again! As like as not it was the memory of Shrewsbury that kept Oxford safe. He let them march out untouched, on condition they dispersed to their homes. He's left the castle well garrisoned and supplied for his own cause, and made off to Winchester with his brother the bishop, to keep Christmas.

And he's sent to call all his midland sheriffs there to keep it with him. It's long since he was in these parts, no doubt he's anxious to look us over afresh, and make sure that all his defences hold fast.'

'Now?' said Cadfael, surprised. 'To Winchester? You'll never make the journey in time.'

'Yes, we shall. We have four days, and according to the courier the thaw's well forward, further south, and the roads clear. I'll be away tomorrow.'

'And leave Aline and your boy to keep the feast without you! And Giles just past his third birthday, too!' Hugh's son was a Christmas babe, and had entered the world in the most extreme of winters, in frost and snow and bitter gales. Cadfael was his godfather and most devoted admirer.

'Ah, Stephen won't keep us long,' said Hugh confidently. 'He needs us where he placed us, to keep an eye on his shire revenues. I shall be home by the year's end, if all goes well. But Aline will be glad if you could pay her a visit or two while I'm gone. Father Abbot won't grudge you leave now and then, and that long lad of yours – Winfrid, is it? – he's getting handy enough with the salves and medicines to be left on his own for an hour or two.'

'Very gladly I'll mind your flock for you at home,' said Cadfael heartily, 'while you're strutting at court. But you'll be missed, all the same. What a turnabout this has been! Five years of it now, and nothing gained on either part. And with the new year, no doubt it must all begin again. All that effort and waste, and nothing is changed.'

'Oh, yes, there's something changed, for what it's worth!' Hugh uttered a brief bark of laughter. 'There's a new contender on the scene, Cadfael. Geoffrey could spare no more than a meagre handful of knights to his wife's aid, but he's sent her something it seems he can part with more willingly. Either that or, as may very well be true, he's taken Stephen's measure shrewdly enough to know past doubt what he dare wager in safety. He's sent over their son in his Uncle Robert's care, to see if the English will rally to him rather than to his mother. Henry Plantagenet, nine years old – or did they say ten? No more than that! Robert brought him to her at Wallingford. By this time I fancy the boy's been whisked away to Bristol or Gloucester, out of harm's way. But if Stephen laid hold of him, what could he do with him? As like as not put him on board ship at his own expense, and send him well guarded back to France.'

'Do you tell me so?' Cadfael's eyes had opened wide in astonishment and curiosity. 'So there's a new star on the horizon, is there? And starting young! It seems one soul at least has a blessed Christmas assured, with her liberty won, and her son in her arms again. His coming will give her heart, no question. But I doubt if he'll do much more for her cause.'

'Not yet!' said Hugh, with prophetic caution. 'We'll wait and see what his mettle is. With his mother's stomach and Geoffrey's wit he may give the king trouble enough in a few years' time. We'd best make better use of what time we have, and see to it the boy goes back to Anjou and stays there, and best of all, takes his mother with him. I wish,' said Hugh fervently, rising with a sigh, 'Stephen's own son promised better, we'd have no need to fear what the empress's sprig may have to show.' He shook off present doubts with an impatient twitch of his lean shoulders. 'Well, I'll be off and make ready for the road. We'll be away at first light.'

Cadfael lifted his cooling pot aside to the earth floor, and went out with his friend through the walled stillness of the herb-garden, where all his small, neat beds slept warmly through the frosts under deep snow. As soon as they let themselves out on to the path that skirted the frozen pools they could see distantly, beyond the glassy surface and the broad gardens on the northern side, the long slope of the guest-hall roof overhanging the drainage channel, the dark timber cage of scaffolding and ladders, and the two muffled figures working on the uncovered slates.

'I see you have your troubles, too,' said Hugh.

'Who escapes them, in winter? It's the weight of the snow that's shifted the slates, broken some of them, and found a way through to douse the bishop's chaplain in his bed. If we left it till the thaw we'd have a flood, and far worse damage to repair.'

'And your master-builder reckons he can make it good, frost or no frost.' Hugh had recognised the brawny figure halfway up the long ladder, hefting a hodful of slates surely few of his younger labourers could have lifted. 'Bitter work up there, though,' said Hugh, eyeing the highest platform of the scaffolding, stacked with a great pile of slates, and the two diminutive figures moving with painful caution on the exposed roof.

'We take it in short spells, and there's a fire in the warming-room when we come down. We elders are excused the service, but most of us take a turn, barring the sick and infirm. It's fair, but I doubt if it pleases Conradin. It irks him having foolhardy youngsters up there, and he'd just as soon work only the ones he's sure of, though I will say he keeps a close watch on them. If he sees any blanch at being up so high, he soon has them on solid earth again. We can't all have the head for it.'

'Have you been up there?' asked Hugh curiously.

'I did my stint yesterday, before the light began to fail. Short days are no help, but another week should see it finished.'

Hugh narrowed his eyes against a sudden brief lance of sunlight that reflected back dazzlingly from the crystalline whiteness. 'Who are those two up there now? Is that Brother Urien? The dark fellow? Who's the other one?'

'Brother Haluin.' The thin, alert figure was all but obscured by the jut of the scaffolding, but Cadfael had seen the pair climb the ladders barely an hour earlier.

'What, Anselm's best illuminator? How comes it you allow such abuse of an artist? He'll ruin his hands in this bitter cold. Small chance of him handling a fine brush for the next week or two, after grappling with slates.'

'Anselm would have begged him off,' Cadfael admitted, 'but Haluin would have none of it. No one would have grudged him the mercy, seeing how valuable his work is, but if there's a hair shirt anywhere within reach Haluin will claim it and wear it. A lifelong penitent, that lad, God knows for what imagined sins, for I never knew him so much as break a rule since he entered as a novice, and seeing he was no more than eighteen when he took his first vows, I doubt if he'd had time to do the world much harm up to then. But there are some born to do penance by nature. Maybe they lift the load for some of us who take it quite comfortably that we're humankind, and not angels. If the overflow from Haluin's penitence and piety washes off a few of my shortcomings, may it redound to him for credit in the accounting. And I shan't complain.'

It was too cold to linger very long in the deep snow, watching the cautious activities on the guest-hall roof. They resumed their passage through the gardens, skirting the frozen pools where Brother Simeon had chopped jagged holes to let in air to the fish below, and crossing the mill-leat that fed the ponds by the narrow plank bridge glazed over with a thin and treacherous crust of ice. Closer now, the piers of the scaffolding jutted from the south wall of the guest-hall across the drainage channel, and the workers on the roof were hidden from sight.

'I had him with me among the herbs as a novice, long ago,' said Cadfael as they threaded the snowy beds of the upper garden and emerged into the great court. 'Haluin, I mean. It was not long after I ended my own novitiate. I came in at past forty, and he barely turned eighteen. They sent him to me because he was lettered, and had the Latin at his finger-ends, and after three or four years I was still learning. He comes of a landed family, and would have inherited a good manor if he hadn't chosen the cloister. A cousin has it now. The boy had been put out to a noble household, as the custom is, and was clerk to his lord's estate, being uncommonly bright at learning and figuring. I often wondered why he changed course, but as every man within here knows, there's no questioning a vocation. It comes when it will, and there's no refusal.'

'It would have been simpler to plant the lad straight into the scriptorium, if he came in with so much learning,' said Hugh practically. 'I've seen some of his work, he'd be wasted on any other labour.'

'Ah, but his conscience would have him pass through every stage of the common apprenticeship before he came to rest. I had him for three years among the herbs, then he did two years more at the hospital of Saint Giles, among the sick and crippled, and two more labouring in the gardens at the Gaye, and helping with the sheep out at Rhydycroesau, before he'd settle to do what we found he could do best. Even now, as you saw, he'll have no privilege because he has a delicate hand with the brushes and pens. If others must slither perilously on a snowy roof, so will he. A good fault, mind you,' admitted Cadfael, 'but he takes it to extremes, and the Rule disapproves extremes.'

They crossed the great court towards the gatehouse, where Hugh's horse was tethered, the tall, raw-boned grey that was always his favourite mount, and could have carried twice or three times his master's light weight.

'There'll be no more snow tonight,' said Cadfael, eyeing the veiled sky and sniffing the light, languid wind, 'nor for a few days more, I fancy. Nor hard frost, either, we're on the edge of it. I pray you'll have a tolerable ride south.'

'We'll be away at dawn. And back, God willing, by the new year.' Hugh gathered his bridle and swung himself into the high saddle. 'May the thaw hold off until your roof's weatherproof again! And don't forget Aline will be expecting you.'

He was off out of the gate, with a sharp echo of hooves ringing from the cobbles, and a single brilliant spark that had come and gone almost before the iron shoe left the frozen ground. Cadfael turned back to the door of the infirmary, and went to check the stores in Brother Edmund's medicine cupboard. Another hour, and the light would be already dimming, in these shortest days of the year. Brother Urien and Brother Haluin would be the last pair up on the roof for this day.

Exactly how it happened no one ever clearly established. Brother Urien, who had obeyed Brother Conradin's order to come down as soon as the call came, pieced together what he thought the most probable account, but even he admitted there could be no certainty. Conradin, accustomed to being obeyed, and sensibly concluding that no one in his right senses would wish to linger a moment longer than he must in the bitter cold, had simply shouted his command, and turned away to clear the last of the day's broken slates out of the way of his descending workmen. Brother Urien let himself down thankfully to the boards of the scaffolding, and fumbled his way carefully down the long ladder to the ground, only too happy to leave the work. He was strong and willing, and had no special skills but a wealth of hard experience, and what he did would be well done, but he saw no need to do more than was asked of him. He drew off some yards to look up at what had been accomplished, and saw Brother Haluin, instead of descending the short ladder braced up the slope of the roof on his side, mount several rungs higher, and lean out sidelong to clear away a further sweep of snow and extend the range of the uncovered slates. It appeared that he had seen reason to suspect that the damage extended further on that side, and wished to sweep away the snow there to remove its weight and prevent worse harm.

The rounded bank of snow shifted, slid down in great folds upon itself, and fell, partly upon the end of the planks and the stack of slates waiting there, partly over the edge and sheer to the ground below. No such avalanche had been intended, but the frozen mass loosed its hold of the steep slates and dropped away in one solid block, to shatter as it struck the scaffolding. Haluin had leaned too far. The ladder slid with the snow that had helped to keep it stable, and he fell rather before than with it, struck the end of the planks a glancing blow, and crashed down without a cry to the frozen channel below. Ladder and snowfall dropped upon the planks and hurled them after him in a great downpour of heavy, sharp-edged slates, slashing into his flesh.

Brother Conradin, busy almost beneath his scaffolding, had leaped clear only just in time, spattered and stung and half-blinded for a moment by the blown drift of the fall. Brother Urien, standing well back, and arrested in the very act of calling up to his companion to stop, for the light was too far gone, uttered instead a great cry of warning, too late to save, and sprang forward, to be half-buried by the edge of the fall. Shaking off snow, they reached Brother Haluin together.

It was Brother Urien who came in haste and grim silence looking for Cadfael, while Conradin ran out the other way into the great court, and sent the first brother he encountered to fetch Brother Edmund the infirmarer. Cadfael was in his workshop, just turfing over his brazier for the night, when Urien erupted into the doorway, a dark, dour man burning with ill news.

'Brother, come quickly! Brother Haluin has fallen from the roof!'

Cadfael, no less sparing of words, swung about, clouted down the last turf, and reached for a woollen blanket from the shelf.

'Dead?' The drop must be forty feet at least, timber by way of obstacles on the way down, and packed ice below, but if by chance he had fallen into deep snow made deeper still by the clearance of the roof, he might yet be lucky.

'There's breath in him. But for how long? Conradin's gone for more helpers, Edmund knows by now.'

'Come!' said Cadfael, and was out of the door and running for the little bridge over the leat, only to change his mind and dart along the narrow neck of causeway between the abbey pools, and leap the leat at the end of it, to come the more quickly to where Haluin lay. From the great court the gleam of two torches advanced to meet them, and Brother Edmund with a couple of helpers and a hand-litter, hard on Brother Conradin's heels.

Brother Haluin, buried to the knees under heavy slates, with blood staining the ice beneath his head, lay still in the middle of the turmoil he had caused.

Chapter Two

WHATEVER THE risks of moving him, to leave him where he was for a moment longer than was necessary would have been to consent to and abet the death that already had a fast hold on him. In mute and purposeful haste they lifted aside the fallen planks and dug out with their hands the knife-edged slates that crushed and lacerated his feet and ankles into a pulp of blood and bone. He was far gone from them, and felt nothing that was done to him as they eased him out of the icy bed of the drain enough to get slings under him, and hoisted him on to the litter. In mourne procession they bore him out through the darkened gardens to the infirmary, where Brother Edmund had prepared a bed for him in a small cell apart from the old and infirm who spent their last years there.

'He cannot live,' said Edmund, looking down at the remote and pallid face.

So Cadfael thought, too. So did they all. But still there was breath in him, even if it was a harsh, groaning breath that spoke of head injuries perhaps past mending; and they went to work on him as on one who could and must live, even against their own virtual certainty that he could not. With infinite, wincing care they stripped him of his icy garments, and padded him round with blankets wrapped about heated stones, while Cadfael went over him gently for broken bones, and set and bound the left forearm that grated as he handled it, and still brought never a flicker to the motionless face. He felt carefully about Haluin's head before cleaning and dressing the bleeding wound, but could not determine whether the skull was fractured. The bitter, snoring breathing indicated that it was, but he could not be sure. As for the broken feet and ankles, Cadfael laboured over them for a long time after they had covered the rest of Brother Haluin with warmed brychans against simple death of cold, his body laid straight and shored securely every way to guard against the shock and pain of movement should he regain his senses. As no one believed he would, unless it was an obstinate, secret remnant of belief that caused them so to exert themselves to nourish even the failing spark.

'He will never walk again,' said Brother Edmund, shuddering at the shattered feet Cadfael was laboriously bathing.

'Never without aid,' Cadfael agreed sombrely. 'Never on these.' But for all that he went on patiently putting together again, as best he could, the mangled remains.

Long, narrow, elegant feet Brother Haluin had had, in keeping with his slender build. The deep and savage cuts the slates had made penetrated to the bone in places, here and there had splintered the bone. It took a long time to clean away the bloody fragments, and bind up each foot at least into its human shape, and encase it in a hastily improvised cradle of felt, well padded within, to hold it still and let it heal as near as possible to what it had once been. If, of course, there was to be healing.

And all the while Brother Haluin lay snoring painfully and oblivious of all that was done to him, very far sunk beneath the lights and shadows of the world, until even his breathing subsided gradually into a mere shallow whisper, no more than the stirring of a solitary leaf in a scarcely perceptible breeze, and they thought that he was gone. But the leaf continued to stir, however faintly.

'If he comes to himself, even for a moment, call me at once,' said Abbot Radulfus, and left them to their watch.

Brother Edmund was gone to get some sleep. Cadfael shared the night watch with Brother Rhun, newest and youngest among the choir monks. One on either side of the bed, they stared steadily upon the unbroken sleep beyond sleep of a body anointed and blessed and armed for death.

It was many years since Haluin had passed out of Cadfael's care to go to manual labour in the Gaye. Cadfael re-examined with deep attention lineaments he had almost forgotten in their early detail, and found now both changed and poignantly familiar. Not a big man, Brother Haluin, but somewhat taller than the middle height, with long, fine, shapely bones, and more sinew and less flesh on them now than when first he came into the cloister, a boy still short of his full growth, and just hardening into manhood. Thirty-five or thirty-six he must be now, barely eighteen then, with the softness and bloom still on him. His face was a long oval, the bones of cheek and jaw strong and clear, the thin, arched brows almost black, shades darker than the mane of crisp brown hair he had sacrificed to the tonsure. The face upturned now from the pillow was blanched to a clay-white pallor, the hollows of the cheeks and deep pits of the closed eyes blue as shadows in the snow, and round the drawn lips the same livid blueness was gathering even as they watched. In the small hours of the night, when the life sinks to its frailest, he would end or mend.

Across the bed Brother Rhun kneeled, attentive, unintimidated by another's death any more than he would be, some day, by his own. Even in the dimness of this small, stony room Rhun's radiant fairness, his face creamy with youth, his ring of flaxen hair and aquamarine eyes, diffused a lambent brightness. Only someone of Rhun's virgin certainty could sit serenely by a deathbed, with such ardent loving-kindness and yet no taint of pity. Cadfael had seen other young creatures come to the cloister with something of the same charmed faith, only to see it threatened, dulled and corroded gradually by the sheer burden of being human under the erosion of the years. That would never happen to Rhun. Saint Winifred, who had bestowed on him the physical perfection he had lacked, would not suffer the gift to be marred by any maiming of his spirit.

The night passed slowly, with no perceptible change in Brother Haluin's unrelenting stillness. It was towards dawn when at last Rhun said softly: 'Look, he is stirring!'

The faintest quiver had passed over the livid face, the dark brows drew together, the eyelids tightened with the first distant awareness of pain, the lips lengthened in a brief grimace of stress and alarm. They waited for what seemed a long while, unable to do more than wipe the moist forehead, and the trickle of spittle that oozed from the corner of the drawn mouth.

In the first dim, reflected snow-light before dawn Brother Haluin opened his eyes, onyx-black in their blue hollows, and moved his lips to emit a hair-fine thread of a voice that Rhun had to stoop his young, sharp ear to catch and interpret.

'Confession . . . ' said the whisper from the threshold between life and death, and for a while that was all.

'Go and bring Father Abbot,' said Cadfael.

Rhun departed silently and swiftly. Haluin lay gathering his senses, and by the growing clarity and sharpening focus of his eyes he knew where he was and who sat beside him, and was mustering what life and wit remained to him for a purpose. Cadfael saw the quickening of pain in the strained whiteness of mouth and jaw, and made to trickle a little of the draught of poppies between his patient's lips, but Haluin kept them tightly clenched and turned his head away. He wanted nothing to dull or hamper his senses, not yet, not until he had got out of him what he had to say.

'Father Abbot is coming,' said Cadfael, close to the pillow. 'Wait, and speak but once.'

Abbot Radulfus was at the door by then, stooping under the low lintel. He took the stool Rhun had vacated, and leaned down to the injured man. Rhun had remained without, ready to run errands if he should be needed, and had drawn the door closed between. Cadfael rose to withdraw likewise, and suddenly yellow sparks of anxiety flared in Haluin's hollow eyes, and a brief convulsion went through his body and fetched a moan of pain, as though he had willed to lift a hand to arrest Cadfael's going, but could not do it. The abbot leaned closer, to be seen as well as heard.

'I am here, my son. I am listening. What is it troubles you?'

Haluin drew in breath, hoarding it to have a voice to speak with. 'I have sins . . . ' he said, ' . . . never told.' The words came slowly and with much labour, but clearly. 'One against Cadfael . . . Long past . . . never confessed . . . '

The abbot looked up at Cadfael across the bed. 'Stay! He wishes it.' And to Haluin, touching the lax hand that was too weak to be lifted: 'Speak as you can, we shall be listening. Spare many words, we can read between.'

'My vows,' said the thread-fine voice remotely. 'Impure . . . not out of devotion . . . Despair!'

'Many have entered for wrong reasons,' said the abbot, 'and remained for the right ones. Certainly in the four years of my abbacy here I have found no fault in your true service. On this head have no fear. God may have brought you into the cloister roundabout for his own good reasons.'

'I served de Clary at Hales,' said the thin voice. 'Better, his lady – he being in the Holy Land then. His daughter . . .' A long silence while doggedly and patiently he renewed his endurance to deliver more and worse. 'I loved her . . . and was loved. But the mother . . . my suit was not welcome. What was forbidden us we took . . .'

Another and longer silence. The blue, sunken lids were lowered for a moment over the burning eyes. 'We lay together,' he said clearly. 'That sin I did confess, but never named her. The lady cast me out. Out of despair I came here . . . at least to do no more harm. And the worst harm yet to come!'

The abbot closed his hand firmly on the nerveless hand at Haluin's side, to hold him fast by the grip, for the face on the pillow had sunken into a mask of clay, and a long shudder passed through the bruised and broken body, and left it tensed and chill to the touch.

'Rest!' said Radulfus, close to the sufferer's ear. 'Take ease! God hears even what is not said.'

It seemed to Cadfael, watching, that Haluin's hand responded, however feeble its hold. He brought the drink of wine and herbs with which he had been moistening the patient's mouth while he lay senseless, and trickled a few drops between the parted lips, and for the first time the offering was accepted, and the strings of the lean throat made the effort to swallow. His time was not yet. Whatever more he might have to heave off his heart, there was yet time for it. They fed him sips of wine, and watched the clay of his features again cohere into flesh, however pale and feeble. This time, when he came back to them, it was very faintly and with eyes still closed.

'Father . . .?' questioned the remote voice fearfully.

'I am here. I will not leave you.'

'Her mother came . . . I did not know till then Bertrade was with child! The lady was in terror of her lord's anger when he came home. I served then with Brother Cadfael, I had learned . . . I knew the herbs . . . I stole and gave her . . . hyssop, fleur-de-luce . . . Cadfael knows better uses for them!'

Yes, better by far! But what could help a badly congested chest and a killing cough, in small doses, or fight off the jaundice that turned a man yellow, could also put an end to the carrying of a child, in an obscene misuse abhorrent to the church and perilous even to the woman it was meant to deliver. From fear of an angry father, fear of shame before the world, fear of marriage prospects ruined and family feuds inflamed. Had the girl's mother entreated him, or had he persuaded her? Years of remorse and self-punishment had not exorcised the horror that still wrung his flesh and contorted his visage.

'They died,' he said, harsh and loud with pain. 'My love and the child, both. Her mother sent me word – dead and buried. A fever, they gave it out. Dead of a fever – nothing more to fear. My sin, my most grievous sin . . . God knows I am sorry!'

'Where true penitence is,' said Abbot Radulfus, 'God does surely know. Well, this grief is told. Have you done, or is there more yet to tell?'

'I have done,' said Brother Haluin. 'But to beg pardon. I ask it of God – and of Cadfael, that I abused his trust and his art. And of the lady of Hales, for the great grief I brought upon her.' Now that it was out he had better control of voice and words, the crippling tension was gone from his tongue, and weak though his utterance was, it was lucid and resigned. 'I would die cleansed and forgiven,' he said.

'Brother Cadfael will speak on his own behalf,' said the abbot. 'For God, I will speak as he gives me grace.'

'I forgive freely,' said Cadfael, choosing words with more than his accustomed care, 'whatever offence was done against my craft under great stress of mind. And that the means and the knowledge were there to tempt you, and I not there to dissuade, this I take to myself as much as ever I can charge them to you. I wish you peace!'

What Abbot Radulfus had to say upon God's behalf took longer. There were some among the brothers, Cadfael thought, who would have been startled and incredulous if they could have heard, at finding their abbot's formidable austerity could also hold so much measured and authoritative tenderness. A lightened conscience and a clean death were what Haluin desired. It was too late to exact penance from a dying man, and deathbed comfort cannot be priced, only given freely.

'A broken and a contrite heart,' said Radulfus, 'is the only sacrifice required of you, and will not be despised.' And he gave absolution and the solemn blessing, and so left the sickroom, beckoning Cadfael with him. On Haluin's face the ease of gratitude had darkened again into the indifference of exhaustion, and the fires were dead in eyes dulled and half-closed between swoon and sleep.

In the outer room Rhun was waiting patiently, drawn

somewhat aside to avoid hearing, even unwittingly, any word of that confession.

'Go in and sit with him,' said the abbot. 'He may sleep now, there will be no ill dreams. If there should be any change in him, fetch Brother Edmund. And if Brother Cadfael should be needed, send to my lodging for him.'

In the panelled parlour in the abbot's lodge they sat together, the only two people who would ever hear of the offence with which Haluin charge himself, or have the right in private to speak of his confession.

'I have been here only four years,' said Radulfus directly, 'and know nothing of the circumstances in which Haluin came here. It seems one of his earliest duties here was to help you among the herbs, and there he acquired this knowledge he put to such ill use. Is it certain this draught he concocted could kill? Or may this truly have been a death from fever?'

'If the girl's mother used it on her, she could hardly be mistaken,' said Cadfael ruefully. 'Yes, I've known hyssop to kill. I was foolish to keep it among my stores, there are other herbs that could take its place. But in small doses, both herb and root, dried and powdered, are excellent for the yellow distemper, and useful with horehound against chest troubles, though the blue-flowered kind is milder and better for that. I've known women use it to procure abortion, in great doses that purge to the extreme. Small wonder if sometimes the poor girl dies.'

'And this was surely during his novitiate, for he cannot have been here long if this child was his, as he supposes. He can have been only a boy.'

'Barely eighteen, and the girl surely no more, if as old. It is some extenuation,' said Cadfael firmly, 'if they were in the same household, seeing each other daily, of equal birth, for he comes of a good family, and as open to love as are most children. In fact,' said Cadfael, kindling, 'what I wonder at is that his suit should have been rejected out of hand. He was an only son, there was a good manor would have been his if he had not taken vows. And he was a very pleasing youth, as I recall, lettered and gifted. Many a knight would have welcomed him as a match for his daughter.'

'It may be her father already had other plans for her,' said Radulfus. 'He may have betrothed her to someone else in childhood. And her mother would hardly venture to countenance a match in her husband's absence, if she went in such awe of him.'

'She need not, however, have rejected the boy utterly. If she had let him hope he would have waited, surely, and not tried to force her hand by forestalling marriage. Though it may be I do him wrong there,' Cadfael relented. 'It was not calculation, I fancy, that brought him into the girl's bed, but too rash affection. Haluin would never make a schemer.'

'Well, for better or worse,' said Radulfus with a weary sigh, 'it was done, and cannot be undone. He is not the first, and will not be the last young man to fall into that error, nor she the first nor the last poor child to suffer for it. At least she has kept her good name. Easy to see why he feared to confide, for her sake, even under the seal of confession. But it is all long ago, eighteen years, his age when it befell. Let us at least secure him a peaceful ending.'

It was the general view that a peaceful ending was the best that could be hoped for for Brother Haluin, and that prayers for him ought not to presume to look towards any other outcome, all the more as his brief return to his senses rapidly lapsed again into a deeper unconsciousness, and for seven days, while the festival of the Nativity came and passed, he lay oblivious of the comings and goings of his brethren round his bed, ate nothing, uttered no sound but the hardly perceptible flutter of his breath. Yet that breath, however faint, was steady and even, and as often as drops of honeyed wine were presented to his lips, they were accepted, and the cords of his throat moved of themselves, docilely swallowing, while the broad, chilly brow and closed eyes never by the least quiver or contraction revealed awareness of what his body did.

'As if only his body is here,' said Brother Edmund, soberly pondering, 'and his spirit gone elsewhere until the house is again furbished and clean and waiting to be lived in.'

A sound biblical analogy, Cadfael considered, for certainly Haluin had himself cast out the devils that inhabited him, and the dwelling they vacated might well lie empty for a while, all the more if there was to be that unlooked-for and improbable act of healing, after all. For however this prolonged withdrawal might resemble dying, Brother Haluin would not die. Then we had better keep a good watch, thought Cadfael, taking the parable to its fitting close, and make sure seven devils worse than the first never manage to get a foot in the door while he's absent. And prayers for Haluin continued with unremitting fervour throughout the festivities of Christmas and the solemn opening of the new year.

The thaw was beginning by that time, and even then it was a slow thaw, wearing away each day, by slow degrees, the heavy wastes of snow from the great fall. The work on the roof was finished without further mishap, the scaffolding taken down, and the guest-hall once again weather-proof. All that remained of the great upheaval was this still and silent witness in his isolated bed in the infirmary, declining either to live or die.

Then, in the night of the Epiphany, Brother Haluin opened his eyes and drew a long, slow breath like any other man awaking without alarm, and cast his wondering gaze round the narrow room until it rested upon Brother Cadfael, mute and attentive on the stool beside him.

'I am thirsty,' said Haluin trustingly, like a child, and lay passive on Cadfael's arm to drink.

They half expected him to sink again into his unconscious state, but he remained languid but aware all that day, and in the night his sleep was natural sleep, shallow but tranquil. After that he turned his face to life, and did not again look over his shoulder. Once risen from the semblance of death he came back to the territory of pain, and its signature was on his drawn brow and set lips, but he bore it without complaint. His broken arm had knitted while he lay ignorant of his injuries, and caused him only the irritating aches of healing wounds, and it seemed both to Cadfael and Edmund, after a day or two of keeping close watch on him, that whatever had been shaken out of place within his head had healed as the outer wound had healed, medicined by stillness and repose. For his mind was clear. He remembered the icy roof, he remembered his fall, and once when he was alone with Cadfael he showed that he recalled very clearly his confession, for he said after a long while of silent thought:

'I did shamefully by you, long ago, now you tend and medicine me, and I have made no amends.'

'I've asked none,' said Cadfael equably, and began with patient care to unfold the wrappings from one maimed foot, to renew the dressings he had been replacing night and morning all this time.

'But I need to pay all that is due. How else can I be clean?'

'You have made full confession,' said Cadfael reasonably, 'you have received absolution from Father Abbot himself, beware of asking more.'

'But I have done no penance. Absolution so cheaply won leaves me still a debtor,' said Haluin heavily.

Cadfael had laid bare the left foot, the worse mangled of the pair. The surface cuts and wounds had healed over, but what had happened to the labyrinth of small bones within could never be put right, they had fused into a misshapen clot, twisted and scarred, discoloured in angry dark reds and purples. Yet the seamed skin had knitted and covered all.

'If you have debts,' said Cadfael bluntly, 'they bid fair to be paid in pain to the day you die. You see this? You will never set this firmly to ground again. I doubt if you will ever walk again.'

'Yes,' said Haluin, staring out through the narrow chink of the window at the darkening wintry sky, 'yes, I shall walk. I will walk. If God allows, I will go on my own feet again, though I must borrow crutches to help them bear me. And if Father Abbot gives me his countenance, when I have learned to use what props are left to me I will go myself to Hales, to beg forgiveness of Adelais de Clary, and keep a night's vigil at Bertrade's tomb.'

In his own mind Cadfael doubted if either the dead or the living would take any great comfort from Haluin's fondly resolved atonement, or still be nursing any profound recollection of him, after eighteen years. But if the pious intent gave the lad courage and determination to live and labour and be fruitful again, why discourage him? So all he said was:

'Well, let's first mend all that can be mended, and put back some of that lost blood into you, for you'll get no leave to go anywhere as you are now.' And contemplating the right foot, which at least still bore some resemblance to a human foot, and had a perceptible and undamaged ankle-bone, he went on thoughtfully: 'We might make some sort of thick felt boots for you, well padded within. You might get one foot to the ground yet, though you'll need the crutches. Not yet – not yet, nor for weeks yet, more likely months. But we'll take your measure, and see what we can fashion between us.'

On reflection, Cadfael felt that it might be wise to warn Abbot Radulfus of the expiation Brother Haluin had in mind, and did so after chapter, in the privacy of the abbot's parlour.

'Once he had heaved the load off his heart,' said Cadfael simply, 'he would have died content if it had been his fortune to die. But he is going to live. His mind is clear, his will is strong, and if his body is meagre it's wiry enough, and now that he sees a life ahead of him he'll not be content to creep out of his sins by way of absolution without penance. If he was of a lighter mind, and could be coaxed to forget this resolve as he gets well, for my part I would not blame him, I'd be glad of it. But penitence without penance will never be enough to Haluin. I'll hold him back as long as I can, but trust me, we shall hear of this again, as soon as he feels able to attempt it.'

'I can hardly frown upon so fitting a wish,' said the abbot reasonably, 'but I can forbid it until he is fit to undertake it. If it will give him peace of mind I have no right to stand in his way. It may also be of some belated comfort to this unhappy lady whose daughter died so wretchedly. I am not familiar,' said Radulfus, pondering the proposed pilgrimage warily, 'with this manor of Hales, though I have heard the name of de Clary. Do you know where it lies?'

'Towards the eastern edge of the shire, Father, it must be a matter of twenty-five miles or so from Shrewsbury.'

'And this lord who was absent in the Holy Land – he can have been told nothing of the true manner of his daughter's death, if his lady went in such awe of him. It is many years past, but if he is still living this visit must not take place. It would be a very ill thing for Brother Haluin to salve his own soul by bringing further trouble and danger upon the lady of Hales. Whatever her errors, she has suffered for them.'

'For all I know, Father,' Cadfael admitted, 'they may both be dead some years since. I saw the place once, on the way from Lichfield on an errand for Abbot Heribert, but I know nothing of the household of de Clary.'

'Hugh Beringar will know,' said the abbot confidently. 'He has all the nobility of the shire at his finger-ends. When he returns from Winchester we may ask him. There's no haste. Even if Haluin must have his penance, it cannot be yet. He is not yet out of his bed.'

Chapter Three

HUGH AND his escort came home four days after Epiphany. Much of the snow was gone by then, the weather grey, the days short and sombre, the nights hovering on the edge of frost, so that the thaw continued its gradual way, and there was no flooding. After such a heavy fall a rapid thaw would have seen a great mass of water coming down the river and draining from every drift, and the Severn would have backed up the Meole Brook and flooded the lower part of the fields, even if the enclave itself escaped inundation. This year they were spared that trouble, and Hugh, kicking off his boots and shrugging off his cloak in his own house by Saint Mary's church, with his wife bringing him his furred shoes and his son clinging to his sword-belt and clamouring to have his new, painted wooden knight duly admired, was able to report an easy journey for the time of year, and a satisfactory reception at court for his stewardship.

'Though I doubt if this Christmas truce will last long,' he said to Cadfael later, after acquainting the abbot with all the news from Winchester. 'He's swallowed the failure at Oxford gallantly enough, but for all that he's on his mettle for vengeance, he'll not sit still for long, winter or no. He wants Wareham back, but it's well stocked, and manned to the battlements, and Stephen never did have the patience for a siege. He'd like a fortress more to the west, to carry the war to Robert's country. There's no guessing what he'll try first. But he wants none of me or my men there in the south, he's far too wary of the earl of Chester to keep me long out of my shire. Thank God, for I'm of the same mind myself,' said Hugh blithely. 'And how have you been faring? Sorry I am to hear your best illuminator had a fall that all but ended him. Father Abbot told me of it. I can hardly have left you an hour, that day, when it happened. Is it true he's mending well?'

'Better than any of us ever expected,' said Cadfael, 'least of all the man himself, for he was certainly bent on clearing his soul for death. But he's out of the shadow, and in a day or two we'll have him out of his bed. But his feet are crippled for life, the slates chopped them piecemeal. Brother Luke is cutting some crutches to his measure. Hugh,' said Cadfael directly, 'what do you know of the de Clarys who hold the manor of Hales? There was one of them was a crusader nearly twenty years back. I never knew him, he was after my time in the east. Is he still living?'

'Bertrand de Clary,' said Hugh promptly, and looked up at his friend with quickening interest. 'What of him? He died years back, ten or more it must be. His son holds the honour now. I've had no dealings with them, Hales is the only manor they hold in this shire, the *caput* and most of their lands are in Staffordshire. Why, what's put de Clary in your mind?'

'Why, Haluin has. He was in their service before he took the cowl. It seems he feels he has left unpaid some debt he still owes in that direction. It came to mind when he made what he took to be his deathbed confession. In something he feels he offended, and has it on his conscience still.'

That was all that could be told, even to Hugh, the confessional being sacred, and if nothing more was offered, Hugh would ask for nothing more, however he might speculate on what had not been said.

'He's set on making the journey to set the account straight, when he's fit to undertake it. I was wondering . . . If this Bertrand's widow is no longer in the land of the living, either, as well Haluin should know it at once, and put it out of his mind.'

Hugh was eyeing his friend with steady interest and a tolerant smile. 'And you want him to have nothing to trouble about, body or mind, but getting back into the way of living as soon as may be. I'm no help, Cadfael. The widow's living still. She's there at Hales, she paid her dues last Michaelmas. Her son's married to a Staffordshire wife, and has a young son to succeed him, and from all accounts his mother is not of a nature to share another woman's household without meddling. Hales is her favourite home, she keeps there from choice and leaves her son to rule his own roost, while she makes sure of ruling hers. No doubt it suits them both very well. I should not be even so well-informed,' he said by way of explanation, 'if we had not ridden some miles of the way from Winchester with a company of de Clary's men, dispersing from the siege of Oxford. The man himself I never saw, he was still delayed at court when we left. He'll be on his way home by now, unless Stephen keeps him for whatever move he has next in mind.'

Cadfael received this news philosophically but without pleasure. So she was still living, this woman who had sought to help her daughter to an abortion, and succeeded only in helping her to her death. Not the first nor the last to come by such a death. But what must the mother's despair and guilt have been then, and what bitter memories must remain even now, beneath the ashes of eighteen years? Better, surely, to let them lie buried still. But Haluin's self-torturing conscience and salvation-hungry soul had their rights, too. And after all, he had been just eighteen years old! The woman who had forbidden him any aspiration to her daughter's affection must have been double his age. She might, thought Cadfael almost indignantly, have had the wisdom to see how things began to be between those two, and taken steps to separate them in time.

'Did you ever feel, Hugh, that it might be better to let even ill alone,' wondered Cadfael ruefully, 'rather than let loose worse? Ah, well! He has not even tried his crutches yet. Who knows what changes a few weeks may bring.'

They lifted Brother Haluin out of his bed in the middle of January, found him a corner near the infirmary fire, since he could not move about freely like the others to combat the cold, and treated his body, stiff from long lying, with oil and massage to get the sinews working again. To occupy his hands and mind they brought him his colours and a little desk to work on, and gave him a simpler page to adorn until his fingers should regain their deftness and steadiness. His mangled feet had healed and fused into misshapen forms, and there was no question as yet of letting him attempt to stand on them, but Cadfael allowed him to try the crutches Brother Luke had made for him, with support on either side, to get accustomed to the heft and balance of them, and the shaped and padded props under his armpits. If neither foot could ever be brought to support him again, even the crutches would not be of any use, but both Cadfael and Edmund agreed that there was every hope of the right foot being restored to use in time, and even the left might eventually provide a grain of assistance, with a little ingenuity in shoeing the invalid.

To that end Cadfael called in, at the end of the month, young Philip Corviser, the provost's son, and they put their heads together over the problem, and between them produced a pair of boots as ill-matched in appearance as were the feet for which they were intended, but adapted as best they could devise to give strong support. They were of thick felt with a leather sole, built up well above the ankles and laced close with leather thongs to support and protect the damaged flesh and make full use of the shin-bones, which were intact. Philip was pleased with his work, but wary of praise until the boots were tried on, and found to be wearable without pain, and blessedly warm in this wintry weather.

And all that was done for him Brother Haluin accepted gratefully and humbly, and went on doggedly refreshing eye and hand with his reds and blues and delicately laid gold. But as often as the hours of leisure came round he would be precariously hoisting himself out of his corner bench with shoulders braced upon his crutches, poised to reach for the support of wall or bench if his balance was shaken. It took some time for the sinews to recover their toughness in his wasted legs, but early in February he could set his right foot firmly on the ground, and even stand on it briefly without other support, and from that time on he began to use his crutches in earnest, and to master them. He was seen again, dutiful and punctual, in his stall at chapter, and in the choir at every office. By the end of February he could even set the blocked toe of his left boot to the ground, to help hold him steady and secure on his crutches, though never again would that foot be able to support his weight, light though he was.

In one thing he was fortunate, that the winter, once that first early snowfall had thawed and vanished, was not a hard one. There were occasional spells of frost, but none that lasted long, and after January such snow-showers as there were were fitful and slight, and did not lie long. When he had his balance and was used to his new gait he could exercise his skills outdoors as well as in, and grew expert, fearful only of the cobbles of the court when they were glazed with frost.

At the beginning of March, with the days lengthening, and the first cautious and reluctant signs of spring in the air, Brother Haluin rose in chapter, when all the urgent business of the day was over, and meekly but resolutely made a plea which only Abbot Radulfus and Brother Cadfael could fully understand.

'Father,' he said, his dark eyes fixed unwaveringly on the abbot's face, 'you know that in my trouble I conceived a desire to make a certain pilgrimage, if I should by God's grace be restored. Great mercy has been shown to me, and if you will give me leave, I wish now to register my vow in heaven. I beg your sanction and the prayers of my brothers that I may fulfil what I promise, and return in peace.'

Radulfus regarded the petitioner in silence for a disturbingly long time, his face revealing neither approval nor disapproval, though the fixity of his gaze brought a surge of blood into Haluin's hollow cheeks.

'Come to me after chapter,' said the abbot then, 'and I will hear what you intend, and judge whether you are yet fit to undertake it.'

In the abbot's parlour Haluin repeated his request in open terms, as to men before whom his spirit was naked and known. Cadfael knew why he himself had been summoned to attend. Two reasons, indeed, stood clear: he was the only other witness of Haluin's confession, and might therefore be admitted into his counsels; and he could speak as to Haluin's fitness to set out on such a journey. He had not yet guessed at a third reason, but he was not quite easy in his mind as he listened.

'I must not and will not hold you back,' said the abbot, 'from what is needful for your soul's health. But I think you ask too soon. You cannot yet have regained your strength. And it is not yet spring, however well we happen to have fared these last weeks. There may still be bitter weather to come. Think how recently you have been close to death, and spare putting yourself in such hardship until you are fitter to bear it.'

'Father,' said Haluin ardently, 'it is because I have been close to death that I must not delay. How if death should reach for me again before I can expiate my sin? I have seen how it can lay its hand on a man in a moment, in the twinkling of an eye. I have had my warning. I must heed it. If I die in paying the penance due from me, that I will embrace as fitting. But to die and not have made any amend, that would be endless reproach to me. Father,' he said, burning up like a stirred fire, 'I truly loved her, I loved her according to the way of marriage, I would have loved her lifelong. And I destroyed her. I have hidden my sins too long, now that I have confessed them I long to complete the atonement.'

'And have you thought of the miles you must go and return? Are you in any case to ride?'

Haluin shook his head vigorously at that. 'Father, I have vowed already in my heart and will repeat the vow on the altar, to go on foot to the place where she is buried, and on foot return – on these feet that brought me to the earth and made me to face the truth of my unshriven offences. I can go, I have learned how the innocent lame must go. Why should not I, who am guilty of so much, suffer the same labours? I can endure it. Brother Cadfael knows!'

Brother Cadfael was none too pleased at being called in witness, and none to happy about saying anything which could promote this obsessed enterprise, but neither could he see any genuine peace of mind for this tormented creature until the expiation was completed.

'I do know he has the will and the courage,' he said. 'Whether he has the strength is another matter. And whether he has the right to force his body to the death in order to cleanse his soul is something on which I will not judge.'

Radulfus pondered for some minutes in sombre silence, eyeing the petitioner with a fixity which should have caused him to stir uneasily and lower his gaze had there been anything false or pretentious in his purpose. But Haluin's wide, earnest eyes sustained the encounter ardently.

'Well, I acknowledgre your desire to atone, late though it comes,' said the abbot at last, 'and I understand the better since the delay of years has not been for your own sake. Go, then, make the attempt. But I will not permit you to go alone. There must be someone with you in case you founder, and should that happen, you must allow him to make such dispositions for your safety as he sees fit. If you endure the journey well, he need not do anything to impair your sacrifice, but if you fall by the wayside, then he stands as my representative, and you must obey him as you obey me.'

'Father,' said Haluin in anxious protest, 'my sin is mine alone, my confession sealed and sacred. How can I let another man come so close, without myself breaking that seal? It would be a violation even to cause wonder and question concerning this penance of mine.'

'You shall have a companion who need neither wonder nor question,' said the abbot, 'since he already knows, at your own telling. Brother Cadfael shall come with you. His company and his prayers can only be of comfort and benefit to you. Your confidence and the lady's memory will be in no danger, and he is well qualified to care for you along the way.' And to Cadfael, turning, he said: 'Will you undertake this charge? I do not believe he is fit to go alone.'

Small choice, thought Cadfael, but not altogether displeased at the instruction, either. There was still, somewhere deep within him, a morsel of the *vagus* who had roamed the world from Wales to Jerusalem and back to Normandy for forty years before committing himself to stability within the cloister, and an expedition sanctioned, even ordered by authority could be welcomed as blessed, instead of evaded as a temptation.

'If you so wish, Father,' he said, 'I will.'

'This journey will take several days. I take it that Brother Winfrid will be competent to dispense whatever may be needed, with Edmund to guide him?'

'For a few days,' agreed Cadfael, 'they should manage well enough. I have stocked the infirmary cupboard only yesterday, and in the workshop there's a good supply of all the common remedies usually called for in the winter. Should something unforeseen be needed, Brother Oswin could come back from Saint Giles to help for a while.'

'Good! Then, son Haluin, you may prepare for this journey, and set out when you are ready, tomorrow if you will. But you will submit yourself to Brother Cadfael if your strength fails you, and do his bidding as faithfully as within these walls you have always done mine.'

'Father,' said Haluin fervently, 'I will.'

At the altar of Saint Winifred Brother Haluin recorded his solemn vow that same evening after Vespers, to leave himself no way out, with a white-faced vehemence which indicated to Cadfael, who witnessed it at Haluin's own wish, that this implacable penitent in his deepest heart knew and feared the labour and pain he was imposing on himself, and embraced it with a passion and resolution Cadfael would rather have seen devoted to a more practical and fruitful enterprise. For who would benefit by this journey, even though it passed successfully, except the penitent himself, at least partially restored to his self-respect? Certainly not the poor girl who had committed no worse sin than to venture too much for love, and who surely was long since in a state of grace. Nor the mother who must long ago have put this evil dream behind her, and must now be confronted by it once again after years. And Cadfael was not of the opinion that a man's main business in this world was to save his own soul. There are other ailing souls, as there are ailing bodies, in need of a hoist towards health.

But Haluin's needs were not his needs. Haluin's bitter years of silent self-blame certainly called for a remedy.

'On these most holy relics,' said Brother Haluin, with his palm pressed against the drapings that covered the reliquary, 'I record my penitential vow; that I will not rest until I have gone on foot to the tomb in which Bertrade de Clary lies, and there passed a night's vigil in prayer for her soul, and again on foot returned here to the place of my due service. And if I fail of this, may I live forsworn and die unforgiven.'

They set out after Prime, on the fourth morning of March, out at the gate and along the Foregate towards Saint Giles and the highroad due east. The day was cloudy and still, the air chill but not wintry cold. Cadfael viewed the way ahead in his mind, and found it not too intimidating. They would be leaving the western hills behind them, and with every mile eastward the country about them would subside peaceably into a green level. The road was dry, for there had been no recent rain, and the cloud cover above was high and pale, and threatened none, and there was a grassy verge such as could be found only on the king's highways, wide on either side the track, easy walking even for a crippled man. The first mile or two might pass without grief, but after that the constant labour would begin to tell. He would have to be the judge of when to call a halt, for Haluin was likely to grit his teth and press on until he dropped. Somewhere under the Wrekin they would find a hospitable refuge for the night, for there were abbey tenants there among the cottagers, and any hut along the way would willingly give them a place by the fire for a midday rest. Food they had with them in the scrip Cadfael carried.

In the brisk hopefulness of morning, with Haluin's energy and eagerness at their best, they made good speed, and rested at noon very pleasurably with the parish priest at Attingham. But in the afternoon the pace slowed somewhat, and the strain began to tell upon Haluin's hardworking shoulders, aching from the constant weight and endlessly repeated stress, and the cold as evening approached numbed his hands on the grips of his crutches, in spite of their mufflings of woollen cloth. Cadfael called a halt as soon as the light began to fade into the windless March dusk, grey and without distances, and turned aside into the village of Uppington, to beg a bed for the night at the manor.

Haluin had been understandably silent along the road, needing all his breath and all his resolution for the effort of walking. Fed and at ease in the evening, he sat watching Cadfael in accepting silence still for a while.

'Brother,' he said at last, 'I take it very kindly that you've come with me on this journey. With no other but you could I speak without conceal of that old grief, and before ever we see Shrewsbury again I may sorely need to speak of it. The worst of me you already know, and I will never say word in excuse. But in eighteen years I have never until now spoken her name aloud, and now to utter it is like food after starvation.'

'Speak or be silent as the need takes you,' said Cadfael, 'and I'll hear or be deaf according to your wish. But as for tonight you should take your rest, for you've come a good third part of the way, and tomorrow, I warn you, you'll find some aches and pains you knew nothing of, from labouring so hard and so long.'

'I am tired,' admitted Haluin, with a sudden and singularly touching smile, as brief as it was sweet. 'You think we cannot reach Hales tomorrow, then?'

'Don't think of it! No, we'll get as far as the Augustinian canons at Wombridge, and spend another night there. And you'll have done well to get so far in the time, so don't grudge the one day more.'

'As you think best,' said Haluin submissively, and lay down to sleep with the confiding simplicity of a child charmed and protected by his prayers.

The next day was less kind, for there was a thin, spasmodic rain that stung at times with sleet, and a colder wind from the north-east, from which the long, green, craggy bulk of the Wrekin gave them no shelter as the road skirted it to the north. But they reached the priory before dusk, though Haluin's lips were fast clenched in determination by then, and the skin drawn tight and livid over his cheekbones with exhaustion, and Cadfael was glad to get him into the warmth, and go to work with oiled hands on the sinews of his arms and shoulders, and the thighs that had carried him so bravely all day long.

And the third day, early in the afternoon, they came to the manor of Hales.

The manor house lay a little aside from the village and the church, timber-built on a stone undercroft, in level, well-drained fields, with gentle wooded slopes beyond. Within its wooden fence stable and barn and bakehouse were ranged along the pale, well maintained and neat. Brother Haluin stood in the open gateway, and looked at the place of his old service with a face fixed and still, only his eyes alive and full of pain.

'Four years,' he said, 'I kept the manor roll here. Bertrand de Clary was my father's overlord, I was sent here before I was fourteen, to be page to his lady. Will you believe, the man himself I never saw, before I came here he was already in the Holy Land? This is but one of his manors, the only one in these parts, but his son was already installed in his place, and ruled the honour from Staffordshire. She always liked Hales best, she left her son to his lordship and settled here, and it was here I came. Better for her if I had never entered this house. Better far for Bertrade!'

'It's too late,' said Cadfael mildly, 'to do right whatever was done amiss then. This day is for doing a right that you have pledged yourself to do now, and for that it is not too late. You'll be freer with her, maybe, if I wait for you without.'

'No,' said Haluin. 'Come with me! I need your witness, I know it will be just.'

A tow-haired youth came out of the stable with a pitchfork in his hands, steaming gently in the chill air. At sight of two black Benedictine habits in the gateway he turned and came towards them, leisurely and amiable.

'If you're wanting a bed and a meal, Brothers, come in, your cloth's always welcome here. There's good lying in the loft, and they'll feed you in the kitchen if you'll please to walk through.'

'I do remember,' said Haluin, his eyes still fixed upon a distant past, 'your lady kept always a hospitable house for travellers. But I shall need no bed this night. I have an errand to the lady Adelais de Clary herself, if she will give me audience. A few minutes of her time is all I ask.'

The boy shrugged, staring them over with grey, unreadable

Saxon eyes, and waved them towards the stone steps that led up to the hall door.

'Go in and ask for her woman, Gerta, she'll see if the lady'll speak with you.' And he stood to watch them as they crossed the yard, before turning back to his labours among the horses.

A manservant was just coming up the steps from the kitchen into the passage as they entered the great doorway. He came to ask their business, and being told, sent off a kitchen boy to carry word to the lady's woman of the chamber, who presently came out from the hall to see who these monastic guests might be. A woman of about forty years, very brisk and neat, plain in her dress and plain in her face, for she was pock-marked. But of her confidence in office there was no question. She looked them over somewhat superciliously, and listened to Haluin's meekly uttered request without a responsive smile, in no hurry to open a door of which she clearly felt herself the privileged custodian.

'From the abbey at Shrewsbury, you come? And on the lord abbot's business, I suppose?'

'On an errand the lord abbot has sanctioned,' said Haluin.

'It is not the same,' said Gerta sharply. 'What other than abbey business can send a monk of Shrewsbury here? If this is some matter of your own, let my lady know with whom she is dealing.'

'Tell her,' said Haluin patiently, leaning heavily on his crutches, and with eyes lowered from the woman's unwelcoming face, 'that Brother Haluin, a Benedictine monk of Shrewsbury abbey, humbly begs of her grace to receive him.'

The name meant nothing to her. Clearly she had not been in Adelais de Clary's service, or certainly not in her confidence or even close enough to guess at her preoccupations, eighteen years ago. Some other woman, perhaps nearer her mistress's years, had filled this intimate office then. Close body-servants, grown into their mistress's trust and into their own blood-loyalty, carry a great treasury of secrets, often to their deaths. There must somewhere, Cadfael thought, watching in silence, be a woman who would have stiffened and opened her eyes wide at the name, even if she had not instantly known the changed and time-worn face.

'I will ask,' said the tirewoman, with a touch of condescension still, and went away through the hall to a leather-curtained doorway at the far end. Some minutes passed before she appeared again, drawing back the hangings, and without troubling to approach them, called from the doorway: 'My lady says you may come.'

The solar they entered was small and dim, for the windward of the two windows was shuttered fast against the weather, and the tapestries that draped the walls were old, and in rich dark colours. There was no fireplace, but a stone hearth laid close to the most sheltered corner carried a charcoal brazier, and between that and the one window that gave light a woman was sitting at a little embroidery frame, on a cushioned stool. Against the light from the window she showed as a tall, erect shape, dark-clothed, while the glow of the brazier shone in copper highlights on her shadowed face. She had left her needle thrust into the stretched cloth. Her hands were clenched fast on the raised arms of the stool, and her eyes were on the doorway, into which Brother Haluin lurched painfully on his crutches, his one serviceable foot sore with use and bearing him wincingly at every step, the blocked toe of his left foot barely touching the floor as a meagre aid to balance. Constant leaning into the crutches had hunched his shoulders and bent his straight back. Having heard his name, she must surely have expected something nearer to the lively, comely young man she had cast out all those years ago. What could she make now of this mangled wreckage?

He was barely within the room when she rose abruptly to her feet, stiff as a lance. Over their heads she spoke first to the waiting-woman, who had made to follow them in.

'Leave us!' said Adelais de Clary. And to Haluin, as the leather curtain swung heavily into place between solar and hall: 'What is this? What have they done to you?'

Chapter Four

SHE MUST, Cadfael reckoned, growing used to the play of light and shadow within the room, be within ten years of his own age, but she looked younger. The dark hair that was coiled in heavy braids on either side of her head was barely touched with grey, and the imperious, fine bones of her face had kept their imperishable elegance though the flesh that covered them was a little shrunken and sapless now, and her body had grown angular and lean as the juices of youth dried up. Her hands, though shapely still, betrayed her with swollen knuckles and seamed veins, there was a languor upon her pale skin at throat and wrist where once the rounded gloss of youth had been. But for all that, in the oval face, the long, resolute lips and large eyes in their deep settings Cadfael saw the ashes of great beauty. No, not ashes, embers, still alive and as hot at least as the coals burning in the heart of the brazier.

'Come nearer!' she said. And when Haluin stood before her with the light upon his face, pale and cold light from the window, flushed from the fire: 'It is you!' she said. 'I wondered. How have you come to this?'

Her voice was low-pitched, full and authoritative, but the first implication of dismay and concern was gone. She looked at him neither compassionately nor coldly, but with a kind of detached indifference, a curiosity of no deep root.

'This is no man's blame but mine,' said Haluin, 'don't regard it! I have what I earned. I came by a great fall, but by the grace of God I am alive, who by this time had thought to be dead. And as I have eased my soul to God and my confessor for old sins, so I come to beg forgiveness of you.'

'Was that needful?' she said, marvelling. 'After so many years, and all this way?'

'Yes, it was needful. I do greatly need to hear you say that you forgive me the wrong I did, and the grief I brought upon you. There can be no rest for me now until the leaf is washed clear of every last stain.'

'And you have told over all the old writing,' said Adelais with some bitterness, 'all that was secret and shameful, have you? To your confessor! And how many more? This good brother who bears you company? The whole household at chapter? Could you not bear to be still a sinner unshriven, rather than betray my daughter's name to the world, and she so long in her grave? I would have gone sinful into purgatory rather!'

'And so would I!' cried Haluin, wrung. 'But no, it is not so. Brother Cadfael bears me company because he is the only one who knows, excepting only Abbot Radulfus, who heard my confession. No other will ever know from us. Brother Cadfael was also grossly wronged in what I did, he had a right to give or withhold forgiveness. It was from his store and after his teaching that I stole those medicines I gave to you.'

She turned her gaze upon Cadfael in a long, steady stare, and her face, for once seen clearly, was intent and still. 'Well,' she said, again turning away into indifference, 'it was very long ago. Who would remember now? And I am not dying yet. What do I know! I shall need a priest myself some day, I could better have answered you then. Well, to put an end to it . . . Have what you ask! I do forgive you. I would not add to what you suffer. Go back in peace to your cloister. I forgive you as I hope for forgiveness.'

It was said without passion; the brief spurt of anger was already gone. It cost her no effort to absolve him, she did it as neutrally, it seemed, and with as little feeling as she would have handed out food to a beggar. Of gentlewomen of her nobility alms could properly be asked, and granting was a form of largesse, the due fulfilment of a rite of lordship. But what she gave lightly came as relieving grace to Haluin. The braced tension went out of his leaning shoulders and stiffly clenched hands. He bent his head humbly before her, and uttered his thanks in a low and halting voice, like a man momentarily dazed.

'Madam, your mercy lifts a load from me, and from my heart I am grateful.'

'Go back to the life you have chosen and the duties you have undertaken,' she said, again seating herself, though she did not yet reach for her needle. 'Think no more of what happened long ago. You say you have a life spared. Use it as best you can, and so will I mine.'

It was dismissal, and as such Haluin accepted it. He made her a deep reverence, and turned carefully upon his crutches, and Cadfael reached a hand to steady him in the movement. She had not so much as bidden them be seated, perhaps too shaken by so sudden and startling a visit, but as they reached the doorway she called after them suddenly:

'Stay if you will, take rest and meat in my house. My servants will provide you everything you need.'

'I thank you,' said Haluin, 'but our leave of absence enjoins a return as soon as my pilgrimage here is done.'

'God hasten your way home, then,' said Adelais de Clary, and with a steady hand took up her needle again.

The church lay a short distance from the manor, where two tracks crossed, and the huddle of village house-plots gathered close about the churchyard wall.

'The tomb is within,' said Haluin, as they entered at the gate. 'It was never opened when I was here, but Bertrand's father is buried here, and surely it must have been opened for Bertrade. She died here. I am sorry, Cadfael, that I refused hospitality also for you, I had not thought in time. I shall need no bed tonight.'

'You said no word of that to the lady,' Cadfael observed.

'No. I hardly know why. When I saw her again my heart misgave me that I did ill to bring before her again that old pain, that the very sight of me was an offence to her. Yet she did forgive. I am the better for that, and she surely none the worse. But you could have slept easy tonight. No need for two to watch.'

'I'm better fitted for a night on my knees than you,' said Cadfael. 'And I am not sure the welcome there would have been very warm. She wished us gone. No, it's very well as it is. Mostly likely she thinks we're on the homeward way already, off her land and out of her life.'

Haluin halted for a second with his hand on the heavy iron ring latch of the church door, his face in shadow. The door swung open, creaking, and he gripped his crutches to ease himself down the two wide, shallow steps into the nave. It was dim and stonily chilly within. Cadfael waited a moment on the steps till his eyes grew accustomed to the changed light, but Haluin set off at once up the nave towards the altar. Nothing here was greatly changed in eighteen years, and nothing had been forgotten. Even the rough edges of the floor tiles were known to him. He turned aside towards the righthand wall, his crutches ringing hollowly, and Cadfael, following, found him standing beside a stone table-tomb fitted between the pillars. The carved image recumbent there was in crude chain-mail, and had one leg crossed over the other, and a hand on his sword-hilt. Another crusader, surely the father of Bertrand, who in his turn had followed him to the Holy Land. This one, Cadfael calculated, might well have been with Robert of Normandy's army in my time, at the taking of Jerusalem. Clearly the de Clary men were proud of their warfare in the east.

A man came through from the sacristy, and seeing two unmistakable Benedictine habits, turned amicably to come towards them. A man of middle age, in a rusty black cassock, advancing upon them with a mildly enquiring expression and a welcoming smile. Haluin heard his steps, soft as they were, and swung about gladly to greet a remembered neighbour, only to recoil on the instant at seeing a stranger.

'Good day, Brothers! God be with you!' said the priest of Hales. 'To travellers of your cloth my house is always open, like this house of God. Have you come far?'

'From Shrewsbury,' said Haluin, strongly recovering himself. 'Forgive me, Father, if I was taken aback. I had expected to see Father Wulfnoth. Foolish of me, indeed, for I have not been here for many years, and he was growing grey when I knew him, but to me in youth it seemed he would be here for ever. Now I dare hardly ask!'

'Father Wulfnoth is gone to his rest,' said the priest, 'seven years ago now it must be. Ten years back I came here, after he was brought to his bed by a seizure, and three years I looked after him until he died. I was newly priest then, I learned much from Wulfnoth, his mind was clear and bright if the flesh had failed him.' His good-natured round face offered sympathetic curiosity. 'You know this church and this manor, then? Were you born in Hales?'

'No, not that. But for some years I served with the lady

Adelais at the manor. Church and village I knew well, before I took the cowl at Shrewsbury. Now,' said Haluin earnestly, observing how brightly he was studied, and feeling the need to account for his return, 'I have good need to give thanks for escaping alive from a mishap that might have caused my death, and I have taken thought to discharge, while I may, every debt I have on my conscience. Of which number, one brings me here to this tomb. There was a lady of the de Clary family whom I reverenced, and she died untimely. I should like to spend the night here at her burial place, in prayers for her. It was long before your time, eighteen years ago now. It will not disturb you if I spend the night here within?'

'Why, as to that, you'd be welcome,' said the priest heartily, 'and I could light a cresset for you, it gives some help against the cold. But surely, Brother, you're under some mistake. True, what you say puts this before my time, but Father Wulfnoth told me much concerning the church and the manor, he'd been in the service of the lords of Hales all his life. It was they helped him to his studies and set him up here as priest. There has been no burial here in this tomb since the old lord died, this one who's carved here on the stone. And that was more than thirty years back, it's his grandson rules now. A lady of the family, you say? And died young?'

A kinswoman,' said Haluin, low-voiced and shaken, his eyes lowered to the stone which had not been raised for thirty years. 'She died here at Hales, I had thought she must be buried here.' He would not name her, or betray more than he must of himself and what moved him, even to this kindly man. And Cadfael stood back from them, watched, and held his peace.

'And only eighteen years ago? Then be certain, Brother, she is not here. If you knew Father Wulfnoth, you know you can rely upon what he told me. And I know his wits were sharp until the day he died.'

'I do believe it,' said Haluin, quivering with the chill of disappointment. 'He would not be mistaken. So – she is not here!'

'But this is not the chief seat of the de Clary honour,' the priest pointed out gently, 'for that's Elford, in Staffordshire. The present lord Audemar took his father there for burial, the family has a great vault there. If there are any close kin dead these last years, that's where they'll be. No doubt the lady you speak of was also taken there to lie among her kinsfolk.'

Haluin seized upon the hope hungrily. 'Yes . . . yes, it could well be so, it must be so. There I shall find her.'

'I have no doubt of it,' said the priest. 'But it's a long way to go afoot.' He had sensed an urgency that was very unlikely to listen to reason, but he did his best to temper it. 'You'd be well advised to go mounted, if you must go now, or put it off for longer days and better weather. At least come within, to my house, and take meat with me, and rest overnight.'

But that Haluin would not do, so much was already clear to Brother Cadfael. Not while there was still an hour or more of daylight left at the windows, and he had still the strength to go a mile further. He excused himself with slightly guilty thanks, and took a restrained leave of the good man, who watched them in wondering speculation until they had climbed the steps to the porch, and closed the door afer them.

'No!' said Cadfael firmly, as soon as they were clear of the churchyard, and passing along the track between the village houses to reach the highroad. 'That you cannot do!'

'I can, I must!' Brother Haluin responded with no less determination. 'Why should I not?'

'Because, in the first place, you do not know how far it is to Elford. As far again as we have come, and half as far after that. And you know very well how hard you have pushed yourself already. And in the second place, because you were given leave to attempt this journey in the belief that it would end here, and we two return from here. And so we should. No, never shake your head at me, you know very well Father Abbot never envisaged more than that, and would never have given you leave for more. We should turn back here.'

'How can I?' Haluin's voice implacably reasonable, even tranquil. His way was perfectly clear to him, and he was patient with dissent. 'If I turn back, I am forsworn. I have not yet done what I vowed to do, I should go back self-condemned and contemptible. Father Abbot would not wish that, however little either he or I expected so long a penance. He gave me leave until I had accomplished what I swore to do. If he were here to be asked, he would tell me to go on. I said I would not rest until I had gone on foot to the tomb where Bertrade lies buried, and there passed a night in prayer and vigil, and that I have not done.'

'Through no fault of yours,' said Cadfael strenuously.

'Does that excuse me? It is a just judgement on me that I must go double the way. If I fail of this, I said, may I live forsworn and die unforgiven. On the blessed relics of Saint Winifred, who has been so good to us all, I swore it. How can I turn back? I would rather die on the road, at least still faithfully trying to redeem my vow, than abandon my faith and honour, and go back shamed.'

And who was that speaking, Cadfael wondered, the dutiful monk, or the son of a good Norman house, from a line at least as old as King William's when he came reaching for the crown of England, and without the irregularity of bastardy, at that. No doubt but pride is a sin, and unbecoming a Benedictine brother, but not so easily shed with the spurs and title of nobility.

Haluin, too, had caught the fleeting implication of arrogance, and flushed at the recognition, but would not draw back from it. He halted abruptly, swaying on his crutches, and detached a hand in haste to take Cadfael by the wrist. 'Don't chide me! Well I know you could, and your face shows me I deserve it, but spare to condemn. I can do no other. Oh, Cadfael, I do know every argument you could justly use against me, I have thought of them, I think of them still, but still I am bound. Bound by vows I will not, dare not break. Though my abbot judge me rebellious and disobedient, though my abbey cast me out, that I must bear. But to take back what I have pledged to Bertrade, that I will not bear.'

The flush of blood mantling in his pale cheeks became him, warmed away the faded look of emaciation from illness, and even stripped some years from him. In stillness he stood upright, stretching his bent back upward between the braced crutches. No persuasion was going to move him. As well accept it.

'But you, Cadfael,' he said, gripping the wrist he held, 'you have made no such vow, you are not bound. No need for you to go further, you have done all that was expected of you. Go back now, and speak for me to the lord abbot.'

'Son,' said Cadfael, between sympathy and exasperation, 'I am fettered as fast as you, and you should know it. My orders are to go with you in case you founder, and to take care of you if you do. You are on your own business, I am on the abbot's. If I cannot take you back with me I cannot go back.'

'But your work,' protested Haluin, dismayed but unwavering. 'Mine can well wait, but you'll be missed. How will they manage without you for so long?'

'As best they can. There's no man living who cannot be done without,' said Cadfael sturdily, 'and just as well, since there's a term to life for every man. No, say no more. If your mind's made up, so is mine. Where you go, I go. And since we have barely an hour of daylight left to us, and I fancy you have no wish to seek a bed here in Hales, we had better move gently on, and look for a shelter along the way.'

Adelais de Clary rose in the morning and went to Mass, as was her regular habit. She was meticulous in her religious observances and in almsgiving, keeping up the old custom of her husband's household. And if her charity seemed sometimes a little cold and distant, at least it was constant and reliable. Whenever the parish priest had a special case in need of relief, he brought it to her for remedy.

He walked with her to the gate after the office, dutiful in attendance. 'I had two Benedictines come visiting yesterday,' he said as she was drawing her cloak about her against a freshening March wind. 'Two brothers from Shrewsbury.'

'Indeed!' said Adelais. 'What did they want with you?'

'The one of them was crippled, and went on crutches. He said he was once in your service, before he took the cowl. He remembered Father Wulfnoth. I thought they would have come to pay their respects to you. Did they not?'

She did not answer that, but only observed idly, gazing into distance as though only half her mind was on what was said: 'I remember, I did have a clerk once who entered the monastery at Shrewsbury. What was his business here at the church?'

'He said he had been spared by death, and was about making up all his accounts, to be better prepared. I found them beside the tomb of your lord's father. They were in some error that a woman of your house was buried there, eighteen years ago. The lame one had it in mind to spend a night's vigil there in prayers for her.'

'A strange mistake,' said Adelais with the same tolerant disinterest. 'No doubt you undeceived him?'

'I told him it was not so. I was not here then, of course, but I knew from Father Wulfnoth that the tomb had not been opened for many years, and what the young brother supposed could not be true. I told him that all of your house now are buried at Elford, where the head of the manor lies.'

'A long, hard journey that would be, for a lame man afoot,' said Adelais with easy sympathy. 'I hope he did not intend to continue his travels so far?'

'I think, madam, he did. For they declined to rest and eat with me, and sleep the night over, but set off again at once.

There I shall find her, the young one said. Yes, I am sure they will have turned eastward when they reached the highroad. A long, hard journey, indeed, but his will was good to perform it.'

His relationship with his patroness was a comfortable and easy one, he did not hesitate to ask directly: 'Will he indeed find the gentlewoman he's seeking at Elford?'

'He well may,' said Adelais, pacing evenly and serenely beside him. 'Eighteen years is a long time, and I cannot enter into his mind. I was younger then, I kept a bigger household. There were cousins, some left without fortune. My lord kept a father's hand on all of his blood. In his absence and as his regent, so did I.'

They had reached the churchyard gate, and halted there. The morning was soft and green, but very still, and the cloud-cover hung heavy and low.

'There will be more snow yet,' said the priest, 'if it does not turn to rain.' And he went on inconsequently: 'Eighteen years! It may be that this monk in his time with you was drawn to one of these young cousins, after the way of the young, and her early death was a greater grief to him than ever he ventured to let you know.'

'It may be so,' said Adelais distantly, and drew up the hood of her cloak against a few infinitely fine spears of sleet that drifted on the still air, and stung her cheek. 'Good day, Father!'

'I will pray,' said the priest after her, 'that his pilgrimage to her grave may bring comfort and benefit to him living, and to the lady dead.'

'Do so, Father,' said Adelais without turning her head. 'And do not fail to add a prayer for me and all the women of my house, that time may lie lightly on us when our day comes.'

Cadfael lay awake in the hay-loft of a forester's holding in the royal forest of Chenet, listening to the measured breathing of his companion, too constant and too tense for sleep. It was the second night since they had left Hales. The first they had spent with a solitary cottar and his wife a mile or so beyond the hamlet of Weston, and the day between had been long, and this second shelter in the early reaches of the forest came very warmly and gratefully. They had gone early to their beds in the loft, for Haluin, at whose insistence they had continued so far into the evening, was close to exhaustion. Sleep, Cadfael noted, came to him readily and peacefully, a restoring mercy to a soul very troubled and wrung when awake. There are many ways by which God tempers the burden. Haluin rose every morning refreshed and resolute.

It was not yet light, there might still be an hour to dawn. There was no movement, no rustling of the dry hay from the corner where Haluin lay, but Cadfael knew he was awake now, and the stillness was good, for it meant that he lay in the languor of ease of body, wherever the wakeful mind within might have strayed.

'Cadfael?' said a still, remote voice out of the darkness, 'Are you awake?'

'I am,' he said as softly.

'You have never asked me anything. Of the thing I did. Of *her*. . .'

'There is no need,' said Cadfael. 'What you wish to tell will be told without asking.'

'I was never free to speak of her,' said Haluin, 'until now. And now only to you, who know.' There was a silence. He bled words slowly and arduously, as the shy and solitary do. After a while he resumed softly: 'She was not beautiful, as her mother was. She had not that dark radiance, but something more kindly. There was nothing dark or secret in her, but everything open and sunlit, like a flower. She was not afraid of anything – not then. She trusted everyone. She had never been betrayed – not then. Only once, and she died of it.'

Another and longer silence, and this time the hay stirred briefly, like a sigh. Then he asked almost timidly: 'Cadfael, you were half your life in the world – did you ever love a woman?'

'Yes,' said Cadfael, 'I have loved.'

'Then you know how it was with us. For we did love, she and I. It hurts most of all,' said Brother Haluin, looking back in resigned and wondering pain, 'when you are young. There is nowhere to hide from it, no shield you can raise between. To see her every day . . . and to know that it was with her as it was with me. . .'

Even if he had put it from him all these years, and tried to turn hands and mind and spirit to the service he had undertaken, of his own will, in his extremity, he had forgotten nothing, it was there within him ready to quicken at a breath, like a sleeping fire when a door is opened. Now at least it could escape into air, into the world of other men, where it could touch other men's sufferings and receive and give compassion.

From Cadfael there were no words needed, only the simple acknowledgement of companionship, the assurance of a listening ear.

Haluin fell asleep with a last lingering word on his lips, murmured almost inaudibly after lengthening silences. It might have been her name, Bertrade, or it might have been 'buried'. No matter! What mattered was that he had uttered it on the edge of sleep, and now would blessedly sleep again after all his harsh labour along the way, perhaps long past the coming of light. So much the better! One day more spent on this pilgrimage might grieve his impatient spirit, but it would certainly benefit his harshly driven body.

Cadfael arose very quietly, and left his companion deeply asleep and virtually a prisoner in the loft, since he would need help to get to his feet and descend the ladder. With the trapdoor left open, a listener below would hear when the sleeper stirred, but by the look of his relaxed body and the thin face smoothed of its tensions he would sleep for some time.

Cadfael went out into the clear, sharp morning, to snuff the still air, redolent of the lingering winter scents of forestland still half asleep. From the forester's small assart among the trees it was possible to see the cleared grey of the track in broken glimpses between the old trunks, for the growth was close enough to keep the ground almost clear of underbrush. A handcart trundled along the road, laden with kindling from the fallen deadwood of the autumn, and the chattering flight of disturbed birds accompanied it in a shimmer of fluttered branches and drifting leaves. The forester was already up and about his morning tasks, his cow lumbering in to be milked, his dog weaving busily about his heels. A dry day, the sky overcast but lofty, the light good. A fine day for the road. By night they could be in Chenet itself, and the manor, in the king's holding, would take them in. Tomorrow to Lichfield, and there Cadfael was determined they should halt for another long night's rest, however ardently Haluin might argue for pressing on the remaining few miles to Elford. After a proper sleep in Lichfield Haluin should be in better condition to endure the next night's vigil pledged in Bertrade's memory, and face the beginning of the return journey, during which, God be praised, there need be no haste at all, and no cause to drive himself to the limits of endurance.

Sounds came muffled and soft along the beaten earth of the track, but Cadfael caught rather the vibration of hooves than the impact. Horses coming briskly from the west, two horses, for their gaits quivered in counterpoint, coming at a brisk trot, fresh from a night's rest and ready for the day. Travellers heading, perhaps, for Lichfield, after spending the night at the manor of Stretton, two miles back along the road. Cadfael stood to watch them pass.

Two men in dun-coloured gear, leather-coated, easy in the saddle, their seats and the handling of their mounts so strongly alike that either they had learned from childhood together, or the one had taught the other. And indeed, the one was double the bulk of the other and clearly a generation the elder, and though they were too distant and too briefly seen to have features, the whole shape of them indicated that they were kin. Two privileged grooms to some noble house, each with a woman pillion behind him. Women warmly cloaked for travelling look all much alike, and yet Cadfael stared after the first of these with roused attention, and kept his eyes on her until the horses and their riders had vanished along the road, and the soft drumming of hooves faded into distance.

She was still within his eyelids as he turned back into the hay-hut, pricking uneasily at his memory, urging, against all his dismissal of the possibility as folly, that he had seen her before, and further, that if he would but admit it he knew very well where.

But whether that was true or not, and whatever it augured if it was, there was nothing he could do about it. He shrugged it into the back of his mind, and went in, to listen for the moment when Haluin should awake and have need of him.

They came through groves of trees into an expanse of level meadows, a little bleached and grey as yet in the cold air, but fertile and well cultivated, a rich little island in a shire otherwise somewhat derelict still after the harsh pacification of fifty years back. There before them lay the sleek curves of the River Tame, the steep-pitched roof of a mill, and the close cluster of the houses of Elford, beyond the water.

In the warm and welcoming hospitality of the clerics of Lichfield they had spent a restful night, and received full directions as to the best road fo Elford, and with the first light of dawn they had set off on the last four miles or so of this penitential journey. And here before them lay the goal of Haluin's pilgrimage, almost within reach, only an expanse of peaceful fields and a wooden footbridge between him and his absolution. A fortunate place, prosperous where much was impoverished, with not one mill by the waterside, but two, for they could see the second one upstream, with ample meadowland, and rich soil where the arable fields showed. A place that might well promise blessing and peace of mind after labour and pain.

The pale thread of the path led them forward, and the roofs of Elford rose before them, circled with trees and bushes still naked and dark at this distant view, not yet so far advanced in bud as to show the first faint, elusive smoke of green. They crossed the bridge, the uneven planks causing Haluin to watch carefully how he placed his crutches, and came into the track between the houses. A neat village, with housewives and husbandmen going cheerfully and confidently about their daily business, alert to strangers but civil and welcoming to the Benedictine habit. They exchanged greetings along the way, and Haluin, cheered and vindicated at the successful completion of his journey, began to flush and brighten with pleasure at being offered this spontaneous omen of acceptance and release.

No need to ask how to reach the church, they had seen its low tower before they crossed the bridge. It had been built since the Normans came, sturdy in grey stone, with a spacious churchyard very well stockaded for sanctuary at need, and full of old and handsome trees. They entered under the round-arched portico, and came into the familiar cool, echoing gloom of all stone-built churches, smelling faintly of dust, and wax candles, and strongly and reassuringly of home, the chosen abiding-place.

Haluin had halted in the tiled silence of the nave to get his bearings. Here there was no Lady Chapel to accommodate a patron's tomb between the altars, the lords of Elford must lie aside, built into the stones of the walls they had raised. The red eye of light from the altar lamp showed them where the tomb lay, a great table slab filling a niche in the right-hand wall. Some dead de Clary, perhaps the first who came over with King William, and got his reward later, showed as a sleeping figure in relief on the sealing stone. Haluin had started forward towards it, only to check and draw back after the first echoing step, for there was a woman on her knees beside the tomb.

They saw her only as a shadowy figure, for the cloak she wore was dark grey like the stone in this dim light, and they knew her for a woman and not a man because the hood of the cloak was thrown back from her head, uncovering a white linen coif and a gauze veil over it. They would have retired into the porch to let her complete her prayers in peace, but she had heard the impact of the crutches on the tiled floor, and turned her head sharply to look towards them. In a single graceful, abrupt movement she rose to her feet, and coming towards them, stepped into the light from a window, and showed them the proud, aging, beautiful face of Adelais de Clary.

Chapter Five

YOU?' SHE said, staring, and turning her startled gaze from one face to the other, seeking, it seemed, some logic in this unexpected visitation. Her voice was neutral, neither welcoming nor repelling them. 'I had not thought to see you again so soon. Is there something more you have to ask of me, Haluin, that you have followed me here? You have only to ask. I have said I forgive.'

'Madam,' said Haluin, shaken and quivering from the apparition of his former mistress in this unexpected place, 'we have not followed you. Indeed I never thought to find you here. For your forbearance I'm grateful, and I would not for the world trouble you further. I have come here only in fulfilment of a vow I made. I had thought to spend a night in prayer at Hales, believing that my lady your daughter must be buried there. But we heard from the priest that it is not so. It's here at Elford she lies, in the tomb of her grandsires. So I have continued this far. And all I have to beg of you is your leave to keep my vigil here through this coming night, in deliverance of what I have sworn. Then we will depart, and trouble you no more.'

'I will not deny,' she said, but with a softening voice, 'that I shall be glad to have you gone. No ill-will! But this wound you have opened again for me I would willingly swathe away out of sight until it heals. Your face is a contagion that makes it open and bleed afresh. Do you think I should have taken horse and ridden here so fast if you had not put that old grief in my mind?'

'I trust,' said Haluin in a low and shaken voice, 'you may find, madam, as I hope to find, the wound cleansed of all its rancours by this atonement. It is my prayer that for you this time the healing may be sweet and wholesome.'

'And for you?' she said sharply, and turned a little away from him, with a motion of her hand that forbade any answer. 'Sweet and wholesome! You ask much of God, and more of me.' In the sidelong light from the window her face was fierce and sad. 'You have learned a monk's way with words,' she said. 'Well, it is a long time! Your voice was lighter once, so was your step. This at least I grant you, you are here at a very heavy cost. Do not deny me the grace of offering you rest and meat this time. I have a dwelling of my own here, within my son's manor pale. Come within and rest at least until Vespers, if you must punish your flesh on the stones here through the night.'

'Then I may have my night of prayer?' asked Haluin hungrily.

'Why not? Have you not just seen me entreating God in the same cause?' she said. 'I see you broken. I would not have you forsworn. Yes, have your penitential vigil, but take food in my house first. I'll send my grooms to fetch you,' she said, 'when you have made your devotions here.'

She was almost at the door, paying no attention to Haluin's hesitant thanks, and affording him no opportunity to refuse her hospitality, when she suddenly halted and swung round to them again.

'But say no word,' she said earnestly, 'to any other about your purpose here. My daughter's name and fame are safe enough under the stone, let them lie quiet there. I would not have any other reminded as I have been reminded. Let it be only between us two, and this good brother who bears you company.'

'Madam,' said Haluin devoutly, 'there shall be no word said to any other soul but between us three, neither now nor at any other time, neither here nor in any other place.'

'You ease my mind,' she said, and in a moment she was gone, and the door drawn quietly to after her.

Haluin could not kneel without something firm before him to which to cling, and Cadfael's arm about him to ease his weight down gently, sharing the burden with his companion's one serviceable foot. They offered their dutiful prayer at the altar side by side, and Cadfael, open-eyed as Haluin kneeled long, traced with measured concern the worn lines of the young man's face. He had survived the hard journey afoot, but not without a heavy cost. The night on the stones here would be cold, cramping and long, but Haluin would insist on the last extreme of self-punishment. And after that, the long road back. As well, indeed, if the lady could persuade him to remain for at least a second night, if only as a concession and grace to her now they had, in a fashion, come to terms with their shared and haunted past.

For it could certainly be true that Haluin's sudden visit had sent her on her own pilgrimage, hotfoot here to confront her own part in that old tragedy. Passing by at a smart trot the forester's assart near Chenet, with only a maidservant and two grooms in her train, and striking an elusive spark in Cadfael's memory. It could well be true. Or would such a seed have borne fruit so fast? The implication of haste was there. Cadfael saw again the two double-laden horses passing in the early morning, going steadily and with purpose. In haste to pay a half-forgotten debt of affection and remorse? Or to arrive before someone else, and be ready and armed to receive him? She wanted them satisfied and gone, but that was natural enough. They had trespassed on her peace, and held up an old, flawed mirror before her beautiful face.

'Help me up!' said Haluin, and raised his arms like a child to be lifted to his feet; and that was the first time that he had asked for help, always before it had been proffered, and his acceptance humble and resigned rather than grateful.

'You did not speak one word throughout,' he said suddenly, marvelling, as they turned towards the church door.

'I had not one word to speak,' said Cadfael. 'But I heard many words. And even the silences between them were not altogether inarticulate.'

Adelais de Clary's groom was waiting for them in the porch, as she had promised, leaning indolently with one shoulder propped against the jamb of the door, as though he had been waiting for some time, but with immovable patience. His appearance confirmed everything Brother Cadfael had elaborated, in his own mind, from the few glimpses he had had of the riders between the trees. The younger of the pair, this, a brawny young man of perhaps thirty years, thickset, bull-necked, unmistakably in the Norman mould. Perhaps the third or fourth generation from a progenitor who had come over as a man-at-arms with the first de Clary. The strong original stock still prevailed, though intermarriage with English women had tempered the fairness of his hair into a straw-brown, and somewhat moderated the brutal bones of his face. He still wore his hair cropped into a close cap in the Norman manner, and his strong jaw clean-shaven, and he still had the bright, light, impenetrable eyes of the north. At their coming he sprang erect, more at ease in movement than in repose.

'My lady sends me to show you the way.'

His voice was flat and clipped, and he waited for no reply, but set off out of the churchyard before them, at a pace Haluin could not well maintain. The groom looked back at the gate and waited, and therefore abated his speed, though it obviously chafed him to move slowly. He said nothing of his own volition, and replied to question or simple civility cordially enough, but briefly. Yes, Elford was a very fine property, good land and a good lord. Audemar's competent management of his honour was acknowledged indifferently; this young man's allegiance was to Adelais rather than to her son. Yes, his father was in the same service, and so had his father been before him. About these monastic guests he showed no curiosity at all, though he might have felt some. Those pale grey, alien eyes concealed all thought, or perhaps suggested thoughts total absence.

He brought them by a grassy way to the gate of the manor enclosure, which was walled and spacious. Audemar de Clary's house sat squarely in the midst, the living floor raised well above a stone undercroft, and to judge by the small windows above there were at least two more chambers over the solar. And his ample courtyard was built round with other habitable rooms, as well as the customary and necessary stables, armoury, bakehouse and brewhouse, stores and workshops, and was populous with the activities of a large and busy household.

The groom led them to a small timber lodging under the curtain wall.

'My lady has had this chamber made ready for you. Use it as your own, she says, and the gateman will see to it you can come and go freely, to go to the church.'

Her hospitality, as they found, was meticulous but remote and impersonal. She had provided them with water for washing, comfortable pallets to rest on, sent them food from her own table, and given orders to tell them to ask for anything they might need or want that had been forgotten, but she did not receive them into her own presence. Perhaps forgiveness did not reach so far as to render Haluin's remorseful presence agreeable to her. Nor was it her house-servants who waited on them, but the two grooms who had ridden with her from Hales. It was the elder of the two who brought them meat and bread and cheese, and small ale from the pantry. Cadfael had not been deceived in their relationship, for this one was clearly father to the other, a tough, square-set man in his fifties, close-mouthed like his son, broader in the shoulders, more bowed in the legs from years spent as much on horse-back as on his own two feet. The same cold, unconfiding eyes, the same bold and powerful shaven jaws, but this one was tanned to a lasting bronze that Cadfael recognised from his own past as having its origin very far from England. His lord had been a crusader. This man had surely been with him there in the Holy Land, and got his burnished gloss there under the fierce, remembered sun.

The elder groom came again later in the afternoon, with a message not for Haluin but for Cadfael. It so happened that Haluin had fallen asleep on his pallet, and the man's entrance, light and soft as a cat for all his bulk, did not disturb his rest, for which Cadfael was grateful. There was a long and unrestful night to come. He motioned to the groom to wait, and went out into the courtyard to him, closing the door softly after him.

'Let him lie. He'll need to be wakeful later.'

'My lady told us how he means to spend the night,' said the groom. 'It's you she bids to her, if you'll come with me now. Let the other brother rest, she says, for he's been mortal sick. I grant him a man's guts, or he'd never have come so far on those feet. This way, Brother!'

Her dower dwelling was built into a corner of the curtain wall, sheltered from the prevailing winds, small, but enough for such occasional visits as she chose to make to her son's court. A narrow hall and chamber, and a kitchen built lean-to against the wall outside. The groom strode in and through the hall with simple authority, as one having privilege here, and entered his mistress's presence much as a son or brother of hers might have done, trusting and trusted. Adelais de Clary was well served, but without subservience.

'Here is Brother Cadfael from Shrewsbury, my lady. The other one's asleep.'

Adelais was sitting at a distaff loaded with deep blue wool, spinning the spindle with her left hand, but at their entrance she ceased to turn it, and lodged it carefully against the foot of the distaff to prevent the yarn from uncoiling.

'Good! It's what he needs. Leave us now, Lothair, our guest will find his own way back. Is my son home yet?'

'Not yet. I'll be looking out for him when he comes.'

'He has Roscelin with him,' she said, 'and the hounds. When they're all home and kennelled and stalled, take your ease, it's well earned.'

He merely nodded by way of acknowledgement, and departed, taciturn and uneffusive as ever, and yet there was a tone in their exchanges of invulnerable assurance, secure as rooted rock. Adelais said no word until the door of her chamber had closed after her servant. She was eyeing Cadfael with silent attention, and the faint shadow of a smile.

'Yes,' she said, as if he had spoken. 'More than an old servant. He was with my lord all the years he fought in Palestine. More than once he did Bertrand that small service, to keep him man alive. It is another manner of allegiance, not a servant's. As bound in fealty as ever lord is to his overlord. I inherited what was my lord's before me. Lothair, he's called. His son is Luc. Born and bred in the same mould. You'll have seen the likeness, God knows it can hardly be missed.'

'I have seen it,' said Cadfael. 'And I knew where Lothair got that copper skin he wears.'

'Indeed?' She was studying him with concentrated interest now, having gone to the trouble to see him for the first time.

'I was some years in the east myself, before his time. If he lives long enough his brown will fade as mine has faded, but it takes a long while.'

'Ah! So you were not given to the monks in childhood. I thought you had not the look of such virgin innocents,' said Adelais.

'I entered of my own will,' said Cadfael, 'when it was time.'

'So did he – of his own will, though I think it was not time.' She stirred and sighed. 'I sent for you only to ask if you have everything you need – if my men have taken proper care of you.'

'Excellent care. And for their kindness and yours we are devoutly grateful.'

'And to ask you of him – of Haluin. I have seen in what sad case he is. Will it ever be better with him?'

'He will never walk as he did before,' said Cadfael, 'but as his sinews gain time and strength he will improve. He believed he was dying, so did we all, but he lives and will yet find much good in life – once his mind is at peace.'

'And will it be at peace after tonight? Is this what he needs?'

'I believe he will. I believe it is.'

'Then it has my blessing. And then you will take him back to Shrewsbury? I can provide you horses,' she said, 'for the way back. Lothair can fetch them to Hales when we return.'

'That kindness he will surely refuse,' said Cadfael. 'He has sworn to complete this penance on foot.'

She nodded understanding. 'I will ask him, none the less. Well – that is all, Brother. If he will not, I can do no more. Yes, one thing I can! I am coming to Vespers tonight, I will speak to the priest, and make certain that no one – no one! – shall question or trouble his vigil. You understand, nothing must be let slip to any soul but us who already know all too well. Tell him so. What remains is between him and God.'

The master of the house was just riding in at the gate as Cadfael walked back to the lodging where Haluin lay sleeping. The ring of harness and hooves and voices entered ahead of the cavalcade, a lively sound, bringing out grooms and servants like bees from a disturbed hive to attend on their lord's arrival. And here he came, Audemar de Clary on a tall chestnut horse, a big man in dark, plain, workmanlike riding clothes, without ornament, and needing none to mark him out as having authority here. He rode in with head uncovered, the hood of his short cloak flung back on his shoulders, and his shock of crisp hair was as dark as his mother's, but the powerful bones of his face, high-bridged nose, thrusting cheekbones and lofty forehead he surely had from his crusader father.

He could not, Cadfael thought, be yet forty years old. The vigour of his movements as he dismounted, the spring of his step on the ground, the very gestures of his hands as he stripped off his gloves, all were young. But the formidable features of his face and the mastery that was manifest all about him, in the efficiency of his management here and the prompt and competent service he expected and got, made him seem older in dominance than he was in years. He had been master, Cadfael recalled, in his father's long absence, beginning early, probably before he was twenty, and the de Clary honour was large and scattered. He had learned his business well. Not a man to be crossed lightly, but no one here feared him. They approached him cheerfully and spoke with him boldly. His anger, when justified, might be withering, even perilous, but it would be just.

He had a young fellow, page or squire, riding close at his elbow, a youth of seventeen or eighteen, fresh-faced and flushed with open air and exercise, and after them came two kennelmen on foot with the hounds on leash after their run. Audemar handed over his bridle to the groom who came running, and stood stamping his booted feet as he shed his cloak into the young man's ready hands. The brief flurry of activity was over in a few minutes, the horses on their way across the court to the stables, the hounds away to the kennels. The young groom Luc came out of the stable-yard and spoke to Audemar, apparently to deliver a message from Adelais, for Audemar at once looked round towards the lady's lodging, nodded understanding, and came striding towards her door. His eye fell on Cadfael, standing discreetly aside from his path, and for an instant he checked as though to stop and speak, but then changed his mind and went on, to vanish into the deep doorway.

Judging by the time that she and her grooms and her maid had passed by in the forest, Cadfael reckoned, Adelais must have arrived here that same day, two days previously. They would have no need to halt for a night between Chenet and Elford, on horseback the distance was easy. Therefore she must already have seen and talked with her son. What she had to communicate to him now, as soon as he returned from riding, might well have to do with whatever was news this day at the manor of Elford. And what was new but the arrival of the two monks from Shrewsbury, and their reason for being here, a reason she would interpret with discretion for him? For he had been here at Elford when his sister died in Hales, for the world's ears – and her brother's also? – of a fever. That must be all he had ever known of it, a simple, sad death, such as may happen in any household, even to one in the bloom of youth. No, that strong and resolute woman would never have let her son into the secret. An old, trusted, confidential maidservant, maybe. She must have needed such a one, now perhaps dead. But her young son, no, never.

And if that was true, no wonder Adelais was taking every precaution to smooth Haluin's way to his atonement, and be rid of him as quickly as possible, warding off all enquiry, even from the priest, offering horses to hasten the departure, and pledging the two pilgrims not to reveal anything of the past to any other being, not to say one word of the import of their errand, or mention the name of Bertrade.

Something, at least, I begin to understand, thought Cadfael. Wherever we turn, there is Adelais between us and all others. She houses us, she feeds us, it is her most loyal servants who approach and wait on us, not any from her son's household. My daughter's name and fame are safe enough under the stone, she had said, let them lie quiet there. Small blame to her for making sure, and no wonder she had ridden in haste to reach Elford beforehand and be ready for them.

And go we will, he thought, tomorrow morning if Haluin is fit to set out, and she can set her mind at rest. We can find another halting-place a mile or two from here, if we must, but at all costs we'll quit these walls, and she need never see or think of Haluin again.

The young squire had remained standing to watch his lord cross to the lady's door, Audemar's cloak flung over his shoulder, his bare head almost flaxen against the dark cloth. He had still the coltish, angular grace of youth. In a year or two his slenderness would fill out into solid and shapely manhood, with every movement under smooth control, but as yet he retained the vulnerable uncertainty of a boy. He looked after Audemar with surprised speculation, stared at Cadfael in candid curiosity, and turned slowly towards the door of Audemar's hall.

So this must be the Roscelin to whom Adelais had referred, thought Cadfael, watching him go. Not a son of the house, by the cut of him and the colouring, but not a servant, either. Doubtless a youngster from the family of one of Audemar's tenants, sent here to his overlord to get his training in arms, and acquire the skills and practices of a small court, in preparation for the wider world. Such apprentice lordlings proliferated in every great barony, the de Clary honour might well be patron to one or two of the same kind.

The early evening had turned cold, and there was a biting wind rising, with a few fine needles of sleet stinging in its touch. The hour of Vespers was not far away. Cadfael went in thankfully from the chill, to find Brother Haluin awake and waiting, silent and tense, for his hour of fulfilment.

Adelais had evidently made her dispositions well. No one

intruded upon their privacy, no one asked any question or showed any curiosity. The young groom Luc brought them food before Vespers, and at the end of the office they were left alone in the church to conduct their vigil as they pleased. Doubtful if any among the household wondered about them at all, being accustomed to random visitors of all kinds, with differing needs, and the devotions of a pair of itinerant Benedictines surprised no one. If monks of the abbey of Saint Peter, elected to spend a night in prayer in a church of Saint Peter, that was no special wonder, and concerned no one else.

So Brother Haluin had his will, and redeemed his vow. He would have no softening of the stone, no extra cloak to ward off the cold of the night, nothing to abate the rigours of his penance. Cadfael helped him to his knees, within reach of the solid support of the tomb, so that if faintness or dizziness came over him he could at least hold fast by it to break his fall. The crutches were laid at the foot of the stone. There was no more he would permit anyone to do for him. But Cadfael kneeled with him, withdrawn into shadow to leave him solitary with his dead Bertrade and a God doubtless inclining a compassionate ear.

It was a long night, and cold. The altar lamp made an eye of brightness in the gloom, at least ruddy like fire if it gave no warmth. The silence carried hour by hour, like an infinitesimal ripple vibrating through it, the gradual heave of Haluin's breathing and the constant whisper of his moving lips, felt in the blood and the bowels rather than audible with the ear. From somewhere within him he drew an inexhuastible wealth of words to be spent for his dead Bertrade. Their tension and passion kept him erect and oblivious to pain, though pain took fast hold of him before midnight, and never left him until his rapture and his ordeal ended together with the coming of the light.

When he opened his eyes at last to the full light of a frosty morning, and laboriously unlocked his cold, clasped hands, the sounds of the customary early activity were already audible from the outside world. Haluin stared dazedly upon the waking day, returning from some place very far off, very deep within. He essayed to move, to grip the rim of the stone, and his fingers were so numbed they could not feel, and his arms so stiff they could give him no help to raise himself. Cadfael wound an arm about him to lift him, but Haluin could not straighten his stiff knees to set his better foot to the ground, but hung a dead weight on the encircling arm. And suddenly there was a flurry of light footsteps, and another arm, young and strong, embraced the helpless body from the other side, a fair head stooped to Haluin's shoulder, and between his two supporters he was hauled upright, and held so as the blood flowed back achingly into his numbed legs.

'In God's name, man,' said the young man Roscelin impatiently, 'must you use yourself so hardly when you have already enough for any sane man to carry?'

Haluin was too startled, and his mind still too far away, to be capable of grasping that, much less answering it. And if Cadfael privately considered it a perfectly sensible reaction, aloud he said practically: 'Keep firm hold of him, so, while I pick up his crutches. And God bless you for appearing so aptly. Spare to scold him, you'd be wasting your breath. He's under vow.'

'A foolish vow!' said the boy with the arrogant certainty of his years. 'Who's the better for this?' But for all his disapproval he held Haluin warmly and firmly, and looked at him sidelong with a frown at least as anxious as it was exasperated.

'He is,' said Cadfael, propping the crutches under Haluin's armpits, and setting to work to chafe life back into the cold hands that could not yet grip the staves. 'Hard to believe, but you had better credit it. There, you can let him lean on his props now, but hold him steady. Well for you at your years, you can sleep easy, with nothing to regret and nothing to ask pardon for. How did you come to look in here so timely?' he asked, eyeing the young man with fresh interest, thus at close quarters. 'Were you sent?'

For this boy seemed an unlikely instrument for Adelais to use in shepherding her inconvenient guests in and out of Elford – too young, too blunt, too innocent.

'No,' said Roscelin shortly, and relented to add with better grace: 'I was plain curious.'

'Well, that's human,' admitted Cadfael, recognising his own besetting sin.

'And this morning Audemar has no immediate work for me, he's busy with his steward. Had we not better get this brother of yours back to his lodging, where it's warmer? How shall we do? I can fetch a horse for him if we can get him mounted.'

Haluin had come back from his distant place to find himself being discussed and handled as if he had no mind of his own, and no awareness of his surroundings. He stiffened instinctively against the indignity. 'No,' he said, 'I thank you, but I can go now. I need not trespass on your kindness further.' And he flexed his hands and gripped the staves of his crutches, and took the first cautious steps away from the tomb.

They followed closely, one at either elbow in case he faltered, Roscelin going before up the shallow steps and through the doorway to prevent a possible stumble, Cadfael coming close behind to support him if he reeled backwards. But Haluin had gathered to his aid a will refreshed and strengthened by achievement, and was resolute to manage this walk alone, at whatever cost. And there was no haste. When he felt the need he could rest on his crutches to draw breath, and so he did three times before they reached Audemar's courtyard, already populous and busy about bakery and mews and well-head. It said much for young Roscelin's quickness and delicacy of mind, Cadfael reflected, that he waited without comment or impatience at every pause, and refrained from offering a hand in help until help should be invited. So Haluin came back to the lodging in Audemar's courtyard as he would have wished, on his own misshapen feet, and could feel that he had earned the ease of his bed.

Roscelin followed them in, still curious, in no haste to go in search of whatever duties awaited him. 'Is that all, then?' he said, watching Haluin stretch out his still numbed limbs gratefully, and draw the brychan over them. 'Then where do you go when you leave us? And when? You'll not set out today?'

'We go back to Shrewsbury,' said Cadfael. 'Today – that I doubt. A day's rest would be wisdom.' By the weary ease of Haluin's face, and the softened gaze turned inward, it would not be long before he fell asleep, the best and best-earned sleep since he had made his confession.

'I saw you ride in with the lord Audemar yesterday,' said Cadfael, studying the youthful face before him. 'The lady mentioned your name. Are you kin to the de Clarys?'

The boy shook his head. 'No. My father is tenant and vassal to him, they've always been good friends, and there's a marriage tie, a while back now. No, I'm sent here to Audemar's service at my father's order.'

'But not at your wish,' said Cadfael, interpreting the tone rather than the words.

'No! Much against my wish!' said Roscelin abruptly, and scowled at the floorboards between his booted feet.

'Yet to all appearances as good a lord as you could hope for,' suggested Cadfael mildly, 'and better than most.'

'He's well enough,' the boy owned fairly. 'I've no complaint of *him*. But I grudge it that my father has sent me away here to be rid of me out of the house, and that's the truth of it.'

'Now why,' wondered Cadfael, curious but not quite asking, 'why should any father want to be rid of you?' For here was undoubtedly the very picture of a presentable son, upstanding, well-formed, well-conducted, and decidedly engaging in his fair-haired, smooth-cheeked comeliness, a son any father would be glad to parade before his peers. Even in sullenness his face was pleasing, but it was certainly true that he had not the look of one happy in his service.

'He has his reasons,' said Roscelin moodily. 'You'd say good reasons, too, I know that. And I'm not so estranged from him that I could refuse him the obedience due. So I'm here, and pledged to stay here unless lord and father both give me leave to go. And I'm not such a fool as not to admit I could be in far worse places. So I may as well get all the good I can out of while I'm here.'

It seemed that his mind had veered into another and graver quarter, for he sat for some moments silent, staring down into his clasped hands with a frowning brow, and looked up only to measure Cadfael earnestly, his eyes dwelling long upon the black habit and the tonsure.

'Brother,' he said abruptly, 'I've wondered, now and then – about the monkish life. Some men have taken to it, have they not, because what they most wanted was for ever impossible – forbidden them! Is that true? Can it provide a life, if . . . if the life a man wants is out of reach?'

'Yes,' said Brother Haluin's voice, gently and quietly out of a waking dream now very close to sleep. 'Yes, it can!'

'I would not recommend entering it as a second-best,' said Cadfael stoutly. Yet that was what Haluin had done, long ago, and he spoke now as one recording a revelation, the opening of his inward eyes just as they were heavy and closing with sleep.

'The time might be long, and the cost high,' said Haluin with gentle certainty, 'but in the end it would not be second-best.'

He drew in a long breath, and spent it in a great healing sigh, turning his head away from them on the pillow. They were both so intent on him, doubting and wondering, that neither of them had noted the approach of brisk footsteps without, and they started round in surprise as the door was thrown wide open to admit Lothair, carrying a basket of food and a pitcher of small ale for the guests. At the sight of Roscelin seated familiarly upon Cadfael's pallet, and apparently on good terms with the brothers, the groom's weathered face tightened perceptibly, almost ominously, and for an instant a deeper spark flashed and vanished again in his pale eyes.

'What are you doing here?' he demanded with the bluntness of an equal, and the uncompromising authority of an elder. 'Master Roger's looking for you, and my lord wants you in attendance as soon as he's broken his fast. You'd best be off, and sharp about it, too.'

It could not be said that Roscelin showed any alarm at this intelligence, or resentment at the manner in which it was delivered, rather the man's assurance seemed to afford him a little tolerant amusement. But he rose at once, and with a nod and a word by way of farewell went off obediently but without haste to his duty. Lothair stood narrow-eyed in the doorway to watch him go, and did not come fully into the room with his burdens until the boy had reached the steps to the hall door.

Our guard-dog, thought Cadfael, has his orders to ward off any others who come too close, but he had not reckoned with having to do as much for young Roscelin. Now could there, I wonder, be some reason why that contact in particular should cause him consternation? For that's the first spark I've seen struck from his steel!

Chapter Six

ADELAIS HERSELF paid a gracious visit to her monastic guests after Mass, with solicitous enquiries after their health and wellbeing. It was possible, Cadfael reflected, that Lothair had reported back to her the inconvenient and undesirable incursion of the young man Roscelin into a preserve she clearly wished to keep private. She appeared in the doorway of their small chamber, prayer-book in hand, alone, having sent her maid on ahead to her dower house. Haluin was awake, and made to rise from his pallet in respectful acknowledgement of her coming, reaching in haste for his crutches, but she motioned him back with a wave of her hand.

'No, be still! No ceremony is needed between us. How do you find yourself now – now that your vow is accomplished? I hope you have experienced grace, and can return to your cloister in peace. I wish you that mercy. An easy journey and a safe arrival!'

And above all, thought Cadfael, an early departure. And small blame to her. It's what I want, too, and so must Haluin. To have this matter finished, neatly and cleanly, with no more harm to any creature, with mutual forgiveness, once spoken, and therefore silence.

'You have had little rest,' she said, 'and have a long journey back to Shrewsbury. My kitchen shall supply you with food for the first stages of the way. But I think you should also accept horses. I have said so to Brother Cadfael already. The stables here can spare you mounts, and I will send for them to Hales when I return there. You should not attempt to go back all that way on foot.'

'For the offer, and for all your kindness, we are grateful,' said Haluin in instant and hasty protest. 'But this I cannot accept. I undertook both to go and to return on foot, and I must make good what I vowed. It is a pledge of faith that I am not so crippled as to be utterly useless and unprofitable hereafter, to God and man. You would not wish me to go home shamed and forsworn.'

She shook her head over his obstinacy with apparent resignation. 'So your fellow here warned me you would argue, when I spoke of it to him, but I hoped you would see better reason. Surely you are also pledged to return to your duty at the abbey as soon as may be. Has that no force? If you insist on going afoot you cannot set out at least until tomorrow, after so hard a night on the stones.'

To Haluin, no doubt, that sounded like true solicitude, and an invitation to delay until he was fully rested. To Cadfael it had the sound of a subtle dismissal.

'I never thought that it would be easy,' said Haluin, 'to perform what I swore. Nor should it be. The whole virtue, if there is any virtue in it at all, is to endure the hardship and complete the penance. And so I can and shall. You are right, I owe it to my abbot and my brothers to get back to my duty as soon as I may. We must set out today. There are still hours of daylight left, we must not waste them.'

To do her justice, she did seem to be taken aback at such ready compliance with what she wished, even if she had not expressed the wish. She urged, though without warmth, the necessity of rest, but gave way pliantly before Haluin's stubborn insistence. Things had gone as she wished, at the last moment she could afford one brief convulsion of pity and regret.

'It must be as you wish,' she said. 'Very well, Luc shall bring you food and drink before you go, and fill your scrip for you. As for me, I part from you in goodwill. Now and hereafter, I wish you well.'

When she was gone, Haluin sat silent for a while, shivering a little in the recoil from the finality of this ending. It was as he had hoped, and yet it left him shaken.

'I have made things needlessly hard for you,' he said ruefully. 'You must be as weary as I am, and I have committed you to leaving thus, without sleep. She wanted us gone, and for my part I heartily wish to be gone. The sooner severed, the better for us all.'

'You did right,' said Cadfael. 'Once out of here we need not go far, you are in no case to attempt it today. But to be out of here is all we need.'

They left Audemar de Clary's manor gates in mid-afternoon, under a sky heavy with grey cloud, and turned westward along the track through Elford village, with a chill, insidious wind in their faces. It was over. From this point on, with every step taken they were returning to normality and safety, to the monastic hours and the blessed daily round of work, worship and prayer.

From the highroad Cadfael looked back once, and saw the two grooms standing in the gateway to watch the guests depart. Two solid, sturdy figures, taciturn and inscrutable, following the withdrawal of the interlopers with light, fierce northern eyes. Making sure, thought Cadfael, that the disquiet we brought to that lady departs with us, and leaves no shadow behind.

They did not look back a second time. The need now was to put at least one safe, alienating mile between themselves and the dower house of Elford, and after that they could look for a night's shelter early, for in spite of his resolution it was clear that Haluin was haggard and grey with exhaustion, and would not get far without danger of collapse. His face was set to endure, he went steadily but heavily on his crutches, his eyes dilated and dark in their deep hollows. Doubtful if even now he enjoyed the peace he should have found at Bertrade's tomb, but perhaps it was not Bertrade who still haunted his thoughts.

'I shall never see her again,' said Haluin, to God, himself and the gathering dusk rather than to Cadfael. And it was hard to say whether he spoke in relief or regret, as at leaving something unfinished.

The first snow of a capricious March burst upon them suddenly out of the lowering sky when they were some two miles from Elford. The air was on the edge of frost, there would be no great or prolonged fall, but while it lasted it was thick and blinding, stinging their faces and confusing the path before them. The premature dusk closed down on them almost abruptly, a murky darkness out of which whirling clouds of white flakes wound about them bewilderingly, veiling even what landmarks they had on a stretch of track open, windswept and treeless.

Haluin had begun to stumble, troubled by the driven flakes filling his eyes, and unable to free a hand to draw the folds of his cowl together against the assault. Twice he planted a crutch aside from the trodden path, and all but fell. Cadfael halted and stood close, his back to the wind, to give his companion breathing space and shelter for some moments, while he considered where they were, and what he could recall of the surrounding country from their outward journey. Any dwelling, however mean, would be welcome until this squall blew over. Somewhere here, he calculated, there had been a side-path bearing north, and leading to what seemed to be a cluster of small houses and the long pale of a manor fence, the only sign of occupation within view of the road.

His recollection was accurate. Going cautiously before, with Haluin close at his back, he came to an isolated clump of bushes and low trees which he remembered clearly in this sparsely treed plain, and a little beyond these the path opened. There was even a flickering spark of torchlight, seen fitfully through the whirling snowfall, to keep them in the direct way towards the distant dwelling. Where the lord of the house showed a beacon for benighted travellers there should be a warm welcome waiting.

It took them longer to reach the hamlet than Cadfael had expected, since Haluin was flagging badly, and it was necessary to go very slowly, reaching back constantly to keep him close. Here and there a solitary tree loomed suddenly out of the spinning whiteness on the left hand or the right, only to be veiled again as abruptly. The flakes had grown larger and wetter, the hint of frost was receding, and this fall would not lie beyond the morning. Overhead the clouds were broken and torn in a rising wind, with a scattering of stars showing through.

The spark of torchlight had vanished, hidden behind the manor fence. A solid timber gatepost heaved out of the dark, the tall palisade running away from it on the left hand, the broad open gateway on the right, and suddenly there was the torch again, across a wide courtyard in a sconce jutting from under the eaves, to light the stair that climbed to the hall door. The usual encrustation of service buildings lined the stockade. Cadfael launched a shout ahead of their lurching entrance, and a man came butting his way through the falling snow from a stable door, shouting to others as he came. At the head of the steps the hall door opened on a welcome glimpse of firelight.

Cadfael brought Haluin stumbling in through the open gate in his arm, and another willing arm took him about the body on the other side, hoisting him vigorously into the comparative shelter within the pale. A voice bellowed heartily through the snowfall: 'Brothers, you chose a bad night to be out on the roads. Hold up, now, your troubles are over. We never shut the gates on your cloth.'

There were others coming forth by then to bring in the benighted travellers, a young fellow darting out from the undercroft with a sacking hood over head and shoulders, a bearded and gowned elder emerging from the hall and coming halfway down the steps to meet them. Haluin was lifted rather than led up the steep flight and into the hall, where the master of the house came striding out of his solar to meet these unexpected arrivals.

A fair man, long-boned and sparsely fleshed, with a short trimmed beard the colour of wheat straw, and a thick cap of hair of the same shade. Perhaps in his late thirties, Cadfael thought, of a ruddy, open countenance in which the blue Saxon eyes shone almost startlingly bright, candid and concerned.

'Come in, come in, Brothers! Well that you've found us! Here, bring him through here, close to the fire.' He had taken in at once the Benedictine habits, the flurries of snow lodged in the folds, and shaken off now hissing into the steady fire in the central hearth of the hall, the crippled feet of his younger visitor, the drawn grey expression of his face. 'Edgytha, have beds prepared in the end chamber, and tell Edwin to mull more wine.'

His voice was loud, solicitous and warm. Without seeming haste he had his servants running here and there on his benevolent errands, and himself saw Haluin installed on a bench against the wall, where the warmth of the fire could reach him.

'This young brother of yours is in very sad case,' said the host, aside to Cadfael, 'to be travelling the roads so far from home. There are none of your order round here – barring the sisters at Farewell, the bishop's new foundation. From which house do you come?'

'From Shrewsbury,' said Cadfael, setting Haluin's crutches to lean against the bench, where he could reach them at will.

Haluin sat back with closed eyes, his grey cheeks slowly gaining a little colour in the warmth and ease.

'So far? Could not your abbot have sent a hale man on his errands, if he had business in another shire?'

'This was Haluin's own errand,' said Cadfael. 'No other could have done it. Now it's done, and we're on our way home, and by stages we shall get there. Always with the help of hospitable souls like you. Can I ask, what is this place? These are parts I hardly know.'

'My name is Cenred Vivers. From this manor I take that name. This brother is called Haluin, you say? And yourself?'

'Cadfael is my name. Born Welsh, and bred up on the borders with a foot either side. I've been a brother of Shrewsbury now more than twenty years. My business on this journey is simply to keep Haluin company and see that he gets safely to where he's going, and safely back again.'

'No easy matter,' agreed Cenred, low-voiced, and eyeing Haluin's deformed feet ruefully, 'the state he's in. But if the work's done and only the way home to venture, no doubt you'll do it. How did he come by such injuries?'

'He fell from a roof. We had repairs to do, in the hard weather before Christmas. It was the slates falling after him that cut his feet to ribbons. Well that we kept him alive.'

They were speaking of him softly, a little aside, though he lay back as eased and still as if he had fallen asleep, his eyes closed, the long dark lashes shadowing his hollow cheeks. The hall had emptied about them, all the bustle of activity withdrawn elsewhere, busy with pillows and brychans and the hospitable business of the kitchen.

'They're slow with the wine,' said Cenred, 'and you must both need some warmth inside you. If you'll hold me excused, Brother, I'll go and hasten things in the pantry.'

And he was off, the flurry and wind of his passing causing Haluin's closed eyelids to quiver. In a moment he opened his eyes and looked slowly and dazedly about him, taking in the warm, high-roofed dimness of the hall, the glow of the fire, the heavy hangings that screened two alcoves withdrawn from the public domain, and the half-open door of the solar from which Cenred had emerged. The pale, steady gleam of candle-light showed from within.

'Have I dreamed?' wondered Haluin, gazing. 'How did we come here? What place is this?'

'Never fear,' said Cadfael, 'on your own two feet you came

here, only an arm to help you up the steps into the house. The manor is called Vivers, and the lord of it is Cenred. We've fallen into good hands.'

Haluin drew deep breath. 'I am not so strong as I believed I was,' he said sadly.

'No matter, you can rest now. We have left Elford behind.'

They were both speaking in low voices, a little awed by the enfolding silence presiding even in the centre of this populous household. When both ceased speaking, the quietness seemed almost expectant. And in the hush the half-open door of the solar opened fully upon the pale gold candle-light within, and a woman stepped into the doorway. For that one instant she was sharply outlined as a shadow against the soft light within, a slender, erect figure, mature and dignified in movement, surely the lady of the house and Cenred's wife. The next moment she had taken two or three light, swift steps into the hall, and the light of the nearest torch fell upon her shadowy face and advancing form, and conjured out of the dim shape a very different person. Everything about her was changed. Not a gracious chatelaine of more than thirty years, but a rounded, fresh-faced girl, no more than seventeen or eighteen, half her oval countenance two great startled eyes and the wide, high forehead above them, white and smooth as pearl.

Haluin uttered a strange, soft sound in his throat, between gasp and sigh, clutched at his crutches and heaved himself to his feet, staring at this sudden glowing apparition as she, brought up abruptly against the intrusion of strangers, had drawn back in haste, staring at him. For one moment they hung so, mute and still, then the girl whirled about and retreated into the solar, drawing the door to almost stealthily after her.

Haluin's hands slackened their hold, dangling inertly, the crutches slid and fell from under him, and he went down on his face in a gradual, crumpled fall, and lay senseless in the rushes of the floor.

They carried him to a bed prepared for him in a quiet chamber withdrawn from the hall, and bedded him there, still in a deep swoon.

'This is simple exhaustion,' said Cadfael in reassurance to Cenred's solicitous anxiety. 'I knew he was driving himself too hard, but that's done with now. From this on we can take our time. Leave him to sleep through this night, and he'll do well enough. See, he's coming round. His eyes are opening.'

Haluin stirred, his eyelids quivering before they rose on the dark, sharply conscious eyes within, that looked up into a circle of vague, concerned faces. He was aware of his surroundings, and knew what had happened to him before he was carried here, for the first words he spoke were in meek apology for troubling them, and thanks for their care.

'My fault!' he said. 'It was presumptuous to attempt too much. But now all is well with me. All is very well!'

Since his chief need was clearly of rest, they were left to make themselves comfortable in their small chamber, though the evening brought them a number of visits. The bearded steward brought them hot, spiced wine, and sent in to them the old woman Edgytha, who brought them water for their hands, food, and a lamp, and offered whatever more they might need for their comfort.

She was a tall, wiry, active woman probably sixty years old, with the free manner and air of authority habitual in servants who have spent many years in the confidence of lord or lady, and earned a degree of trust that brings with it acknowledged privilege. The younger maidservants deferred to her, if they did not actually go in awe of her, and her neat black gown and stiff white wimple, and the keys jingling at her waist bore witness to her status.

Late in the evening she came again, in attendance on a plump and pleasant lady, soft-voiced and gracious, who came to enquire kindly whether the reverend brothers had all that they needed for the night, and whether the one who had swooned was now comfortably recovered from his faintness. Cenred's wife was rosily pretty, brown-haired and brown-eyed, a very different creature from the tall, slender, vulnerable young thing who had stepped out of the solar, to be startled into recoil from the unexpected apparition of strangers.

'And have the lord Cenred and his lady any children?' Cadfael asked when their hostess was gone.

Edgytha was close-lipped, possessively protective of her family and all that was theirs, to the point of rendering every such enquiry suspect, but after a moment's hesitation she answered civilly enough: 'They have a son, a grown son.' And she added, unexpectedly reconsidering her reluctance to satisfy such uncalled-for curiosity: 'He's away, in service with my lord Cenred's overlord.'

There was a curious undertone of reserve, even of disapproval, in her voice, though she would never have acknowledged it. It almost distracted Cadfael's mind from his own preoccupation, but he pursued delicately:

'And no daughter? There was a young girl looked into the hall for a moment, while we were waiting. Is she not a child of the house?'

She gave him a long, steady, searching look, with raised brows and tight lips, plainly disapproving of such interest in young women, coming from a monastic. But guests in the house must be treated with unfailing courtesy, even when they fall short of deserving it.

'That lady is the lord Cenred's sister,' she said. 'The old lord Edric, his father, married a second time in his later years. More like a daughter to him than a sister, with the difference in years. I doubt you'll see her again. She would not wish to disturb the retirement of men of your habit. She has been well brought up,' concluded Edgytha with evident personal pride in the product of her own devotion, and a plain warning that black monks cast by chance into the household should keep their eyes lowered in a young virgin's presence.

'If you had her in charge,' said Cadfael amiably, 'I make no doubt she does credit to her upbringing. Had you Cenred's boy in your care, too?'

'My lady would not have dreamed of trusting her chick to any other.' The old woman had warmed into fond fervour in thinking of the children she had nursed. 'No one ever had the care of better babes,' she said, 'and I love them both like my own.'

When she was gone Haluin lay silent for a while, but his eyes were open and clear, and the lines of his face alert and aware.

'Was there indeed a girl who came in?' he said at last, frowning in the effort to recall a moment which had become hazy and uncertain in his mind. 'I have been lying here trying to recall why I so started up. I remember the crutches dropping away from under me, but very little besides. Coming into the warmth made my head go round.'

'Yes,' said Cadfael, 'there was a girl. Half-sister, it seems, to Cenred, but younger by some twenty years. If you were thinking you dreamed her, no, she was no dream. She came into the hall from the solar, all unaware of us, and perhaps not liking the look of us, she drew back again in haste and closed the door between. Do you not remember that?'

No, he did not remember it, or only as an unconnected

snatch of vision comes back out of a dream, and is gone again as soon as glimpsed. He frowned after it anxiously, and shook his head as if to clear eyes misted by weariness. 'No . . . there's nothing clear to me. I do recall the door opening, I take your word for it she came in . . . but I can recall nothing, no face . . . Tomorrow, perhaps.'

'We shall see no more of her,' said Cadfael, 'if that devoted dragon of hers has any say in the matter. I think she has no very high opinion of monks, Mistress Edgytha. Well, are you minded for sleep? Shall I put out the lamp?'

But if Haluin had no clear recollection of the daughter of the house, no image left from that brief glimpse of her, first a dark outline against candlelight, then lit from before by the ruddy glow of the torch, Cadfael had a very clear image, one that grew even clearer when the lamp was quenched and he lay in the dark beside his sleeping companion. And beyond the remembrance he had a strange, disquieting sense that it bore for him a special significance, if he could but put his finger on it. Why that should be so was a mystery to him. Wakeful in the dark, he called up the features of her face, the motion of her body as she stepped into the light, and could find nothing there that should have been meaningful to him, no likeness to any woman he had ever seen before, except as all women are sisters. Yet the sense of some elusive familiarity about her persisted.

A tall girl, though perhaps not so tall as she gave the impression of being, for her slenderness contributed to the image, but above the middle height for a girl just becoming woman. Her bearing was erect and graceful, but still with the tentative and vulnerable springiness of the child, the suddenness of a lamb or a fawn, alert to every sound and motion. Startled, she had sprung back from them, and yet she had closed the door with measured softness, not to startle in return. And her face – she was not beautiful, except as youth and innocence and gallantry are always beautiful. An oval face she had, tapered from broad brow and wide and wide-set eyes to the firm, rounded chin. Her head was uncovered, her brown hair drawn back and braided, still further emphasising the high white brow and the great eyes under their level dark brows and long lashes. The eyes consumed half the face. Not pure brown, Cadfael thought, for in spite of their darkness they had a clarity and depth and brightness perceptible even in that one glimpse of her. Rather a dark hazel shot with green, and so clear and deep it seemed possible to plunge into them and drown. Eyes utterly candid and vulnerable, and quite fearless. Young, wild, mettlesome creatures of the woods, never yet hunted or harmed, may have that look. And the pure, fine lines of her cheekbones Cadfael remembered, elegant and strong, after the eyes her chief distinction.

And in all of this, sharply defined in his mind's eye, what was there to trouble him, to pierce him like an elusive memory of some other woman? He found himself summoning up, one by one, the faces of women he had known, half the population of a long and varied life, in case some cast of features or carriage of head or gesture of hand should strike the chord that would vibrate and sing for him. But there was no match, and no echo. Cenred's sister remained unique and apart, haunting him thus only because she had appeared and vanished in a moment, and he would probably never see her again.

Nevertheless, the last fleeting vision within his eyelids as he fell asleep was of her startled face.

By morning the air had lost its frosty bite, and most of the snow that had fallen had already thawed and vanished, leaving its tattered laces along the foot of every wall and under the bole of every tree. Cadfael looked out from the hall door, and was inclined to wish that the fall had persisted, to prevent Haluin from insisting on taking to the road again immediately. As it turned out he need not have worried, for as soon as the manor was up and about its daily business Cenred's steward came looking for them, with the request that they would come to his lord in the solar after they had broken their fast, for he had something to ask of them.

Cenred was alone in the room when they entered, Haluin's crutches sounding hollowly on the boards of the floor. The room was lit by two deep, narrow windows with cushioned seats built into them, and furnished with handsome benchchests along one wall, a carved table, and one princely chair for the lord's use. Evidently the lady Emma ran a well-regulated household, for hangings and cushions were of fine embroidery, and the tapestry frame in one corner, with its half-finished web of bright colours, showed that they were of home production.

'I hope you have slept well, Brothers,' said Cenred, rising to greet them. 'Are you recovered fully from last night's indisposition? If there is anything my house has failed to offer you, you have but to ask for it. Use my manor as you would your own dwelling. And you will, I hope, consent to stay yet a day or two before you need set out again.'

Cadfael shared the hope, but was all too afraid that Haluin would rouse his over-anxious conscience to find objections. But he had no time to do more than open his mouth, for Cenred went on at once:

'For I have something to ask of you . . . Is either of you ordained a priest?'

Chapter Seven

'YES,' SAID Haluin, after a moment of blank silence. 'I am a priest. I studied for minor orders from the time I entered the abbey, and became full priest when I reached thirty years. We are encouraged to do so now, those who enter young and are already lettered. As a priest, what is there I can do to serve you?'

'I want you to conduct a marriage,' said Cenred.

This time the silence was longer, and their concentration on him more wary and thoughtful. For if a marriage was contemplated in this house, surely provision would already have been made for a priest, and one who knew the circumstances and the parties, not a chance Benedictine benighted here by a fall of snow. Cenred saw their doubts reflected in Haluin's attentive face.

'I know what you would say. This must surely be the proper business of my own parish priest. There is no church here in Vivers, though I intend to build and endow one. And it so happens that our nearest parish church is at this moment without a priest until it pleases the bishop to name his choice, for the advowson is with him. I had meant to send for a cousin of our house who is in orders, but if you are willing we may spare him a wintry journey. I promise you there is nothing underhand in this matter, and if it is being arranged in some haste, there are sound reasons. Sit down with me, at least, and I'll tell you freely all you need to know, and you shall judge.'

With the impulsive and generous vehemence that seemed to be natural to him, he strode forward himself to support Haluin by the forearms as he lowered himself to the cushioned bench built against the panelled wall. Cadfael sat down beside his friend, content to watch and listen, since he was no priest, and here had no hard decision to consider, and the delay came gratefully to him for Haluin's sake.

'In his old age,' said Cenred, coming bluntly to the business in hand, 'my father married a second time, a wife thirty years younger than he was. I was already married, with a son a year old, when my sister Helisende was born. Those two children grew up in this house, boy and girl together, like brother and sister, and close at that. And we, their elders, have taken them for granted and been glad they should have each other's company. I have been much to blame. I never noticed when they began to be more than playmates. I never thought how childish companionship and affection could change so after years, into something more perilous by far. I do not blink away facts, Brothers, once I have seen them, and been forced to see them. Those two were left alone to play too long and too lovingly. They have slipped into an inordinate affection under my very nose, and I stone blind to it until almost too late. They love each other in a fashion and to a degree that is anathema between two so closely kin. Thanks be to God, they have not sinned in the flesh, not yet. I hope I have awakened in time. God knows I want what is best for them both, I would have them happy, but what happiness can there be in a love which is an abomination? Better by far to tear them apart now, and trust to time to take away the pain. I have sent my son to serve his apprenticeship to arms with my overlord, who is a good friend, and knows the reason and the need. And sore as he is at being banished so, my son has pledged himself not to return until I give him leave. Have I done right?'

'I think,' said Haluin slowly, 'you could have done no other. But it is a pity it went so far unchecked.'

'So it is. But when two grow up from babes together as brother and sister, that in itself is commonly enough to put away from them without grief all thought of affection after the way of marriage. I have wondered sometimes how much Edgytha noticed that I did not. She indulged them always. But never, never did she say word to me or my wife, and whether I have done well or not, I must go on.'

'Tell me,' said Cadfael, speaking for the first time, 'is not your son's name Roscelin?'

Cenred's eyes flashed to Cadfael's face, astonished. 'So it is.

But how can you know that?'

'And your overlord is Audemar de Clary. Sir, we came hither directly from Elford, we have spoken with your son there, he lent Brother Haluin here a strong arm to lean on when he needed it.'

'You have talked with him! And what did my son have to say, there at Elford. What had he to say of me?' He was alert and ready to hear bitter rumour of complaint and estrangement, and to swallow that grief if he must.

'Very little, and certainly nothing you could not have heard with a quiet mind. No word of your sister. He mentioned that he had left home at his father's wish, and that he could not refuse you the obedience due. We had no more than a few minutes' talk with him, by pure chance. But I saw nothing there of which you should not be glad and proud. Consider, he is barely three miles away, and against his own wish, but he keeps true to his word. There is but one thing I remember him saying,' pursued Cadfael with sudden probing intent, 'that perhaps you have a father's right to hear. He asked us, very solemnly, whether our order could provide a worthwhile life for a man – if the life he most longed for was forbidden to him.'

'No!' cried Cenred in sharp protest. 'Not that! I would not for the world he should turn his back on arms and reputation and hide himself away in the cloister. He is not made for that! A youth of such promise! Brother, this does but confirm me in what I am asking. There is no putting off what must be done. Once done, he will accept it. As long as the loss is not final he will go on hoping and hankering after the impossible. It is why I want her married, married and out of this house, before ever Roscelin enters it again.'

'I understand your reasons very well,' said Haluin, opening his hollow eyes challengingly wide, 'but it would not be right to make them reasons for a marriage, if the lady is unwilling. However hard your plight, you cannot sacrifice the one to preserve the other.'

'You mistake the case,' said Cenred without heat. 'I love my young sister, I have talked with her openly and fairly. She knows, she acknowledges, the enormity of what threatened them both, the impossibility of such a love ever coming to fruit. She wants this terrible knot severed, as truly as I do. She wants a career of honour for Roscelin because she loves him, and rather than see it blighted through her she agrees to seek refuge in marriage with another man. This has been no forced surrender. And no wanton choice, either. I have done the best I could for her, it is a match any family would welcome. Jean de Perronet is a well-endowed, well-conditioned young man of good estate. He is due here today, so you may see him for yourself. Helisende already knows him, and likes if she cannot yet love him. That may come, for he is greatly drawn to her. She has fully consented to this marriage. And de Perronet has this one inestimable advantage,' he added grimly, 'his seat is far away. He will take her home to Buckingham, out of Roscelin's sight. Out of sight, out of mind I will not say, but at least the lines of a remembered face may fade gradually over the years, as even stubborn wounds heal.'

He had become eloquent by reason of his own deep disquiet and distress, a good man concerned for the best interests of all his household. He had not remarked, as Cadfael did, the gradual blanching of Haluin's thin face, the tight and painful set of his lips, or the way his linked hands gripped together in the lap of his habit until the bones shone white through the flesh. The words Cenred had not deliberately chosen to pierce or move had their own inspired force to reopen the old wound he had come all this way to try and heal. The lines of a remembered face, surely somewhat dimmed in eighteen years, were burning into vivid life again for him. And wounds that have not ceased to fester within cannot heal until they have again broken out and been cleansed, by fire if need be.

'And you need not fear, and neither need I,' said Cenred, 'that she will not be cherished and held in high regard with de Perronet. Two years back he asked for her, and for all she would have none of him or any suitor then, he has waited his time.'

'Your lady is in agreement in this matter?' asked Cadfael.

'We have all three talked of it together. And we are agreed. Will you do it? I felt it a kind of blessing on what we intend,' said Cenred simply, 'when a priest came to my door unsummoned on the eve of the bridegroom's coming. Stay over tomorrow, Brother – Father! – and marry them.'

Haluin unlocked his contorted hands slowly, and drew breath like a man awaking in pain. In a low voice he said: 'I will stay. And I will marry them.'

'I trust I have done right,' said Haluin, when they were back in their own quarters. But it did not seem that he was asking to be confirmed in his decision, rather setting it squarely before his own eyes as a responsibility he had no intention of hedging or sharing. 'I know only too well,' he said, 'the perils of proximity, and their case is more desperate than ever was mine. Cadfael, I feel myself listening to echoes I thought had died out long ago. It is all for a purpose. Nothing is without purpose. How if I fell only to show me how far I was already fallen, and force me to make the assay to rise afresh? How if I came to life again as a cripple, to make me undertake those journeys of body and spirit that I dreaded when I was strong and whole? How if God put it into my mind to go on pilgrimage in order to become some other needy soul's miracle? Were we led to this place?'

'Driven, rather,' said Cadfael practically, remembering the blinding snow, and the small beckoning spark of the torch in the drifting dark.

'It's true, to arrive on the eve of the bridegroom's coming is very apt timing. I can but go with the burden of the day,' said Haluin, 'and hope to be led aright. These second marriages in old age, Cadfael, have sorry tangles to answer for. How can two babes playing together in the rushes of the floor know that they are aunt and nephew, and fruit forbidden? A pity that love should be spent to no end.'

'I am not sure,' said Cadfael, 'that love is ever spent for no end. Well, at least now you can be still and rest for a day or so, and all the better for it. That, at any rate, comes timely.'

And that was plainly the best use Haluin could make of this halt on the way home, since he had already tried himself very near the end of his endurance. Cadfael left him in peace, and went out to take a daylight look at this manor of Vivers. A cloudy day with a fitful wind, the air free of frost, and occasional fine drifts of rain in the air, but none that lasted long.

He walked the width of the enclave to the gate, to see the full extent of the house. There were windows in the steep roof above the solar, probably two retired rooms were available there. Haluin and his companion had been accommodated considerately on the living floor. No doubt one of those upper chambers was being prepared at this moment for the expected bridegroom. The daily bustle about the courtyard seemed everywhere to be in hand without haste or confusion; things were well ordered here.

Beyond the pale of the stockade the soft, undulating landscape extended in field and copse and sparsely treed upland, all the greens still bleached and dried with winter, but the black branches showed here and there the first nodules of the leaf-buds of spring. Faint frills of snow outlined all the hollows and sheltered places, but a gleam of sun was breaking through the low cloud, and by noon all the remnant of last night's fall would be gone.

Cadfael looked into the stables and the mews, and found both well supplied and proudly kept by servitors ready and willing to show them off to an interested visitor. In a separate stall in the kennels a hound bitch lay curled in clean straw with her six pups around her, perhaps five weeks old. He could not resist going into the dim shed to take up one of the young ones, and the dam was complacent, and welcomed admiration of her brood. The soft warmth of the small body in his arms had a smell like new bread. He was just stooping to lay the pup back among its siblings when a clear, cool voice behind him said:

'Are you the priest who is to marry me?'

And there she was in the doorway, again a shadowy form against the light, so composed, so assured that she might easily be taken for a mature and stately woman of thirty, though the fresh, light voice belonged to her proper age. The girl Helisende Vivers, not yet decked out to receive her bridegroom, but in a plain housewifely gown of dark blue wool, and with a gently steaming pail of meat and meal for the hounds in one hand.

'Are you the priest who is to marry me?'

'No,' said Cadfael, slowly straightening up from the wriggling litter and the crooning bitch. 'That is Brother Haluin. I never studied for orders. I know myself better.'

'It's the lame man, then,' she said with detached sympathy. 'I am sorry he suffers such hardship. I hope they have made him comfortable, here in our house. You do know about my marriage – that Jean comes here today?'

'Your brother has told us,' said Cadfael, watching the features of her oval face emerge softly from shadow, in every plaintive, ingenuous line testifying to her youth. 'But there are things he could not tell us,' he said, watching her intently, 'except by hearsay. Only you can tell us whether this match has your consent, freely given, or no.'

Her brief silence at that did not suggest hesitation so much as a grave consideration of the man who raised the question. Her large eyes, dauntlessly honest, embraced and penetrated, quite unafraid of being penetrated in return. If she had judged him so alien to her needs and predicament as to be unacceptable, she would have closed the encounter there and then, civilly but without satisfying what would then have been mere intrusive curiosity. But she did not.

'If we do anything freely, once we are grown,' she said, 'then yes, this I do freely. There are rules that must be kept. There are others in the world with us who have rights and needs, and we are all bound. You may tell Brother Haluin – Father Haluin I must call him – that he need have no qualms for me. I know what I am doing. No one is forcing my hand.'

'I will tell him so,' said Cadfael. 'But I think you do it for others, not for yourself.'

'Then say to him that I choose – freely – to do it for others.'

'And what of Jean de Perronet?' said Cadfael.

For one instant her firm, full lips shook. It was the one thing that still disrupted her resolute composure, that she was not being fair to the man who was to be her husband. Cenred would certainly not have told him that he was getting only a sad remainder after the heart was gone. Nor could she tell him so. The secret belonged only to the family. The only hope for this hapless pair was that love might come with time, a kind of love, better, perhaps, than many marriages ever achieve, but still far short of the crown.

'I will try,' she said steadily, 'to give him all that he is asking, all that he wants and expects. He deserves well, he shall have the best I can do.'

There was no point in saying to her that it might not be enough, she already knew that, and was uneasy about a degree of deception she could not evade. It might even be, that what had already been said here in the dimness of the kennels had re-opened a deep abyss of doubt which she had almost succeeded in sealing over. Better let well alone, where there was no possibility of rendering the load she carried any lighter.

'Well, I pray you may be blessed in all you do,' said Cadfael, and drew back out of her way. The bitch had uncoiled herself from among her puppies and was nuzzling the pail, and waving a feathered tail in hungry expectation. The ordinary business of the day goes on through births, marriages, deaths and festivals. When he looked back from the doorway the girl Helisende was stooping to fill the bitch's bowl, the heavy braid of her brown hair swinging among the scrambling litter. She did not look up, but for all that he had the feeling that she was deeply and vulnerably aware of him until he turned and walked softly away.

*

'You'll miss your nurseling,' said Cadfael, when Edgytha came at noon to serve food and drink for them. 'Or will you be going south with her when she's married?'

The old woman lingered, taciturn by nature but visibly in need of unburdening a heart by no means reconciled to losing her darling. Within the stiff folds of her wimple her withered cheek trembled.

'What should I do at my age, in a strange place? I am too old to be of much value now, I shall stay here. At least I know the way of things here, and everyone knows me. What respect should I have in a strange household? But she'll go, I know that! She'll go, I suppose, as go she must. And the young man's well enough – if my lamb had not another in her eye and in her heart.'

'And one placed so far out of reach,' Haluin reminded her gently, but his own face was pale, and when she turned and looked at him in silence for a long moment he averted his eyes and turned away his head.

Her eyes were the pale, washed blue of fading harebells. Once, shadowed by lashes now grown thin and meagre, they might have resembled more the colour of periwinkles. 'So my lord will have told you,' she said. 'So they all say. And if there's no help, she might do much worse. I know! I came here in attendance on her mother, all those years ago, and that was no lover's match, neither, her so young, and him nigh on three times her age. A decent, kind man he was, but old, old! She had good need, poor lady, of someone from home, someone she knew well and could trust. At least they're marrying my girl to somebody young.'

Cadfael asked what had been preoccupying his mind for some little while, since no word had been said on the matter: 'Is Helisende's mother dead?'

'No, not dead. But she took the veil at Polesworth, it must be eight years ago now, after the old lord died. She's within your own order, a Benedictine nun. She had always a leaning towards it, and when her husband died, and she began to be talked about and bargained about as widow ladies are, and urged to marry again, rather than that she left the world. It's one way of escape,' said Edgytha, and set her lips grimly.

'And left her daughter motherless?' said Haluin, with more reproof in his voice than he intended.

'She left her daughter very well mothered! She left her to the lady Emma and to me!' Edgytha smouldered for a moment, and subdued the brief fire within lowered eyelids. 'Three mothers that child has had, and all fond. My lady Emma could never be harsh to any young thing. Too soft, indeed, the pair of them could always get their will of her. But my own lady was given to solitude and melancholy, and when it came to a new marriage, no, she would not, she took the veil gladly rather than marry again.'

'Helisende has never considered that refuge? asked Cadfael.

'Not she, God forbid she ever should! My girl was never of that mind. For those who take to it kindly it may be bliss, but for those who are pressed into it, it must be a hell on earth! If you'll pardon my tongue, Brothers! You know your own vocation best, and no doubt you took the cowl for the best of reasons, but Helisende . . . No, I would not want that for her. Better by far this Perronet lad, if there has to be a second-best.' She had begun to gather up the platters and dishes they had emptied, and took up the pitcher to refill their cups. 'I did hear say that you've been at Elford, and seen Roscelin there. Is that true?'

'Yes,' said Cadfael, 'we left Elford only yesterday. We did, by chance, have some brief talk with the young man, but never knew until this morning that he came from this neighbouring manor of Vivers.'

'And how did he look?' she asked longingly. 'Is he well? Was he down in spirits? I have not seen him for a month or more, and I know how ill he took it that he should be sent away like some offending page from his own home, when he had done no wrong, nor thought none. As good a lad as ever stepped! What had he to say?'

'Why, he was in excellent health at any rate,' said Cadfael cautiously, 'and very fair spirits, considering all. It's true he did complain of being banished, and was very ill-content where he is. Naturally he said little about the circumstances, seeing we were chance comers and unknown to him, and I daresay he would have said no more to anyone else who had as little business in the matter. But he did say he had given his word to abide by his father's orders, and wait for leave before he'd venture home.'

'But he does not know,' she said, between anger and helplessness, 'what's being planned here. Oh, he'll get leave to come home fast enough as soon as Helisende is out of the house, and far away south on her way to that young man's manor. And what a homecoming that will be for the poor lad! Shame to deal so behind his back!'

'They think it for the best,' said Haluin, pale and moved. 'Even for his best interests, they believe. And this matter is hard even for them. If they are mistaken in hiding this marriage from him until it is over, surely they may be forgiven.'

'There are those,' said Edgytha darkly, 'who never will be.' She picked up her wooden tray, and the keys at her girdle chimed faintly as she moved towards the door. 'I wish this had been honestly done. I wish he had been told. Whether he could ever have her or not, he had a right to know, and to give his blessing or his ban. How was it you were brought in touch with him there, to know the half of his name but not the whole?'

'It was the lady mentioned his name,' said Cadfael, 'when de Clary came in from riding, and the young man was with him. Roscelin, she called him. It was later we spoke with him. He saw my friend here stiff from a night on his knees, and came to lend him an arm to lean on.'

'So he would!' she said, warming. 'To anyone he saw in need. The lady, you say? Audemar's lady?'

'No, our errand was not to him, we never saw his wife and children. No, this was his mother, Adelais de Clary.'

The dishes jangled momentarily on Edgytha's tray. With care she balanced it on one hand, and reached to the latch of the door. 'She is there? There at Elford?'

'She is. Or she was when we left, yesterday, and with the snow coming so shortly after, she is surely there still.'

'She visits very rarely,' said Edgytha, shrugging. 'They say there's small love lost between her and her son's wife. That's no uncommon thing, either, I suppose, so they're just as well apart.' She nudged the door open expertly with an elbow, and swung the large tray through the doorway edgewise. 'Do you hear the horses, outside there? That will be Jean de Perronet's party riding in.'

There was nothing clandestine or secretive, certainly, about Jean de Perronet's arrival, though nothing ceremonious or showy, either. He came with one body-servant and two grooms, and with two led horses for the bride and her attendant, and pack-horses for the baggage. The entire entourage was practical and efficient, and de Perronet himself went very plainly, without flourishes in his dress or his manner, though Cadfael noted with appreciation the quality of his horseflesh and harness. This young man knew where to spend his money, and where to spare.

They had gone out, Haluin and Cadfael together, to watch the guests dismount and unload. The afternoon air was again clearing towards a night frost, but there were scudding clouds in the upper air, and might be further flurries of snow in the dark hours. The travellers would be well content to be under a sound roof and out of the chilly wind.

De Perronet dismounted from his flecked roan horse before the door of the hall, and Cenred came striding down the steps to meet him and embrace him, and lead him by the hand up to the doorway, where the lady Emma waited to welcome him as warmly. Helisende, Cadfael noted, did not appear. At supper at the high table she would have no choice but to attend, but at this stage it was fitting that the honours of the house should rest with her brother and his wife, the guardians of her person and the disposers of her marriage. Host, hostess and guest vanished within the great hall. Cenred's servants and de Perronet's grooms unloaded baggage and stabled horses, and went about the business so practically that within a matter of minutes the courtyard was empty.

So that was the bridegroom! Cadfael stood considering what he had seen, and so far could find no fault in it except that it was, as Edgytha had said, a second-best. And a second-best was all that boy would gain. A young man of perhaps twenty-five or twenty-six, already accustomed to authority and responsibility by his bearing, and well capable of handling them. His men, these favoured ones at least, were easy with him. He knew his business as they knew theirs, and there was an air of mutual respect between them. Moreover, he was a goodlooking young man, tall and shapely, of open, amiable countenance, and by the look of him in the happiest possible humour on the eve of his marriage. Cenred had done his best for his young sister, and his best promised to turn out very well. A pity it could not have been what her heart desired.

'But what else could he have done?' said Haluin, betraying in few words the depth of his own dismay and doubt.

Chapter Eight

IN THE late afternoon Cenred sent his steward to ask the two Benedictine brothers if they felt able to join his household at supper in hall, or if Father Haluin preferred to continue his rest in retirement, and be waited on in his own chamber. Haluin, who had withdrawn into a dark, inward meditation, would certainly rather have remained apart, but felt it discourteous to absent himself any longer, and made the effort to emerge from his anxious silence, and do honour to the company at the high table. They had given him a place close to the bridal pair, by virtue of his office as the priest who was to marry them. Cadfael, seated a little apart, had them all in view. And below, in the body of the hall, the whole household assembled in its due ranks, under the glow of the torches.

It occurred to Cadfael, watching Haluin's grave face, that this would be the first time his friend had ever been called upon to be go-between for God. It was true that the young brothers were being encouraged to aim at orders, more now than ever in the past, but many of them would be, as Haluin was, priests without pastoral cares, who in a long life would probably never christen, never marry, never bury, never ordain others to follow them in the same sheltered paths. It is a terrible responsibility, thought Cadfael, who had never aspired to ordination, to have the grace of God committed to a man's hands, to be privileged and burdened to play a part in other people's lives, to promise them salvation in baptism, to lock their lives together in matrimony, to hold the key to purgatory at their departing. If I have meddled, he thought devoutly, and God knows I have, when need was and there was no better man to attempt it, at least I have meddled only as a fellow-sinner, tramping the same road, not as a vicomte of heaven, stooping to raise up. Now Haluin faces this same terrible demand, and no wonder if he is afraid.

He looked along the array of faces which Haluin, being so close beside them, could see only as overlapping profiles, each briefly seen as the ripple of movement flowed along the high table, and lit deceptively by the falling glow of the torches. Cenred's broad, open, blunt-featured countenance a little drawn and taut with strain, but resolutely jovial, his wife presiding over the table with determined amiability and a somewhat anxious smile, de Perronet in happy innocence, shining with evident pleasure at having Helisende seated beside him and all but his already. And the girl, pale and quiet and resolutely gracious at his side, doing her gallant best to respond to his brightness, since this grief was no fault of his, and she had acknowledged that he deserved better. Seeing them thus together, there was no question of the man's attachment, and if he missed the like radiance in her, perhaps he accepted that as the common ground on which marriages begin, and was ready and willing to be patient until the bud came to flower.

This was the first time Haluin had seen the girl since she had startled him to his feet here in the hall, and brought him down in that crashing fall, half-dazed as he already was by the stinging wind and the blinding snow. And this stiff young figure in her best, gilded by the torchlight, might have been a stranger, never before seen. He looked at her, when chance brought her profile into clear view, with doubt and bewilderment, burdened by a responsibility new to him, and heavy to bear.

It was late when the women withdrew from the high table, leaving the men to their wine, though they would not sit here in hall much longer. Haluin looked round to catch Cadfael's eye, agreeing in a glance that it was time for them to leave host and guest together, and Haluin was already reaching for his crutches and bracing himself for the effort of rising, when Emma came in again from the solar with a flustered step and an anxious face, a young maidservant at her heels.

'Cenred, here's something strange happened! Edgytha is

gone out and has not returned, and now it's beginning to snow again, and where should she be going, thus in the night? I sent for her to attend me to bed, as always, and she's nowhere to be found, and now Madlyn here says that she went out hours ago, as soon as it was dusk.'

Cenred was slow to turn his mind from his hospitable duty towards his guest to an apparently small domestic problem, surely the women's business rather than his.

'Why, Edgytha may surely go out if she so chooses,' he said good-humouredly, 'and will come back when she chooses no less. She's a free woman, knows her own mind, and can be trusted to mind her duties. If she's once missing when she's called for, that's no great matter. Why should you worry over it?'

'But when does she ever do so without saying? Never! And now it's snowing again, and she's been gone four hours or more, if Madlyn says true. How if she's come to harm? She would not stay away so long of her own will. And you know how I value her. I would not for the world that any harm should come to her.'

'No more would I,' said Cenred warmly, 'nor to any of my people. If she's gone astray we'll look for her. But no need to fret before we know of any mishap. Here, girl, speak up, what is it you know of the matter? You say she went out some hours ago?'

'Sir, so she did!' Madlyn came forward willingly, wide-eyed with half-pleasurable excitement. 'It was after we'd made all ready. I was coming in from the dairy, and I saw her come forth from the kitchen with her cloak about her, and I said to her that this was like to be a busy night, and she'd be missed, and she said she'd be back before she was called for. It was just beginning to get dark then. I never thought she'd be gone so long.'

'And did you not ask her where she was going?' demanded Cenred.

'I did,' said the girl, 'though it was little enough she was ever likely to tell about her own business, and I should have known she'd make a sour answer if she made any at all. But there's no sense to be made of it. She said she was going to find a cat,' said Madlyn in baffled innocence, 'to put among the pigeons.'

If it meant nothing to her, it had a meaning for Cenred and for his wife, who plainly heard it now for the first time. Emma's startled gaze flew to her husband's face as he came abruptly to his feet. The look they exchanged Cadfael could read as if he had the words ringing in his ears. He had been given clues enough to make the reading easy. Edgytha was nurse to them both, indulged them, loved them like her own, resents even their separation, whatever the church and the ties of blood may say, and much more this marriage that makes the separation final. She is gone to enlist help to prevent what she deplores, even at this last moment. She is gone to tell Roscelin what is being done behind his back. She is gone to Elford.

None of which could be said aloud, here in front of Jean de Perronet, who stood now at Cenred's side, looking from face to face round the circle, puzzled and sympathetic in a domestic trouble which was none of his business. An old servant gone missing in the evening, with night coming on and snow falling, called for at least a token search. He made the suggestion ingenuously, filling a silence which at any moment might have caused him to look more narrowly at what was happening here.

'Should we not look for her, if she's been gone so long? The ways are not always safe at night, and for a woman venturing alone. . .'

The diversion came as a blessing, and Cenred seized on it gratefully. 'So we will. I'll send out a party by the most likely way. It may be she's only been delayed by the snow, if she intended a visit in the village. But this need not give you any concern, Jean. I would not wish your stay to be marred. Leave this matter to my men, we have enough in the household. And rest assured she cannot be far, we shall soon find her and see her safe home.'

'I will gladly come out with you,' de Perronet offered.

'No, no, I will not have it. Let all things here go as we have planned them, and nothing spoil the occasion. Use my house as your own, and take your night's rest with a quiet mind, for tomorrow this small flurry will be over and done.'

It was not difficult to persuade the helpful guest to abandon his generous intention, perhaps it had been made only as a courteous gesture. A man's household affairs are his, and best left to him. It is civil to offer help, but wise to give way gracefully. Cenred knew very well now where Edgytha had set out to go, there would be no question of which road to take in hunting for her. Moreover, there was some genuine call for concern, for in four hours she could have been there and back even in snow. Cenred quit his supper-table purposefully, driving the men of his following before him to muster within the hall door. He bade de Perronet an emphatic goodnight, which was accepted pliantly as dismissal even from this domestic conference, and issued brisk orders to those of his servants whom he chose to go with the search party, six of the young and vigorous and his steward with them.

'What must we do?' Brother Haluin wondered half-aloud, standing with Cadfael a little apart.

'You,' said Cadfael, 'must go to your bed, like a sensible man, and sleep if you can. And a prayer or two will not come amiss. I am going with them.'

'Along the nearest road to Elford,' said Haluin heavily.

'To find a cat to put among the pigeons. Yes, where else? But you stay here. There is nothing you could do or say, if there has to be speech, that I cannot.'

The hall door was opened, the party tramped down the steps into the courtyard, two of them carrying torches. Cadfael, following last, looked out upon a glittering, frosty night. The ground was covered but meagrely, small, needle-sharp flakes out of an almost clear sky, brittle with stars and too cold for a heavy fall. He looked back from the doorway, and saw the women of the house, gentlefolk and servants alike, drawn together in mutual uneasiness in the far corner of the hall, all eyes following their departing menfolk, the maids huddling close, Emma with her smooth, gentle face wrung in distress, and pulling nervously at her plump fingers.

And Helisende standing a pace apart, the only one not clinging to her kind for comfort. She was far enough back from one of the sconces for the torchlight to show her face fully, without exaggerated shadows. All that Emma had reported to her husband, all that Madlyn had told, Helisende surely knew now. She knew where Edgytha was gone, she knew for what purpose. She was staring wide-eyed into a future she could no longer foretell, where the results of this night's work hid themselves in bewilderment and dismay and possible catastrophe. She had prepared herself for a willing sacrifice, but she found herself utterly unprepared for whatever threatened now. Her face seemed as still and composed as ever, yet it had lost all its calm and certainty, her resolution had become helplessness, and her resignation changed to desperation. She had arrived at an embattled ground she believed she could hold, at whatever cost to herself, and now that ground shook and parted under her feet, and she was no longer in control of her own fate. The image of her shattered gallantry, disarmed and vulnerable, was the last glimpse Cadfael carried out with him into the darkness and the frost.

Cenred drew his cloak close about his face against the wind, and set out from the gate of the manor on a path that was strange to Cadfael. With Haluin he had turned in from the distant highway, straight towards the gleam of light from the manor torches, but this way slanted back to strike the road much nearer to Elford, and would probably cut off at least half a mile of the distance. The night had its own lambent light, partly from the stars, partly from the thin covering of snow, so that they were able to go quickly, spread out in a line centred upon the path. The country here was open, at first bare of trees, then threading a belt of woods and scrubland. They heard nothing but their own footsteps and breath, and the soft whining of the wind among the bushes. Twice Cenred halted them to have silence, and called aloud to the night, but got no answer.

For one who knew this path well, Cadfael calculated, the distance to Elford would be roughly two miles. Edgytha could have been back in Vivers long ago, and by what she had said to the maid Madlyn she had intended to return in ample time to be at her mistress's disposal after supper. Nor could she have strayed from a known way on so bright a night, and in barely more than a sprinkling of snow. It began to seem clear to him that something had happened to prevent either her errand, or her safe return from it. Not the rigours of nature or the caprice of chance, but the hand of man. And on such a night those outcast creatures who preyed upon travellers, even if any such existed here in this open country, were unlikely to be out and about their dark business, since their prey would hardly be eager to venture out in such a frost. No, if any man had intervened to prevent Edgytha from reaching her goal, it was with deliberate intent. There was, perhaps, one better possibility, that if she had reached Roscelin with her news, he had persuaded her not to return, but to remain at Elford in safety and leave the rest to him. But Cadfael was not sure that he believed in that. If it had happened so, Roscelin would already have been striding indignantly into the hall at Vivers before ever Edgytha had been missed from her place.

Cadfael had drawn close alongside Cenred, pressing forward in haste in the centre of his line of hunters, and one dark, sidelong glance saluted and recognised him, without great surprise. 'There was no need, Brother,' said Cenred shortly. 'We are enough for the work.'

'One more will do no harm,' said Cadfael.

No harm, but possibly none too welcome. As well if this matter could be kept strictly private to the Vivers household. Yet it seemed that Cenred was not greatly troubled by the presence of a chance Benedictine monk among his search party. He was intent on finding Edgytha, and preferably before she reached Elford, or failing that, in time to negate whatever mischief she had set afoot. Perhaps he expected to meet his son somewhere along the way, coming in haste to prevent that marriage that would destroy his last vain hopes. But they had gone somewhat more than a mile, and the night remained empty about them.

They were moving through thin, open woodland, over tufted, uneven grass, where the frozen snow lay too lightly to flatten the blades to earth, and they might have passed by the slight hummock beside the path on the right hand but for the dark ground that showed through the covering of white lace, darker than the bleached brown of the wintry turf. Cenred had passed it by, but checked sharply when Cadfael halted, and stared down as he was staring.

'Quickly, bring the torch here close!'

The yellow light outlined clearly the shape of a human body lying sprawled, head away from the path, whitened over with a crust of snow. Cadfael stooped and brushed away the crystalline veil from an upturned face, open-eyed and contorted in astonished fright, and a head of grey hair from which the hood had fallen back as she fell. She lay on her back but inclined towards her right side, her arms flung up and wide as if to ward off a blow. Her black cloak showed darkly through the filigree of white. Over her breast a small patch marred the veil, where her blood, in a meagre flow, had thawed the flakes as they fell. There was no telling immediately, from the way she lay, whether she had been on her way outward or homeward when she was struck down, but it seemed to Cadfael that at the last moment she had heard someone stealing close behind her, and whirled about with hands flung up to protect her head. The dagger her attacker had meant to slip between her ribs from behind had missed its stroke, and been plunged into her breast instead. She was dead and cold, the frost confounding all conjecture as to when she must have died.

'God's pity!' said Cenred on a whispering breath. 'This I never thought to see! Whatever she intended, why this?'

'Wolves hunt even in frost,' said his steward heavily. 'Though what rich traffic there can be for them here heaven knows! And see, there's nothing taken, not even her cloak. Masterless men would have stripped her.'

Cenred shook his head. 'There are none such in these parts, I swear. No, this is a different matter. I wonder, I wonder which way she was bound when she was struck dead!'

'When we move her,' said Cadfael, 'we may find out. What now? There's nothing now can be done for her. Whoever used the knife knew his grim business, it needed no second stroke. And whatever footprints he left behind the ground's too hard to show, even where the snow has not covered them.'

'We must carry her home,' said Cenred sombrely. 'And a sorry matter that will be for my wife and sister. They set great store by the old woman. She was always loyal and trustworthy, all these years since my young stepmother brought her into the household. This must not pass without requital! We'll send ahead to see if she ever came to Elford, and what's known of her there, and whether they have any word of chance marauders haunting these ways, perhaps on the run from other regions. Though that's hard to believe. Audemar keeps a firm hand on his lands.'

'Shall we send back and fetch a litter, my lord?' asked the steward. 'She's but a light weight, we could make shift to carry her back in her cloak.'

'No, no need to make another journey. But you, Edred, you take Jehan here with you, and go on to Elford, and find out what's known of her there, if anyone has met and spoken with her. No, take two men with you. I would not have you in any danger on the road, if there are masterless men abroad.'

The steward accepted his orders, and took one of the torches to light him the rest of the way. The small, resiny spark dwindled along the pathway towards Elford, and vanished gradually into the night. Those remaining turned to the body, and lifted it aside to unfasten and spread out on the path the cloak she wore. As soon as she was raised one thing at least was made plain.

'There's snow under her,' said Cadfael. The shrunken shape of her was dark and moist where contact had been close enough for her body's lingering warmth to melt the flakes, but all round the rim where the folds of her clothing had lain only lightly, a worn border of lace remained. 'It was after the snow began that she fell. She was on her way home.'

She was light and limp in their hands. The chill of her body was from frost, not rigor. They wound her closely in her cloak, and bound her safely with two or three belts and Cadfael's rope girdle, to give hand-holds for the servants who carried her, and so they bore her back the mile or so they had come, to Vivers.

The household was still awake and aware, unable to rest until they knew what was happening. One of the maids saw the lamentable little procession entering at the gate, and ran wailing to tell Emma. By the time they brought Edgytha's body up into the hall the whole fluttered dovecote of maids was again assembled, huddled together for comfort. Emma took charge with more resolution than might have been expected from her soft and gentle person, and swept the girls into service with a briskness that kept them from tears, preparing a trestle table in one of the small chambers for a bier, composing the disordered limbs, heating water, bringing scented linen from the chests in the hall to drape and cover the dead. The funeral ceremonies do as much for the living as for the dead, in occupying their hands and minds, and consoling them for things left undone or badly done during life. Very shortly the murmur of subdued voices from the deathchamber had softened from distress and dismay into a gentle, almost soothing elegiac crooning.

Emma came out into the hall, where her husband and his men were warming their chilled feet at the fire, and rubbing the sense back into their numbed hands.

'Cenred, how is this possible? Who could have done such a thing?'

No one attempted to answer that, nor had she looked for an answer.

'Where did you find her?'

That her husband did answer, scrubbing wearily at his furrowed forehead. 'Past the halfway to Elford by the short road, lying beside the path. And she'd been there no long time, for there was snow under her. It was on her way back here that someone struck her down.'

'You think,' said Emma in a low voice, 'she had been to Elford?'

'Where else by that path? I've sent Edred on there, to find out if she came, and who has spoken with her. In an hour or so they should be back, but whether with any news, God alone knows.'

They were both of them moving delicately about and about the heart of the matter, avoiding the mention of Roscelin's name, or any word of the reason why Edgytha should go rushing out alone on a wintry night. True, word had gone round even in the kennels and mews by then, and the entire household of Vivers was gathering uneasily, the indoor servants hovering in an anxious group in the corners of the hall, those from without prowling and peering over their shoulders, unable to withdraw to their own proper business or their normal rest until something should happen within here to scatter them. Few of all these, if any, could be in their lord's confidence in the matter of Roscelin's outlawed love, but many of them might have guessed at the undercurrents sweeping Helisende into this hasty marriage. Some reserve in speech would have to be observed in front of all this clan.

And here, to complicate matters further, came Jean de Perronet from the chamber above, where he had retired out of courtesy, but not to sleep, for he was still in his supper-table finery. And here, too, was Brother Haluin from his bed, anxious and silent. All those under the roof of Vivers that night had been drawn gradually and almost stealthily into the hall.

No, not quite all. Cadfael looked round the assembly, and missed one face. Where all others foregathered, Helisende absented herself.

By the look of his face de Perronet had been doing some serious thinking since he bowed to his host's wish, and let the search party go out into the night without him. He came into the hall with a face composed and grave, revealing nothing of what went on in his mind, took his time about looking all round the mute and dour circle of them, and looked last and longest at Cenred, who stood with his boots steaming in the ashes of the hearth, and his head bent to stare blankly into the embers of the fire.

'I think,' said de Perronet with deliberation, 'this has not ended well. You have found your maidservant?'

'We have found her,' said Cenred.

'Misused? Dead? Do you tell me you have found her dead?'

'And not of cold! Stabbed to death,' said Cenred bluntly, 'and left by the wayside. And no sign of another soul have we seen or heard along the road, though this befell no long time ago, after the snow began to fall.'

'Eighteen years she has been with us,' said Emma, wringing her hands together wretchedly under her breast. 'Poor soul, poor soul, to end like this – struck down by some outlaw vagabond to die in the cold. I would not for the world have had this happen!'

'I am sorry,' said de Perronet, 'that such a thing should be, and at such a time as this. Can there be some link between the occasion that brought me here, and this woman's death?'

'No!' cried husband and wife together, rather resisting the thought already in their minds than lying to deceive the guest. 'No,' said Cenred more softly, 'I pray there is not, I trust there is not. It is of all chances the most unhappy, yet surely no more than chance.'

'There are such unblessed chances,' admitted de Perronet, but with evident reserve. 'And they do not spare to mar festivals, even marriages. You do not wish to put off this one beyond tomorrow?'

'No, why so? It is our grief, not yours. But it is murder, and I must send to the sheriff, and loose a hunt for the murderer. She has no living kin that I know of, it is for us to bury her. What's needful we shall do. It need not cast a shadow upon you.'

'I fear it already has,' said de Perronet, 'upon Helisende. The woman, I believe, was her nurse, and dear to her.'

'The more reason you should take her away from here, to a new home and a new life.' He looked round for her then for the first time, startled not to find her there among the women, but relieved that she was not there to complicate a matter already vexed enough. If she had indeed been able to fall asleep, so much the better, let her sleep on, and know nothing worse until morning. The maidservants were drifting back from the room where they had been busy making Edgytha's body seemly. There was nothing more they could do here, and their uneasy presence, mute and fearful in hovering groups, became oppressive. Cenred stirred himself with an effort to be rid of them.

'Emma, send the women to their beds. There's no more to be done here, and they need not wait. And you, fellows, be off and get your sleep. All's done that can be done till Edred gets back from Elford, no need for the whole household to wait up for him.' And to de Perronet he said: 'I sent him on with two others of my men to inform my overlord of this death. Murder in these parts is within his writ, this will be his business no less than mine. Come, Jean, with your leave we'll withdraw to the solar, and leave the hall to the sleepers.'

Doubtless, thought Cadfael, watching the harassed lines of Cenred's face, he would be happier if de Perronet chose to draw off once again from all involvement, and stand apart, but there's no chance of that now. And however he hedges round the truth of why his steward has pushed on to Elford, the very name of that place has now assumed a significance there's no evading. And this is not a man who likes deception, or practises it with pleasure or skill.

The women had accepted their orders at once, and dispersed, still whispering and fearful, to their quarters. The menservants quenched the torches, leaving only two by the great door to light the way in, and fed and damped down the fire to burn slowly through the night. De Perronet followed his host to the door of the solar, and there Cenred, turning, waved Cadfael to join them within.

'Brother, you were a witness, you can testify to how we found her. It was you showed how the snow had begun to fall before she was struck down. Will you wait with us, and see what word my steward brings back with him?'

There was no word said as to whether Brother Haluin should consider this invitation as applying equally to him, but he caught Cadfael's eye, deprecating rather than recommending such a move, and chose rather to ignore it. Enough had already happened to exercise his mind, if he was to join two people whose imminent marriage was at least suspect of bringing about a death. He needed to know what lay behind these nocturnal wanderings, and withdraw from his commitment if he saw reason. He set his lips, and followed the company into the solar, his crutches heavy and slow in the rushes, and starting a dull echo as he stepped on to the floorboards within. He took his seat on a bench in the dimmest corner, an unobtrusive listener, as Cenred sat down wearily at the table, and spread his elbows on the board, propping his head between muscular hands.

'Your men are on foot?' asked de Perronet.

'Yes.'

'Then we may have a long wait yet before they can be here again. Had you other parties out on other roads?'

Cenred said starkly: 'No,' and offered no further words by way of explanation or excuse. Not a quarter of an hour ago, thought Cadfael, watching, he would have evaded that, or left it unanswered. Now he is gone beyond caring for discretion. Murder brings out into the open many matters no less painful, while itself still lurking in the dark.

De Perronet shut his lips and clenched his teeth on any further questioning, and set himself to wait in uncommitted patience. The night had closed in on the manor of Vivers in hushed stillness, ominous and oppressive. Doubtful if anyone in the hall slept, but if any of them moved it was furtively, and if any spoke it was in whispers.

Nevertheless, the wait was not to be as long as de Perronet had prophesied. The silence was abruptly shivered by the thudding of galloping hooves on the hard-frozen earth of the courtyard, a furious young voice yelling peremptorily for service, the frantic running of grooms without, and the hasty stirring of all the wakeful retainers within. Feet ran blindly in the dark, stumbling and rustling in the rushes, flint and steel spat sparks too brief and hasty to catch the tinder, the first torch was plunged into the turfed-down fire, and carried in haste to kindle others. Before the listeners in the solar could burst out into the hall a fist was thumping at the outer door, and an angry voice demanded entry.

Two or three ran to unbar, knowing the voice, and were sent reeling as the heavy door was flung back to the wall, and into the brightening flurry of torchlight burst the figure of Roscelin, head uncovered, flaxen hair on end from the speed of his ride, blue eyes blazing. The cold of the night blew in with him, and all the torches guttered and smoked, as Cenred, erupting out of the solar, was halted as abruptly on the threshold of the hall by his son's fiery glare.

'What is this Edred tells me of you?' demanded Roscelin. 'What have you done behind my back?'

Chapter Nine

FOR ONCE paternal authority was caught at a disadvantage, and Cenred was all too aware of it. Nor had he the past reputation of a family tyrant to fall back on, but he did his best to wrest back the lost initiative.

'What are you doing here?' he demanded sternly. 'Did I send for you? Did your lord dismiss you? Has either of us released you from your bond?'

'No,' said Roscelin, glittering. 'I have no leave from any man, and have not asked for any. And as for my bond, you loosed me from it when you played me false. It's not I who have broken faith. And as for the duty I owe to Audemar de Clary, I'll return to it if I must, and abide whatever his displeasure visits on me, but not until you render me account here openly of what you intended in the dark behind my back. I listened to you, I owned you right, I obeyed you. Did you owe me nothing in return? Not even honesty?'

Another father might well have felled him for such insolence, but Cenred had no such option. Emma was plucking anxiously at his sleeve, troubled for both her menfolk. De Perronet, alert and grim, loomed at his shoulder, eyeing the enraged boy confronting them, and already apprised of an inevitable threat to his own plans. What else could have brought this youngster haring through the night? And by all the signs he had come by the shortest road, dangerous in the dark, or he could not have arrived so soon. Nothing that had happened this night was accident or chance. The marriage of Helisende Vivers had brought about all this coil of murder and search and pursuit, and what more was to come of it there was as yet no knowing.

'I have done nothing,' said Cenred, 'of which I need to be ashamed, and nothing for which I need account to you. Well you know what your own part must be, you have agreed to it, do not complain now. I am the master in my own house, I have both rights and duties towards my family. I will discharge them as I see fit. And for the best!'

'Without the courtesy of a word to me!' flared Roscelin, burning up like a stirred fire. 'No, I must hear it only from Edred, after the damage has already begun, after a death that can surely be laid at your own door. Was that for the best? Or dare you tell me Edgytha is dead for some other cause, by some stranger's hand? That's mischief enough, even if it's no worse than that. But whose plans sent her out into the night? Dare you tell me she was on some other errand? Edred says she was on her way to Elford when someone cut her off. I am here to prevent the rest.'

'Your son refers, as I suppose,' said de Perronet, loudly and coldly, 'to the marriage arranged between the lady Helisende and me. In that matter, I think, I too have a say.'

Roscelin's wide blue stare swung from his father's face to the guest's. It was the first time he had looked at him, and the encounter held him silent for a long moment. They were not strangers to each other, Cadfael recalled. The two families were acquainted, perhaps even distant kin, and two years ago de Perronet had made a formal offer for Helisende's hand. There was no personal animosity in Roscelin's glare, rather a baffled and frustrated rage against circumstance than against this favoured suitor, to whom he could not and must not be a rival.

'*You* are the bridegroom?' he said bluntly.

'I am, and will maintain my claim. And what have you to urge against it?'

Animosity or not, they had begun to bristle like fighting cocks, but Cenred laid a restraining hand on de Perronet's arm, and frowned his son back with a forbidding gesture.

'Wait, wait! This has gone too far now to be left in the dark. Do you tell me, boy, that you heard of this marriage, as you heard of Edgytha's death, only from Edred?'

'How else?' demanded Roscelin. 'He came puffing in with

his news and roused the household, Audemar and all. Whether he meant me to hear when he blurted out word of this marriage I doubt, but I did hear it, and here am I to find out for myself what you never meant me to question. And we shall see if all is being done for the best!'

'Then you had not seen Edgytha? She never reached you?'

'How could she if she was lying dead a mile or more from Elford?' demanded Roscelin impatiently.

'It was after the snow that she died. She had been some hours gone, long enough to have reached Elford and been on her way back. *Somewhere* she had been, from somewhere she was certainly returning. Where else could it have been?'

'So you thought she had indeed reached Elford,' said Roscelin slowly. 'I never heard but that she was dead, I thought it was on her way. On her way to me! Is that what you had in mind? To warn me of what was being done here in my absence?'

Cenred's silence and Emma's unhappy face were answer enough.

'No,' he said slowly, 'I never saw hide or hair of her. Nor did anyone in Audemar's household as far as I know. If she ever was there at all, I don't know to whom she came. Certainly not to me.'

'Yet it could have been so,' said Cenred.

'It was not so. She did not come. Nevertheless,' said Roscelin relentlessly, 'here am I as if she had, having heard it from another mouth. God knows I am grieved for Edgytha, but what is there now to be done for her but bury her with reverence, and after, if we can, find and bury her murderer? But it is not too late to reconsider what was intended here for tomorrow, it is not too late to change it.'

'I marvel,' said Cenred harshly, 'that you do not charge me outright with this death.'

Roscelin was brought up short against an idea so monstrous, and stood open-mouthed with shock, his unclenched hands dangling childishly. Plainly such a notion had never entered his ingenuous head. He stammered a furious, half-inarticulate disclaimer, and abandoned it halfway to turn again upon de Perronet.

'But you – *you* had cause enough to want her stopped, if you knew she was on her way to warn me. *You* had good cause to want her silenced, so that no voice should be raised against your marriage, as now I raise mine. Was it you who did her to death on the way?'

'This is foolery,' said de Perronet with disdain. 'Everyone here knows that I have been here in plain view all the evening.'

'So you may have been, but you have men who may be used to do your work for you.'

'Every man of whom can be vouched for by your father's household. Also, you have been told already it was not on the outward way this woman was killed, but returning. What purpose would that have served for me? And now may I ask of you, father and son both,' he demanded sharply, 'what interest has this boy in his close kinswoman's marriage, that he dares to challenge either her brother's rights or her husband's?'

Now, thought Cadfael, it is all as good as out, though no one will say it plainly. For de Perronet has wits sharp enough to have grasped already what particular and forbidden passion really drives this unhappy boy. And now it depends on Roscelin whether a decent face is kept on the affair or not. Which is asking a lot of a young man torn as he is, and outraged by what he feels as a betrayal. Now we shall see his mettle.

Roscelin had blanched into a fixed and steely whiteness, his fine bones of cheek and jaw outlined starkly in the torchlight. Before Cenred could draw breath to assert his dominance, his son had done it for him.

'My interest is that of a kinsman close as a brother lifelong, and desiring Helisende's happiness beyond anything else in the world. My father's right I never have disputed, nor do I doubt he wishes her well as truly as I do. But when I hear of a marriage planned in haste and in my absence, how can I be easy in mind? I will not stand by and see her hustled into a marriage that may not be to her liking. I will not have her forced or persuaded against her will.'

'This is no such matter,' protested Cenred hotly. 'She is not being forced, she has consented willingly.'

'Then why was I to be kept in ignorance? Until the thing was done? How can I believe what your own proceedings deny?' He swung round upon de Perronet, his blanched face arduously controlled. 'Sir, against you I have no malice. I did not even know who was to be her husband. But you must see how hard it is to believe that all has been done fairly, when it has not been done openly.'

'It is in the open now,' said de Perronet shortly. 'What hinders but you should hear it from the lady's own lips? Will that content you?'

Roscelin's white face tightened yet more painfully, and for a moment he struggled visibly against his fear of inevitable rejection and loss. But he had no choice but to agree.

'If she tells me this is her choice, then I am silenced.' He did not say that he would therefore be content.

Cenred turned to his wife, who all this while had clung loyally to her husband's side, while her troubled eyes never left her son's tormented face.

'Go and call Helisende. She shall speak for herself.'

In the heavy and uneasy silence after Emma had departed it was not clear to Cadfael whether any or all of this disturbed household had found it as strange as he did that Helisende should not long ago have come down, to discover for herself the meaning of all these nocturnal comings and goings. He could not get out of his mind the last glimpse he had had of her, standing solitary among so many, suddenly lost and confounded on a road she had believed she could walk to the end with resolute dignity. In a situation so grimly changed she had lost her bearings. A wonder, though, that she had not, in defence of her own integrity, come down with the rest to discover the best or the worst when the searchers returned. Did she even know yet that Edgytha was dead?

Cenred had advanced into the half-lit hall, abandoning even the seclusion of the solar, since there was no longer any privacy to be found behind a closed door. A woman of the household had been killed. A lady of the family found her marriage the occasion of conflict and death. There was no possibility here of any separation between master and man, or mistress and maid. They waited with equal disquiet. All but Helisende, who absented herself still.

Brother Haluin had drawn back into the shadows, and sat mute and still on a bench against the wall, hunched stiffly between the crutches he hugged to his sides. His hollow dark eyes passed intently from face to face, reading and wondering. If he felt weariness, he gave no sign. Cadfael would have liked to send him away to his bed, but there hung on everyone here a compulsion so strong that there could be no departure. Only one had resisted the pull. Only one had escaped.

'What keeps the women?' fretted Cenred, as the moments dragged by. 'Does it take so long to pull on a gown?'

But it was long minutes more before Emma reappeared in the doorway, her round, gentle face full of consternation and dismay, her linked hands playing agitatedly at her girdle. Behind her the maid Madlyn peered warily, round-eyed. But of Helisende there was no sign.

'She is gone,' said Emma, too shaken and bewildered to make many words of it. 'She is not in her bed, not in her chamber, nowhere to be found in all this house. Her cloak is gone. Jehan has been out to the stables. Her saddle-horse and harness are gone with her. While you were absent she has saddled up for herself and ridden away secretly, alone.'

For once they were all alike silenced, brother, bridegroom, frustrated lover and all. While they schemed and agonised and wrangled over her fate she had taken action and fled them all. Yes, even Roscelin, for he stood stricken and amazed, utterly at a loss like all the rest. Cenred might stiffen and frown at his son, de Perronet swing round upon him in black suspicion, but plainly Roscelin had had no part in this panic flight. Even before Edgytha's death, thought Cadfael, her secret errand and failure to return had shatteered all Helisende's arduously assembled certainty. Yes, de Perronet was a decent man and an honourable match, and she had pledged herself to him to remove herself from Roscelin's path, and deliver herself and him from an unbearable situation. But if that sacrifice was to bring only anger, danger and conflict, even short of death, then all was changed. Helisende had drawn back from the brink, and cut herself free.

'She has run!' said Cenred on a gusty breath, not questioning, accepting. 'How could she do it, all unseen? And when can she have set out? Where were her maids? Was there never a groom about the stable to question her going, or at least give us warning?' He passed a helpless hand over his face, and looked round darkly at his son. 'And where would she run but to you?'

It was out now, and there was no taking it back.

'Have you hidden her away somewhere in secret, and ridden here with your false indignation to cover up the sin?'

'You cannot believe that!' said Roscelin, outraged. 'I have not seen her, not had any word from her, nor sent her any, and you know it. I'm newly ridden from Elford by that same way your men came there, and if she had been on that path we should have met. Do you think I would then have let her go anywhere alone in the night, whether on to Elford or back here? If we had met we should have been together now – wherever that might be.'

'There is a safer way by the highroad,' said de Perronet. 'Longer, but as fast on horseback, and safer going. If she did indeed set out for Elford, she may have ridden that way. She would hardly risk the same path your men had taken.'

His voice was dry and cold, and his face set in forbidding lines, but he was a practical man, and intended wasting no energy or passion on a green boy's mistaken affections. They did not threaten his position. The match he desired was arranged and accepted, and need not and would not be abandoned. What mattered now was to recover the girl unharmed.

'So she may,' agreed Cenred, encouraged. 'So most likely she would. If she reaches Elford she'll be safe enough there. But we'll send after her by the highroad, and leave nothing to chance.'

'I'll ride back by that way,' offered Roscelin eagerly, and was off towards the door of the hall with a bound, if de Perronet had not plucked him back sharply by the sleeve.

'No, not you! What we might see of either of you again, if once you met, I much mistrust. Let Cenred seek his sister, and I'm content she'll come back to speak her own mind when all this coil is over. And when she does, boy, you had best abide it, and keep your tongue within your teeth.'

Roscelin did not like being handled, nor much savour being called 'boy' by a man whose height and reach he could match, if not his years and assurance. He wrenched his arm free strongly, and stood off further affront with a blackly lowering brow.

'So Helisende be found safe and well, and let alone in very truth to speak her own mind, and not yours, sir, nor my father's, nor any other man's, overlord or priest or king or whatever he may be, I am content. And first,' he said, turning on his father between defiance and pleading, 'find her, let me see her whole and well and used with gentleness. What else matters now?'

'I am going myself,' said Cenred with reviving authority, and strode back into the solar to reclaim the cloak he had discarded.

But there was to be no more riding out from Vivers that night. Cenred had scarcely pulled on his boots again, and his grooms were no more than hoisting down saddle and harness in the stables, when there arose the purposeful stir of half a dozen horsemen riding into the courtyard, the ring of challenge and answer at the gate, the jingle of harness and dull tramping of hooves on the frozen earth.

All those within came surging to open the door and see what company this might be, so late in the night. Edred and his companions had gone on foot, and might be expected to return on foot, and here was a well-mounted troop arriving. Out went the torches into the darkness, out went Cenred, with Roscelin and de Perronet hard on his heels, and several of his menservants following.

In the yard the flickering torchlight flared and guttered and flared again on the strongly-boned countenance and massive body of Audemar de Clary, as he swung himself down from the saddle and tossed his bridle to a scurrying groom. Behind him came Edred the steward and the grooms who had been sent on with him to Elford, mounted now at de Clary's charge, along with three of Audemar's own men.

Cenred came hurrying down the steps to welcome them. 'My lord,' he said, for once formal with his friend and overlord. 'I never looked to see you tonight, but you come very timely and are more than welcome. God knows we're like to be causing you trouble enough, for we have murder here, as Edred will have told you. Murder within your writ is hard to believe, but so it is.'

'So I've heard,' said Audemar. 'Come within, and let me hear the whole tale from you. There's nothing to be done now before morning.' His eye fell on the truant Roscelin as he entered the hall, recorded the boy's grim and unrepentant countenance, and acknowledged tolerantly: 'You here, lad? That at least I expected.' Clearly the deeper reason for Roscelin's banishment was no secret from Audemar, and he had a certain easy sympathy for the boy, short of indulging his folly. He clouted him hard on the shoulder as he passed, and drew him with him into the solar. Roscelin resisted the urging, gripping his lord's sleeve urgently.

'My lord, there's more to be told. Sir,' he appealed to his father passionately, 'tell him! If she did make for Elford, where can she be now? My lord, Helisende is gone, she has ridden out alone, my father believes she must have set out for Elford – because of me! But I rode here by the rough track and saw nothing of her. Has she indeed come safely to you? Put me out of this anxiety – did she go by the highroad? Is she safe at Elford now?'

'She is not!' Brought up short against this new vexation, Audemar looked sharply from son to father and back again, well aware of the tensions that plagued them. 'We have just come by the highroad and never a sign of her or any woman have we seen. One road or the other, one of us would have met with her. Come, now!' he said, sweeping Cenred along with him in his free arm. 'Let's within, the few of us, and see what knowledge we can put together, to be used with good sense tomorrow by daylight. Madam, you should take some rest, all's done that you can do before morning, and I will make myself accountable from this on. No need for you to watch out the night.'

There was no question now as to who was master here. At his bidding Emma folded her hands thankfully, shared a glance of harried affection between her husband and her son, and departed docilely to such rest as she could hope to get before dawn. Audemar looked round once from within the solar, a sweeping glance amiable enough but unmistakable in its dominance, that dismissed all further attendance. His eye lit upon the two Benedictines, waiting unobtrusively on the edge of the scene, recognised them with a nod of easy reverence for their habit, and smiled.

'Goodnight, Brothers!' said Audemar, and drew the solar door firmly closed at his back, shutting himself in with the troubled Vivers household and their aspiring kinsman.

Chapter Ten

HE IS right!' said Brother Haluin, stretched on his bed in the pre-dawn twilight, wakeful still and loosed now from his long silence on the fringe of other men's chaos. 'Goodnight, Brothers, and goodbye! There will be no marriage. There can be no marriage, there is now no bride. And even if she should come back, this match cannot now go forward as if nothing had happened to cast it into such bitter doubt. When I accepted the burden – for even so it was burdensome – there was no call to question that it was for the best, grievous though it might be. There is good reason to question now.'

'I think,' said Cadfael, listening to the muted, deliberate voice, as Haluin felt his way towards a resolution, 'you are not sorry to be delivered from your promise.'

'No, I am not sorry. Sorry enough, God knows, that a woman has died, sorry that these children should suffer unhappiness without remedy. But I could not now be answerable to God for joining the girl to any man, unless I could recover the certainty I have lost. As well that she is gone, and I pray into some safe refuge. And now it only remains,' said Brother Haluin, 'for us to take our leave. We no longer have any part to play here. De Clary has plainly told us so. And Cenred will be glad to see us go.'

'And you have a vow to complete, and no further cause to delay. True!' said Cadfael torn between relief and regret.

'I have delayed too long already. It is time I acknowledged,' said Haluin inflexibly, 'how small are my own griefs, and how great the part I have chosen. I made the choice for my own craven sake, now with what life I have left I will make it good for a worthier reason.'

So this journey, thought Cadfael, has not been in vain. For the first time since his flight from the world, sick with his guilt and loss, he has ventured back into the world, and found it full of pain, into which his own pain has fallen and been lost, like a raindrop in the sea. All these years he has been outwardly dutiful, keeping every scruple of the Rule, and agonised in solitude within. His true vocation begins now. Once enlightened, Haluin may well prove the stuff of which saints are made. As for me, I am unregenerate man.

For in his heart he did not want to leave Vivers, thus with nothing resolved. Everything Haluin said was true. The bride was gone, there could be no marriage, they had no excuse for remaining here any longer, nor had Cenred any further use for them. He would indeed be glad to see them go. But Cadfael would not go gladly, turning his back upon a murder unavenged, justice out of kilter, a wrong that might never be set right.

True also, Audemer de Clary was overlord here, a man of force and decision, and with such crimes as fell within his writ he must deal. There was nothing Cadfael could tell him that Cenred would not already have told him.

And what, after all, did Cadfael really know in this matter? That Edgytha had been absent several hours before she died, since there was already snow on the ground when she fell. That she must have been on her way back to Vivers, as she had intended. That she had had ample time to go as far as Elford. That she had not been robbed. The murderer had simply killed and left her, not the way of footpads living wild. If not to stop her from warning Roscelin – for that would have been credible only on the outward journey – then to stop her mouth for another reason, before ever she could get back to Vivers. Yet what connection was there between Elford and Vivers except young Roscelin's banishment to Audemar's service? What other secret to fear betrayal but that of the planned marriage?

But Edgytha had never reached Roscelin, never had speech with him, nor had she gone to Audemar or any of his household. So if she had been to Elford, why had no one there seen her? And if she had not been to Elford, where had she been?

So if it was not what he along with his host and hostess had supposed, what was the cat Edgytha had gone to find, to put among Cenred's pigeons?

And in all probability he would never learn the answer to these questions, or learn what fortune awaited the lost girl and the unhappy boy, and the elders distressed and torn with concern for both of them. A pity! But no help for it, they could no longer trespass on Cenred's disrupted family and burdened hospitality. As soon as the household was astir they must take their leave and set out for Shrewsbury. No one would miss them. And it was high time they went home.

The morning came greyly, under a sky lightly clouded over but lofty, and threatening no further falls of snow. Only a few threads and traceries of white lingered along the bases of walls and under the trees and bushes, and the frost was yielding. It would not be a bad day for travellers.

The household was up and in ferment early. Cenred's servants rolled out of their brief sleep bleary-eyed and grim, well aware that there would be no rest for them that day. Whatever else had been decided in the solemn conference in the solar overnight, whatever possible asylums had been suggested as safe havens for Helisende, it was certain that Audemar would have patrols working every road in the countryside, and enquiring at every cottage, in case someone, somewhere, had seen and spoken with Edgytha, or seen anything of a solitary and furtive figure lurking along the path she had taken. They were already gathering in the courtyard, saddling up, tightening girths and waiting stoically for their orders, when Cadfael and Haluin, booted and girded for the road, presented themselves before Cenred.

He was deep in colloquy with his steward in the middle of the bustle in the hall, when they approached him, and he turned to them courteously but blankly for a moment, as if in these graver preoccupations he had forgotten he had ever before set eyes on them. Recollection came at once, but brought him no pleasure, only a gesture of hospitable compunction.

'Brothers, I ask your pardon, you have been neglected. If we have troubles here to deal with, don't let that disturb you. Use my home as your own.'

'My lord,' said Haluin, 'we owe you thanks for all your kindness, but we must be on our way. There is now no way I can serve you. There is no more haste, since there is no more secrecy. And we have duties waiting for us at home. We are come to take our leave.'

Cenred was too honest to pretend any reluctance to part with them, and made no demur. 'I have delayed your return for my own ends,' he said ruefully, 'and all to no purpose. I am sorry I ever drew you into so vexed a business. Believe me, at least, that my intent was good. And go with my goodwill. I wish you a peaceful journey.'

'And to you, sir, the safe recovery of the lady, and the guidance of God through all perplexities,' said Haluin.

Cenred did not offer horses for the first stage of the journey, as Adelais had done for the whole of it. He had need here of all the horses at his disposal. But he watched the two habited figures, the hale and the lame, make their way slowly down the steps from the hall door, Cadfael's hand on Haluin's elbow ready to support him at need, Haluin's hands, calloused now from gripping the staves of his crutches, braced and careful at every tread. In the courtyard they threaded the bustle of preparation, and drew near to the gate. Cenred took his eyes from them with relief at being rid of one complication, and turned his face doggedly if wearily upon those remaining.

Roscelin, chafing at delay, stood bridle in hand at the gate, shifting restlessly from foot to foot, and peering impatiently back for his father or Audemar to give the word to mount. He gave the two monks a preoccupied glance as they drew near, and then, warming, bade them a good morning, and even smiled through the grey distorting mask of his own anxiety.

'You're away for Shrewsbury? It's a good step. I hope you'll have easy travelling.'

'And you a blessed end to your search,' said Cadfael.

'Blessed for me?' said the boy, again clouding over. 'I don't look for it.'

'If you find her safe and well, and no man's wife until she so pleases, that's a fair measure of blessing. I doubt if you may ask for more. Not yet,' said Cadfael cautiously. 'Take the day's measure of good, and be thankful, and who knows but more may be added?'

'You talk of impossibilities,' said Roscelin implacably. 'But you mean me well, and I take it as you mean it.'

'Where will you ride first, to look for Helisende?' asked Brother Haluin.

'Some of us back to Elford, to make sure she has not slipped between us and made her way there, after all. And to every manor around, for any word of her, or of Edgytha. She cannot have gone far.' He had truly grieved and been angry for

Edgytha, but the 'she' that drove all others from his mind was Helisende.

They left him chafing and agonising, more restless than the horse that shifted and stamped to be off. When they looked back from outside the gate his foot was already in the stirrup, and behind him the rest of the hunters were gathering the reins and mounting. Back to Elford first, in case Helisende had slipped through their fingers, eluding the riders on both tracks, and come safe to shelter. Cadfael and Haluin must go in the opposite direction, towards the west. They had turned some way north from the highroad to reach the lights of the manor. They did not return that way, but turned due west at once, on a trodden path that skirted the manor fence. From the limit of the enclave they heard Audemar's hunters ride forth, and turned to watch them stream out from the gate and lengthen out into a long, many-coloured thread, dwindling into the east and vanishing among the trees of the first belt of woodland.

'And is that the end of it?' wondered Haluin, suddenly grieved. 'And we shall never know what comes of it all! Poor lad, and his own case beyond hope. All his comfort in this world must be to see her happy, if that will ever be possible without him. I know,' said Brother Haluin, in compassion untainted by any lingering self-pity, 'what they suffer.'

But it seemed that it was indeed over for them, and there was no sense in looking back. They set their faces towards the west, and went forward steadily on this untested path, with the rising sun behind them, casting their elongated shadows along the moist grass.

'By this way,' said Cadfael, taking his bearings thoughtfully when they halted to eat their midday bread and cheese and strip of salt bacon in the lee of a bushy bank, 'I think we shall miss Lichfield. I judge we're already passing to the north of it. No matter, we shall find a bed somewhere before nightfall.'

Meantime, the day was clear and dry, and the country through which they made their way was pleasant, but sparsely populated, and afforded them fewer human encounters than they had met with on the direct highway through Lichfield. Having had so little sleep they made no haste, but went steadily, and took whatever rests offered along the way, wherever a solitary assart provided the hospitality of a bench by the hearth, and a few minutes of neighbourly gossip in passing.

A light wind sprang up with the approach of evening, warning them it was time to look for a night's shelter. They were in country still wasted from harsh usage fifty years past. The people of these parts had not taken kindly to the coming of the Normans, and had paid the price for their obduracy. There were the relics of deserted holdings to be seen here and there, collapsing into grass and brambles, and the ruins of a mill rotting gently into its own overgrown stream. Hamlets were few and far between. Cadfael began to scan the landscape round for any sign of an inhabited roof.

An elderly man gathering firewood in a stand of old trees straightened his bent back to answer their greetings, and peered at them curiously from within his sacking hood.

'Not half a mile on, Brothers, you'll see to your right the pale of a nunnery. They're still building, it's mostly timber yet, but the church and the cloister are in stone, you can't miss it. There's but two or three holdings in the hamlet, but the sisters take in travellers. You'll get a bed there.' And he added, eyeing their black habits: 'They're of your own persuasion, it's a Benedictine house.'

'I knew of none in these parts,' said Cadfael. 'What is this house called?'

'It's like the hamlet, called Farewell. It's no more than three years old. Bishop de Clinton set it up. You'll be made welcome there.'

They thanked him, and left him to bind up and hoist his great bundle of wood, and make off for home in the opposite direction, while they went on, encouraged, towards the west.

'I remember,' said Haluin, 'hearing something of this place, or at least of the bishop's plans for a new foundation somewhere here, close to his cathedral. But I never heard the name Farewell until – do you recall? – Cenred spoke of it, that night we first came to Vivers. The only Benedictine house in these parts, he said, when he asked where we were from. We're fortunate, it's well we came this way.'

By this time, with the twilight closing in, he was beginning to flag, in spite of the easy pace they had set. They were both glad when the path brought them to a small open green flanked by three or four cottages, and they saw beyond these the long pale fence of the new abbey, and the roof of the church above it. The track led them to a modest timber gatehouse. Both the stout gate and the grille set in it were closed, but a pull at the bell sent a succcession of echoes flying away into distance within, and after a few moments brought light, flying footsteps skipping towards them from within the pale.

The grille slid open, and revealed a round, rosy, youthful face beaming through at them. Wide blue eyes surveyed their habits and tonsures, and recognised kindred.

'Good even, Brothers,' said a high, girlish voice, joyously self-important. 'You're late on the road tonight. Can we offer you a roof and a rest?'

'We were about to ask it,' said Cadfael heartily. 'Can you lodge us overnight?'

'And longer if you need,' she said cheerfully. 'Men of the Order will always be welcome here. We're off the beaten track, and not yet well known, and with the place still building we offer less comfort, I daresay, than some older houses, but we have room for such guests as you. Wait till I unbar the doors.'

She was about it already, they heard the bolt shot back and the latch of the wicket lifted, and then the door opened wide in exuberant welcome, and the portress waved them in.

She could not, Cadfael thought, be more than seventeen, and new in her novitiate, one of those superfluous daughters of poorly endowed small nobility for whom there was little to spare by way of dowry, and little prospect of an advantageous marriage. She was small and softly rounded, plain of face but fresh and wholesome as new bread, and blessedly she glowed with enthusiasm in her new life, with no apparent regret for the world she had left behind. The satisfaction of trusted office became her, and so did the white wimple and black cowl framing her bright and candid face.

'Have you travelled far?' she asked, viewing Haluin's laboured gait with wide-eyed concern.

'From Vivers,' said Haluin, quick in reassurance. 'It is not so far, and we have taken it gently.'

'And have you very far still to go?'

'To Shrewsbury,' said Cadfael, 'where we belong to the abbey of Saint Peter and Saint Paul.'

'It's a long way,' she said, shaking her head over them. 'You'll be needing your rest. Will you wait here in the lodge for me, till I tell Sister Ursula she has guests? Sister Ursula is our hospitaller. The lord bishop asked for two experienced elder sisters to come to us from Polesworth for a season, to instruct the novices. We are all so new, and there's so much to learn, besides all the work we have to do in the building, and the garden. And they sent us Sister Ursula and Sister Benedicta. Sit and warm yourselves but a few minutes, and I'll be back.' And she was off, with her light, dancing step, as blithe in her cloistered calling as any of her secular sisters could have been in approaching a more worldly marriage.

'She is truly happy,' said Brother Haluin, wondering and pleased. 'No, it is not a second-best. So I have found it in the end, but she from the beginning. The sisters from Polesworth must be women of wisdom and grace, if this is their work.'

Sister Ursula the hospitaller was a tall, thin woman perhaps fifty years old, with a lined, experienced face at once serene, resigned and even mildly amused, as if she had seen and come to terms with all the vagaries of human behaviour, and nothing could now surprise or disconcert her. If the other borrowed instructress measures up to this one, Cadfael thought, these green girls of Farewell have been fortunate.

'You're warmly welcome,' said Sister Ursula, sailing briskly into the lodge with the young portress beaming at her elbow. 'The lady abbess will be happy to receive you in the morning, but you must be most in need now of food and rest and a bed, all the more if you have such a long journey before you. Come with me, there's a chamber prepared for chance comers always, and our own brothers are all the more welcome.'

She led them out from the lodge into a narrow outer court, where the church lay before them, a modest building of stone, with the traces of the continuing work, ashlar and timber, cords and scaffolding boards, stacked neatly under its walls, in token that nothing here was finished. But in only three years they had raised the church and the entire frame of the cloister, but for the south range, where only the lower floor which housed the refectory was completed.

'The bishop has provided us the labour and a generous endowment,' said Sister Ursula, 'but we shall be building for some years yet. Meantime we live simply. We want for nothing that's needful, and hanker after nothing beyond our needs. I suppose when all these timber housings are replaced in stone my work here will be done, and I should be returning to Polesworth, where I took my vows years ago, but I don't know but I'd rather stay here, if I'm offered a choice. There's something about bringing a new foundation to birth, you feel towards it as towards a child of your own body.'

The enclave fence, doubtless, would eventually be replaced by a stone wall, the wooden buildings that lined it, infirmary, domestic offices, guest-hall and storehouses, gradually rebuilt one by one. But already the glimpse they had into the cloister in passing showed that the garth had been grassed, and a shallow stone basin in the centre held water to attract the birds.

'By next year,' said Sister Ursula, 'we shall have flowers. Sister Benedicta, our best gardener at Polesworth, came here with me, the garth is her preserve. Things grow for her, birds come to her hand. That gift I never had.'

'And has Polesworth also provided you your abbess?' asked Cadfael.

'No, Bishop de Clinton brought Mother Patrice from Coventry. We two must go back to our own house when we're no longer needed here, unless, as I say, they let us remain for life. We should need the bishop's dispensation, but who knows, he may see fit to grant it.'

Beyond the cloister a small private court opened, and the guest-hall stood on the further side of it, close to the pale fence. The small room that awaited the first travellers was dim and full of the warmth and fragrance of wood, furnished simply with two beds and a little table, with a crucifix on the wall and a prayer-desk below it.

'Use it as your domain,' said Sister Ursula cheerfully, 'and I'll have supper brought to you here. You come too late for Vespers, but if you please to join us at Compline later, you'll hear the bell. Use our church for prayer as you wish. It is but young yet, the more good souls it harbours under its roof, the better. And now, if you have all you need, I'll leave you to your rest.'

In the blessed virginal quiet of this new abbey of Farewell Brother Haluin fell rapturously asleep as soon as he returned from Compline, and slept like a child all through the night and deep into the dawn of a soft, clear morning, free of any touch of frost. He awoke to find Cadfael already up, and preparing to go and recite the morning office and offer his private prayers in the church.

'Has the bell sounded for Prime?' asked Haluin, rising in haste.

'No, nor will for half an hour yet, by the light. We can have the church to ourselves for a while, if you're so minded.'

'A good thought,' said Haluin, and went with him gladly, out into the small court, and across it to the south door into the cloister. The turf in the garth was moist and green, the bleached pallor of winter vanished overnight. The shy mist of buds that had barely showed a few days ago along the branches of the trees now had a positive colour, grown into a tender green veil. It wanted only a few more such mild days and a glimpse of the sun, and suddenly it would be spring. In the clear shallow water in the stone bowl small birds were fluttering and shrilling, aware of change. Brother Haluin approached the little church of Farewell through evidences of hope. Certainly this first church would be enlarged or replaced later, when the abbey's immediate building needs were met, its endowment assured, and its prestige established. Yet this first edifice, small and plain as it was, would always be remembered with affection, and its supplanting a matter of regret to those, like Sister Ursula and Sister Benedicta, who had been present and served at its birth.

They said the office together in the dim, stony quietness, kneeling before the small spark of the altar lamp, and made their private prayers in silence afterwards. The light softened and brightened over them, the first veiled ray of the rising sun stole through the pales of the enclave and touched the upper stones of the eastern wall into pale rose, and still Brother Haluin kneeled, his crutches laid beside him.

Cadfael was the first to rise. It could not be long now to Prime, and it might be an inconvenient distraction to new young sisters to have two men in evidence at their morning service, even two monks of the same order. He crossed to the south door, and stood there looking out into the garth, waiting until Haluin should need his help to rise.

There was one of the sisters standing beside the stone bowl in the centre, very slender and erect and composed, feeding the birds. She crumbled bread on the broad rim of the bowl, and held fragments of it out on her open palm, and the flurry and vibration of hovering wings span fearlessly about her. The black habit became her slenderness, and her bearing had a youthful grace that stabbed piercingly into Cadfael's memory. The poise of the head on its long neck and straight shoulders, the narrow waist and elegant, long hand offering alms to the birds, these he had surely seen before, in another place, by another and deceptive light. Now she stood in open air, with the soft morning light upon her, and he could not believe that he was mistaken.

Helisende was here at Farewell, Helisende in a nun's habit. The bride had fled her unbearable dilemma to take the veil rather than marry anyone but her unfortunate lover Roscelin. True, she could not have taken any vows as yet, but the sisters might well see fit, in her stressful circumstances, to give her the instant protection of the habit, even before she entered on her novitiate.

She had quick hearing, or perhaps she had been expecting

and listening for a light footstep in the western range of the cloister, where the sisters' dortoire lay. For plainly she caught the sound of someone approaching from that direction, and turned to meet the newcomer, smiling. The very movement, measured and tranquil, in itself cast doubt on the youth he had seen in her but a moment earlier, and showed him fully a face he had never seen before.

Not a young, unpractised girl, but a serene, worn, mature woman. The revelation in the hall at Vivers came about full circle, from illusion to reality, from the girl to the woman, as then it had spun headily backwards from the woman to the girl. Not Helisende, not even very like Helisende, but for the tall white ivory brow, and the sweet and plaintive oval shape of the face, and the wide-set, candid, gallant and vulnerable eyes. In figure and bearing, yes, the very same. If she had turned her back again, she would again have become the image of her daughter.

For who else could this be but the widowed mother who had taken the veil at Polesworth rather than be harried into a second marriage? Who else but Sister Benedicta, sent here to the bishop's new foundation to help to establish a secure tradition and a blessed example for the fledgling nuns of Farewell? Sister Benedicta who could charm flowers to grow and birds to come to her hand? Helisende must have known of her move, if the rest of the household at Vivers had not. Helisende had known where to look for refuge in her need. Where should she go but to her mother?

He had been concentrating so intensely upon the woman in the garth that he had heard nothing from within the church, until he caught the tapping of crutches on the flagstones within the doorway, and swung about almost guiltily to return to his bounden duty. Haluin had somehow got to his feet unaided, and emerged now at Cadfael's side, gazing out with pleasure into the garth, where misty sunlight and moist shadow mingled.

His eyes fell upon the nun, and he halted abruptly, swaying on his crutches. Cadfael saw the dark eyes fix and widen, their arrested stare burning hollowly into the glowing stillness of vision or trance, and the sensitive lips move almost soundlessly, forming the slow syllables of a name. Almost soundlessly, but not quite, for Cadfael heard it.

In wonder and joy and pain, and all in extremes, as one driven and wracked by religious ecstasy: 'Bertrade!' whispered Brother Haluin.

Chapter Eleven

THERE WAS no mistaking the name, and no questioning the absolute certainty with which it was uttered. If Cadfael clung to sane, sensible disbelief for one moment, he discarded it the next, and it was swept away once for all in a great flood of enlightenment. In Haluin there was no doubt or question at all. He knew what he saw, he gave it its true, its unforgotten name, and stood lost in wonder, trembling with the intensity of his knowledge. Bertrade!

The first glimpse of her daughter had struck him to the heart, the dimly-seen copy outlined against the light was so true to the original. But as soon as Helisende had stepped forward into the torchlight the likeness had faded, the vision dissolved. This was a girl he did not know. Now she came again, and turned towards him the remembered and lamented face, and there was no more questioning.

So she had not died. Cadfael grappled silently with enlightenment. The tomb Haluin had sought was an illusion. She had not died of the draught that robbed her of her child, she had survived that peril and grief, to be married off to an elderly husband, vassal and friend to her mother's family, and to bear him a daughter the image of herself in build and bearing. And she had done her best to be a faithful wife and mother as long as her old lord lived, but after his death she had turned her back on the world and followed her first lover into the cloister, choosing the same order, taking to herself the name of the founder, binding herself once for all to the same discipline into which Haluin had been driven.

Then why, argued a persistent imp in Cadfael's mind, why did you – *you*, not Haluin! – find in the face of the girl at Vivers something inexplicably familiar? Who was it hiding from you deep in the caverns of memory, refusing to be recognised? You had never seen the girl before, never in life set eyes on this mother of hers. Whoever looked out at you from Helisende's eyes, and then drew down a veil between, it was not Bertrade de Clary.

All this came seething through his mind in the instant of revelation, the brief moment before Helisende herself emerged from the shadows of the west range and came out into the garth to join her mother. She had not donned the habit, she wore the same gown she had worn the previous evening at her brother's table. She was pale and grave, but had the calm of the cloister about her, safe here from any compulsion, with time for thought and for taking counsel.

The two women met, the hems of their skirts tracing two darker paths in the silver-green of the moist grass. They turned back together at leisure towards the doorway from which Helisende had come, to go in and join the rest of the sisterhood for Prime. They were going away, they would vanish, and nothing be answered, nothing resolved, nothing made plain! And still Haluin hung swaying on his crutches, stricken motionless and mute. He would lose her again, she was all but lost already. The two women had almost reached the west walk, the cords of deprivation were drawn out to breaking point.

'Bertrade!' cried Haluin, in a great shout of terror and despair.

That cry reached them, echoing startlingly from every wall, and brought them about to stare in alarm and astonishment towards the door of the church. Haluin tore himself out of his daze with a great heave, and went hurtling forward recklessly into the garth, his crutches goring the soft turf.

At sight of an unknown man lurching towards them the women had instinctively recoiled, but seeing at second glance his habit, and how sadly he was crippled, in pure compassion they halted their flight to permit his approach, and even came a few impulsive steps to meet him. For a moment there was no more in it than that, pity for a lame man. Then abruptly everything changed.

He had been in too much haste to reach them, he stumbled, and swayed out of balance for a moment, on the edge of a fall, and the girl, quick to sympathy, sprang forward to support him in her arms. His weight falling into her embrace swung them both about, to steady and recover almost cheek to cheek, and Cadfael saw the two faces for a long moment side by side, startled, bright, dazzled into wonder.

So now at last he had his answer. Now he knew everything there was to be known, everything except what fury of bitterness could drive one human creature to do so base and a cruel a thing to another. And even that answer would not be far to seek.

It was at that moment of total enlightenment that Bertrade de Clary, staring earnestly into the stranger's face, knew him for no stranger, and called him by his name:

'Haluin!'

There was nothing more, not then, only the meeting of eyes and the mutual recognition, and the understanding, on either part, of past wrongs and agonies never before fully understood, bitter and terrible for a moment, then erased by a great flood of gratitude and joy. For in the moment when the three of them hung mute and still, staring at one another, they all heard the little bell for Prime ringing in the dortoir, and knew that the sisters would be filing down the night stairs to walk in procession into the church.

So there was nothing more, not then. The women drew back, with lingering glances still wide with wonder, and turned to answer the summons and join their sisters. And Cadfael went forward from the porch to take Brother Haluin by the arm, and lead him gently, like a sleep-walking child, back to the guest-hall.

'She is not dead,' said Haluin, rigidly erect on the edge of his bed. Over and over, recording the miracle in a repetition nearer incantation than prayer. 'She is not dead! It was false, false, false! She did not die!'

Cadfael said never a word. It was not yet time to speak of all that lay behind this revelation. For the moment Haluin's shocked mind looked no further than the fact, the joy that she should be alive and well and in safe haven whom he had lamented so long as dead, and dead by his grievous fault, the bewilderment and hurt that he should have been left so long mourning her.

'I must speak with her,' said Haluin. 'I cannot go without having speech with her.'

'You shall not,' Cadfael assured him.

It was inevitable now, all must come out. They had met, they had beheld each other, no one now could undo that, the sealed coffer was sprung open, the secrets were tumbling out of it, no one now could close the lid upon them ever again.

'We cannot leave today,' said Haluin.

'We shall not. Wait here in patience,' said Cadfael. 'I am going to seek an audience with the lady abbess.'

The abbess of Farewell, brought by Bishop de Clinton from Coventry to direct his new foundation, was a dumpy round loaf of a woman, perhaps in her middle forties, with a plump russet face and shrewd brown eyes that weighed and measured in a glance, and were confident of their judgement. She sat uncompromisingly erect on an uncushioned bench in a small and Spartan parlour, and closed the book on the desk before her as Cadfael came in.

'You're very welcome, Brother, to whatever service our house can offer you. Ursula tells me you are from the abbey of Saint Peter and Saint Paul, at Shrewsbury. I intended to invite you and your companion to join me for dinner, and I cordially extend that invitation now. But I hear you have asked for this interview, forestalling any move of mine. I take it there is a reason. Sit down, Brother, and tell me what more you have to ask of me.'

Cadfael sat down with her, debating in his mind how much he might tell, or how little. She was a woman quite capable of filling in gaps for herself, but also, he judged, a woman of scrupulous discretion, who would keep to herself whatever she read between the lines.

'I come, Reverend Mother, to ask you to countenance a meeting, in private, between my brother Haluin and Sister Benedicta.'

He saw her brows raised, but the small bright eyes beneath them remained unperturbed and sharp with intelligence.

'In youth,' he said, 'they were well acquainted. He was in her mother's service, and being so close in the one house, and of an age, boy and girl together, they fell into loving. But Haluin's suit was not at all to her mother's mind, and she took pains to separate them. Haluin was dismissed from her service, and forbidden all ado with the girl, who was persuaded into a marriage more pleasing to her family. No doubt you know her history since then. Haluin entered our house, admittedly for a wrong reason. It is not good to turn to the spiritual life out of despair, but many have done it, as you and I know, and lived to become faithful and honourable ornaments to their houses. So has Haluin. So, I make no doubt, has Bertrade de Clary.'

He caught the glint of her eyes at hearing that name. There was not much she did not know about her flock, but if she knew more than he had said of this woman she showed no sign and made no comment, accepting all as he had told it.

'It seems to me,' she said, 'that the story you tell me bids fair to be repeated in another generation. The circumstances are not quite the same, but the end well could be. It's as well we should consider in time how to deal with it.'

'I have that in mind,' said Cadfael. 'And how have you dealt with it thus far? Since the girl came running to you by night? For the whole household of Vivers is out by now for the second day, scouring the roads for her.'

'I think not,' said the abbess. 'For I sent yesterday to let her brother know that she is here and safe, and prays him to be left in peace here for a while for thought and prayer. I think he will respect her wish, in the circumstances.'

'Circumstances which she has told you,' said Cadfael with conviction, 'in full. So far, that is, as she knows them.'

'She has.'

'Then you know of a woman's death, and of the marriage arranged for Helisende. And the reason for that marriage, you know that, too?'

'I know she is too close kin to the young man she would liefer have. Yes, she has told me. More, I fancy, than she tells her confessor. You need not fear for Helisende, as long as she remains here she is safe from all harassment, and has the company and comfort of her mother.'

'She could not be in a better place,' said Cadfael fervently. 'Then, as to these two who most concern us now – I must tell you that Haluin was told that Bertrade was dead, and has believed her so all these years, and moreover, taken her death to himself as blame. This morning by God's grace he has seen her before him alive and well. They have exchanged no words but their names. But I think it would be well that they should, if you so grant. They will serve better in their separate vocations if they have peace of mind. Also they have a right to know, each one, that the other is whole, blessed and content.'

'And you think,' said the abbess with deliberation, 'that they *will* be blessed and content? After as before?'

'More and better than before,' he said with certainty. 'I can speak for the man, if you know as much of the woman. And if they part thus without a word, they will be tormented to the end of their days.'

'I would as soon not be answerable to God for that,' said the abbess, with a brief, bleak smile. 'Well, they shall have their hour and make their peace. It can do no harm, and may do much good. Do you purpose to remain here some days longer?'

'This one day at least,' said Cadfael. 'For I have one more prayer to make to you. Brother Haluin I leave to you. But there is a thing I must do, before we set off for home. Not here! Will you let me borrow a horse from your stable?'

She sat studying him for a long moment, and it seemed that she was guardedly satisfied with what she saw, for at length she said: 'On one condition.'

'And that is?'

'That when time serves, and all harm is spent, you will tell me the other half of the story.'

Brother Cadfael led out his borrowed horse into the stableyard, and mounted without haste. The bishop had seen fit to provide stabling adequate for his own visitations, and two stout cobs for remounts should any of his envoys travel this way and make use of the abbey's hospitality. Having been given a free hand, Cadfael had naturally chosen the more likely looking of the two, and the younger, a lively, solid bay. It was no very long ride he had in mind, but he might as well get out of it what pleasure he could along the way. There would be little pleasure at the end of it.

The sun was already high when he rode out at the gate, a pale sun growing brighter and clearer as the air of the day warmed into palpable spring. The fatal snow at Vivers would be the last snow of the winter, appropriately completing Haluin's pilgrimage, as the first snow had begun it.

The filigree green gauze of buds along the branches of bush and tree had burst into the tender plumage of young leaves. The moist grass shimmered, and gave off a faint, fragrant steam as the sun reached it. So much beauty, and behind him as he rode lay a great mercy, a just deliverance, and the renewal of hope. And before him a solitary soul to be saved or lost.

He did not take the road to Vivers. It was not there he had

urgent business, though he might well return that way. Once he halted to look back, and the long line of the abbey fence had disappeared in the folds of land, and the hamlet with it. Haluin would be waiting and wondering, groping his way through a confused dream, beset with questions to which he could have no answer, torn between belief and disbelief, fearful joy and recollected anguish, until the abbess should send to summon him to the meeting which would make all things plain at last.

Cadfael rode on slowly until he should encounter someone from whom he could ask directions. A woman leading sheep and lambs out to pasture at the edge of the village stopped willingly to point him to the most direct road. He need not go near Vivers, and that was well, for he had no wish to meet Cenred or his men as yet. He had nothing at this moment to tell them, and indeed it was not he who must tell what finally had to be told.

Once on the track his informant had indicated, he rode fast and purposefully, until he dismounted at the gate of the manor of Elford.

It was the young portress who tapped at the door and entered Brother Haluin's haunted solitude, later in the morning, when the sun had shed its veil, and the grass of the garth was drying. He looked round as she came in, expecting Cadfael, and gazed at her with eyes still wide and blank with wonder.

'I am sent by the lady abbess,' said the girl, with solicitous gentleness, since it seemed he might be almost beyond understanding, 'to bid you to her parlour. If you will come with me, I'll show you the way.'

Obediently he reached for his crutches. 'Brother Cadfael went forth and has not returned,' he said slowly, looking about him like a man awaking from sleep. 'Is this bidding to him also? Should I not wait for him?'

'There is no need,' she said. 'Brother Cadfael has already spoken with Mother Patrice, and has an errand he says he must do now. You should wait for his return here, and be easy. Will you come?'

Haluin thrust himself to his feet and went with her, across the rear court to the abbess's lodging, confiding like a child though half his mind was still absent. The little portress tempered her flying steps to his laboured gait, bringing him with considerate gentleness to the door of the parlour, and turning upon him on the threshold a bright, encouraging smile.

'Go in, you are expected.'

She held the door open for him, since he had need of both hands for his crutches. He limped across the threshold into the wood-scented, dimly lit room, and halted just within to make his reverence to the Mother Superior, only to stand motionless and quivering as his eyes adjusted to the subdued light. For the woman who stood waiting for him, braced and still and wonderfully smiling in the centre of the room, her hands extended intinctively to aid his approach, was not the abbess, but Bertrade de Clary.

Chapter Twelve

THE GROOM who came unhurriedly across the courtyard to greet the visitor and enquire his business was neither Lothair nor Luc, but a lanky lad not yet twenty, with a shock of dark hair. At his back the courtyard seemed emptied of its usual lively activity, only a few maids and manservants going back and forth about their work in a casual fshion, as if all constraints were slackened. By the look of things, the master of the house and most of his men were still out and about on the hunt for any word that might lead to the murderer of Edgytha.

'If you're wanting the lord Audemar,' said the boy at once, 'you're out of luck. He's still away to Vivers about this woman who was killed a couple of nights back. But his steward's here, if you want lodging you'd best see him.'

'I thank you,' said Cadfael, surrendering his bridle, 'but it's not the lord Audemar I've come to see. My errand is to his mother. I know where her dower apartments are. If you'll see to the horse I'll go myself and ask her woman to enquire if the lady will be good enough to see me.'

'As you please, then. You were here afore,' said the lad, narrowing his eyes curiously at this vaguely familiar visitor. 'Only a few days back, with another black monk, one that went on crutches and very lame.'

'True,' said Cadfael. 'And I had speech with the lady then, and she will not have forgotten either me or that lame brother. If she refuses me a hearing now, I will let her be – but I think she will not refuse.'

'Try for yourself, then,' agreed the groom indifferently. 'She's still here with her maid, and I know she's within. She keeps within, these last days.'

'She had two grooms with her,' said Cadfael, 'father and son. We were acquainted, when we stayed here, they had come from Shropshire with her. I'd willingly pass the time of day with them, afterwards, if they're not away to Vivers with the lord Audemar's people.'

'Oh, them! No, they're her fellows, none of his. But they're not here, neither. They went off yesterday on some errand of hers, very early. Where? How should I know where? Back to Hales, likely. That's where the old dame keeps, most of her time.'

I wonder, thought Cadfael, as he turned towards Adelais's dwelling in the corner of the enclave wall, and the groom led the cob away to the stable, truly I wonder how it would suit Adelais de Clary to know that her son's grooms speak of her as 'the old dame'. Doubtless to that raw boy she seemed ancient as the hills, but resolutely she cherished and conserved what had once been great beauty, and from that excellence nothing and no one must be allowed to detract. Not for nothing did she choose for her intimate maid someone plain and pockmarked, surrounding herself with dull and ordinary faces that caused her own lustre to glow more brightly.

At the door of Adelais's hall he asked for audience, and the woman Gerta came out to him haughtily, protective of her mistress's privacy and assertive of her own office. He had sent in no name, and at sight of him she checked, none too pleased to see one of the Benedictines from Shrewsbury back again so soon, and so unaccountably.

'My lady is not disposed to see visitors. What's your business, that you need trouble her with it? If you need lodging and food, my lord Audemar's steward will take care of it.'

'My business,' said Cadfael, 'is with the lady Adelais only, and concerns no one beside. Tell her that Brother Cadfael is here again, and that he comes from the abbey of Farewell, and asks to have some talk with her. That she shuns visitors I believe. But I think she will not refuse me.'

She was not so bold that she dared take it upon herself to deny him, though she went with a toss of her head and a disdainful glance, and would have been glad to bring back a dismissive answer. It was plain by the sour look on her face when she emerged from the solar that she was denied that pleasure.

'My lady bids you in,' she said coldly, and opened the door wide for him to pass by her and enter the chamber. And no doubt she hoped to linger and be privy to whatever passed, but favour did not extend so far.

'Leave us,' said the voice of Adelais de Clary, from deep shadow under a shuttered window. 'And close the door between.'

She had no seemly woman's occupation for her hands this time, no pretence at embroidering or spinning, she merely sat in her great chair in semi-darkness, motionless, her hands spread along the arms and girpping the carved lionheads in which they terminated. She did not move as Cadfael came in, she was neither surprised nor disturbed. Her deep eyes burned upon him without wonder, and he thought without regret. It was almost as though she had been waiting for him.

'Where have you left Haluin?' she asked.

'At the abbey of Farewell,' said Cadfael.

She was silent for a moment, brooding upon him with a still face and glowing eyes, with an intensity he felt as a vibration upon the air, before ever his eyes had grown accustomed to the dim light, and watched her lineaments grow gradually out of darkness, the chosen darkness in which she had incarcerated herself. Then she said with harsh deliberation: 'I shall never see him again.'

'No, you will never see him again. When this is done, we are going home.'

'But you,' she said, 'yes, I have had it in mind all this time that you would be back. Sooner or later, you would be back. As well, perhaps! Things have gone far beyond my reckoning now. Well, say what you have come to say. I would as lief be silent.'

'That you cannot do,' said Cadfael. 'It is your story.'

'Then be my chronicler. Tell it! Remind me! Let me hear how it will sound in my confessor's ears, if any priest takes my confession ever again.' She stretched out one long hand suddenly, waving him imperiously to a seat, but he remained standing where he could see her most clearly, and she made no move to evade his eyes, and no concessions to the fixity of his regard. Her beautiful, proud face was composed and mute, admitting nothing, denying nothing. Only the burning of her dark eyes in their deep settings was eloquent, and even that in a language he could not quite translate.

'You know all too well what you did, all those years ago,' said Cadfael. 'You executed a fearful punishment upon Haluin for daring to love your daughter and getting her with child. You pursued him even into the cloister where your enmity had driven him – all too soon, but the young are quick to despair. You forced him to provide you with the means of abortion, and you sent him word, afterwards, that it had killed both mother and child. That awful guilt you have visited upon him all these years, to be his torment lifelong. Did you speak?'

'No,' she said. 'Go on! You have barely begun.'

'True, I have barely begun. That draught of hyssop and fleur de luce that you got from him – it never was used. Its purpose was only to poison him, it did no harm to any other. What did you do with it? Pour it away into the ground? No, long before ever you demanded the herbs from him, as soon as you had driven him out of your house, I daresay, you had hustled Bertrade away here to Elford, and married her to Edric Vivers. It must have been so, certainly it was done in time to give her child, when it was born, a credible if unlikely father. No doubt the old man prided himself on still being potent enough to get a child. Why should anyone question the birth-date, since you had acted so quickly?'

She had not stirred or flinched, her eyes never left his face, admitting nothing, denying nothing.

'Were you never afraid,' he asked, 'that someone, somehow, should let fall within reach even of the cloister that Bertrade de Clary was wife to Edric Vivers, and not safely in her grave? That she had borne her old husband a daughter? It needed only a chance traveller with a gossiper tongue.'

'There was no such risk,' she said simply. 'What contact was there ever between Shrewsbury and Hales? None, until he suffered his fall and conceived his pilgrimage. Much less likely there should ever be dealings with manors in another shire. There was no such risk.'

'Well, let us continue. Living you took her away and gave her to a husband. Living the child was born. So much mercy at least you had on the girl – why none for him? Why such bitter and vindictive hate, that you should conceive so terrible a revenge? Not for your daughter's wrongs, no! Why should he not have been considered a suitable match for her in the first place? He came of good family, he was heir to a fine manor, if he had not taken the cowl. What was it you held so much against him? You were a beautiful woman, accustomed to admiration and homage. Your lord was in Palestine. And I well remember Haluin as he first came to me, eighteen years old, not yet tonsured. I saw him as you had been seeing him for some few years in your celibate solitude – he was comely . . .'

He let it rest there, for her long, resolute lips had parted in deliberate affirmation at last. She had listened to him unwaveringly, making no effort to halt him, and no complaint. Now she responded.

'Too comely!' she said. 'I was not used to being denied, I did not even know how to sue. And he was too innocent to read me aright. How such children offend without offence! So if I could not have him,' she said starkly, 'she should not. No woman ever should, but not she of all women.'

It was said, she let it stand, adding nothing in extenuation, and having said it, she sat contemplating it, seeing again as in another woman what she could now no longer feel with the same intensity, the longing and the anger.

'There is more,' said Cadfael, 'much more. There is the matter of your woman Edgytha. Edgytha was the one trusted confidante you needed, the one who knew the truth. It was she who was sent to Vivers with Bertrade. Utterly loyal and devoted to you, she kept your secret and abetted your revenge all these years. And you trusted in her to keep it for ever. So all was well for you, until Roscelin and Helisende grew up, and came to love each other no longer as playmates, but as man and woman. Knowing but forgetting that the world would hold such a love as poisoned, guilty, forbidden by the church. When the secret became a barrier between them, where no barrier need have been, when Roscelin was banished to Elford, and marriage with de Perronet threatened a final separation, then Edgytha could bear it no longer. She came running here in the night – not to Roscelin, but to you! To beg you to tell the truth at last, or to give her leave to tell it for you.'

'I have wondered,' said Adelais, 'how she knew that I was here within her reach.'

'She knew because I told her. All unwitting I sent her out that night to plead with you to lift the shadow from two innocent children. By merest chance it was mentioned that here in Elford we had spoken with you. *I* sent her running to you and to her death, as it was Haluin who caused you to come here, in haste to ward him off from any dangerous discovery.

We have been the instruments of your undoing, who never wished you anything but well. Now you had better consider what is left to you that can be saved.'

'Go on!' she said harshly. 'You have not finished yet.'

'No, not yet. So Edgytha came to plead with you to do right. And you refused her! You sent her running back to Vivers in despair. And what befell her on the way you know.'

She did not deny it. Her face was bleak and set, but her eyes never wavered.

'Would she have come out with the truth, even against your prohibition? Neither your nor I will ever know the answer to that. But someone equally loyal to you overheard enough to understand the threat to you if she did. Someone feared her, followed and silenced her. Oh, not you! You had other tools to use. But did you speak a word in their ears?'

'No!' said Adelais. 'That I never did! Unless my face spoke for me. And if it did, it lied. I never would have harmed her.'

'I believe you. But which of them was it followed her? Father and son alike, they would die for you without question, and without question one of them has killed for you. And they are gone from here. Back to Hales? No, I doubt that, it is not far enough. How distant is your son's remotest manor?'

'You will not find them,' said Adelais with certainty. 'As for which of them did the thing I might have prevented, I do not know, I want never to know. I stopped their mouths when they would have spoken. To what end? That guilt, like all the rest, is mine alone, I will not cede any scruple of it. Yes, I sent them away. They will not pay my debts for me. Burying Edgytha with reverence is poor atonement. Confession, penance, even absolution cannot restore a life.'

'There is one amend that can still be made,' said Cadfael. 'Moreover, I think a price has been exacted from you, no less than from Haluin, all these years. Do not forget that I saw your face when he presented his ruined body before you. I heard your voice as you cried out on him: "What have they done to you?" All that you did to him you did also to yourself, and once done, it could not be undone. Now you may be free of it, if you choose to deliver yourself.'

'Go on!' said Adelais, though she knew well enough what was to come. He recognised it by the composure with which she had borne herself throughout. Surely she had been waiting here in her half-lit room for the finger of God to point.

'Helisende is not Edric's daughter, but Haluin's. There is not a drop of Vivers blood in her veins. There is nothing to stand in the way if she wishes to marry Roscelin. Whether those two would do well to marry, who knows? But at least the shadow of incestuous affection can and must be lifted from them. The truth must out, since it is out already at Farewell. Haluin and Bertrade are there together, making their peace, making each the other's peace, and Helisende their child is with them, and the truth is already out of its grave.'

She knew, she had known ever since the old woman's death, that it must come to that at last, and if she had deliberately averted her eyes and refused to acknowledge it, she could no longer do so. Nor was she the woman to delegate a hard thing to others, once her mind was made up, nor to do things by halves, whether for good or ill.

He would not prompt her. He drew back from her to leave her space and time, and stood apart, watching her disciplined stillness, and measuring in his mind the bitter toll of eighteen years of silence, of pitilessly contained hate and love. The first words he had heard from her now, even at this extreme, had been of Haluin, and still he heard the vibration of pain in her voice as she cried aloud: 'What have they done to you?'

Adelais got up abruptly from her chair and crossed with long, fierce steps to the window, to fling back the shutter and let in air and light and cold. She stood for a while looking out at the quiet court, and the pale sky dappled with little clouds, and the green gauze veiling the branches of the trees beyond the enclave wall. When she turned to him again he saw her face in full, clear light, and saw as in a dual vision both her imperishable beauty and the dust time had cast upon it, the taut lines of her long throat fallen slack, the grey of ashes in her coiled black hair, the lines that had gathered about mouth and eyes, the net of fine veins marring cheeks which had once been smooth ivory. And she was strong, she would not lightly relinquish her hold of the world and go gently out of it. She would live long, and rage against the relentless assault of old age until death at once defeated and released her. By her very nature Adelais's penance was assured.

'No!' she said, with abrupt, imperious authority, as though he had advanced some suggestion with which she was in absolute disagreement. 'No, I want no advocate, there shall no man rid me of any part of what is mine. What now needs to be told, *I* will tell. No other! Whether it ever would have been told, if you had never come near me – you with your hand for ever at Haluin's elbow, and your temperate eyes that I could never read – do I know? Do you? That is of no account now. What is left to be done, *I* will do.'

'Command me to go,' said Cadfael, 'and I will go. You do not need me.'

'Not as advocate, no. As witness, perhaps! Why should you be cheated of the ending? Yes!' she said, glittering. 'You shall ride with me, and see it ended. I owe you a fulfilment as I owe God a death.'

He rode with her, as she had decreed. Why not? He had to return to Farewell, and by way of Vivers was as good a road as any. And once she had resolved upon action there could be no delay and no denial.

She rode astride, booted and spurred like a man, she who in the common progressions of her recent years had been content to go decorously pillion behind a groom, as was fitting for a dame of her age and dignity. She rode with the lordly confidence of a man, erect and easy in the saddle, her bridle hand held low. And she rode fast but steadily, advancing upon her losses as vigorously as upon her gains.

Cadfael, riding at her side, could not but wonder whether she still felt tempted to hold back some part of the truth, to cover herself from the last betrayal. But the smouldering calm of her face spoke against it. There would be no evasion, no appeal, no excuse. What she had done she had done, and would as starkly declare. And if she repented it, only God would ever know.

Chapter Thirteen

THEY RODE in at the gate of Vivers an hour after noon. The gate stood open, and the turmoil within had subsided, there was no more than the normal to-and-froing in the court. Evidently the abbess's messenger had been received and believed, and whether gladly or reluctantly, Cenred had fallen in with Helisende's wish to be left alone for a while in her sanctuary. With one search abandoned, Audemar's men would be free to pursue a murderer. One they would never find! In the night and the snow, who could have been abroad to witness that knife-stroke in the woods, and put a name or a face to the slayer? Even if there had been a witness, who in these parts, apart from Audemar's own household, would recognise a groom from distant Hales?

Cenred's steward was crossing the court when Adelais reined in, and he came in haste, recognising the mother of his lord's overlord, to help her down, but she was out of the saddle before he could reach her. She let down her kilted skirts, and looked about her for any of her son's people. Cadfael had seen for himself that the hunters had not returned to Elford, nor were they in evidence here. For a moment she frowned, impatient at the prospect of having to wait and contain still all that she had to say. Once resolved, it displeased her to be baulked. She looked beyond the steward's deep reverence towards the hall.

'Is your lord within?'

'He is, madam. Will you be pleased to enter?'

'And my son?'

'He, too, my lady. He came back only some minutes since, his men are still out with ours, questioning in every house for miles around.'

'Waste of time!' she said, rather to herself than to him, and shut her lips grimly on the reason. 'Well, so much the better! They are both here. No, you need not tell them I have come. That I'll do for myself. As for Brother Cadfael, this time he comes in attendance on me, not as a guest.'

Doubtful if the steward had even cast a glance at the second rider until this moment, but he did so now, speculating, Cadfael supposed, what had brought one Benedictine visitor back so soon, and in particular without his companion. But there was no time for enquiry. Adelais had set off vigorously towards the steps that led up to the hall, and Cadfael followed dutifully, as if he were indeed her domestic chaplain, leaving the steward staring after them in doubt and wonder.

In the hall the midday meal was past, and the servants busy clearing away the dishes and stacking the tables aside. Adelais walked through them without a word or a glance, straight to the curtained door of the inner chamber. A murmur of voices, dulled by the hangings, came from within, Cenred's deep tones distinguishable beneath the lighter, younger voice of Jean de Perronet. The suitor had not withdrawn, but intended to wait out his time doggedly if not patiently. Just as well, Cadfael reflected. He had a right to know how formidable an obstacle was now placed in his way. Fair is fair. De Perronet had done nothing dishonourable, fair dealing was his due.

Adelais swept the curtain aside and flung open the door. They were all there, in muted conference over a situation which left them frustrated and helpless, trapped in inaction, since even the gesture of sending out men to try and trace Edgytha's murderer was by this time foredoomed to be fruitless. Had any man in the region known anything, it would have been told already. And if Audemar ever thought to number over his mother's household servants, and level a suspicious finger at the missing, she would stand immovably between him and them. Wherever Lothair and Luc might now be, however confounded and chastened by her revulsion from what they had mistakenly done for her, she would not let the price be charged against them which she held to be her debt.

At the sound of the door opening they had all turned their

heads sharply to see who came in, for her entrance was too abrupt and confident by far for any of the servants. Her gaze swept round the circle of surprised faces, Audemar and Cenred at the table with wine before them, Emma apart at her embroidery frame, but paying no attention to the work, rather waiting with strung nerves for events to unfold in some more comfortable form, and life to return to its level course. And the stranger – Cadfael saw that Adelais could never before have set eyes on Jean de Perronet. On him her glance halted, considering and identifying the bridegroom. Very faintly and briefly her long lips contorted in a dour smile, before her eyes passed to Roscelin.

The boy sat withdrawn into a corner where he could hold all the assembled company in his eye, as if he contemplated imminent battle, and sat prepared and armed, stiff and erect on the bench against the tapestried wall, head reared and lips tightly set. He had accepted, it seemed, however much against his will, Helisende's wish to be left in peace at Farewell, but he had not forgiven any of these conspirators who had planned to match her in secret, and cheat him of even the perverse hope he had to sustain him. His grievance against his parents extended by contagion to de Peronnet, even to Audemar de Clary, to whose house he had been banished to remove the obstacle to their plans. How could he be sure Audemar had not been a party to more than that banishment? A face by nature open, good-humoured and bright now stared upon them all closed, suspicious and inimical. Adelais looked at him longer than at any. Another youth too comely for his own good, attracting unfortunate love as the flower draws the bee.

The moment of blank surprise was over. Cenred was on his feet in hospitable haste, advancing with hand outstretched to take the visitor by the hand, and lead her to a seat at the table.

'Madam, welcome to my house! You do me honour!'

And Audemar, less pleased, half frowning: 'Madam, what brings you here? And unattended!' It suited him better that a mother of so formidable a character should exile herself to the distant manor of Hales, and keep her own court there. Seeing them thus face to face, Cadfael found a strong likeness between the two. Doubtless there was affection between them, but once the son was grown it would be hard for these two to live together in one household. 'There was no need,' said Audemar, 'for you to ride over here, there is nothing you can do that is not already being done.'

Adelais had let Cenred's attentive hand persuade her into the centre of the room, but there she resisted further movement and stood to be seen clearly and alone, with an authoritative gesture freeing her hand.

'Yes,' she said, 'there is need,' and again cast a long glance round all the watching faces. 'And I am not unattended. Brother Cadfael is my escort. He comes from the abbey of Farewell, and will be returning there when he leaves us.' She looked from one young man to the other, from the favoured bridegroom to the frustrated lover, both of them eyeing her warily, conscious of impending revelations, but unable to hazard at what might be coming.

'I am glad,' said Adelais, 'to find you all assembled thus. I have that to say that I will say only once.'

It could never have been a problem for her, thought Cadfael, watching, to hold the attention of everyone about her, wherever she went. In every room she entered she was at once the focal point, the dominant in every company. Now they were silent every one, waiting on her word.

'As I have heard, Cenred,' she said, 'you intended, two days ago, to marry your sister – your half-sister I should say – to this young gentleman. For reason enough, the church and the world would agree, seeing she had become all too dear to your son Roscelin, and he to her, and a marriage that would take her far away removed also the shadow of such an unholy attachment from your house and from your heir. Pardon me if I use too plain words, it's late for any others. No blame to you, knowing only what you knew.'

'What more was there to know?' said Cenred, bewildered. 'Plain words will do very well. They are close blood-kin, as you know well! Would not you have taken the same measure to ward off such an evil from your grandchild, as I intended from my sister? She is as close a charge to me as my own son, and as dear. She is your grandchild. I well remember my father's second marriage. I recall the day you brought the bride here, and my father's pride in the child she bore him. Since he is long gone, I owe Helisende a father's care no less than a brother's. Certainly I sought to protect both her and my son. I still desire the same. This is but a check on the way. Messire de Perronet has not withdrawn his suit, nor I my sanction.'

Audemar had risen from his place, and stood eyeing his mother with close-drawn brows and an unrevealing face. 'What more is there to know?' he said levelly, and for all his voice was equable and low there was doubt and displeasure in it, and a woman of less implacable will might have found it menacing. She stared back at him eye to eye, and was unmoved.

'This! That you trouble needless. There is no barrier, Cenred, between your son and Helisende but the barrier you have conjured up. There is no peril of incest if they were wedded and bedded this very night. Helisende is not your sister, Cenred, she is not your father's daughter. There is no drop of Vivers blood in her veins.'

'But this is foolishness!' protested Cenred, shaking his head over so incredible a claim. 'All this household has known the child from birth. What you say is impossible. Why bring forth such a story, when all my people can bear witness she was born to my father's lawful wife, in their marriage bed, here in my house.'

'And conceived in mine,' said Adelais. 'I can't wonder if none of you thought to count the days, I had lost no time. My daughter was already with child when I brought her here to her marriage.'

Then they were all on their feet, all but Emma, shrinking appalled behind her embroidery frame, shaken by the outcries of anger and disbelief that clashed about her like contrary winds. Cenred was stricken breathless, but de Perronet was clamouring that this was false, and the lady out of her wits, and Roscelin had sprung to confront him, glittering, half incoherent, swinging about from his rival to Adelais, pleading, demanding, that what she said be truth. Until Audemar pounded the table thunderously with his fist, and raised an imperious voice over all to demand silence. And throughout, Adelais stood erect and unmoving as stone, and let the outcries whirl about her unacknowledged.

And then there was silence, no more exclaiming, not a sound, hardly a breath, while they stared upon her intently and long, as if the truth or falsity of what she said might be read in her face if a man held still and unblinking long enough.

'Do you fully know, madam, what you are saying?' asked Audemar, his voice now measured and low.

'Excellently well, my son! I know what I am saying, I know it is truth. I know what I have done, I know it was foully done. It needs none of you to say it, *I* say it. But I did it, and neither you nor I can undo it. Yes, I deceived the lord Edric, yes, I compelled my daughter, yes, I planted a bastard child in this house. Or, if you choose, I took measures to protect my daughter's good name and estate and ensure her honourable status, as Cenred wills to do for a sister. Did Edric ever regret his bargain? I think not. Did he get joy out of his supposed child? Surely he did. All these years I have let well or ill alone, but now God has disposed otherwise, and I am not sorry.'

'If this true,' said Cenred, drawing deep breath, 'Edgytha knew of it. She came here with Bertrade, if you are telling truth now, so late, then she must have known.'

'She did know,' said Adelais. 'And sorry the day I refused her when she begged me to tell the truth earlier, and sorrier still this day when she cannot stand here and bear me witness. But here is one who can. Brother Cadfael is come from the abbey of Farewell, where Helisende now is, and her mother is there with her. And by strange chance,' she said, 'so is her father. There is nowhere now to hide from the truth. I declare it in my own despite.'

'You have hidden from it long enough, madam, it seems,' said Audemar grimly.

'So I have, and make no virtue of revealing it now, when it is already out of its grave.'

There was a brief, profound silence before Cenred asked slowly: 'You say he is there now – her father? There at Farewell with them both?'

'From me,' she said, 'it can only be hearsay. Brother Cadfael will answer you.'

'I have seen them there, all three,' said Cadfael. 'It is truth.'

'Then who is he?' demanded Audemar. 'Who is her father?'

Adelais took up her story, never lowering her eyes. 'He was once a young clerk in my household, of good birth, only a year older than my daughter. He desired to be accepted as a suitor for her hand. I refused him. They – took measures to force my hand. No, perhaps I do them both wrong, what they did may not have been calculated, but done in desperation, for she was as lost in love as he. I dismissed him from my service, and brought her away here in haste, to a match the lord Edric had mooted a year or more earlier. And I lied, telling the lover that she was dead. Very blackly I lied to him, saying both Bertrade and her child had died, when we tried to rid her of her burden. He never knew until now that he had a daughter.'

'Then how comes it,' demanded Cenred, 'that he has found her out now, and in so unlikely a place? This whole wild story comes so strangely, thus out of nowhere, I cannot believe in it.'

'You had better come to terms with it,' she said, 'for neither you nor I can escape the truth or amend it. He has found her by the merciful dispensation of God. What more do you need?'

Cenred swung upon Cadfael in irritated appeal. 'Brother, as you have been my guest in this house, tell what you know of this matter. After so many years, is this indeed a true tale? And how came these three to meet again now, at the end of all?'

'It is a true tale,' said Cadfael. 'And truly they have met, by now they will have talked together. He has found them both because, believing his love dead, and having touched hands with his own death a few months ago, and been spared, he turned his thoughts to mortality, and determined at least, since he could never see her again in this world, to make a pilgrimage to her grave and pray for her peace in the next. And not finding her at Hales, where he supposed she must be, he came here, my lord, to your manor of Elford, where those of your line are buried. Now, on the way home again, by the grace of God we asked lodging last night at the abbey of Farewell. There the lady who was your sister is presently serving as instructress to the novices of the bishop's new foundation. And there Helisende fled for sanctuary from too painful stresses. So they are all under one roof at last.'

After a moment of silence Audemar said softly: ' "*We* asked lodging last night at the abbey of Farewell" – You have said almost enough, yet add one thing more – name him!'

'He entered the cloister, long ago. He is a brother with me in the abbey of Saint Peter and Saint Paul, at Shrewsbury. You have seen him, my lord, that same brother who came to Elford with me, on crutches every step of the way. Monk and priest, the same, my lord Cenred, whom you asked to marry Helisende to the man you had chosen for her. His name is Haluin.'

Now they had all begun dazedly to believe what they could not yet fully grasp in all its implications. With glazed glances they stared within at the slow realisation of what this must mean to them. To Roscelin, quivering and glowing like a newly lighted torch, the sudden dizzy lightness and liberty of guilt and grief lifted from him, the very air of the day intoxicating as wine, the world expanded into a vast brightness of hope and joy that dazzled his eyes and muted his tongue. To de Perronet, the stinging challenge of finding himself faced with a formidable rival where he had looked for no conflict, and the instinctive stiffening of his pride and determination to fight for the threatened prize with all his might. To Cenred the overturning of all his family memories, a father made to seem belittled, even senile, by his fond acceptance of such a deception, a sister abruptly withdrawn into a stranger, an interloper without rights in his house. To Emma, silent and fearful in her corner, the grief of an offence against her lord, and the loss of one she had looked upon almost as her own daughter.

'So she is no sister of mine,' said Cenred heavily, rather to himself than to any other, and as quickly repeated it with sudden anger to them all: 'She is no sister of mine!'

'None,' said Adelais. 'But until now she believed herself so. It is not her fault, never cast blame on her.'

'She is not kin to me. I owe her nothing, neither dowry nor lands. She has no claim on me.' He said it bitterly rather than vengefully, lamenting the abrupt severance of a strong affection.

'None. But she is kin to me,' said Adelais. 'Her mother's dower lands went to Polesworth when she took the veil, but Helisende is my granddaughter and my heiress. The lands I hold in my own right will go to her. She will not be penniless.' She looked at de Perronet as she spoke, and smiled, but wryly. No need to make the lovers' path too smooth by rendering the girl less profitable, and therefore less attractive in the rival's eyes.

'Madam, you mistake me,' said Cenred with muted fury. 'This house has been her home, she will still think of it as home. Where else is there for her? It is we here who are suddenly cut off, like lopped limbs. Her father and mother, both, are in the cloister, and what guidance, what care has she ever had from you? Kin to us or not, she belongs here at Vivers.'

'But nothing prevents now,' cried Roscelin triumphantly. 'I may approach her, I may lawfully ask for her, there is no barrier now. We've done no wrong, there's no shadow over us, no ban between us. I'll go and bring her home. She'll come, blithely she'll come! I knew,' he exulted, his blue eyes brilliant with vindicated joy, 'I knew we did no wrong in loving, never, never! It was *you* persuaded me I sinned. Sir, let me go and fetch her home!'

At that de Perronet took fire in his turn, with a hiss like a sulphur match flaring, and took two rapid strides forward to confront the boy. 'You leap too soon and too far, my friend!

Your rights are no better than mine. I do not withdraw my suit, I urge it, I will pursue it with my might.'

'And so you may,' exulted Roscelin, too drunk with relief and delight to be ungenerous or take offence. 'I don't grudge any man his say, but on fair terms now, you and I and any who come, and we shall see what Helisende replies.' But he knew what her reply would be, his very certainty was offence, though it meant none, and de Perronet had his hand on his dagger and hotter words mounting in his throat when Audemar smote the table and bellowed them both into silence.

'Hush your noise! Am I overlord here, or no? The girl is not without kin, for she is niece to *me*. If there is anyone here who has rights in her and a duty towards her – any who has not farmed out both upon another man long since! – it is I, and I say that if Cenred so wishes, then I place her here in his fosterage, with all the rights he has exercised as her kinsman all these years. And in the matter of her marriage both he and I will take good care what is best for her, but never against her will. But now, let her be! She has asked for time untroubled, and she shall have it. When she is ready to return, I will fetch her home.'

'Content!' said Cenred, breathing deeply. 'I am content! I could ask no better.'

'And Brother . . .' Audemar turned to Cadfael. He had the entire issue in his hands now, over all matters here his writ ran, and what he ordained would be done. The least damage was his design, as his mother's had been the ultimate destruction. 'Brother, if you are going back to Farewell, tell them there what I have said. What's done is done, all that waits to be done shall be in daylight, openly. Roscelin,' he ordered sharply, turning on the boy restless and glittering with the joy of his release, 'have the horses readied, we ride for Elford. You are still in my service until I please to dismiss you, and I have not forgotten that you went forth without leave. Let me have no further cause for displeasure.'

But his voice was dry, and neither words nor look cast the least shadow upon Roscelin's exultant brightness. He bent his knee in the briefest of reverences by way of acknowledging the order, and went blithely to do his lord's bidding. The wind of his flight swung the curtain at the door, and sent a current of outer air floating across the chamber like a sigh.

Audemar looked last and longest at Adelais, who stood with eyes steady and dark upon his face, waiting his judgement.

'Madam, you will ride back with me to Elford. You have done what you came here to do.'

Nevertheless, it was Cadfael who got to horse first. No one was any longer in need of him here, and whatever natural curiosity he might feel concerning the family adjustments still to be made, and perhaps less easily accomplished than decreed, must be for ever contained, since he was unlikely to pass this way again. He reclaimed his horse without haste, and mounted, and was ambling towards the gate when Roscelin broke away from the grooms who were busy saddling Audemar's horses, and came running to his stirrup.

'Brother Cadfael . . .' He was lost for a moment for words, since his wonder and happiness were beyond words, and shook his head and laughed over his own incoherence. 'Tell her! Tell her we're free, we need not change, there's no one can blacken us now . . .'

'Son,' said Cadfael heartily, 'by this time she knows it as well as you.'

'And tell her soon, very soon, I shall come for her. Oh, yes, I know,' he said confidently, seeing Cadfael's raised brows, 'but it's me he'll send. I know him! He'd rather a kinsman he knows and can rely on, his own man, with lands bordering his own, than any lordling from distant parts. And my father won't stand between us now. Why should he, when it solves everything? What's changed, except what needed changing?'

And there was something in that, Cadfael reflected, looking down from the saddle into the young, ardent face. What was changed was the replacement of falsity by truth, and however hard the assimilation might be, it must be for the better. Truth can be costly, but in the end it never falls short of value for the price paid.

'And tell him,' said Roscelin earnestly, 'the lame brother . . . her father . . .' His voice hung on the word with wonder and awe. 'Tell him I'm glad, say I owe him more than ever can be repaid. And tell him he need never fret for her happiness, for I'll give my life to it.'

Chapter Fourteen

AT ABOUT the same time that Cadfael dismounted in the court of Farewell, Adelais de Clary sat with her son in his private chamber at Elford. There had been a long and heavy silence between them. The afternoon was drawing to its close, the light dimming, and he had sent for no candles.

'There is a matter,' he said at length, stirring out of his mourne stillness, 'which has hardly been touched on yet. It was to you, madam, that the old woman came. And you sent her away with a short answer. To her death! Was that at your orders?'

Without passion she said: 'No!'

'I will not ask what you know of it. To what end? She is dead. But I do not like your manner of dealing, and I choose to have no more ado with it. Tomorrow, madam, you shall return to Hales. Hales you may have for your hermitage. But do not come back to this house, ever, for you will not be admitted. The doors of every manor of mine except Hales are henceforth closed to you.'

Indifferently she said: 'As you will, it is all one to me. I need only a little space, and may not need it long. Hales will do very well.'

'Then, madam, take your leave when you will. You shall have a safe escort on the road, seeing,' he said with bitter meaning, 'that you have parted with your own grooms. And a litter, if you prefer to hide your face. Let it not be said that I left you to travel defenceless, like an old woman venturing out alone by night.'

Adelais rose from her stool and went out from him without a word.

In the hall the servants had begun to kindle the first torches and set them in there sconces, but in every corner, and in the smoky beams of the lofty roof, darkness gathered and clung, draped cobwebs of shadow.

Roscelin was standing over the central fire on its flagged hearth, driving the heel of his boot into it to tease it into life after the damped-down hours of the day. He still had Audemar's cloak over his arm, the capuchon dangling from one hand. The light from the reviving flames gilded his stooping face into gold, smooth-cheeked, with elegant bones and a brow as fair as a girl's, and on his dreaming lips the softest and most beguiling of smiles bore witness to his deep happiness. His flaxen hair swung against his cheek, and parted above the suave nape of his neck, the most revealing beauty of the young. For a moment she stood apart in the shadows to watch him, herself unnoticed, for the pleasure and the pain of experiencing again the irresistible attraction, the unbearable bliss and anguish of beholding beauty and youth pass by and depart. Too sharp and sweet a reminder of things ended long ago, and for years believed forgotten, only to burn up into new life, like the phoenix, when a door opened, and confronted her with the ruin the years had left of the beloved being.

She passed by silently, so that he should not hear, and turn upon her the too radiant, too exultant blue eyes. The dark eyes that she remembered, deeply and delicately set beneath arched black brows, had never looked so, never for her. Always dutiful, always wary, often lowered in her presence.

Adelais went out into the chill of the evening, and turned towards her own apartments. Well, it was over. The fire was ashes. She would never see him again.

'Yes, I have seen her,' said Brother Haluin. 'Yes, I have spoken with her. I have touched her hand, it is warm flesh, woman's flesh, no illusion. The portress brought me into her presence all unprepared, I could neither speak nor move. She had been so long dead to me. Even that glimpse I had of her in the garth among the birds . . . Afterwards, when you were gone, I could not be sure I had not dreamed it. But to touch her, to have her call me by my name . . . And she was glad . . .

'Her case was not as mine, though God knows I would not say her burden has been any lighter. But she knew I was man alive, she knew where I was, and what I was, and for her there was no guilt, she had done no wrong but in loving me. And she could speak. Such words she offered me, Cadfael! "Here is one," she said, "who has already embraced you, with good right. Now with good right embrace her. She is your daughter." Can you conceive such a miracle? Giving the child to me by the hand she said it. Helisende, my daughter – not dead! Alive and young and kind and fresh as a flower. And I thought I had destroyed her, destroyed them both! Of her own sweet will the child kissed me. Even if it was only from pity – it must have been pity, how could she love one she never knew? – but even if it was only from pity, it was a gift beyond gold.

'And she will be happy. She can love as it best pleases her, and marry where her heart is. Once she called me "Father", but I think it was as a priest, as first she knew me. Even so it was good to hear and will be sweet to remember.

'This hour we three have had together repays all the eighteen years, even though there was so little said between us. The heart could hold no more. She is gone to her duties now, Bertrade. So must I to mine, soon . . . very soon . . . tomorrow . . .'

Cadfael had sat silent through the long, stumbling, eloquent monologue of his friend's revelation, broken by long pauses in which Haluin was rapt away again into a trance of wonder. Not one word of the abominable thing that had been done to him, wantonly, cruelly, that was washed clean away out of mind by the joy of its undoing, without a lingering thought of blame or forgiveness. And that was the last and most ironic judgement on Adelais de Clary.

'Shall we go to Vespers?' said Cadfael. 'The bell has gone, they'll all be in their places by now, we can creep in unnoticed.'

From their chosen dim corner in the church Cadfael scanned the young, clear faces of the sisters, and lingered long upon Sister Benedicta, who had once been Bertrade de Clary. Beside him Haluin's low, happy voice intoned the responses and prayers, but what Cadfael was hearing in his own mind was the same voice bleeding words slowly and haltingly, in the darkness of the forester's hay-loft, before dawn. There in her stall, serene, fulfilled and content, stood the woman he had tried to describe. 'She was not beautiful, as her mother was.

She had not that dark radiance, but something more kindly. There was nothing dark or secret in her, but everything open and sunlit, like a flower. She was not afraid of anything – not then. She trusted everyone. She had never been betrayed – not then. Only once, and she died of it.'

But no, she had not died. And certainly at this moment, devout and dutiful, there was nothing dark or secret in her. The oval face shone serene, as she celebrated with joy the mercy of God, after years. Without any lingering regret; her contentment was without blemish. The vocation she had undertaken unblessed, and laboured at against the grain, perhaps, all these years, surely reached its true wholeness only now, in the revelation of grace. She would not have turned back now even for that first love. There was no need. There are seasons of love. Theirs had passed beyond the storms of spring and the heat of summer into the golden calm of the first autumn days, before the leaves begin to fall. Bertrade de Clary looked as Brother Haluin looked, confirmed and invulnerable in the peace of the spirit. Henceforth presence was unnecessary, and passion irrelevant. They were eased of the past, and both of them had work to do for the future, all the more eagerly and thoroughly for knowing, each of them, that the other lived and laboured in the same vineyard.

In the morning, after Prime, their farewells made, they set out on the long journey home.

The sisters were in chapter when Cadfael and Haluin took scrip and crutches and went out from the guest-hall, but the girl Helisende went with them to the gate. It seemed to Cadfael that all these faces about him had been washed clear of every shadow and every doubt, they had all of them that stunned brightness, astonished by the good that had befallen them. Now it could be seen more clearly how like were father and daughter, so many of the marks of the years having been smoothed from Haluin's face.

Helisende embraced him without words at parting, fervent but shy. However they had spent the previous day, whatever confidences had been exchanged, she could not so quickly know him of her own knowledge, only through her mother's eyes, but she knew of him that he was gentle and of pleasing person and address, and that his eruption into her life had freed her from a nightmare of guilt and loss, and she would always remember and think of him so, with pleasure and gratitude not so far distant from love. Profit enough, even if he never saw her again.

'God keep you, Father!' said Helisende.

It was the first and the last time that she gave him that title not as a priest but as a man, but it was a gift that would last him a lifetime.

They halted for the night at Hargedon, where the canons of Hampton had a grange, in a countryside slowly being recovered out of the waste that had followed the Norman settlement. Only now, after sixty years, was ploughland being resurrected out of the scrub, and an occasional hamlet being raised where tracks crossed, or rivers provided water for a mill. The comparative security offered by the presence of the canons, steward and servants had drawn others to settle close by, and there were now assarts being hewn out of the neglected woods by enterprising younger sons. But still it was sparsely populated territory, level, lonely and in the evening light melancholy. Yet with every laboured step taken westward across this mournful plain Brother Haluin's brightness increased, his pace quickened, and his colour flushed into eagerness.

From the narrow unshuttered window in the loft he looked out westward into a night full of stars. Nearer to Shrewsbury, where the hills began to heave their fleeces towards the mountains of Wales, earth and sky balanced in harmony, but here the vault above looked immense, and the earth of men suppressed and shadowy. The brilliance of the stars, the blackness of the space between, spoke of a touch of frost in the air, but promised a fine day for the morrow.

'And you never feel,' said Cadfael quietly, 'any desire to look back over your shoulder?'

'No,' said Haluin tranquilly. 'No need. There behind me all is well. All is very well. There is nothing now for me to do there, everything where I am bound. We are sister and brother now. We ask nothing more, we want for nothing more. Now I can bring a whole heart to God. I'm glad beyond measure that he cast me down, to raise me renewed to his service.'

There was a long, untroubled silence, while he continued to stare out into the clear night with a kind of bright hunger in his face. 'I left a leaf half-finished when we set out for Hales,' he said meditatively. 'I thought to be back to complete it long before this. I hope Anselm has not given it to someone else. It was a capital N for the 'Nunc Dimittis', still wanting half the colours.'

'It will be waiting for you,' Cadfael assured him.

'Aelfric is good, but he doesn't know my intent, he might overdo the gold.' His voice was soft and practical and young.

'Leave fretting,' said Cadfael. 'Possess your soul three days more in patience, and you'll have brush and pen in hand again, and get back to work. And so must I to my herbs, for the medicine cupboards will be running low by this time. Lie down, lad, and get your rest. There are more miles waiting for you tomorrow.'

A soft wind from the west blew in through the open window, and Haluin lifted his head and sniffed the air like a high-bred horse scenting his stable.

'How good it is,' he said, 'to be going home!'